MOSQUITO

ROMA TEARNE

HarperCollins*Publishers*Ltd

For Barrie, who understood,
and for Oliver and Alistair and Mollie

Published by HarperCollins Publishers Ltd

First Canadian Edition

HarperCollins books may be purchased for educational, business, or sales promotional use through our Special Markets Department.

Quote on p. 63 © Andrew Spielman and Michael d'Antonio, *Mosquito* (Faber and Faber: London, 2002).

HarperCollins Publishers Ltd
2 Bloor Street East, 20th Floor
Toronto, Ontario, Canada
M4W 1A8

www.harpercollins.ca

Library and Archives Canada Cataloguing in Publication

Tearne, Roma
Mosquito / Roma Tearne.—1st Canadian ed.

ISBN-13: 978-0-00-200770-2
ISBN-10: 0-00-200770-3

I. Title.

PR6120.E27M68 2007   823'.92   C2007-901686-3

HC 9 8 7 6 5 4 3 2 1

Printed and bound in the United States
Set in Minion with New Baskerville display

. . . they are places that don't belong to geography but to time.

SAUL STEINBERG, *Reflections and Shadows*

1

THE CATAMARAN, ITS BLUE-PATCHED SAILS no longer flap-
ping, its nets full of glistening catch, came in after the night's
fishing. The breeze had died down, the air had cooled, and the
fishermen's sarongs slapped wet against their legs as they swung
the boat above the water, to and fro, and up and along the empty
beach, scoring a dark, deep ridge in the sand. Often, before the
monsoon broke, the sea was like a mirror. The sky appeared
joined to it with barely a seam, there was a faint vibration of
thunder and along the shoreline the air hung in hazy folds,
suspended between land, and sea, and sky. In a few hours the
heat would spread insidiously, hovering with the mosquitoes and
the spiders that waited motionless and lethargic, trapped by their
own clammy inertia. But still there was no storm. Every year it
was like this, before the monsoon, for three or four days, sometimes even longer. Every year, around the third week in June, a
yellowing stickiness, a blistering oppression clung everywhere,
so that even the bougainvillea lost its radiance.

Theo Samarajeeva walked back from the beach with fresh
fish for lunch. It was still early. The manservant, Sugi, had

brought breakfast out on to the veranda. A black-and-gold lacquered tray with a white cloth was placed on the cane table. There was a silver teapot, a jug of boiled milk, one cup and a saucer. There was some freshly cut pineapple and some curd and roti.

'You had better get the lime juice ready, Sugi,' said Theo Samarajeeva wryly, hearing the gate click shut. The manservant grinned and went inside.

'You see, by a process of elimination I knew you would be coming here,' Theo said, turning towards the gate by way of greeting.

'How?' asked Nulani Mendis, appearing, sitting down opposite him, and helping herself to the glass the manservant held out to her. Theo Samarajeeva watched as she drank. He watched her gasp as the cool, sharp liquid caught in her throat. He noticed that her fingernails had small slivers of paint under them. She wore a green skirt wrapped tightly around her waist, and a soft faded white blouse of some thin opaque fabric. The skirt was old, and almost exactly the colour of the lime juice.

'How did you know I would come today?' she demanded again when she had finished drinking.

'Well,' said Theo, 'I saw you walking on the beach earlier, and as I hadn't seen you for at least twenty-four hours I told Sugi: Ah! Miss Nulani will be here later so don't forget her lime.'

Nulani smiled guiltily, remembering she was meant to go straight home.

'So, poor Mrs Mendis still waits for her daughter, no?' he guessed.

Inside, in the dark interior of the house, music was playing on the radiogram. It floated out through the open windows, tripping effortlessly down the steps from the veranda before dispersing into the trees.

'I've been drawing,' said Nulani, taking out a small notebook from her satchel. 'Look!'

She moved her chair closer to his, giving him the book. Images rose out of it, they fell hither and thither, marvellously, on to his knees. A man sat under a tamarind tree, another squatted in the narrow spit of shade afforded by a house. A woman stretched out on a makeshift bed staring at the rough edges of a palm roof through the bars of the window. Someone, a middle-aged man, lean legs stretched in front of him, was writing, head bent at a table. He had a cigarette in his left hand and behind him was the blur of tropical trees.

'This is me, no? When did you do this one?'

'Yesterday,' said Nulani, laughing. 'I was hiding over there, you didn't see me.'

'You little pest! Why didn't you make yourself known? Sugi had made a fine red mullet curry. You could have eaten with me.'

'You are not angry?'

'I feel the bushes have eyes,' he teased her. 'I shall have to watch everything from now on. No talking to myself any more! But seriously, these are good. Are you going to use them in a painting?'

'I don't know,' said Nulani, frowning. 'Do you really like them?' And boldly, 'I want to paint you. But . . .'

Theo considered her. For a moment he felt lost for words. Nulani Mendis had been visiting him for nearly three months now. It had begun when he had first moved to this part of the island. The convent school had invited him to give a talk on his latest book. He had not long been back from the UK, some perversity making him give up the modest success he enjoyed there. People thought him mad. The Liberation Tigers had been demanding a separate Tamil state for years with no success. Civil unrest grew daily. Then, after Singhala was made the national language, discrimination against the Tamils became commonplace. A potential guerrilla war was simmering. Why did he want to go back to that hell? they asked. Was he off his head? An established writer, with a comfortable life in London, his own flat, his work, what could he want with Colombo? Was it not enough writing books on the impending violence, did he want to *live* it too? But, he had no ties. Perhaps it was sentimentality in early middle age? Perhaps the terrible events from the past had finally got to him, they said.

Theo could not explain. He himself barely understood this sudden compulsion, this urgency to go home. It was a time when everyone who could was escaping. Perhaps simply because he no longer had anything to escape from, going back was not a problem. So he told his agent he would work better if he had some sun and, putting his flat on the market, he left. The agent said nothing, thinking privately that what Theo really needed was some distraction, danger even. Do him good, thought the agent; add richness to this next book. Other men might have given up writing altogether after what he had been through, but Theo had carried on. He probably needed a complete change of scene, needed to put the past finally behind him. So, with this in mind, the agent encouraged him to go back, for a time at least.

It was 1996. While he had been away Sri Lanka had changed. The change confused Theo. He found himself remembering the liberal atmosphere of his youth. Where was it? In England, whatever corruption there was, was kept discreetly out of sight. Or maybe he was less critical because the British were not his own people. It was a different matter in Colombo where every small injustice, every appalling act of violence seemed a personal affront. The civil unrest he had predicted in his books, the beginnings of rage seemed to have been nurtured in his absence, and spread, like a newly germinated paddy field. He left Colombo, moved to a backwater, and began writing his fourth novel. His second book was being made into a film and an article about him appeared in one of the papers. The local schools, having noticed it and having registered his arrival in the town, asked him to speak to the pupils. At first he had hesitated, worrying. But what was there worth worrying about in these troubled times? People had been garrotted for less outspoken views, so why did he care? His life would go on for as long as it would, or it simply would cease. Why worry? He was no longer a Buddhist, but Buddhism had worked on him like milk and honey nonetheless. He agreed to give two talks, one at the boys' school and the other at the convent. Nulani Mendis had been one of the students. She had held her hand up and asked him several questions.

'The girl hardly speaks,' the teacher had told him afterwards. 'Since her father was murdered she has become silent. The mother has given up trying to make her talk. All she does is draw, draw, draw.'

But on that day she had spoken to Theo and later, on one of his early-evening walks along the narrow strip of beach behind the house, he saw her again. He had smiled slightly, registering her good looks, and remembering the story of her father, he waved. But she seemed to vanish into the darkness. After that he kept seeing her and he guessed she lived nearby. Then Sugi caught her in the garden. She was drawing his stone lions. Sugi began complaining loudly.

'Sir, sir, these local children are pests. They've started coming into the garden again. We need to get rid of them or they will multiply!'

Surprised, Theo came out and, recognising her, asked her name. Then he invited her, in spite of Sugi's protest, to come over at any time and draw. This had been nearly three months ago. She never called him anything except Mr Samarajeeva. He supposed, wryly, that this was out of a sense of respect for his age. But she came back, again and again, and, if she did not appear for a few days, he became inclined to drift into bad temper.

'Can I go now?' she asked, breaking into his reverie. 'I want to draw the house from over there.'

She had been with him since breakfast.

'Won't you be late for school?' he asked. 'Does your mother know you are here?'

'No,' she said, disappearing around the side of the house. Her voice reached him from another part of the garden, vague and indistinct. 'No, she's out. And I've finished the jobs she gave me so I can go straight to school from here.'

Theo shook his head, amused in spite of himself. The man-servant gave him a look that said clearly, 'I told you, these local children are pests.' But she's different, thought Theo.

At first she came only once a week, barely speaking, staying further back in the garden. But as she grew bolder she seemed to be there all the time. Then, one day, out of the blue, she showed him her notebook for the first time. The sketches were all of him, delicate, and with a clear unwavering likeness. Startled, he took down his book of Picasso drawings and talked to her about the artist. After that she began to talk to him.

'I will be seventeen in three months,' she said.

On another afternoon she told him about her brother Jim. He was only eighteen months younger. She told him, they were not close.

'It is our karma,' she said solemnly. 'We have brought it into this life.'

Their father, she said, had known most of this long before the astrologer came to visit. He told their mother, soon after the birth of Jim, he had seen it in a dream; the children would never be close. He could see it written on their faces, he had said, the girl child, and his infant son. Their mother, hearing this pronouncement, had begun wailing. After all her labours was this the future? But their father told his wife sternly to stop her noise. Be thankful, he said, for the fact that both children were healthy. After puberty, he suspected, after they came of age, they would cross a great expanse of water, leave Sri Lanka. Go to mainland India even. It would be a good thing, he had said, for peace in this country was always uncertain. Thus had her father predicted, long before the astrologer came to plot their horoscopes, walking up the steps of the house. With his saffron robes and his sandals dusty with beach sand, and his black umbrella faded with the heat. Their father, not foreseeing his own death in the riots of the following June, felt the future of his children grow large in his own mind.

How long was it before she realised the strange masculine world inhabited by her brother was not for her, wondered Theo. Was it when she was still small? Did her understanding come, as all unshakeable beliefs do, not at any given moment but slowly, like seawater seeping into a hole dug on a beach? Lucky Jim could pace his domain freely, marking his undisputed territory, certain of his own image of the future. But what of Nulani?

Sometimes while her brother slept, before the father's unpredicted death, when they were younger, Nulani told Theo, she would bend over Jim and smell the sugar-sweet baby scent of greenness on his skin, run her finger across an old scar that straddled the rounded grubbiness of his brown leg. Later when she was older, she told Theo, she stole a box of Venus B pencils (Made in Great Britain) from the house of their English neighbour, to draw her sleeping brother. But the neighbour found out and demanded she be punished for stealing. She returned the pencils; two of them were used and broken.

'All right, Mrs Mendis,' the neighbour, the Englishman, told her mother angrily, 'I know it must be hard for you, with your husband dead. But "render unto Caesar" and all that!'

He had laughed, without rhythm. Nulani had wondered if that was how the English laughed. She knew she would not be allowed into the Englishman's house again. She would not be able to play with his daughter Carol any more; she would never be able to touch her shining golden hair.

'Why did you take them?' her brother had demanded. 'Render unto Caesar,' he had said, sounding like the Englishman.

Nulani's uncle came. Because her father was no longer alive, it was his duty to beat her with an *ekel* stick.

'Render unto Caesar,' he had said. They were ashamed of her. The whole family avoided the neighbours now, eyes cast down whenever the jeep drove them about, into the city, to the beach, shopping.

'See what you've done to us.'

Nulani could see. She stopped drawing her brother when he slept. She just looked at him. Her little brother. She was his *loku akka*, his big sister. Her father had said they would not be close. But no one, she told Mr Samarajeeva, not even the astrologer, had said she would not love him.

And now she came here to draw. Arriving early, leaving late. Always talking. Transformed.

'Child,' Theo said suddenly now, drifting back from his thoughts and realising the time, 'you'll be late for school.'

When there was no answer he went to look for her at the back of the garden, but then he heard the gate click again.

'I'm late,' she called, grinning at him, hurrying off. 'But I'm coming back!'

And she disappeared up the hill with a wave of her hand.

They swarmed so thickly that they might easily have been mistaken for smoke. Rising swiftly from the water-filled holes dug by the

*gem miners in their search for sapphire, the mosquitoes seemed
suspended in reflected light. For a moment the holes appeared as
mirrored surfaces, blue as the sky. Further out towards the coast
the rainwater filled the upturned coconut shells, as they lay scattered across the groves. Here the beautiful female anopheles
mosquitoes, graceful wings glinting in the sun, landed lightly and
prepared to create a canoe of death for their cargo of eggs. The
Ministry of Health sprayed the coconut groves with DDT to prevent
outbreaks of malaria. The metallic smell drifted and mixed heavily
with the scent of frangipani and hibiscus. There had been no
epidemic for nearly five years.*

Theo liked to spend the morning writing, but lately it had been
difficult to concentrate with the girl present. She sat against a
wall, almost in the bushes, drawing him. He had tried to make
her come inside but she was stubborn and stayed where she
was, far back along the veranda, crouching beside the lilies and
the ferns.

'How can you draw like this? You can't see me,' he had
protested. 'Why do you want to crouch so low?'

She had refused his invitation and in the end he had just
shrugged, leaving her alone, going back to his typewriter in the
cool of his study. It was hot. For some reason the fans had all
stopped working. Perhaps the generator had broken down again.
He would have to get Sugi to look at it. Every now and then
as he worked he would look up and catch a glimpse of her
faded lime-green skirt translucent against the extraordinary
light of the untamed garden. She folded and rearranged herself
until from where he sat she was a smudge of green and white
and black. He could not see her face; it was hidden by her dark
hair. He found her presence disturbing. How was he supposed
to work? Surely it must be lunchtime? He half hoped she would

stay to eat with him. Sometimes she did; at other times, although she hesitated, an inner tempo seemed to call her, guilt perhaps, a sudden memory of an uncompleted errand for her long-suffering mother. Every time Theo asked her to stay for lunch. He waited, unaware that his breath was bated, for her reply, knowing only his irrational disappointment if she went home.

He had decided then, the best thing to do was to commission her to paint him. It was clear that, once voiced, she would not give up the idea, so one evening he strolled over to Mrs Mendis with the suggestion. Mrs Mendis welcomed him with some *aluva* and coffee. He told her he wanted to commission Nulani to paint his portrait. He would like to pay her if Mrs Mendis did not mind. Mrs Mendis did not mind. Mr Samarajeeva was extremely kind. She just hoped Nulani would do a proper job.

'The girl is a dreamer,' said Mrs Mendis. 'She does not talk much and she is stubborn. If you can get her to do anything it will be a miracle. Most of the time, if there is any work to be done, she disappears. She won't help in the house or with any of my sewing. How am I to make a living, with no one to help me?'

Having started her complaints, Mrs Mendis found it curiously difficult to stop. Her thin, high voice rose like the smoke from a mosquito coil.

'I am a widow,' she said. 'Has Nulani told you? Has she told you my husband was set fire to during the rioting in the seventies? They threw a petrol bomb at him. Aiyo, we watched as he went screaming down the Old Tissa Road. Fear kept all the people hidden behind closed doors.' Mrs Mendis waved her hands about in distress. 'Everyone watched through the shutters of their houses,' she said. 'But no one came to help.'

Harsh sunlight had pressed itself on the edges of the house and then Mrs Mendis had run screaming into the street, chasing hopelessly after her husband, but it was too late. He lay blackened and burnt; clear liquid oozing out from his staring eyes, his body charred, the stench of flesh filling her open-mouthed screams.

'The neighbours came out of the houses then and pulled me away,' she said.

They had been fearful she might throw herself on to the flames. By the time the ambulance came he was beyond help.

'Luckily,' said Mrs Mendis, lowering her voice, 'my son Jim was somewhere else and did not see his father's life as it left this world.'

Lucky Jim. 'He had been so close to his father,' she said. 'The shock is still with him.'

Only the girl had been at home. Mrs Mendis wasn't sure how much she had seen. Always quiet, she became mute after that.

'She's difficult,' said Mrs Mendis, 'obstinate and odd.'

Theo Samarajeeva, who had not meant to stay for long, looked around for escape. There was no sign of Nulani, but something about the stillness of the air made him certain she was listening.

Walking home he turned several times, convinced he was being followed. But the road was empty. The air was choked with the heavy scent of frangipani. As he entered his house he noticed Sugi had lit some oil lamps. Theo could see him fixing a few cheap Chinese lanterns to the trees. He poured himself a whisky, and was still listening to the ice crackling in the glass when he saw her. Standing in his doorway holding out a branch of blossom, the rich scent filling the room, her smile wide, her eyes as bright as the new moon.

She came almost daily after that, before school, after her evening meal, at odd unexpected hours, nearly every weekend. A notebook was filling up with small studies of him. Sometimes she showed him what she had done. She seemed to be trying to record every slight movement of his face, he thought, amused. Such was the minute detail of the drawings. He was astonished by her perception. Thin pencils, stubs of charcoal, delicate brush-strokes, whatever she used, all had the same fluid quality, the same effortless logic as they moved across the page. Each time she showed him what she had done, he was astonished all over again.

'Nulani,' he asked once, after looking at these drawings for a long time. 'Why me? Why draw me? Why not someone younger, your brother's friends perhaps?'

He was genuinely puzzled. But she had only laughed.

'Wait till you see the painting!' she promised.

Now he watched her as she drew him from the corner of the veranda.

'Why don't you sit somewhere better, child?' he asked again. 'You can't possibly see me clearly from where you are!'

'I don't want to see you, Mr Samarajeeva. I'm learning to draw you from memory.'

'Will you please stop calling me Mr Samarajeeva.'

'OK, Mr Samarajeeva.'

He never knew if she was teasing him. He had a feeling she could read his mind, that she liked to make him feel older than he felt already, because it amused her, because in fact his age made no difference whatsoever to her.

'I want to be able to draw you from memory, with my eyes closed,' she said, 'so I will never forget you.'

Startled, he stood up. Sugi came in to announce lunch was ready. Lunch was some fresh *thora-malu*, seer fish, from today's catch.

'When will you start painting?' he asked while they ate. A small beam of sunlight fell on her face. Her skin glowed with a sheen of youthfulness. Through the curtain of thick hair her eyes were as bright as a pair of black cherries. He thought of all the years of living that lay between them, as heavy and as sweet as a piece of sugared coconut jaggery, irreplaceable, unexchangeable, for ever between them.

'I have already started the painting, but I must draw more. Can I come here and paint?'

Theo laughed. 'At this rate you will always be here. What will your mother say? She won't be happy with that idea. She must want to see her daughter *sometimes*.'

'I want to be here all the time,' she said.

Theo looked at her. The beam of sunlight had moved and rested on the top of her head. Her hair was a sleek smoky black; it reminded him of the blue-black cat he and Anna had once had, in that other life. But all he said was: 'I have to go to Colombo tomorrow, is there anything you need? Any paints I can try to get you?'

He did not tell her that he had done no work since she had been drawing him; he did not tell her that her presence in his house, like a beautiful injured bird, was distraction enough without the drawing. London seemed far away.

'Has your mother seen the painting?'

'No. Amma, my mother, worries too much all the time. She doesn't have time to look.' She seemed to hesitate. 'Her worry is because she hopes.'

'She hopes?'

'She hopes things will not get worse than they already are. She hopes my brother does not leave, go to England. But she also hopes he *does* go because he will have a better life there. She hopes she will never see the things she saw once. So she does not look.'

It was the first time she had made reference to her father's murder.

'We are not like you,' she said.

'But you paint,' said Theo, '*you* still look.' And he thought how it was, that this beautiful place, with its idyllic landscape

13

of sea and sky and glorious weather, had lost its way. Both through the lack of human intervention and, also, because of it. How many generations did it take before all the wondrous things of the island could be described again? Twenty years? Fifty years? Would a whole generation have to grow and be replaced before that could happen?

'You must never stop looking,' he said firmly. 'Never. Even when it becomes hard you must never stop. Also, you are a woman. It is important for women to do something about what they see. Only then will there be change. My wife was like that, she would have loved your drawings.'

'Your wife? Where is she?'

'She's dead,' said Theo.

He kept his voice steady; surprisingly he did not feel the usual sharp stab of bitterness. The beam of sunlight had moved and now shone against the edge of the huge mirror that stood above the Dutch sideboard, reflecting the fine golden sea dust that foxed its surface. Sugi came in with some mangoes. The afternoon heat, dazzling and yellow, was at its worst. It stood in abeyance outside the open door.

'What was her name?' asked Nulani, after Sugi had gone.

'She was called Anna.'

He noticed they had both slipped into their native Singhalese. Was pain easier to deal with in one's mother tongue? Nulani was thinking too.

'My brother has a long scar on his leg,' she said.

When he cut it he had cried. She could remember how his leg had bled, she told Theo. The blood had poured out like rain.

'There was no blood when Father died. After the ambulance took him away to the mortuary I went back to look at the road. I wanted to see the black dust. It was his dust, his body dust. That was all there was of him.'

14

She had rubbed the palm of her hand in it, she told Theo, until someone, some neighbour, had pulled her away. She still knew the exact spot where it was. There was a traffic island there now. It was her father's headstone. It was her scar.

'You have a scar, no?' she said. 'While I have been drawing you I have felt it. It is all over you, no?' She traced the shape of his spine in the air. 'It is under your skin, between the back-bones,' she said.

'It was a long time ago now.'

'Is that why you came back?'

'No, yes . . . partly.'

'It will get better here,' said Nulani softly.

She was too young to give him firm comfort but her certainty, though fragile, comforted him anyway. He was twenty-eight years older than her. Mango juice ran down her arm as she ate. Her lips were moist. Anna would have loved a child, he thought. Her generosity would have rushed in like waves, enveloping Nulani. Why had they never come here when Anna was still with him? Fleetingly, he thought of his old home in London, with its books and rugs and old French mirrors that filled the apartment with the light that was always in short supply. How different it was now, where they shuttered out the light instead.

The sun had moved away from the glass as they finished their meal and Theo lit a cigar. Nulani was fidgeting, wanting to get on. She remembered she had to go home. Her uncle, her mother's brother, was coming to see how his niece and nephew were. He was all they had for a father these days.

'Sugi will clear the space at the back for you to paint,' said Theo finally. 'You can come any time you like, but I shall be in Colombo tomorrow.'

He waved, watching her walk away, the dust from the garden washing brown against her open-toed sandals.

* * *

After he had cleared the room Sugi polished the floor with coconut scrapings. He rubbed as hard as he could, using first his left and then his right foot until the house smelt of it and the floor shone like marble. Then he went outside into the backyard and chopped open a *thambili*, an orange king coconut, and drank from it. After that he went back to work. There were several jobs he hoped to finish before Mr Samarajeeva returned from Colombo. He liked to surprise him with some small task or other well done. Last time it had been the fixing of the stone lions to the garden wall. The time before that he had painted the shutters.

Mr Samarajeeva was always weary when he returned from Colombo. He looked as he did when Sugi had first seen him, on the day he came to live here, walking from the station with his bags, a piece of paper in his hand, the address of the beach house on it. He had asked for directions and Sugi had brought him to the house, and stayed ever since. At the time he thought Mr Samarajeeva was a foreigner, in his fine tropical suit, with his leather suitcases and his hat. But then Theo had spoken to him in their mother tongue with such fluency that Sugi had grinned.

'I have been away a long time,' said Mr Samarajeeva. 'But my Singhala isn't bad, is it?'

He had wanted Sugi to work with him, help him set up his life here in the house. He would need some cooking, some domestic chores and some house maintenance. Could Sugi manage all that? Sugi could. As there was no one else to talk to, Mr Samarajeeva talked to Sugi. When his things arrived from London he unpacked them with Sugi and talked about his life there. He unpacked several framed photographs. They were of the same woman, blonde, curly-haired, smiling at the camera.

'My wife Anna,' he told Sugi.

Then he unpacked his books. There seemed to be hundreds of books. There were other things from his old life. Later Sugi found out more about his wife. He tried to imagine the type of woman who had collected all these things. The mirrors, the plates, the cutlery. She must have been a fine woman, thought Sugi. When he found out Mr Samarajeeva was famous, the books he had written, and soon the film, he felt it his duty to warn him. These were troubled times. Envy and poverty went hand in hand with the ravaged land, he said. Even though he was a Singhalese, Mr Samarajeeva should be careful. His sympathy for the Tamil children was too well known. The house should be made more secure. Locks were needed for the shutters and the doors. The garden wall needed to be repaired in order to keep intruders out. Sugi made a list. Theo smiled lazily. He did not stop Sugi but he did not care much either.

'Sir,' said Sugi genuinely puzzled, 'you don't understand. There can be sudden outbreaks of trouble here. When you least expect it. You must be careful. People know who you are and they talk too much in these parts. It's not as you remember, no?'

All this was before the Mendis girl started visiting. Sugi knew the family.

'The boy is the only son, Sir,' he said. 'He is arrogant, and clever. There is talk of him getting a British Council scholarship in spite of what happened to the father. The father was warned several times, you know. Before they killed him, they warned him. But he was a fearless man who spoke out against the injustice done to the Tamils long ago. So, even though he was warned, he ignored the warnings.'

He paused, remembering.

'He was an educated man, too. He wasn't a fool. But in the end it did him no good. He was very handsome, and he had strong principles. Always campaigning for the Tamil underdog.

What they did to him was a terrible thing. But you know, Sir, he should have been more careful. Someone should have advised him. That silly wife of his, someone.'

'And the girl?' asked Theo.

'Oh, the girl looks just like him,' said Sugi, misunderstanding. 'But you know the whole family is being watched now. They were never popular. And the boy is very selfish. He is only interested in himself.'

It was clear Mr Samarajeeva was not interested in the boy, thought Sugi, disapproving of the girl's visits.

'She comes here too often, Sir, now,' he warned. 'There are certain people in this town who are very interested in that family.'

She was friendly enough, thought Sugi, but still, she might bring trouble with her. Someone had once told him she had stopped talking after her father died, but from what he could hear she never stopped when she was with Theo. Her drawings, he reluctantly admitted, were another matter. They were good. Sir had them scattered all over the house and now, in this latest development, the girl was going to work on Mr Samarajeeva's portrait in the house. Sugi shook his head. He could not understand how the mother could care so little that she let her daughter wander around in this way. How could a respectable Singhalese woman be so negligent? Rumour was that Mrs Mendis had become unhinged since the tragedy. But then, thought Sugi, going off on another track, everyone is strange nowadays. The things that had happened in this place were turning people mad. It was not possible to have normal lives any longer. It was not possible to walk without looking over your shoulder at all times. Without wondering who was a friend and who a new enemy. Fear and suspicion was the thing they lived off, it was the only diet they had had for years. Almost every family he knew was touched in some way by the troubles, living with the things they were too frightened to talk about. There was no point, no point to anything. One just waited, hoping. Dodging the curfew. Hoping not to put a foot wrong, thought Sugi, hoping not to tread the rusty barbed wire hidden in the sea sand.

A few nights previously Sugi had cautioned Theo again. Not that it was any use, but he had tried.

'You must not walk on the beach when there is a curfew. The army is watching. Or if they are not, then there are thugs who will watch for them. Believe me, Sir. And another thing, you shouldn't have given your talk about your book at the schools. They won't like that.'

'It is no way to live,' said Theo Samarajeeva frowning. 'No one owns the beach. Sugi, there are many countries all over the world that have trouble like this. We must not give in to the bullies.'

'Ours is a very small country,' Sugi said, shaking his head. 'No one cares about us. Why should they? Only we care about the differences between the Singhalese and the Tamils. No one understands what this fight is about. We hardly understand ourselves any more.'

Theo nodded. He brought out his pipe and began tapping it.

'When the British brought the Tamils here from India, some people thought they brought trouble to this island,' Sugi said.

Theo was trying to light his pipe but the breeze kept whipping the flame so that he had to turn away. Sugi continued to stare into space. When he spoke at last he sounded agitated.

'What is wrong with us that we behave in this way?' He watched as Theo struggled to relight his pipe. 'Isn't it possible for us to solve this thing peacefully?'

'It will take longer than we think,' Theo said, He put his match into the ashtray Sugi handed him. 'Why should the world care, Sugi?' he asked gently. 'We aren't important enough for the British any more. And unlike the Middle East, we have no oil. So we can kill each other and no one will notice. That's why things will take longer than we think.'

He knew from his life in England, people thought Sri Lanka was a place spiralling into madness; and yes, he thought, it was true, no one cared.

They had taken to having these conversations in the evening when the curfew was on. The girl never came after the curfew. Sugi was thankful that at least her mother had the sense to keep her in at night. So Theo had only Sugi to talk to. Sugi was always careful to keep a respectful distance from Mr Samarajeeva during these discussions. Occasionally he accepted a cigarette or a beer but never anything else. He stood a little away from the chairs; he would never accept a seat. Sometimes he squatted on the step, the end of his cigarette glowing in the dark.

'I would like to see England,' he said one night. 'I think the people there are not like us.'

'No, they're not. But they have their own problems, Sugi, their own battles. Just as pointless in their different ways. And I never really felt I belonged there.'

'Even after all that time, Sir?'

'No,' said Theo with certainty. 'These are my people. *This* is where I belong.'

But Sugi was doubtful.

'Don't mistake our friendliness, Sir. We are Buddhists but these days we have forgotten this,' said Sugi. 'We are quite capable of killing. It isn't like before. When you were last here. Things are complicated now. These days we don't know who we are.'

Theo nodded in agreement. 'They should have known it wouldn't end simply,' he murmured.

'Who? The Tamils?'

'No, Sugi,' Theo said. He sounded sad. 'I mean those who conquered us. I mean the British. Their presence casts its shadow on this island. Still.'

'Cause and effect, Sir. Just as the Buddha said.'

But Theo was following his own thoughts.

'Why are we surprised by this war, Sugi? Has there ever been a country that, once colonised, avoided civil war? Africa? India? Burma?'

Night flowers appeared everywhere in the garden, blooming in ghostly clusters, their branches pouring scent into the air. Frogs croaked, small bats moved silently in the trees, and here and there, in the dull light of the lamp, silvery insects darted about. On one occasion Sugi shone a torch into the under-growth, convinced a nest of snakes lurked close by. He advanced with his axe but then the moon had gone behind a cloud and he could not find a single one. At other times, on certain nights, suddenly there were no sounds at all. No drums, no radios, no sirens. Nothing moved in the darkness and at such moments Sugi's nervousness would increase. The silence, he complained, was worse than all the noise, the atmosphere created by it, terri-fying in a different way. Suspense hung heavily in the air; at such moments anything could happen. For in Sugi's experience, most murders were committed in the lull before the full moon. Whispers alighted as softly as mosquitoes on unsuspecting flesh; whispers of torture. And the smell of death brought the snakes out. Theo listened to Sugi's fears without speaking. But then, sometimes, on these faceless nights, as they sat talking in the garden, they would catch the unmistakable sigh of the great ocean drifting towards them. They would hear it very clearly, rushing and tugging, to and fro and across, in an endless cycle as it washed and rewashed the bone-white shore. And as always, as they listened, the sound of it comforted them both.

By the time Theo Samarajeeva returned from Colombo the back room of his house had been cleared, the walls lime-washed, and Nulani Mendis was installed with her canvases, her paints and her cheap thinners. The house smelt of coconuts and linseed oil. He knew she was there even as he approached, even as the bougainvillea cascaded into view over the new garden wall. The light from the mirrors in this hastily devised studio flickered in a dazzling way, casting intermittent reflections on everything in the room. Theo watched through the open window as Nulani crouched on the ground working on the painting. She used rags to mix the paint, and rags to layer it smoothly on to the canvas. All around were her pencil drawings of him. He could not see her face. Slivers of light danced on her hair. He did not know how long he stood watching her. Time stood still.

After a while she moved, placing the painting against the wall beside a chair where the reflections continued to tremble, uninterrupted. There was an old jug made of thin dusty glass nearby on a shelf. Shadows poured endlessly into it where once it must have held liquid. The heat was impossible. Before he could say anything she turned suddenly and saw him. Her instantaneous smile caught them both unawares. It must have been a trick of the light, thought Theo surprised, but the day seemed exceptionally pierced by the sun.

'So you are back,' she said. 'Sugi said you wouldn't be back till later.'

How to tell her that Colombo seemed unbearably hot and crowded? That what he thought he had needed to look up in the university library had in fact been irrelevant? That he knew, if he hurried, he would be able to catch an earlier train and be back before she went home, thereby seeing her a day sooner? How to tell her all this when he was unable to understand these thoughts himself?

'I have brought you a present,' he said instead, handing her a paper bag. Inside were all the colours she wanted but did not have. Cobalt blue, crimson lake, Venetian red. A bottle of pure turpentine, refined linseed oil. The paints were good-quality pigments, made in England, of the sort she had seen long ago in the English neighbour's house when she had stolen the pencils. The tubes were clean and uncrushed by use. She opened them and watched as traces of oil oozed slowly out; the colour was not far behind. They looked good enough to eat. Her bright red dress was new.

'It's my birthday today,' she said delighted, seeing him look at her dress. 'I was hoping you would come back today.'

'I know!' he said. 'Happy seventeenth birthday!'

Again the day seemed suffused by an inexplicable green lightness, of the kind he remembered in other times, in other places. Maybe there will be rain later, thought Theo, confused.

She had begun to paint him against a curtain of foliage. There were creases in his white shirt, purple shadows along one arm. She had given his eyes a reflective quality that hinted at other colours beyond the darkness of the pupils. Was this him, really? Was this what *she* saw? In the painting he paused as he wrote, looking into the distance. Aspects of him emerged from the canvas, making certain things crystal clear.

'You were looking at *me*,' she said laughing, pointing to one of the drawings.

He did not know what to say. Her directness left him helpless. Perhaps it was this simplicity that he needed in his new book. Once he had been able to deal with all kinds of issues swiftly, cut to the heart of the matter. Now for some reason it seemed impossible for him to think in this way. Had fear and hurt and self-pity done all this to him? Or was this the uncertainty of middle age? Suddenly he felt small and ashamed. He stood looking at the painting and at the girl framed by the curtain of green light, aware vaguely that she was still smiling at him. He stood staring at her until Sugi called out that lunch was ready.

'Tell me about Anna,' she demanded, over lunch. 'I have been looking at all the pictures of her. They are very beautiful.'

So he told her something about Anna.

'I used to see her every morning in a little café where I went for breakfast.'

'In London?'

'No, in Venice. She was Italian. We used to glance at each other without speaking. It was bitterly cold that winter. The apartment I was renting was so cold that I would go to this little dark café for breakfast. And I would drink a grappa,' he said smiling, remembering.

'What happened then?'

'One day she came in with some other people. Two women and a man. The man was clearly interested in her.'

'So what did you do?'

Theo smiled, shaking his head. 'Nothing. What could I do? My Italian was not very good in those days. But then she turned and waved at me. Asked me if I would like to join them. I was astonished, astonished that she should notice me.'

'But you said you used to look at each other every morning.'

'Yes,' said Theo. 'I suppose I mean I was surprised she noticed me enough to want to talk to me.'

He was silent again, thinking of the fluidity of their lives afterwards, the passion that never seemed to diminish as they travelled through Europe. Then he described the high tall house in London with the mirrors and the blousy crimson peonies she loved to buy. He spoke of the books they had both written, so different yet one feeding off the other.

'She was very beautiful,' he said, unaware of the change in his voice. 'Now *she* was someone you should have drawn.'

Nulani was listening intensely. He became aware of her curious dark eyes fixed on him. He did not know how much she understood. What could Europe mean to her?

'My brother Jim wants to go to Europe,' she said at last. 'He says, when he is in England studying it will be easy to travel.'

'And you? What about you?'

But he knew the answer even before she told him. Who would take her? What would she make of Paris. And Venice?

'I will go one day,' she said as though reading his mind. 'Maybe we will go together.'

He felt his chest tighten unaccountably, and he wondered what her father had been like. What would he have made of this beautiful daughter of his, had he lived? Nulani had told him he had been a poet. She remembered him, she told Theo, but only as a dreamer. Always making her mother angry as she, Nulani, did now. What fragile balance in their family had been upset by his death? The afternoon had moved on but the heat showed no sign of letting up. The sun had moved to another place.

'You should go home,' he said, suddenly anxious, not wishing to keep her out too late. 'I'll get Sugi to walk you home.'

But she would have none of it; standing close to him holding her paints, so close he could smell the faint perfume that was her skin, mixing with the oils.

'Thank you,' she said and she went, a splash of red against the sea-faded blue gate, and then through the trees, and then taking in glimpses of road and bougainvillea before she disappeared from view around the bend of the hot empty road. Taking with her all the myriad, unresolved hues of the day, shimmering into the distance.

2

THEO HAD NOT SEEN THE GIRL for five days. He waited, watching the geckos climbing haltingly across the lime-washed walls. He walked on the beach most evenings, much to Sugi's alarm, ignoring the curfews, hoping she might be doing the same. He sat on the veranda smoking; he wandered into the room strewn with her paints. The smell of turpentine and oil remained as strong as ever. It was the way of smells, he knew. It had been this way when Anna had died. All the smells of beeswax and red peonies, of lavender-washed cotton and typewriter ribbon had gathered together, bringing her back to him in small concentrated fragments. So he knew about smells, the way they tumbled into the air, falling softly again, here and there, like confetti without the bride. The sunlight seemed suddenly to have lost its brilliance. His old anger returned. He had thought he was over it, but bitterness attacked him in waves. Ugliness remembered. Sugi watched him surreptitiously, serving his meals, bringing a tray of morning tea, cooking a redfish curry in the way he liked it. The fans had stopped working again and the lights often failed at night. Sugi watched him in the light of the coconut-oil lamps.

There did not seem to be much evidence of Sir working. Across the garden Theo felt the silence stretch into eternity. The leaves on the pawpaw tree looked large and malevolent.

'Sir,' said Sugi finally, 'Sir, why are you not writing?'

Beyond the light from the veranda the undergrowth rustled vaguely. Two mosquito coils burned into insubstantial columns. A black-spotted moth circled the lamps, mesmerised. Sugi looked at Theo. This is a fine state of affairs, he thought. It was as well he was here.

'Maybe there is trouble at her house, no?' he ventured tentatively. 'Shall I go and find out?'

'No,' said Theo quickly.

Such an intrusion was unbearable and he could not allow it. Sugi fell silent again. Maybe he should talk about something else instead. Sir was a grown man after all. He had lived all over the world. Given the things he had been through, his innocence was surprising.

'There is a shortage of food in the market this week,' Sugi said. 'I don't know why. I could only get river cress, a coconut and a bunch of shrivelled radishes.'

It was true. The rice was appalling too, and there were no fresh vegetables to be had.

'Of all the places on this island,' he continued, complaining loudly, hoping to distract Theo, 'this should be the place for fresh fish. But the day's catch had vanished by the time I got into the town. There's been some kind of trouble further along the coast; maybe that's got something to do with it. Someone told me the army drove their jeeps on to the sands, chasing a group of men. And then they shot them. They were all young, Sir. Nobody knows what they had done.'

He spread his hands helplessly in front of him.

'The army left the bodies on the beach, and the local people cleared up the mess. There is always someone prepared to clean up after them. Either a Buddhist or a Christian. They will always find someone to do the dirty work.'

Theo shifted uneasily in his chair. Sugi's anxiety was different from his.

On the fifth evening of Nulani's absence, in spite of Sugi's entreaties, Theo decided to walk along the beach again.

'Look,' he said, 'nothing can happen to me. It's not people like me that interest them. I'm too well known. I'm safe.'

And he went out. A full moon spilled a continuous stream of silver on to the water. An express train hooted its way along the coast, rushing towards Colombo. But there was no sign of the girl on the empty beach. What *is* the matter with me, he thought, exasperated. Am I going mad? She's probably busy, helping her mother, sewing, being seventeen. And she never said when she would be back, he reasoned silently. He was puzzled by this disturbance to his equilibrium. Time was passing, in a few months it would be winter in England. His agent would not wait for ever. He had not written much. As he watched, the moon spread its phosphorescent glow into the sea.

'Look,' Sugi said when he returned.

He held out a piece of paper. Thick heady blossoms glowed white under the lamplight while Theo unfolded it quickly. It was from the girl. She had drawn a picture of a man. The man was sitting on one of the cane chairs on her veranda. There was a cup of tea on the table beside him; it was placed on a heavily embroidered cloth. The man's face was in profile, but still, it was possible to see the fine lines of dissatisfaction and anger and suppressed cruelty. It was possible to see all this on the small piece of paper, clearly marked by the stub of a pencil.

'It's her uncle, Sir,' said Sugi when Theo showed him. 'I know this man. He is a bad man. The talk is he betrayed Mr Mendis.

That it was because of him, the thugs came. He never liked his sister's choice of husband. There are seven brothers in that family, you know, and they like their women to do as they are told.'

Theo felt anger tighten its belt around him. His anxiety for the girl intensified.

'I think I'll take a walk over to Mrs Mendis's house,' he said.

But Sugi was alarmed. He would not let Theo be so foolish.

'Are you crazy, Sir? Leave that family alone, for God's sake. I'm telling you, you don't understand the people here. You must not meddle with things in this place. Please, Mr Samarajeeva, this isn't England. The girl will be OK. It's *her* family, and she is no fool. She will come here, tomorrow or the next day, you'll see.'

He sounded like a parent, quietening a restless child. In spite of his anger another part of Theo saw this and felt glad. He was amazed at the easy affection between them. They had slipped into a friendship, Sugi and he, in spite of the rising tide of anxiety around them, perhaps because of it.

'Sugi,' he said softly into the darkness, feeling a sudden sharp sense of belonging. 'You are my good friend, you know. I feel as if I have known you for ever.'

He hesitated. He would have liked to say something more. Moved by their growing affection for each other, he would have liked to speak of it. But he could not think of the right way to express himself. Sugi, too, seemed to hesitate, as though he understood. So Theo said nothing and instead poured them both a beer. But the warmth between them would not go away, settling down quietly, curling up like a contented animal. He looked at the note again. Underneath the drawing Nulani had captioned it with two exclamation marks. What did *that* mean?

'I told you, Sir, the girl understands her family better than you. She is probably laughing at her uncle right now. You must not worry so much. She'll be able to take care of herself. And

29

tomorrow she will be back, you'll see,' he added, cheerfully, for he could see that Theo was less worried now. 'I'll squeeze some limes and make a redfish curry. Tomorrow.'

'I would have liked children, Sugi,' Theo said later on, calmer now than he had been for days.

Sugi nodded, serious. 'Children are a blessing, Sir, but they are endless trouble as well. In this country we seem to have children only to carry on our suffering. In this country it's only one endless cycle of pain for us. Some terrible curse has fallen on us since we became greedy.'

Startled, Theo looked sharply at him. He had forgotten the slow and inevitable philosophy of his countrymen. But before he could speak, Sugi put his hand out to silence him. The moon had retreated behind a cloud and a slight breeze moved the leaves. It reminded Theo of other balmy nights long ago with Anna, spent in the fishing ports along the South of France. Something rustled in the undergrowth; Sugi disappeared silently along the side of the house. Thinking he heard the gate creak Theo stood up. A moment later there was a muffled grunt, the sound of a scuffle and Sugi reappeared, emerging through the bushes, pushing a boy of about fourteen in front of him. He had twisted the boy's arm behind his back and was gripping him hard. In the light of the returning moon a knife glinted in his hand.

'He was trying to break in, Sir, from the back. With this,' he added grimly.

And he held up the knife. He pushed the boy roughly towards Theo, speaking to him in Singhalese.

'He says he was only doing what he was told.'

'What were you trying to steal?' Theo asked him, also in Singhalese.

But the boy would not reply. In another moment, with a swift jerk of his elbow he broke free and vaulted over the garden wall, vanishing into the night. And although they ran out into the darkened road there was no sign of him anywhere. Sugi began bolting the windows and checking the side of the house, shining a torch on the dense mass of vegetation.

'Tomorrow,' he said, shaking his head, looking worried, 'I will cut some of it back.'

Tomorrow he would rig up a garden light to surprise any further intruders. The boy was probably just a petty thief, stealing things to sell in order to buy drugs. But still, one could not be too careful. Tomorrow he would make some enquiries in the town. Meanwhile, Sir should go to bed.

After he had lit another mosquito coil and closed the net around himself, just at the point of sleep, Theo realised he had forgotten to ask Sugi who had delivered the drawing from the girl. And he thought with certainty, Sugi was probably right; the girl would reappear in the morning.

She was waiting for him the next morning in her usual spot on the veranda, drawing his lounge-backed cane chair.

'So,' he said sitting down, filling her view, smiling, 'so, welcome back!'

And he seemed to hear the faintest flutter of wings. Small banana-green parrots hopped restlessly in the trees, music floated out from the house, and the air was filled with beginnings and murmurings. Last night seemed not to have happened at all. Her uncle had just left, she said. It was Saturday; there was no school so she had escaped from home. She wanted to work on the painting. Too much time had been wasted by her uncle's visit. He had come to discuss Jim's future. The days had been filled with squabbling and the thin raised voice of her mother. Her uncle had not cared about his sister's distress. He merely wanted Jim to join the organisation he ran.

'It's something to do with the military,' Nulani said scornfully. 'I think they spy on people, for the army. My uncle said Jim is old enough and it was time for him to give up his studies. He said there's no time for studying right now, when Sri Lanka needs him.'

'What?' said Theo. 'Are you serious?'

'Yes, but Amma does not want this kind of future for her son. She is frightened, she has lost my father, she does not want to lose a son as well.'

Sooner or later, Nulani's uncle had told them, sooner or later Lucky Jim's luck would run out. Then what would he do? Better to start now, show which side of the fence he was on. Before questions were asked.

'So he was threatening your brother?' Theo asked.

'Yes, but Amma will not allow it. So they were fighting.'

Sugi brought out a dish of pawpaw. He had been preparing the table for breakfast. He covered it with an indigo cloth. Then he brought out some freshly made egg hoppers and some *seeni sambol*. And a small jug of boiled milk with the tea. A band of sunlight had escaped from the roof and bent across the table, stretching across the floor. Theo went inside to turn the record over.

'And you? What did your uncle have to say to you,' he asked, coming back.

Nulani pulled a face, laughing up at him. 'I dropped two dishes yesterday,' she said. 'I was in a hurry. I thought if I cleared up quickly I might be able to come here. But then I dropped the dishes and Amma shouted at me. So I couldn't escape.'

'What happened then? Were you punished or something?' It all sounded ludicrous.

Nulani shrugged. 'No. Amma just said, "What's wrong with the girl?" and that started my uncle off again, only this time

he began to shout at *me*. He said I hadn't been trained properly and I needed a husband!'

'What?' asked Theo in alarm.

'Oh, he's full of talk,' Nulani said dismissively. 'He can't do
anything. And I just ignore him anyway. He told Amma he
would find someone suitable for me to marry, but Amma was
too angry about what he had said to Jim to worry about me.'

The sky seemed cloudless and suddenly overbright.

'I don't have to do what he tells me,' said Nulani. 'My father
hated him.'

But her father could no longer help her, Theo thought
uneasily. Thinking also, in spite of this new threat from the
uncle, how glad he was she was here now, and how empty the
days had been while she had stayed away, wondering too, what
he might do that would be of any help to her. Wondering if
the chasm of age and life and experience left room for giving
her anything on his part.

'I haven't seen you for five days,' she said, suddenly, and in
that moment, it seemed to Theo, the sky had changed and was
now the timeless blue of the tea-country lakes.

'But I have been drawing you from memory. Look, they're
nearly perfect,' she told him, moving her chair closer and
handing him her book. Once again images rose from the pages,
tossed carelessly out, those aspects of himself that he barely
intuited. There he was smiling, pensive, staring owlishly into
the distance, cleaning his glasses. Oh Christ, he thought, Christ!
What was this? He looked at the drawings helplessly, feeling
his heart contract painfully. Lighting his pipe he drank his tea
in silence. Then he stood up and held the door of her new
studio open, smiling down at her.

'Work,' he said firmly, wanting for some aching, unaccountable reason to touch her long dark hair.

What remained of the morning was spent in this way. Nulani worked on the two canvases that would eventually be the portraits of Theo. The smell of her colours, mixed with the turpentine, filling the house. Outside a monkey screamed and screamed again. The heat draped itself like a heavy leaded curtain across the veranda. They would have to take their lunch indoors. Somewhere in the kitchen Sugi was scraping coconuts. Theo had so far written two sentences towards his new book. The image of the girl wove into his thoughts; it ran with the sound of the piano music from the record, it merged confusingly with the heat outside. Why had he ever imagined he could work in this place? I need the cold, he thought, restlessness stirring in him. He thought of the muffled noise of traffic rising up towards the tops of the plane trees in Kensington. A memory of his wide airy flat returned to him with the mirrors and the pale duck-egg walls, broken by patches of Kandyan red and orange cloth. Once he had been able to work among all that elegance, once he had had another life. Perhaps, thought Theo, perhaps I have no more to say; perhaps this latest book is doomed? Perhaps the sun has sapped my inspiration?

But then he went to get the girl, for the lunch was ready, and he saw the light flickering against the walls of the room where she worked. Her small face was smudged with paint, and it struck him forcefully that no, his book was not doomed at all. For the early-afternoon sun seemed to turn and pivot on a new axis of optimism. Sugi too seemed to have excelled himself with the lunch. All he said was that the market had been good as he set the jug of lime juice down and brought in the curries; *murunga*, bitter-gourd, *brinjal*, fish and boiled rice. He was smiling broadly and his previous disapproval of the girl seemed to have evaporated. Nulani, unaware of any difference, chattered happily with him as he brought in the food. But he would not stay while they ate, shyly asking instead if he might take a look at the painting of Sir.

'Yes, yes,' the girl said delighted. 'But Mr Samarajeeva must not see it yet.'

'Will you stop calling me that!' Theo laughed. 'Come back and tell me what you think.'

But Sugi could not be persuaded. He had work to do, he said. He was going to put barbed wire over the back-garden wall, whether Sir liked it or not.

So that it wasn't until much later, when they were alone and he smoked his cigarette on the veranda with Theo, that he said, 'She is very talented, Sir.'

They sat for a moment in companiable silence.

'And she has become too attached to you,' Sugi said.

All afternoon he had been working on the garden. The heat had eased off slightly, and then the girl, having cleared up her paints, had gone home. Huge tropical stars appeared between the leaves of the plantain trees. The garden was as secure as it was possible to make it, he told Theo. It had not been easy to get barbed wire; in the end, hoping no one had seen him, Sugi had picked up what had been lying around the beach. He was still worried about the boy from the night before, he told Theo.

'You worry too much,' said Theo, smiling at him. His affection felt clumsy. Again he recognised his own inability to speak of the growing bond between them.

He is like a brother to me, he thought with amazement. If I believed in it, I would say we had known one another in a previous life. It occurred to him that he would like to give Sugi something to mark his feelings, some tangible thing, a talisman for the future that was nothing to do with payments or employment. But he did not know how, or even what. And then, once more, he found himself thinking of the girl and her extraordinary quiet ability to make sense of all she saw, with delicate pencil lines overlaying more lines. The evening, and the night ahead, seemed suddenly interminably long until the morning. He hoped she had reached her home safely. He worried that she let neither Sugi nor him walk her back. He worried that her uncle was waiting for her. What on earth is *wrong* with me, he muttered, half exasperated, half amused at himself. I'm acting like her mother. And then he thought, Am I simply being sentimental? Perhaps this is what middle age is about. As he lit the mosquito coil, before he got under the net, he remembered again that he had forgotten to ask Sugi who had delivered Nulani's drawing the night before.

One morning, some weeks later, Theo decided to visit the temple on the hill. The girl had told him it was very beautiful.

'You should go,' she had said. 'We held my father's funeral there.'

He had sensed she wanted him to go for this reason and he thought of the irony of it. Burning the man who had already been burned. Mrs Mendis was leaving the temple as he entered. He heard her calling him and looked around for an escape but there was none.

'I have brought an offering for my son,' she said. 'He sits his scholarship exam this morning. I think his karma is good but I want to be sure he passes. I don't want him to join the army. I don't want him to die like my husband,' she said, talking too loudly.

Theo looked at the woman with dislike. She had not mentioned her daughter once. Inside the temple it was cool and dark, and further back, out of sight, the monks sat in rows, their chants rising and falling in slow, low folds. The air was crowded with sounds, like the hum of hundreds of invisible birds. It reminded him of his childhood, of his mother. He had not been in a temple for many years. He stood in the coolness, thinking of Mr Mendis, wondering what he might have been like. And then he thought of the girl, wishing he had known her as a small child. Thinking how fleeting glimpses of that lost time often emerged in her mischievous laugh. Certain, too, that her father would always remain within her, however long she lived.

That afternoon, Nulani talked about her brother's probable departure.

'I think he will be happier in England,' she told Theo. 'And maybe he will come back to see us when the trouble is over.'

By now she was working on the larger portrait. She wanted it to be a surprise, she said. But she was less happy, he saw. Something was ebbing out of her, some vitality moved away leaving her drawn and hurt. Watching this, Theo felt unaccountably depressed.

'That boy will never come back,' Sugi said quietly, when he heard. 'He only thinks about himself. Once he leaves he will forget about them.'

Sugi watched Theo. Although he said very little he knew all the signs were there. If he is not careful, he worried, Sir will get hurt. Why doesn't he see this? Why, after all he has been through, is he not more careful? He's a clever man, but . . . And Sugi shook his head.

'Maybe,' Theo said, 'things will be easier for her when Jim goes. Maybe the mother will care more.'

'The Mendis woman has only ever cared about the son, I tell you, Sir,' Sugi said. 'I know all about her. After the father was murdered, she used to talk to my friend who works in Sumaner House. And it was always the boy she worried about. Lucky Jim! That's her name for him. She hardly notices her daughter.'

They were sitting on the veranda once again. It was late and the heat had finally moved a little distance away. Most nights now Theo listened to the menace of the garden, the rustlings and unknown creepings that scratched against the trees. He was hardly aware of doing so, but since the intruder, both he and Sugi were watchful.

'And her father?' he asked. 'What was he like?'

'People used to watch them,' Sugi remembered. 'Mr Mendis used to walk with his daughter every evening, up and down the beach. They used to say you could set your clocks watching those two. They always walked at five o'clock, every day, except when the monsoons came. He used to hold her hand. She was devoted to him.' Sugi's eyes moved restlessly across the garden. 'It must have been terrible for her after he died. She must have felt so alone.'

They were both silent. Then Sugi went off for his nightly surveillance of the perimeter walls and gate, testing his barbed wire, wandering silently through the undergrowth. When he was satisfied that everything was in order, he came back and accepted a beer.

'She needs to go from this place,' he continued. 'There is nothing here for her. Her uncle is a very unpleasant man. And, Sir, I know I've said it before, but you should be careful with this family. The girl is good but you are a stranger to these parts. Please don't forget this.'

The night, once again, was quiet. There were no sounds of gunshots or sirens. Nor were there street lights here, for it was too far away from the other houses. The scent of blossom drifted in waves towards them. Occasionally the plaintive, lonely hoot of a train could be heard in the distance, but that was all.

'You can't change anything,' said Sugi. He sounded sad. 'You are right, things will take longer than we expect. Life is just a continuous cycle. Eventually, of course, at the right time there will be change. But however hard we try to alter things ourselves, what must be will be. Who knows how long it will take, Sir. Sri Lanka is an ancient island. It cannot be hurried.'

Theo watched the headlights of a car disappeared from view. The yellow beam stretched through the trees, bending with the road, piercing the darkness, searching the night. Then it was gone. It occurred to him there had been no car along that particular stretch of road for weeks.

Someone had thrown a plucked chicken over the wall into the garden. They had tossed it over, cleverly missing the barbed wire. It was trussed; legs together, smeared with yellowish powder, a thin red thread wound tightly round its neck. Even though death had come swiftly, leaving traces of blood, staring at it Theo imagined the frenzy of anger that had brought it to this state. A whole pageant of slaughter lay here, he thought, in this one small carcass. Mesmerised, he gazed at a half-remembered history, of sacrifice both ancient and bloodied. The turmeric had given the chicken's skin the appearance of a threadbare carpet. He touched the bird with his foot; it was so long since he had seen something like this he had almost forgotten what it was meant for. And as he stood gazing at it, he remembered, in a rush of forgotten irritation, the reasons he had never made this country his home. Impatiently, for the waste of energy angered him, he kicked the chicken across the garden, and in doing so crossed a hidden boundary. For in that moment, it seemed to the horrified Sugi looking on, he did what no man should ever do: he tampered with those laws that could not be argued with.

'Don't touch it, Sir, for God's sake,' implored Sugi, but he was too late. The deed was done.

'Don't touch it, Sir, please. I will see to it. Someone is trying to put a curse on this place.'

Theo grinned. He has been away too long, thought Sugi, distressed. He questioned, instead of accepting. Twenty-odd years living away had made Theo forget. He was trying to single-handedly alter the inner structure of life. And seeing this, Sugi was frightened. His fear clung to the barbed wire that was pressed against the garden wall. Fear had been stalking Sugi daily for years.

'This town is not as it used to be,' he said. 'We used to know everyone who lived here. We knew their fathers and their grand-fathers too. We knew all the relatives, Sir. Many people have moved into this area, thinking it is safer here. But the trouble is, this has made it *less* safe. There are thugs in the pay of the authority, and there are thugs working for those who would like to be rid of the authority. Singhalese, Tamils, what does it matter who they are, everyone spies on everyone else.' A nation's hatred has split open, he said, like two halves of a coconut. 'People are angry, Sir. They can barely hide it.'

Theo was silenced. Other people's jealousies spilled out around him, dismembered bodies, here and there they scat-tered randomly, saffron yellow and cochineal. He could say nothing in the face of Sugi's certainty. He did not want to hurt his feelings. Only the girl, arriving soon afterwards, expressed contempt. The dead chicken did not bother her, she said; she had seen so many before. Her father, she told Theo, had laughed at such nonsense. Her father had been full of peace, she told him. He did not believe violence answered anything, and so Nulani Mendis believed this too. She drank the lime juice Sugi had made for her and it was she who tried to reassure him. She was wearing her faded green skirt wrapped even more tightly around her slender waist and her skin appeared flawless through the thin cotton blouse. Sunlight fell in straight sheets behind her, darkening her hair, shadowing her face, making it difficult to read her expression. For a moment she seemed no longer a child. Had she changed since yesterday? puzzled Theo.

When she finished working on her painting she discarded her overall. There were still some slivers of paint in her finger-nails. Today they were of a different colour. However hard she scrubbed her hands there was still some paint left, thought Theo amused. The day righted itself. The soft smell of colour still clung to her and seemed to Theo sweeter than all the scent of the frangipani blossoms. The picture was nearly finished, she told him, and she wanted to do another one. She needed one more sketch of him. Would Theo be able to sit still, please? He hid his amusement, noticing she had become a little bossy. Her notebook of drawings had grown and she wanted to use them in one more painting. She wanted to paint Theo in his dining room with its foxed mirrors, its beautiful water glasses, its jugs. She wanted to paint him surrounded by mirror-reflected light. Light that moved, she said. This was what interested her, not the trussed chicken. And no, she did not want him to sneak a look at the portrait, she added, laughing at him.

'You can see it soon,' she promised, as though *he* was the child. 'When it's finished.'

For now, she told Theo, he could look at her sketchbook instead. Once again she gave him the fragmented stories she had collected. And again they fell from the pages in a jumble of images.

'Look,' she said laughing, 'my uncle!'

She stood too close, confusing him, making him want to touch her hair. Their conversations were a running stitch across her notebook, holding together all that he could not say.

'There's no one at home,' she volunteered. 'Jim has gone to Colombo with his teacher and Amma is visiting a friend. So I'm all on my own.'

She did not say it, but it was clear she was free to do what she pleased. How can I encourage her to defy her mother in this way? wondered Theo.

'Jim has to get all the documents he needs to leave.' Her brother's departure was never far from her thoughts.

'Doesn't he want to wait?' asked Theo. 'Doesn't he want to be sure he has passed the exam first?'

But, Nulani told him, Jim was certain. His teacher too believed he would pass the examination and be awarded the British Council scholarship. Such certainty, thought Theo, raising an eyebrow. He said nothing, watching as the thought of Jim's certain departure darted and fluttered across her face.

'He wants to leave Sri Lanka by October,' Nulani said. She dared not think what that would mean for her.

For the moment, though, with the absence of her family, something, some unspecified tension seemed to ease up. She would stay late and the mornings were fresh and unhampered by the heat. The days stretched deliciously before them, slipping into an invisible rhythm of its own. By now Theo had become used to her presence, and he worked steadily on his manuscript, distracted only occasionally. Perhaps, he thought, Anna had been right. She had always insisted they needed a child to give purpose to their lives. A child was an anchor. It brought with it the kind of love that settles one, she used to say. When she had died Theo had remembered this, thinking, too, how useless a child would have been when all he wanted had been her. Now he wondered if Anna, wise, lovely Anna, had been right after all.

3

THERE WERE FLEETS OF ENORMOUS ORANGE MOTHS in Sumaner House where Vikram lived. Moths and antique dust that piled up in small hills behind the coloured-glass doors. The beetles had drilled holes in the fretwork of the frames and sawdust had gathered in small mounds on the ground. It was a useless house really, everything was broken or badly mended, everything was covered in fine sea sand, caked in old sweat and unhappiness. Objectively, it might have made a better relic than a house, but relics were plentiful and houses of this size not easily found. The fact was Sumaner House was huge. Once it must have been splendid. Once, rich Dutch people would have lived in it and crossed the Indian Ocean in big sailing ships, carrying spices and ivory and gold back to their home. Once, too, the filigree shutters, and the newly built verandas, and the black-and-white-tiled floors must have looked splendid. The green glass skylight would have filtered the sun down into the dark interior. But what was the use? Time had passed with steady inevitability, washing away the details of all that had gone before, leaving only small traces of glory. Now the furniture was scratched and full of decay. These days only Vikram and his guardian and the servant woman lived here. Most of the time it was only Vikram and the servant woman who were in the house. She stayed in her quarters, cooking or cleaning, and Vikram came and went as he pleased. There was no one to stop him. No one to ask him questions or argue with him, for Mr Gunadeen, his guardian, was hardly ever present. He was in Malaysia. Why he had ever wanted to be Vikram's guardian was a mystery. Perhaps he had wanted to protest against the exploitation of child soldiers. Perhaps, he had hoped, that by adopting a Waterlily House orphan he would build up good karma. No one knew, because after that one act of enigmatic charity, Vikram's guardian went off to work, first in the Middle East and then in Malaysia. Supervising telecommunications systems in other developing countries. Perhaps the war had made him restless, the people in the town said. At least by adopting Vikram he had done something to counteract the work of those murderous Tamil bastards. For, it was said, he was a good Singhala man.

Having picked Vikram more or less randomly from the Waterlily orphanage, Mr Gunadeen put him in the local boys' school.

'He needs a good education,' he told the headmaster privately, without noticing the irony of his words.

The headmaster knew, but chose to forget, that in the wake of independence the Singhalese had slowly denied the Tamils any chance of a decent education. Well, things had changed and these were desperate times. The headmaster knew nothing about child soldiers or their psychological scars. He thought Vikram was an orphan without complications. He knew nothing of his soldiering past.

'I shall be gone for a few months,' Vikram's guardian had said.

'Don't worry,' said the head. 'He'll be fine. You'll notice a change in him when you return, I promise.'

Vikram's guardian paid him handsomely. Next, Mr Gunadeen instructed the servant woman, Thercy.

'You know what to do,' he said. 'The boy's a little restless, but just feed him well and make sure he goes to school. I'll be back in a few months or so.'

And then he went, giving Vikram a contact address and a phone number. He did not think things needed to be any more complicated than that. So Vikram had a home now, a new school and plenty of food. What more could an orphan boy expect? He was far away from the brutal place where they recruited underage children into the military. What more could be done? The people in the town shook their heads in disbelief. What a good man Mr Gunadeen was, they said again, hoping Vikram would be worth the effort put into him. That had been four years ago.

But Vikram seemed not to realise the significance of his good fortune. Right from the very beginning he did not appear to *care* about anything. At first, when he came to live in Sumaner House, he used to kick the walls, treating the house as though it were a person, scuffing the furniture slyly, gouging holes in the doors when no one was looking, and cracking the fine-coloured glass into as many lines as he could, without breaking it completely. Torturing the house. Only the servant woman knew what he was up to. Thercy the servant woman saw everything that went on.

Then later, as he grew into adolescence, Vikram quietened down. The servant woman noticed this too. Almost overnight Vikram became monosyllabic and secretive. Whenever Thercy looked at him she noticed how expressionless his face was. In the last four years, since the random killings here in the south,

45

the troubles had worsened. Nothing was certain any more but Thercy had learned to keep silent. Privately, she thought Vikram was disturbed. His disturbance, she was certain, lurked, waiting to pounce.

The only person the servant woman trusted in the whole town was Sugi. She knew Sugi was a good man. Often when they met at the market they would walk a little way together (not so far or so often as to attract attention) and exchange news. Thercy often talked to Sugi about the orphan from Waterlily House.

'He has everything he needs and nothing he wants,' she liked to say. 'It's his karma. To be saved from his fate in the orphanage, and given another sort of fate! But it won't work,' she added gloomily.

Sugi would listen, nodding his head worriedly. He had heard all this before. Vikram hadn't been a child soldier for long but Sugi knew: once a child soldier always a soldier. Why had Vikram's guardian tampered with the unwritten laws of the universe? What had happened to him was unimaginable and because of this he should have been left alone, in Sugi's opinion. Thercy had told Sugi the whole sorry story many times and each time Sugi had been convinced, Vikram should not have been brought here. The army entered Vikram's home in Batticaloa and raped his mother and his sister. They raped them many, many times, Thercy had said, beating the palm of her hand against her forehead as she talked.

'Then they took them away,' she had said. 'The army never thought to look under the bed. Vikram was hiding there. His father was away at the time. Someone went to find the poor man, bring him the news. They told him, his whole family had been wiped out.' Thercy had sliced the air with her hand. 'Just like that,' she had said. 'Gone! What could the man do? His

46

grief must have been a terrible thing. He found some poison and, God forgive him, he swallowed it. It was only afterwards, when it was too late, that the people in the village thought of looking under the bed.'

She shook her head recalling the story. Sugi had heard it many times. Each time he was shocked. So much for our wonderful army, he thought each time.

'So much for our wonderful army,' he said again today, when they talked. 'What d'you expect?'

'We'd better go,' Thercy said, noticing how long they had been standing together and suddenly becoming nervous. 'There he is, over there. I don't want him to see us talking together.'

'Who's that man he's with?' asked Sugi, looking at Vikram, stealthily.

The boy was standing with an older man at the *kade*, the roadside shop. They were both drinking. Sugi had heard other rumours about Vikram. After his parents had died the Tigers were supposed to have got hold of him. But then, as luck would have it, the Singhalese army rounded up some of the Tiger cubs and handed them over to the orphanages a few months later. Vikram was one of them. He was only seven. He had already been carrying equipment for the guerrillas. Sugi could hardly believe that. A boy of seven, being a runner for the Tigers.

'And what would all that have done to him?' asked Sugi, watching Vikram now.

How could his past be changed? How could he be given new thoughts simply by being adopted? Thercy agreed.

'Aiyo!' she said, remembering. 'You should have seen him when he first came here. Mr Gunadeen wasn't around of course. He just went off and left me with the boy. I had to deal with everything all alone. Vikram used to run riot in the house. He's calmed down a lot now. In fact . . .' She paused.

'What?' asked Sugi.

'Well . . .'

Thercy hesitated. The truth was, there was a kind of emptiness to the boy. He seemed such a strange, mysterious creature, silent and friendless. Well, almost. Today she had some new information for Sugi.

'You know he's made friends with the Mendis girl?'

'What?' cried Sugi in alarm.

Thercy shook her head quickly. She hadn't wanted to alarm Sugi.

'No, no, I didn't mean to worry you. I know what you're thinking. He's not likely to visit you. And anyway the girl doesn't speak to many people either, and I only saw her talking to him once. I shouldn't have said anything.'

Sugi relaxed slightly, although he still looked distracted.

'It isn't good,' was all he said, not knowing how to express his disquiet. How much would Nulani Mendis tell Vikram about her visits? About Theo?

'His Singhalese is faultless, you know,' continued Thercy. 'Not many people around here realise he's a Tamil. Mr Gunadeen didn't want that to be common knowledge. For his own safety.'

'That's exactly what I mean,' said Sugi, uneasily. 'He could be working for the Tigers, couldn't he, for all we know?'

'Who, Vikram?' Thercy laughed. 'Is that what you're worrying about? No, no, Sugi, he's harmless really, I promise you. In that way, anyway. He's just a little strange, that's all. I can't explain it . . .' Again she hesitated. 'And he has a temper. To tell you the truth, of late I feel *sorry* for him. What chance is there for him to ever have a normal life?' she said, adding, 'He's so disturbed.'

Vikram had no idea that people were talking about him. Even had he known he would not have cared much, for Vikram lived in a world without people. The space inside his head was so empty that it almost echoed. Long ago, when he was at Waterlily House, he had begun to cultivate indifference. Nobody knew of course, but indifference had become a way of life for him. By the time he was twelve, before his guardian had arrived on the scene, he had learned not to make a fuss. What was the point? He could manage his life with ease without noise or fuss. He did whatever random thing he wanted, took what he liked the look of, unrestrained by anyone, neglected and unloved. By the time he reached the age of sixteen, he had grown enormously, was not bad-looking and was more or less friendless.

Sumaner House stood on the crest of a rise away from the immediate town; there were no other houses nearby. The view of the sea was uninterrupted. Vikram had his own room in the house. For nearly four years he had lived like this. He went to school and worked hard. For four years, while his guardian dipped in and out of his life, he studied. He soaked up knowledge like a sponge. The head was pleased. He wrote to Mr Gunadeen.

'*It's been a success,*' he wrote. '*And, it proves these children can be rehabilitated,*' he added triumphantly.

So Vikram was a success story. He was good at English and his Singhalese was brilliant.

'He writes beautifully too,' his teachers said.

In this way they continued to encourage Vikram. For, as everyone knew, whichever way you looked at it, the boy had had a bad start to life.

Every morning Vikram walked to school. It was the same school that Jim Mendis attended. It was generally expected that Lucky Jim, in spite of having no father, would one day go to the UK because he was so clever. And so, because of his luck, and quite possibly also his loss, the boys all wanted to be Jim

Mendis's friend. All except Vikram, that is. Vikram watched the Mendis boy quietly. Nobody noticed, because he was so quiet, but Vikram watched him idly, wondering if there was a chink in Jim's luck. But it seemed Lucky Jim was luck-tight. Soon after this, Vikram began to notice Jim Mendis's sister. She too walked to school and now Vikram noticed with some surprise that she was sweetly pretty. Something about her puzzled him. Then one day, as they stood at the crossroads, she turned and smiled absent-mindedly at him. Startled, he stared at her, his uneasiness growing. And then, because he couldn't think of anything to say, he looked quickly away. His heart was pounding as though he had been running. The Mendis girl reminded him vaguely of someone else. He could not think who it might be. After that he began to hear little things about her, little bits of gossip.

People said she did not talk. And she had no friends. All she did was draw, draw, draw. Vikram began to watch her secretly and with new interest. One day he saw her go over to the road island on the Old Tissa Road. He saw her touch the ground, rubbing her hand slowly in the dust. And then she looked up and down the road. Vikram hid behind a tree. What on earth was she doing? he wondered curiously. Again the girl reminded him of someone but he could not be sure whom. He felt an unaccountable fear bubble up in him. He did not see her again for a long while after that. He was busy doing other things. Having discovered furtive sex with the daughter of a local shop-keeper, he was often occupied. The shopkeeper's daughter had not wanted his advances, but Vikram had told her calmly, he would kill her if she told anyone. He had only meant it as a joke but she took him at his word. Pleased with his success, he took her to the back of the garages, close by the railway line. After a while she stopped struggling and accepted the inevitable, crying silently and allowing him to do whatever he wanted. Once, he brought her to Sumaner House, but the servant woman had stared meaningfully at him and although he behaved as though he did not care, the woman's look had put him off. He took the girl back to the garages after that.

Then, as Vikram approached his sixteenth birthday, he met Gerard.

Gerard was not his real name, he was really Rajah Buka, but no one knew this. He owned a gem store in the high street, and although there was an intermittent war on, he did good business with the foreigners who occasionally passed through. Gerard had seen Vikram on several occasions, loitering at the junction buying cheap alcohol. He had struck up a conversation with the boy. He appeared interested in everything Vikram had to say. How well he was doing at school, whether he had any friends. He found out that Vikram talked to no one, and so he invited Vikram to his rooms above the shop and he gave him some *vadi*, a special Tamil sweetmeat. Vikram was pleasantly surprised.

'Where did you get this from?' he asked.

Gerard laughed and gave him a Jaffna mango by way of answer. Vikram was amazed.

'How did you get to Jaffna?' he asked. 'Isn't it impossible to cross Elephant Pass because of the army blocks?'

'Nothing is impossible,' said Gerard meaningfully.

He paused and lit a cigarette.

'How do you feel about being adopted by a Singhala?' he asked casually. 'They killed your family, I heard. And they hate the Tamils, don't they?'

Gerard flicked ash on the floor and waited.

'How d'you feel about that?'

Vikram said nothing. He had been told by his guardian never

to mention the fact he was Tamil. So how did Gerard know? Gerard watched the boy's face and he laughed, finding it hugely funny.

'Don't you want to avenge your family, then?' he asked softly, easily.

Still Vikram said nothing. He felt as though a large cloven-hoofed animal had clambered on his back. The feeling sent a small shiver running up and down his spine. He felt as though his back might break under the strain. The palms of his hands became moist. An image of a young girl pounding spices flashed past him. Gerard smoked his cigarette and continued watching the boy with interest. There was the faintest hint of a smile on his face. When he had finished his cigarette, he went over to a desk and took out a key.

'Come,' he said. 'I want to show you something. Don't worry,' he added, seeing Vikram's wary look. 'We're on the same side.'

Gerard knew he had been right all along. He had told them many times at headquarters, the advantage of boys like Vikram were that they were halfway to being recruited already. Lupus, of course, had been sceptical. He was sceptical of everything Gerard proposed. Naturally he saw Gerard as a threat. Naturally anyone with independent thoughts worried Lupus. Which was precisely why Gerard did not want to operate from the north. There were terrorists and terrorists, Gerard knew. Not all of them were bright. Not all of them had had the kind of university education that Gerard had, or his never-ending passion and capacity for rhetoric. Not everyone had his vision, he decided regretfully. Having declared war on the Singhalese government, Lupus and his guerrilla organisation wanted a separate Tamil state. But they have no plan, thought Gerard, inclined to laugh, no strategy. Except to blow up as many people, and make as many enemies as possible in the international community. No diplomatic skills, sneered Gerard, whose own plans were far more ambitious. His plan was about *unity*. Of course he *wanted* a different government, what Tamil didn't. But the difference was that Gerard wanted the new government to be central, not separate. And he wanted the Singhalese *out*! He wanted a single, powerful Tamil government for the entire island. *He* wanted majority rule for the minority. Actually, what he really wanted was to be Prime Minister! But first things first, thought Gerard. He was a patient man and he was prepared to wait. There was a little groundwork to be completed, a government to be destabilised. It was work that needed a certain amount of brute force. Which was where the likes of Lupus came in, Gerard believed.

Long ago, when he had been on one of his recruiting visits to Waterlily House, Gerard had noticed Vikram. The boy had been small then, traumatised, but bright. On his next visit to the orphanage he had seen Vikram's guardian-to-be. And that was when he had laid his plan. For as he had noticed instantly, most of the spadework had already been done for Gerard on that memorable afternoon when the Palmyra toddy was on the kitchen table and the red dhal was in the clay pot. Later he heard about the day that Vikram had played hide-and-survive while the sunlight mingled with the screams of his mother and his big sister. The day the sky had boiled and the light had fallen, harsh and green and terrible, down through the rattan roof, and Vikram's sister prepared an offering of pawpaw and king coconut washed with saffron water. On the fateful day when his sister had never made it to the temple, what had to happen, happened. So now, guessing correctly, fully understanding, Gerard earmarked Vikram for greater things. He knew he had picked a winner. Backed by Gerard, Vikram would go far.

Gerard unlocked the drawer and watched Vikram's face.

'Well,' he said very gently. 'Don't tell me you're scared? Don't tell me you won't avenge your family, given a chance?'

'Will you teach me to use it?' asked Vikram, startled from his usual reverie, staring at the gun.

'Patience, patience,' Gerard laughed, closing the drawer, amused by Vikram's sudden interest, preferring it to the boy's usual indifference.

'All things come to those who wait. You must learn to clean it first.'

It was the best way to start; it would keep Vikram's interest alive. Cleanliness was next to godliness, he told the boy, and God was the gun. Vikram liked the idea of the power of God. He liked the mantras Gerard was always reciting. For a moment he felt as though he had a purpose in life. Most of the time the empty, shut-down feeling in his head made him lethargic. But now, for the first time in ages, he felt a stirring within him. A new energy. Avenge your family, Gerard had said. Vikram looked at him and thought, Gerard likes me. The notion was oddly pleasing.

One morning soon after all this happened, having decided he had no need for school, Vikram was on his way to Gerard's gem store when he saw the Mendis girl again. He had forgotten all about her. But she stopped and began to speak to him.

'Don't you go to school any more?' she asked.

Vikram was confused. He thought she didn't speak. And how did she know he was not at school? He stared at her.

'I'm Jim's sister, Nulani, remember?' she said, clearly thinking he did not recognise her. 'You live at Sumaner House, don't you?'

Vikram nodded. Nulani Mendis fumbled in her satchel. She took out a small battered notebook.

'Look,' she said, showing him a drawing.

She was laughing. He could see her teeth, white and very even. Vikram took the book reluctantly. Then, in spite of himself, he too grinned. It was a picture of a teacher no one liked. Nulani Mendis had drawn a caricature, catching his likeness perfectly. Suddenly, Vikram felt shy. The girl was standing close to him. He could smell a faint perfume.

'You're good,' he ventured at last, hesitantly.

For some reason she scared him. There was an air of determination, a certainty about her that confused him. He felt as though she might ask him for something he could not give. He saw she was still smiling at him and again he felt an urge to run away. Then he noticed that close up she was even prettier than she had appeared from a distance. Tongue-tied, he continued to stare at her, hardly aware she was still speaking.

'Has your brother gone to the UK?' he asked finally, with some difficulty, not understanding and wanting to distract her.

The girl shook her head. 'Not yet,' she said.

She smiled again, but this time it was she who hesitated. Then she seemed to withdraw slightly. He thought she appeared older than he remembered, and he saw her eyes were very dark and deep and sad. They seemed full of other puzzling and unnamed things. He stared at her for a moment longer and nodded. Then, making up his mind, he loped off.

That afternoon, after he had finished his target practice with the silencer on the gun, Gerard told Vikram he had something important to say.

'First,' he said, 'well done!' He took the gun from Vikram. 'Congratulations! You've worked hard and as a reward I shall take you on a little operation with me at the end of the month. If you do well at that, there will be bigger and more interesting assignments ahead, OK? And then, in a few months' time you will go to the Eastern province for something extremely important.'

'What?' asked Vikram. 'The Eastern province? Isn't that where the Tigers are trained?'

'Vikram,' said Gerard, 'you must learn not to ask too many questions. You'll be told everything. But, all in good time. Don't ask questions. You aren't going to be an ordinary member of the Tigers, believe me. *You* are both intelligent and a good shot. So now you're going to be trained for something top class. Trust me, men.'

'When?' demanded Vikram.

'Patience, patience,' said Gerard, holding up his hands mockingly, shaking his head. 'Patience is what's required now. We've both waited a long time to prepare you for this. Don't ruin things. I promise you the time is coming when you *will* avenge your family. I fully understand how you must feel. Just wait a little longer. And for heaven's sake, Vikram,' he added, 'do me a favour. Go back to school for your exams. You don't want to attract any notice at this stage. If the Mendis girl knows you're absent, then others will too.'

Vikram picked up the gun and held it below his crotch. He stroked the tip of the barrel. He laughed, a high-pitched out-of-control scurrilous screech.

'That's enough,' said Gerard sharply. 'Put it down. It's not a toy. You can have all the things you want if you show restraint. You've been earmarked for great things. Now, go back to school.'

Gerard was aware that underneath his silent exterior Vikram was coiled like a spring. He knew whatever simmered in Vikram was dangerously near the surface. And that it was best to keep a tight control over him. Just in case.

A few days after his exams, Vikram saw the Mendis girl once more. She did not see him. She was hurrying in the direction of the beach. Interested, he decided to follow her. He watched her body move darkly beneath the lime-green skirt, in the sunlight. Her hair was tied up and it swung to and fro as she walked. Where is she going? Vikram wondered curiously.

The road went nowhere in particular. In fact, it was not possible to reach the beach this way without scrambling over the giant cacti. Then the road curved, and suddenly it was possible to see the sea. The beach was completely empty and scorched. Just before the road came to an end, there appeared a long, low house, surrounded by a flower-laden wall and flanked by two stone lions. The top of the wall was covered in barbed wire. Vikram remembered now. It was the house where the UK-returned writer lived. He had seen the man once when he had come to the school. The teachers had shaken their heads, saying he was a Singhalese who was pro the wretched Tamils. What kind of a Singhalese was he? they asked. Still, they had said, he was famous. Misguided, but famous. So they had invited him because of that.

A large jackfruit tree overhung Theo Samarajeeva's garden wall. Its leaves were thick and succulent, and the girl, stopping outside the gate, began to draw in her notebook. She had no idea she was being followed. Nor did she seem to notice there was no shade. Nulani Mendis sat on the withered grass verge absorbed in her drawing, as the low hum of mosquitoes and the drowsy buzz of other, more benign, insects slowed to a halt in the baking air. Across the sun-drenched garden Vikram could just make out the writer, in his pale linen trousers and his white shirt, working at a table on the veranda. The veranda had been bleached white by the sun and appeared dusty in the dazzling light. Then the manservant came out to fetch the girl in for lunch, and shut the gate. And that was all Vikram saw of any of them that day.

* * *

Nulani had almost finished the portrait. In a week she would be ready to show both Theo and Sugi.

'I will cook *kiribath*, some milk rice,' Sugi said. 'And buy the best fish.'

'I shall decide where it must be hung!' said Theo.

An air of gaiety descended. Sugi replaced the lanterns in the trees. And Theo declared the day of the unveiling a holiday from his writing. His work was progressing slowly. In October the film of his second book would be out. He would have to go to London for the premiere.

'For how long will you be gone?' asked Nulani, her eyes suddenly anxious. 'Will they let you come back?'

Her hair was coiled against the back of her neck and a frangipani blossom quivered just above her ear. Theo watched it shake as she moved her head, wondering when it would fall. Once, he nearly put his hand out to catch it. How could he explain to her that no one could stop him coming home? When had he started to call this place home again?

His agent had rung him complaining. It was impossible to get a call through to him, did he know that? The lines were always down. How could he live in a place with no access to the outside world, where the lines were always down? The agent hoped he was working. Through the crackle on the line the agent sounded like a peevish nanny. The summer in London, he told Theo, was disappointing. Wet, cold and miserable. The only consolation, he supposed, was that the telephones worked!

Because the curfew was not in operation just now Theo walked openly on the beach. The sand, ivory and unblemished, seemed to stretch for ever, smooth and interrupted only by his footsteps. One evening Nulani went with him. She had told her mother she was working late on the painting. They walked the wide sweep of beach without seeing anyone, with only the slight breeze and the waves for company. It felt as though they had walked this same beach for an eternity. She walked close to him, like a child, her hand brushing against his arm. He felt her skin, warm against him. He had an urge to take her hand and cradle it in his two hands. He knew she was worrying and he wanted to tell her to stop. But he felt helplessly that he had no right to intrude.

'I feel as if I have known you for ever,' the girl said suddenly. 'D'you think we knew each other in our last birth?'

He swallowed. Her eyes were large and clear. They seemed to mirror the sky. Looking at her he could not think of a single thing to say. Twenty-eight years between them and still he was lost for words, he thought, amazed. They walked the length of the beach and he watched the frangipani in her hair, marvelling that it did not fall; half hoping it would, so that he might catch it.

4

'WHEN CAN I SEE WHAT YOU'VE DONE?' asked Theo impatiently. He sat squinting at the sun. His white shirt was crumpled and the light cast purple shadows against the creases of the cloth.

The girl smiled. 'What if you don't like the painting?' she asked, teasingly. 'What if the money you are paying my mother is wasted?'

'I will love it,' he said, certain. 'No question. I can't wait. Don't forget, I saw it when you began. And another thing, while I remember, I want the money to be kept for your work only. Should I tell your mother that?'

She laughed. What did she need the money for? She had wanted only to paint him. It will soon be October, thought Theo. The rains would come then, he knew. When they broke he would be in London. He did not tell her but he no longer wanted to go. The film had no significance for him. It was all part of another life. A life he seemed to have discarded with alarming ease. Living among his own people, here in this amorphous heat, seeing the mysterious and uneasy ways in which one day flowed into another, he felt as though he had never left.

The girl was sitting close to him on the veranda, staring dreamily at the garden. She was so close her arm brushed against his. She had the ways of the very young, he mused. Physical closeness came naturally. He could see the shadows of her breasts, small dark smudges, rising and falling through her thin white blouse. She looked very cool and self-possessed. And she seemed happier. He realised with shock that loneliness had clung to her like fine sea dust when he had first met her. But now she's content, he thought. Now she is happier.

He wanted to think he had given her something, some comfort for the loss of her father. Even if all he did was offer her a space and encouragement to paint, surely that was better than nothing? He felt a growing certainty in his desire to help her. He felt it rise above the anxieties of this place.

'You must work here when I am in London,' he said.

An idea was forming in his mind. He did not know whether to tell her. He wanted to organise an exhibition of her paintings. But she had opened her notebook and was drawing again, her eyes half shut against the glare. Green and red splashed against him, other stories unfolded. He saw she was drawing his outstretched foot.

'You can't keep drawing me!' he said laughing, moving his foot out of sight. 'Now look, I've been thinking, I want to organise an exhibition of your paintings. I can't do that if you only draw me!'

'Where? Colombo?' Her head was bent over her notebook.

'Yes, maybe,' he said, suddenly wanting to take her to London with him in October.

Thinking, what was wrong with him that he could not bear to be parted from her? He knew nothing about art but even he could see the astonishing things that were conjured up by her hands. They were the hands of a magician. Like shadow puppets they illuminated other dimensions of the world, probing the edges of things and those corners where drifts of light revealed all that had been concealed from him until now.

'You must work hard until I get back,' he said instead, trying to look stern.

So that she threw her head back and burst out laughing. And he saw, how in spite of everything she had been through, her youth could not be contained but was mirrored in her laugh. It was low and filled with happiness. October is still a long way off, he reassured himself. I'll feel differently then.

The hot season was coming to an end and the full moon was ten days away. Twenty kilometres from the town was a sacred site where the festivities were beginning. It had been at the time of the festival that her father had been murdered, Nulani told him. Just before the water-cutting ceremony, in the build-up to *poya,* the religious festival on the night of the full moon. All across the town fear mushroomed in polluted clouds, hanging over two thousand years of faith. Fear seemed inseparable from belief. Men with bare feet walked over red-hot coals or swung themselves on metal hooks across the coconut trees. And all the while, interwoven with the sounds of drums and conch shells, the *nada* filled the air.

'You must be careful,' said Sugi. 'Not everyone is a believer. These are troubled times. And even if,' he added, 'even if they are believers, some people still have evil intent.'

Every year Sugi went to the festival. He always met his family there; he had done this for as long as he could remember. But this year he was worried about leaving Theo on his own.

'This is the time when some people try to put curses on their enemies.'

62

'Sugi, for heaven's sake, what d'you think is going to happen? No one's interested in *me*. I'll be perfectly fine.'

'But the girl won't be here either,' said Sugi worriedly.

Theo laughed. The girl was going with her mother to the festival. They were going to pray for her brother Jim. To be certain he would get the scholarship.

'Well, I thought you'd be pleased about that,' he teased, giving Sugi a sly look.

'Sir!' said Sugi reproachfully.

'Oh, Sugi, I'm only pulling your leg. I'm going to work like mad while you're away. No distractions, no chatting, you know. No stopping for tea. Just work. I shall have most of this next chapter finished by the time you both get back. You'll see.'

In the now skeleton-staffed Department of Tropical Diseases, a conference, planned two years previously, had to be cancelled because of lack of funds and resources. Many eminent scientists from all over the world, having been invited to give papers, were now told the unstable situation on the island made it impossible to guarantee the safety of their stay. It was a disappointment for all those who had worked tirelessly to eradicate the threat of an epidemic. An article appeared in a scientific journal. 'No animal on earth has touched so directly and profoundly the lives of so many human beings. For all of history and all over the globe the mosquito has been a nuisance, a pain and the angel of death.'

Deep within the jungle the festival was in progress. A god with many hands sat inside the dagoba. The monks had placed him there, hoping he would give an audience to the crowds. This happened every year; it was the highlight of the festival. People came from far and wide to pray to him. The hands of this many-handed god were empty apart from his spear. He looked neither right nor left. If he heard the prayers of the tormented he gave no sign. There were peacocks at his side and sunlight shone on his burnished anklets. Young girls brought him armfuls of offerings, walking miles in the boiling heat. Young men came carrying hope. He received each of them without a word. All day long the drumming and the sounds of elephant bells filled the air in a frenzy of noise and movement. Trumpeters and acrobats walked the roadsides while men with tridents chalked on their foreheads paid penance for ancient inexplicable sins. Elsewhere the ground was strewn with red and yellow flowers and the heavy smell of cinnamon was underfoot. There were giant mounds of sherbet-pink powders and uncut limes piled up on silver platters everywhere.

The many-handed god watched them all. He watched the backs of the women bent in devotion. Who knew what they prayed for? Was it for abundance in their wombs? Or was it simply peace for the fruits of these same wombs that they desired? The crowds came with their coins tied in cloth, with their ribbons of desires, their cotton-white grief and their food. As night approached a full moon arose across the neon sky silhouetting the dagoba, white and round, with a single spike pointing at the stars. Hundreds of coconut flames fanned an unrelenting heat.

Midnight approached and the temple drums grew louder, announcing the arrival of the Kathakali Man of Dance. The crowds gasped. With his pleated trousers and beaded breast-plates, the Kathakali Man pointed his fingers skywards. He seemed to be reaching for the stars. With ancient gesture and sandstone smile, he danced for the gaping, amazed gathering. The Kathakali Man had a many-faceted jewel that gleamed in his navel and a peacock's cry deep in his throat. His drum tattooed yet another ancient tale, telling of those things which were allowed and those which were forbidden. His was a dance of warning. History ran through his veins, giving him authority. Everyone heard him in the neon-green night but not everyone was capable of interpreting what he said. Those who ignored him did so at their peril, he warned.

Long ago, in the days before the trouble, people from England used to come to see him. They came simply because they knew they could find native colour and because, in this sacred place, even the statues smiled. They did not understand the real meaning of a sacred site. They came for rest, for healing herbs and pungent oils. And sometimes the many-handed god welcomed them, and sometimes he did not. Now that the troubles were here no one came from England. Nothing but a steady stream of hope walked through the jungle to the dagoba. Nothing but despair showed through the brave colours of the processions.

Sugi stood in the crowds watching the festival. He was waiting for his relatives. While he waited he looked around him to see if there were others he knew. He noticed Mrs Mendis. Ah, observed Sugi, she is here for her son Lucky Jim. Born with the kernel of luck that Mrs Mendis protected with the husk of her own life. No doubt she wanted the kernel to grow. She's a true believer and so she knows, true believers had a better chance. She wants nothing for herself, thought Sugi. But then, he noticed, Mrs Mendis had forgotten about her daughter. Sorrow, like too much sun, has blinded her. Mrs Mendis left her clay curd pots, her crimson flowering pineapple and her *kiribath*, milk rice, at the feet of the god. Without a doubt, thought Sugi, watching silently, the god will grant her wish. For it must surely have been decided in another life that Jim's luck could only grow. Then Sugi glanced at Nulani Mendis. The child was lost in thought. What future will *she* have? he wondered, pity flooding his heart. With a mother like this! Sugi had been watching the girl for months. He was astonished at how she had changed. When she had first come to the beach house she had been silent and unhappy. Then slowly she had begun to blossom. In the beginning, he remembered, her unhappiness had blotted out her light. But gradually she changed. Her eyes shone, she laughed. And she talked all the time. Sometimes she drove Sir mad, Sugi knew. Sometimes they would exchange looks of amusement. And recently, thought Sugi, pensive now, Sir had a different look in his eyes. But Sir himself seemed unaware of this. Only Sugi knew.

A sudden harsh sound in the trees sent a flock of iridescent blue magpies bursting into the sky as though being lifted by a gust of wind. Several people threw themselves to the ground, crying. Was this an ill omen? Sugi looked uneasily around him. There was no wind. Ancient laws were written all over this sacred site. Sugi was a man of simplicity. And he was afraid. He saw the girl ahead of him in the procession look up at the magpies. She was smiling at some secret thought of her own. Yesterday she had let Sugi look at her latest painting. It was nearly finished and was a remarkable painting, of glossy greens and quiet violets. It was full of something else as well, Sugi saw. Something Nulani Mendis had no idea of. Painting was what she had brought into this life, Sugi told himself, watching her now. It was her fate. He knew her talent would never leave her. He watched as she bent her head and prayed. He knew she was praying for her brother. And he knew there were other undiscovered longings in her heart.

The procession had brought all sorts of people out. Some of them were not the kind of people who usually went on pilgrimages.

One of the people in the crowd was Vikram. Gerard had told him about the sacred site.

'Go and see it,' he had said. 'Mingle, learn what goes on there. Watch the Buddhist monks and look out for the army check-points. You should always talk to the army. Get them used to your face. Could be useful for the future.'

And he winked at Vikram. Then he put his hand on the boy's shoulders, never noticing how he winced, not realising Vikram did not like being touched.

So Vikram went to the festival. The anniversary of the massacre of his family was approaching. Every year around this time he had nightmares. He would wake up to the sound of grinding teeth and discover they were his own. He would wake with an erection or with his sheet wet. And, always, he would wake with a skullful of anger punctured as though by knives. In the morning he was fine again, back to his usual indifferent self, with all disturbance forgotten. But for a couple of nights, close to the anniversary of the deaths, things were bad. On these occasions, Vikram heard, quite clearly, as if from a distant part of Sumaner House, his mother's muffled screams, his sister's voice crying out in Tamil. Why had they cried so much? What had they hoped to achieve? Mercy, perhaps? Had they not realised they were about to die? That no amount of crying would help them in the long dark place they had reached? From where he crouched, rigid under the bed, all Vikram had seen were their hands waving in a gesture of helplessness. The hands that had held him moments before, and had stroked his head, were now waving their goodbye. From his hiding place he could see fingers threshing and flaying the air, engaged in some ancient struggle, and in his dreams, so many years later, it was this image, of those hands forever beating the air, that he still saw. Gerard had reminded Vikram that his family needed to be avenged. They were waiting for the day, Gerard said, when, like a half-finished jigsaw, they would be made whole again.

So Vikram walked through the jungle, following the sound of the drums like everyone else. Thinking his own thoughts. On the way he passed a Coca-Cola lorry and a black Morris Minor. They were tangled and smashed together in a crash. Curious, he stopped to investigate. Bodies were tossed carelessly across the overgrown path, reddish-brown liquid frothed from under the lorry. Just looking at it made Vikram thirsty. Other people had visited the site of the crash before him. They had plundered the victims, taken their money and their jewellery. There was nothing left to take. Vikram stared. One of the bodies was that of a woman. A long deep ridge exposed the tendons and muscles across one part of her face. Bone jutted out. A fountain of blood flowed from her mouth. Her hands moved feebly like an ant on its back, clawing the air. Vikram looked at her impassively. She was beginning to bloat and her lips reminded him of the blood-swollen bellies of mosquitoes he was forever swiping. But, thought Vikram walking on, she did not look in *so* much pain. How long would it take for her to die? he wondered idly. Would she be dead by the time he had walked two dozen steps, or half a mile? Would she be dead by the time he reached the sacred site? Vikram continued on his way, following the distant noise of drums and the monkeys that swung in front of him from tree to tree. He could hear the bells of the Kathakali dancers somewhere in the distance.

He came to a reservoir. When he had been quite small, his mother had taken him back to the village where she had been born. There had been a reservoir there too. It was so large that Vikram had thought it was the sea. In those days Vikram had not yet seen the sea. There were trees all around the banks of this great stretch of water, frightening jungle vegetation, tangled and ugly. Branches and creepers trailed succulently along the forest floor. Small emerald birds flew harshly about. Vikram was three years old and he had been frightened. His aunt or his sister, he could not remember which, held him up in the water, someone else bathed him. Vikram had cried out. They told him the water was pure and clean. Later, sitting on the steps of a now forgotten house, the same girl, whoever she was, taught him to knit. Knit one, purl one.

'See,' she had said, laughing. 'Look, he has learned to knit. Baby is very clever.'

The sun had beaten down on his head as he sat on the step of the house.

'I'm thirsty,' he had said in Tamil and instantly they had brought him a green plastic cup of king coconut juice and held it while he drank thirstily.

They had called him Baby; it was the only word of English they knew and they were proud they too could speak English, even though they had not been to school. Vikram knew they had loved him. Their excited voices had encircled him, round and round, picking him up and kissing him until he laughed with pleasure. He supposed it was pleasure.

The reservoir near his mother's house was smooth and clean, and aquamarine. A mirror reflecting the sky. The one he was passing now was brown and mostly clogged with weed. There had been no rain here for a long time.

After he had prayed for his sister's family and for his mother's health, Sugi took his leave of them. He needed to get back home. His mother, who was old and frailer since he saw her last, kissed him goodbye. She was glad her son was doing so well, working for Theo Samarajeeva. A decent man, she said, a man for the Sri Lankan people, the kind of man that was desperately needed. They had heard all about his books and now there was to be a film too, about the terrible troubles in this place. It was good, she told her son, the world needed to hear about their suffering.

'But you must be careful, no?' Sugi's brother-in-law asked him privately. 'This man will make enemies too. You must advise him, he will have forgotten how it is here. He has lived in the UK. They are honourable there. And you must be careful. You too will be watched.'

Sugi knew all this. He left his red and silver offerings and his temple blossom for the many-handed god and just as he was about to leave a monk gave him a lighted lamp to carry back in. Perhaps, thought Sugi trustingly, this was a good omen.

Overhead, huge firework flowers and tropical stars filled the heavens as he rode home on his bicycle. Because it was so late, instead of taking the coast road he cut across the outskirts of the jungle. He kept close to the path; in the distance he could see the reservoir gleaming in the moonlight. He passed a largish village on his left. There were green and red lights threaded among the branches of the trees and a small *kade* was still open selling sherbet and plantains. Because of the festivities there was no curfew here, and people strolled along the street. A smell of gram and hot coconut oil drifted towards him. Children shouted, dogs barked, youths loitered. Had it not been for two army tanks and armed soldiers at either end of the village forming a makeshift checkpoint, it would have been impossible to know there was a war on. Soon Sugi was through the village and heading for home.

Night stretched across the road. The sky glowed like polished glass. He would have been back in less than twenty minutes but for the obstruction. The Coca-Cola lorry no longer frothed liquid; the corpses lay naked and silvery, bathed in moonlight.

Everything from the Morris Minor had been stripped bare. Seats, steering wheel, wing mirrors, even the windscreen wipers had gone. All that remained was the skeleton of a car. Suddenly a jeep roared round the bend of the road. Sugi, who had stopped, wheeled his bicycle quickly towards a clump of trees and hid. A soldier leapt down and took out a can. He began to pour petrol over the bodies. Another jeep skidded to a halt and then another. Camouflage soldiers spilled noisily out. Sugi froze. The soldiers poured petrol over the Morris Minor. Someone was shouting orders in Singhala. His face seemed familiar. For a moment Sugi puzzled over this. Then the smell of fuel drifted across the narrow deserted road. It was strong and metallic. In another minute there was an explosion as the Morris Minor blew up. Black smoke choked the edges of the trees. The whole jungle seemed on fire, awash with the sour smells of tamarind and eucalyptus, and something else, something rotten and deep and terrifying. Hiding behind the clump of trees, Sugi recognised the smell. It had never been far from his life since the war had worsened. He waited, knowing there was nothing he could do. He had wanted to see if anyone was, by some miracle, still alive, to raise the alarm if this was so, but he knew now it was an impossibility. The flames would burn for a long time. He felt the heat from where he stood, banking up against him, taut and terrible against his body. Sweat and fear poured down his face and mixed with his despair. There was nothing he could do now. The soldiers stood at a safe distance from the bonfire. For a while they strutted around their vehicles, laughing hollowly, slapping each other on the back. In the moonlight Sugi could see their Kalashnikovs glinting. Then, after what seemed an eternity, they piled into the jeeps and went with a screech of tyres, leaving skid marks on the road, their voices receding swiftly. All that was left were the outstretched arms of the flames, the moon as witness, and an unmarked, communal grave. Far away in the distance he could hear a faint lonely trumpeting. Somewhere, in some impenetrable corner of the jungle, an elephant was preparing to charge. Turning his bicycle towards the road Sugi began to peddle furiously, chasing the moonlight. Carrying his distress with the slapping motion of his sarong, freewheeling down the hill. Silently. Riding his bicycle, accepting his pain. The witness to all that had passed.

The festival was over and the procession had dispersed. The two-toned chanting hung loosely in the air, floating above the white dagoba and away towards the primeval jungle. The monks packed up the many-handed god as though he were a puppet. His anklets made no sound, his paper arms were crushed by the many prayers thrust in them. The monks put away his silver sword. It was time for him to rest. As always after days of observing human nature and all its eternal struggle, the monks were exhausted. Collecting up the prayer papers they packed them into a satinwood box. Then they burned some cinnamon sticks for good luck. The smoke rose thin and beautiful like a mosquito net. Fragments of temple powders and yellow saffron-stained offerings remained on the ground. Somewhere in the forest the devil-bird screeched, but most of the sacred site collapsed like a concertinaed paper lantern, returning to normal. An ordinary village in the jungle; there were so many of them. Overhead, storm clouds walked the telegraph poles, electric blue as magpie wings. As yet nothing happened but the sea currents close by the shore had changed and the fishermen, wisely, did not put out to sea. They were waiting for the storm to arrive.

* * *

From his bedroom Theo Samarajeeva had an uninterrupted glimpse of the beach. The wind had begun to die down and although the coconut palms still beat themselves in a frenzy, the sky had changed colour. It was seven o'clock in the morning and a patch of blue had begun to spread across the horizon. While Sugi and the girl had been absent Theo had worked hard on his book. They had seemed to be away for an eternity. Because he had not liked the silence or their absence, he had worked furiously. The book would be finished on time. The girl would come this morning, Theo knew. She would be here soon. Then they would have the great unveiling of the paintings. There were three paintings now. He could hardly wait.

For days after Nulani had left for the festival, the smells of linseed oil and colours had hovered around the house but then it had grown fainter. Theo, remembering once more the loss of other smells, other memories, had buried himself in his work. But then Sugi came back; he had returned late last night. Theo had waited up for him, anxiously, listening out for the squeak of his bicycle brakes and the sound of the gate. He came in and they had shared a beer, although Sugi had seemed exhausted and had not wanted to talk.

'There are many, many more thugs about now,' was all he had said when Theo asked him about the festival. 'Much more than last year. They are all men in the pay of the army. You must not drive out into the jungle.'

'Did you see anyone you knew? Did you see Nulani?'

'Yes,' Sugi had said. He had been unusually silent. 'I think I saw her uncle too.'

'What? With her?' Theo had asked, alarmed. Talk of the uncle always made him uneasy.

'No, no. I saw him on my way back. He was with other people.'

Sugi had looked strained and unhappy in the light from the veranda. There had been something worn and nervous about him, something hopeless.

'Are you all right?' Theo had asked finally, wondering if there was trouble with his family. He had been lonely without him but perhaps Sugi needed some time to himself?

'Yes. I am fine. A little tired. It was a long ride back. And I am tired with how this country has become.'

Theo had become alarmed, then. Sugi had sounded more than tired. He had sounded depressed. They finished their beer to the plaintive sounds of the geckos and the thin whine of swarming mosquitoes that inhabited the humid night. There was no doubt, a storm had been brewing and so, partly because of this and partly because Sugi clearly was not in a mood to talk, Theo had gone to bed.

Towards dawn it had begun to rain. Hot broken lines of water, clear blue shredded ribbons, curtains of rain. The view from the window was fragmented by it, changed and coloured by the water. Smells like newly opened blossoms rose up and lifted into the air. Here and there they flew, rough earth and mildew smells, caterpillar green and plantain savoury. The smells woke Theo, who dressed hurriedly, breathing in the scent of gravel and insects, of hot steam and rainy-morning breakfast. Now, sitting out on the veranda, he lit his pipe and the musty smell of pleasure joined the day. He could hear Sugi moving around making egg hoppers. The noise suggested that Sugi was happier this morning. Whatever had bothered him last night had passed. Relieved, Theo listened to the coconut oil sizzling as it rose in clouds above the blackened pan and it seemed to him as though it had been years and years since he had last seen Nulani Mendis. He knew she would not arrive until the rain had stopped.

5

SHE CAME AS SOON AS SHE COULD. It was later than she had meant it to be but the rain, and the news that her brother had won his scholarship, and her uncle's sharp eyes following her suspiciously, had all contrived to make her late. But she came, with the last of the raindrops trailing the hem of her red dress and her long hair swinging loosely as she hurried. He was out on the veranda, waiting with barely concealed impatience, just as he had told her he would be, smoking his pipe. He watched her as she rushed in through the unlatched gate, caring nothing for the rain drumming the ground or the branches that shook and showered drops of water on her. Her dress was stained with dark patches of water. And she was smiling.

'Well,' he said, coming swiftly towards her, his worries all ironed out by the sight of her. 'Are you going to stand there for ever?'

He made as if to touch her but then, changing his mind, smiled instead. The rain vanished and the previous day's vague anxieties disappeared with it. The leaves shone as though they were studded with thousands of precious stones. And the whole day suddenly seemed extraordinarily iridescent and beautiful.

'Well,' he said again, and he felt, without quite understanding, the light touch of her gladness.

The girl was smiling at him with barely suppressed excitement. Taking his hand she led him back to the veranda, making him sit down, laughing, making him wait. She gave him her latest notebook to look through, while she went to fetch the paintings. But where was Sugi?

'Wait,' said Theo, but then Sugi appeared from nowhere and he too was smiling, for Sir's face had suddenly become transformed.

Sugi came out with the tray on which was a beer for Theo and a jug of Nulani's favourite lime juice. There was a small plate of *boraa*. Theo would not look at the paintings until Sugi had poured himself a beer. Sugi grinned. Sir was impossible of late. Sunlight danced across the canvases as she turned them round.

They were smaller than he expected. In one, Theo sat at his desk in front of a lacquered bowl of bright sea urchins and red coral. The mirror, scratched and marked with age, reflected a different interior. It was of his flat in London. There were peonies in the mirror-interior but none beside the bowl of sea urchins. A small mosquito with spindly legs rested on the edge of the polished wood. Theo sat working at his typewriter. The portrait he had glimpsed months earlier was the largest of them all. It too was finished. The girl had painted herself in one corner of it, as a splash of green and white and black hair. A thin glass jug, cracked and brittle, stood on a corner of the shelf beside Theo. Sunlight poured into it. His face was turned towards the light, looking out at the trees, caught in the moment between thinking and writing. And with an expression in his painted eyes that now confused him. It was the expression of a younger man, he felt; himself perhaps in another life. How had she caught it? How had she even known of it? Oh! Christ, he thought. Oh! Christ. He felt a wave of something, some rush of clumsy tenderness wash over him. It left him suffused with certainty so that when finally he could speak again the day poured its endless light over him too.

'You are a truly beautiful painter,' he said at last, feeling the weightlessness of his words, the mysterious nature of the language as it floated dreamily, tumbling into the thick and languid air. 'Others must see your work,' he said, taking in her shining eyes, thinking, no, there were no words for what he felt. No language, however many civil wars were fought, was fine enough to describe his thoughts. Thinking too, certain also, that her paintings must go to England. It was the thing he could do. Somehow.

The rain was terrible. It filled the upturned coconut shells that littered the ground everywhere. Clear, round mirrors of water reflecting patches of the sky. The Buddhist monks, when they remembered, kicked them over, spilling water. But mostly they did not remember. The curfew was back and there were new things on their minds. Although they knew it was the time when the swarms of mosquitoes appeared, thick as smoke and deadly as flying needles, they were busy with other matters. Language was on their minds, the importance of Singhalese as opposed to Tamil. The army too, who in peacetime might have been employed to spray every house with DDT, now had more important preoccupations. So the rains fell largely unheeded, forming glassy ponds in the shade of the coconut palms, in ditches and in stagnant tanks. Reflecting the sky. It was a mosquito's paradise. They floated their dark canoes on these ponds among the lotus flowers and the water lilies. Waiting for the night. But for humans this was no paradise, and those foolish enough to think this a place to toy with, did so at their peril.

Two British journalists were shot dead. A third man, a photographer, escaped with his life, having lost his left eye. Two Indian students had limbs mutilated. Their stories eventually made news and the international press issued a worldwide warning. Stay away, for the unseen laws that governed this place were not to be tampered with. But the rains, unheeding in the midst of all that was terrible, fell indifferently, and many people thought this was a blessing.

Later, after they had hung the paintings and the girl had gone home, Theo went back to look at them. Paint and linseed oil gathered in the room where they were hung and her presence was everywhere. Again he felt the dull ache of it. He remembered her, in her red dress, with patches of rain falling on it, looking at him, alert as a bird that had evaded a storm. He thought of her silent concentration over the past months as she worked in the studio, and once again he was filled with wonder. At her youth, at her unwavering certainty, and her talent. Staring at the smudges of paint, the light and shade that transformed into the edges and corners of things, he felt privy to her thoughts. He noticed she had placed the framed photograph of Anna in the reflected mirror room. Petals from a vase of peonies fell beside it. She had painted not just a likeness; she had painted some other dimension, some invisible otherness of how he must once have been. And the look on his face, where was that from? Closing his eyes, Theo felt the heat and intimacy of the moment. Sugi, coming in just then, stood looking silently with him. He too saw the face of a much younger man. How had this happened, so quickly?

'I must take her to Colombo,' Theo said, 'to meet a painter friend of mine. I must ask her mother if she will allow it. We could go up on the train.' He nodded, his mind made up.

'Sir,' said Sugi, but then he hesitated.

What could he say? It was too late, what had not meant to be had already happened. He saw it clearly; Sir's eyes were shining like the girl's. Trusting like a child's, full of unspent love. So what was there to say? What was there to stop?

'Be very careful, Sir,' was all he said in the end. 'I told you this girl's family is watched. You do not yet fully understand this ruined place. The uncle does not know you yet but, now that the boy is going to the UK, he is there all the time of late.'

Sugi hesitated again, not knowing how to speak of those things lodged in his heart.

'You do not see how we have changed,' he said eventually. 'We are so confused by this war. Sometimes I hear people arguing that it is the fault of the British. That even though they have gone, we still have an inferior feeling in us. Who can tell?' He shrugged, helplessly. 'Our needs are so many, Sir, and our attitudes have changed because of them.'

A paradise that has been lost, thought Theo, staring out to sea. Before he could speak, Sugi remembered the chicken.

'Who knows where the enemy is, Sir?' he told Theo. 'There are many people who will envy you, who might put the evil eye on you.'

Sugi spoke earnestly, even though he knew his words fell on deaf ears. Sir, he saw, would take no notice. He knew it was not in Theo's nature to be careful. He had been away for too long and too much living in alien places had affected him; it had made him fearless. And he had no time for these dark, point-less evil eyes that could decide what should and could not be. So he watched as Theo went to see Mrs Mendis.

It was as Sugi said: the uncle was there but there was no sign of the girl. The uncle listened without comment. Theo talked quickly, drinking only milk tea, refusing offers of beer, as he tried to impress on them the girl's talent.

'My friend teaches at the British School, he is a well-known painter. He has many contacts in the art world. He is an elderly

Singhalese,' he added, speaking to the uncle directly, knowing the man's politics, his prejudices. The uncle said nothing.

'If she is taken on at the art school she'll be funded by a scholarship,' Theo continued, not knowing if this was really the case.

The uncle swirled his beer. His face was set. What is wrong with me? thought Theo. I am behaving as though he frightens me, when in fact he's harmless, just a provincial man. Sugi's anxiety has rubbed off on me, that's all. The uncle looked at Theo. Then he squashed and tossed the empty can out into the darkening garden. Mrs Mendis began to scold him, calling the servant to pick it up. The uncle stood up, tightening the belt of his khaki trousers. He looked across at Theo; he was smaller than Theo but wider, fatter. His lips were soft mounds of flesh, well defined and full of blood. He laughed a strange high-pitched laugh, ironic and humourless.

'Art!' he said. His voice was falsetto with amusement. 'We are a country at war, trying to survive in spite of the Tamils. What do we need art for, men?' He looked briefly and threateningly towards the house. 'It isn't art she needs. At this rate, she will have a serious problem finding a husband. But it is not up to me, it's up to her mother, no?' And then he went, down the veranda steps, into the threatening rain and out to his waiting jeep, his headlights probing the silent road ahead like yellow sticks of dynamite.

Well, thought Theo, breathing a sigh, that wasn't so bad after all. The man is harmless enough. They would go to Colombo the next morning. Because the paintings were still wet he decided they would go by car. He would pick the girl up early and, with luck, they would be at his friend's studio by mid-morning. And because of the curfew they would be back by dark.

'Tell her to bring her notebooks,' he said to Mrs Mendis.

*   *   *

Sugi lit the paper lanterns. They cast a trelliswork of patterns on the walls of the house. Geckos moved between the shadows. He fastened a shutter against the breeze. Then he went into the girl's studio to look at the paintings of Theo. He was alone; Sir was still over at the girl's house. He seemed to have been gone for a long time. Sugi's unease was increasing. He remembered the first time he met Sir, on that afternoon as he walked from the station, carrying his smart leather bags. Sugi had had a good feeling about Mr Samarajeeva. He had thought, ah, here is a real gentleman. He had not known what an important man he was then, of course. But he had seen in him the kind of person that no longer existed. Someone fine and just and clever, thought Sugi, staring at the paintings. Someone who had not been corrupted by the war. It had all been there, quite plainly in Sir's face, even on that very first day. Which was why Sugi had agreed to work for him. When he had found out that Theo was a widower, he began to wonder what had driven him to come back to this place. And later, when he knew more, he had hoped the old home would heal him.

'They are my people here, Sugi,' Theo had told him many times in the following months, as they sat drinking their beer late into the night. 'I have nothing more in Europe.'

'Did your wife have family, Sir?'

'Oh yes, but . . . well, she was not close to them, and after she died they had nothing more to say to me. Anna and I were too bound up in each other, you see. Perhaps it was a bad thing, I thought afterwards it probably was. I don't really know.'

He had fallen silent, straining to remember her voice. Bullfrogs croaked in the undergrowth and in the distance the Colombo express hooted as it rushed past.

'We never seemed to need other people much,' he had continued, lighting his pipe. 'That was part of the trouble. So that even the absence of children did not matter in the end. Only our friends Rohan and Giulia understood.'

Sugi had made no comment. He would not pry. The shadows from the oil lamp had lain in a dark band across Theo's eyes. It had the curious effect of making him look as though he wore a blindfold. His voice had been barely audible, suddenly without energy.

'We had wanted children. But then she died. After that, what was there to want? I was glad we had none.'

He had spread his hands helplessly in front of him as the silence between them lengthened. The air had been soft with unspoken affection.

'You know, Sir, you will meet her again,' Sugi had said finally. 'These things are not lost. Loving someone is never wasted. You will find her again some day, when you least expect. I have heard of such things happening.'

Theo had sighed. He was tired, he'd said. Tired of running.

'I simply had to come back home, Sugi,' he had said again. 'It was the only place I could think of. After she died everything I did, every place I went to reminded me of all I had lost. I was like a man suffering from burns. Even breathing was difficult.'

He had shaken his head, unable to go on. In the distance the sea, too, had sighed. At last he had roused himself.

'In the end, I knew, if I were to survive I would have to come back. I thought I might make sense of events once I was here.'

Sugi had nodded, moved. He understood. Underneath the mess they had created for themselves, the land still had powerful ancient roots. It was still capable of healing. One day it would go back to what it had been before.

'I know. I can wait,' Theo had said as they had sat surveying the garden. 'I'm in no hurry.'

Sir is an idealist, thought Sugi, now, going over the

conversation in his mind, staring at the painting, astonished all over again at the Mendis girl's talent. The child has seen into Sir's heart. She knew. Because she felt it too. Sugi shivered; in spite of the heat, he shivered. They are both such children, he thought. The girl is too young, and he is too innocent. It is left to me to look after them. This is a fine state of affairs. And then Sugi went to fetch a glass of cold beer, thankful that the sound of the gate being opened meant, at least, that Sir had returned from Mrs Mendis's house unscathed.

There had been no problem with Nulani leaving. Contrary to what Sugi had said, the uncle did not return in the morning, and Mrs Mendis had been friendly enough. She asked Theo if Nulani was likely to get another commission. The money was always useful and what with Jim leaving for the UK there were even more expenses. Theo continued to dislike the woman but, folding these thoughts, he slipped them out of sight. He smoothed them down like a sheet on an unmade bed. And then the girl came out with her bouquet of excitement, her dress a scarlet splash across the day, and all his momentary irritation with the mother, and his anxiety over the uncle, all of it vanished and the morning shifted and changed into a different, glorious focus. He turned the car around on the gravel and they left. The edges of her hair were still damp from her early-morning shower.

Theo thought it was best to take the coast road. In spite of the checkpoints and occasional roadblocks, it was quicker and more straightforward. He had wedged two of the paintings in the boot of the car but the third, being so much larger, rested on the back seat. The girl was trying to hide her excitement and failing. It escaped in little green tendrils, curling itself around him, rising like the wisps of mist that were coming in from the sea. It was going to be another scorching day. The girl's excitement was such that Theo was certain she had not slept much.

'You'll be exhausted by lunchtime,' he said looking at her, thinking she looked as though it was Christmas. As though she was about to open her presents. He hid his own excitement at having a whole day with her, talking to her, having her paintings looked at, keeping his delight quiet and cool, even though all he wanted was to hold her small hand. The day lay ahead of them, as clear as the sea emerging from its mist. It felt, for Theo, a snatch-back from his youth. He did not think all this, not in so many words. All he saw was the smoothness of the beach and the shining excited eyes of the girl.

'Why don't you try to take a nap?' he said, pretending to be tired, trying to sound bored. 'It will take an hour to reach Colombo, maybe longer. Why don't you have a little sleep, no?'

And then he burst out laughing, looking at her astonished face and her total incomprehension.

'Well,' he said, smiling, pretending to yawn, teasing her some more, 'It's what you would do if you were *my* age!'

And he thought again how her eyes were like dark cherries.

'Your friend, what is he like?' asked Nulani.

The road wound its way along a picturesque stretch of the coastline. Groups of rocks thrust their way into the sea. Giant cacti clung to the edges of the sand. Coconut palms fringed the beach, sometimes so densely that only glimpses of sea could be seen. At other places whole stretches of white sand, empty and clean, unfolded before them, fringed by the lacy edge of the waves and marked by the empty railway line.

'Rohan? He is a fine painter. He used to live in London, which was where I met him. He was my wife's friend to start with. She knew him long before I did; she used to buy his paintings. Then, after I met Anna, I saw one of them hanging in her apartment and I wanted to meet him too. Because I liked the painting, and because he was my countryman.' Rohan, he thought, how to describe Rohan? How to describe the times they had spent together? Rohan, with his Italian wife Giulia, and Anna, in that other, distant life. The years of holidaying together, in Venice, in the Tuscan hills. The evenings spent arguing and drinking wine, the affection. And afterwards, Rohan and Giulia at the funeral, beside him as he stood blinded by the unnatural brightness of his pain, rejecting all offers of friendship. But they had not minded. Like the true friends they were, they had understood, had waited patiently, year upon year, writing to him, telling him about their lives, their decision to return to Rohan's home in Colombo, in spite of the trouble. So that slowly, given time, Theo began to write back to them. They were his dearest friends. Nulani was watching him intensely.

'You will like them both,' he said, knowing that they would love the girl.

The sun was climbing to its hottest point as they reached the first checkpoint. The currents had subsided and the sea was calm. There were hardly any waves now. The fishing boats had put out to sea again. At the checkpoint a woman soldier examined their passes and searched the car.

'The paintings are wet,' Nulani said, but it was too late, she had already touched them.

'You can't go much further,' the soldier told them flatly. 'The road is blocked. You will have to leave the A2 and go inland through the coconut groves until you get to the ruined city and then you can pick up the Colombo road again after that. There is another checkpoint further up. After that you will have to turn right.'

The detour would add half an hour to their journey.

'There has been an incident,' the woman soldier continued. 'It's over now but it will take some time to clear.'

'An accident?' asked Theo.

'No, an incident,' she repeated shortly. And then she smiled, a swift flash of uneven white teeth, from some other long-vanished and different kind of life.

'Look for the ruined city,' she said abruptly. 'It's very beauti-ful. If you are an artist,' she glanced briefly at Nulani, nodding her head, 'you will like it there. You can make a *pujas*, pray for a safe journey.'

And she waved them on.

Further along the road, about a mile away, the land swept into a wide long bend. A whole stretch of beach lay before them. Then the road forked, turning sharply to the right, heading into the coconut grove; suddenly the roadblock the soldier had promised was in front of them. Two army trucks acted as a barrier. A police car was parked to one side, its light flashing pointlessly. On the edge of the cliff, overlooking the sea, there were two limousines piled into one another. It looked at first as though there had been an accident. But there was no ambulance present. Only uniformed men with sub-machine guns paced the road. In the high bright morning light the dead strewn across the side of the road bore the strangest resemblance to piles of scattered dirty laundry, bundled up and ready for washing. All around was the sweet drenching smell of an invisible blossom. There was, too, a curious dry odour, dead and chemical, which Theo knew could only have come from explosives. He stopped the car and a soldier, a man of about twenty-five, came up to the open window. Theo handed over their documents.

'What happened?'

His voice, flanked by the waves and the sound of a train rushing suddenly past, seemed to come from a long way away.

'Open the boot!'

Theo was aware of the girl's anxiety. All the time he was

opening the boot and holding the pictures for the man to see, telling the soldier the paint was not dry and that they were taking them to the university to show Professor Fernando, all that time, while the huge seagulls wheeled overhead, her anxiety drifted towards Theo. When they were finally dismissed, with a sharp movement of a rifle butt, the day itself had acquired a sour hard taste to it. Turning the car into the coconut grove, Theo saw a slender brown arm, fingers curled slightly. It was severed below the rolled-up sleeves of an otherwise clean white shirt. An ordinary white shirt, the sort he owned.

It was another quarter of an hour to the ruined city with its votive dagoba. A woman selling king coconuts stood bare-headed in the burning sun. She knew nothing about the roadblock or the massacre at the crossroads, but the detour meant she had sold nearly all her coconuts even before ten o'clock. They drank the cold coconut water and wandered around the dry earth-caked ruins. Theo watched the girl, a flutter of scarlet cloth against the orange lichen-covered statues. She stood with her head bent, eyes closed, and the sickness and horror and the pity of what he had just seen was touched with the sweetness of her presence, turning slowly within him. They were due at Rohan's place by eleven.

Through the wing mirror Vikram watched them drive off. He was dismantling a Kalashnikov. Gerard had moved the car to a wooded area not far from the ruined city. Now he rubbed the dust from the wing mirror so he could see the Mendis girl more clearly. He swatted a mosquito on his arm and wiped the blood off.

'The mosquitoes are back,' he told Gerard.

Gerard grunted and mopped his brow. They had had a successful morning. Seven dead and the Singhalese army in a quandary. What could be better? Nobody knew there were any Tigers in the locality.

ROMA TEARNE

'They didn't see us,' was all he said as the car disappeared round the bend of the road. 'Now you should go back. Walk around the town, talk to people, let them see you. D'you understand? Vikram, are you paying attention?' he added sharply.

Gerard was still a little jumpy. He knew he was happiest when he did not have to do the dirty work. But he had not wanted Vikram to tackle it alone. Not this time anyway. Now all he wanted was to get rid of the boy. He was not interested in his chatter. Vikram's calmness had stunned Gerard. To his astonishment, the boy had hardly batted an eyelid. He's a tough nut, thought Gerard, tougher than even I expected. Handled properly, he could be quite dangerous. Vikram was nodding. He was vaguely aware that Gerard was nervous but by contrast he felt suddenly exhilarated and ready for more action.

'It's important you don't blow your cover. So make sure as many people as possible see you. Pity you don't have more friends. Can't you talk to that Mendis girl?'

'Maybe,' said Vikram, instantly scowling.

'I would take you over to that fellow, you know, Theo Samarajeeva, but the servant is suspicious of me.'

'I'll talk to her,' Vikram said, rather too quickly. He did not want Gerard to get involved with the girl.

'OK, now go,' said Gerard. 'I'll take the gun back to my place. No, Vikram,' he said firmly, before the boy could protest. 'It's for your own safety. You don't want to get caught carrying a weapon. I'll see you back at the shop after dark.' He placed the two dismantled Kalashnikovs in his rucksack. 'It'll take you about an hour on foot,' he said. 'Take the track through the jungle and go straight to the town and have a beer. I'll see you later. And, Vikram,' he added as the boy got out of the car, 'well done!'

Vikram slunk into the trees. He knew this path well, having gone over it many times with Gerard after dark. He would follow

88

the track until he reached the river and then it would be another quarter of a mile until he reached the outskirts of the town. After he had had his beer he would go and find the shopkeeper's daughter, and take her to the back of the garages, he decided. The day had left him with an unexpectedly pleasant feeling. He had not lost his nerve and he knew Gerard had been impressed. It was the first time he had used the gun, the first time he had killed anyone. Gerard had looked at him curiously and not without a certain admiration. Once, long ago, Vikram remembered his father looking at him in this way after he had recited some verse he had learned in school. As he hurried through the trees, lowering his eyes to the ground, watching out for snakes, his mind was momentarily caught in a contented daydream. Then he remembered the Mendis girl. What had she been doing in that car just now, so far from home? Why was she always with that old man? He wanted to see her again, for there was something mysterious about her that eluded him. Gerard was right; he should talk to her, although for some reason, not entirely clear, Vikram did not want *him* to have anything to do with her.

'Nulani,' he said, experimentally.

Perhaps, thought Vikram, perhaps I should talk to her uncle. Yes, that's what I'll do, he decided. I'll make friends with the uncle. Then maybe I'll get invited to the house. Tearing a branch off a tree, clearing a path, he continued on his way.

Rohan was drawing in the garden behind his studio, shaded by a murunga tree.

'Come in, come in. We have been waiting for you fellows. Giulia is preparing a feast. She has engaged the entire service of the black market in your honour!'

He beamed at them and the girl smiled. Rohan was exactly as Theo had described him.

'Now then,' said Theo, watching Nulani, 'don't start drawing the poor man yet!'

In the last part of their drive the day had righted itself somehow. The girl's quiet voice talking lightly about insubstantial things had soothed him. He knew she was talking simply to distract him. He was amazed once again by her intuition and her insight. He knew this quality was also in her work. He hoped Rohan would see it too. Then he caught sight of Giulia hurrying towards them. She was laughing and balancing a tray of soft drinks and ice as she walked. For a second Theo was struck by the returning past. In this way had she come towards him when he had first met her. Again he felt a shift of focus towards all that had gone before, so that the memory of Anna returned to him again. The cuttlefish pasta, the wine, the clove-scented cigarettes. He saw, from the outside looking in, all he had denied himself for so long. And in that instant, the many thoughts he had punished himself with smoothed out and became simple and calm. In this way he remembered it, with a sudden rush, sweetly, and without bitterness. Somewhere nearby were the faint cries of seagulls, and he heard these too, coming back to him hauntingly, as though from another, different, Adriatic sky.

'This is Nulani,' he said, his hand on the girl's cool arm, feeling in that instant a poignant sense of belonging.

The afternoon wove around them. After a lunch of fresh crab curry and mallung, brinjal and *parippu*, of excellent curd and plantain, and beans, after an endlessly long and slow meal filled with banter, Rohan held up his hand.

'Enough!' he said, teasingly. 'This will *not* do. We have serious business. We are here to look at Nulani's paintings, you have all talked rubbish for long enough!'

And he covered his ears at their protestations. Sunlight danced on the walls. The war seemed something they had only heard about.

'I shall clear a space in my studio,' announced Rohan, handing Theo a cigar.

'My God!' said Giulia. 'It isn't often I hear him saying anything about clearing his studio. This is your doing, Nulani!'

'Maybe he has reached a turning point in his career?' suggested Theo. 'Come, Giulia, it's what you've been waiting for. Don't say you're not excited!'

'Yes, yes,' said Giulia earnestly. 'Perhaps meeting Nulani will make him tidy at last!'

'That's quite enough from both of you. Come, Nulani, ignore these philistines. Bring your work in.'

'Well,' sighed Giulia, 'I shall make some milk tea, for Theo and myself. It's clear we're not wanted by these artists!'

'And I shall get the paintings out of the boot,' said Theo. 'It's all I'm capable of doing!'

With a flourish of his hand, he held the door open for the girl and they went outside.

'You're different today,' the girl said, laughing up at him.

They walked along the side of the house keeping out of the sun. The air was hot and still.

'It's good,' she said softly, standing close to him. 'This is the first time you have looked really happy since I met you.'

Theo looked at her. He felt the air, delicate and white, like a gull's egg, charged with unspoken thoughts. Still and unbearable. The heat balanced precariously on the edge of an unknown precipice, so that, hardly conscious of what he did, he reached out and touched her hair. Crossing some invisible boundary, suspending them both in the moment. And Giulia, glancing up through the curtain of creepers growing outside the window, thought, I have seen that look on his face once, long ago, just before Anna died. Looking at Anna, in just this way. Does he know?

Rohan loved the paintings.

'Art school isn't what you need,' he said. 'Art school will only spoil what you already have. You already paint from the inside out. No, what you need is simply to paint. All the time, every *thing* you want to paint, until you have a body of work.'

He paused, staring intensely at the paintings, lost in thought.

'What you need is discussion about your work. You can have that with me. But most of all you must continue working in this way. And we should try to organise an exhibition for you. Here, and also in England, no? What do you think, *putha*? Tell me? Would you like that?'

Theo had left them alone to talk, and after he had looked at Nulani's paintings, Rohan brought out his own work. They were large semi-abstracts in oils. Vast grey canvases. He talked to her of the daily practice of painting.

'Some say art is our highest form of hope,' he said absently. 'Perhaps it's our only hope. Living has always been a desperate business.'

He paused, thinking of Theo, remembering the time when his friend had been lost to him when Anna had died.

'Life is full of pointlessness. Not just now there is a war, but always, before. It's the nature of living. And the wounding of beauty, that's all part of it, no? First you possess it and then you lose it. Art represents that aesthetically. To a certain extent your paintings are already doing this, you know, Nulani. But still, you must push your boundaries even further. On and on, don't stop whatever you do; keep looking, always, for the happy accident, for the things that move you. And don't just paint that bugger Theo, either!'

He smiled at her, for she was so lovely. And so pitifully young. The young, he felt, had little hope in this place. He wanted to give her something to take with her. He knew how hard it would be for her to follow her chosen path. What will she paint in ten years' time? he wondered. Or twenty? What *would* her life be like, in this backwater, married off, worn down by poverty and children? If the war doesn't get to her first, of course. He felt only shame and bitterness for his country. Already he could see she had captured the fragility in Theo, the threads of what he had lost. Already she had achieved something soft and fluid and painterly. If colour *does* express something of our deepest emotions, then these painstakingly beautiful paintings have begun to touch that mysterious thing, he thought. What other things will age and experience bring to her work?

'He is a good man,' he said, suddenly, of his friend. 'And he has suffered.'

He wondered how much she intuited. Probably she knew, possibly she understood more than Theo himself. Women were quicker, thought Rohan. Especially in this country, they were quicker.

'So, now you have lifted that greyness from his life. That is all really, and still it's also everything,' he said, as though she had replied.

They were silent, preoccupied, while the afternoon moved the light slowly around the huge white room. The smell of thick paint and bitumen was everywhere. Rohan's studio was cluttered with objects. Many of the things he chose to paint were those from his daily life. An empty carafe that had once held Tuscan wine, a cast-iron bird bath from their small Venetian garden, three shades of grey Fortuny silk, colours from a museum city. A blackened crucifix resting against the whitewashed wall.

'I myself,' said Rohan, seeing her look at his props, 'I myself, love grey. You may say this is a little ridiculous of me. To come all this way back home to paint with grey? But, grey has no agenda. And that's what really interests me. Its neutrality. Grey has the ability, that no other colour has, to make the invisible

visible. So I paint with grey. I need some spirituality to keep going in this place. For, you see, my heart is saddened by what's happening to our beautiful country.'

He paused, appearing to forget she was in the room. He was thinking he understood what Theo had meant. The girl sat without moving, silently. She had the calmness of an injured bird, he saw. As if some instinct told her, there was no point in struggling. And then Rohan saw that no one had talked to her in this way about painting.

'They are killing each other,' he said softly. 'Day after day. Over which language is more important. Can you credit these stupid bastards!'

Bitterness crossed his face like an ugly scar. The light was fading.

'Where it gets interesting for us, as painters, is in the absence of language,' he said a bit later on, getting excited again. 'You are a good painter. But you know all that, I hardly need to tell you.'

Then he remembered something else.

'Your notebooks,' he warned. 'They should never stop. No matter whatever happens in your life. Remember that. Always, *always*, no?'

The sun had almost gone, unnoticed by them. Deep shadows fell in through the window. In another part of the garden, Theo sat talking to Giulia. They had been drinking milk tea. Giulia had trained the plants to form a shady covering. She had placed some cane chairs and a small table underneath it. Orange blossom and jasmine tangled together overhead. A hosepipe trailed across the small immaculate lawn and somehow the garden had acquired an Italianate feel to it. Theo paused, looking at the terracotta pots of lilies, the cacti and the pink and white oleanders. It reminded him of the walled garden in Venice, where he and Anna had been such frequent visitors. How had

Giulia managed to bring her home here, into the untamed tropics? He began talking about the girl. Words poured out; he could not stop. It was as if a dam had burst in him.

'She is very young and with such extraordinary talent. I wish I knew what the future held for her,' he said.

I have seen this face in so many moods, thought Giulia, marvelling at the flexibility of the human heart. Marvelling that at last the torrent of grief over Anna seemed to have passed. Did he know? Had he any idea at all, of how he had changed?

'So, my friend,' Rohan said quietly, some time later, after they had put the paintings back in the car. 'You look a little better than the last time I saw you. Thank God, no?' And he placed his arm around Theo's shoulder, for he had hated the unhappiness and the anger that he had seen for so many years.

It was time for them to leave. Darkness was descending and soon the heat would lessen. Rohan and Giulia leaned against the gate. They stood arm in arm, smiling at Theo, kissing the girl goodbye.

'Bring her back to us very soon,' said Rohan. 'And, Nulani, remember what I said. I want to see some new paintings. But not just paintings of this fellow, you understand!'

They drove along the coast following the perfect disc of the moon. There were no remains from the day's bloodshed, nothing stirred under the steady beam of the headlights of the car. Theo drove with all thoughts suspended, cocooned within a glow of contentment. Their talk was languid and desultory. In this short intermission between twilight and darkness, a mysterious transformation had occurred. An unusual cast of light made the girl seem both real and yet unbelievable. As they passed along the lonely stretch of road, the sea appeared to drift towards them, so that Theo could not easily distinguish the sound of the water from their voices. A gentle connection seemed to exist between them, invisible until now, yet somehow already present. How this was he could not tell. He heard the girl's voice rise and fall to the sound of the waves; he heard the rustle of the coconut palms and the rush of cool air as they passed. In that moment of neither night nor day it was as though all of it, the girl, the moon and Theo himself, moved together in some mysterious harmony of their own.

By the time they got to the lane that led to her house they were late. She wanted him to stop the car before they reached it. Pockets of fragrance exploded everywhere, jasmine opened into the night, carried on the breeze. The fifth sense, thought Theo, is a forgotten one. Yet for most of us, memory comes with smell.

'My uncle will be at the house,' the girl was saying. 'I want to thank you here, for taking me to meet your friends, without my uncle listening. He does not like to hear talk about my painting. He is a fool.'

It was the first time he had heard this tone in her voice. He thought how far she had come since he had first met her and how much older she seemed in so short a time. How happy she sounds, he thought, filled with gladness. Helplessly, he looked at her and as she smiled, he saw that her eyes reflected the moonlight. Slowly, with unhurried tenderness, hardly aware of what he did, he bent down and kissed her. He felt her tremble as he touched her, and he felt, too, his own sweet shock of surprise. He had never thought to feel this way again. He had been running for so long and now it was as though at last his heart had stilled. Something invincible seemed to settle within him. And then he was driving on, towards the bright lights of the house, and her brother Jim's *baila* music, and her uncle's snaking dislike. And all around, the Milky Way appeared to unfold in an endless canopy above them, scattering its stars far and wide, like fireflies rising in the dark tropical sky.

6

IT RAINED IN THE NIGHT BUT towards dawn the mist began rolling in from the sea. When it finally cleared, the day would be hot and dry as an elephant's hide. The news on the radio was not good. Two Cabinet ministers and their families, returning to Colombo after the weekend, had been machine-gunned down. All that was left of them were limbs, studded with bullet holes, crushed to the edge of bone, brittle, like coral. No one knew who might have committed such a crime. This part of the island had always been considered safe. So it was a mystery how this could have happened. The army began putting up roadblocks everywhere in the hope of catching the terror-ists. But so far no one had been arrested. Rumours were, the railway line would be the next target. In the main part of the town, further along from where the Mendis family lived, small groups of men gathered to talk of this latest, unaccountable act of violence. The air of nervousness, even here in this backwater, was no longer possible to hide. A few fights had broken out in the streets and Mrs Mendis begged her son to stay away from the town. He was leaving at the end of August. The priest at the boys' school had organised his visa. Mrs Mendis did not want anything to ruin his future. She was torn between her desperation for Jim's safety and her agony at the thought of his imminent departure. Fear and anxiety, and also irritation towards Nulani, mixed confusingly within her. There was so much to do for Jim and all the girl had wanted was to go to Colombo to talk about her paintings. Why was she such a selfish child? Why did she care so little for what was left of her family? Here was her mother, working night and day to make ends meet, and all Nulani could do was paint. Mrs Mendis complained loudly about her daughter to the servant. She complained about her to the clients who came with sewing. And she insisted Nulani stay in and help her.

'You've had your day gallivanting with that poor gentleman,' she told Nulani firmly. 'He's a good man to take such interest in you, but today you can finish the jersey for your brother to take to England. And then you can clean the house.'

Jim cycled off to his tutor's house. He had some final preparations. And Nulani Mendis sat alone on the veranda step watching him go.

It was how Vikram saw her, spying through the branches of the mango tree. He had been preoccupied for the last week, busy doing important things, being seen by as many people as possible, taking the shopkeeper's daughter to the back of the garage, drinking. Of late the shopkeeper's daughter had begun to irritate him. She had, he realised, become too fond of him and had stopped fighting and started smiling instead. As a result Vikram was becoming bored. He knew he would have to wait a while before Gerard gave him his next task. Gerard was lying low for a few days, he guessed, waiting until the news had died down, until someone had been caught and hung. So with no other excitement ahead Vikram was at a loose end. On his way back from the *kade*, he passed the Mendis house. Idly he decided to see who was in. Perhaps this was the moment to get to know the uncle.

But it was the girl he saw instead. She was knitting her brother a jersey to take to England. Knit one, purl one went her hands, binding the dark green wool together. They were painter's hands, moving quickly, making work. Vikram paused. He had come to see her uncle and found himself staring at Nulani Mendis instead. He watched her cautiously from this safe distance. Something about her made him careful. As always, whenever he caught sight of her, he felt uneasy without quite knowing why. Perhaps it was the tranquillity of her manner; perhaps it was the mysterious certainty in her face. He knew she might suddenly look up and see him, so he held his breath, hiding behind the *ambarella* tree. Her smile gave him the oddest of feelings. It made him remember things best forgotten, things that were no longer his to remember. But the girl did not look up. She was absorbed in her knitting. Knit one, purl one went her hands. Vikram was shocked to see her knitting. His shock was mixed with confusion, for thus had his sister knitted in that other, abundant life that once belonged to him too. The garden was filled with the sound of small birds. An underripe fruit thudded to the ground but still the girl did not look up. She bent over the dark green wool and for a moment, a mere fraction of a second, it seemed to Vikram as though the day had stopped. Shadows crossed the ground. A child's voice could be heard in the distance, repeating a question over and over again, high and clear. The rich hum of a passing mosquito vibrated in Vikram's ear. There were mosquitoes everywhere since the rains had begun. But the girl did not see them; she did not see Vikram either. She had a soft look on her face, like the nearly ripe mango that had fallen too early. She looked beautiful and dark, and mysterious. When she had finished all she meant to do, Nulani stood up and glanced swiftly across the lane. Then she sighed, and, folding up her knitting as though it were a precious thought, went inside.

Vikram watched her retreating back. He saw that even when she walked there was a peacefulness about her. His curiosity grew. What was it about this girl that drew him to her? He knew nothing more about her than the idle gossip surrounding Mr Mendis's death. From where he was, he could see the cool, dark interior of the house quite clearly. He could see also that it was shabby and withered and, in a way, hopeless too. None of this surprised him. Someone had told him that the family had slowly disintegrated after Mr Mendis had died. He could not remember who had said it. Perhaps it had been a student at the school, knowing of his dislike for Jim Mendis. But anyway he sensed this house had seen better times. Vikram imagined Mr Mendis, before his outspoken poetry had killed him, walking the beach with his daughter, carrying his young son. And the young Mrs Mendis, what had she been like? People said in those days she was always smiling. He imagined the house would have had energy then. Now, from where he crouched, he could see the place was a mess. Cricket bats and shoes, he supposed they belonged to Jim, shed like a gecko's skin, strewn everywhere. Vikram edged a little closer and he saw there were empty cotton reels and bits of thread and cloth lying on the floor. He could hear the sound of the sewing machine rattling on and, further back, through the closed doors, he heard raised voices. He watched as Nulani Mendis, ignoring everything, began to tidy up the room. There was something oddly dreamlike in the way she moved, he thought, puzzled. It was as though the girl was somewhere else entirely. She began folding her brother's clothes. She gathered up his books and picked up his shoes. Vikram watched. She moved his cricket bat and his kneepads. And she knocked the mirror over.

The mirror, shattering the light, crashing against her brother's shoes, his cricket bat, his kneepads. It fell to the ground, breaking into many pieces of silver, fragmenting the room, spewing dust, bringing Mrs Mendis in. Mrs Mendis let out a cry, a thin wail of despair, a long whine of sorrow. Broken-mirror dust was everywhere.

'There is no escape,' cried Mrs Mendis, 'Aiyo! My brother was right.'

Misfortune lay across the room. The girl stood looking at her hands while her mother's fears clogged the air. Vikram could feel her fears, even from where he stood, prickling against his own skin. He felt them, darkly unbending. Only Jim's cricket bat remained unharmed. Only Jim, out at the time doing whatever came easiest to him, did not witness the broken glass. Lucky Jim.

Theo had not slept. Happiness stopped him from sleeping. It was no longer possible to hide from his thoughts. The truth washed bare, rising to the surface, clear and clean like the beach. Had it only been a matter of hours? he wondered in amazement. He felt as though he had been travelling for aeons. Sugi had been waiting for him when he finally got back. The lights in the veranda shone, the beginnings of rain dampened the air, and the sound of the waves seemed louder. Sugi had gone for his beer as soon as he heard the gate and Theo insisted he join him. So they had sat and smoked in companionable silence for a while.

'I will set the table, Sir,' said Sugi. 'You must be hungry.'

But he had not wanted food. And Sugi seeing this, waited patiently.

'Have I changed, Sugi?' he asked. 'Since I first arrived here, do you think I am different?'

'Of course, Sir,' said Sugi. 'You have been changing for months now.'

'How?' asked Theo, wonderingly, smiling, wanting to be told.

'You are happier, Sir, you know; really, so much happier. You were very sad when you arrived, but . . .'

'What? Tell me.'

'I . . . Sir . . . you must be careful. I understand and I'm glad to see you this way.'

He did not ask how the day had gone. He knew it had gone well. So he nodded gently instead. For Sir was being blessed by the gods in some way. What was there for him to say?

'I'm no longer . . . a young man, you know, Sugi,' Theo said hesitantly. 'You know that . . . it isn't . . . I'm worried about this. I will grow old long before her . . .' He laughed.

Again Sugi hesitated. The effort of denial had been great, he knew. Now that barrier had been removed. Sir's face was radiant. It made Sugi both sad and happy.

'Some time has been lost, Sir, that's true,' he said at last. 'You had to wait for her to be born, to grow. But she is here now. In your life. I think, for ever,' he added.

'Ah, Sugi,' said Theo, looking up at the star-spangled sky.

He felt overcome, he felt happiness detach itself from him and float towards the trees. Filled with a sudden burst of energy, he wondered if perhaps he should do some work. And then, he thought, perhaps he would simply go to bed. Sugi smoked his cigarette. He was silent. Sir's happiness was such that it should not be disturbed. The darkness enfolded them both.

'Sugi!' said Theo at last, looking at him. 'If only you knew . . . how lucky I was that day to meet you! What would I have done had I not? It was as if you were waiting for the train I was on, waiting for the last passenger to walk up the hill.'

He shook his head, smiling broadly, wanting to say more, unable to express all he felt, his optimism for the future, and his affection for Sugi. But there was no need.

'Perhaps I was,' said Sugi. 'Without realising!' In the light his face looked tired.

'You mustn't worry about me, Sugi,' said Theo, gently. Tonight, he felt his heart was overflowing with almost unbearable gladness. 'Things are simpler than you think. You know I have to go back to England briefly, don't you? For the film?'

Sugi nodded.

'But I'll be back as soon as I can.'

'Everything will be fine here. Don't worry, Sir. I will look after things here,' he said, meaningfully.

There is no finer friend to be wished for, thought Theo. I hardly need to say anything, he knows already. And he smiled in the darkness.

'I think I might go for a walk on the beach. I'm not sleepy. And the day was a success, you know. Rohan loved her. And her paintings!'

'Be careful, Sir,' said Sugi, out of habit. But he spoke softly, as though afraid of breaking some spell.

Twenty-eight years, thought Theo walking across the smooth sand, listening to the screams of the wide-mouthed gulls. All the madness and hell of this country seemed nothing beside the astonishment of what he felt. The last love of my life, he murmured, that's what you are. There, he thought, I've faced it; that's what you are. Beyond reason, beyond practicality, that is what you are. And then he remembered her hands and the ways in which they made sense of the material world. Where has this talent come from? Will you love in the same effortless way that you draw? How *will* you love? Dare I even ask the question? I am forty-five, an old man by your standards. And in spite of the implausibility of our two ages, even as I hear the warning bell, I know it is too late, I will never let you go. He saw that he had arrived at a point of no return and that the girl had left her imprint on his imagination in ways he could never have foreseen. Throwing his head back, breathing in the fresh salty air, laughing out loud, he understood with the utmost certainty there were no more journeys for him to travel. Gazing up at the stars, dizzy with happiness, he cried: 'This is where I shall stay, until I die. Here in this place, with you.'

And as he watched, the ships on the horizon seemed sharply defined, glittering like diamonds against the night sky. Yes, he loved her. And yet, he thought, wistful now, you who are only just beginning to close the gate on your childhood, how could you understand the wonder of loving so late?

Looking out across the water, into the distance, he imagined her father speaking to her. She had told him that her father used to say: 'There's nothing except Antarctica from here. Nothing, no land, nothing.' Staring into the darkness, Theo tried to imagine her six-year-old incomprehension. And then his thoughts turned slowly towards Anna, seeing her with fresh understanding. Remembering too how once, many years ago, he had walked across another, wilder stretch of beach with her. They had been newly married. He had not known that after she died time would stop. But now, at last, he began to understand the indestructibility of things. Overnight almost, the memory of her had shifted and changed and miraculously, no longer cluttered by pain, become a peaceful thing. And it felt, in that moment, that Anna and their time together threaded like the strong ribbon on a kite, running through all he had just discovered, anchoring him. In this way, thought Theo, the dead return to bless us. In this way, through the new, will I remember the old.

He stayed out almost until dawn. And went back to sleep. When he woke Sugi had set the tea things outside on the table and he told Theo that the talk in the town was all about the murder of the two ministers and their families.

'We saw it,' Theo said quietly.

Not wanting to talk about it, not wanting the day to be spoiled, he told Sugi about Colombo and the lunch with his friends, and the girl. The day was hot. Sugi bought some fish. He cooked lunch and squeezed lime juice for the girl. But she did not appear.

'I expect her mother has got some jobs for her,' said Sugi, noticing Sir was not working. Noticing he had walked to the gate and was looking up the deserted dirt track for the fourth time.

The afternoon dragged on. The sounds of the cicadas filled the air and the mosquitoes too were back with a vengeance. But there was still no sign of the girl. They both began to listen out for the click of the gate. Theo had found a place to hang the paintings, away from the light, and Sugi took a hammer and put them up. But still, there was no sign of her. What had happened to her? wondered Theo uneasily.

'Don't worry, Sir,' said Sugi soothingly. 'My friend said Mrs Mendis is very upset the boy is leaving. She's probably given her some work to do.' The afternoon was nearly over.

'Perhaps I should go over there,' said Theo.

'Sir,' said Sugi, and he shook his head. 'It will do no good and it might even do harm. She will come. As soon as she can, she will come, I am certain.'

Towards evening, just before it became dark, Theo slipped out to the beach. Sugi watched him go.

'Don't be too long, sir,' he said. 'There's talk of a curfew. If you see the searchlights, come back immediately. These army types won't stop to look. They simply shoot, you know.'

As always at this time the beach was deserted. Theo was trying to light his pipe, bending away from the wind, when he saw her. Hurrying across to him in headlong flight, running heedlessly along the empty stretch of sand. Carrying her mother's wails of superstitions, chased by unseen demons, straight into his arms. And for the first time, as he held her like a child, relieving her of her fear, he saw how much she had begun to depend on him. And he saw also from her eyes that she was beginning to understand, too sharply and too finely perhaps, the many things that had not worried her until now. At last she saw what there was to be afraid of in this war. And he felt his own feelings for her break open and flower in some unbearable and inexplicable way.

Mirror dust fell everywhere, sparkling between them. Looking at her face he thought, once again with amazement, how it was that in so short a time, she seemed both older and yet so young. And then he knew, without a shadow of doubt, that he could never live in England again. So he laughed at her, teasing her about her mirror-fears, holding her as though she was a child woken from a nightmare, telling her it was all nonsense.

'Will you come back?' she asked anxiously, reading his mind a little. 'No one will stop you from coming back, will they?' Thinking with dread of his trip to London, for the premiere of his film. 'You *will* be allowed back in, no?'

They were sitting side by side on a broken catamaran. Half of it had sunk in the sand, brown-whiskered coconut husks filled its broken base, weather-beaten planks were all that were left of its seats. Her bare legs were close to his. One worn straw sandal had burrowed into the sand and come undone. He bent and fastened the strap, his hands fumbling and unfamiliar in their new task, brushing the traces of fine grains that clung to her leg. He felt her tremble and he knew she was thinking that he had never touched her in this way before. And all the things he had held in check, all the happiness of the past few days, gathered with great sweetness in that touch, of his hand on her skin.

'I will always come back,' he said fiercely, placing his hand against her face. 'You must never doubt that. If anything happens, if my visa is delayed, or the trouble worsens here, or the flights are cancelled, you must *not* worry. You must remember that I have told you I *will* come back. No matter how long it will take I *will* come back. I can't live away from you now. You must take no notice of the news,' he added, with the new urgency he had begun to feel. 'And promise me you will paint while I am away.' And he had kissed her again, for he could not bear the look on her face.

She had gone back then, to listen to her mother's complaints, with the caress of his hand on her legs, her red dress fluttering like a flag in the breeze, trailing the mist coming in from the sea, leaving the night to descend. Leaving the beach to him.

Walking back, Theo heard the sound of police sirens in the distance, rising and falling in time to the rhythmic gnawing of the sea.

On the edge of Aida Grove, on a slight incline not far from Sumaner House was an area where coconut trees would not grow. The earth was bare and wasted, without grass, without bushes, without life. There was nothing there except a lone straggling tamarind tree. Once this patch of land had been part of a larger grove of coconuts. It had belonged to the owners of Sumaner House, but with time, neglect and some erosion it had become common land, useless and uncultivated. Superstition abounded. Local legend had it that long ago a servant girl was ravished by a wandering shaman, here in this spot, and then left for dead. Eventually, according to the story, after many days of searching, the girl's distraught father found her body. His grief was so terrible that the gods, pitying the girl, turned this once fertile grove into barren land. Later on the place was used for human sacrifice. One evil deed precipitated others, and this became a spot avoided by most people. Cattle would not graze, children would not fly their kites and no one walked here after dark. Occasionally, in the hope of changing the atmosphere, the locals would offer *pujas*, prayers to the gods. But to no avail, Aida Grove would never become popular. In recent times the army had tried to make it their own, parking their trucks and using it as a lookout post, staring at the ships through their binoculars, but Aida Grove defeated even them, and after a while they too stopped coming. Only Vikram frequented the place, idly observing the votive offerings, the stray soldiers, the local carrion. Sometimes he would go to Aida Grove in the hottest hours of the afternoon simply to sit under the tamarind tree and watch the dappled light as it flickered on the ground. He was drawn to the place without knowing why. At seventeen he was the size of a fully-grown man. In spite of everything that had happened to him, he thrived. Such was the virulence of youth; such was the ability of unhappiness to grow. These days he kept busy in unexplained ways. He was still waiting for Gerard to give him his next task. But although he had returned to the town, and although someone else was helping the army with their murder inquiries, Gerard told him things were held up for the moment.

'Patience, patience,' Gerard had said. 'I'll let you know in a few weeks' time. When the Chief sends his orders. Now stop pestering me and circulate around the town, will you.'

One evening, as he walked home full of arrack, Vikram heard the usual sound of temple chants filling the air. The sounds floated across Aida Grove and the sky, he noticed, was filled with hundreds of small insects. There was hardly a breeze, the heat lay heavy and close to the ground. In some parts of the island, as Vikram was aware, in places where there was no curfew, Deepavali, the festival of light, was being celebrated once more. When they had been alive Vikram's family had always celebrated Deepavali. Vikram staggered on. Huge, blue magpies chattered a warning in the tamarind tree. The darkness grew stronger. Inside Sumaner House the servant woman Thercy had switched off the naked electric bulb in the kitchen. There had been no news from Vikram's guardian for months now. Thercy had given up wondering if he would ever return. He still paid her wages and he still sent money to Vikram. Everyone was content with the arrangement, so what did she care? All evening police sirens had been screaming. Fighting had broken out further up the coast. Tomorrow, thought Thercy, she would go into the town and meet her friend Sugi. He would know the latest news. Vikram was nowhere in sight. She imagined he was somewhere in the town getting drunk as usual. Thercy had no control over him. It was late, so, turning off the lights, all but the one on the veranda, she retired to bed.

Meanwhile, Vikram paused at the edge of Aida Grove. Something was different about it tonight. At first he couldn't think what it was. The light from the veranda shone faintly on the tamarind tree. Something was swinging from its highest branch. The movement caught Vikram's eye. He looked across the length of the tree trunk and saw the thing hung awkwardly, like a broken doll, swinging in the slight breeze. Slowly, making no sound, Vikram walked towards the tree. What appeared to be a giant pendulum moved backwards and forwards, swinging to an invisible beat. In the darkness, rocking gently, it appeared like an image from a painting.

In the dead of night, before the carrion came, when the air had cooled slightly and the dawn was still some way off, someone took the body down. It was dead-weighted and black-booted, hooded and bound. There were electrodes fixed to the palms of its hands. The hands were still young. A palmist might have identified the dark lines that crossed and recrossed it. A palmist would have seen the history in its fingers. The life and love that had lodged there once. But no such palmist was present. There was no one to display a single gesture of pity. And in the morning, when the light returned to the tamarind tree, the body had gone. Resurrected perhaps, moved to another place maybe. Blood had been spilt, thought Sugi when he heard, and the earth was soaked with it. Behind the tamarind tree and far away through the coconut grove were broken glimpses of the sea. It was blue like the sky, and the horizon was dotted with ships.

Nothing changed. The sea still scrolled restlessly up the beach. The catamarans remained half buried under the sand. When they could, after the curfew was lifted again, Theo and the girl walked on the beach. For Nulani there were two departures ahead.

'My brother goes to England in three weeks,' she told Theo.

He saw she could hardly bear what lay ahead. When would she see her brother again? Theo at least would be back. He tried to comfort himself with this thought, saddened by all that lay ahead for her. Remnants of her superstition had worked on him by some process of osmosis, he now realised. Am I going mad? he wondered uneasily. All this nonsense about broken mirrors; it's crazy. But he could see very clearly how her life rested on shifting sand. Why had he not seen this before?

Sugi watched his struggle. Sugi was his rock.

'Don't worry, Sir,' he said again, and again as they smoked together.

The generator had broken down again. Bullfrogs croaked but otherwise all was quiet.

'I will look after her for you. Always.'

They shared the silence.

110

'Do you remember when you first walked up the road, Sir, looking for this house?'

He still calls me Sir. That will not change either, thought Theo, his affection lengthening like the shadows.

'She will be fine, Sir. I will make sure of that, not to worry.'

There was money and a forged passport for the girl, hidden in a secret place.

'If there is any trouble, with the uncle, with anything, take her to Rohan,' said Theo in an agony of worry.

Time was passing relentlessly.

'Sir,' said Sugi, 'you must trust me. I will take care of her with my life. She will be fine. You and she are precious to me.'

Theo looked at him; Sugi had never expressed his feelings in quite this way before. His trip was still a month away.

Because of her brother's imminent departure the girl had stopped painting for the moment. These days she was often needed at home, sewing on buttons, and packing, or labelling the jars of lime pickles. How many jars of pickle could the boy take in his suitcase? wondered Sugi. But he refrained from comment. Since the trip to Colombo, Mrs Mendis kept her daughter occupied most of the time, adding to the girl's distress. When she could Nulani would escape to walk with Theo along the beach, and Sugi as always watching with his anxious eyes could see: they were getting closer daily. Sugi looked out across the horizon. The sea is full of fish, he thought. And the fruit is ripening in the trees, but still that isn't enough. Still we fight.

'Will they have egg hoppers for breakfast in England?' the girl asked Theo.

'You *will* see him again,' Theo told her, understanding in a new and mysterious way what she was thinking.

He had begun to feel the leave-taking of her brother almost

as keenly as she did. Her pain had become a terrible thing for
him to watch.

'Will you take me to England then?' she asked, and her eyes
were very large and dark and full of light in the way children's
eyes are. However much she aged in years to come, he thought,
she still would remain beautiful because of them. They were
the eyes of someone from another age, deep and wise and very
lovely. Oh Christ, how he wanted to take her to England, and
to Paris and to Venice. He could not bear to leave. When I
return, he decided, determined, I will never leave her again.
And one day, I will even take her to see that wretched brother
of hers and, when the war is over, I will bring her back home
again. For I know her heart will always remain here, in this
place, her home. So thought Theo as he watched her tenderly,
as she drank the lime juice Sugi still served in the tall glass. So
thought Theo watching her anxiously and waiting for the rains
to come, marvelling at how only last year she had turned seventeen – so young, yet already it felt as though he had known her
for a lifetime.

By Christmas there was to be a general election. From all he
could glean, in the brief talks with his agent in London, this
war no longer interested the foreign newspapers. Sri Lanka was
no longer news these days. It was a shipwrecked land. A forgotten
place. Lately, Theo noticed, since the curfew had been lifted, a
car headlight crossed the top of the sea road each night. It
happened always at nine o'clock, every night, sweeping its beam
across the road. But it never came any further and their peace,
such as it was, remained for the moment undisturbed.

7

'How long will it take,' she asked him, 'to get to London?'

Her brother had gone a few weeks earlier, leaving for the airport in the schoolteacher's car, with his unwavering belief in the new life ahead.

'Gone to the UK,' her mother had told everyone proudly, through her tears.

The house had shrunk. And now, another departure hung over Nulani.

'About a day. From door to door,' said Theo. 'Tomorrow, by this time, I will be in the hotel.'

'And you would have travelled halfway around the world,' she said in a small voice, picking up his passport and reading the names stamped in it.

'Frankfurt, Vienna, Amsterdam, Paris, Venice. You have been everywhere,' she said. 'And I have only been to Colombo, once!'

Theo, who had been gathering his notes for his tour, his money and his documents, stopped and looked at her. He took her hands in his. They were cold. He had been trying to keep busy but he saw now that it was useless.

'I'm so much older than you,' he said finally. 'It's hardly surprising. And you will go to all of these places one day, I promise you. *I* will take you, you'll see.'

She was silent, not looking at him, staring at the patch of sea through the open window. Impassively, accepting. He felt a moment of sickness at the thought of abandoning her. Seagulls circled the sky outside. He thought of how her father left her, not meaning to, but doing so anyway. Then, because he could not bear it, he looked at his watch. In less than an hour he would be gone, sitting on the fast train to Colombo. And he needed to talk to her. He could hear Sugi moving in the kitchen.

'Let's go to the catamarans,' he said quickly.

It was still so early that mist lay in thin patches on the beach. There would be no one about. First her father, then her brother Jim, he thought, and now me. But I shall come back, he reminded himself firmly.

'Listen to me,' he said, his hands gentle on her face. 'You must not worry. I'm coming back. I've promised you. I *will* keep my word. Just look after yourself, for me. Will you? And when I get back . . .'

He hesitated, not knowing how to go on. Her face looked drawn in the faint dawn light. She looked terrified.

'Look at me,' he said. 'Nulani, listen. You know I don't want to go but . . . You must not be afraid. The six weeks will go quickly, I promise you.'

Again he hesitated.

'When I get back . . . I want to talk to you about something. I want to ask you . . .'

He didn't have much time. He couldn't miss his train. There would not be another one today. But he needed to ask her something.

'Please, Nulani,' he said, 'look at me. Are you listening? I want us to get married. Would you like that too? Will you be prepared to do this crazy thing? With me?'

He went on smiling at her, hiding his desperation, holding on to her, knowing she was nearly crying, knowing too he could not bear to let her. For he knew that if she did, he would not be able to leave.

When she spoke at last, her voice was carried by the wind and caught up in the roar of a train rushing past. The sun was moving slowly through the mist; a few fishermen were coming in from the night. The air smelt sweetly of sea and sand and old fishing nets and tobacco as he kissed her.

'Yes,' she said, faintly. 'I want it too.'

Sugi squeezed some limes. Then he strained the juice into the tall glass jug and took it out onto the veranda where Nulani was drawing. Almost four days had gone since Theo had left and his absence was like a chasm between them. They had had a brief talk to him on the telephone but the line was bad and most of the time they only heard an echo of their own voices.

'Don't worry if you haven't heard from me,' Theo had said. 'Sometimes it's hard to get a connection.'

They had told him that everything was fine, that there was no trouble.

'Miss Nulani is here all the time, Sir,' Sugi had grinned. 'She's looking after me in exchange for lime juice! So don't worry. Just look after yourself.'

'And come back soon,' the girl had said. 'I have been drawing you from memory. Please come back.'

Afterwards she had been very upset. Sugi had not known what to do. He could see the signs of strain stretch taut against her. She was becoming silent, as she had once been. He told her she should do what she had always done. Each morning, until Theo returned, she should go into her studio and paint. In this way she could surprise Sir when he returned. Six weeks was not too long, looked at in this way, said Sugi firmly, talking to her as though she was a child.

Thus began a routine. Every morning as soon as she had helped her mother, she went over to the beach house and worked. Her mother no longer complained about her absence. Mrs Mendis too had grown quiet. Life had defeated her. She did not know when she would have word from her son. They did not have a telephone and although Nulani had written a letter there had been no reply as yet. Jim Mendis had vanished, swallowed up by the sky, as far as she could see. There was no longer any purpose to her life. The future held no interest for Mrs Mendis. By now Nulani had stopped going to the convent school. Most of the girls of her age were preparing for marriage, or leaving the country if they could. Those who were serious about their studies had moved to Colombo to a larger school. There was nothing to do except paint. The days crawled on. Soon a whole week had passed and there were only five weeks left.

One afternoon she arrived at the beach house later than usual. Her mother had gone to visit someone in a neighbouring village so she had found she was free. But she was restless. The light was wrong, she said, it was not possible to paint. Sea-damp had curled her notebook, she told Sugi, showing him the pages. Her drawings were ruined, she said sadly. Perhaps she could not paint after all. Sugi looked at her. She looked as though she had been crying and there were dark circles around her eyes. He brought out a plate of sweetmeats and some curd and jaggery. Then he sat down on the step and, in order to distract her, he told her a story.

Once long ago, when he was a young man, Sugi told her, he

had wanted to go to America. The idea of a neon life, Pepsi cola and cars seduced him. Once.

'When I was young I worked for a while in the Mount Lavinia Hotel in Colombo, carrying the bags that had just arrived off the passenger boats. America seemed glamorous in those days, and the women were tall and confident. So healthy-looking,' he said. 'Their teeth were large and white, their smiles spelt happiness.'

He had fallen in love with such a one, a woman called Sandy. He thought she might have been older than him. She had had a fiancé in Germany. Sandy had stayed in the hotel for nearly three months waiting for a passage to Europe.

'During that time we had only four conversations,' said Sugi. And he smiled at the memory.

'The first time was when I took her bags to her room. I read the labels on her bag and saw that her name was Miss Sandy Fleming, from Buffalo. I tried to imagine such a place,' he said. 'She saw me reading the label and smiled at me.'

He saw that her smile was even-toothed and confident. Such confidence frightened him a little. But it also fascinated him. Then the woman had thanked him and given him a tip. The second time she spoke was a few days later. She was poring over a map but, catching sight of him, she asked him for directions instead, saying that maps were too confusing. She smiled at him again and it was then that he had noticed her eyes.

'They were like green marbles,' said Sugi.

He could remember them still. Startled, caught unawares, Sugi had smiled back and Sandy Fleming had touched his arm lightly saying he ought to be coming with her on her trip. He had held the door open and, as she passed through into the blinding sun outside, he smelt the perfume on her skin. Again she touched him, lightly on the cheek.

'After that I was unable to stop thinking of her,' Sugi said. 'I didn't see her again for ages; my shift changed and I was needed to work in the kitchens.'

Often after he finished work he would loiter in the corridor near to Sandy's room in the hope of catching sight of her, but she was never around.

'Then about six weeks later,' Sugi said, 'the manager found he was short-staffed. He asked me to serve in the dining room.'

It was late afternoon; most of the guests had retired to their rooms to lie under their ceiling fans until the worst of the heat had passed. Outside, the sea was an unbelievable swimming-pool blue and the sand was bleached white. The breeze masked the blistering heat. Only fools would have ventured out but Sandy was on the terrace, her yellow straw hat providing her with a slight filigreed shade.

'I went to ask if she would like a drink,' said Sugi. 'A Lanka lime, a gin and tonic? You see, I knew how the Americans loved to drink.'

But in reality he had wanted only to talk to her. So he went out with his silver tray, his clothes a white flag in the sun, and he saw that she was crying. He had been about to move away quickly, eyes downcast so as not to intrude, when she turned and, seeing him, began a conversation as though she had left off a moment before.

'She told me that her fiancé had called off their engagement. She told me he had fallen in love with a German. Imagine that, she said. I didn't know what to say, so I was silent.'

He had seen that her eyes were smudged and greener than the cat's-eye gemstones mined in Ratnapura.

'He prefers Germans!' she had laughed with heavy sarcasm.

She asked Sugi if he had a girl. She was sure he did for he was such a handsome boy, she told him. And if by any chance he did not have a girlfriend, she had said, then he should tell her, because she would not like to think of him being wasted. Sugi saw that she was drunk.

Later, in his room in the servant quarters he thought about her, wishing he had not been so tongue-tied.

'I never asked myself what a woman like her would want with a boy like me,' he told Nulani.

He did not see her the next day, or the day after that, even though he looked for her everywhere. He asked the chamber-maid if the American lady had checked out and found that she was still there but her bed had not been slept in for two nights. The chambermaid wondered why he wanted to know this.

'I pretended I had found a brooch of hers but the chamber-maid was no fool, she told me to hand it in at the office and not have anything to do with the American.'

'She is a loose woman,' the chambermaid had said, showing her betel-stained teeth, fanning Sugi's interest further.

Then late one evening, after he had descended into a state of despair, when he was working on the reception desk, she had come in with a British Army officer in tow. They were laughing noisily, and Sandy was swaying slightly. She asked for her key, looking past Sugi. Much later she called up for a bottle of champagne and when he took it up himself she tipped him, complaining to the manager afterwards that he had looked at her in a manner that was too familiar.

'Some weeks after,' said Sugi, 'I left Colombo. I felt everyone was judging me. I didn't know if they thought I was a thief or a fool. Or both. So I left and went into domestic service in the south.'

He stopped speaking. In the distance a train thundered by. It was the afternoon express from Colombo. The sun had moved away from the house as he had talked and a cool breeze had sprung up. All of it had happened so long ago, in the days when the war had been something they had hoped would be avoided. He had been young then and his mother and sisters had constantly tried to find a woman for him. But the planets had been fixed in such a way when he was born that his horoscope revealed them to be in discordant houses, so that it had proved impossible.

'I seemed to be attracted only to unsuitable women,' he said wryly. The war and time had eroded his desire, he told Nulani, so that before he realised it, he was too old care any more.

Sugi fell silent. All this had happened long ago. Now his interest lay elsewhere. How many lives does a man have to live before he can finally be at peace? he thought, thinking too of Mr Samarajeeva. These days he wanted only to help Sir. There was something very fine and very noble about Theo Samarajeeva, something that had not been seen in this country for a long time. We are a Buddhist country, thought Sugi, turning things over in his mind. But what has happened to us? Where has our compassion gone? He would do anything for Sir, he knew. Help him in any way. Before he had left Theo had told Sugi he wanted to marry Miss Nulani.

'Do you think it's wrong of me, Sugi?' he had asked.

Sugi had been amazed. Why was Sir asking him?

'You are a wise man, Sugi,' Sir had said warmly. 'So tell me, *am* I doing the right thing?'

'It is the best thing you can do, Sir,' Sugi had said. 'Nothing else will do, for either of you, now. It is meant to be. You were meant to meet, your ages do not matter. At first I was worried, but now, I am certain of it.'

Sir had smiled at that, his anxieties momentarily smoothed out. And then, because he could not say all he felt, he had tried to joke.

'I take it I have your blessing, Sugi,' he had said.

'A thousand blessings, Sir.'

And they had sat in this way, in the darkness, sipping their beers, wrapped lightly in all that was left unsaid. Later, Sugi again said, 'I'll look after her. She'll be safe until your return.'

'I know,' Theo had replied, with calm certainty. 'I know you will, Sugi, you are my friend.' And then early the next morning he had gone.

'Sir is different,' Sugi told the girl, now. 'Sir is a wonderful man. And soon,' he said gently, smiling encouragingly at her, 'when he returns, I hear you'll become his wife. So be patient, have faith. It will be a blessing for you both, you'll see.'

His words settled between them, like the flock of white birds that sat in circles on the empty beach.

While he had been talking, the girl had been drawing him. She had never drawn him before. She did not know why this was, she said. But she had drawn him now. She showed him the sketch. Then she tore it out of her notebook and gave it to him. Tomorrow, she told him, she would start a small painting. It would be of Sugi and it would be finished by the time Theo returned home. It would be her welcome-home present for him, she said, smiling at last.

Vikram was finally preparing to leave for the east coast. He told the servant woman Thercy that he was going away for a time. He told her to pass the message on to his guardian should he contact her. Thercy nodded without questioning him. It was none of her business and Vikram was old enough to please himself. She was glad to have the house to herself for a while. Once he goes, she thought, I will give the place a good clean.

Vikram packed a rucksack. He shouted to Thercy to give him some ironed shirts. Then he went into the town. There had been no trouble for weeks, no curfew, no murders. The army seemed to have gone to ground. It was as good a time as any for Vikram to disappear. Gerard told him the Chief should not be kept waiting. So Vikram went over to the gem shop. As soon as Gerard saw him, he closed the door and shuttered up the shop. Then they both went upstairs.

'Can I have some arrack?' asked Vikram.

Gerard hesitated for a fraction of a second. Since the business at the crossroads, he noticed, Vikram was less polite, more confident and full of demands. But he got two glasses and poured some arrack for them both. He handed Vikram his travel documents. The papers stated that Vikram was a Singhalese man of twenty.

'You shouldn't have a problem with that,' Gerard said easily. 'Your Singhala is perfect, you even look Singhalese. In fact, if I didn't know better I would say you were one of these bastards!'

Vikram grinned. Gerard noticed he downed his arrack in one gulp.

'You know what to do, huh? Take the train to Colombo. Then go to this address and ask for Rajah. Say Singh sent you. Give him this packet of tea. Be careful how you hold it. There's no tea inside it, remember!' He laughed heartily, amused at his own joke. 'Rajah will take you to Batticaloa. You'll have to travel by night because of the daytime roadblocks. But that shouldn't be a problem as there's no curfew at the moment. When you get to Batticaloa you will be given over to a man called Lakshman. You can speak Tamil with him, safely. Lakshman will take you to the Chief. He'll blindfold you for security reasons, OK? Now, any questions?'

Vikram said nothing, looking meaningfully at the arrack bottle.

'No,' said Gerard shortly. 'Not in the middle of the day. I

can't afford to have you drunk in broad daylight. Now, listen carefully. You'll be at the training camp for a couple of weeks, maybe a bit longer. I'll see you only after that. By that time you'll have been briefed for your next assignment. Then there'll be nothing you won't be able to do for the Tamil people. You'll get your chance to avenge your family at last. OK?' He paused. 'Again, any questions?'

'Can I have my gun back?' asked Vikram.

Gerard sighed. The truth was he was getting a little bored with the boy and his monosyllabic ways. After the initial eagerness at the crossroads shootout, Vikram had sunk back into his usual morose silence. Well, anyway, thought Gerard, this latest little job will put some life back into him. Brute force was fine for a foot soldier but Gerard hoped for better things from Vikram. He knew the work ahead would be punishing and rigorous, the assignment the most ambitious the Tigers had undertaken yet. It remained to be seen if the boy was up to the task. Vikram was looking at him expectantly. Oh yes, thought Gerard wearily, the gun. I almost forgot.

'Vikram,' he said patiently, 'you can't take it with you. You will have your own gun once you get to the camp, men. A more up-to-date model. You can't travel with a thing like that across enemy territory. Why can't you understand?'

For a moment he thought the boy would argue. But then Vikram picked up his pass and his papers and left. Silently, as he had come.

Outside, the afternoon was gelatinous with the heat. It was the mosquito season once more. Everywhere the drains were clogged with rotten fruit that had burst open. The sun, dust-laden and harsh, lay with bright indifference over the shuttered town. An occasional bicyclist passed by. Vikram crossed the main road and turned through the coconut grove heading towards Sumaner House and the last of his things. Bony cattle grazed on the common land, chewing a frothy cud, gazing into the distance. A stray dog barked at the breeze. Otherwise the town rested from the heat. Vikram passed by a water pump, stopping to quench his thirst. A few overripe mangoes lay squashed on the ground among a scattering of cigarette stubs and smashed beer bottles. The stench of garbage was everywhere. Since the war had advanced to this corner of the island, even the refuse was not collected. The market stalls had sold out long ago and moved on but the stray cats remained, skimming the ground for a phantom lick of fish, staring sleepily at the flies that swarmed on their sores. Vikram passed the road island and cut across through the temple grounds. Ahead of him was Nulani Mendis. He could see her talking to the local doctor. The doctor was writing something on a piece of paper. Then he nodded and went towards the temple. Seeing Vikram the girl raised her arm in greeting and waited. She was wearing a white dress and she had tied her hair in a coil at the back of her head. She looked cool and very pale. She waited and as he came closer fell into step with him. Vikram was startled. He saw that today she did not smile.

'My mother is not very well,' she said as though she was picking up a previous conversation. She pointed in the direction in which the doctor had gone. 'And I can't get this prescription until four o'clock.' She looked around as though she expected to find what she needed.

'What's the matter with her?' asked Vikram.

'I don't know. I think she misses my brother. It is a terrible thing to lose a son.'

Vikram said nothing, remembering the story of Lucky Jim's departure. Mrs Mendis had thrown a party and most of the school had gone to it.

'I looked for you at my brother's party,' the girl was saying. 'But you didn't come. Have you left school?' she asked, adding, before he could say anything, 'I have. There seems no point. I'm no good at anything.'

She sounded lost. Vikram looked at her curiously. Something, some desperation, uncoiled itself from her and moved towards him. Did she mind that much about her useless brother? He could not think whom she reminded him of.

'You can draw,' he said and the girl smiled so suddenly that Vikram stopped walking, startled.

'Yes,' she nodded. 'I can draw.'

But she spoke flatly, reminding him of the rumours that had once circulated about her silences. He had the strangest of urges to tell her not to mind so much, but the heat and her prox- imity confused him. Her apparent ease, as though it was an established fact that they were friends, unnerved him too. They walked a little way saying nothing. The girl seemed lost in thoughts of her own.

'What's it like in Sumaner House?' she asked at length. 'Do you get lonely in such a big place?'

She was looking at him. Her eyes were huge and unhappy. He saw that they were very clear, like the eyes of a small child.

'My father was killed too,' she said softly, unexpectedly. 'I expect you've heard. Everyone gossips about it. We never found out who poured petrol over him. The police came, but they never caught anyone. I was in the house when it happened. I saw everything.'

They had come to the top of the lane where her house was. Vikram did not know what to say.

'Don't let gossip worry you,' she continued.

He had the oddest feeling they were talking of something else entirely, that they had spoken in this way before. It seemed to him they were picking up threads from another conversation.

'Everyone does it,' she went on. 'It doesn't mean anything. It's just the way things are.'

'You're friends with the old man at the beach house,' he blurted out unthinkingly.

He knew she would leave in a moment, but he wanted to keep her here, wanted to keep her talking to him. Suddenly he could not bear the thought of her going home. The girl stood for a moment longer, looking at him. Vikram saw that in fact she was exhausted, that possibly she had been crying. Small beads of perspiration had gathered on her brow and there were dark rings under her eyes. And although her hair was coiled up she wore no flower in it as he had often seen her do.

'He has gone away,' she said flatly.

She stared out at the sea. He thought she might say something else but she seemed to change her mind and smiled instead. The smile didn't quite reach her eyes and he wished he hadn't mentioned the old man. Confused, he scuffed the ground with his feet. She put out her hand and touched his arm.

'Don't do that,' she said absent-mindedly. 'You'll ruin your shoes.'

Vikram could think of nothing to say.

'I must go,' she was saying. 'I must make my mother some coriander tea. See you.'

And the next moment she was gone.

Time crawled slowly like the geckos that came out of the cracks in the walls. Every day Nulani returned to the beach house and painted under the watchful eyes of Sugi. He tried to make her eat a little, knowing that when she was at home all her energies were directed towards caring for her mother. Theo had been away for three weeks.

'Halfway there, already,' said Sugi encouragingly.

But it was no use, Sugi could see that her unhappiness was growing and her energy fading like the colour in her green skirt.

'How is your mother today?' he asked. He knew from his friend Thercy that Mrs Mendis was very unwell.

'Must be her broken heart,' Thercy had said. 'Even though her daughter looks after her so lovingly, it's the boy she wants. It was always the boy as far as she was concerned.'

Jim Mendis wrote one letter home. The day the letter arrived the girl came rushing down the hill to Sugi, wanting to tell him the news.

'He shares a house with an English boy,' she said. 'They have become good friends. And he plays cricket,' she said delighted for him.

Sugi listened. Jim Mendis had not asked a single question about his mother or sister.

Theo wrote. Without any hope that the post would reach her, still he wrote. '*I'm longing to come home,*' he said.

Every night, he told her, he put a tick in his diary. He hoped she was missing him as much as he missed her. And, he said, smiling as he wrote, everywhere he looked he saw only her face. Distance had focused his thoughts, stripped him of diffidence. Slowly he wrote his first words of love and, having started, found he could not stop.

> *The party for the film premiere was very grand, very important, I suppose, but, without you, I didn't have the slightest interest in it. All I could think of was how much I miss you and wonder what you would make of so many*

strange people, all dressed in their finery. How you would have wanted to draw them all! Everywhere I go I seem to see things with your eyes. You see what you've done to me? And incidentally, have I told you how lovely your eyes are? Or, when you used to sit at the back of the veranda in your lime-green skirt, how impossible it was for me to work? All I wanted to do was to keep you talking so I could stare at you! And now you are so far away. Last night I woke in a panic worrying about whether you were all right. I had to force myself to remember you had Sugi looking after you. I trust Sugi with my life, you know, and so can you. I calmed down when I remembered that. I have told him we are going to get married when I return. I know you won't mind. Sugi only wants us to be happy.

I've been telling my agent a little about you too. Well, he was questioning me. He knew Anna, you see. And he saw how I was after she died. In fact, he was very good to me at the time. Now of course he could see I was different and he was curious to know the reason for this. Transformed, was what he said. Who has done this to you? he asked me. So I told him a little. Not too much, you understand. I'm not ready to share you with too many people yet! But I told him I feel as though a light has been switched on in my life. The light that is you! Three weeks, less, if you don't count the last weekend, and I will be home.

'I can't hear his voice any more,' the girl said to Sugi, panic-stricken. 'He's been away for so long I'm frightened.'

'Draw him, *putha*,' said Sugi soothingly, comforting her as though she was his own child. 'Have faith. He'll be back very soon. You must not be afraid.'

And by some miracle, when she calmed down, she saw that indeed she could draw him from memory. Perfectly.

'See,' said Sugi, triumphantly, 'all those months of practising have been worth it. His likeness is perfect!'

And then, suddenly, her mother's illness was not just simply a broken heart. She had malaria. The doctor was reluctant to admit her to hospital. Conditions were not good there. It would be better, and safer, he told Nulani, if they could nurse her here at home. So Nulani and the servant changed the sweat-sodden sheets and tried as best they could to deal with the deadly sickness as Mrs Mendis's body twisted and turned in agony.

'Soon, very soon, Sir will be back,' said Sugi, who had begun to shop and cook for them.

By the time the first case of malaria occurred Vikram was already in the eastern province at the special camp. The camp was near an underground cave, deep in the jungle. Close by was a river that overflowed in the rainy season. Once this had been a place of pilgrimage but now the ground was full of newly dug graves. The leader of the camp, who was not much older than Vikram, told him the dead were mostly women and children.

'First they were raped,' he told Vikram, 'then we were brought in to shoot them.'

'Who were they?' asked Vikram.

'Muslims.'

The boy told Vikram that the dead amounted to 270. They were people who should not have been living there, it was not their land, it was Tamil land. And their husbands and sons were all in the Singhalese army. The Tigers had turned their sub-machine guns on them, sending bullets buzzing like bees. And then afterwards the rains had washed the bodies into the river.

Later, the boy told Vikram, the bodies had surfaced, bloated and stinking like cattle, with stiffened limbs. Some soldiers still thought the place was haunted with the souls of the dead, others, that Muslims had no souls to speak of. But that was some weeks ago, the boy told Vikram. Now the whole place had been cleaned up for their camp.

'Were you at Waterlily House?' asked the boy.

'How did you know?'

'I was there with you,' the boy said, grinning. 'You don't remember me, no?'

Vikram shook his head. But he was interested in spite of himself.

'Somebody from your village brought you there after the army killed your family.'

'I don't remember,' Vikram said slowly. 'I've been living in the south.'

The boy nodded. 'My name is Siva Thruban,' he said. 'But everyone calls me Gopal.'

Gopal told Vikram he had been in the camp a long time, perhaps four years.

'After you left, I got moved from Waterlily House. We were on our way by truck to another orphanage when we were ambushed by the Tigers and I was taken to a camp. I was trained there for four months. We did many things,' he added proudly. 'We blew up army jeeps, we carried messages for the Chief, we stole motorcycles and we threw hand grenades.'

He told Vikram the worst fighting was in the north but he had only been on one trip up there.

'What happened to your family?' asked Vikram.

Gopal had no idea. 'The Tigers came in the night to my village,' he said. 'They asked my father where my older brother was. My family had sent my brother away because they knew the Tigers were coming. But the man told my father if they couldn't have my brother then I would have to go with them. I was asleep. They woke me up. My mother was crying, my father was crying too.'

They had taken him away, he said. He had never seen his parents again. He did not know where his brother had gone either. At some point he had been told his family did not want him back. To start with this had angered him.

'It wasn't like your family. *Your family* died. Mine didn't want me.'

But now he no longer cared. Vikram made no comment. He took a can of Coca-Cola from his rucksack and drank it.

'It's not so bad here,' Gopal said after a while. 'It isn't as bad as people think. This is my home now. I wouldn't want to go back to my village. We were forced to pour petrol on the cattle there, and set fire to them. So after that I could never return.'

'You went back to your village?' asked Vikram.

'Oh yes. I had to. It was important that it was my own village. It was my initiation ceremony. Otherwise they told me I would not be able to join the Leopard Brigade. You have to show you don't care about anything! Your family, your village, anything from the past. So, you see, men, I survived all the campaigns,' he said grinning, ticking an imaginary list on his fingers. 'I have been a spy, a courier, a front-line fighter. I have survived all of it.'

They had put him in this special unit because of this ability to court good luck, he said.

'This time we're getting very different kind of training, you know. You've been brought here specially. They told me you are a very good shot, is it true? We're going to be working together on this new campaign.'

Vikram nodded.

'I've been using Type 52 and 58 up to now. But this ambush is different. We'll be told about it tomorrow.'

Gopal took Vikram to his sleeping quarters. They would each have a hammock in a tent on the far side of the camp.

'Have you had suicide training?' he asked Vikram later, when they were alone. 'When I first joined the Tigers I was given a suicide bodysuit with explosives. I wore it when we carried out the attack on Elephant Pass.'

Gopal grinned. He looked for a moment like a small boy. He had been frightened at first, he said, even though he knew they were doing it for the glory of the oppressed. At one point, two of his team stepped on a landmine and were blown up.

'I was very upset at the time,' he continued chattily. 'But, you know, now I've almost forgotten what they looked like. It's the way things are in this business.'

He paused, then made up his mind.

'Look, let me show you something.'

Pulling out a box he showed Vikram his treasures. He had collected razor wire and explosives, wire-cutting tools and a small radio. Then he showed Vikram a pair of designer trainers. They were hardly worn. He had stolen them, he said.

'If my luck runs out,' he said. 'Take them!'

Mrs Mendis was admitted into hospital. Her condition had worsened. All night long Nulani watched as her mother shuddered with the ice-cold chill that shook the bed and sent her body into desperate spasms in its attempt to generate heat. Then, after the terrible cold, came the raging fever. Slowly it became clear that Mrs Mendis was becoming weaker by the hour. Sugi came. He brought food, but Mrs Mendis was beyond eating. So he fetched the doctor instead. The doctor saw the hopelessness of the situation. Where were Mrs Mendis's relatives, her brother? Surely the girl could not make decisions alone? The doctor was not an unsympathetic man but the girl did not seem to understand, the hospital was not necessarily the answer. The wards were overcrowded and understaffed; there was hardly any medicine. Still, something of the girl's distress penetrated some part of the doctor's numbed mind. He found a bed and sent Mrs Mendis there. He could see that Nulani Mendis was at the point of collapse. This was a family well known to him. He had watched as it slowly shrank and dis-integrated. Now, as far as he could see, the daughter had no one left except her thuggish uncle. The doctor had been fond of Mr Mendis; he had seen the children change after his death. The girl had become withdrawn. She has grown very beautiful, he thought, looking at her tiredly. But what use were her looks without her family to protect her? So he admitted Mrs Mendis to hospital in the hope that she would recover. And Nulani, travelling in the ambulance, glad that her mother would get well quickly, thought, in less than a week Theo will be back from the UK.

They were biding their time. In between the training sessions at dawn the Leopards spent endless hours of intolerable boredom. Waiting. Waiting for what? No one would say. They knew the next mission would be dangerous, but that was hardly surprising. Nearly everything they did in this unit was lethal. Only twelve of the original thirty recruits from Waterlily House had survived. The rest were all new and therefore younger.

'Would you swallow the cyanide?' asked Gopal as they began to pack. Finally the orders had come that the operation was to begin. 'If you get caught, I mean.'

'No.'

'What, not even if they tortured you?'

Vikram shook his head. He frowned and continued to reload his gun. This new model was smaller and deadlier. It was light-weight even with the silencer fitted. But he preferred his old one.

'I would,' said Gopal cheerfully. 'What's the point of suffering?'

They had finished their preparation. In a few hours they would move from the camp and head through the jungle for Katunayake Airport. Vikram and Gopal had worked closely together during the past few weeks. As the oldest in the group, they were the leaders. The youngest were only ten. They were the runners and would carry the explosives.

'Your father took cyanide, didn't he? That's what they said at Waterlily House.'

'Yes,' said Vikram shortly.

He clicked the safety catch on. Then he wiped the back of his hand across his face. The humidity had risen to unbearable levels since the morning. The swampy ground was a hotbed of mosquitoes and other insects. Gerard had told him he could go back to the south once this job was done. He glanced at his watch. They were due at the airport by four. It was now midday. Gopal was still talking. He didn't seem to be in any rush.

'Did you have brothers?' he asked.

The appalling heat did not seem to bother Gopal.

'No,' said Vikram. 'Gopal, aren't you ready?'

'Almost,' said Gopal. 'I thought you said you had a brother.'

'I only had a sister.'

Had she lived she would have been twenty-eight now. The thought came to Vikram quite calmly, without effort, as though it was an everyday occurrence for him to think of his sister. There had been a man who visited them, he remembered suddenly. Somehow, even though he had been small, he had known the man only visited because of his sister. He remembered nothing else of the man, except that he was always at their house and his sister was always happy when he was there. She used to smile in a secret, inexplicable way at these times. She laughed when she played with Vikram and she was happy when she helped their mother. But with the man, she had been different. Vikram had not understood the difference, only that it was not how she looked at any of them. He frowned, thinking all this suddenly. Seeing the vivid green of the plantain trees near their house, the walk to the well and the schoolteacher who had taught him his alphabet. H for hollyhocks, the schoolteacher had written on his slate.

'I think I saw my brother when we were at Elephant Pass,' Gopal was saying. 'Just before we blew up the bridge. If it was him he didn't see me, or didn't want to.'

Vikram blinked. For a moment he had forgotten where he was. He looked pointedly at his watch and Gopal laughed good-naturedly.

'OK, OK, men. Have you become our new Chief or something?' He began to collect together the last of his things. He was in charge of the two boys who would carry the explosives. He would see to it they planted them in the correct spot. Unusually, everything had been organised with precision. Vikram would detonate the bombs. For once headquarters wanted to reduce the number of casualties among the Tigers. Gopal opened his box and took out the pair of Adidas trainers. He wiped them with his shirt. Then he put them back in the box. Their belongings were to be loaded into a different truck. The camp was being dismantled for security reasons and would regroup elsewhere. Their possessions would be moved on while they were at the airport.

'What d'you think of Meera?' Gopal asked suddenly, jerking his head in the direction of the girls' camp.

Vikram finished loading his gun and began clearing out his pockets.

'D'you think she's pretty?'

'She's all right,' said Vikram. 'She's a good shot,' he added. 'For a girl.'

Gopal laughed, a high-pitched excited laugh. Vikram looked sharply at him.

'D'you like any of them here, Vikram?'

'No,' said Vikram. 'Not here.'

'Where then?'

'Somewhere else,' Vikram said shortly.

'Really?' Gopal was interested. 'Have you got a photo, men?'

His sharp eyes darted feverishly about and he moved his head from side to side, grinning. He reminded Vikram of a stray mongrel he had once seen. He thought of the temple on the hill, near Sumaner House. The breeze had been clean and fresh, not at all like the heavy, rancid air they breathed in the camp. Through the trees he had glimpsed small cameos of the sea. And the girl's dress had been piercingly white in the sunlight, absorbing the heat, changing it into something sweet and very calm. He heard her voice, over and over in his head. He had seen her twice more before he left. On one occasion, she had been standing in the queue at the dispensary in the lime-green skirt he had often seen her wear. She had not seen him. She stood quietly staring at the ground, patiently waiting her turn in the queue. And her face in profile had such a look of accept-ance that it had hit him like a spasm of pain. He had moved away, not wanting her to see him, not understanding why he felt this way. And then there had been the last time on the way to the station when he was leaving. It had been early in the morning and he had been in a hurry. On an impulse he had decided to walk along the sea road and over the hill, as Gerard had advised and in order to avoid being seen. And then he had come across her standing motionless staring at the railway line. She had turned and he saw she was deep in thought and did not recognise him. But then she had come towards him and touched his arm asking him where he was going.

'I like to watch the train from Colombo,' she had volunteered. 'When I can't sleep it's what I like to do. My mother is in the hospital at the moment, and I like to wake early so I can visit her.'

Vikram told her he was going to Colombo. 'To meet a relative,' he lied, and at that she had said she was glad he had someone left from his family. Even in his confusion he had felt the sincerity of her words.

'Hurry or you'll miss the train,' she had said. 'I'll wave to you when it goes.'

She had smiled at him and then, just as he had turned to go, she had reached up and kissed him on the cheek. Gopal was staring at him.

'No,' said Vikram. 'No, I've no photo. And we'd better go.'

They crouched, watching as it came into view. It appeared as a small speck in the sky, glinting in the sun, descending fast, heading for the runway, graceful as a gull. The sun was on its wings and it had travelled seven thousand miles. In spite of the tension Vikram was mesmerised by the sight of the aeroplane. He lay flat on the ground clutching his radio, holding it to his mouth. From where he was he could just make out the outline of the others as they waited for the plane to land. The two boys were already close to the runway, under some airport trucks. Gopal, the most experienced of them all, was not far behind with the silencer fitted on his revolver. He would have to shoot the driver of the fuel tanker and possibly some of the ground staff. The stationary fleet of empty aircraft were dotted around in bays and the two boys placed a small black box close to the base of each fuel tank. So far everything had been straightforward. Someone had provided them with access to the enclosed grounds, and now, Vikram knew, the runners were waiting tensely for the oncoming plane to land. Once the passengers had disembarked the runners would plant the final cache of explosives under it before taking cover. Vikram had had his own private briefing. The Chief had shaken Vikram's hand and told him he had great plans for him. If at the given moment there were still people on the tarmac, he had said, it did not matter. If they did not move quickly enough, Vikram was to trigger the bombs regardless. It was his priority, the Chief had emphasised, somehow making it sound as though he was giving Vikram a warning. Did Vikram understand, the Chief asked? This was a war, not a game of cricket.

'Your responsibilities are to the Tamil people, not to individuals,' he had said.

Then the Chief shook Vikram's hand warmly again.

'We shall grind this country to a halt,' he had said, loudly. 'We have to let the world see that we mean business. Only then, after we've taught them a lesson, will they listen. There will be no aircraft, no runway, no way out! What will they do then, men?'

Having glared at Vikram, he smiled suddenly and reminded him once again of his family, and what had been done to them.

'Don't forget that, Vikram, not even for one single moment. It is your duty to avenge their memory.'

He told Vikram he would be listening to the news all day. And if it was a success, it would be Vikram's doing.

'There will be plenty of rewards,' he promised. 'Plenty, plenty, men.'

Vikram began his countdown, slowly, as the wheels of the aircraft touched the ground. He would wait exactly eight minutes. Eight minutes for it to clear itself of passengers and crew. There would be no time for the baggage trolleys. Anything or anyone still on the tarmac after that had only their karma to blame. The passengers began to disembark. From where he was they were merely a collection of unrecognisable shapes of brightly coloured saris, and the tropical suits of Westerners refusing to believe in warnings. Vikram could not see their faces. He counted silently, staring at his watch, his mind perfectly clear now. He did not look up, he did not see if the small boys had cleared the fence. He could not see Gopal or any of the others. He simply pressed the button.

Turning as he reached the airport doors, hearing the noise, feeling the blast of heat, Theo Samarajeeva saw the plane he had just arrived on become a coffin of flames. There was a shout of warning as another explosion went off. And another, and another. People screamed and begun running towards the building in blind panic. Two more explosions followed. Glass and metal were flying in all directions and smoke poured across the runway. In the chaos no one could tell if it was the airport itself that was burning. The revolving doors became jammed with passengers caught in the rush to escape. As more glass shattered the police appeared and began their stampede on to the tarmac, accompanied by firefighters and ambulance men. The public address system pleaded for calm in English and in Singhalese but there was no calm to be had. A wall of black smoke arose, blotting out the sun, muffling the sounds of the screams of sirens and guns and those who were trapped outside.

He was running through the long grass. Four of them were missing already and Gopal was bleeding. Part of his arm had been ripped off and now hung limply. A piece of metal was embedded in his leg. He was panting and his face was slowly draining of all colour. Vikram was half dragging and half carrying him but he was a deadweight.

'Try to walk,' he said harshly. 'We've got to make it to the trees. Then at least we will be hidden.'

'I can't,' Gopal said faintly. 'You go.' He was fumbling in his shirt pocket.

'It's not much further. Come on. I'm going to put you on my back.' Vikram hoisted Gopal up. 'Put your arm around my neck,' he said with gritted teeth.

But Gopal struggled against him and slid to the ground. There was the sound of something moving in the bushes. Vikram turned swiftly, cocking his gun, looking around him.

'Vikram,' hissed Gerard appearing in front of him on all fours. 'Get to the trees,' he said. 'The army has arrived. They're everywhere. We'll have to go south to avoid the roadblocks. Quickly, now!'

Vikram turned back to Gopal. He was struggling with something in his mouth. Before he could reach him, Gerard whispered sharply, 'Leave him, Vikram! He's finished. Leave him. Come. Now! Before it's too late.'

Through the sour odour of explosives and sweat Vikram caught the unmistakable scent of almonds, and in that instant he realised Gopal had bitten into his cyanide capsule. And he saw too that Gerard was running towards the covering of trees.

By the time the army helicopters were hovering over the airport, Vikram was already heading for the east coast of the island. It had not been an easy journey and they had changed vehicles three times in order to avoid being seen.

'You've got me to thank for saving you,' said Gerard grimly.

'You bloody sentimental fool! A few more minutes and they'd have spotted you.'

Vikram was silent.

'They would have strung you up,' said Gerard. 'You damn idiot! They would have tortured you and made you talk. And then they would have killed you. D'you realise that?'

Vikram was coughing. The smoke had filled his lungs and he was covered in cuts. The bittersweet smell of almonds seemed everywhere, in his clothes, on his hands, in his mouth. The smell came back to him from some place deep within his past. It was now past midnight. He had been without sleep or food for almost a day. Gopal was dead.

'At least he had the sense to take his capsule,' said Gerard pointedly. 'This had better not get back to the Chief. Although,' he added, as Vikram continued to say nothing, 'it was a success in spite of the fact that only you survived. I expect you think you're immortal, no?'

Laughing in a loud and jerky way, his gestures oddly un-coordinated, Gerard turned the radio on. Again Vikram smelt almonds. The news, in Singhalese, was of nothing else except the airport bombing. The runway was unusable. Any refuelling was out of the question; nothing could take off or enter the country. Those foreigners still on the island would be flown from the army airbase to the Maldives where they would wait for any available international flights. Gerard laughed again and switched channels.

'See,' he said proudly. 'My planning and your operation. We're quite a team!'

Vikram was searching the radio stations. He ignored Gerard.

'In Sri Lanka a series of explosions that set fire to seven aircraft in the international airport of Katunayake has brought the country to a standstill. The Foreign Office has advised against travel within

the region. Tamil separatists have claimed responsibility and the
Sri Lankan government has declared a state of emergency.'

'So the Chief has made a statement,' said Gerard. He spoke
very quietly. His good mood had evaporated and he clenched
his fists. His whole body was tense again. 'He might have told
me,' he muttered darkly. 'Who made the tape? Who delivered
it, huh? Which ignorant Tamil bastard?'

'What happens next?' asked Vikram.

'We go down south,' said Gerard shortly. 'I have a job for
you. Only you can do it. And, Vikram,' Gerard said, 'it won't
involve guns, I'm afraid. Not yet. You'll need to lie low for a
while. Anyway, I've already told the Chief you're working for
me. It's a waste using you as a foot soldier.'

They were reaching the camp.

'Get some sleep,' said Gerard.

'I need to get Gopal's things.'

'What?' asked Gerard. 'Oh, they were probably dumped. Did
you really believe anyone would come out alive from this operation? Count yourself lucky.' He paused. 'You're working for
me from now on,' he said at last. 'Get some sleep. I'll pick you
up in a couple of hours.'

And he stopped the car.

8

SHE WAS WAITING FOR THEO ON the brow of the hill, wearing the red dress that she had first worn on her seventeenth birthday. She looked smaller than he remembered. Her dark hair was loose, and he saw she had been crying. He knew then that she had heard of the bombings on the radio. She had heard it and had not known if he was safe. But he was here now, even though it seemed as though he had been away for years. Suddenly all his tiredness, his anxieties for her safety in his absence, the horror of all he had just seen, and the pity, all of it vanished as he hurried towards her. He could see the house in the distance with the late-afternoon sun, warm and golden on the stone lions, the faded blue gate, the bougainvillea that cascaded over the wall, all exactly as he had left it. The weeks in London, the fuss of the film premiere, the press, none of it was of the slightest significance. The sea swung into view, unchanged and un-utterably beautiful, and the day became fixed in this one moment, with the view and the black eyes of the girl, as he came towards her. Why had they worried?

'I'm home,' he said tenderly, laughing a little, thinking how like this place she was, unchanged and so lovely. 'I told you I would be back, no?' he said taking her in his arms. 'So why are you crying?' he asked. 'And tomorrow,' he continued, smiling at her, delighting in the words, 'tomorrow we will speak to your mother.'

She had begun to cry in earnest then, and he had said nothing. Letting her cry, listening to the sound of the terrible desperation that came of living through a war that had torn apart her family. He said nothing, stroking her hair, thinking of all that she had lost in her short life, and all that she might yet lose, of all the hurt that had come too early, and would now mark her for ever. But she had gone on crying, for how could she tell him, after all the horror he had seen, and her terror that he might have been caught up in it somehow, how could she tell him that her mother had died that morning?

Later, he watched her face, silvery pale in the flight path of the moon. She had not slept properly for weeks, he knew, but now she slept, as trusting as a child. Behind them the sea whispered in the darkness, shimmering like wild silk, and the night returned to him in a series of disconnected moments, with all the rush and touch of unfamiliar love. He could smell the sea as he had kissed the pebble smoothness of her shoulder. So close, they had never been this close. Time had unfolded. The palms of his hands had felt calloused and rough against the hollow of her throat, the lobe of her ear, the corners of her mouth. She kissed him back. She pulled his head down towards her and kissed his mouth. Instinct had kept him still when she touched him; it kept him silent as he watched her shed the last remnants of her childhood. He stroked her back; his hands went on forays of their own, until at last she was naked. They lay on the edge of the moon-white bed and he drew her towards him then, and kissed her breasts and the soft places that had belonged until now only to her young-girl aloneness. He waited, and only when he saw the knot inside her had eased a little did he enter her, moving as though he were a hummingbird, travelling deeper and deeper into the forest. Further and further he travelled until at last, when he could go no further, when all his longings could no longer be contained, when he had touched her deepest, most secret part, he dissolved within her. The lights were out, the darkness was complete and he could hear the sound of the sea rising out of a new distance. The girl had looked up at him with a grave and beautiful smile as they lay on the crumpled sheets and he saw that from now on he would see himself for ever defined by her eyes.

They slept then. And all the sad, terrible events of the day, the bombs at the airport, the hours sitting by her mother's bedside, the agony of waiting, her brother's absence, all these things slept with them. And in this way, serenely and at peace, the night had ebbed away, unnoticed as the sea rocked against the shore. When he woke again Theo knew some rain had fallen. He could smell the fresh green wetness of the garden drifting in through the window. Of such moments was paradise made, he thought, smiling in the darkness. He felt as if he had been travelling for ever, through eternity and through many lives. He thought again of the useless weeks in London, his film, the people he had met, the pointlessness of all of it. He would never leave her again. After her mother's funeral, they would go to Colombo and he would marry her. Sugi had been relieved when he heard. Rohan and Giulia would be delighted. He would ring them again in the morning. Last night had been too fraught, too frantic. Last night he had thought only of her needs. And of his. Tomorrow would be time enough.

The moon had slipped behind a cloud. He had woken and now he was thirsty. The long flight back had dehydrated him.

Something had woken him, some rustle in the garden. He listened, thinking he had heard the gate creak. There were no lights, the moonlight had moved over the sea and the garden. The house was still. But something had woken Theo. Slowly a thread of awareness uncurled itself with the rapidity of a snake. No one could have entered the garden without the light going on, but he decided to check the veranda anyway; and get a glass of water. Outside, the sea breeze moved uneasily with a soft murmur and suddenly he saw a car headlight, thin and sulphurous, on the road. The light was stationary. Sugi too must have seen it for he was up and had moved to the window.

'It's her uncle, Sir,' he whispered.

Sugi was wide awake and holding a crowbar. How long had he been standing there?

'He's been back twice in the night already, while you were asleep. He's looking for her, I think. We must get her out of here quickly. It's a very bad thing that he should be here at all.'

'How long have you been awake?'

'Most of the night. I was worried they would come looking for her. She should have gone home tonight, Sir. Have you hidden the money in the well?'

'Yes, don't worry. I don't think it's money he's after anyway. I'm sorry you were woken, Sugi. Go back to bed. I'll talk to him.'

'No, Sir,' said Sugi sharply, alarmed. 'You don't understand. If the uncle has come here it isn't good. You must not let him see you. With any luck he'll think there's no one in.'

But Theo had lived too long by different rules. It had made him foolish. Nothing of what he had ever witnessed had changed that. He had smudged the boundaries between what he saw and what he wanted to see. He had been an exile for so long that it had altered his judgement, leaving him vulnerable in ways he did not understand. And he had underestimated the nature of things. So he would not listen to Sugi.

'I will go out,' he said, 'I will talk to him. I want to marry Nulani; there is nothing for the man to worry about. I will tell him that. It will make all the difference, you'll see.'

And all Sugi's whispered pleadings were of no use. Theo went out, unarmed and hopefully, towards the uncle.

There were others there, Sugi knew. He could hear their voices, the uncle and Theo and then the voice of another man. They were out of Sugi's field of vision, their voices raised and agitated. Then he heard a sound. In some part of his mind he knew it was the crack of a sharp object as it met bone. He heard a long, hollow scream and a shot, then another shot, and then the sound of a car reversing swiftly up the lane. Standing rooted to the spot, Sugi felt sickness spreading coldly through him, his mind bludgeoned with horror. He heard a voice, whimpering from somewhere nearby, but it was a moment longer before he realised that it was the sound of his own heart, crying.

Sugi bent over the girl. He could see the moonlight on her face as she slept, innocent of what had just occurred. That she was in danger, that she was alone once more. That last night was the last carefree moment of her life; that only minutes before she had held everything she ever wanted. Whoever had brought her the news of her father's death would have known, thought Sugi, how he felt now. Sleep marked her face like a caress as he shook her awake. Three times in her short life, he thought, his whispers fluttering towards her, confused and urgent. In the distance a train hooted, reaching far into the night, a sound of infinite loneliness, hauntingly sad. Sugi could see she was still half asleep. He could see his words shifting in and out of meaning, elusive and insubstantial. He saw that her sleep-filled limbs were still disconnected from her mind, that she could not yet be prepared to feel Theo's absence. Perhaps, he thought, with a feeling of terrible pity, perhaps she never would be prepared. So thought Sugi as he finally shook her awake, seeing also, by the way in which his words fixed in her mind, that she understood in the clearest moment of horror that she would not hear Theo Samarajeeva's voice again.

The moon, like a searchlight, shone relentlessly over the room. It silhouetted the chair, the corner of the wardrobe mirror and Theo's shoes. Staring at them in the second before the girl's despair broke open and he put his hand over her mouth, Sugi remembered also, as though it was an ordinary matter, that her mother had died yesterday. He held the passport Theo had left, and told her swiftly what they must do. They had no time to lose. At any moment the men might return. Sir had wanted her to be taken to Colombo, to safety. He had not wanted her uncle to find her here. It had been Sir's biggest fear, Sugi told her.

'Quickly,' he said, helping her to gather her things, locking up the house, hurrying her out of the back gate and across the moonlit beach. 'There's a train that passes the level crossing by the next cove. It's the mail train to Colombo and it passes in twenty minutes.' Her uncle might be back at any moment. 'I will come with you to Colombo,' Sugi said. 'After I get you to the house of his friends, I will come back with Mr Rohan and find Sir. I promise you,' he said.

Theo had made emergency plans many months ago, Sugi told her. Should there be trouble Sugi was to take her to Rohan and Giulia. She would be safe there. She *must* come, Sugi insisted, desperate now, for the girl refused to move.

'They must not find you here,' he pleaded. 'It will be worse for Sir. I will come back and find him. I *will* find him. You must believe me. Let's not waste any more time, please.'

He would find Theo, he told her again and again, cajoling her across the endless stretch of sand. Dead or alive, he thought grimly, he would find Theo. He saw the moon reflected in her frightened eyes, as she protested.

'I promise, I promise,' Sugi murmured, holding her cold hands in his, knowing only that he should follow Theo's wishes. Knowing only that he could not break his promise.

'Once you are with Sir's friends, I will go back and find him. I promise. I promise. Please, Miss Nulani, Sir did not want your uncle to harm you.'

The beach was cool and smooth, their footsteps clearly visible as they walked in an endless line of steps towards the next bay. They passed the catamarans half sunk into the sand; the places where the coconut palms bent low and local children had rigged a swing once, long ago. The sea and the sky were joined as one tonight as they walked the beach unheeding, looking neither to right or left. Sugi's anxiety propelled them on. The girl carried a small bag with a few things; a comb, her earrings, a change of clothes. It was all she had now. Pity flooded Sugi's heart. He dared not voice his thoughts but he feared Theo was dead.

Memories criss-crossed his mind. Once long ago, when Mr Mendis was alive, before things had become bad, Sugi had seen him take his small daughter out in a fishing boat. They were going out to the reef, he had said. The fishermen had begun to sing a *kavi* and they had waved at Sugi, asking him if he wanted to come with them. The sea was calm, they had said, they could make a fisherman of him yet, they joked. But Sugi had not gone and they had vanished slowly into the night. A few days later he had seen Mr Mendis again. He was walking on the beach with the child. He had stopped to tell Sugi about the trip. He had wanted his daughter to understand the lives of the fishermen who lived here, he had said. Only then, he told Sugi, only when she understands the traditions of her home will she truly love it. Mr Mendis had spoken with a passion that had surprised Sugi. He loved this land, he had said, and he wanted his daughter to love it too. And now, thought Sugi, his daughter was hurrying away, leaving it all behind.

Sugi walked on, his mind darting backwards and forwards in a confusion of thoughts. He desperately wanted to get the girl to safety and return as quickly as he could. He wanted to get help, to find Theo. Dead or alive, he thought, I must find him. But first they must stop the train. If they missed it as it slowed down at the crossing there would not be another one until the morning. Her uncle, or his friends, anyone, might spot them later on.

'I promised him I would get you out,' he said again, in a voice barely above a whisper. 'But I *will* find him.'

As they rounded the corner of the bay they heard the train hooting. The moon had disappeared as they scrambled up and across the dunes to a place where giant cacti grew beside a cluster of coconut trees. They were almost at the crossing now. The coast road, narrow and completely empty, stretched beside the railway line. Sugi was calling hoarsely to her, urging her to hurry for they were in an exposed and vulnerable position. At any moment the train could come thundering towards them, or an army convoy might appear. The moon reappeared, and at the same instant Sugi saw the signal was still green. He needed to get to the signal box beside the level crossing several minutes before the train reached the first bay if he was to stop it. He ran on the last hundred yards shouting to Nulani to keep off the track. His voice whipped across the breeze telling her to be careful. Hardly had he reached the barrier and lowered it, when the tracks began to vibrate. Instantly the lights changed and they heard the train beginning to slow down. In order to scramble on to the truck with the mail bags they needed to run back along the line to a point where they could board the train more easily. They had only a minute to do this. The headlights stretched across the tracks and the train roared into view, hissing and slowing down. It would not stop moving completely, Sugi, shouted again. She must wait until he told her to jump. They were crouching beside the giant cacti as the wheels screeched and the brakes locked. All of a sudden two army jeeps careered across the bend of the road and some figures stepped into the headlights of the train. Two men walked over to the crossing. Two more followed them. Out of the corner of his eye Sugi recognised one of them. He was shining a torch on the track, and under the wheels. The lights had not changed yet.

'Now,' hissed Sugi. 'Jump! Now! Now!'

He pushed a small bag into her hands and in one swift move-ment she was up and over into the mail truck. The train began to move and as she turned in the darkness of the carriage to see where he was she heard a sharp volley of gunfire. Through the small gap left in the slats she could see Sugi. He had slipped down on to the tracks and had begun to run towards the beach. He zigzagged crazily, shouting at the men, waving his hands, drawing attention to himself. The men turned sharply and began to shoot at him even as the lights changed. The girl stood rooted to the spot, watching with horror, unaware that the train was moving, as they emptied a steady stream of bullets into Sugi, and in that moment she realised that one of the men was her uncle. The train began to gather speed and she saw that Sugi had given her the bag containing her passport and money, moments before he decided to distract her uncle from searching the train. And, as she watched through her blinding tears, as the train rattled noisily along the coast, she saw also that the dawn was beginning to appear faintly from the east, enduring and very beautiful.

At daybreak the seagulls returned with the fishermen trawling their catamarans. The night had been full of fish, silvery-stiff in death, and plentiful. Dragging their nets along the beach, they saw the body. It was completely unrecognisable, blackened and filled with holes, in its stomach, on its legs and what were once arms and face. When the fishermen's gaze reached up to the head, they saw that grey substance had seeped out. In the early-morning light it spread like delicate fronds of coral on the sands. The sea began to edge around, nudging against it, foaming and darkly red. Overhead the seagulls screamed, circling in great wild swoops above the day's catch, while the fishermen watched as Sugi's body rocked gently on its journey out to sea.

9

Only afterwards did they ask themselves, why had they not been more prepared? Many days later, when she could think a little, Giulia had remembered, a knock on the door at that hour was never good. Knowing all they did, they should have seen how much there was to lose. Did they think they were exempt from loss? Did they think this war was meant for others than themselves? Somehow, thought Giulia in the small hours of the sleepless nights that followed, we should have been prepared. But they had not seen it, lurking in wait, ready to pounce, sweeping them along in the wave of insanity that characterised this civil war. Theo had rung them briefly earlier the day before. He had told them he had been at the airport but was safe now. He would ring them, he had said, in the morning. And soon he would bring the girl to visit them. There was something, he had told them, laughing excitedly, that he wanted to tell them. They had not heard him sound this way in years. Guessing his news, teasing him, they too had been glad. But Theo, they now realised with horror, had simply come home to die.

The girl stood at their door. She was etched palely against

the moonlight, carved as though in sandstone, surrounded by the sounds of geckos and bullfrogs, and even in her grief her face remained beautiful. Why had this shocked them so much? Here was proof, they whispered, here was evidence of the fragility of life. She had found them by some miracle; she had come, because, she cried, there was nowhere else for her to go. Rohan was the quickest to understand. And he saw in a moment, reading Sugi's hastily scribbled note, that it was all over. Finished.

'Come back with me,' Nulani had begged them. 'Please! Quickly, come and talk to my uncle.'

But, Rohan asked, what about Sugi? Where was he?

And it was only then, with a voice barely above a whisper, that she had cried, 'He's dead.' That was what she had said. 'They *killed* him! I saw him die!'

Wanting to hide their shock, folding it up tightly, they had tried to tuck it out of sight; but it remained, untidily, visible. Forcing them to confront the unthinkable. Rohan, always the quickest, saw the girl still hoped Theo was alive. He saw she was still warm with the touch of him and would not unclasp herself from it. Sugi, it seemed, had known the only way to get her to Colombo was to let her believe this. Giulia sent the servant to fetch the doctor. The doctor had many contacts all over the island, he could make some enquiries in the morning, he promised. For now he sedated Nulani Mendis and together they reread Sugi's note.

'If I don't contact you in a day, you must send her to safety. You mustn't let them find her. It was what he wanted.'

Theo, they saw, had taken care of everything. There was a passport for the girl, money for a ticket, instructions in case of an emergency. They were stunned, fearful for her safety. The enormity of their task frightened them.

'But how can we do this, Rohan?!' Giulia said. 'Theo might still be alive. He might be held captive somewhere. We can't just send her away. It's too big a decision for us.'

The sedative had begun to work; at last the girl's eyes began to close. Their whispers were low and vaporous in the darkened room.

'Keep her with you,' the doctor murmured. 'Don't let her out. You don't know what could happen. I'll see what information I can find among my patients. Theo Samarajeeva was well known. But so, unfortunately, were his pro-Tamil views, he should not have come back to live here. It was such a foolish thing to do.'

'This was his home,' Rohan said angrily. 'Where else should he have gone? He wrote the truth, about things we all believed in.'

'Shh!' Giulia said, glancing nervously at the girl.

They watched over her, listening to her breathing, thinking of their friend, knowing that at least while she slept, her pain was held in abeyance.

'He should have lived in Colombo,' the doctor said. 'He might have had better protection here.'

'It's no good talking about what he should have done,' said Rohan. 'We need to find him now.'

The doctor shook his head, sorrowfully. 'I will see what I can do. But I have to say, in my experience . . . once they get into the hands of the army, there's not much hope, you know.'

They fell silent then, their minds numbed as much by the lateness of the hour as the horror of what they were facing.

That had been three days ago. Three unimaginable days of watching Nulani Mendis's descent into hell. On the evening of the third day the doctor returned. It was true, he said, what the girl had said was true. Someone, an unidentified man, had been shot on the beach, beside the level crossing. It must have been the manservant, the doctor supposed. And Theo Samarajeeva had indeed disappeared without trace. Local people had heard the sounds of a shoot-out, but had stayed indoors, not wanting to be mixed up in it. Someone had told him the man who was the girl's uncle terrorised the town.

'Better send her to the UK then,' he said at last, into the silence. 'At least she'll be safe there. Get her out if you can.'

He smiled wearily, waiving his fee. Leaving them with some pills for her before stepping out once more into the night.

'You know she won't go, Rohan,' Giulia murmured. 'Can you see her leaving without him? She'll never leave.'

'She has a brother in England. We'll have to tell her what the doctor said. She'll have to know the truth, if she doesn't already guess it. I think she does, I think in her heart she under-stands she'll never see him again. So what is there for her to stay for, tell me? What is there for any of us here now?' he asked.

Bitterness formed a crust over his words. Bitterness mixed with betrayal. Until now he had always loved his home.

Later Rohan went out, dodging the curfew, hurrying along the darkened alleyways of the city with the girl's forged pass-port in his pocket. Somehow, using his contacts, he managed to get a seat on the last remaining flight out. It was on a plane that touched down briefly at the private airport reserved for short local flights. That the girl was Singhalese helped. That she had forged documents stating British citizenship also helped. Theo had thought of everything, it seemed. Everything except his own death. The flight was in the evening of the following day. She would fly to Chennai and change planes there.

But they had reckoned without her. Nulani Mendis did not want to go. Clinging to Giulia, desperate, refusing all sedatives, refusing food, her face swollen with tears, she refused to go. Today her mother was to be cremated, she told them piteously, how could she go? She begged them, and then she argued with them, screaming in a way they would not have believed possible. They began to fear for her sanity. She had come here, she said, believing they would help her. Believing Sugi would find Theo, that he would follow her to Colombo. That was why she came, she said. Didn't they understand? How could they betray her in this way? She was going back, now. No one could stop her. She was going back to find him.

'I don't care what happens to me,' she cried wildly. Anger overtook grief. Why had Sugi lied to her? she demanded. Why had he not told her that Theo was dead?

In the end it was left to Rohan to persuade her.

'Nulani, listen,' he said, stroking her hair, holding her as she struggled. 'Sugi did the best he could. He was frightened. And he had to make a quick decision. He didn't want you to die as well. It had been Theo's last wish, should anything happen, that Sugi would get you out. Sugi was only keeping his promise. Please, Nulani, understand, he loved you both.'

She said nothing.

'Theo always worried something like this might happen. He made emergency plans some months ago, you know. In his heart, I think he knew it wasn't really safe here. If he was forced to leave he wanted to take you with him. Why else would he have got these travel documents for you? It wasn't an easy matter getting a false passport. It took months of negotiation; it was a dangerous business. And he had an instinct, a sixth sense, you know. So that with him, or without him, he needed to be certain you would be safe. So you see, *putha*, you *must* go. For his sake you must. Even more so now your mother has died.'

157

She covered her ears, weeping.

'It's true,' Rohan said. 'While your mother was there you had some protection. Now you have none.'

He paused, shocked by what he was doing but determined nonetheless. She became silent.

'Can't you see, child?' Rohan said more gently, as the storm of weeping showed no sign of abating. He felt the weight of what he had to do grow dark and rotten inside him. He was shocked to the core of his being by it, but still he continued. 'Sugi only did what he believed Theo wanted. He paid a terrible price. But *we* will keep looking. We'll *never* stop looking. And you know that if he is still alive, he'll find you, somehow. *You* know that. So you see, you must go.'

She gave in then, the pointlessness of her struggle leaving her speechless for the second time in her life. And Giulia sitting beside her, holding her, thought, first her father and now this. How will she ever recover from *this*? But Rohan, having seen what he must do, did not waver. He kept talking; about Theo, and what she had meant to him, and the bleakness of his life after Anna had died, before he had met her.

'We, none of us, could give him what you did, Nulani. You were a sort of gift. He told me, I promise you, the last time we spoke. He said it many times; you were the last gift in his life. Hold on to that. Like a coconut palm in the monsoon, you must bend *with* the wind.'

And, he thought, one day, many years from now, please God, you will paint away your grief. One day all this will find its way into your work. An orphan, Giulia thought, giving her the last of the sedatives, waiting with her until she slept the drug-induced sleep of utter exhaustion.

'I can't stay in this place much longer,' Rohan said finally, watching as she slept. He felt utterly desolate and alone, it seemed he had been fighting this war for ever. 'We must go back to Europe. I can't live with this savagery.'

Far away, in another life, were other seagulls sitting on the boat posts, the *briccole*, that marked out the waters of Giulia's home. Now, overcome with longing she wanted to go back to them. She had been away for too long. Lately, even before recent events, the sickness in her husband's country had begun to defeat her. She felt homesickness, never very far away, returning.

'We are all she's got, you know,' Rohan was saying.

I can't take any more, thought Giulia.

'In Europe at least we will be able to keep an eye on her.'

'There's her brother too.'

'Him! Well, I'm not so sure, you heard what . . . she will have no help there.' Suddenly he felt he could no longer bear to say his friend's name out loud.

The girl lay drugged and inert, watched over by them. Twice during that night the telephone rang, slicing into the silence, but when Rohan answered it, no one was there. The drive to the airport skirted the jungle on a road that had been ambushed many times. Their car was old, there were no street lights and they would have to leave well before the curfew. But what if they broke down, on that lonely stretch of road, what if the plane was delayed or her passport did not hold up to scrutiny? What if someone knowing her connection with Theo saw them? Anything was possible.

'This was done because of his books,' Rohan said, at last. They had hardly slept, hardly eaten. Both of them were beyond weeping. 'And the film, of course. That couldn't have helped. They had warned him, you know. He told me this when they visited. He knew they had wanted him for a long time, but he took no notice.'

'I don't understand,' said Giulia. 'He had everything to live for, everything to be careful for. Why did he take so many risks?'

'A man has to survive, Giulia. You cannot expect a man to skulk in fear of everything, especially a man such as Theo.'

Giulia was silent. Truly, she thought, it was time they went back to Europe. Rohan had not been Theo's friend for nothing. He could not skulk either; now less so than ever. And Giulia was afraid.

The cremation of Mrs Mendis, unlike that of her husband, went according to plan. Her brothers, who had shown no interest in her welfare since her marriage, turned up in full force. They sat, all together, with their wives, their children, the neighbours, the schoolteacher, the Buddhist monks and the Catholic priests in the seldom used sitting room. There were so many of them that they spilled out on to the veranda and down the steps into the garden. The servant had so much work that someone had paid for extra help. The woman Thercy, from Sumaner House, helped the servant. Mrs Mendis, in her white sari and the jacket that her daughter had embroidered long ago, was lying in her coffin for all to see. She was surrounded by flowers. There was a wreath from her son with love to his amma. The boy could not get back for his mother's funeral. Everyone understood that. What with the airport closed because of the bastard Tamils and poor Jim's poverty, he was forced to stay away. It was a tragedy. But he had sent flowers, said the aunts and the cousins, he had hardly any money but he had sent flowers. What a loving son. How proud Mrs Mendis had been of him. How lucky she had been with her son Jim. One of the uncles took a photograph of everyone around the open coffin, standing close, as though it was a giant birthday cake, surrounded by flowers and candles. The difference with *this* party was their faces were sad. Another difference was the marked absence of Nulani Mendis.

'What a bitch she is,' said the cousins.

'She was always so stuck-up, too good to speak to any of us. And now she can't even come to her mother's funeral, aiyo!'

'Let's hope she is happy, no?'

'I doubt it. Have you heard the rumour? They were saying in the convent that she's gone off with that man, the one who lives in the beach house! You know, the writer fellow.'

'Twice her age, it's a terrible shame. I'm glad her mother didn't live to feel the disgrace.'

'Well, you know, girlie,' said a distant relative, 'her mother asked for it by marrying that Mendis man in the first place. What do you expect? She left her decent home and went after a pretty face. What d'you expect, huh?'

'Now, now, let's not talk ill of the dead!'

'Aiyo! I'm not talking ill, I'm just *telling* you, men. We all make our own karma, I say.'

Nulani Mendis's uncle listened to the women arguing. He did not put them right. Nulani Mendis was of no interest to him in any case. No doubt she was hiding somewhere, shame keeping her away. What did he care, his sister's family were a dead loss. The monks placed a statue of the many-handed god beside the coffin. The statue watched over the monks as they chanted, their voices rising and falling in sweeping hypnotic drones, backwards and forwards. The air in the room curdled with the stench of over-scented flowers, stagnant water and coconut oil. The monks chanted in low cadences, their saffron robes arranged in bright folds. Their black umbrellas piled outside. Someone brought a silver tray with a jug of water and a silver goblet. A rustle of whispers crossed the room as a priest began to pour the water from the jug to the goblet. He poured the water slowly and the whispers increased. The elderly folk shook their heads in sorrow. The eldest child should have been holding the tray while the water filled and overflowed the goblet. Nulani Mendis should have been there while the waters of her mother's life rose and spilled out on to the tray. What karma was so bad that a woman could not have her own daughter present at her funeral? Nobody deserved such neglect!

Then the brothers closed the lid of the coffin, nailing it down and Mrs Mendis was fully prepared to begin her journey into the afterlife. Mrs Mendis's struggles were over, she had done what she had been meant to do, in so far as she was able. The monks picked up their many-handed god. They folded him up. They would take him back to the temple. There was no point in this statue being here, staring at the dead. This god was for the living. The coffin would travel on its journey alone, and the smell of incense rose and spread indifferently across the grieving house. There were some who smelt it as it passed and thought it was a blessing, but mostly no one noticed.

In certain parts of the jungle, there grows an insect-eating plant not found anywhere else on the island. If disturbed, its elegant leaves close down, like eyelashes. When this happenes, the butterflies or bees, flies or mosquitoes drawn to its scent, are trapped in its vice-like grip, killed in an instant. In this remote part of the rainforest, tucked away among the curious plant life, there appeared an incongruous building surrounded by a thick high concrete wall, covered in barbed-wire circles. It had been there for many decades. No other building was within sight of it. There were no sounds except the faint rush of a waterfall some distance away cascading into a deep ravine. The jungle, in these parts, was mostly impenetrable and dense, although on close observation it was possible to see the tracks of some large vehicle, a tank or a heavy truck of some kind. Such was the density of the vegetation that the afternoon sun could only filter in a diffused way through the branches of the trees. A few birds flew harshly about. That was all.

Perhaps it was the eeriness of the silence after all the noise, or perhaps the pain on his left shoulder had finally penetrated his consciousness, for slowly, Theo found himself awake. And lying in a pool of liquid. It was still light. Although he was blindfolded, the cloth was of a flimsy material, so that he could see faint glimmers, and the movement of shadows through it. His face was wet. When he licked his lips he felt the salty stickiness of it. He knew from this, his face was covered in blood. Because his hands were tied he could not stand. He heard a sound, half groan, half gasp, which seemed as though it came from near him. Nothing happened and he drifted back into unconsciousness. When he next awoke it felt much later. The sun had vanished and it was dark. The pain in his shoulder was much worse and as he struggled to take the weight away from it he felt his face, stiff and caked over, and again he felt the wetness, although most of it had hardened like mud. The blood was congealing. The rope tied to his wrists cut into him, and his chest, his back and his lips, everything in fact, ached. He wondered how long he had lain here. It was surprising how clear his thoughts were. He was without fear, merely curious. With difficulty he began to piece together the information he had. His legs seemed fine, even though he could not stand up. His back ached but that was probably because of the way he was lying, twisted, and slightly at an angle. His shoulder was the worst and as he ran his tongue across his mouth again, he wondered if his lip was split. Where were his glasses? He desperately needed a drink.

The door opened. He could not see it open of course, but

there was a creaking and then something metal, a tray maybe, scraped the floor. Something, a boot probably, prodded him in the small of the back and he was yanked roughly to his feet. He screamed and passed out. The next time he surfaced he found himself pushed against the wall and his blindfold removed. His hands were free. Theo shielded his eyes for this sudden sight hurt them.

'Your food,' a voice said pleasantly in Singhalese.

He stared into the gloom and saw the butt of a gun as it pointed to the tray of food. Beyond the gun was the blurred outline of a face.

'Where am I?' asked Theo.

His voice sounded strained. As though he had been using it too much.

'Eat!'

Again he saw the butt of the gun.

'I want some water,' he said. 'Please, I'm thirsty.'

The man who came towards him out of the gloom was holding a chipped enamel cup and he took it with both hands and drank the cool water. It was so cold that he knew it had come from a well. The door closed and he was alone and in darkness once more. He did not have the faintest idea what he was doing here.

Suddenly, as though a light had been turned on in his head, Theo thought of the girl. It was the first time he thought of her. A single thought that, once it started, ran on through his head like an alarm bell. He could not turn it off. He felt his mind turn with slow and clumsy sickness. He was not yet afraid. Where was he? What had happened to him? Outside the door a rod of light flicked on and off. Was it night? He realised with something like relief that his hands were free. But where was the girl? He noticed there were bars up across the window and at last fear began to spread itself coldly, flatly over him. How long he had been here was unclear. In spite of the heat he began to shake. He touched his head, feeling where the skin had split open. He thought for a moment and remembered, as though from a long, hollow distance, that someone had hit him across his forehead. The memory came towards him jerkily, rushing up with the ground. When he steadied himself, he remembered a little more. He had walked out into the garden. But then, he could remember nothing else. He blacked out again.

The next time he came to he heard Sugi's voice. Sugi was telling him something. The words were slurred and indistinct. Theo frowned. But although he concentrated as hard as he could, he could not make out the words.

'What did you say?' he asked.

But there was only silence. His head was throbbing and he wondered why his trousers were wet. The thought of Sugi had calmed him a little. If he could find Sugi, he felt, things might get better. He began to edge his way around the room banging against the wall but the sounds were feeble and no one answered. Panic overtook him again and he thought of the girl once more. Who the hell has done this to me? Who the hell do they think they are? I need the police, he thought. I need a lawyer, he decided, frantic. How dare they do this?

'Let me out,' he yelled, as loudly as he could. 'Let me out. There's been some mistake. Let me out! Sugi, Sugi, where are you?'

His voice echoed hoarsely around the room. His hands beating against the concrete walls were bleeding again. But no one came.

Gerard and Vikram watched the funeral procession as it wound its way across the town.

'It's the Mendis woman,' said Gerard. 'Killed by a mosquito,' he giggled. 'One less of them!'

Vikram looked at the guests as they walked behind the coffin. He could not see the girl.

'Oh, you won't find her!' said Gerard, noticing the look. 'If the rumours are anything to be believed, *your* girl has gone off with Theo Samarajeeva. No one knows where she is. Too busy to come to her mother's funeral!'

In spite of himself, Vikram was shocked.

'It can't be true,' he said slowly, shaking his head.

He could kill Gerard, he thought, surprised at the pleasure the thought gave him. Not now, but one day, he might do it. Gerard deserved to die, he decided. Lately, for some unspecified reason, he had begun to detest him. But all he said was, 'She looked after her mother.'

'Really? How d'you know?'

Gerard was laughing at him. Vikram said nothing.

'You like her, don't you? The Mendis girl, ah? No use denying it, it's obvious!' he laughed.

Still Vikram said nothing.

'Well, in that case,' said Gerard, seeing the expression on his face, making up his mind, 'I've a job for you that you'll like. I need to find Theo Samarajeeva. Between you and me, I'm not happy with the image the Chief is getting for us Tamils. We're losing a huge amount of international sympathy these days.' He glanced at Vikram. 'Don't get me wrong, the Chief makes a good soldier, you understand, but . . .' He paused, wondering how much the boy understood. 'It's diplomats who move things along, get what's wanted. Not soldiers. And at the moment, the Tamil image is being destroyed.' He spoke with great friendliness. 'I need to change all that,' he said, more to himself now than to Vikram. 'I've been meaning to do something about it but the time's never been right. I might need your help, Vikram, in the future, huh? So what d'you say? People abroad are getting sick of this Tiger cub business. I have an alternative plan to the Chief's grand scheme that involves our writer friend. I want you to go to his house, find out where he has gone. I need to get hold of Theo Samarajeeva. As you're so friendly with the girl, I'm sure you'd like to know where she's gone! You could go now, while the whole town is at the funeral, huh?'

Vikram hesitated. His face was completely blank. What the hell is he thinking? wondered Gerard uneasily.

'OK,' he said finally, and began to walk away.

Gerard watched him go. He hadn't expected such a swift response. It was the first time Vikram had shown any interest in another person. Perhaps, he thought, perhaps the Mendis girl was the key. The boy's inscrutability got on his nerves.

'There's a manservant living there,' Gerard shouted after him. 'I think his name is Sugi. He'll know where they've gone.'

The house was empty. There was no music playing. In the past, on the few occasions Vikram had snooped around the garden, music was always playing. Now the silence of abandonment crossed the veranda to greet him. He walked around the back and forced open a window. The faintest smell of paints led him to a room full of paintings. Notebooks lay open, and images spilled out; supple limbs, eyes that creased in smiles, fragments of happiness discarded hither and thither, the careless accumulation of memories. Vikram turned, startled. What was this? He knew she drew, but this? Confused, he followed the trail. Tubes of paint, ultramarine and vermilion, fused together, for ever purple now, were discarded everywhere. In the bedroom a crumpled white sheet lay on the floor. There was a pair of shoes, straw sandals with the straps broken. And close by, a picture of the girl, eyes shaded from the sun, smiling.

Vikram was taken aback. And for a split second, with shocking unexpectedness, he thought he was looking at his sister, as he remembered her, long ago, under a banyan tree, green-glazed light, against the sun. She had been learning to knit, he remembered. Knit one, purl one, she had chanted, making a scarf for Vikram, for when he was older, she had said, teasing him; for when he went to England to study. Now, with unnerving clarity, he saw her again, as he had not seen her for years. He saw her long beautiful fingers moving deftly. Vikram picked up the photograph. He saw that it was of the Mendis girl. His head spun dazzlingly, and sitting down abruptly, he slipped the photograph out from under its frame. Then he tucked it inside his pocket in one swift movement. The smell of oil and turpentine drifted around. In the dining room, beside a gilded mirror, was a vase of flower stalks, the crimson petals fallen away. Beside the typewriter were a sea urchin and some pale pink shells. The sea moved queasily behind him while seagulls on the telegraph pole outside split their cry into two sounds. Something moved and Vikram swung round sharply, but it was only the last petal in the vase, falling. He sat at the table and touched the typewriter keys. The heat shimmered. It was so great that the trees seemed to drip with it. He felt suddenly very tired. The tension of the airport, the lack of sleep, Gopal's death, all of it had worn him out. Hastily he turned his thoughts away from Gopal. His head was throbbing badly. Vikram realised he was hungry and then, for the first time in many years, he thought of the *vadi* his mother used to make.

He shook his head trying to dislodge the thought. The girl, it was patently clear, was not here. Neither was Theo Samarajeeva. Vikram did not think they had been here for some time. He went back to the room with the paintings. One of them, a small canvas, was propped against a table leg. The paint was not quite dry. It was a perfect likeness of the manservant whose name escaped Vikram, but whom he had often seen in the town. Just then he heard the sound of the gate being closed and swiftly he crossed to the window. It was the servant woman Thercy. Hesitating, not sure he wanted to be seen by her, he looked around for escape. But Thercy was hurrying up the steps and it was too late.

'What are you doing here?' she asked, with a sharp intake of breath. 'I didn't know you were back.'

She didn't ask where he'd been. He could do as he liked. Vikram saw she was trembling a little. It dawned on him that she was frightened of him, that she must have always been frightened, but that he had never noticed before. What was she scared of? he wondered, surprised. What does she think I will do to her?

'I'm looking for the owner,' he said.

'You won't find him,' she said shortly, her breath coming out in gasps. 'He's gone, I don't know where.'

'And the girl?' asked Vikram. He felt some unaccountable bitterness, mixed with something else. 'She isn't at the funeral, is she?'

'Something must have happened to her,' said Thercy quickly. 'You mustn't think ill of her. She would have been at her mother's funeral if she could. Something must have stopped her. She was a loving child, you understand. Nothing would have kept her away. I knew the whole family. The boy was useless; the girl was the best of all, although not many people noticed.' She pulled a face. 'You should have seen how she cared for her mother at the end. I was there, I watched. She would have been here today, if she could. I am certain of it.'

The servant woman stood too close to Vikram.

'Don't listen to gossip,' she said sharply.

Her voice rose in a thin harsh sound, complaining and frightened. Vikram frowned. The woman was like an insect, her voice got on his nerves.

'Like what?'

Thercy hesitated.

'Who knows what happens in this place?' she said instead. 'People disappear. That poor child was unprotected, uncared for. Who knows what has happened to her? Ask her uncle. He'll know.'

'Has she gone somewhere with the writer?'

Thercy glared at him. Then she laughed wearily, without humour.

'Who told you that? It isn't true. Listen to me; Nulani Mendis was a lonely child. She never got over her father's death. She was different from her brother. Mr Samarajeeva was a widower. He was much older than her. He became like a father to her. Can you understand that? You know what it's like to be alone.'

She stopped. She hadn't meant to say so much and she was uncertain of the boy. But still, she couldn't bear him joining in with the vicious judgement on the Mendis girl that circulated the town today. Vikram was taken aback.

'Why d'you think something has happened to her?'

'Can't you see? She would never have gone anywhere with Mr Samarajeeva and missed her mother's funeral. And I can tell you, even if she had wanted to, *he* would not have let her. He was a good man.'

She stopped talking. The boy was looking at her as though he wanted to hit her. She was suddenly very scared.

'Look . . .' she said uneasily, but Vikram moved across the room and was barring her exit.

'Who would want to hurt her?' he asked.

His face was so close to hers that she broke out in a sweat.

170

Vikram smelt like an animal, she thought. He smelt of rancid sweat. He's been drinking, she thought in alarm.

'Vikram,' Thercy said quietly, even though her heart was pounding, 'who knows why anything happens in this town? There were many people who hated her father. And so they hated her too. Ask her uncle.'

Vikram moved away abruptly. He had hardly exchanged more than a few words with this woman in all his years at Sumaner House. Mostly they ignored one another. But he felt an urgent desire to find the girl. He had the strangest feeling that if he found her again anything might be possible. The servant woman, seeing his distracted look, began speaking again. There had been too many deaths on the beach lately, she said. Too many people had gone missing. Mr Samarajeeva had disappeared too.

'And someone killed my friend Sugi,' she added and, without warning, she began to cry. 'He was such a good man. He was my only friend in this town. Now I too have no one. The fishermen found his body on the beach. He was a jewel of a man. I don't know who could have wanted to harm him. He never did anything wrong. That's why I think something has happened to Nulani Mendis. Go and ask that wretched uncle of hers, will you? Please. Ask him where she is. Say you are a friend and you want to know.'

Outside on the veranda the heat had risen again and the afternoon clamoured with a cacophony of sounds as, deep within the crematorium, Mrs Mendis's coffin began, slowly, to be licked by flames.

The end when it came was quick and decisive. The girl had been totally silent during the drive. They had been quiet, for what was there left to say? Giulia sat in the back of the car with her, holding her hand, guiding her through this last journey. It had still been light when they set out, the smallest glimmer of sun fading rosily into the sky. They drove through the outskirts of the jungle. Dark branches brushed against the sides of the car. Occasionally they saw the headlights of some other vehicle but it was always in the distance, on some other dirt track that never crossed their path. Only the wind, rustling the trees, disturbed their thoughts. It was a clear night for flying, Rohan saw. But he said nothing. The visibility would be good because of the moon. She would see the island from above as she left, if she found a window seat. Giulia was thinking too. How much will she remember of this? she wondered. Sorrow spilled across the night, varnishing her thoughts. In all the endless years to come how much of it will remain to comfort her? What can her life possibly be after this? Rohan was silent. His bitterness had become a heavy thing, filling the car, impenetrable as an ancient rock. I wish we were going on this plane with her. We have to get out, he decided. There is nothing more for us here. By now they had skirted the perimeter of Katunayake Airport and darkness had fallen. The radar antennae turned slowly in the sky, a bowed dagoba. Journey's end, thought Giulia sadly, remembering the day Theo had brought Nulani to them. And how, it had been she, Giulia, who had seen, before anyone else, that he had loved her.

Then, in an unmarked space of time, in the swift way of significant events, Nulani Mendis left them, going through the barrier into the area restricted to passengers. Barely registering the last moments, or fully understanding as they took their leave of her, she was gone, her passport checked and stamped, herded along with the other travellers into the waiting area. They watched the plane through the window. The refuelling had finished. The ground staff moved away, the engines started up. The great bird was ready for flight. They watched helplessly as a fly buzzed endlessly against the window. Giulia stared at it with unfocused eyes, thinking of the long dark shadow of this moment, and all the other moments that had led up to this. And of the cost on what was about to become of Nulani Mendis's life.

The tarmac was hot with the smell of fuel, and the air filled with the drift and swell of the sea, hidden just beyond the trees. The plane began to taxi across the runway, it hurried through the darkness gathering speed, and then swiftly, too swiftly, even as they watched, it was airborne, flying briefly over the thick covering of coconut palms. She would see a few roads, some twinkling violet neon lights, thought Rohan, before the aircraft would bank gently and turn out towards the sea. And, he thought, feeling as though his heart might at any moment break, then she would see the moon stretch far across the crumpled water, and catch the last lingering sweep of coastline. Bone-white and beautiful and all that remained of her home.

10

BEFORE THE DUST COULD SETTLE ON Mrs Mendis's ashes,
Gerard began making his enquiries. The town had sunk back
into its usual apathy of heat and sleepy indifference. The house
where the Mendis family had once lived, where children had
played and the sounds of voices were heard, was no more.
Empty coconut shells lay scattered everywhere, overripe
mangoes still thudded to the ground, and cane chairs faded
dustily in the sun. Someone had thrown a broken mirror out
with the rubbish, and the two sewing machines that Mrs Mendis
had made her living by had been sold. Mrs Mendis's brother
had seen to all of this. He had installed himself on the veranda
and in the house. He was sleeping on his dead sister's bed,
eating off his dead brother-in-law's plates, enjoying himself. He
told Gerard, the house was his now. Possession was everything,
he said defensively, draping himself across a planter's chair. He
was an odd-jobbing man, he said, in his falsetto way. Odd and
jobbing, he had said, laughing at his own joke. Well, a man had
to make a living. The army had offered him good money for
Mr Samarajeeva, he added, helping himself to Gerard's arrack.

174

No, no, the man wasn't dead, at least not when he delivered him to the headquarters in Colombo.

'I say, what d'you think I am?' he asked. 'A murderer?'

And he laughed again. Gerard apologised. But he had got what he wanted, he had got his information; Theo Samarajeeva had been alive when they caught him. And the girl? Who knows, said the uncle. The army hadn't wanted her. The uncle laughed, she must have found another man by now! Anyway, she needn't think of coming back. The house was his.

'I want you to go to Colombo,' Gerard told Vikram later. 'I want you to find Theo Samarajeeva. He's our man. Someone will talk, if you hang around long enough. The uncle doesn't know any more.'

Vikram waited. He knew if he stayed silent Gerard would say more than he should.

'We need Samarajeeva,' said Gerard. 'He writes eloquently. Foreigners respect him. We need him to speak out against the government. What the Chief is doing isn't working. *I* should be in charge of the Tamil image. The Chief is just a soldier.'

He paused, absent-mindedly pouring them both another drink.

'If you are successful, Vikram, I promise you, I shan't forget,' he lied. 'If we form the kind of government I have in mind, you'll be part of it. My right-hand man, no? Understand?'

He stared at Vikram. The boy was getting on his nerves. Sluggish and constantly sullen, today he looked particularly mulish. Gerard had had enough. The boy was no longer of any use to him. After the airport bombings he had shown telltale signs of stress, wanting to save one of the team, risking his life for a lame duck. And afterwards, he had been upset. Then he had trailed Gerard back to the south in a state of exhaustion and apathy. Gerard hadn't forgotten any of this. He knew that

Vikram had come to the end of his usefulness and that his battle fatigue and his nervous exhaustion had made him a liability even to the Tigers. Added to which it would be difficult to use Vikram in any further high-profile activities. He's finished, Gerard decided.

Vikram had no idea what Gerard was thinking. Lately, he had not been sleeping well. He had begun to dream again. Those things once hidden had risen to the surface; his sister's face growing out of a plantain tree, his mother's death cry. He would go to Colombo, he decided. There was nothing for him here any more. It would take a few days for him to get ready. He was tired and in any case he needed the necessary papers. Good, thought Gerard, satisfied, watching his face. That's settled then. Of late, Vikram had become transparent about certain things.

'The Mendis girl is probably in hiding,' he said out loud. 'If you find Theo Samarajeeva for me, he will probably lead you to her,' he added cunningly.

So Vikram left, taking with him a package from Gerard to be delivered to someone in Colombo. The air was oppressive. The sea lay like a ploughed field before him. All along the coast the fishermen were back on their stilts, delicate nets fanning out like coral beneath the green water. Nothing much had changed. As the train pulled out of the station Vikram caught a glimpse of the writer's house. It sat snugly at the edge of the bay, overlooking the sea. The carriage was empty. Vikram opened his wallet and took out the photograph of the girl he had stolen. He stared at it and the girl stared back at him. The corners of her mouth were turned up with the beginnings of a smile and her eyes were dark and unfathomable. The last time he had seen her she had been standing on the brow of the hill, staring at the railway line. He had startled her, he realised, but then she had seemed glad to see him. It occurred to Vikram

176

suddenly that she might have been planning to throw herself on the railway line. He had no idea why he had thought this. The train rattled and swung round a bend, and suddenly, without warning, Vikram saw his sister's face again. Twice in one week, calling out a warning to him. Her face stared at him like the face in the photograph, caught by a lens, cactus-sharp, rock solid and frozen for ever. Staring at the horizon, at the point where the sky met the sea, he counted the ships, idly, out of habit. His family had been dead for over a decade. In a rare moment of retrospection he supposed he had come a long way. And although he had no idea where he might be going, he was certain the Tigers no longer interested him. He saw now that they had never really interested him, they had simply been all there was on offer. Gerard too had ceased to interest him, Gerard couldn't give him anything much. Avenging his parents was not possible, he saw. Briefly, feeling strangely light-headed, Vikram remembered Gopal. And again his sister's face rose up, issuing some warning he did not understand. Or was it the face of Nulani Mendis? Had his sister really looked like the Mendis girl? he wondered, confused. He couldn't remember any more, he was too tired, everything was blurred by the heat. The train lurched its way into the central station in Colombo and Vikram took down his suitcase from the luggage rack, handling it with care. He reached for the handle of the carriage door. As he opened it there was a blinding yellow flash followed by a distant thud and the sound of breaking glass. Then, seconds before he felt the pain in his face, the handle was wrenched from his hand as the compartment buckled and collapsed to the ground, dragging him with it.

Seventeen people were killed in the bomb blast that day, including Vikram. The Tiger separatists claimed responsibility.

*　*　*

The river running through parts of the jungle was a wide gaping mouth. It cut deep into the interior like a gangrenous wound, neglected and rotten. Too wide to cross, to swollen to ignore, it provided a natural barrier around the low-slung concrete building that was the army headquarters. Because of the existence of the river this part of the jungle was wet and rich with vegetation. Brilliant tiger-striped orchids sprouted everywhere. Lilies grew wild, choked by the scented stephanotis, and huge creepers tangled with the trees. Birds rustled in the dense mass of leaves, their cries echoing across the valley. Everywhere, in every pocket of light, there were small clouds of tiny butterflies hovering above the flowers, slipping through the hard scalloped leaves of the *belimal* trees. For the forest was teeming and heaving with life. Close to the wall of this makeshift barracks, resting in the sun, was a lyre-headed lizard. It paused for a moment, head darting swiftly, waiting for some mysterious signal before moving on. This part of the jungle was still an area of outstanding natural beauty, but the army traffic that moved backwards and forwards throughout the day was blind to all it offered.

On the fourth day of Theo Samarajeeva's captivity and solitary confinement the guard came in. He told Theo that he had orders to move him.

'Where to?' cried Theo hoarsely. His lips were cracked and caked with dried blood. His throat was closing up, he could hardly speak. 'I want to speak to whoever is in charge.'

His voice sounded unnatural even to his own ears. The guard spoke to him in his native tongue, handcuffed him, pushing him roughly out of the cell. He told him, when they got to their destination, there would be plenty of time to speak.

'But where are we going?' demanded Theo.

He wanted to appear determined, but he heard his voice

rising in panic. The light flooded painfully into his eyes, making them water. He could not shield them. All his questions, all his pleas during the last four days had remained unanswered. Although the knock on his head had confused him at first, some of his memory was returning shakily. He remembered it had been the girl's uncle who had hit him in the garden. He remembered walking out on to the veranda, wanting to talk to the man. He had wanted to stop the man entering the house. Did the uncle know the girl was with him that night? Had he in fact come for her? The thought chilled Theo. He had wanted to question the guard but did not know the uncle's name and in any case he had not wanted to implicate the girl further. With his returning memory, his anxiety for Nulani had risen steeply. It was worse than the pain in his head. He felt weak; the wounds across his face and back ached dully. He had not eaten or drunk much. And he suspected that his whole body had been repeatedly kicked and beaten. But for what reason? thought Theo, bewildered. For loving the girl? He knew he was running a fever. As he stumbled and was pushed towards the waiting truck, the day pressed against him as though tuned to some high-pitched frequency, feverish and urgent. The light too seemed excessively bright, and although the heat was relentless he shivered violently with cold. Again, he guessed the time to be about seven o'clock in the morning but he had no idea what day it was or how long he had been in this state. Again, he tried talking to the guard.

'Look,' he said in Singhala, 'will you at least tell me where we're going?'

He tried to sound reasonable, confident, his old self. But the guard did not answer. He was too busy negotiating the rough dirt track across the jungle. They began to follow the river and Theo wondered whether it was the Mahiyangana and if they were in fact moving towards Koddiyar Bay. He saw suddenly that he might not survive what was to come. With painful clarity, he saw the girl's face, close up and very beautiful. The image was disconnected to the dull throb in his body. He knew, in some part of his brain, that capture such as this seldom led to release, and that his only hope was in finding ways to endure the minutes and hours of what was left of his life. These were his people. And now, for the first time, he felt the shock of double betrayal.

In front of them was an army jeep. Behind, following closely, were two more.

'Who brought me here?' he asked in vain. 'Tell me his name, let me speak to him.'

The guard ignored him. The jungle was full of its morning activities. It occurred to Theo with a detached, surreal irony that here, in this very spot, was the location for his film. But the film had been made in another rainforest, in another country, for there had been no possibility of entering any part of Sri Lanka at that time. He had not thought of the film since leaving England. Now, in order to stay calm, he forced himself to think about it. The premiere, his time in London, all seemed long ago, already in some other life. The critics had been appreciative; the reviews would be good. Good for the box office and good for sales of his book. But none of it had mattered. It had passed in a blur of nothingness and all his energy had been spent in getting back to the girl. He shied away from any thought of her and concentrated instead on the book. It had been written before Anna died.

Anna, he thought, with a rush of relief. He would think about Anna. Thinking about Anna would save him. He would focus on their life together, their travels around Europe, the memories they had made, the happiness. And now he recalled the hazy, halcyon days of summer when youth had been a mere careless thing, full of endless possibilities. Where had it gone? Happiness, he saw, had left silently, slipping through a crack in the door, an open window, vanishing into the night, unnoticed, going even as death arrived. Remembering how it had begun, that first night when he had missed the last train, Theo closed his eyes. The pain in his back was unbearable. The truck bounced and rattled along the dirt track road. He had stayed with Anna, that first night, and she had taken a bath with the door ajar. Provocatively, knowing he would *have* to look in. He forced himself to conjure up the moment as the truck lurched and swayed around a bend. The road appeared to be climbing upwards. Theo sat dully staring at the flickering light by his feet, his mind moving restlessly, recalling other times, other things. They had established themselves as a couple, rented their first flat, and decided to start a family. All their plans, she had laughed, wrapped around the lovemaking that followed. That night was the future, they had declared. Their future! How lovely she had looked. He could remember it still. Could he have imagined any of what followed? Some time after, the next day perhaps, they had gone for a walk and seen long-legged herons fishing gracefully on the mudflats near the lagoon, and she said she knew, she was pregnant. She had been laughing, but she meant it too. And so he tried photographing her and the heron together, but they had disturbed it and it flew away.

Remembering Anna in this way, he managed to avoid thinking of the girl, knowing instinctively that this would push him into a more urgent, immediate despair. He saw his only hope lay in staying calm. His other hope was Sugi, and this too gave him courage. Sugi would be looking for him, he was certain. And more importantly, Sugi would make sure the girl was safe. The jeep carrying him through the jungle lumbered on. Most of the windows had been blacked out and what little he could see made no real sense. Leaf-green, delicate light filtered down through the canvas roof. The moment was dreamlike and undefined, the future full of shadows and some other terrible reality he was unable to comprehend. His thoughts rushed by in this way, careering against each other in a confusion of past events. What was the past, he wondered, shivering, but only the substance of present memory? Time had lost all meaning. Staring at his bare feet he saw, from some great blurred distance, his shoes, placed neatly beside the wardrobe in the bedroom of the beach house. Already, he intuited, it had become another life. His hands were not visible to him. And he wondered at the kind of life that denied a man the use of his own hands.

Far away in the distant tangle of trees, the sound of the yellow-green iora arose, calling to its mate over and over. From this he knew they were moving deeper into the rainforest. Then this too vanished and all that was left was the steady ache of his limbs, and the throbbing sound of the engine.

Giulia listened to Rohan's breathing. Since Nulani had left he had not rested but now she hoped he was asleep. The doctor had told him it was too soon to visit the beach house.

'Wait a little,' he had said. 'I'll be able to find out more from a reliable source soon,' he had said. 'Be patient. It might be dangerous if you go now.'

Giulia was frightened. She was frightened for Rohan. She couldn't believe Theo was still alive. People didn't survive disappearances in this place. It was well known. The army came for them in the night, and then they vanished. Years later, having waited in vain, having finally given up all hope, the relatives received news. Years later the clothes of the missing were sent back. A bundle of torn and bloodied cloth, a pair of shoes with soles hardly worn, a wallet with a photograph in it was all the word they had of an unmarked death. It had happened so many times. Nobody said anything any more, no one dared. Giulia felt grief, suppressed and lead-weighted as a curtain, held back until now for Nulani's sake, beginning to break. Theo had been their closest friend. And now she had another secret worry. Supposing something were to happen to Rohan, too? It was selfish of her, she knew, but she was paralysed by fear. I want to leave this place, she thought. I hate it here. She knew Rohan was still too angry, too hopeful of finding Theo to have planned much beyond this point. When the enormity of what had happened really hit him his reactions would be unpredictable. She was frightened of this and also of her treacherous, selfish thoughts. She wanted to go back to Italy. The idea having taken hold of her ate away, unnoticed. Like acid on one of Rohan's etching plates, it corroded her days. Was it so wrong that she wanted them to survive?

Since Nulani had left, Giulia had slept badly, waking in the small hours of the morning thinking of the girl flying thirty-four thousand feet above the Italian Alps, dry-eyed, bewildered and alone. Imagining her watching Europe unfold, passing over Lake Geneva, the vastness of France, Paris, the English Channel, and then across the Thames estuary, following the tailwind to line up towards London's Heathrow. What sense could Nulani possibly make of any of it? What sense *was* there to be made, catapulted as she had been from one life to another? I can't stand any more, thought Giulia. She was reaching breaking point, she knew, despair was closing around her, walling her in. All I want is to go home.

Rohan, lying awake beside her, facing the wall, remained silent, grappling with thoughts of his own.

*   *   *

Towards late afternoon the convoy of jeeps began to slow down. The sun had moved and the light filtering through the slats was muted. As the trees thinned out, patches of sky became visible. Theo guessed it must be about four o'clock. Hunger gnawed at him and his arms ached from being tied behind his back. Finally, after another hour, they came to a standstill. The driver opened the back of the jeep and placed a black hood roughly over his head. Immediately Theo felt he was suffocating. He began to pant. As he shuffled forward he smelt the sweat of the fabric. He was still struggling with the nausea that enveloped him, when an unexpected slap sent him reeling. He felt his right eye open up. For some reason he had thought he was standing on the edge of some stairs and feared he would fall, but instead he hit a wall. He felt a warm stickiness gluing the hood against his face. In the distance he could hear the muffled sound of crying.

When he came to, he was sitting on the floor. Someone was talking to him. It was a man's voice but for a moment Theo did not understand which language it was. His thinking seemed to have completely slowed down and he asked for some water in English. The words continued, pleasantly questioning. He struggled to understand. The voice dropped to almost a whisper.

'*Tiger Lily*?' asked the Singhalese voice, pleasantly. 'A good name for a book, ah?' The man laughed easily. 'You must sign my copy when you can.'

Theo tried to speak but his lips would not move properly.

'I understand,' said the man soothingly. 'It's a great pity of course, because you write so well.'

The voice went on repeating something, over and over again, and dimly he knew the word being used was 'traitor'. But he still had no idea which language he was being addressed in. He asked in English for some water again, and again a hand slapped him across the face. Sharp pains shot across his lips. He was pulled up by his arm and handcuffed to a hook high above his head. He felt as though his arm was being pulled out of its socket and this time he knew that the screaming came from deep within him. Then he passed out again.

When he regained consciousness he was in a cell with a number of others. It was dark, apart from a sickly neon light that seeped in from the outside. The air was thick with the humidity made worse by the overcrowding; it was fetid with the smell of the overflowing hole in the ground that was the only latrine. In that moment, in the fading light, surrounded by the curious stares of his fellow prisoners, he knew with chilling certainty that he had entered a dark and terrible place where an ineluctable and malevolent fate had swallowed him whole. Survival of this nightmare depended solely on his ability to keep his mind clear. Nothing else remained except his faltering sanity. How long he would keep it depended only on his instincts. And luck. But luck, he saw with slow realisation, was in short supply.

Sleep was impossible in the cramped painful position he was in. Towards dawn the guard unlocked the door and called out the name of four prisoners. When they had left, the others reshuffled in the space, squatting or leaning against the wall or each other. The fraction of extra room brought a false atmosphere of optimism. The opening of the door had let in a small rush of fresh air and breathing was marginally easier for a brief moment. Daylight arrived unnoticed. A heavy-jawed, thickset man of about thirty stared at Theo.

'Are you Burgher?'

Theo shook his head. 'No,' he said. His voice was barely above a whisper. He no longer recognised it as his own. 'I'm Singhalese.'

185

'Don't say anything,' someone cried warningly from the back of the cell. 'They are all bloody spies here. Don't tell anyone *anything*.'

For the first time he became aware of the number of people packed into the small cell. A very old man in a dirty sarong and bare feet, head bowed silently, stared at the ground. Two Tamil men with broken noses were looking curiously at him. After a while they introduced themselves. They were brothers, they said. Theo stared blankly. He had no idea what they were saying.

'We were at the medical school in Colombo,' one of them said. 'But new laws forced us to leave just as we were about to be qualified, you know.'

There had been medics in their family for generations, they told Theo. Their father and their grandfather before them had been surgeons. 'Our younger sister managed to escape to England. She's training to become a doctor there,' they said.

One day, someone had approached them with a view to recruit them to the Tigers, they told Theo. They had refused but after that their house had been watched. Then the Singhalese army arrived with a warrant for their arrest.

'They said we were Tamil spies.'

Their mother had watched as her sons were taken away. They had been here for three months now. The beatings had stopped after a while and they were optimistic that their release would come soon.

Theo stared without responding. Nothing in this conversation made any sense. Nothing of what was happening seemed real. Sweat poured from his face.

'Let me look at your eye,' said one of the brothers.

'He's our own house doctor,' chuckled the old man, rousing

himself suddenly, grinning at Theo. 'Go on, let him, men. He knows what he's talking about!'

The medical students looked uncertainly at Theo, then one of them shuffled towards him and peered at his eye.

'You're in shock,' he said quietly. 'Everyone arrives like this. But don't worry about the eye. It will heal naturally. I promise you. I won't touch it,' he added, 'in case I hurt you.'

Someone, a small, bald-headed man standing in the far corner by the latrine, hooted with manic laughter. 'It'll heal so long as you don't get beaten again!'

Still Theo said nothing.

'I've seen your photo in the papers,' continued the student. His voice was gentle. 'Are you a politician?'

'I know who he is,' the man by the latrine cried. 'You're that novelist fellow, aren't you? Didn't you write a book about the war, huh?'

'Leave him,' the student said. 'He'll tell you when he's ready.'

At that the others in the cell lost interest. Only the man by the latrine kept grumbling. He had been arrested for reasons he did not understand, he said. That was nearly a year ago. He was still waiting for a trial. Each time he asked about his case, he got nowhere.

'I keep asking them when I will be released but of course they're only guards. How do they know?' But at least, he admitted, he had never been beaten.

'It is because you're a Singhalese, men. You are one of them,' said the student.

'No, no,' the man disagreed, chuckling as though the thought amused him. 'That's the last thing I am.'

11

THEO SAMARAJEEVA REMAINED IN THE SAME cell for nearly fourteen months. Apart from the overcrowding, the complete lack of privacy and the stench of the latrine, the main peril was utter boredom. Nothing changed. Day after endless day passed in interminable monotony. Time stood still. He could barely eat. The foul odours of sweat and filth, and the cramped conditions made the very act of eating repugnant. A few prisoners were removed; others arrived. Several contracted dysentery, and with the return of the mosquitoes there was a constant fear of fever. Most of the inmates soon had faces covered with bites and at night, often the worst time of all, the groaning and cursing were combined with the sound of frantic scratching. The medical students begged the guards for clean water so at least they could wash their hands, but any water they were allowed was for both drinking and washing in. Next the students tried to organise a rota, asking everyone to drink first from the bucket before washing, but inevitably this did not work either. Added to this, the tension and the inactivity caused arguments to erupt suddenly and with ferocious unpredictability, turning, occasionally, from verbal attacks to full-scale fights. When this happened a guard would simply unlock the cell door, drag out whoever was nearest and beat him relentlessly. Once or twice an innocent bystander was reduced to a bloodied pulp before being thrown into solitary confinement.

As far as they were able, the Tamil brothers, the medics, tried to prevent these incidents. But without any outlet to their frustrations this, too, was not easy. Yet in spite of this they remained optimistic, full of stories of their life before the arrest and of their younger sister in England. When she had been a little girl, they said, she had wanted to train as a Kandyan dancer. But then one day she had seen a man soaked in kerosene and left to burn in a ditch. It was the end of her dancing days. From then on she had wanted only to study medicine. She had wanted to save the lives that others tried to destroy, she had told her parents. The whole family had been amazed but she had never wavered in this decision. For the sounds of a man's screams, her brothers told their cell audience, could not be erased so easily. She had been thirteen at the time. Now she was almost twenty.

'When the war is over she will come back and marry her childhood sweetheart.'

The war could not last for ever, the brothers said. They could not be left in this place indefinitely. Soon, all of them would be released.

'We have only to be patient,' they said. 'There is talk of peace negotiations, and there *will* be the general election in the new year. However long it takes, men, things can't stay this way for ever.'

In the beginning Theo did not join in any of these conversations. His shock and sense of disorientation were so great he barely registered what was going on. All his anger had been wiped out, crushed by agonising anxiety for the girl's safety. The intensity, and the violence of his recent experiences, had sapped him of his usual optimism. His fearlessness seemed a thing of the past. He no longer recognised himself. Having become a prisoner, he began to behave as though he had been one for ever. The conditions in the cell were so appalling that survival was all he had energy for. Paralysed by his situation, terrified by what might happen next, he was unable to go beyond the one, unanswered question of why he was here. Added to this was the sense of being on a roller-coaster. He was trapped in a nightmare from which there appeared no possible escape. At night endless shadows flickered across the cell wall and the shrill cries of monkeys from some distance outside confused him further, making him shake convulsively.

After the brutality of the first hours and days following his arrival, he had lost track of how long they had beaten him. The guards ignored him, and he was too cowed, too grateful at being left alone, that he could not bring himself to ask them for any explanation. The everyday had receded to a point out of sight. In fact, he had stopped thinking in days for at any moment he expected to be hauled out and beaten again. By now, his capacity to respond had slowed down, made worse by the fact that his glasses had been broken. He could no longer focus on anything any more.

During all this time, the heat did not let up. And at night, when it cooled slightly, Theo began to experience blinding headaches. But he felt safer at night, more private, less exposed. There were fewer sounds to startle him so that in the darkness he began, fearfully and at last, to piece together his thoughts about the girl. What had his disappearance done to her? Where was she; what was she thinking now? What *could* she think, except that he was dead? Sugi would by now believe he was dead. Sugi would have heard what had happened and assumed the worst. Theo was tormented by these thoughts. The agony of not knowing what the girl would have done when she woke continued to haunt him. Had she slept at all since he left her? Was she at this very moment searching for him? Was she too in danger? And then he thought, I am to blame, this is all my fault. Nothing could take away his guilt. Questions chased around his head, refusing to be stilled. He imagined her waking, bewildered, then slowly becoming distraught. He imagined her running across the beach, staring at the sea; not knowing what she should do next. And he thought with sickness of how he had left her, sleeping, peacefully, bathed in moonlight , believing that at last she was safe. Fear twisted in him like a sand worm burrowing in the ground. Fear washed him like a wave on a shell. It broke against the brittle spine of his sanity. His only hope was that Sugi had taken her to Colombo. But what if in the panic he had forgotten the documents or the money? What then? There had been a passport. It was forged; if Sugi had been found with it on his person then he would go to prison. Briefly Theo was struck by the irony of this. The passport had only been a last resort. Oh God, he thought, what is happening to them? And then, the one terrible thought he had been avoiding all this time, unleashed at last, broke free and devoured him. Will I *ever* see her again?

Every night the questions marched towards him, relentless as an army of soldiers, drumming against his head, leaving him with no respite. During the day he managed somehow to block all thoughts of the girl, but then as darkness fell, in the stifling air, he conjured her up like a magician, and walked an imaginary beach with her. In this way he both sustained and punished himself every night. And at these moments, under cover of the unlit cell, he broke down soundlessly. He thought he was silent.

One night, as he was beginning his slow agonising discourse, he felt a hand on his shoulder.

'Why don't you talk to us?' a voice asked.

Theo froze.

'We're all the same, men, in this wretched place. Why are you so proud? Everyone understands, there's no shame in what you feel, you know.'

In the darkness Theo felt a hand, roughened and sand-papery, move across his face.

'I've read your book,' the voice continued. 'The one they say has been made into a film. You're a courageous man.'

Caught unawares, Theo shook his head. He felt himself unravel swiftly, sliding out like a thread from a piece of cloth. Silently, he shook with sobs. Something small and hard and bitter, deep within him, dissolved. The others in the cell moved uneasily.

Soon after this they began to speak to him, and for the first time Theo understood they were addressing him in Singhalese. The medical students too shuffled over and began asking him about his film. Was it like the book? Where was it shot? Who acted in it? Were they Sri Lankan actors? Would it ever be shown in this country?

They sensed he both was, and was not, one of them. So they turned, all together, standing close to him, like weary cattle waiting for a storm to break, nudging him with their hot breath, giving him comfort in the only way left to them. After a while, unasked, he began to talk a little about his life. The very act of speech ignited some hope.

'My wife,' he said, 'was Italian.'

He saw it suddenly, as though it were a thousand years ago. Anna, and the watery city. Italy was a puzzle to them, further maybe than the moon. Italy had no history to offer them, no tradition, either good or bad. But England was another matter.

England interested them. So he talked about London instead. In the darkness he talked of the greyness and the poverty of the big city. He told them that it was possible to find warmth in spite of the cold but that you had to hunt for it and some luck was always necessary.

'It is not luck,' said the old man who had first spoken to him. 'It's just a person's karma.'

He talked of his novels.

'Writing them was easy. Once I started I realised I had many things inside me that needed to be said. In fact, later on,' he added, slowly, 'when things were bad, writing was easier than living.'

Old memories stirred in him and he remembered with unforgiving clarity all that had happened. An animal, he said, he had been like an animal, howling for its dead. Then, because he had started, and also because the night made these things possible, hesitantly, he told them how Anna had died.

'There was no warning,' he said. 'She was walking home on an ordinary winter's night. It was not very dark; she had been working late. She often worked late. I had cooked a meal, nothing much. Pasta, tomato sauce, cheese. That's all. I turned the lights on and waited. But she never came.'

Even after so long he felt the power of that moment reaching down through the years. Like starlight, he thought, wistfully.

'She was mugged,' he told them, speaking quietly. 'It happened quickly. On an empty street in London, robbed for twenty pounds and a credit card. There was one witness, that's all. She died on a hospital bed, on a white sheet, as a result of a massive brain haemorrhage. They never caught the men. It was an unsolved crime.'

He had come home to Sri Lanka, he said, because he felt it was better to put his energy into his own country than waste it on foreign soil.

The cell fell silent. Somehow the telling had shocked those who listened. I can speak of all this now, he thought, detached. As though it happened to someone else, as though I had only read about it. I can say the words. And nothing in the words can convey how I felt, what I still feel. But he did not mention the girl. *Her* name was an impossibility. He had folded his thoughts of the girl into a secret petition and dropped it at the feet of a god long given up for lost.

Things changed imperceptibly after that. As the weeks lengthened into months Theo began to invent a routine for himself. There was no paper. He tried asking the jailer but in return narrowly missed a kicking. So he began to construct a story in his head. And after a while he began to tell his stories out loud. The brothers were impressed. Soon it became a daily entertainment that was looked forward to by the whole cell. He talked mostly at night, feeling as though he was following the tradition of Buddhist oral storytelling. It reminded him of his childhood and the servants who had cared for him. Softly, fearful of being overheard, fearful of being thrown into solitary confinement, he told his stories. Then as he became bolder he began to recite poetry as well. He recited long passages of *The Rime of the Ancient Mariner*. The brothers, loving it, joined in with poems they had learned in school. And so the days inched by.

One morning a boy of about ten was suddenly brought in. He had been captured during an ambush, his cyanide capsule cut off and now he waited questioning. Slumping in a corner of the cell he simply shivered, refusing to speak. There were burn marks along the lengths of his legs and across his chest. He was bleeding from his head. The brothers immediately began to look him over but moments later the door burst open again and they were both ordered out. There was no time for goodbyes.

Night descended and with it there arose sounds of screaming. The sounds came from a grating that drained the water from the latrine. At first they thought it was chanting until a shift in key, a small inflection of voice made it clear that they were screams. The noise was intermittent but clearly audible. No one spoke as it rose in a lament so pure, so full of pain, that it was obvious; sleep would be impossible. The boy continued to whimper, huddled up in a corner, snarling at anyone who came near him. Whenever there was a pause in the unearthly sounds from below, everyone breathed a sigh. But then, there would be another long cry of such agony, a cry so low and so filled with suffering that they knew it was not over yet. Pity filled the small airless cell, and silently, out of respect for what they were witness to, every man bowed his head. Towards dawn the sounds became feebler. Footsteps could be heard walking away. A light was switched off. Inside the cell the geckos continued to move haphazardly across the walls, and the boy drifted off to sleep.

In the first few days after Nulani Mendis had left, Giulia and Rohan had been hopeful. They had made enquiries; frantic now, Rohan had gone to see someone he knew vaguely in the Cabinet, but there was no help to be had there. He had tried driving over to Theo's beach house but the roadblocks made it impossible. Then he had rung an acquaintance who lived in the next bay but the phones were down and there was no response. A journalist they approached refused to run a story about Theo in the daily newspapers. It was more than his job was worth, he told Rohan apologetically, avoiding his eye. Finally, they began to believe the worst.

'We should contact his agent in London,' said Rohan. 'He'll make a fuss.'

But they had no phone number and in any case they suspected their phone was tapped.

A month after she left, a letter arrived from the girl. She had written it almost immediately on reaching London. But it had taken a month to arrive.

'Look at this,' said Rohan, bringing it in to Giulia, pointing at the envelope. It was clear the letter had been opened.

'I want to leave,' said Giulia, insistent now. 'Theo's gone, Nulani's gone, I want us to go too, before it's too late.'

Rohan did not answer. Theo Samarajeeva had been like a brother to him. He could not accept he was dead. He could not bear the thought of leaving without him. He wanted to go over to the beach house but he knew how frightened Giulia was. He had not told Giulia, but their own house was being watched. And a few days ago he was certain he had been followed home. Rohan had not mentioned any of this to Giulia. She was already overwrought, and on edge. He did not like leaving her alone in the house for too long. In his heart, he knew, it was time for them to leave.

Giulia began reading Nulani's letter out loud. The words erupted across the page, confused and desperate.

I don't know what I'm doing here. I feel I can't go on living. Everything is finished for me. Yesterday I was eighteen. How many more years of my life must I live? Have you no news for me? Have you nothing at all? I tried ringing you many times but the lines were down. Jim met me at the airport. He took me to the place where I'm now staying and a friend of his said he knows of a job close by. I haven't gone out much since I got here. It's so cold and I'm so tired, Giulia. I want to come home. Jim is busy, he is happy with his studies but what is there for me here? All I really want to do is sleep. Waking is terrible. Will my whole life pass as slowly as this?

The writing meandered on in this way, starting and stopping, repeating itself, full of pain. full of the absence of Theo, understated, desperate. She talked a little about her brother. Giulia was alarmed.

Yesterday I saw Jim again. He is pale, the same, but paler. He's my brother but we have nothing left to say to each other. Although he has been good to me we hardly speak. The astrologer was right. Jim talked about Amma. Why didn't I go to the funeral? What could I say? Jim says I'm selfish. We met in the railway station café because he was in a hurry. Then he went back to Sheffield. He can't see me until next term he said. I'm staying at the address you gave me. Using the money you gave me. I don't know what else to say.

Nulani.

That was all. When she had finished reading it Giulia sat staring into space.

'Perhaps we shouldn't have sent her,' she said uneasily. 'She's in a bad way.'

'What was the choice?' asked Rohan.

Giulia sighed. Why had they thought it would be that simple?

'I know. I thought her brother might have helped her, somehow.'

Rohan made a sound of disgust. Then he took the letter from Giulia. Yes, he thought, it has been opened. Tomorrow he would make some enquiries about leaving.

'If only they had married before this happened,' Giulia said, beginning to cry. 'She would at least have had his name.'

'She would have had the royalties from his books too. Although,' Rohan stared at his hands, 'it's only money. It won't bring him back. She'd still be alone.' He stared bleakly at some point above her head.

'One day she'll make money, you'll see. That much I believe. She's a damn good painter, you know. It won't go to waste. You watch, it *will* surface. Give it time.'

He nodded, sounding more certain than he felt. Outside, the curfew had just begun. Thank God I still have a British passport, thought Rohan. And thank God Giulia was an Italian citizen. He wondered if it was possible to buy two tickets to London on the black market. Before it was too late.

After the disappearance of the Tamil brothers the atmosphere in the prison cell quickly turned to one of despair. The next day the small boy captured during the guerrilla fighting was taken out to the firing squad and shot. No one in the cell uttered a word. If they said nothing, maybe they could believe nothing had happened. On the afternoon of the following day, the metal door opened and the warden came for Theo. A simple interrogation, he said, just a few minutes. But first, a short journey. The old man shouted his goodbye first.

'May God protect you,' he said. 'You're a good man!'

Some of the others joined in.

'Maybe we'll meet in the next life.'

Before he could answer Theo was pushed outside.

He had lost track of how many months had passed. Barbed wire stood silhouetted in drums across the sky. It was late afternoon. Long shadows stretched across the ground. A fresh breeze lifted the edges of the heat as they began the drive to the army headquarters. Perhaps because of the happiness he felt from being in the open, Theo experienced a sharp stab of optimism. He did not have the blindfold on this time, the warden was driving him personally instead of some thug. Could it be his release was imminent? Here and there he caught sight of a flash of colour. Birds, he thought excitedly, he hadn't seen a bird in months. Then he saw glimpses of acid-green paddy fields and guessed they were somewhere in the eastern province. How he had got there was a mystery. He had been certain the first prison camp had been close to Colombo.

They drove on. Occasionally Theo thought he smelt the sea somewhere in the distance, but again, he could not be sure. Every now and then they passed the burnt remains of a village. They passed a truck overturned by the roadside, pockmarked and riddled with bullet holes. Once, this had been a fertile land with rice and coconut as the economy. Once, this had been a tourist paradise, lined with rest houses. The port had been an important naval base. Now there was not a single person in sight. He was hungry. They had left before the daily ration of food and uncertainty and hope were making him light-headed. After about an hour or so, he sensed rather than saw they were heading away from the coast towards the interior. Hunger gnawed at him and anxiety too began to grow. Where were they going? The warden had said it would be a short journey. Theo judged they had been driving for about two hours.

Suddenly the truck swerved and braked violently. In front of them was a roadblock. He had just enough time to register this before there was a loud explosion and a volley of gunfire. He ducked and the engine strained into reverse. There was shouting and then more gunshots. The truck swung backwards along the track they had just driven on, swerving and lurching. He tried to stand up, tried to shout to the driver, but the violence of the movement sent him flying towards the door, hitting his head against the handle. He must have passed out.

It was dark when he came to. A foul chemical smell hung in the air and he could not see clearly. His head seemed to have a tight band holding it together. Slowly as he began to focus in the half-light he saw four lengths of thick rope attached to blocks of wood screwed to the ceiling. On the opposite walls were some metal plates attached to some electric wires. Someone was shining a torch directly into his eyes and his mouth seemed full of foam. He tried to speak but his tongue was unaccountably leaden and stuck to the roof of his mouth. Still the torch continued to be directed at his left eye and he realised that, once more, his hands were tied behind his back. They were talking to him in Tamil. They asked him a question. When he didn't reply they spoke in English.

'So, you Singhala bastard, so, you dog, what d'you say to us now?'

'You thought you were in safe territory, did you? Oppressor of the Tamil people, why are you silent?'

'Where's your wonderful army to defend you now?'

'The only good Singhalese is a dead Singhalese!'

'Go on, beg. Beg!'

Again Theo tried to speak, tried in vain to say his name. He opened his mouth but no words came. In that moment it seemed that all the resistance within him, all that had kept him sane over the last months began to crumble. He could stand it no more. His mind had reached its limits. He saw a pair of hands coming towards him and a black sack was pulled over his head. The stench of foul-smelling chemicals grew stronger and was mixed with another smell, something that he vaguely recognised. Then they hit him. Soon he was suspended from the ceiling. His handcuffs were taken off and he felt something cold being stuck to the palms of his hand and to the back of his neck. He knew, with the part of his mind still functioning, that he had entered a hell like no other. That this tunnel he was being forced down was narrowing to a point where every last glimmer of hope was being extinguished. He knew that the best option for him was that he should die now, here, and instantly. Someone peeled his trousers off amid hoots of laughter, and he hung for a moment while a flash bulb went off in his face. Something wet and putrid was smeared all over his nakedness. Laughter surrounded him like baying dogs, high and inhuman. Although the heat in the room was oppressive he was shivering and although he was crying no sound came from him. They hosed him down and the metal plates began to burn steadily into his hands. He felt the heat rise through him, swiftly reaching a point where he could no longer bear it. In a flash of understanding, moments before his body jerked into the air, he saw in the distance the stone face of a god he had once believed in, turning away. Then, mercifully, he passed out.

12

ROHAN WENT TO THE BEACH HOUSE. The doctor had found a man to drive him there. Giulia didn't want him to go but he went, promising her that if there were signs of trouble he would turn back. The driver was a patient of Dr Peris's.

'You can trust him,' the doctor said. 'He's helped other people for me. He'll take you along the side roads. It's safer than the coast road.'

The doctor spoke calmly, not wanting to alarm them. Knowing they were incapable of doing anything in their grief, he managed to make the house secure through a local contact. But he did not tell them this. Neither did he tell them that he had received a warning that the house was likely to be looted and probably vandalised. He did not tell them he had paid a man to watch over the place. He saw no point in upsetting them further. The doctor had admired Theo Samarajeeva's books and he felt it was the least he could do.

'It shouldn't take more than a couple of hours to get there. He'll come for you early. Take everything of value.'

So Rohan went. In spite of Giulia's fears he went. In the end it had taken fourteen months for the doctor to think it safe. On the morning before he left, a letter arrived from the girl. It was only her second letter, written months before, and this too, Rohan observed, had been opened. England, she wrote, suited Jim. He did not miss his home, she said. Unlike Nulani herself who thought of nothing else. The letter meandered disjointedly on.

Jim says home is a place full of foolish superstitions, best forgotten. He wants me to stop being so useless. But useless is what I am. I started to tell him a little about Theo, but I don't think he really understands.

'Well, that's a surprise,' said Rohan, grimly.
'Listen to this, Rohan,' said Giulia uneasily.

What use is anything without Theo? How can I say this to my brother? How can I tell Jim that everything I do, even eating, is a betrayal, because I live and he does not? Jim will never understand. How could he, he didn't know him. I'm glad there's no sun in this place. I'm glad it's grey. I've never seen so many shades of grey. The sky, like my heart, is full of greyness.
* The worst thing of all is that already, so soon, I have started to forget things. What is happening to me? All our memories, all the things we shared, those last hours, are not clear any more. Things I should not have forgotten are evaporating. And then, at other times, everything reminds me of him. But yesterday I couldn't remember his face. However hard I thought, my mind stayed a blank. I have left all my notebooks in the beach house. All my drawings of him. My life. Everything.*

'Rohan, I'm worried. D'you think she's . . .'

'Why doesn't she draw him from memory?' murmured Rohan. He couldn't bring himself to mention Theo's name.

Some time later Rohan reached the beach house without a hitch. Bypassing the town the driver went towards the railway station and down a dirt track towards the beach. Nothing stirred. Flat-webbed fronds of fishing nets dried in the sun. Rubber tyres hung like nooses on trees waiting for men to swing for unknown crimes. Rohan looked nervously about. There were bullet holes everywhere.

'I'll turn the car around,' the driver said.

Rohan saw him look sharply up and down the empty road. Something must have caught his eye.

The house, when Rohan entered it, had changed subtly. The outside had come in. Small plants grew in cracks; fine sand had blown in with the gales, bringing salty smells and scraps of rubbish. The house had an air of haste and sea grass. Three large terra-cotta urns stood half in shadows growing tired cacti. Nothing moved. The sea-moistened woodwork had small patches of mould. Months of wind and monsoon rain had left telltale marks of destruction everywhere; on the dust that fingered the pages of the many books lying around, in the open record player. A typewriter stood on a small table, one key, the letter 'E', stuck down as though in mid-sentence. Rohan passed into another room full of dried-up paint tubes. Stiffened rags, moulded into the shape of the fingers that had once held them, were scattered everywhere. Sunlight poured into an old glass jug. Two sea urchins and a pink conch shell sat on a shelf. There was a photograph of Anna smiling out at eternity. Rohan stared at it. It had been a beautiful day when it had been taken. The house, the place, the day, all seemed insub-stantial suddenly. Rohan felt his stomach churn. He felt unutter-ably depressed. Sitting on a stool he lit a cigarette. He should not have come. Every part of Theo's life was public property here; stories fell open around him. The girl's notebooks, the paintings, how many had she done, Rohan wondered with a sense of paralysis. He felt unable to move, the heat seemed to immobilise him. A typewriter ribbon spooled on the table. He felt grief, suppressed for too long swell inside him like seawater. But whatever he had hoped to find was not here. Bastards, he thought, bastards! He took those things he could carry, three paintings of his friend, the photograph of Anna, the girl's notebooks. He began loading up the car. She must have what little is left of him, he thought grimly. He had not noticed the half-finished portrait of Sugi tucked away behind the mirror. They will be her memories now, he thought. And in that moment, he knew, he would leave for Europe soon.

Afterwards Theo Samarajeeva had no idea how many days or nights he spent in that place. Or how often they beat him with the hose, nor how many times he was burned. He did not recall being dragged by his feet to a cell where, semi-naked and bleeding, he was left for dead. Trauma locked his memory out. His hands were almost paralysed and there were great weals across his back. If he had had a wish it was simply to die. That he survived at all was a miracle, for in those lost hours, without pity and without witness, humanity itself was violated and what was left of his spirit was broken. Nothing in ordinary life had prepared him for this journey. Moving in a blur of constant pain to some sealed spot, silent, isolated and alone, he dreamt of the sea. It was blue and huge and the horizon rose before him, moving as one with the sky. Although he was unaware of it his body had finally given way to a fever. He shook uncontrollably, sweat poured from him and he grew weaker. But still, he remained only semiconscious. He had no idea if there were others around; he heard voices but they were indistinct. Lights flickered on and off. Sometimes he dreamt the sea was on fire and he burned alive. And he dreamt of the girl. In his dream she told him her father had burned like a tiger, running through the streets. He saw her face, very serene and certain, her eyes large and very lovely. And he heard her talk to him. Her father, she said, had been running forever. It was time he stopped. And then, she reached down and touched the great wounds on Theo's body. Screaming, he opened his eyes and found that he was lying on a bed in a white room. The sun had forced its way to the edge of the blinds. It slipped through the veiled slats in the windows and a cool breeze lifted the edges of the sheet. His body ached. Someone, some indistinct figure, stood over him offering him a glass of water. He drank it and the water tasted clean.

'It was a mistake,' the figure said. 'I am sorry to say they got the wrong man. You aren't one of them. It was a mistake. Some idiot was left in charge. So now, you must rest here and when you are better you will be released.'

The man addressed him in English. A bowl of hot rice was held out to him. Seeing it, Theo felt his stomach contract. He vomited before passing out once more.

It was several days before he was awake enough to under-stand that he was in a makeshift hospital in Kandy. This time when he woke, it was a different voice that talked to him.

'We're sending you to a safe house,' the voice said. 'To rest. All you need to do now is rest and eat and not worry. It's been a bit of a mix-up.'

The voice made it sound very easy. He, it was a man, Theo saw, smiled thinly, showing gold-capped teeth. He told Theo that he had pardoned two other prisoners that very morning.

'Nothing to worry about,' he said. 'It was an unfortunate mistake. You are our guest now. Just ask if there's anything special you want to eat. We have a very good cook here! Tamil cooks are the best in the world.'

The man laughed good-humouredly. Outside the sun shone tight against the khaki blinds.

'We are fighting for recognition and freedom,' the man said, his eyes glazing over. 'We're fair-minded people. But sometimes in these troubled times, we make mistakes. It is impossible not to make mistakes during a war. Don't forget,' he said as though Theo had argued with him, 'this is a war brought on by others. But you know all that!'

Two small boys holding Kalashnikovs stood guarding the doorway. They wore camouflage and around their necks were cyanide necklaces.

'See,' said the man, 'they are your personal bodyguards. If there is anything you want just ask them.'

He smiled again and ruffled the heads of the boys, who grinned. Then he left. Theo stared after him, unaware that his face was wet. Outside the Kandyan heat simmered gently. He stared at a patch of uninterrupted sunlight. It was dazzling and very clear and also, for some reason, unbearable and full of life. Then he turned his face to the wall, away from the bright luminous heat outside, folding himself against the cool parts of the bed. Slowly, like the leaves of the nidikumba plant, he closed his eyes.

In Colombo, the dark face of the army was on alert for the beginning of the election campaign. White uniforms paraded the streets. They marched purposefully among the monks, the rickshaws and the propaganda blasting out of loudhailers. Angry mobs formed and re-formed like armies of beetles. Riots were hastily staunched only to spill out in other places. Outside the parliament buildings, and in between the cool water sprays of Cinnamon Gardens, the limousines glided like stately barges.

'I simply cannot stand this any longer,' shouted Rohan.

He had not painted for months. He had not stretched a single piece of linen on its frame. His dead friend's life spilled across every empty canvas. On their return from the beach house, the driver had noticed they were being followed. Later on, someone had tossed the bones of a chicken into the garden. Luckily Rohan had been outside when this had happened and he had managed to remove them before Giulia became aware of anything amiss. Then one morning a roadside spirit offering was left outside the gate. Rice and fish and pineapples were placed in a coconut woven basket, threaded with crimson shoe-flowers. Passers-by crossed the road to avoid it. Later on, Dr Peris came to visit. Two bombs had gone off in his part of town and his days had been spent dealing with the victims. The first blast had been the result of a suicide bomber. Dr Peris had come to talk privately to Rohan.

'You should leave,' he said. 'While you still can. I can get you two tickets. One of my patients has a source . . . it isn't safe here for you both.'

He looked meaningfully at the painter. His friend the driver had been watching their house, he said. There might be trouble ahead.

'My advice is go. While you can.'

Two days later the telephone rang several times in the middle of the night. But when they answered it there was no one there. They had not heard from Nulani again. The post was no longer getting through. Rohan got the tickets. They would fly, via Singapore, to Milan. Then they would take the train to Venice. They had no place to stay in Venice yet, but it no longer mattered. Something would come up.

'This place has defeated me,' Rohan said. 'Ultimately, even I have given up on my country.'

The new year had not brought peace. They were being buried alive. Someone threw a petrol bomb into a crowd and death stalked the city in a monk's saffron robe. Petrol was in short supply, except when it was needed for random burnings. How had two thousand years of Buddhism come to this? A Cabinet minister was assassinated, seventeen members of the public injured, three killed on a bus. Glass rose like sea spray, shattering everywhere. But the radio stations still played *baila* music in a pretence of normality although no one knew what was normal any more. They packed. Hastily, frightened to speak of their imminent departure, frightened to use the telephone, frightened to leave the house for long, they packed.

They were to leave at night. But because of the curfew and the unpredictability of the journey they decided to leave in early evening. They hoped there would be less likelihood of ambush if they left while there was still some light. The last of the sun was disappearing rapidly, the evening had a rosy glow, and the air was filled with the distant cry of birds. The plane would take off at midnight. Once in the airport their tension eased slightly. No one knew they were here and for the first time since Theo had gone they felt they were safe. The airport itself was subdued and empty. Security was much heavier since the bombings of eighteen months previously. There was only one flight out of the country and they had hours to wait before they could board the plane. But it was worth it, they told each other. Better than driving through the jungle in the dark, they said. The trip with Nulani had been enough, they added, remembering the last time they had come here. That too was already a lifetime away. And already, Giulia thought sadly, they had accepted Theo's death.

'I'll never return,' Rohan said with finality. 'This time I'm finished with this place for good.'

He told her he had worried they would never be able to leave. He had been afraid, he said, that something would have stopped them, that one of them might have been captured.

'The house was watched, you know,' he told her, in the safety of the airport lounge. 'Every time I went out I knew I was watched and I wondered if I would return home again. Or if you were all right on your own.'

Giulia shivered. Now he tells me, she thought.

'There was a man on the hill above the bay, watching us through binoculars. I'm not sure if he saw me take the paintings from Theo's house. Not that I cared. I wanted Nulani to have something of him. But we were followed all the way back to Colombo.'

He did not tell her he had been suspicious of their neighbours too. What was the point in letting her lose all hope in the place? But the cheapness of life in this paradise was more than he could stand any more. At eleven o'clock they were allowed to board the plane. Night had fallen unnoticed while they sat in the airport, and outside the sea moved darkly, for there was no moon tonight. Ten minutes to twelve, thought Giulia. Ten more minutes left, thought Rohan, and still I feel nothing. Theo had been dead for nearly eighteen months.

In the darkness, as the plane began to taxi, in a house that appeared occupied, in a leafy suburb in Colombo, a fire started. It was uncertain what might have caused it. Arson was commonplace enough. The fire rushed through the empty rooms, taking everything in its path. Burning canvas, melting tubes of oil paint, cracking mirrors, incinerating the furniture. It tore through the corridors in a fury of heat; it destroyed pictures and documents, and the paraphernalia of the recently departed. When it had burned itself out, when all that was left was blackened rubble, the fire brigade arrived. And the neighbours came to gaze in awe at all that remained of the house where the painter and his Italian wife once had lived.

13

HE SAW IT ALL IN COLOUR, dark green with a touch of blue. The images fragmented, like rushes from an uncut film, full of light and sharpness. But every time, before his mind could investigate them further, he drifted back into sleep. Whenever he regained consciousness he drank the water that arrived, by mysterious means, in his hand. It was cool and fresh and he drank it without thought or question, without pleasure. He drank it simply because it presented itself. And then he slept again. Something had happened to the seal on his eyelids because all the time the light seeped through to his eyes, so that while he slept he dreamt of sun, dazzling on the sea. He could not have been further from the ocean.

Other things happened while he slept. Voices flitted across his brain, like fruit bats. Words circled him like gulls; words like, 'in the beginning', and 'flailing', biblical words, words that had no end. In the background was the sound of artillery moving in and out of focus.

At night, the single light bulb, unshaded and comfortless, cast an aching, dull glow. It reflected the slow tortuous routes of the geckos and the cockroaches that crawled past him. He watched them through a curtain of pain and sweat, these routes that crossed and criss-crossed along the wall, passing through imaginary enemy lines. Although they came from the hole in the broken window they never went back that way. They would always disappear from his sight line somewhere to the left of his bed. He never turned his head to find out where they went. He never turned his head for anything. He was simply not interested. Like the beetles, he seemed to have arrived here through a broken skylight, crashing in from some other life, never knowing that this place, this spot, would be where he would land. Here in this bed, with this small pile of sodden cloth, his only possession.

Some time later, he woke once more, to walls that were bare of beetles. The sun was raking long fingers through the blinds and the voices were back.

'How long has he been this way?' Gerard asked.

The man in the doorway shrugged. Ten days, two weeks? 'There's nothing much the matter with him now. His wounds are healing well. He could walk out of here if he wanted to.'

'No,' Gerard said hastily, 'that's not what we want. He needs to stay here for a while.'

'He can't stay here. The Chief doesn't want him. You'll have to move him.'

'Yes, all right,' said Gerard. 'But you'll have to give me time. I can't work miracles.'

'Look, he's waking again. Now he'll have a drink of water and stare at the ceiling. Then he'll go back to sleep. We can't spare the bed much longer.'

'OK, OK. I'll move him.'

They watched curiously as Theo finished drinking. He was unaware of their presence. Secretly, though, Gerard was shocked. The writer had taken a severe beating, far worse than he had expected. The fingernails on both his hands were ripped and blackened and he looked smaller than Gerard remembered. He lay motionless, like a broken fishing boat.

'Can he hear us, d'you think?'

They moved closer, watching him in silence.

'Who knows? It was a mistake.'

'Yes, yes, I know, men.'

'These things happen. All the time. He's lucky someone found out before it was too late. He's lucky they didn't finish him off.'

Luck, thought Gerard, laughing inwardly. No, you fool, it wasn't luck. It was my doing. While you rush around in circles with your machine guns, shooting at shadows, I pick up the pieces. Louts in charge won't make a government. But he said nothing. He wondered if Theo would be useful in the way he had hoped. Would his mind be too damaged to write again? Well, the first thing would be to move him down the valley, into a remote part of the hills and give him some peace. Then we'll see, thought Gerard. Rome wasn't built in a day. Let them slaughter each other for a bit longer.

'OK,' he said, making up his mind, 'we'll move him in the morning.' And he went out.

The next time Theo looked at the sky it seemed more intensely blue. And the green of the leaves were dark and succulent. As always, the smell of food made him want to vomit. A man came into view.

'Hello, Theo,' said Gerard. 'I'm here to make sure you're looked after until you get better. You're in a safe house, now, OK? You've nothing to worry about. All you have to do is get better. Do you understand? You're safe now. We've got you away from that place.'

There was a pause. Outside a bird cried harshly and repeatedly.

'I'm not sure how much he understands,' said Gerard. Perhaps they went too far, he thought. Perhaps I'm wasting my time. He's become a cripple, with a cripple's mind. Broken and rubbish-can empty.

'I want to sleep,' said Theo, faintly.

'That's OK, men,' said Gerard heartily. 'You have a sleep. But you must eat something when you wake up. I shall be gone for a few days, but everyone here will take care of you. And I'll see you soon. OK?'

There was no reply. Theo had shut his eyes again. He had become a curvature of bones across the bed, bereft of words. Violence had washed away his hope, robbed him of speech.

'Make sure he eats,' was all Gerard said. And he left.

Days sifted by. Nights passed without notice. Theo moved uneasily between consciousness and sleep. At night the darkness cocooned him and he hardly stirred, moving from one dream to another. He dreamt as once he had read, sifting through images as once he had turned pages. He was neither happy nor unhappy. Mostly these dreams were nebulous things filled with people he did not know. One in particular repeated itself night after night. He saw himself sitting at a desk beside a long, high window, working. He was writing furiously. In his dream the rain fell heavily from a leaden sky and leaves drifted, like flocks of birds, towards the ground. But he had no idea what he was writing. And the dream never went any further. Then one night, without warning, he saw a face that was vaguely familiar. He was sitting with a woman on the balcony of a funny little flat. The balcony was filled with pots of bright red geraniums. Somehow he knew the flat was in London. He remembered the place being called Shepherd Market. But that was all.

'Write it down,' the woman urged him. 'Write it down, Theo. That way you won't forget.'

In the dream, the woman peeled a fruit. He could see the yellow insides of the fruit as she ate. The juice ran down her arm and on to her white dress. He thought he had seen that image somewhere else. The woman frowned and licked her arm, then, seeing him looking at her, she laughed.

'Why d'you never listen to me?' Her eyes were sharply focused and very blue. 'You're a writer, Theo. You should be writing all of this down.'

He woke feeling agitated and found the sunlight sleeping on him, heavy as a dormant cat. A little later, how much later he couldn't say, he had the same dream again. And on that same day he remembered the name of the fruit the servant brought him. It was a mango. He must have moved about a little after that, because he began to notice there were other rooms leading on from his. His whole body ached and the wound across his back bled as he walked. The servant woman came and went, nodding at him, occasionally speaking to him. The man he knew was called Gerard visited almost daily. One afternoon he handed Theo an exercise book and a pen.

'Yes,' he said, as though he was continuing some previous conversation with Theo, 'it's a good idea to try to start writing again.'

A bit later Gerard returned, bringing a doctor with him. Why are you here? Theo wanted to say. But he could not bear to hear the sound of his own voice, so he said nothing. The doctor looked him over. He felt his arms and examined the wound on his back. Theo flinched when he came near him. But the doctor was smiling. Don't smile, thought Theo. I'd rather you didn't smile. But again he remained silent. The doctor told him he was fine, his ribs and pelvis were mending, as were his collarbone and arms.

'With time, the scars will all fade,' the doctor said. He sounded pleased.

'Good,' Gerard said, heartily. 'Good. You see, Theo, you'll soon be fit and ready to start your new book.'

Theo looked at him blankly.

'You don't remember, do you?' Gerard said, laughing. 'Well, I think you should reread one of them, in that case. Your most famous one, perhaps!'

And he handed Theo a book. *Tiger Lily*, it was called. So, he *had* been a writer. Inside the book, he read, *For Anna*. He stared at the name blankly. There was a photograph on the back cover that he supposed was of him. He squinted at it.

'Of course!' Gerard said. 'You wore glasses, of course. How stupid of me! Wait, men, let me see if we can replace them.'

Maybe it was because of the new glasses that had been found for him, not quite perfect but usable, that he began to move around more. The house, he saw, was large and shabby, though not uncomfortable. There were two other people in it, the Tamil woman who cooked for him, and outside, discreetly out of sight, was an armed soldier, a boy of about fourteen.

On the second day that Theo was up and walking, the servant woman came into his room and lifted the blind. Soft light poured in. The woman gave him a mango. She spoke to him in a low voice. Theo did not speak Tamil. He asked her for the time in English.

'Up, get up,' she said, pointing at the sun. 'Morning.'

Later on that same day, she brought him a clock. He had been sleeping for hours, he realised. Maybe days. Fully conscious now, he thought he heard voices. But the gaps in his memory distressed him more than his aching body. He could not leave them alone, probing and fretting over them. Something gnawed away at him, constantly. Or was it *someone*? He had a feeling there was a missing person somewhere in all this. He decided to read *Tiger Lily*. Perhaps the answer was in the book. And the name Anna.

During the long, solitary day, he had discovered an urge to write. But what about, or who to, he couldn't say. In any case he was easily tired, easily frightened. And his fingers ached constantly. Something marked time in his head like a metronome. It moved almost on the threshold of his thoughts so that he felt himself edging towards an abyss. The sight of his face in the mirror, the man called Gerard, all these things both terrified him and left him curious. Maybe I should read the book, he thought at last, reluctantly opening it.

'*No one should be an exile,*' he read. '*For it is an indignity curiously difficult to overcome.*'

Theo shuddered. A sliver of memory uncoiled itself silently. He read on.

'*What can I tell you about the boy? He was a Tamil, brought over from the Indian subcontinent, olive-skinned and handsome. It was meant to be the perfect solution. Except it didn't work out that way.*'

He felt the stirrings of suspicion. And interest too. The sunlight on the wall beside him fell in a slanted disc. Outside the window the branches of the mango tree drooped heavy with fruit. Something has happened, thought Theo. Again his skin grew taut with fear. He began to smell colours. Crimson lake, he thought. Cobalt blue. The greens and yellows, the browns of the yard outside the window filled him with nausea and intense panic. They were army-camouflage colours, he thought, unaccountably depressed. Suddenly he had the urge to write all this down.

'*There is no such thing as freedom,*' he wrote. '*Nor do I want to have an ideology. I see no sense . . . To have an ideology means having laws; it means killing those who have different laws.*'

He looked at what he had written. He had no idea why he had written this. Something was scratching away inside his head, struggling to get out.

'*Man kills as no other animal kills,*' he wrote. '*He kills himself, as if under a compulsion, not out of hunger, not because he is threatened, but often out of indifference. We live in a jungle . . .*'

Again he paused. A thought crawled along the rim of his brain and then slipped maddeningly away. Perhaps, he thought, perhaps it's to do with the woman I keep seeing. Outside a bird pecked at the air as if it were puncturing it.

'Oh good,' said Gerard, walking in. 'You're up! And writing too!' His friendliness was terrifying.

'I've been trying to remember,' said Theo slowly. 'Perhaps you're right, perhaps I was a writer.'

Speech, the smallest utterance, was distressing. Every word quivered on the edge of a scream. But Gerard seemed perfectly friendly and one night, after his visit, Theo determined to finish reading *Tiger Lily*.

'*At last he knew the meaning of what had occurred. That the things he had been through were too terrible to utter out aloud. That one part of him had gone ahead while the rest of his mind remained frozen. And he knew too that he had been tipped into an inexplicable no-man's-land, not of his making.*'

Theo stared at the words, knowing with sudden, sharp shock how the novel resolved itself. Fragments from the past detached themselves and floated towards him. He stopped reading and saw again, with perfect ease, the high-ceilinged room, with its vases of peonies and his desk, littered with papers. There was a cup of coffee beside him; hot, rich, strong coffee. A hand lingered on his arm. And then he saw what must have been his own hand touch the silky cloth, and then the arm, and finally the face of the woman it belonged to. And in the clearest of moments of certainty, he understood that the woman's name was Anna. Memory flooded over him.

The house had been shut up for the night. The guard sat near the gate, his footsteps occasionally crunching on the gravel.

'Why am I a prisoner here?' he said out loud. 'What else have I forgotten?'

Panic rose out of nowhere, with a new urgency. He turned out his light and lay rigid in the darkness listening to his own heartbeats and to the faint sound of a waterfall in the distance, thinking of the woman in the silky dressing gown, certain now that Anna had been his wife.

Towards dawn he slept a little. When he woke it was morning. He saw again that something had been working silently within him. Like a spool of tape threaded through a machine, it replayed itself in slow motion. Anna, he thought. She had died. He had marked the place where she had fallen like a leaf to the ground. He had marked it with flowers. Bunch after bunch, wrapped in foil to stop them withering. Week after week he had gone to the spot, marking it so it no longer remained an unmarked grave. Month after month, long after they said he should have stopped going, long after they said was healthy. He had wondered what was unhealthy about loving. Should his love for her have ceased when her life did? He had gone home after they'd told him she had died. It had been an early-spring day, sharp and cold and with splashes of crocus colour. A day full of birdsong and fresh air. He had registered all that with the curiously detached other part of his brain. Then he had seen her small delicate bra, suspended like some strange beautiful flower, pegged out on the washing line. Hanging out to dry. And without thinking he had taken it down out of habit, and even though it had been washed, even though the sun had dried it, still he could smell the secret parts of her. All this he

remembered now. Seeing it like a photograph, still and deceptive, and potent. Opening his notebook he began to write of
Anna. Lest he forget.

*I saw you for many days before I spoke to you. In those
days you were always laughing. I sat at a table with my
book, occasionally glancing up at the blue shirts of the
vaporetto drivers. This was their café too, after all. They
gathered here whenever they came off duty, shouting at
the barmen for their 'cappuccini' and their 'cornetti' as
they walked in through the door. You were there every
morning; what you did or where you went afterwards was
a mystery to me, but I was struck by the blueness of your
eyes and your curly blonde hair among all the dark
heads. Beyond us lay the lagoon, blue-green, grey, yellow-
tinged, depending on the currents. I didn't know this
then, but the currents had different colours that changed
several times a day in spring.*

*It was March when I first saw you; still cold but with a
hint of the warmth that would come. I remember your
long, slim leg, and your small foot balancing precariously
in its red shoe. You were Italian, so of course you had no
time for sitting. You simply knocked back your macchiato
and then you went away again tossing your hair in the
breeze. Across the water the sunlight fell on the island of
San Michele, the island of the dead. Had I been the true
child of my mother, had I remembered the warnings of
my country, I would have taken this to be an omen of
what was yet to come. But the East, and my troubled
homeland, was a thing of the past. I had shed old habits
like a lizard sheds its skin. In those days in Venice, I was
full of expectations, thrilled by my own discoveries, like*

*any romantic foreigner. Only later would I discover how
bored you were by all of it! But to start with, in those
first weeks, I knew none of this. And so I watched you,
day after day. In reality it was probably only a week
before you spoke to me, joining me at my table. You, and
Gianni, and Sara. All chatting, all laughing, talking to me
in Italian.*

'Sei un studente?'

*No, I said, I was writing a novel set in the
Renaissance. At this you burst out laughing. A tricky
subject, you said. After that I saw you every morning,
either by chance or deliberately. I hoped it was the latter
of course. Sometimes you were with your friends and
sometimes you were alone. When you walked in, your
eyes searched the bar, looking for me. Then, when you
caught my eye, you pretended not to see me, but I knew,
you were glad I was there.*

*I found out that you too were writing a book, on the
sculptures of Ulysses. I found out you had lived mostly in
Rome but that you were here for the spring. And that
Gianni was in fact not your boyfriend. Somehow, in the
days that followed, I saw a lot of you. We talked, we
walked along the Lido, we ate together and finally,
inevitably, I went back to your tiny flat, glowing with its
art-nouveau lamps, its threadbare velvets, its warmth.
And I knew then, this was serious. Afterwards, even years
afterwards, after you died and all the flowers I placed on
the pavement had been swept away by the road sweepers,
still I could remember that first night with the utmost
clarity. How could I have forgotten it now?*

*And so we continued, you and I. We had both loved
others; we had both been disappointed. Maybe that was*

the reason we felt so complete, together. Maybe that was why our lovemaking was so candid. At the time it was a revelation to me. You were almost as tall as me and as I peeled off the layers of your clothes, revealing the pale glow of your skin, the small mole on your back, the soft downy blonde hair at the entrance to your secret chamber, I knew that for you too, this time would be different. I lost myself in you after that, in the visceral perfume of our two bodies, and the small murmurings and gasps of our limbs together. Later, we both slept but it was I who woke first to stare at you, delighting in watching the innocence of your sleep. How was I to know that many years later you would look this way as you lay dying? Sleeping, not in my arms but alone on a hospital bed. With the same curl of eyelashes, the same fit of lips against each other. This time your eyes never opened. This time I knew I would never again see that flash of piercing blue. This time there would be no tomorrow.

Theo closed his exercise book. Memory was rushing towards him as though he was parachuting to the ground. He felt his life hung on a thread which at any moment might break. He felt the tension within the house stretch tightly around him. His body seemed to be weeping from an invisible wound. What was love but a memory? How could he have forgotten so much? He was aware that something else, something he could not quite grasp, fluttered vainly within him. But what it was he could not say. What more was there to remember? he wondered fearfully.

The intrusive roar continued for a moment longer and he realised a radio had been turned on in the next room. There had been a tragedy at Mannar, the voice intoned. Hundreds were left to drown. Villages along the northern coast had been burnt down; women and children hacked to death. A British journalist, some foolish man in search of a human story, having strayed in through the security system, had his eyes plucked out. His captors had released a photograph of him. Appalled, Theo listened.

'Ah,' said Gerard, walking in, making him jump. 'You're up! Good, good. You're on the mend. Soon you'll be well enough to start working.'

'Why am I here? When can I leave?'

Perhaps it was the unfamiliar sound of a foreign voice speaking English on the radio, but he felt some assertiveness, something he might have possessed in another life, return.

'I told you, Theo,' Gerard said easily, watching him, 'you're here for your own safety. Have you begun to remember what the Singhalese did to you yet? No? Well, I'm afraid we need to keep you out here for a while. Consider it a bit of a holiday, if you like, a chance for you to do some writing, to rest, get your memory back even. Don't worry about it. And try to eat a little,' he added, with all the appearance of friendliness.

14

Wherever he looked, Rohan saw the sea. Every time he thought of beginning to paint again, the sight of it distracted him. But when he looked closer it was the tropical waters of his home that he saw. The perversity of the human mind never failed to amaze him. He remembered the beach, whitewashed, picked clean, pared down and smooth, a strong breeze scuffing the waves. The water had always looked benign enough, but underneath there were shark-toothed currents lurking. He knew those currents well enough to know that they could pull a man under in seconds. He tried to imagine the catamarans, hide-grey and rotten, half buried in the sand. Husks from long ago, withered and crumbling, was how he recalled them from this distance. Like his life, he thought, staring into space. If he were honest, if he allowed himself a moment's truth, away from Giulia's anxious eyes, this was what he believed. And the beach that Rohan saw was always empty. No one fished in that sea any more. No fishermen lifted their boats up and along the sands. The small, dark-limbed urchin boys who had played there no longer filled the landscape, and the sea and the sky

belonged only to his dreams. I must paint it, he thought, daily.
But he was too apathetic to do anything.

They had been in Venice for several months and had returned
to the old routine of crossing and recrossing the bridges every
day, on trips to the fish market, to the bar, to an old favourite
restaurant. For hadn't they lived here together, once, long ago?
At first the relief on reaching Venice had outweighed everything else. Sorrow was to come slowly. So at first Giulia was
glad. She was glad to be back in an ordered world again. Putting
the water on to boil for the pasta, making the *sugo* of toma-
toes, delighting in the fragrant perfume of basil plants. Yes, she
was glad of all these things. But then she saw, something had
happened to them both.

On their arrival, desperate to meet up with the girl, they
wrote several letters. They had brought her paintings and her
notebooks with them and they wrote, giving their new address,
telling her they longed to see her again, telling her they had
talked about nothing else. At first, they hadn't worried when
there was no reply. Rohan had tried phoning the doctor to find
out if he had heard from her. But as usual the line was dead.

Unpacking their luggage, they reread her letters more carefully, now that they had time on their hands. The letters felt
old, as though they had been written in another life. They were
full of other time zones.

> *Jim has found me a room in a house. Here is the address.*
> *There are five other people living here but I never see*
> *them. It is dark and very cold. Next week, Jim's friend has*
> *promised to get me a job. The money you gave me will be*
> *enough for the moment but soon I will have to find some*
> *work. Jim's friend says there is a newsagent nearby where*
> *I can work. I am very tired all the time. But at least*

because I am so exhausted I can sleep and that helps to numb the pain. Only sleep releases me.

Reading the letters from this distance made them uneasy. There were things that had slipped their notice before.

'Oh God, Rohan, it's much worse than we realised,' Giulia said urgently. 'We *must* find her.'

'Sure, sure,' he agreed. 'She'll write, don't worry. We are her only real family now. Her brother is a useless fellow.'

'She's young. She should meet someone else,' said Giulia, 'make another life.'

And Rohan had agreed again, although he been less certain. He too looked at the letters once more, with fresh eyes.

Yesterday, I was staring out of my window at some yellow flowers in the garden next door. Something, the old habit I suppose, made me want to draw them. Without thinking, I found a pencil and some paper. I began to draw quite fast, not taking my eyes off the flowers, but my mind must have been somewhere else. And then to my horror I saw that I had been drawing his face again. From memory, as I used to. Do you remember?

Months passed and their uneasiness grew. Why had she not responded? In all they had written six letters and all of them remained unanswered. Giulia's distress had grown, so that, really anxious now, Rohan booked two flights to London.

'Wait,' he calmed her, 'we'll go over and find her. We'll be able to speak freely then. Things will become clearer, you'll see,' he promised.

So they had packed up Nulani's paintings and put the notebooks into a small bag and left with a confidence that would astonish them afterwards. They had no telephone number for her, just an address. Perhaps, reflected Giulia with hindsight, that was when things in their own life began to fall apart.

For London was not as they remembered. And the house where the girl had lived was full of new tenants. Bills and circulars sat together in the letter box, but their own letters were not among them. No, they were told, there's no one of that name here.

'Sorry,' said the lodger shivering at the entrance, 'I can't help you, I'm afraid. Never heard of her. Try the next house.'

They took the tube to Kensington and walked the street where the Samarajeevas had once lived. There was a new owner in the top flat. A new name on the bell, curtains at the window. The woman who opened the front door looked at them in surprise. What had they wanted? They could not for the life of them say. Giulia shook her head, confused. Rohan apologised, hurriedly. They must have got the wrong address. What had possessed them to knock on *that* door? After that, they looked in the telephone directory. But what name did they want? Samarajeeva? Mendis? Passing the place where Anna had been murdered, they saw, without comment, the unmarked, flowerless pavement. Time had passed with steady inevitability and they took what comfort they could from this fact. London traffic moved with swift indifference all around. They felt small, angry, gagged. Then, silently, for what else was there to do, they took the plane back to Venice.

Depression enveloped them, and gradually, Giulia saw that this was the price they had paid. Rohan changed. Slowly, like the tide submerging the beach, Rohan began to drown. He became morose and irritable. Giulia did not like to dwell on it, but leaving Sri Lanka had broken him in a way that she had been unprepared for. She feared the worst. She feared he would never paint again. And she noticed he was for ever cold. Even in that first high summer, when Venice overflowed with humidity, even then, she saw, he hated the climate. *She* had come home but Rohan was somewhere else. Every time she delighted in her native tongue she felt his loss keenly. He had escaped with his life but other things had been lost instead. Something had severed his spirit, broken his determination and cast him adrift. And now a strong current was taking him away from her. Helplessly, unable to follow, she watched as he stared out across the Adriatic Sea. She knew it was some other stretch of water that he longed for. Guilt cemented their relationship where once there had been love. Guilt served to make matters worse. And although the Lido filled with the sound of children's laughter, still he complained, there was not a single conch shell to be found on the beach. However beautiful it was, still this was not his home. Giulia said nothing.

One day she caught him looking through the girl's notebooks.

'Let me see,' she said eagerly, wanting to break the silence, longing to talk.

They had never mentioned their failed trip to London. It had joined all the other untouchable subjects.

'Look,' he said grudgingly. 'All she had were crude graphite sticks, but look at the line of his hand.'

'Theo was all she ever wanted to draw,' said Giulia sadly.

'She's a better painter than I could ever be.'

He would not have it otherwise. There was nothing she could do. He simply said he could no longer paint.

'Perhaps when I've settled in this place,' he said restlessly.

But how can he settle, Giulia worried, if he never paints? All around, the lagoon reflected the milky sky. They were surrounded by light, surrounded by safety. There was no curfew. What more do I want? thought Rohan impatiently, trying to shake this sickness off.

'Maybe she lost our address?' Giulia said. 'Or maybe she's busy now and wants to forget.'

It was possible. But they both knew she was not the sort of girl to forget. And the lurking fear, the unspoken horror, that she might have ended her life finally, added to their guilt.

The year turned. Spring tides came and went and the swallows departed, leaving the city to its storms of mosquitoes.

'Just like home,' murmured Rohan, knowing it was not.

That spring they gave up hoping for news, waiting for the letter that never came. Nulani Mendis is a thing of the past, Giulia chided herself sternly. We must learn to live with only our memories. And she cooked fresh fish for Rohan in the way she used to, in Colombo, serving it with hot rice and chilli, hoping to bring some small comfort to him. Meanwhile, he began to go for long walks on the Lido. He wanted to listen to the mewing seagulls, he told Giulia. He wanted to be alone, he said, to think. And Giulia took some comfort in this, hoping his solitude might inspire him to paint again.

The weather changed and it began to rain at night. After days of silence, the rain fell in persistent folds, not like tropical rain at all, but gently, lingeringly. Theo lay awake listening to it. Once he slept all the time, but since he had begun to write things down, sleep eluded him. Often he would remain awake until dawn, thinking, or scribbling in his exercise book, and then falling into an uneasy sleep as the light appeared. He felt safer that way. His memory was returning slowly. A few nights previously he had remembered the post-mortem after Anna's death. She had been pregnant, he remembered.

His memory had come with the rain. Lying on his bed

listening to the house breathe and creak, listening to the heavy drip of water, he longed for some kind of peace. For although his wounds were healing, the tension within him was increasing. He had been here for months. Gerard continued to visit. But the visits had become less friendly. Gerard watched him with open hostility. Instead of asking after his health, instead of bringing him newspapers to read, he had only one question now.

'You did a good job for the Tamils with *Tiger Lily*. You're a local hero, you know. So when are you going to start your next book about our plight?'

Yesterday, annoyed at Theo's continuing silence, Gerard had asked to see his exercise book.

'There's nothing in it to interest you,' Theo had said. 'Just things about my wife.'

'Now, you listen to me,' Gerard had threatened, flinging the book across the room. He advanced towards Theo who'd shrunk. 'You are trying my patience a little too much. I don't care about your precious memory loss. I'm not interested in your deceased wife. If you want to leave this place alive, if you have any hope for the future, then you are going to have start working fast. D'you understand?' He had paused. And lowered his voice.

'Start with something small.' he said quietly. 'Write me an article for a British newspaper. About the things the Singhalese bastards have done to us. Something with your name attached to it. Forget about your damn memory. I'm trying to help you, Theo, but if you refuse to cooperate, I'm afraid you'll be removed. Understand? Things will be out of my control then.'

Theo had broken out in a sweat. Gerard stared at him.

'If you can write another book,' he said at last, reasonably, breathing deeply, 'if you can contact your publishers we'll be able to let you go. If not . . .' His voice trailed off.

So he knew now. But what could he write about. That night he lay awake, terrified, imagining metal hooks were screwed into the walls above his bed. Finally, Theo slept fitfully. Then towards dawn something woke him. A sentence was repeating itself in his head.

'Now that there are no priests or philosophers left, artists are the most important people in the world. That is the only thing that interests me.'

And then suddenly, as the dawn light filled the sky, he knew. As though he were retrieving a lost language, he saw them. Rohan and Giulia, standing grey-black in the rain. Coffin-rain, made for the dead. Astonished, he thought, But how could I have forgotten them? Unravelling their names from the tangle of forgotten things, he saw Giulia against a waterlogged sky, wintry and far away. Because there was no one to share his new discovery with, he paced the floor of his room. The Tamil woman, hearing his footsteps came in, curious to see what he was doing.

'I've remembered something else,' he shouted. But his excitement was tempered with fear. 'What else is there?' he cried, forgetting the woman did not understand.

Outside, the upcountry rain, which had held off in the night, began falling again. It brought with it the faint smell of tea bushes and blossom. Sharp bird calls stabbed the air, and dark clouds hid the trees.

Giulia had not meant to spy on him. At least that was what she told herself later. She had been on her way to the fish market when she had decided to take a boat out to the Lido instead. The foolishness of it did not strike her until afterwards, but by then it was too late and she had seen Rohan. He was not walking on the beach and he was not alone. She stared mesmerised, uncaring that he might look up and notice her. Rohan was laughing. At least, it seemed that way to Giulia from where she stood, drinking her coffee. The woman looked vaguely familiar. As her heart constricted with a sharp stab of betrayal, Giulia saw Rohan reach over and light the woman's cigarette. Then he lit one for himself. But he's given up smoking, thought Giulia, bewildered. And she flushed with pain. Moving closer, she searched Rohan's face. It appeared as that of a stranger. What is it? she thought. What is he laughing about? She could not remember the last time she had seen him laugh. And try as she might she could not see happiness in his face.

Back in their flat, she opened the suitcase with Nulani's things in it and looked at them. All the small, useless tokens they had brought for her lay untouched, along with the letters she had sent. Some bangles, a lime-green skirt, neatly folded, a bottle of cheap perfume. The sum of a life. There were a few photographs of Theo, one of Theo with Anna, and another one of Nulani's brother Jim. Giulia stared at them. Suddenly she began to weep, thick heavy sobs.

'Will he leave me?' she cried.

This, then, was how it was to end. Anna gone, Theo dead, our marriage finished. Is this how he means to forget all that we have been through together? Throwing me out with all that has hurt him? Is this my fate, now? She had been unable to foresee such an ending. How foolish of her. In the old days, she remembered, when she had first wanted to go to Sri Lanka, he had refused, saying nothing good would come out of it.

'Oh, Giulia, don't you understand?' he had said. 'My country is damaged. This war will go on and on in the minds of the people long after it is over. They will try to pretend it's forgotten but how does one forget when your father and your mother and your brother have been slaughtered before your eyes?'

The aftermath of a war was mostly scars, he had told her bitterly. Giulia was crying more quietly now, rocking gently, sitting on the floor beside the tokens from Nulani Mendis's life. Remembering his warning words. At least, she thought, neither Anna nor Nulani had been betrayed in this way. At least they were loved until the end. Picking up the last letter they had received from the girl, she unfolded it for the hundredth time and stared blindly at it.

'*Jim won't see me for a while,*' Nulani had written. '*He is busy with his final exams. Then he has to look for a job. I miss you.*'

Suddenly Giulia was galvanised into action. Nulani's brother had been at Sheffield University, she was certain of it. Someone had mentioned it, Theo maybe, or the girl herself. Why had they not thought to follow this lead? I will find her, thought Giulia. Closing the suitcase, wiping her eyes on her skirt, she picked up the phone. She would ring Sheffield University. And find Jim Mendis.

Later, after the rain had cleared, the light retained a softness, not unlike a spring day in England. And in the afternoon the sun came out. The old woman brought in a plate of fruit. She had placed it on a tarnished metal tray covered with drawings of Hindu gods. As she walked towards Theo something else seemed to come with her but then she grinned her discoloured, toothless grin and he lost the wisp of it again. All afternoon, after that, he was agitated and restless. Something was very wrong. Blood throbbed at his temples, and he started to shudder. Gerard had said he would be visiting but after the scene of the day before Theo was reluctant to see him. By mid-afternoon he had curled into a tight ball of worry, glancing at the door, expecting Gerard to walk in at any moment. But still he did not appear and terror, never far from the surface, rose in Theo. He had begun to feel sick. His leg ached constantly and he wondered if the glasses they had found him were, in fact, the cause of his never-ending headaches. Glancing towards the door, straining for the slightest sound, he paced the floor nervously. A bit later on he vomited. Then he lay on his bed and slept, moaning and tossing feverishly. When he woke the old woman was standing over him saying something. Her voice was insistent and harsh and there was another sound that puzzled him. The woman was talking to him in Tamil. She stood too close for his liking. He felt hot and faint and wondered if a mosquito had bitten him. The woman pointed towards the roof. Theo looked at her through a wave of sickness. He had no idea what she meant. He tried asking her to fetch the radio. But either she did not want him to have it, or she could not understand him. In the end he gave up. In any case the woman was getting too friendly and he felt the need to keep a distance. As there was still no sign of Gerard, Theo picked up his notebook. Rohan, he thought, I must not forget Rohan. I mustn't lose that thought.

He was staring at his notebook thinking of the books Anna used to keep, filled with her small beautiful handwriting, crushed all together on the page. The look of things had always struck him forcefully. Rohan's paintings with their faulty horizons sitting uneasily on the canvas, rich and luminescent, had had the same effect. Making the invisible visible, Rohan had said. Had it been Rohan? Or had it been someone else? He felt as though his face was on fire. The sun had gone down completely. The walls of his room, flat and empty of objects, had the effect of cutting him off from the world on the other side. He felt not merely alone but ejected into dangerous isolation. It struck him that he was hardly human, locked up, pounding away in a twilight hell of gunshots and violence. He was *certain*, something was terribly wrong. Perhaps he was ill with malaria? He began to shake then, with an awful sense of premonition, feeling a clamouring inside him, some struggle beyond his control. And then, in the purest moments of shock, without warning or sound, without preparation, the thought came forward, crashing against him with the roar of the sea. His memory of Sugi. And of the girl.

He must have collapsed. When he came to, it was dark again and he was sitting on the floor. The girl's face appeared clear and very serene, framed in light, made sharper by his own exhaustion. And he felt at last with shattering horror, the true weight of his loss. He heard a noise approaching from a very long distance and felt it vibrate against him in slow, nauseating waves. It dissolved into the sound of a king coconut being cracked open with a machete. Held between two hands. Liquid gushed between long fingers, cloudy and plentiful. Small, rough-papered notebooks lay on a table, unwavering stories drawn in black lifted off its pages and came towards him. Hither and thither they fell, clamouring for his attention. Sunlight poured into a cracked glass jug, an arm, bare to the elbow, rested by a typewriter. And all around was the fragrance of linseed oil, of turpentine and colour. Rooted to the spot, Theo saw all this as if he watched through a mirror, rising darkly, out of the piano music that tripped down the steps into the tangle of garden light. Somewhere out of sight a gate was clicked open. A silver tray was placed on a table. It held a cup of tea and a glass of lime juice. He saw a man standing beside the table, smiling broadly. Still the noise approached. It was coming from the sky. Voices rose in confusion.

'I haven't seen you for four days,' the girl was saying, her eyes shining, her black hair a curtain against her face, and all the heat of the afternoon gathered into a moment of such sweetness that Theo gasped for air.

'Where have you been?' he mumbled, struggling to stand up. The noise was getting louder. It drummed in his head.

'Sir, you have been away too long. But not to worry, I have looked after Miss Nulani.'

'Sugi,' he said, tentatively. 'Sugi?'

'You have a scar. I can feel it as I draw you.'

'Draw, draw, draw. . .'

The voices were indistinct. They were muddled with other sounds that he could not understand. He saw the treetops being whipped up by a wind. Maybe a storm was brewing. The beach flashed past him like a mirage, scorching white, lace-edged by water. Someone had knocked the stone lions off their plinth; someone had picked a great branch of blossom and placed it in a jug of water on his table.

'Was it you, Sugi?' he asked urgently.

'Yes, it was me,' Sugi admitted. 'We were worried, you were away for so long. We thought something might have happened.'

'But you're here, now,' the girl seemed to say. Her face appeared strangely distorted, and part of the whirling noise outside. He wanted to speak, but his mouth would form no words. He could not move.

'I have been tortured, Sugi,' he wanted to say. 'What do you say to that?'

He wanted to shout, to catch his attention, but the image of Sugi had become indistinct.

'They showed me no mercy,' he tried to say, 'and once that has happened, once you have been tortured, you can never belong in this world. There is no place that can ever be your home again.'

But the words that had remained locked within him for so many months could not be voiced. And the pain that he had carried for so long, unknowingly and fearfully, seemed an impossible thing, too elusive and too raw to speak of. A slab of meat. That was what he wanted to say, that was what he had been. That was what he was.

In the darkness that had descended unnoticed, at last, he understood the sound was that of a helicopter. It whirled and chopped the air, swinging closer and closer. Unable to move, he watched as the beam of light swept across the jungle outside.

Oh Christ! he thought. Oh Christ!

And the only real thing that remained forcing itself upon him was the roaring of an engine in his ears, and the heavy sound of falling rain.

15

THE TAMIL WOMAN SCREAMED AND DARTED into the room.

'Helicopter,' she said in English. 'Singhala army.'

The noise was deafening and directly overhead. Theo froze, his heart was racing, his leg a lame weight against his body. Then with one swift movement, with catlike speed, the youth on guard duty was standing beside him. Theo drew his breath in sharply but the youth shook his head violently, putting his hand out to stop him.

'Quiet, no more noise,' he hissed. 'They look for Gerard.'

'What?'

The helicopter's rotor blades whirled closer. It was about to land. The noise was so great that it wasn't possible to hear anything else and then the boy threw himself on to the ground.

'They have guns,' he said, through clenched teeth.

Theo braced himself, shrinking into a corner of the room. But the whirling continued without attack and the searchlights moved in a circular fashion across the trees again.

'What's happening?'

'They look for Gerard,' the boy whispered from the floor. He began crawling towards the window.

'Who?' asked Theo. 'Who's looking for him? Who are these people?'

'The Chief. He wants Gerard. He told the Tigers, Gerard is traitor. He wants find him. All day they are looking for him. They kill him when they find him.'

The boy spoke in a matter-of-fact way now, as though none of this frightened him.

'But he's not here,' Theo said. He was sweating badly. 'He hasn't visited today.'

'I know. He and Chief have big fight. Big fight!' The boy seemed to be relishing this. 'Gerard wants finish from Tigers. He tells world. Now, everyone look for him. Tigers, Singhalese, everyone.'

The boy stood up. The searchlights were back, close up, by the house and the helicopter blew a hurricane of air over the trees. Then they heard a different sound and seconds later a truck drew up. The Tamil woman was whimpering quietly. She had moved closer to the boy and was plucking at his arm but he pushed her away roughly and spoke to her in Tamil. Dimly, in spite of his state of shock, Theo realised the boy must be her son. Through the haze of fear and confusion, he saw she was frightened for the boy and he saw for the first time that the boy was very young. All the time he had been guarding the house the woman must have been frightened for his life. All the time she had served Theo his meals, or grinned at Gerard, she had been worried for the boy's future. And then he thought, in however many months I have been here, I never cared to ask her name. The thought came to him simply, without the complications of grief or the fear of the past months. The boy was crouching by the window and had cocked his gun. The idea that they were about to die fixed itself firmly in Theo's mind. Again the thought was uncluttered by fear. Outside the rain increased. It fell in small dashes on to the glare of the searchlights. Someone was moving against the darkest parts of the garden. Fleetingly he remembered the girl again. She appeared in his mind unsullied by the moment's sudden real violence and by its terror. He sensed, rather than saw, a figure inch its way along the corner of the bungalow. Somebody, screened by the creepers, was breathing hard, close by. The sound was very loud and rasping as if whoever it was had been running for a long time. As if they were very frightened. Theo understood the sound, and the feeling that went with it. Next to him, the Tamil woman and the boy stood absolutely still, waiting, listening. Suddenly there was a shout, followed by running footsteps and Gerard appeared briefly in the beam of the headlights. Two men in camouflage uniform were dragging his arms back as the helicopter rose swiftly and disappeared above the trees. Now Theo could see Gerard clearly. At some point in the scuffle he had been blindfolded and his hands tied together. His mouth was working but no sound came out of it. As he watched, Theo saw two men force Gerard to his knees and in the light from the truck he saw one of them pull out a cigarette, smoking it silently and with an air of calm. Then the man threw his half-smoked cigarette away and picked up an axe from the back of the truck. With a swift movement, a wide arc of his arm, he brought the axe down sharply on Gerard's bowed neck. Once, twice, at the third attempt, Gerard's head rolled to the ground like a coconut.

Afterwards he had no idea for how long the three of them stood there, rooted to the spot. Silent as the dead, themselves. Luck had entered the arena and saved them. Fate had given them a hand. The men dragged Gerard's body into the back of the truck. They wrapped his head in a green cloth, as if it were a trophy, and tossed it in. Then they drove off. Not a single shot had been fired. All was darkness once more as the rain continued to fall unnoticed. The old woman began to weep quietly.

'We must go,' the boy said at last. In the darkness his face looked unearthly. 'They will come back. You must leave here. Go!'

Theo stared at him. He was incapable of moving, incapable of speech. His mind and body had seized up as though in rigor mortis.

'Come,' the boy urged again, his face calm. 'I take you to the border. Then we leave. You must go. They might find you here. Just go. Back to your home.'

The old woman nodded. She wiped her eyes and Theo saw, without surprise, that her face too was devoid of expression.

'Come,' the boy said again, seeing Theo could not understand. 'Before they return.'

The old woman began to speak in Tamil.

'What's she saying?' asked Theo. He was terrified.

'She says we are not normal. We cannot speak in normal voices ever again. Even if the peace comes,' the boy said, 'there is no peace for us.'

Together they stepped out into the rain, and hurried away from the house, towards the gate, where a battered jeep was hidden in the undergrowth. The old woman was still muttering and the boy turned to Theo.

'She says, peace is a jack tree that grows on the blood that has been spilt,' he said. 'It is an old Tamil saying.'

All around was an eerie silence. Above was a splattering of stars. The jungle appeared before them in the headlights of the jeep, immense and impenetrable. And as they drove into it, Theo saw that all the time he had been standing at the window, all the time his heart had been tied up with fear, he had been clutching the exercise books in which were the salvaged remains of his life.

Rohan had begun to paint. Giulia was not sure how this happened, but he had found a small warehouse in Dorsoduro and turned it into a studio. His early-morning trips to the Lido had stopped as abruptly as they had begun. And he was working seriously again. Too much time had been lost already, he told Giulia. He didn't want any more distractions.

'People will come and go. Only art survives,' he told her, airily.

Giulia said nothing. In the end even she had been unable to trace the girl. On the day Giulia had seen Rohan laughing with the unknown woman she had rung Sheffield University in search of Jim Mendis. But there she had drawn a blank. Jim Mendis had graduated a year earlier and moved on. He had left no forwarding address. Next, Giulia had tried contacting a fellow student, a contemporary of his. But the student had only known Jim slightly, and had no idea where he could be or if he had a sister. With no other clue there was nothing else Giulia could do. Perhaps, she thought, sadly, Rohan was right, and it was time to give up on this hopeless cause. The girl had been swallowed up by an indifferent world.

'Time has passed, events have moved on,' Rohan said briskly, seeing her looking at the notebooks. 'Put them away, forget about it now.'

Giulia smiled, agreeing, but the smile did not reach her eyes. Although she did not blame him, Rohan's coldness towards her brought an unbearable loneliness in its wake. She was glad he was painting again; glad to see him so busy. But every night when he returned home exhausted and preoccupied with his work, she looked for signs of other distractions, fearful of what she might see.

Outwardly Rohan appeared happier. He was relieved to be painting at last. He had missed his work. When he stretched his first canvas he hoped he would be able to pick up exactly where he had left off, using the colour grey, painting the large, soft abstracts he once had. But he found this was impossible. Life had taken him to a different place. So instead, he began to paint in dark austere tones. He painted blocks of flats from which light seeped out and formless human presence, ghosts sitting patiently, waiting for or guarding some unseen treasure. He hardly knew what he was doing. The size of his canvases had become smaller too, partly because of the cramped nature of his studio and partly because what he wanted to say was more intimate, more secretive. He had the strangest feeling of living in a closed box, from which no light could escape. Loneliness preoccupied him, and the blank empty spaces of loss. The twilight world of the displaced interested him in a way quite different from before, the slow disquiet of the home- less. All that had been familiar and certain vanished from his work. The war was embossed on Rohan's life like a watermark, visible only under close scrutiny. His palette changed. Ignoring the soft tones of the Adriatic, the blues and the greens, he began to use crimson and pink. He refused to look at other colours. Giulia thought the surfaces of his paintings were like bruised flesh, visceral and close to death. But fearful of Rohan's sudden bursts of anger, she dared not say anything. She was aware he was drinking too much, but she could not stop this either, and whenever they were alone together he became bad-tempered and argumentative. Dimly aware of his new, unspoken dislike of her, Giulia merely hid her own unhappiness under an air of false cheerfulness, refusing to question it. Privately, she believed, the war in Sri Lanka had become her war too. Sometimes on a busy *calle*, in broad daylight, she would become lost in a daydream, caught up in some unresolved memory. She would stop walking and stand absolutely still as passers-by stepped around her irritably. I'm no use, she would think, rising from her reverie, scurrying home with pounding heart. And it was at these moments that she saw clearly how her husband's country had wormed its way under her skin, invading her life, incapacitating her. It had carved out its violence on her too, so although she still loved Rohan, showing this love was gradually becoming a complicated and reluctant thing.

When Rohan had done about a dozen paintings, he told Giulia he had decided to find a gallery to represent him. Venice was a small town filled with tourists and the contemporary art available mostly serviced this industry. It was easier to find a meaningless painting in Venice than not, Rohan complained. Then one day he introduced Giulia to a woman. He had met her in the piazza, he said, where he took his morning coffee. The woman ran a small gallery tucked away behind the Calle del Forno. She represented only Venetian artists, serious artists, but, because he lived here, because his wife was from these parts, the woman told Giulia unsmilingly, she was prepared to take Rohan's work. They were sitting in his studio sharing a bottle of wine. Giulia had a feeling she had seen the woman somewhere before.

A month later two of Rohan's paintings sold for a substantial sum of money.

'I'm so proud of you,' Giulia said, after that first sale. 'See, there's hope.'

She spoke sadly, for she now remembered where she had seen the woman before. Rohan pulled a face. He had banished hope.

Two storks nested on the roof of the beach house. There had never been storks there before. Mother, father and the nest waited patiently for the egg to hatch. Maybe they felt the house was

vacant so they felt safer here, or maybe they liked the uninterrupted view with nothing as far as the eye could see. Only
Antarctica lay beyond the ocean. The seagulls left them alone;
they were too big to be argued with. Inside the house all was
quiet but not empty. Inside the house was a life, of sorts. There
were small signs, small stirrings of living, ebbing and flowing
feebly. For inside the house was Theo Samarajeeva. He was home
at last. It had taken almost four years but he was back. He had
been back for some time, days, months. Time did not matter
much, he had no train to catch, no appointment to keep. Mostly
he slept on a bed, *the* bed; it had belonged to him once long ago.
It was his again. And he was back now and sleeping on it, all
day and all night, hardly ever getting up. There was no one to
recognise him and no one to care. There wasn't a soul around,
just the storks. Soon the egg hatched and the baby stork breathed
fresh sea air. It breathed the same air as Theo. Neither of them
cared much if the air was free. They both just breathed it.

Had Sugi been there he would have told Theo it was good
luck to have storks nesting on the roof. Sugi would have seen
it as an omen. He would have cleaned the house and polished
the floor with coconut scrapings, and made Sir some milk tea,
bringing it out to the veranda on a silver tray. He would have
fixed the doors and shutters that hung limply on their broken
hinges, and then he would have picked up the stone lions that
had crashed to the ground. But Sugi wasn't there. And the
house, neglected and vandalised, remained uncared for.

On that first day of his return, Theo waited for Sugi. He had
been patient for nearly four years, another day or so made no
difference. Sugi would be back soon, he was certain. The girl, he
hoped, was somewhere safe, waiting for news of him. He was too
nervous to try the lights on that first night; he simply waited.
When Sugi did not appear the next day or the next or even the

day after that, he began to stumble around the house, dragging his lame leg against what furniture remained. He opened the tins of food in the larder, which by some miracle had not been stolen, and when he could no longer stop shaking he tried to eat a little. But his throat had closed up to food. Only the bottles of whisky, hidden away with a few documents inside the covered-over garden well, held his interest. And this was how Thercy found him.

Thercy still lived in the town. She was no longer the person she once was, and the town, too, had changed. With new developments further up the coast most of those who lived here now were newcomers, indifferent to its history. Four years and two assassinated prime ministers had altered the way the war was fought. Loyalties had changed, and changed again. Blood had cooled. Four years had buried the past. Only the ghosts stayed on. Thercy was like a ghost, she had meant to leave long ago, but apathy had stopped her. She had aged, walking up the hill wasn't easy any more, but when she saw a light in the beach house something stirred within her. Something she had never thought to feel again. Thinking of her dead friend, panting, she walked slowly towards the house.

'Aiyo!' she said. 'Mr Samarajeeva!' and then she stopped, unable to go on.

She had recognised him, but only just. Theo looked back at her. He was frightened. The woman stood in the doorway, blocking his escape.

'I was Sugi's friend,' Thercy said, barely above a whisper, staring at this remnant of a man. Mr Samarajeeva looked like a ghost. 'What has happened to you?'

'Sugi? Where has he gone? Tell him, I'm home.'

'Aiyo!' said Thercy softly. 'Sugi is gone, my Sir. He's dead.'

It was the word 'Sir' that Theo heard first. And it was the first notch of his undoing.

'Nulani,' he said. 'Nulani Mendis . . .'

'I . . . don't know, Sir. Maybe she's . . .' and Thercy caught his crumpled body as he fell.

Later, she cleaned the house for him and made some mulligatawny chicken soup. Later, when he was less frightened, she talked some more. Soothingly, as though he was her child.

'Nulani's uncle has gone,' she said. 'The people who bought the house have divided it up. There are two families who share the garden now.'

It seemed that the lane down which Theo had driven, on that carefree distant night, was almost unrecognisable. Someone had cleared the path of all but memories. The Mendis family might as well not have existed. Other things, Thercy told him, had changed too. The convent school and the boys' school, having joined forces under new staff, had moved up the coast. Nothing remained of its former self. New schoolchildren took the bus to school now. Young girls in faded skirts and with ribbons in their hair walked chattering down the road.

'And the traffic island, Sir,' Thercy said, 'd'you remember, Miss Nulani used to say it was her father's headstone? Well, that has gone too.' Even the hospital, she told Theo, had been relocated to another place. Theo listened. He hardly responded, but he watched her as she served his broth, and swept the floor, and collected the empty arrack bottles. Then she told him she would be back tomorrow with some food.

Thercy came every day, after that. She came with rice, and with dhal and with string-hopper pancakes. She made more mulligatawny soup, and she asked Theo if there was anything else she could buy for him. She went to the bank at his request and drew out the money he wanted. She told him, no one had been in the least interested in his name. And all the while she talked to him, telling him about the changes in the town.

'Sumaner House is changed, Sir,' she told Theo one day. 'The owner had it boarded up and now it's waiting to be sold. I never liked it much, although when the orphan was there at least it was a good job. Plenty of money for me, then. But after the boy disappeared, his guardian saw no point in returning to our useless island. Why should he, when work was plentiful elsewhere? He gave me a pension and I now live in Bazaar Street, behind the railway station.'

Thercy talked determinedly on. She hid her shock, having quickly got accustomed to the frailness of this man, and did whatever she could to help him. Besides, she felt he was getting stronger daily. Every time she visited, she thought of another little snippet of information. To waken his interest in life.

'D'you remember the gem store, Sir?' she asked him one morning. 'It used to be so popular with tourists. One night, about a year ago, the police came without warning, raided it, and shut it up for good.' She raised her hands heavenwards, shrugging. 'There were stories about what had gone on in there for a while, terrible rumours about the man who owned it. But so many things have happened in this wretched town that one more story means nothing. No one is surprised for long.'

She was silent, not wanting to say more, aware of Theo's unspoken desire to know how Sugi had died.

At night, because there was no longer a curfew, when he was alone, Theo would walk for hours on the beach, listening to the sea. Then, the depression he had held in check all day descended. In his headlong flight, chasing his freedom to the coast, snatching at its tail feathers, touching but never quite catching it, he had not thought about the future. After the Tamil boy dropped him at the border, he had simply headed for the sea, the sound of it, the smell of it. His heart had yearned for the girl; his arms had ached with the need to hold her. But now all he had was a pair of broken straw sandals and a notebook lying open with all its stories gone. The wind had whisked them away; the rain had washed them out. Time had rendered them useless, making them old stories from long ago. It dawned on him that recovery would not be easy, maybe even that these stories were un-recoverable. At moments like this, despair grew like sea cacti, piercing his heart. He stared at the sea; it was a blank canvas of nothingness. It moved with the richness of silk but, he felt, underneath it was cruel. Often at night, after Thercy left, reality rocked against the walls of the beach house, and at these times, Theo discovered forbidden thoughts. They rotted like fruit beside his silent typewriter where once his manuscript had been. Then, staring at the undulating phosphorescent water, he understood at last that freedom was a double-edged thing, which, like inno-cence once lost, was unrecoverable.

Towards dawn always, after these wanderings, he would return to lie like an emaciated stain on the bed where once his love had slept. Wearing a thin sarong that had belonged to Sugi, two legs placed carefully together, the soles of his feet worn and smashed, his face turning of its own accord to the wall. So that Thercy, coming in to sweep out the night, would stare at the scar across his back and heave another little sigh of pity. And fill a vase with shoe-flowers from the garden, for time, she knew, was what he needed most.

One day Thercy found the half-finished portrait of Sugi behind the bookshelf.

'Sir,' she had said, 'Mr Samarajeeva, I . . .'

It had been too much for him, days of bottled-up emotions gushed out.

'All the other paintings she did have gone,' he said after-wards, when he could speak calmly again. 'Why would anyone want to steal them?'

'Maybe,' Thercy suggested, tentatively, 'maybe your friends in Colombo came and collected them. What d'you think? I heard that someone came to this house after Sugi was gone.' She frowned, not wanting to be impertinent, but anxious to help. 'Why don't you contact your friends? How are they to know you are still alive if you don't contact them?'

There, she thought, she had said the thing utmost in her mind. But the idea filled Theo with horror. All day it worked in him, all day he gazed at the painting. And that night, having finished off a whole bottle of arrack, he decided to go for a swim. Throwing off his clothes on the deserted beach, he waded into the water, swimming slowly, thinking he might head out towards the rocks. There had been a storm the day before and the sea was still rough. Within minutes he was out of breath but, deciding to turn back, Theo found he was further away from the shore than he realised and an under-current was pulling at him. The harder he swam, the further away from the beach he seemed to get. A train hooted, appearing suddenly around the bay. Theo shouted and waved, but the beach itself was empty. By now he was panting. The alcohol had made him dizzy and his legs were beginning to give out. He realised that unless he could reach the shore soon he would drown. A wave rose and hit him, pushing him further out. He was struggling so much and the roar in his ears was so loud that he did not hear the shout until the catamaran was alongside him and a hand hauled him up and over the side of it. Two pairs of eyes stared at him in the thin light of a lantern.

'There's no point in drowning,' a voice chided him sternly. 'You'll only have to come back to live another life.'

'It's a good thing we saw you,' the second fisherman added. 'Are you new here, or are you just a fool? This isn't a place for swimming. The currents are treacherous. You have to go to the next bay if you want to swim.'

They shook their head in amazement and took him back to find his clothes, joking with him that they would have better fish for sale in the morning. And then they left him, putting out to sea, vanishing into the darkness.

That night, for the first time in years, he slept uninterrupted and when he woke at last it was from a dream of the girl and their single night together. The mist was already beginning to clear on the horizon and he could hear the '*malu, malu*' cry of the fishermen in the distance. Thercy stood unsmiling beside his bed, holding out a cup of morning tea.

'I heard what happened to you last night,' she said, shaking her head.

She waited while he took a sip of tea.

'I have to say something to you, Mr Samarajeeva. I have said nothing all this time but now I won't be quiet any longer.'

She made a small gesture of anger. She was breathing deeply and her voice, when she spoke, was rough and close to tears. It surprised him into listening.

'Sir, you are a clever man,' said Thercy grimly. 'Sugi told me all about the books you wrote and your film. Sugi was full of admiration for you. And love. He was my friend, so I knew about the things that were in his heart. And I must tell you, Sir, the fishermen were right. I am sorry, Mr Samarajeeva, you *are* behaving like a fool! Go and find your friends in Colombo, find out what happened to Miss Nulani. She was a loving girl. I know how you have suffered, how you feel, but can't you *see*? She would want to know you are safe. What is wrong with you? At least go and talk to them.'

Her voice had risen and she was gesticulating wildly. Theo handed her his empty cup.

'Twice in one day,' he said faintly, with the barest movement of a smile, 'there must be some truth in it. You are right, Thercy, and thank you for saying it. I must try to overcome this fear. I must stop being a coward. I will go to Colombo. Tomorrow, I'll go tomorrow and find Rohan and Giulia. I promise. I know that only they can tell me what happened to her in the end.'

16

In Colombo the mosquitoes were back. Thin, fragile and deadly, they coated the walls of buildings in their thousands, filling the waterlogged coconut shells, turning the surfaces of everything they alighted on into a living carpet. They fed on the flesh of rotting fruit, sucking out what remained of the honeydew nectar. Arriving with the mosquitoes was a new breed of women from the north of the island. Like the mosquitoes, they came with the rains. But unlike the mosquitoes, the women were full of a new kind of despair and a frightening rage. Their desire for revenge was greater than their interest in life. They had been trained; a whole army of psychologists working tirelessly on them had shaped their impressionable minds. The female mosquitoes' purpose in life was the continuation of their species, but the suicide bombers cared nothing for the future. Steadily they changed the shape of the battle lines, appearing everywhere, in government buildings, at army checkpoints, beside long-abandoned sacred sites. They appeared in churches when mass was being said, at roadside shrines and during Buddhist funerals. Neither place nor time mattered much to these women. Nature had not designed their limbs to grow once broken. Killing was what interested *them*. For these women were the new trailblazers, the world epidemic slipping in unnoticed, just as the malaria season returned.

Unaware of this and eventually after much procrastination, Theo dragged himself to Colombo. Thercy watched him pocket his reluctance and go, pleased, but saying nothing. She had thought he would change his mind. Thercy understood the shame he felt, she had seen it before in others. She knew what torture did. But she knew also the desire to find the girl and his friends was greater. Speech was not necessary; all he wanted was to catch sight of her. If his karma is good, Thercy thought, then he will.

'She must have a chance to forget me,' he said out loud. 'I know my age never worried her but, well, things are different now. Now I am old in an inescapable way.'

He looked at Thercy but she didn't seem to be listening. She was cleaning the mirror.

'I have lived on the edge of an abyss for so long that the world and I are separate. I have nothing to offer her, even if she has been waiting for me. Even if she still wanted me I have no more to give.'

Thercy finished her cleaning and went outside. She knew he liked cut flowers, so she cut some of the jasmine creeper and brought it in. Then she found a vase and trailed the branch in it.

'All I want is the chance to see her from a distance,' Theo told her, watching her arthritic hands. 'Out of curiosity really, nothing more. Just to know that she's happy, that she's painting. That she has retained her hope.'

'Yes,' Thercy said.

The scent from the jasmine began to fill the room.

'After all, I must face reality. Probably she has married, by now. Who knows, she might have several children.'

The scent filled Theo with unbearable sadness. All gone, he thought. Every single one of them. Thercy looked at him. She pursed her lips and wiped the table. Then she went into the kitchen to make him some tea.

The train hugged the coastline, running parallel to the road. It was a journey he had made many times before. Wide sandy beaches unfolded before him, a few scattered villages screened by coconut palms. Staring out of the window he saw that nothing had changed; everything was as it had been yesterday. But the man who had once rested his eyes on the view had vanished. He had held this view within him during all the terrible years in prison. The girl's face and the view had been so closely linked, so connected that they had been inseparable in his mind. He had imagined her waiting for him on the brow of the hill and all of this, and Sugi, had been the sum of his hope. Somehow, he realised, he had kept the hope alive. Now at last he was free, and the beach and the sea had waited for him, but the view he had dreamt about in prison was no longer as he imagined. And he was no longer that man who had been able to dream. A sense of loss, terrible in its hopelessness, washed over him. You will not recognise me, he thought, staring at the sea. I have been to places I can no longer describe. And he thought again, no, she must not see me. Better for her to remember me as I was.

In Colombo there had been a temporary clean-up. During Theo's imprisonment most of the heaviest fighting had moved away from the capital and was now concentrated elsewhere in the north. Only the suicide bombers operated with a disregard for boundaries. Because of them, the outside world had woken up to what was taking place and had become interested in the country at last. The suicide bombers, it seemed, had started a cult following. Muslims in the Middle East were beginning to follow suit. At last, Sri Lanka was newsworthy. A few days earlier the ex-Governor from Britain had visited briefly. After meeting the Prime Minister he travelled north to shake hands with the head of the insurgents. Peace was a long way away, but it was what he had in mind. The ex-Governor left a trail of bunting behind him. They still lined the streets, while elsewhere, wilted flowers covered up the bullet holes as best they could. Whitewash brightened the bombed-out buildings. All was sunlit activity. Colombo, Theo saw, was like him, struggling with the pretence of normality. But the army was still a presence, and seeing a truck Theo panicked. He rushed into a shop to hide, his heart pounding. No one followed him and gradually he became aware that he was being stared at. Then, as the shopkeeper approached, he ran out. Like a petty thief, he thought, fleetingly, unable to stop himself. He should not have come. Outside in the glaring light, looking around for escape, he became frantic. How long would it be before someone caught up with him? Hurrying across the road he expected a roadblock, or the sound of gunshot, at any moment, but still nothing happened. Forcing himself to calm down, to breathe deeply, he lost his way. He looked at a passing bus, but such was his anxiety that he was unable to read the sign. This, then, was what it meant to be hunted.

Eventually, he found his bearings. After the near drowning Theo had begun to realise how weak his legs were, yet in spite of this, rather than take a bus and be stared at, he decided to walk. Rohan's house was fifteen minutes away. Four years and two months away. A lifetime away. Theo walked slowly now, head down against the sun, remembering. The smell of limes and frangipani filled the air. It was five o'clock. Rohan would have finished work. He would be cleaning his brushes, wiping his hands absent-mindedly on a rag, staring at his painting. And Giulia, most probably, would have brought in the tea. Theo would be the last person they would expect to see. Once again he began to wonder at the wisdom of this trip. What if he were not welcome? The idea had not occurred to him before, but time, he knew, changed things. *He* had changed. What if they had too? As he turned the corner into their road, he hesitated. His bad leg was throbbing and he was shaking all over. What if the girl was there? What if he frightened them? He was no longer as they remembered. And the enormity of what he would need to say to make them understand struck him suddenly and forcefully. He was sweating heavily, partly from the heat but mostly from fear. Maybe, he thought, they would simply not believe him. In *Tiger Lily* he had written about a man whom no one believed. The man had gone from one village elder to another, telling of atrocities done to him, but no one believed him. In the end, doubting himself, hounded from his home, followed by demons, the man had thrown himself into the river and drowned.

Feeling unutterably exhausted, Theo walked the length of the road. Rohan's house was nowhere in sight. Although he peered into gardens, walking halfway along driveways he could not, for the life of him, see the canopied terrace that Giulia had pain-stakingly made. Rohan's studio was at the front of the house. In the past, whenever Theo had arrived at their house, Rohan had always been the first to spot him, rushing out with a greeting. But today, although he retraced his steps several times, Theo could no longer see the studio. Perhaps he had mistaken the road, he thought, momentarily distracted. Some construction work was going on nearby. Puzzled, he stood watching the workmen on the scaffolding. A lorry passed through what must have once been a driveway. Theo could have sworn this was where Rohan and Giulia had lived. It dawned on him that they might have moved. Then a black VW Beetle pulled up in the driveway of the house next door.

'Are you looking for someone?' the driver asked, getting out.

Theo stared. The man half smiled at him, uncertain. 'I know you, don't I?' he asked. 'Haven't I met you before?'

'I'm looking for someone by the name of Rohan Fernando,' Theo said reluctantly. 'I thought he lived here but . . .'

'Rohan? You knew Rohan?'

'Where is he?'

'You haven't heard?'

'No,' said Theo.

'You from around here?'

'No,' said Theo.

'Ah, I see. You've been overseas,' the man said, nodding, understanding.

Theo nodded too.

'I'm sorry. In that case you wouldn't have heard. About two years ago, there was a fire in their house, one in Rohan's studio, and one on their veranda. Two years ago. It tore through their house, men. We were in bed, my wife and I, when we heard it . . . there was no chance, none whatsoever. I'm sorry to tell you this. You aren't a close friend, are you? I can't understand it really. This whole road was puzzled. They were quiet people, and Rohan's wife wasn't even Sri Lankan.' The man shrugged apologetically, his pleasant features puzzled. 'Things were very bad two years ago, very savage. Now, thank God, this new government is trying to negotiate peace talks. The first in decades. Everyone is hopeful, you know. Now that the ex-Governor has visited. It can only be a good thing. You recently returned?' he asked.

And when Theo said nothing, the man continued, pointing at the building site: 'There, that was where their house stood, over there.'

17

WITHIN A YEAR THE GALLERY IN Calle del Forno offered
Rohan a solo show. The demand for his small paintings had
grown. The urgency, the intensity of the colour, their size, all
added to their odd charm. He had been an abstract painter for
years but now slowly he found himself propelled towards empty
interiors, furniture and unclothed figures. The rooms he painted
were always dark. Wardrobes opened out in them like gaping
holes, beds remained unmade, figures were silhouetted against
barred windows. And all the time, small glimmers of light
escaped through cracks in the canvas.

In the past Rohan had always talked to Giulia about his work.
When they lived in Colombo she used to come into his studio
at the end of each working day and they would drink tea
together. And then they talked. In those days Rohan moved his
vast canvases around the room and they would look at them
together. He used to do all this energetically. Giulia, given half
a chance, would tease him about his seriousness. Afterwards
they would go back to the house for dinner. Now all this had
changed. Now Rohan did not joke. These days he hardly said

anything. Neither of them could say when it had happened but they had established separate rhythms to their life. Giulia had begun to teach English, making friends with several people in the neighbourhood. And she had taken up her translation work again. Often when Rohan worked late she would have supper with a neighbour. Once or twice she had tried including Rohan in these visits but it had never been successful. Both of them knew they were drifting apart; neither knew how to stop the change. Whenever Giulia attempted to talk about their past, Rohan blocked her. So now they never mentioned Theo or the girl. Their life in Sri Lanka might never have happened. Lying awake at night while he slept, Giulia wondered if this was all they had escaped for, this empty void they called freedom. Months passed. Rohan's exhibition was mentioned in an Italian newspaper. An unknown critic praised his work. The paintings, he said, reminded him of a shared grief, of dreams vaguely remembered, furniture that served as receptacles of memory. All of human life, in fact, reduced to memory. Rohan walked in to find Giulia reading the review. She was crying.

'Don't start,' he shouted. 'Don't start all that again. I paint what I paint. It's not my fault if they want to interpret it in this obvious, puerile way.'

'Rohan,' began Giulia, but then she stopped. What was the use? Grief had solidified into a wall between them; it had hardened and set in stone. There seemed little point to anything. When things were at their worst they had shared everything, every thought, every anxiety. Now all they had was bitterness to drown in. And yet, she thought wistfully, Theo was my friend too, my loss too. And then again, she thought angrily, your country is nothing to do with me. Resentment filled up the cracks. It covered everything they touched in fallout dust. *You were the one to take me there*, remember, thought Giulia, her eyes following him around the small flat. But she did not say it out loud. She was afraid of damaging what little they had. And she asked herself, has he forgotten my friend, Anna? No one mentions her any more, but I lived through that too. Yet in spite of this, still Giulia was unable to hurt Rohan further. Nor did she tell him that she was toying with the idea of going to London in the spring, to make one last attempt to look for Nulani Mendis. After Christmas, she decided, in the new year, I'll go over there. Alone.

'Next year, I'm having a show in Munich,' was all Rohan said.

Six years is a long time by any standards. Six years is like a steep mountain. Theo Samarajeeva climbed his mountain almost without noticing. He did not set out to do so but he began to write. What else could he do, he was a writer. He had been writing all his life, how could he stop now? At first it could hardly be called writing. At first it was more ramblings. Because his fingers had been broken, he could not type easily. Everything ached. His back, the soles of his feet, his leg. He never went in the water again. He no longer had any desire to swim. Nevertheless, the will to live remained in some strange and unaccountable way. And so he began to write again. Slowly, because he was uncertain, because his fingers were unsteady and the typewriter was too painful to use, he wrote by hand. It was Thercy who had encouraged him. Thercy who still came over to cook for him, walking slowly down the hill with her bunches of greens, her coconut milk and fresh fish. She had become less formal with him and he was no longer frightened of her. She was part of his landscape. Whenever his depression descended on him like a smoky cloud of mosquitoes, it was Thercy who would talk to him, cajoling and distracting him as best she could.

'You are a writer,' she would say. 'So why don't you write?'

There were things he could not write about, he told her. Thercy did not think this was a problem. She had seen too many things herself to be shocked, she told him. But she could understand, he was not ready to write about his experiences.

'Maybe,' she said, 'you will never be ready for that. So write of other things.'

She had only a vague knowledge of his books. It pleased him that she had not seen the film in Colombo. It pleased him that she knew very little about his past. Picking up his notebook he began to write. As always he started with Anna. Nothing could be counted before her. It was she who had led him to the girl. And it had been her voice he heard first.

After a while, unasked, he began to tell Thercy things.

'I was blindfolded,' he told her cautiously. 'And I was hit. Sometimes I was hit so hard that I fell forward. Then they gave me electric shocks. They put chilli inside me. They were laughing. Later, I'm not sure when, but another time I was hit with the butt of a rifle. They broke my fingers. See, three of them are broken! A writer without fingers, they laughed. They found this funny.'

Thercy was polishing the floor with old coconut scrapings. Watching her he felt his heart contract with grief. Sugi had polished the floor in this way.

'If you have a wound that you can't heal,' Thercy said very quietly, not looking at him, 'it will get bigger. You must try to heal it yourself.'

She no longer called him Sir. In fact, she seldom addressed him in any specific way. But her eyes followed him when he wasn't looking and she understood his moods. Long ago, she told him, in the early days of the war, she had had a son.

On another occasion, Theo told her, 'They played psychological games when I was blindfolded. I thought I was standing at the top of some steps and if I moved forward I might fall. But when they hit me I smashed against the wall instead.'

'Yes,' Thercy said. 'What happened then?'

But he could not say. Later, after she had gone slowly up the hill again, he went back to his notebook.

'*I have been tortured*,' he wrote.

He looked at what he had written. The ink was black. Four simple words. Changing a life for ever. He needed to write it in red ink. Who would believe me, he thought, when *I* can hardly believe it happened? But Thercy seemed to believe him, all right. Why should she not? she had asked, surprised. Violence had been done to her, why could it not happen to him?

'*Self-pity*,' he wrote, '*is all that's left. When I arrived I brought it with me. And now I'm in possession of it once again.*'

He paused, thinking. And then he wrote again.

Only the girl made a difference, coming back like a stray cat. At first I had no idea why this was so. I was worn out by your death, unable to believe in the future. And suddenly, there she was, appearing day after day. The war, although I didn't realise it then, was gathering momentum and all she did was draw. Everything made sense by illusion. Fabulously. Stories appearing under her fingers, stories I never knew existed, even. What took me twenty words, she achieved in an unwavering drift of a line. It was astonishing, really.

Thercy brought him some milk rice. It was a *poya* day. She had been to the temple earlier because it was the anniversary of Sugi's death. She did not tell Theo this but Sugi was on her mind.

'He was frightened for you,' she said, chewing on a piece of jaggery. 'You and Miss Nulani, both.'

263

They were drinking a cup of tea together. Theo had been writing all morning and he was glad to see her. If she was ever late he became anxious. But Thercy was seldom late.

'Sugi saw where it could all lead long before I did,' he agreed. 'It was only afterwards, after she painted me, that I realised. My wife's death had left me with a set of beliefs too naive to be of use. Sugi must have known that. He must have watched me and seen what was happening. He didn't like the way I talked about this country. He wanted me to be more cautious.'

Theo glanced at her. He wasn't sure how much she understood, but Thercy nodded. He's better than he used to be, she thought.

'I had never seen anyone draw as she did,' Theo said, 'nor will I again.'

Wondering, how would she draw my life now? That evening, after Thercy went home, he continued to write.

Of course, she was so much younger. I always knew that. Who could say what might have happened had we been together? Perhaps she would have tired of me and found a younger man? After a while I would have become a millstone. You had been my whole life until that moment, Anna. Your death had robbed me of many things, I felt spent, finished, over. And then she arrived. What was I to think? Now of course I see more clearly how great the need was, to fill the gap you left. She was different from you, yet the same. You see, Anna, the truth is, the shameful admission is, that I have always defined myself by someone else. First you, and then the girl. When we met, you and I, I had the strangest feeling that I was enveloped by your identity. Then later I wanted to be supported by her. Can I be brutally honest? I went to her

*for the renewal of my courage, and for help with all I had
to bear. I was so afraid, so alone, so needing from the
outside for the assurance of my own worthiness to exist.
There, I have written the shameful truth. Have I given
you pain? Is it possible to love again, with a different
intensity, without losing what went before? Some would
say so. In prison, I was filled with guilt. Each time they
beat me, when I could breathe again it was guilt that
always rose to the surface.*

A little later on he wrote:

*In my worst moments I felt as though I had tried to wipe
you out with her. So, you see, I deserved to be punished.
And now you have both vanished. Although in the end, it
is perhaps I who has disappeared.*

Alone in the broken beach house, with its blue-faded gate,
and its endless glimpses of the sea, silence swooped down on
Theo like the seagulls. Time had passed without a sound. Time
had gathered in pockets in the landscape but he never noticed.
He walked the beach and watched the sea rise and heave
unmoved. Like memory, the sea had a life of its own. Sun and
rain came and went regardless. Further up the coast, where
once a man had been hung, a huge high-rise hotel was going
up. Daily it grew, thrusting its scaffolding into the blistering
sky. Workmen in hard hats drove on the beach where once
army jeeps had patrolled. A beach restaurant was being built,
and an oyster-shaped swimming pool with fresh water was
planned for those tourists who did not want the sea.
International cuisine was all that was needed. New glass-
bottomed boats began to appear and old ones were being

painted over. It was many years since the coral reef held such interest. Suddenly paradise was the new currency. The island began to rescue itself, hoping to whitewash its bloody past. Theo Samarajeeva watched from afar. He was writing steadily now, almost all of the time. When he had filled up three note-books he walked the beach, thinking. He wanted to approach his old agent, he told Thercy, but he was nervous.

'Don't be silly,' Thercy said. 'Yes, yes, it's a good idea. I've told you. The only way you'll survive this life is to refuse to let them beat you down.'

Looking at Thercy, he was reminded more and more of the old ayah who had looked after him as a child.

'But I have nothing more to say about Sri Lanka. Everything has been pushed so far back inside me that I can't dislodge it. I don't want to.'

'So? That's fine,' Thercy said firmly. 'Write about the way we survive then. Tell them how we live. Miss Nulani gave you hope, didn't she? She showed you that you were still a person, capable of loving, of living. I think she gave you back yourself. What more d'you want?'

She was right. Walking along the beach that evening, he searched the sea for a sign. But the sea could not answer him and the moonlight on the empty beach unrolled silently like a bolt of silk across the sands.

Lately his eyesight was beginning to mist over. He was loath to visit an optician. It would mean another trip to Colombo and he could not face going back. Nor did he want to think of Rohan or Giulia, shying away from the thought that they too might have died because of him. But he had reckoned without Thercy. Insistently, day after day, she cajoled him until at last, reluctantly, he wrote a letter to his agent. He wrote cautiously, taking days to find the right words, hesitating, rewriting it. In the end, with a sigh, he gave it to Thercy to post. His book was growing and a certain urgency because of his eyes made him write furiously. For the first time he was attempting a book that was not politically driven. He had no more to say about injustice. Having lived it, he saw the hopelessness of defining it. This book, he saw, was about loving. This book was about something he could speak of. Every night he walked the beach, waiting for the monsoons, watching the clouds gather across the sky, seeing a new generation of children fly their box kites. Local people knew him, now. He was that writer fellow, they said, who had once been famous. Once he had been a handsome man who came from the UK to live among his people. But then he had gone away to England and returned mad. He had gone mad for love, they told their children. He was crazy now, they said. Better if he had stayed in England and been happy. Foolish man, coming back to this place! Let this be a warning, the mothers told their children. If you are lucky enough to get to England, stay there. So the village children flew their kites and rode their bicycles, taking care to stay away from the madman in the beach house, careful always to avoid the place after dark.

A lifetime passed. Objects marked the years on Theo's table. Each was from another life, each irreversibly linked to the next. They were all his possessions. A penknife from his childhood, that was one. He had been six when he had been given it. Many words had been carved with its blade. An oil lamp, given to him by his mother, left over from the days when he used to visit the temple. He had always taken it on his travels and somehow it had never broken. A small beaded bag belonging to Anna. They had found it on the ground where she had been mugged. He had kept it all these years. Inside was the wedding ring he had taken from her finger before he buried her. A palm leaf, kept between the pages of a book. He had picked it on a trip down the Nile. A mollusc shell from the Adriatic, indigo blue and black, and pearl white. A rag, moulded and stained with vermilion, and a small hand-sewn notebook, unused and torn.

The agent was astonished to hear from him.

'For God's sake, Theo, I thought you were dead. I sent you letter after letter, but you never replied. I tried phoning you but the lines were constantly down. What sort of hole have you been living in?'

Theo laughed. It was the first time he had laughed in years.

'I've been writing,' he said.

'Theo,' said the agent, sounding hysterical, 'what do you mean? You ring me up after years and tell me you've been writing. You can't do this to me. Do you know the trouble I've gone to trying to get hold of you? I even thought of coming out to that wretched place in search of you but the Foreign Office gave out a warning against travel. Your countrymen seemed such bloody savages that I gave up. *Well*, what happened? And another thing,' the agent rushed on, 'you're a rich man now, you know. The film was a runaway success. And did you say you're writing again? Tell me all about it.'

'I'll put it all in a letter,' Theo said faintly, not wanting to talk.

So Theo wrote to him. For talking wore him out and his own voice could not be trusted. So he wrote.

'*The book is about hope,*' he wrote, '*and survival. About war, and also indifference. But you're wrong,*' he added, surprising himself by the strength of his convictions, '*they are not* all *savages here. There are savages everywhere, not just here.*'

Then he sent the agent the first part of his story.

18

AFTER HIS SHOW IN MUNICH ROHAN had had two more shows in Venice. In the four years since he had started painting again, he had worked with dogged determination, spending all the available hours of daylight possible in his studio. Giulia had begun collecting his reviews in a book. She was glad he was working properly again; glad he had picked up where he had left off in Colombo. It appeared they had shaken off their turbulent years in the tropics, outwardly it might have been said they had recovered. Rohan was mellower, less bad-tempered, and for her part Giulia expected less. Old age had crept up on both of them, she noticed, thinking, too, this suited them in many ways. All in all they were more content these days. Occasionally Giulia even managed to make him socialise with the few friends she had made, and they had stopped sniping at each other as they had when they first arrived in Italy. The difficult patch in their marriage appeared to have passed, but, Giulia saw with sad acceptance, the optimism had gone from it also. They lived quietly, seriously, no longer taking risks and were wary of new things. And the past with all its light and shade was never mentioned. Only in Rohan's paintings, strange, elegiac and ghostly, could it be glimpsed. Threadbare like a carpet, all his memories showed in his pictures with a transparency that Giulia found at times unbearable. He was an exile; he would remain an exile always. Once, in a rare moment of admission, he read Giulia a small notice in an English newspaper.

A spate of credit-card crimes involving a gang of Sri Lankans has erupted in London. The Home Office has confirmed that these underaged youths, currently facing trial, could also face deportation back to Sri Lanka despite the spasmodic violence still taking place in some parts of the island. Young Tamil boys, who left their homeland hoping to provide for their impoverished families, could soon be returning in disgrace often to a worse situation than the one they left behind. It is well known that Tamils who evaded the guerrilla army by escaping abroad often face execution on their return.

'So it goes on,' Rohan said. 'Once an outcast, always an outcast. Memory is all we have to rely on. Let's hope the girl is holding on to hers.'

Reviews of his paintings were appearing with marked regularity in the Italian papers. They spoke of his depiction of loss and alienation, and of warmth remembered. Giulia read them without comment. And so the years had passed. This was their life now, neither so good nor so bad. And at least, they both thought privately, they were free.

One day towards the end of summer Rohan was introduced to an Englishwoman from London. Her name was Alison Fielding, she told him, and she ran a small gallery called London Fields. Having seen his paintings in Art Basel, she contacted him, inviting him to submit slides of current work.

'London?' said Giulia, surprised. 'I thought you didn't want to show in London?'

He had not been back since that day, seven years ago, when he and Giulia trawled the city looking for Nulani. Giulia too had never returned. Somehow it had never happened. The small difficulties, the shifts and changes in their relationships, all the minutiae of the everyday, had made her reluctant to disturb the past. Too much had been lost, too much remained precarious for either of them to open old wounds. But now, as summer began to recede, before the sharp forerunners of winter winds stirred the leaves, Rohan finally had a reason to visit. Alison Fielding was enthusiastic.

'*Do come,*' she wrote. '*Bring some work. We can talk it over. I liked your paintings very much.*'

Giulia could not leave her work, so Rohan went alone to a city still basking in an Indian summer. The land was brown through lack of rain and the city glowed with an alert bustle that he had never noticed before. The gallery was smaller than he had expected, tucked away in a corner of Clerkenwell. He almost walked past it. In the window were two paintings, one black on red, thick impasto, marked and stained, and another white as marble. Small numbers were stencilled along the edges of the canvas. Something about them caught Rohan's eye. He gazed, puzzled.

'Ah,' said Alison Fielding, greeting him, smiling. 'You've noticed my other Sri Lankan artist!'

Blue flew out from a canvas. Followed by another, deeper shade, more piercing, hinting gold beneath it and something else, some unidentifiable movement of light. Rohan stared. A line, excavated, as it were, in the dark, seemed slightly muffled, bringing a mysterious sense of intimacy to the whole. Another painting hung alone on a far wall. He found himself thinking

271

of the inner chamber of ancient, sacred tombs. Stars showed faintly through a midnight sky. The canvases glowed; there was no other way to describe them. They were both luminescent and extraordinarily still. The contradictions of this vast, aerated space within the density of the blues were magical. Darkness and light, together in the most unlikely place of entombment, appeared to sink to the depths of the earth, to the human body itself, metaphorically binding two impossible worlds. The paintings had no names, only numbers. There were more, stacked in corners. Rohan followed them around the room, mesmerised. Downstairs, the images were of carefully drawn objects, glimpsed and then rubbed out even at the moment of recognition; hinting at the ways in which the past inhabits us, shaping us at some level hovering below conscious thought. And all the time anxiety and claustrophobia remained inescapably part of the whole.

'You like them?' asked Alison Fielding. Rohan stared.

'They're wonderful,' he said. 'Did you say . . . ?'

'Yes, the artist is Sri Lankan. A woman.'

'There is only one,' said Rohan slowly, 'only one Sri Lankan artist that I can think of. Only one who . . .' He broke off, unable to go on.

'Her name is Nulani Mendis,' said Alison Fielding, smiling broadly. 'D'you know of her? Good! I was thinking of showing you both together actually. You must meet her. But first, let me see what you have brought me.'

'And that was how I met her, finally,' said Rohan.

He was back, with the promise of an exhibition with Nulani. His excitement was infectious. Since he had returned he had been unable to stop smiling. All evening they had sat drinking wine and he had talked non-stop. Giulia could not get a word in edgeways. She felt light-headed, drunk with astonishment and unanswered questions. When would Giulia see her? How was she? How did she look? What did she say when she met Rohan? Rohan laughed, delighted, remembering.

'She simply could not believe it when Alison rang her. It was comical really,' he said, pausing. 'If it wasn't so sad,' he added. 'Alison picked up the phone and just called her up. "There's a painter friend of yours from Sri Lanka," was all she said. Just like that. Can you imagine it? And half an hour later there she was, little Nulani Mendis, changed and yet not so changed, at all. Breathless with shock and beautiful as ever.' He paused, again. 'We spent the whole evening together. In the end Alison had to send us tactfully away, so she could shut the gallery.'

They had stepped out into the street. The weather had changed. He had noticed it had been raining. Fine, autumn rain, bringing a few leaves down. The air was edged with a sharp chill, but they had not cared, for home cried out to them. The smell of it, the sounds. It had been a low and haunting call, insistent and lovely, refusing to be ignored. They had gone into a pub and he had bought her a lemonade.

'She doesn't drink,' Rohan said. 'And she's very thin, and . . .' He hesitated, not knowing how to go on. How to describe the dark eyes that had looked back at him, unfathomable and softened, with a distant cast of pain.

'She's a wonderful painter,' he said instead. 'Alison's going to arrange the exhibition. She'll be in touch soon. And d'you know what her first words were? "Where's Giulia?"'

He grinned. Tears pricked the back of Giulia's eyes. Was it really true?

'So when can I see her?'

'Whenever you want,' said Rohan, laughing boyishly. 'I can't believe it either. It felt as though we had been talking together only moments before, as though no time had elapsed at all. Well . . .' he hesitated, 'almost.'

They had gone on in this way all evening, saying everything and nothing. Feeling the slow ebb and flow of memory thread lightly between them, drawing them closer. How had they lost touch? At some point Rohan had sensed she had no desire to go back to her flat. He had asked her about her brother then.

'Jim?' asked Giulia. 'Theo used to call him Lucky Jim.'

Rohan nodded, his face inscrutable. Yes, they had talked about her useless brother.

'She never sees him. Hardly, anyway. Once a year perhaps.'

And then, he told Giulia, they had alluded to other things; the years that had passed. And Rohan had felt admiration rise up and astonish him and he had understood, perhaps for the first time, her terrible struggles, and the acceptance of what had happened to her life.

'You were the one who told me to accept,' she had reminded him. '"Like a coconut palm in the monsoon," you said. "You must bend in the wind." D'you remember?'

Rohan remembered. Why had he not been able to take his own advice?

'She's given me her telephone number,' he told Giulia. 'Naturally she's frightened of losing us again. I said you'd want to ring. I said, knowing you, you'd ring whatever the time was tonight!'

They both laughed and Rohan poured more wine.

'Oh, it's good to be back,' he said, meaning something else entirely.

The air was charged with unspoken things. Refreshed, reborn. They felt alive in ways only dimly remembered.

'And she's all right?' asked Giulia, eventually, as they sat in companionable silence, forgetting to turn the lights on. She did not want to probe too much, too soon, but the memory of Theo stretched in a long, sorrowful shadow between them. As it always will, reflected Giulia. Rohan sighed deeply. They continued to sit without speaking in this way. At last he stirred himself.

'Yes and no.' He was silent for a moment longer. 'She's living with some man. It doesn't sound as if it's working. She wants to leave. I think. They . . . haven't much in common except, she said, maybe a mutual loneliness at the beginning. Anyway, it's been wrong for some time. They are both aware of this.'

Once again shadows passed between them.

'But habit has kept them together. For how much longer, who can say?'

'Like us,' said Giulia softly, before she could stop herself.

Startled, Rohan glanced sharply at her. Outside the window the twilight was fading fast. Giulia's face, silhouetted against it, looked tired. She had aged, he saw, but still there was something infinitely lovely about her. Shocked, he looked at her anew and saw the light which once, many years ago, had shone faintly and transparently within her, was now very clear and very pure. As if the shaping and chiselling of all the years of her life was revealed at last, in the many fine lines of her face. Why had he not seen this before? Why had he taken her for granted? And then, with sudden insight, he knew she had very nearly given up. But how long has she looked this way, without me caring? he thought with amazement. They had embarked on a journey together. It had not been easy. Giulia had not been able to have children yet somehow they had weathered *that* storm. And he paused for a moment, head bowed, recalling again the friendship, first with Anna, and later with Theo. Anna's death, he saw, had been the foreshadow of what was to come. How happy they had been once, he thought, how young! They would never be young again. And in that moment, halfway between evening and night, with a feeling of great sweetness, he saw, at last, they had reached a different kind of peace. She was his wife. He loved her, still. After all these years, after all they had been through, he could *still* say this and mean it. In the bluish half-light reflecting the surface of the canal water, he reached out and clasped her hand. It was soft and warm and it carried within it a lifetime of touch.

'No,' he said at last, his voice firm. 'Not like us. We have come through this together. What happened to Anna and then to Theo was terrible but I no longer look for explanations. I accept, Giulia. This is life. These are the fruits of war, inescapable and terrible. I see now how important it is to end this struggle, to accept my own helplessness in all that has happened. My problem was that I always thought it was my fault and I carried the burden alone. But,' he gestured towards his paintings, 'I can't do any of this without you, you know. You have borne witness with me. We tell this tale together. You, Giulia, you are the mainstay of my life.'

She smiled at him, and he saw her eyes still shone with the grace he had always associated with her. He saw in that smile, mellow and very wonderful, that she understood. And, he thought with astonishment, she had always understood.

Later she rang the girl. Bridging the years, hearing again the voice that sounded the same, yet was not. Guessing at all the invisible changes that must have taken place. All that probably could never be spoken of now. First excitement gave way to caution.

'We brought your notebooks,' she said, hesitantly. 'We had no address to send them to.' She paused, waiting.

'And your paintings, did Rohan tell you?'

And in a rush of emotion, Giulia remembered how she had longed to find her, how the absence had served only to compound the other losses, of Anna and of Theo. Of her own marriage. So many lives unravelled by the chain of terrible events. So much destroyed by war. They talked for a while longer, laughing, interrupting each other, and slowly, imperceptibly, she began to hear the subtle changes in the girl.

'She's grown up,' she told Rohan afterwards. 'It isn't anything she says, specifically. It isn't *what* she says. More how she says it.'

'She's a serious artist, now,' said Rohan. 'People have begun to notice her. D'you remember what I told you, on that terrible night? How it would all feed into her work?'

Giulia nodded. How could she forget that night?

'I wish it could have happened in a different way, but . . .'

They had promised to meet in a few weeks, just as soon as Giulia could arrange some time off. When they had finished talking she offered Rohan something to eat. It was late but he showed no sign of tiredness.

'I could hear someone, a man's voice in the background, calling her,' Giulia said. 'But she ignored him.'

'Yes,' Rohan said, slowly. 'And, you know, the feeling I had was that all the time we were talking about other things really we were talking about him. All the time.' He wouldn't say Theo's name. Still. That hadn't changed. 'She hasn't got over him. Why should she? She was never that kind of person. They were similar in that way.'

'Yes.'

In the semi-darkness Rohan's face was gentle.

'It will never fade, Giulia. I can tell you, she will always love him. And the threads that bound them together will weave through her work for ever. Not in any physical presence, you understand. In fact, Alison Fielding was very interested when I told her of the earlier portraits. She would like to see them. I'm not sure Nulani will ever part with them, of course, but she might show them, she might be persuaded.'

'Poor Nulani,' said Giulia softly. 'How old is she now? About twenty-eight?'

'Twenty-seven.'

'All those years in London, grieving. Alone. Did she talk about them?'

Rohan shook his head.

'Not much. Her brother found her a place to live and then more or less abandoned her. She got a job in a café; she painted. She was cold.' He shrugged. 'What is there to say after all? When I asked her about that time, she just said she painted what she felt. Everywhere she looked, everything she caught sight of, she said, reminded her of how she felt. Staining the light, catching at the colours, moving her to mark it. She said she felt as though her whole body was branded by it.'

He smiled, suddenly, brilliantly.

'An abstract painter, that's what she is now. Who would have thought it!'

'And us? Did she wonder why we never wrote?'

'She didn't say. I think she assumed the letters didn't get through. She loves us, Giulia, in that trusting, straightforward way that was always hers. She knew we would get in touch if we could and the fact that we didn't could only mean one thing. You know what she was like.'

'Oh God!' said Giulia. 'Tomorrow I'll book a flight to London.'

19

THEO'S AGENT LIKED WHAT HE READ.

'At last!' he said, jokingly.

Privately, Theo astonished him. Having read his letter, having known his past, he was amazed by what he read. *Tiger Lily* had been a bleak novel, successful perhaps because of its bleakness. The film had brought a short-lived fame for its author. But *this* manuscript was different. The agent had a hunch that this new book, when finished, would be a success in a different kind of way. Yes, thought the agent, confidently, a slow burner. Slow and steady. It was an elegiac book, filled with optimism and awash with tenderness.

'The language is very beautiful,' he said, when he finally got through to Theo on the telephone. 'Your best work yet,' he enthused. 'I recognise the character of Irene, but Helena, where's she come from? Honestly, Theo, you're a marvel. I thought you'd disappeared and then up pops another book! You must never stop writing, d'you hear me? When you're ready, I'm going to sell this book at the Frankfurt fair. So will you come back to Britain, now?'

'You should go,' was all Thercy said when he told her.

But Theo had no interest in travel, to Britain or anywhere. He continued rewriting sections of the book, honing it painstakingly. It would be ready by October. Every morning, before sitting at his desk and opening the manuscript, he tried to conjure up as true a picture of the girl as possible.

I want to see you objectively. In the way you appeared to others. You see how far I have moved since that day I lost you? How time has changed me? You, the last love of my life, would understand that. If you could see me now, what would you think? Would you remember how I worried over the difference in our ages! How I agonised. You were the child I never had, the wife I had lost, but most importantly of all, you were yourself. They said we were destined to find each other. What we didn't know was that our time was wrong, the planets discordant or whatever they call it here. Karma, I suppose. Prison made me believe that. All the endless violence I witnessed has convinced me. And as I see you now, quietly sitting within the pages of what I write, distanced by words and time, detached and perfect, I know it was a gift; you were the gift.

He paused, staring out into the garden, overgrown and neglected. He wondered why, in spite of all his understanding, he was still weak with sadness? He told himself, had she returned to him both of them would have suffered. What had been taken from him was too great and because of this, he knew, he would have in turn taken too much from her. So much had changed; even his own soul had changed. He felt a stranger to himself.

'Some day,' he told Thercy, 'perhaps I might bump into her, in Colombo, on a train, somewhere by chance.'

Months passed. The new novel continued to grow with a logic and a rhythm of its own. It took its time, following a path of its own. The atmosphere of brooding darkness in a jungle of noxious violence and superstitions had developed in a manner that had nothing to do with him. And always in the midst of it was the figure of the girl, steeped in sunlight. It was, he told himself again and again, a novel about love. Anna would have been proud of him. Finally, then, it was finished. He had settled it to his satisfaction. Life in this paradise, he felt, was exactly as the beautiful mosquito that lived here, composed in equal parts of loveliness and deadliness. And he felt, too, that at the heart of all he had written, remained the puzzle of humanity. Long ago Rohan had said that only art could change evil. It was art, he had said, that changed people's perceptions. How they had disagreed in those light-hearted days, when a good argument was all there was to win. But perhaps Rohan had been right.

Later, when he had finished the last correction, replaced the last words with those he had wanted, Theo sent his manuscript reluctantly to England.

'It's over,' he told Thercy.

The agent was right. It was the best he had ever written. Anna and Nulani, he thought. A novel about them both. Why couldn't I see this before? And he thought, pouring himself a glass of arrack, I will dedicate this book to Nulani. The girl who painted the invisible.

That night, he slept dreamlessly, and without effort. And the bed where briefly love had once slept, and the room where a pair of straw sandals still remained, watched him sleep the gentle sleep of peace. The monsoons were almost over. Thercy was going to visit her sister-in-law for a while. She felt she could leave him, now. Soon it would be October and the weather would be cooler. Then I will paint the front of the veranda, thought Theo, I will make that my next task. And he remembered Rohan and Giulia. And he remembered Sugi, whom he had loved, and the girl and Anna and all the things that had made up his other life. And he thought, I have lived, I have loved, what more can a man ask for?

In London, Alison Fielding, working on a hunch that their paintings would sell, was getting excited. The exhibition was called 'Two Sri Lankan Painters'.

'They're very different,' she said. 'Similar experiences, I think. Pretty grim, actually, civil war is no joke. Things have calmed down a little, but they've suffered. Lost friends, relatives, become displaced.' She was talking to someone from an art journal.

'They're haunting,' the man from the magazine said. 'Darkly atmospheric, grainy, overcast. Every gesture is eloquent.' He thought for a moment. 'They reflect the spirit rather than the outer world,' he added, nodding, thinking of what he would write later.

'I've decided to show some of their earlier work as well, by the way,' said Alison. 'It gives the current work more context. But none of the earlier pieces by Nulani are for sale.'

'Pity,' said the reviewer, looking at them closely. 'They're beautiful. They'd be snapped up.'

He paused, looking at the three small portraits, all of the same man, still and arrested against a dazzling tropical blur of light. Caught with the sun in his eyes. Smiling.

'Who is it?' asked the journalist, curiously. 'He seems vaguely familiar.'

Alison Fielding shrugged. 'Someone she knew, I think. Her father, an old friend, she won't say, and I don't like to pry too much. She's a private person. And anyway, it doesn't matter. With some portraits, that sort of information is important, but

282

with these, I somehow don't think it matters. There is a quality, an essence, a . . .' She tailed off.

In fact, she thought the portraits stunning. The man sat with his back to the mirror. His eyes were extraordinarily expressive and beautiful. On the table were some objects. Two sea urchins, a pink conch shell, a photograph of a blonde woman. Sunlight fell in long streaks against his arm and in the distance, shimmering like sapphires, was the sea.

'They're powerful,' agreed the journalist. 'I think we'll include an image. My editor said only one illustration, but I think we need one of the portraits as well. Have you a slide we could use?'

'Of course,' said Alison, delighted. 'Will you give me a double spread?'

Later Alison Fielding saw her intuition was right. The paintings of these two artists complemented each other. And nearly all of them sold during the private view of the show.

'They're beautiful,' Giulia said, when she saw them. 'I'm so proud of you both. Can anyone doubt the suffering that country has endured, after seeing this?'

'And I always knew,' said Rohan smiling at them both, 'Nulani would triumph.'

Yes, she had lost Theo, he thought, yet miraculously here he was appearing again, just as Rohan himself had once predicted. Here in her paintings. Astonished by the maturity of this work, astonished by its breath and scope, its certainty, Rohan beamed at Giulia. So young, he thought. It's only the young who can change things. And what would he say? thought Rohan. If he could see her now, how proud would *he* be? Feeling as though he was coasting along on a breeze, Rohan watched Giulia link arms with Nulani. The two of them were deep in conversation, unaware of him for the moment, talking as though they would never stop. The girl has saved us, thought Rohan, for the hundredth time. She has pulled us back from the abyss. And it wasn't over yet by any means. One day, he was certain, she would be a truly great painter.

After the private view Rohan and Giulia returned to Venice. But not before they had extracted a promise from Nulani to visit them before winter settled in. She would come, she promised. She did not want to lose them again. And so it was, as they boarded the plane bound for Italy, someone, a man who received regular invitations from the London Fields Gallery, but who had been away on holiday, opened his invitation and stared, puzzled at the portrait of Theo Samarajeeva. The man stared at the uncanny likeness; he had been reading Theo Samarajeeva's manuscript only the night before. And here was his portrait. Just as it was described in the book. The man, Theo's literary agent, went over to see Alison Fielding. To find out who had painted the writer with such power and conviction.

20

GIULIA HURRIED ACROSS TO THE WAREHOUSE space in Dorsoduro where Rohan had a small studio. Normally she never disturbed him when he was working, normally she would have been working on her translations, but the arrival of the postman was too much. Excitement swelled in her like the spring tides coming in from the sea. Sunlight sparkled under the bridges, church clocks chimed, lions flew and pigeons walked, as Giulia hurried on, head bowed, carrying her letter.

'What d'you mean?' asked Rohan in a whisper, staring at her. 'What do you mean?'

'Read it, read it,' said Giulia, thrusting it into his hand.

'What are you talking about? It's a hoax. Some idiot.'

'Read it!'

Rohan continued to stare at her.

'Read it,' shouted Giulia. 'Rohan, for God's sake, read it.' She was almost crying. 'It's from his agent. Look at it. I'm telling you, Theo's *alive*. He's at the beach house. He's been there for years! Read what the agent says.'

But he had never thought of that. He had never thought of

285

an alternative. Even in his wildest dreams, he had not doubted what he had been told. Theo had been dead for years. Like Sugi. Hadn't they *all* thought that? The girl, he thought, the girl had been certain. Sugi had seen it happen. The same people had killed Sugi, hadn't they? So now what were they telling him? Theo alive, Theo tortured? What was the matter with Giulia?

'How long was he a prisoner?' demanded Rohan, angrily, disorientated. 'Who is this person? How do we know he really is his agent?'

It was only when I saw the invitation for the exhibition that I knew who the painter could have been. She's in his book, his latest book. I'd just finished reading the manuscript. So of course I spoke to Alison Fielding, who's an old friend. I've known her for many years. I always support her exhibitions. So now, I'm contacting you. I think he might like to hear from you. I've read the book, you see. I know the story, or at least some of it. Here's his address. Write to him. Try to persuade him to come back to Britain. Be less of a hermit! This last book is possibly his best yet.

'Write to him?!' said Rohan. '*Write to him?!*' he asked, hysterically. 'What the hell are you talking about? He must come *here*! *He must come here!*' he shouted.

Rohan threw his head back and roared, and then he threw his brushes into the jar of white spirit and whirled Giulia around in an impromptu dance. But it was Giulia who suddenly became the cautious one. Theo had been hurt. He would be changed. If Anna's death had scarred him what would torture have done? And the girl, what about his feelings for the girl? Why had he not contacted them himself? All he had to do was write to their old address and word would have got to them somehow. Perhaps he did not *want* to contact them. Had Rohan thought of that?

'No!' bellowed Rohan. He was laughing, taking in great gulps of air, as though he could not breathe. 'No, no, *no*. He is my friend! How can you *say* that! Maybe he wrote, maybe the letters went astray, maybe they were never forwarded, maybe they *were* forwarded but someone, some bastard, intercepted them. Who knows in that wretched, foul country of mine? Who knows?'

They argued all that evening and late into the night. The next day they were still discussing it endlessly.

'Wait,' said Giulia, who was frightened. 'Wait, wait, let's think of the best way to do this. And what do we say to Nulani? What will she say when she hears? She has to be told and then what might happen?'

'I know what will happen. I'll tell you. If we don't strap her down she'll be on the first plane back to Sri Lanka!'

So they talked and shouted through the night, opening another bottle of wine. For was this not a cause for a celebration? And then as they paused, as the first shock faded slightly, as they looked at each other with amazement, it was as though a terrible evil that had hung over them had begun to pass away. Theo, they cried. Theo! They had never thought to say his name again.

21

THE FOLDS OF THE ITALIAN ALPS appeared in the distance, creased like a silk handkerchief. Snow had come early and would stay late. As they flew towards it there were no clouds and the view was clear for miles. Below was the intense blue of the glacier lakes, the dark mountain rivers, the beginnings of Alpine forests. He had flown this route many times in years gone by. Now he was flying it again. The other passengers in the aircraft were restless. It had been a long flight.

'Hello again, ladies and gentleman. If you look to the right of the aircraft you will see a clear view of the Alps. In about ten minutes we will begin our descent. The weather in Venice is exceptionally warm for this time of year. The earlier thunderstorms have passed, the air has cleared and we have made up the time we lost earlier. You should be able to get a good view of the city as we land. The local time is twelve minutes past four, if you want to adjust your watches. So sit back and relax, and enjoy the rest of the flight.'

They had been flying for nearly twelve hours. He had not slept.

Ten years, thought Theo. Ten years of longing and now she was somewhere below him in the very place he had wanted to take her to. Giulia's letter was in his pocket. He unfolded it again and reread it although by now he knew every line off by heart.

'We have found you both again. What else is worth saying?' Rohan had written and then Giulia had continued, 'Come, Theo, please you must come. She has suffered enough. She wants to see you. If anything can bring you here it is this. That she has not once, not for one moment, forgotten you. Everything she has done, every way she has lived has been in the shadow of the loss of you. So come.'

And here he was, flying, flying through the light, crossing oceans, leaving everything, walking out through the sea-blue gate, never looking back, unwavering as a seabird, rushing towards her, carrying in his hand luggage a tightly closed temple flower. It was as though he was a younger man. Over India he had flown, crossing the Middle East, uncaring of the meals they served, uncaring that they were flying over other war zones now. He had carried a war not of his making for so long, paid for it with the years of his life and the lives of others, that he could no longer carry anything more. Others would have to carry the burden. Again he took out the small cutting Rohan had sent him.

A REMARKABLE SRI LANKAN ARTIST BRINGING THIS
FORGOTTEN WAR TO OUR NOTICE.

Nulani Mendis is a Sri Lankan artist who paints jewel-like abstract paintings. Filled with the colours of her homeland, with luminescent blues, phosphorescent greens and hints of gold, they are paintings scarred by war. In one, a vague smudge suggests a figure under an electric light.

Above are marks that appear to be stitching. Faint lines reminiscent of a hangman's noose hover overhead. The surface is slashed and broken, rivets of paint-smeared pain seem to hold another canvas together. Elsewhere, another painting, the only one with a title, *In the key of 'E'*, has a small typewriter key drawn into the paint, embedded like cattle branding. Beautifully crafted, with slow delicate glazes, this particular canvas was instantly snapped up. When invited to speak about her work, Mendis merely smiled, saying only that she was pleased they had been so well received. But about the work itself she had nothing to say. The viewer is left with the conundrum: are these hauntingly beautiful paintings directly related to the troubles that have being going on in Sri Lanka, or a feminist statement perhaps? In the end, in the words of her dealer Alison Fielding, what does it matter? These are simply very, very good paintings.

There were two colour photographs of the paintings. That was all. Here it was then, this was how she had developed, he thought, staring at the cutting, reading and rereading the words tenderly as they flew over the Alps. His typewriter had always stuck on the letter 'E'. He had forgotten how it had always infuriated him. Smiling, he stared out of the window, his heart brimming with gladness. She would have heard his annoyance. While she sat in the corner of the veranda, drawing him, she would have listened. Giulia had said she had wanted desperately to see him but that she was frightened. She had gone reluctantly to Venice, fearing, what? *She is frightened you won't come*, Giulia had written, *she is frightened it isn't true, that it is all a hoax and you are not really alive. She has believed for so long she would never see you again and now she is terrified. She has dreamt of you for so many years, so hopelessly, that she can't face a mistake. And she is afraid of all the time that has passed, afraid it has made her old! She is not old at all, Theo, she's lovelier than we remember and full of a maturity that was not evident before.*

And, he thought with astonishment, what is she *like* now? How had those years been for her, when his self-pity had got the better of him? He felt small and ashamed beside the thought of her and her courage, in the way he once remembered she had made him feel; ashamed that it was only his terrible loss that filled his thoughts; his pain. It was he who was old now, thought Theo wryly, even older than when she first knew him. And damaged, he thought fearfully. In her last letter Giulia had laughed when he said this to her. *Nulani does not care, Theo; I don't think you understand how she has longed for you. I don't think you can imagine the woman she has become. Just come. See for yourself.*

So here he was, clutching his temple flower. The plane turned towards its final descent. While he had been thinking, the sea and the lagoon had come into view. Below was the shining dome of St Mark's. The sound of the engine changed as it hurried on, swooping down towards Torcello with its Byzantine tower, its marshlands where once mosquitoes had flourished. And there beneath him, spread like a glorious painting itself, hanging like a Renaissance pendant, was the watery city. Happiness caught at his throat. This was not his home; why, then, did he feel he was coming home?

22

ROHAN WATCHED THE PLANE COMING IN, its wings tipped with the light from the sun. Graceful as a swan it descended towards the runway, growing larger as he watched. Steadily it dropped, swift as an arrow it flew, landing with a rush and thrust of tyres and airbrakes. For a moment he stood rooted to the spot, watching all the business of the gangway and luggage trolleys. He watched as the passengers began to pour out of the aircraft. Holidaymakers with their children, Italians, some coming home, others coming to visit the city, American tourists. And suddenly he saw him. The gaunt figure of a man in a light linen suit, still with the round-rimmed spectacles he remembered, only now his hair was white. He was walking slowly. As he came towards the airport building it was possible to see he had a slight limp that he was trying his best to hide. Swallowing, Rohan hurried towards the arrivals lounge.

'So, you old bugger, you've managed to stay thin, unlike me!' he said in English as they embraced and he felt the bones that jutted out from under his friend's jacket. For a moment neither of them could speak. Then Theo took off his glasses and wiped them.

'How is she, Rohan?' he asked helplessly,

'I knew there was a woman behind this visit, men,' joked Rohan, looking at the temple flower. Adding softly, 'She's fine. I left her with Giulia in the flat. I wanted to have a few minutes with you alone, knowing we'll not see you once you set eyes on her!'

He took Theo's luggage and guided him to the exit, hiding his shock.

'I thought you might be tired so we're going back in style, by water taxi,' he said, waving his arm at Theo's protest. 'Hang the expense. It's not every day you visit, men.'

And that was how they came into La Serenissima, by water, as people had done for centuries, past the small nameless islands, following the seabirds that nestled like white blossom among the reeds. Everywhere around him was the melodious sound of Italian. Theo had forgotten how he loved to listen to it, how like an opera it was here, just like a land of make-believe. And then they arrived at the Fondamenta Nuove and there was Giulia standing on the bridge and then hurrying towards them. And she was laughing and crying and wiping her eyes as she greeted him half in Italian and then in Singhalese and now in English. Just as he remembered.

'Steady on, Giulia,' said Rohan, smiling broadly. 'Wars have been fought over this kind of language mix-up!'

'She's asleep,' said Giulia, knowing what he wanted most to hear. 'It is her first proper sleep since she heard, since she arrived. *Poverina*. She is exhausted with waiting.'

'Is she all right?'

'Yes, yes, now you are here she will be. Oh Theo, oh my dear, thank God. Thank God you came. I was so afraid you would not come.'

And she took his face in both her hands and kissed him, leading him towards the house where they rented a flat on the *piano nobile*. He handed Giulia the temple flower. It had travelled well and was now fully open.

'I will put it in water,' she said. 'She'll see it when she wakes. Now go. She's in there,' she whispered, pointing towards the door.

He opened the door slowly and went in. The room was L-shaped, and a large gilded mirror stood immediately before him. The glass was old and foxed and beautiful, and the light reflected in it was thin and dusty. It gave the half-shuttered room an air of unreality. He caught a glimpse of himself before he saw her. It felt as though he was looking at one of her paintings, softened and made remote by an invisible and intractable past. Only now it was he who observed her. All that had vanished, all those small memories he had carried unnoticed within him, the longings that even he had forgotten, now surfaced and fused. Shaken, for nothing could have prepared him for this moment, he stood looking at her through the glass. Astonished too, for he saw, as no photograph could ever have shown him, the promise of youth fulfilled at last.

It had been in this way that he had left her. Sleeping. Only then it had been with the moonlight on her face and the rustle of the sea close by. Now she slept fully dressed, lying across the bed with its washes of blue light. He stood looking at her reflection, silent, rooted to the spot. She slept quietly, her body rising and falling gently as she breathed. She was wearing a soft skirt of some grey fabric. Dimly, he could see the shadows marking her breasts through the thin white shirt. Her hair was cut short and its tendrils framed all the delicate bones of her face. Her dark lashes swept down over her closed eyes. He had forgotten how small she was, how fragile, how terribly lovely. Time, he saw, had stolen clarity, blunted his memories. Time could not be trusted. What had seemed sharp and certain was in fact a pale shadow of the present.

The girl slept without moving, her brow clear and untroubled as a child, one arm raised above her head. But her wrists, he saw, were no longer the wrists of a child and peering at the glass he noticed her fingernails still had small slivers of paint under them. Seeing this, he felt his heart rise and break open with all the unspoken years between them. Softly, so as not to disturb her, he bent down and took his shoes off. His fingers trembled and as he straightened up he closed his eyes. When he opened them again he could see the reflection in the mirror had altered and the girl's face was now beside his own. Staring uncomprehendingly he watched her for a moment longer, seeing her lips move. Unable to speak he watched her frightened eyes as she said his name again. Then helplessly, hardly aware of what he did, blindly, he turned towards her, resting his face against her hair, letting her cry, holding her as he once had done. Knowing instinctively she was not crying for the horror that had passed, or the years that could never be recovered, or Sugi, or her parents, or even the home she had loved and lost. He knew she was crying for something else, something deeper and more enduring than he had thought possible. Something that had not occurred to him until now. And in that instant he saw, in spite of what had happened, and all that had been lost for ever, what mattered was the thing that somehow had remained. Unharmed and indestructible. And as he held her sleep-warmed body against his, letting her cry, knowing what she was thinking, thinking it too, he breathed again the faint fragrance of her hair, from some other time and some other place of long ago.

Outside the evening was just beginning in Venice. The orchestra in St Mark's square was playing again. Great seagulls perched jauntily on the *briccole* dotted across the lagoon, watching as the fishermen brought in their catch. And all around, between sea and sky and land, was the gentle sound of lapping water as the sun, golden and full of autumn warmth, sank softly into the reeds.

ACKNOWLEDGEMENTS

My agent Felicity Bryan, who knew my paintings long before she read my words, for her unwavering encouragement and her determination to keep me going.

Kathy van Praag, who read the manuscript and was so whole-heartedly enthusiastic.

And Clare Smith, my editor at HarperPress, who loved the book enough to make it happen.

Also at HarperPress, Annabel, Julian and Mally, all of whom made life easier for me.

To Michele Topham, at the Felicity Bryan Agency.

To my exhuberant Italian friends Rosy Colombo and Anna Anzi for their support, seminars and summer retreats during the writing of the book.

To Loretta Innocenti for her support in Venice, and Daniele Lombardi for his wonderful recording of *Preludes Fragiles*, which I listened to endlessly whilst writing.

To Vishvarani Wanigasekera, who corrected my Singhalese.

And finally to my long-suffering family, sternest and wisest of critics.

Thank you.

To Woody –
With Warmest regards
and very best Wishes –
Many thanks for being
a Giant!
Andy Robustelli

ONCE A GIANT, ALWAYS...

ONCE A GIANT, ALWAYS...

My Two Lives
with the
NEW YORK
GIANTS

Andy Robustelli
with Jack Clary

Quinlan Press
Boston

Library of Congress Cataloging-in-Publication Data

Robustelli, Andy.
  Once a Giant, always—.
  1. Robustelli, Andy. 2. Football players—
United States—Biography. 3. Football—United
States—Coaches—Biography. 4. New York Giants
(Football team)—History. I. Clary, Jack T. II. Title.
GV939.R59A3 1987   796.332′092′4 [B]   87-42762
ISBN 0-933341-26-1

Front jacket photograph by Jon Naso
Back jacket photograph by Dan Rubin

Printed in the United States of America
August 1987

To Jeanne, all the kids...my family...Fr. St. Martin...all my teammates, the fans and all whom I depend upon so much: I always tried to be the best.

A.R.R.

To Pat, who shares my feelings for the Giants and this great sport...and to Andy and his teammates, who helped to nurture those feelings.

J.T.C.

Acknowledgements

My special thanks and appreciation must go to Pat Walsh and Howard Wolven for meticulously keeping and filing all of my records and making the organization of this book so much easier; to Diane Bocchetta, of DB Business Services, Stamford, Connecticut, and Karen Metro of WordsPlus, Acton, Massachusetts, for transcribing countless hours of tapes and typing the final manuscript; to the New Jersey Sports Authority for its courtesy in arranging the site of our cover photo; to photographer Jon Naso of Sports Action Photography, Princeton, New Jersey; and to my editor, Kevin Stevens of Quinlan Press, who allowed me the fullest expression and was very sensitive in his handling of this special project.

Andy Robustelli
Stamford, Connecticut

Contents

Introduction

Since leaving the Giants following the completion of the 1978 season, I have been asked several times to detail what really happened to the organization and its ownership. The plea was always the same: tell what transpired under the conditions that existed. I always declined because I didn't want to focus attention on the attendant problems lest they intrude on the stated goal of producing a championship team.

That goal has been achieved with the Super Bowl victory, bringing the Giants great national attention. That attention has also focused on a part of the past that was good...and a part of the past that was not so good, with all of its conflicts and even some misconceptions about what brought them about. Since so much has been discussed about those two facets of the team's history, I believe the time is now right for presenting my side of the ledger concerning those periods, and doing so without affecting either the current players or the continuing goals of the football operation.

The first half of this book was a delightful exercise, for the most part, because it enabled me to recapitulate some tremendous personal experiences, especially those involving my teammates, first during my five seasons with the Los Angeles Rams, where we won an NFL title, and then with the Giants from 1956 through 1964, when the great surge of Giants popularity swept the Metropolitan area and created the unprecedented public love affair the team has known ever since. Those great seasons with the Giants were ones I shared with some of the sport's greatest players and coaches, and I believe that for the first time ever the public will have a solid view of exactly what we were about, why we were so successful and even why we broke a lot of hearts, including our own, when NFL titles were at stake.

The second half of the book is a presentation of the events that transpired during my five often-tumultuous seasons as director of operations for the Giants, a time when the team had hit rock bottom and was searching for a way to reclaim former glories. In laying out all that occurred during those years, I have relied on a substantial file of daily notes and memos which were the exchange of ideas, problems, solutions and viewpoints between Wellington and Tim Mara, the team's co-owners, and myself. The matter contained thus is as fresh as the day it happened, and the facts can be viewed in the context of how they happened at the time—and also from the perspective of events that transpired after I left.

There is little doubt that I am more sensitive about this period of my life with the Giants than my years as a player and coach. Much of what occurred was in direct contradiction to the positive achievements that had always marked both my athletic and business careers. There is also little doubt that I took my own measure of satisfaction, along with many of my teammates, in becoming a part of the Giants' resurgence in 1986, if only because so many of us were called on by the media to recount our feelings of past glories and present achievements. This attention brought back many fond memories to a group of guys who knew how to carry the torch of victory.

But long after that torch has passed, I've learned that one can sometimes lose perspective. It is important that all the Giants—past, present and even those of future teams—realize that there is a responsibility in wearing that world championship ring.

Shortly after the Giants won Super Bowl XXI, Phil Simms noted to some of the media that he hoped that achievement would put an end to all of the comparisons between his team and our teams of the fifties and sixties. Sorry about that Phil, but it just doesn't work that way. Once you become part of a great Giants team you are stamped indelibly, and some day there will be other media-making comparisons between a future Giants team and your 1986 champions.

The Super Bowl victory restored at last a sense of excellence on the field that was so much a part of our teams. I don't believe in making absolute comparisons between teams; the game has changed somewhat since our day, as have the people who administer, play, coach, report and watch, but there is a fiber that connects our two generations.

From my vantage point it was pride and determination that helped harness the talent of the Super Bowl team, the same principal forces that drove us to our success. Our teams in the fifties and sixties were never the most talented in the NFL, but we may have been the most determined not to lose. We were not the closest in the locker room—indeed, for most of my years with the Giants we really were two teams, the offense and the defense, wearing the same uniform. Once we hit the field in practice, and on Sunday, we became *the* Giants, and all that really mattered was the final score.

I know in this age of cynicism that sounds almost corny, but to understand it totally, perhaps you have to go through an entire season where every effort is directed toward winning. There can be no deviations...no excuses...no substitutions for the tightly focused view that you cannot lose. I often believed during our seasons that the fans began to share those feelings, that they were as much involved as we were. I have never forgotten the surge of emotion that gripped me whenever we played at Yankee

Stadium, how I could literally feel the need to excel. I was not alone among my teammates in that regard.

Some of that dedication came from within us as players, and the way we played transmitted it to the millions who watched. It didn't happen only in one game against the Colts in 1958, or in our great battles with the Browns. It didn't begin when Y. A. Tittle and Del Shofner joined us in 1961, or when we were coached by Tom Landry and Vince Lombardi. It happened before, during and after each of these men made their contributions...and it happened when others made their contributions as well.

I still believe that our defensive teams were the catalyst for the success of those great Giants teams—even the Tittle teams that produced so much offensive power—because we had set a standard by which the Giants have been measured. Why us? We used a defensive system where success depended upon every player in the game carrying out his assignment—teamwork in the truest sense. This defensive strategy did not allow for glory-seekers, prima donnas or guys looking for great statistics. Everyone was the same on the field, on every play and in every postgame film session. The fact that Sam Huff got so much of the public glory was simply the result of the work of Jim Katcavage, Dick Modzelewski, Rosie Grier, John Lovetere, Swede Svare, Bill Svoboda, Cliff Livingston, Tom Scott, Bill Winter and Jerry Hillebrand, as well as Jimmy Patton, Em Tunnell, Dick Lynch, Lindon Crowe, Dick Nolan, Erich Barnes, Allen Webb and myself—yes, and others who may have played only two plays or two games. As far as we were concerned, the game was ours to win or lose, and that was all that mattered.

I believe our teamwork showed in the way we revolutionized the game. For the first time, defense had as much recognition as offense had historically received. Thousands who had once cheered long runs and arching touchdown passes now stood and cheered goal-line stands, sacks of quarterbacks and our repeated forcing of an offense to punt after just three plays. They recognized that holding great running backs like Jim Brown, Ollie Matson, Rick Casares and John Henry Johnson to relatively few yards in crucial games was quite a feat. Our defensive unit helped to educate them to recognize that football has more than one dimension. In a true sense, the cheers that greet today's Giants defensive team are an echo of a tradition—and what has become an expectation—that great defense has become the soul of all Giants teams. It all began beneath that hallowed facade that once ringed Yankee Stadium's roof, and now it thrives in the beauty of Giants Stadium.

If the Giants of today, and their new fans, wonder why many of their brethren still hark back to those days for their comparisons, they should understand that we helped begin that historic love affair in which the ardent supporters of one franchise never stopped caring for—or adoring—a bunch of guys who also cared for them. We are still openly thankful for all those supporters did to help us gain the recognition that exists more than a quarter-century after our crowds stopped roaring. Perhaps our greatest legacy was building pro football to such peaks in the hearts and minds of those who saw us play that they have passed that torch to those who have come after, fans who never saw Tittle throw and Shofner catch, Alex Webster and Frank Gifford run behind Jack Stroud, Rosey Brown and Ray Wietecha... fans who never understood the gritty play of Charlie Conerly, Joe Walton, Greg Larson and Hugh McElhenny... fans who never saw Katcavage and Huff stuff a quarterback, who never witnessed the athletic grace of Jim Patton, the guile of Dick Lynch, the tenactiy of Erich Barnes, the splendor of Em Tunnell on pass defense or punt returns or the soaring kicks of Don Chandler that often were a defensive unit's best friend.

We'll take the blame for all of those comparisons (gladly I might add) because we also got so much of the glory. Some of us have our busts dusted regularly in the Hall of Fame in Canton, Ohio, and we know there are people who see them and wonder just who we were and what we did to be so exalted, particularly the young, who are so immersed in their heroes of today. Unlike their elders, who had to learn about blitzes and sacks, strongside and weakside, these new fans are familiar with all aspects of the game. Sometimes they even take too much of it for granted without stopping to try and understand exactly what the Giants' tradition really means. They are not unlike some of my own kids, who once stood in our backyard in Stamford and told me they were bored, while around them was a swimming pool, basketball court, volleyball net and a garage filled with bikes. When I took them to my old neighborhood to give them an object lesson in what life can be like without such pleasures, one of them said, "But we don't live here."

Giants fans now live in Giants Stadium, and some day they may be telling future generations about the feats of "their" teams. I hope so. The continuity of the Giants' mystique is as special as all of the victories and the titles. After all, a title only lasts from the end of one season to the beginning of the next; the emotional ties last forever.

However, it is just as important for those who guide the destinies of the team to realize they have an obligation to sustain this relationship between generations as much as they do to put the very best team on the field. It would be nice to say that the love showered on the Giants by those who have played and who have watched has been matched in equal parts by those who administer, but that has not always been true. At times it has sullied a great tradition. Self-interest on any level or by one part of a team's ownership is not a square deal to those who are unbending with their support year after year, and whose emotional fuel really generates the success that this great franchise has known.

I have seen all four sides of this structure—as player, coach, executive and fan—and that unique perspective allows me to present the facts and make the judgments that are contained within this book. Underlying all that I have written is the realization that everything in our society is imperfect because all of us are imperfect, and I have taken into account all that is contained in that idea. I continually marvel that over the three decades I have been associated with the Giants, our success has resulted from the achievements of ordinary people, who believed—as we did when we played—that nothing counts more than making a total effort to win. Lack of success has been the result of a failure to forge a united effort to guide the team's destiny.

That truism was really driven home to me when I thought back to the seasons when Y. A. Tittle played for us. Within his personality were the components that knitted two distinct units into one team. His presence helped all of the feelings for the Giants coalesce and did more to produce three unforgettable seasons than any so-called strategical innovations. It also underscored what I first saw in my rookie season with the Los Angeles Rams when we won the NFL title: football may be a game of X's and O's, but more than anything it is a game of people, and success is bred in the hearts of the players, not on the blackboards of the coaches or in the meeting rooms of the front office. The history of the game teaches us one thing: selfishness is a cancer that makes potentially great teams ordinary at best; selflessness can make ordinary teams champions.

That is the legacy which should guide the Giants of today because it will be the link with the Giants of the future. . .and always with the Giants of the past as part of pro football's greatest tradition. It is a tradition of which I'm proud to be a part, and for which I still have the deepest feelings.

Part 1
The Way We Were

1 Prepping for the Giants

On an average day, it takes about an hour to drive to Yankee Stadium from my home in Stamford, Connecticut, and a bit more to drive to Giants Stadium in the Jersey Meadowlands. For fourteen years of my life I put thousands of miles on any number of cars traveling to both places to be a part of a team that has my heart forever.

On the other hand, back in 1951 it took nine hours to fly to Los Angeles, and of all the trips I ever made from Stamford, one that began in mid-July of that year has been the most significant because it started my professional football career with the Los Angeles Rams. It is a long way from Stamford, Connecticut, to Los Angeles, light-years in many respects, but distance is not a factor when I consider all that trip has meant over a lifetime. Had I given in to the misgivings about coming from tiny Arnold College in Milford, Connecticut, to the Rams, then all of the success that I have achieved—with the Rams, with the Giants and in my own business life—might never have happened, and my involvement in professional football might have been limited to television viewing.

I know it may be difficult for many who associate me only with the Giants to understand what being a member of the Los Angeles Rams really has meant to my life. On a personal basis, I made the team in my rookie year as a starting defensive end and was a part of a world championship. There is no bigger thrill because, while we didn't call it the Super Bowl back then, the prize was the same, made all the sweeter because I was a nineteenth-round draft pick accorded little chance, even by some of my close friends, of succeeding.

The 1951 Rams were one of the greatest teams in NFL history, and I say that with no apologies to my former Giants teammates and all that we accomplished. The players represented the best that professional sports ever had to offer, on and off the playing field. Like the old New York Yankees, they left a mark forever on anyone who played for them, with their special tradition of absolute professionalism and excellence where winning with style, class and total dedication and effort was appreciated above all else. I brought those qualities from the Rams, and as much as my playing skill, they were my most important contributions to the Giants.

1

The Rams, under owner Dan Reeves and his general manager Tex Schramm, who has gained such renown as president and general manager of the Dallas Cowboys, also developed their own style of football after Reeves moved the team to California from Cleveland shortly after it won the 1945 NFL title. This style fit perfectly into an environment that really had few traditional barriers. The wide-open offense, with Bob Waterfield and, later, Norm Van Brocklin, throwing long, arching passes to Tom Fears, Elroy Hirsch, Bobby Boyd and others who were the fastest group of receivers in professional football on warm, sunny afternoons, was a refreshing contrast to the slogging, mud-spattered, frozen-field style of the other NFL teams at that time. Certainly the Rams were in perfect harmony with California's best-known export—entertainment—with all of the flash and dash conjured up in their next-door neighborhood, Hollywood.

All of this was in deep contrast to my own past existence. The west side of Stamford, Connecticut, the high school and college practice fields, the sparse crowds who watched Arnold College and the harrowing adventures aboard a destroyer escort during the war in the Pacific were far removed from the glitz and glitter of southern California, though all of that background really prepared me to accept the changes and challenges faced in professional sports.

My grandfather had come from Italy, saved his money and purchased some homes in Stamford's west side. My parents and five brothers and sisters lived with him in one of those homes, and we were the only white family with five other black families. Looking back, I probably spent more time with one or two of those black families than anyone else. In that environment, no prejudices ever entered into our lives. We all played sports together, and when it was football season, we tucked a couple of pieces of cardboard into the shoulders of our shirts to act as makeshift shoulder pads. Religion also played a dominant part in our lives, and though both of my parents worked full-time, my mother always found time on Saturdays to clean Sacred Heart Church without pay, and thus brought all of us into close affiliation with the church's activities, including sports. I often short-shrifted Stamford High School to play for the church's teams.

I played end at Stamford High School, was a catcher in baseball and a pretty good basketball player, good enough in all three sports that when I graduated I got a scholarship to LaSalle Military Academy, in Oakdale, Long Island, to prep for Manhattan College or Fordham. Before I could enroll at either, World War II got in the way. All of my friends enlisted, but my mother refused to sign a waiver, so I spent four months at LaSalle until I was eighteen years old. The day after my birthday I went to the draft board and told them I wanted to be drafted, and then I told my mother I had been drafted. Ironically, the good thing to come out of the LaSalle enrollment was being placed as a drill instructor in the Navy's basic training school because of my so-called "military background."

I spent two and a half years in the Navy, the first part as a water-tender

2

and a 20-mm. antiaircraft gunner aboard the destroyer escort William C. Cole, old DE641. Most of that time we were in the Pacific, where we were part of the invasion of Okinawa. Destroyer escorts were very fragile ships, and there was always the gnawing fear that the plane we might not shoot down would sink us with one good hit. We all got our share and we survived, though I could not help wishing for the 20-mm. antiaircraft gun on that very bad afternoon at Giants Stadium in 1978 when a plane was towing its sign demanding the team become an instant winner. But more about that later.

Following the war, I wanted to enroll at Fordham, but I had to wait for admittance. Two of my best friends, Carmine Tosches and Lou Thomas, had enrolled in Arnold College, so I said, "To hell with it, I'll take a chance and go there."

Arnold, now the University of Bridgeport, was a small college with fewer than three hundred students, including women, which offered degrees in physical education. Since I wanted to coach and teach that was just right for me. We also played football against such small Eastern schools as the Merchant Marine and Coast Guard Academies; New Haven State Teachers College, now Southern Connecticut State; American International; Wagner College; and St. Michael's College in Vermont. I was a two-way end who had pretty good speed and good hands for catching the ball. I also had the talent to play our very rudimentary defenses, where being quick and tough got you a lot of tackles and big plays. Near the end of my final game, against St. Michael's, I broke my leg, but I had made some big plays beforehand, and that probably sold the Rams. In those years they were ahead of everybody in scouting players because they rated many different categories, such as blocking a punt and then picking up the ball and running for a touchdown. I led every player in the nation in that particular category, and I had also made the 1951 Little All-America Team, so I was not exactly an unknown quantity. Lou DeFillipo, then the line coach at Fordham and a Rams scout, also gave me a great recommendation, so the Rams selected me on the nineteenth round of a thirty-round draft. Ironically, I never was seriously considered by the Giants.

Being drafted by the NFL wasn't the big deal that it is today, in terms of money, prestige or notoriety. My college football career was not totally directed at playing professional football, so when I had to make a decision about whether to play for Los Angeles there were several factors of equal importance.

The first was my family. I had married my childhood sweetheart, Jeanne Dora, after my freshman year in college, and when I graduated, our oldest son, Rick, was a year old. I had to think about supporting them. I received just ninety dollars per month on the GI Bill when I was in school, and I had to pursue any number of odd jobs to make ends meet. I had an opportunity to become a teacher and coach where there could be some future stability.

3

Then there was professional baseball. I suppose I was more thrilled at getting a tryout from the New York Baseball Giants than being drafted by the Rams because I was a lifelong Giants fan and had dreamed, as a kid, of some day playing for them in the Polo Grounds. I had batted over .400 during four varsity seasons as a third baseman at Arnold, but I also had been a good catcher in high school, so two days before I was to leave for the Rams' training camp the Giants brought me to the Polo Grounds to catch batting practice prior to offering me a minor league contract for their Class B farm club in Knoxville, Tennessee.

That same day, they also had recalled a young outfielder named Willie Mays from their Trenton (N.J.) farm club, and he was getting ready to make his major league debut.

I laid out all of these options to my good friend, J. Walter Kennedy, a sports columnist for the *Stamford Advocate*, who had also worked in various sports jobs. Walter later became the very successful commissioner of the National Basketball Association, and following retirement from that post in 1975 he accepted a job with my firm in Stamford. Sadly, before we could ever enjoy the fruits of a long-sought mutual association, he died of cancer.

"Stick to the teaching and coaching by all means," Walter told me. "You've got a wife and baby so you can't afford to gamble on something as chancy as professional football, certainly not with your small-college background."

His arguments certainly were compelling, so I asked my dad for his advice. He really didn't understand sports, but he told me, "You've got to take a chance. If you don't, you'll spend the rest of your life wondering whether you could have made it."

That sold me. I figured that I would go out and give the Rams a shot, and if I didn't make it I could always come home and try to get a teaching job or go back to the Giants and try life in the minor leagues. Before I left, though, I called Walter Kennedy and told him, "I appreciate your advice, and I've wrestled with it because I don't know if I'm good enough for the big time. But I'll never know if I don't give it a shot."

As soon as I arrived at training camp I was told flat out that I had to make the team as a defensive end since no rookie had a chance to displace Fears, Hirsch and Boyd. As it turned out Norb Hecker, a rookie from Baldwin-Wallace and later a very successful defensive coach in the NFL, including a tour with the Giants, and I were the only two ends to make the team, and Norb played primarily in the secondary.

We trained in Redlands, California, about twenty miles from Palm Springs. It was hotter than a blast furnace, and I was a typical rookie, always a little afraid, a little homesick, a little embarrassed at my lack of football knowledge. All of that was magnified a bit by my small-college background. What helped most of all, at one point, was a friendship with

Harry Thompson, a one-year guard from UCLA who had a relative married to Jackie Robinson. Since Jackie was playing with the Dodgers—he also had gone to UCLA—and was living in Connecticut, I had some kind of bond to home, tenuous to be certain, but important to me.

On the practice field I controlled some of my own destiny. Joe Stydahar, the head coach, ran a very tough, disciplined camp, much like Jim Lee Howell when he coached the Giants. I didn't mind because I always had been very disciplined. Further, I never questioned my ability to compete against anyone, even if he came from Notre Dame, the Big Ten, UCLA or the other schools with big football programs. I also saw there were other veterans from small schools, which proved to me that achievement, not background, really counted.

Still, training camp was a lonely existence for a young married guy with a wife and son three thousand miles away; who got ten dollars a week for laundry money; and who had to go through tortuous two-a-day practices. It really tested my desire to play football, and there were times when I wondered whether I had it. About five days after camp opened—five days during which I ate little and slept even less—I finally went to Stydahar and told him I didn't think I was making too much progress, and that I might be better off going home and getting a full-time job to support my family.

Joe just glared at me, and then he exploded:

"If you go home, you'll cheat yourself, and that Polish wife of yours will break a broomstick over your head. And she should, too, if you don't stick it out and give it a full shot. You can't quit now, I won't let you quit. Get out of here."

I guess I needed to hear that I still had a chance, but it still took a mighty break—Jack Zilly's leg, to be exact—to give me the opening I needed. Jack was a four-year veteran from Notre Dame and the incumbent right defensive end. I jumped in, really winning a job with a good day in our final team scrimmage. Even if Jack came back, I felt I would have a job as third defensive end behind him and Larry Brink.

Zilly was a helluva guy. Though he was hurt and saw a rookie taking his job, for good as it turned out, he really helped me. Jack was a cute player who combined his intelligence with his physical skills, and he taught me to do much the same. We spent hours, including many evenings, talking about all that went into the position. As it turned out, Jack became the third defensive end that season, and he was traded to the Eagles in 1952. We had established quite a rapport, and I saw him from time to time when he was head coach at the University of Rhode Island in the sixties and seventies.

Linebacker Don Paul was another veteran who went out of his way to help me. He was the toughest player on that team, just a mean competitor on the line of scrimmage. He got a runner any way he could, and if necessary that included using a very mean elbow. "It's not what you do, it's what they see you do," he would say. In fact, Don was one of the first players to begin wearing a face mask because everyone was trying to work him over with their own elbows. Don kind of protected me and taught me to be a pretty good player by impressing on me the necessity of sticking my nose in and never backing off, regardless of the matchup. And I never did.

One thing I still remember from that first preseason is the getaway from Redlands to Los Angeles for our exhibition games. LA was a long drive, and the players left the night before to stay in a hotel. Getting out of camp became a big deal because Stydahar wouldn't allow anyone to leave until five o'clock. But well before then, the players lined up their cars, engines revving, as if it were a Grand Prix race. The moment that clock hit five they all took off. Our guys had some pretty good cars. Waterfield had a Jaguar, Hirsch a Cadillac. It became a competitive thing to see who could get to town first. One time Don Paul even swerved up on an embankment to get out in front.

The hallmark of that team was that great competitiveness. It formed its backbone, to which was added great talent at every position, fine character, and the unquestioned leadership of Bob Waterfield, though Norm Van Brocklin was beginning to push a bit when I arrived. They were a great contrast, Waterfield always so ice-cool and Van Brocklin so red-hot.

Bob was the greatest all-around football player I ever saw. He did everything: he was a superb passer; he kicked field goals and extra points; he punted and played defense; and he was a great runner, having been an All-America tailback at UCLA in the early forties. He even kicked off. Imagine today, the starting quarterback kicking off...or playing defense! And if Bob played now, he would still be able to do it all.

He also was unparalleled as a leader, on and off the field. His style was quiet, yet he was tough. Once one of the Ram backs whined in the huddle about carrying the ball on a particular play. Bob said nothing. Instead, he stepped inside the huddle and slapped the guy in the face. No more complaints. Another time, Hirsch suggested a pass pattern and Waterfield threw it, only to see it read perfectly and intercepted. As they met at the sidelines, Waterfield told him, "Elroy, if you don't know what you're talking about, keep your damn mouth shut."

But it was away from the field that he first impressed me. It was customary for veterans to ride the rookies pretty hard, but Waterfield had none of that. In fact, he went out of his way to make new players feel comfortable and do all he could to help them succeed. When Bobby Boyd joined the team in 1950, he was a 9.5 sprinter but not a very good receiver. When he asked Bob to work with him, Old Buckets, as we called him, stayed out for hours helping Bobby develop into a fine end. He believed in people, and he instilled confidence in everyone.

The first weekend of training camp, we all knew that Jane Russell, Bob's wife and one of Hollywood's most beautiful stars, would drive out to pick him up, and we just waited around to get a glimpse of her. When she appeared, they got into her car and Bob then tossed his car keys to the rookies. "It's yours for the weekend," he said. "Have fun." Another time, he gave Dan Towler his car to use, as well as his gasoline credit card, because he knew Dan had very little money.

Bob was as quiet as Dutch Van Brocklin was gregarious. No one got inside him, and Jane affectionately called him "Old Stone Face." When the controversy of which of the two star quarterbacks should start ripped apart Ram fans, Bob never reacted. Dutch really was embarrassed by the furor, and while he wanted to start and really was pushing Bob on the field for the job, he never rocked the boat in the locker room, nor made public waves. Contrary to what many claimed at the time, the team did not split into separate camps. Waterfield, for as long as he stayed, was the undisputed leader.

While Van Brocklin kept his cool on the quarterback matter, he was never a stone face. Dutch was like a volcano at times, and he never hid it from anyone, friend or foe. Once, offensive tackle Tom Dahms, a rookie with me, missed a block, and the opposing player sacked Dutch. When they reached the sidelines, Van Brocklin grabbed a cup of water and tossed it into Dahms's face. Tom, who outweighed Van Brocklin by fifty pounds, blinked, and then shrugged, but he missed no more blocks that day.

When an opposing tackle once roughed him up, Dutch challenged him to meet under the Coliseum stands after the game. That tackle might have shown up, but Dutch never did. "I may have a hot head," he said, "but it's not empty."

Perhaps his greatest nonfootball asset was his frankness. It made enemies among some in the media, and rubbed some players the wrong way because he never sugarcoated anything that was important to him. Yet he was great fun to be around. He always giggled when something struck his fancy, so we dubbed him "Laughing Boy." Dutch also was a master at handing out nicknames. Glenn Davis, one of the greatest collegiate running backs ever up to that time, was tagged with "Buttercups." Fears was becoming prematurely bald, and sensitive about it, but that didn't stop Van Brocklin from tabbing him "Skinhead." He called rookie offensive tackle Bobby Cross "Look Out," and when asked why, Dutch replied, "Because whenever Cross sees a defensive player go past him, he always yells, 'Look out, Dutch.' "

He was unparalleled as a passer. He could throw the ball as far as anyone could run, and yet he had great accuracy with a marvelous feathery touch that made it easy to catch. Once a teammate challenged his accuracy.

"Toss a football down the field and let's see where it lands," he told Dutch. "Each time you hit the ball where it is laying, I'll buy you a Coke." The ball was 35 yards away, and Norm hit it six times in ten throws.

"Thanks for the Cokes," he said and walked away giggling.

But it was his great competitiveness, his singlemindedness and toughness that complemented his great talent so well. Yet late in 1951, that determination to get his own way cost him the NFL passing championship, and almost cost us the title.

When we played Green Bay in the final game of the year, Stydahar sent in a pass play, but Dutch ignored it. Joe pulled him, and Waterfield played the rest of the game, racking up enough statistics to win the NFL passing title; and then Stydahar started him in the title game against the Browns. Finally, seeing the need to make a big play, Stydahar inserted Van Brocklin in the fourth quarter, and he threw the game-winning TD to Tom Fears.

With a great football mind, Van Brocklin was a quarterback who really was a coach on the field, as he later proved in leading the Eagles to the NFL title in 1960. I urged John McVay to hire him as an offensive coordinator when I was the Giants' director of operations because we really needed someone to fire up our offense. There was no one in my mind more qualified than Van Brocklin, both as an innovator and as a teacher for our young quarterbacks. My advice was ignored, and I believe it hurt us.

Ironically, with all of the hoopla that surrounded Waterfield and Van Brocklin during their time together with the Rams, both of them passed away within days of each other a few years ago, and I couldn't help thinking that some Divine Plan must have meant them to be linked together for all time.

On a more personal note, Dutch and I were in the same class of inductees into the Pro Football Hall of Fame in 1971. Ten years later, we returned to the Hall for a tenth reunion, and Dutch and his wife, Gloria, and my wife Jean and I, had a marvelous reunion. It was the last time I saw him alive, and I miss him very much.

While no team ever has been simultaneously blessed with two quarterbacks of the Waterfield-Van Brocklin caliber, few also have had receivers of the Fears-Hirsch talent. Elroy was nicknamed Crazylegs for good reasons—he was a tremendous runner after he caught the ball, part of that coming from his college years as a great running back at Wisconsin and Michigan. Everything he did was super, on and off the field. We never expected him to flatten someone every time he blocked, but we expected him to win games for us with his pass receiving, and he did. He could run all out and catch the ball as it came over his head without breaking stride. Del Shofner, when he played with the Giants, was the only other receiver I knew who was so adept at that skill.

Hirsch was a total producer. In our championship 1951 season, he caught 17 touchdown passes in 12 games and the average length was 50 yards; and he won at least four games that year for us. He nearly knocked me off my chair one day when he said, "I never really had confidence as a player. I always had a fear I'd drop a ball right out in the open." I never saw him do it.

8

"Legs" also was our chief gagster. When it was smoggy, he put on a gas mask. Or if he wanted a drink of water, he crawled around on the field screaming like some B movie actor dying of thirst on the back lot at Paramount.

Not only was Fears an almost effortless long pass-route runner, he was also a great "move" receiver who specialized in catching all of the curls, hooks and turnarounds—those punishing inside patterns of five to 15 yards. Tom once noted that catching them was like "committing suicide a little at a time." Defensive backs time their hits to occur the instant the ball arrives, to force an incompletion and mete out enough hurt so the receiver won't concentrate on the ball the next time he comes into that territory.

None of that bothered Fears because his concentration, and courage, were unparalleled. Many still claim he is the greatest pass receiver of all time, and I'll not dispute that, if only because he never missed a beat in working with Waterfield and Van Brocklin, quarterbacks with two distinct styles. The single catch I'll always recall was his 73-yard reception of Dutch's pass in the final five minutes of our 1951 title game against the Browns. He split two defenders and then outran them into the end zone.

Taken together, Hirsch and Fears were an ideal combination, though both also had their distinct styles. Elroy was outgoing and gregarious; Tom quiet, rather intense. They were good friends off the field, yet with each aware of his own importance there was a bit of a rivalry on the field. Still, we considered Fears as our bread-and-butter guy who always came up with the first down. Though he ran so many short patterns, he had very deceptive speed, seeming to glide rather than run. He didn't have sprinter's speed, but he had enough, as he proved in that title game.

Hirsch had the speed. He also caught the short passes very well, so defenses never could establish definite tendencies on either. "Legs" could catch the quick out and then turn it into a big gain. In short, take the bomb away from Hirsch and Fears killed defenses with first-down catches; if Tom was double-teamed, Elroy had the deep area for his own. Perhaps records also tell some of the story. More than thirty years after they finished playing, Fears still holds Ram team records for most career receptions (400) and Hirsch is second (343); Fears has the single-season record (84 in 1950), the third-best mark (77 in 1949), and most in one game (18 against Green Bay in 1950). Hirsch still is the all-time yardage leader (6,289), most yards in one season (1,495 in 1951), most touchdowns (53), and most TDs in one season (17 in 1951). Tom later coached the Rams and New Orleans Saints and then went into the restaurant business in the LA area. Hirsch just concluded a distinguished tenure as athletic director at the University of Wisconsin.

Waterfield, Van Brocklin, Hirsch and Fears were only parts of an overall offensive philosophy that was revolutionary in its time. After we were beaten, 44-17, by the San Francisco 49ers in the sixth game of the 1951 season, Stydahar faced a dilemma. We had to play the 49ers again the following week, and their coach, Buck Shaw, had found a way to contain some of our speed backs by using two fast halfbacks as outside linebackers.

Our offensive coach, Hampton Pool, a tremendously creative guy, came up with the solution. He developed the Bull Elephant Backfield, placing Dick Horner and Deacon Dan Towler, who had been alternating as fullbacks, and Tank Younger, who had been used mostly as a linebacker, into one backfield. Each of them weighed over 220 pounds; each had sprinter's speed; and besides their ability to crunch inside, all were splendid pass receivers, particularly Horner. We knew that two skinny halfbacks disguised as linebackers could not last very long against this group. The experiment worked and we beat San Francisco. A few weeks later we played the Bears with first place at stake, and the three of them combined for 205 yards of rushing and another 133 in pass receiving.

In one of their favorite plays, called "27-M Sockem," Hirsch turned out the defensive end, the tackle turned in his man, while Horner and Younger, shoulder-to-shoulder, barreled through on the linebacker with Towler on their heels. Deacon rolled up many, many 15-yard gains with that play.

Towler got his Deacon Dan nickname because he started the custom of leading us in prayer before every game, and he ended his pro career prematurely to become an ordained minister, his life's goal. He was a Larry Csonka-type runner; the more work he got, the better he became, and he just punished people who got in his way. He led the NFL in rushing in 1952, and he had a bit of philosophy to fit any occasion. One that always stuck with me concerned how running backs had to be aware of blindside tackles. "Them that don't hear footsteps, feel 'em," Deacon said.

Younger, though nicknamed "Tank," was anything but tanklike—his six-foot, three-inch frame hid his 226 pounds very compactly. Even though he became part of the Bull Elephant Backfield, he still did not relinquish his linebacking duties, and in that victory over the Bears he played sixty minutes, including time on every special team. Tank had one other distinction: he was the first player from Grambling College to play in the NFL.

In contrast to the Bull Elephants was our Pony Express Backfield, again a revolutionary concept because no team in football had three world-class sprinters in one backfield. This group was comprised of Glenn Davis, Tom Kalminir, a hard, tough runner, and Vitamin T. Smith. They were smaller, none over 170 pounds; but not only could they outrun a defense, each of them was a superb pass receiver.

Among the Pony guys, Glenn Davis, a splendid person, was the most renowned because of his years with the great Army teams in the mid-forties, where he teamed with Doc Blanchard. Glenn, like Doc, won a Heisman Trophy, and when he joined the Rams, so the story goes, he became good friends with Tom Harmon and Les Horvath, both former

Ram players. They also were Heisman Trophy winners, at Michigan and Ohio State respectively, and helped Glenn find a home in their neighborhood.

One evening, a guest in Glenn's home, seeing the Heisman Trophy displayed on a mantle, gushed about it being so special. "I don't know about that," Glenn is supposed to have replied. "They seem to be all over our neighborhood."

After I joined the Rams a knee injury sapped Glenn's skills, though you could see an occasional flash that showed how spectacular he was when healthy.

Vitamin Smith was something else. He was V.T. Smith, the V standing for Verda, but Frank Finch of the *Los Angeles Times* nicknamed him "Vitamin" because, Finch said, he had the energy of six guys and was always wound up. That he was, a five-foot, eight-inch bundle of concentrated energy who exploded into action. Hirsch said Vitamin had the finest burst of speed he ever saw during his first two years with the Rams, but Smith was at his best on punts and kickoff returns, and he still holds the Rams' best kickoff season average with 33.7 yards in 1950, and is among the top five in all other club punt and kickoff lifetime marks.

We also had one other combination. Often, Fears, Hirsch and Bobby Boyd would line up together as receivers, and defenses at that time simply weren't geared to play against a three wide receiver concept. Sometimes we threw a couple of the Pony guys in with them for a pure speed attack. This was made for Van Brocklin with his wonderful arm strength, distance and feather-touch. His receivers simply ran under those deep passes without ever slowing a step.

The architect of these revolutionary offenses was Hampton Pool, our offensive coach. He was a very clever, inventive person who was allowed full rein with the offense by Joe Stydahar. Joe was much like Jim Lee Howell when he coached the Giants. Jim Lee allowed Vince Lombardi total control of the offense and Tom Landy full responsibility for the defense. Joe and Jim really were administrators who gave full support to their coaches and were fair in their dealings with all the players. Joe, Hamp Pool, defensive coach Red Hickey and line coach Ray Richards were tough on the players. You toed the line or you didn't stay around.

Inventive, clever coaches can thrive under such conditions, and Pool certainly did. He took many of the revolutionary concepts that Clark Shaughnessy installed when he coached the team in the late forties, and added men in motion, spread formations and, of course, the Bull Elephant and Pony Express Backfields.

Hamp, who also was in charge of the defense, also was a bug on positive thinking. In our 1951 training camp, he read to us every day on the subject, partially to get us in good mental state when we played the Philadelphia Eagles in an exhibition game in Little Rock, Arkansas. The Rams had not beaten Philadelphia since moving to Los Angeles in 1946, and it had become a sore point, particularly after the Eagles won the 1949 NFL title game, 14-0. I don't know whether his readings were the key, but we beat them, and afterward most of the veterans went out and celebrated.

Stydahar gave the players a one a.m. curfew, and when these veterans failed to show at that time, he called some of their rooms. No one answered and he was furious. He recalled hearing about a nightclub that stayed open late, so he called it, disguising his voice to resemble one of the players, and asked for Jack Finlay, an offensive lineman.

"Any Rams there Jack?" he asked in his disguised voice.

"Most of 'em," Finlay replied. "Come on down."

Stydahar exploded. He told Finlay that everyone was fined one hundred dollars, and it would be three hundred if they weren't back to the hotel in a half-hour. None made it at that time, so twenty-six veterans and two rookies were nailed for a total of $7,900—an NFL record.

Pool was unruffled, and resumed his inspirational readings, guaranteeing they would help us beat the Cardinals the following week in Salt Lake City. He even promised to try and have the fines rescinded. Everyone worked like hell, as much to get their money back as to win the game. But the Cardinals must have read the same book because we lost, 36-21, and Hamp's positive thinking campaign lost some of its impact. However, two days before the season began Stydahar rescinded the fines, and that bit of positive thinking worked best of all because we beat the New York Yanks, 51-14. Van Brocklin gained 554 yards passing, the all-time, NFL one-game record, and Hirsch caught four of his five touchdown throws.

Red Hickey was my position coach, and he was a tough, no-nonsense person who had finished playing for the Rams just a couple of seasons before I arrived. He had a line on everyone's thinking and took no guff from anyone. Red later became the head coach of the 49ers, and he has worked for the NFL scouting combines and Dallas Cowboys for many years.

My closest friends on the club in 1951 were three other rookies: Leon McLaughlin, a center from UCLA; Don Simensen, an offensive tackle from St. Thomas College in Minnesota; and Herb Rich, our second-round pick and defensive back from Vanderbilt, who was later my teammate with the Giants. Simensen was my roommate for the first two years, but in 1953 he suffered a cerebral hemorrhage while pushing his car out of the slush and snow in Minnesota. After six hours of brain surgery he was partially paralyzed and had to learn to walk again. He later taught conservation studies in St. Paul. Leon and I then roomed together for the rest of my time with the Rams. He was a very, very smart center who made up with his mental agility what he lacked in size, and he was a great team leader. We have remained close friends, and Mac has been a fine line coach for several NFL teams since his retirement as a player.

Our defensive team in 1951 didn't get the rave reviews of the offense, but with players such as Don Paul, Larry Brink and Stan West, as well as Tom Keane, Rich, Jerry Williams and Woodley Lewis in the secondary, we more than held our own. I was the right end and Brink played the left. Larry was six-five, 240 pounds, which was big for those days, and he was ideal for his position, which in the 5-4 defense meant he basically flew down the line of scrimmage to get to the play. When the team switched to the 4-3 concept a few years later, Larry's lack of agility hurt him, and he was traded to the Bears after the 1953 season.

West was a roving middle guard–linebacker. He lined up over the center in our 5-4, but occasionally he dropped off and formed a 4-3 alignment. Stan had the ideal build for the middle guard, a roly-poly guy who was six-two and 258 pounds, and a very tough, hard-nosed player who gave smaller centers fits.

Our number-three draft pick in 1951 was Charley Toogood, from Nebraska. All the rookies envied him because he got five hundred dollars to sign his contract, and we all thought he was a millionaire. But Charley was a very good player who fit right in at defensive tackle, and only a leg injury a few years later kept him from having a fantastic career.

Among those players, and others whom I haven't mentioned, there was no dead wood, which is rare because nearly every team has a couple of guys who don't belong. But those Rams were a total professional team—in the way we played, the way we practiced, and the way we comported ourselves off the field. In fact, only three or four players wore low-cut football shoes, which were just coming into vogue, and most of us had jersey sleeves right to our wrists. If the sleeve only went to the elbow, you were considered a hot dog.

There really was something special about being a member of the Rams, and the club treated us that way. Bill Granholm, now an administrative assistant to NFL commissioner Pete Rozelle, was our equipment manager, and every day that we went to practice everything was meticulously laid out. Socks were pressed, uniforms were placed perfectly in our lockers, our shoes were shined. Teams don't even do that today.

We were seen as something special away from the field as well. While Hollywood celebrities abounded, none held more esteem and popularity than the Rams players, and whenever we went to the same clubs and restaurants in the Los Angeles area that were frequented by such stars as Frank Sinatra, Dean Martin and Don Rickles, we got the most attention. In fact, the Hollywood set always sought us out rather than the other way around.

We were very comfortable in this environment. Of course, Bob Hope, one of the team's owners, was around us quite a bit, and no one in Hollywood was any bigger. And the Hollywood scene rubbed off on the team itself when the film, *Crazylegs—All-American,* was produced. It was

13

Hirsch's screen biography and many of the players were in it. We really never gave it a second thought.

All of this mainly was a result of our 1951 championship. Going into the final game, we were tied for second place in the National Conference with the Bears, a half-game behind Detroit. But the 49ers upset the Lions, the Bears lost to the Cardinals, and we smothered the Packers to finish with an 8-4 record, while Detroit and the 49ers were 7-4-1. That season we produced 5,506 yards in just 12 games, an average of 458 yards per game. No NFL team ever has bettered it.

The title game was a rematch against the Cleveland Browns, who had beaten the Rams on Lou Groza's field goal in the final seconds of the 1950 championship. The Browns stayed in Pasadena, at the Green Hotel, and worked on a nearby open practice field, so Stydahar sent a scout to watch them. Our guy returned with sketches of a six-man defensive front, plus a couple of other new things. We worked all week preparing for them, but one thing was wrong: Paul Brown, Cleveland's coach, had set us up. He knew someone would be watching so he devised the bogus formations for our benefit, and in the game it took us a while to become untracked because we trailed, 10-7, at the half.

Early in the third quarter, Brink blindsided quarterback Otto Graham at his 30 yardline. He lost the ball, and I scooped it up and headed for the end zone. I never had complete control of the ball, so I couldn't run all out, and Marion Motley caught me at the two yardline. Three plays later Towler's touchdown gave us a 14-10 lead. Waterfield added a field goal for a 17-10 advantage before the Browns tied it with about six minutes to play in the fourth quarter. A minute later, Van Brocklin worked his magic with Fears and we won the game, 24-17.

That game marked the first of many encounters with the Browns, Paul Brown and his great Cleveland teams. It also was the first of many one-on-one battles between me and tackle Lou Groza, who is in the Hall of Fame. Lou never got all the credit he deserved for his tackle play, probably because his great kicking skills got him more notoriety. But while other offensive linemen rested, Lou kicked off and ran down to make tackles; kicked field goals and extra points; and then played left tackle on every offensive play, a truly remarkable achievement. He was a superb tackle, whose strong point was pass blocking. Take it from someone who played against him, there is no denying his Hall-of-Fame spot.

I saw much more of the Browns after joining the Giants, though I had one more memorable joust against them in 1955 when they beat us for the NFL title. Cleveland always was a well-conditioned team, methodical and precise, and almost perfect in what they did. Play execution was their hallmark. They were never the toughest physical team, but being so precise and talented they didn't have to win on toughness. That is not to say they didn't have some very tough, physical players. They did, which belied their image because they always appeared so clean-cut, wearing uniforms that seemed so neat, and in public they looked like a group of bankers. Everything about the Browns was first class, which mirrored their coach, Paul Brown.

Otto Graham was responsible for much of their offensive success. He was a master of throwing on the break to Dante Lavelli, Mac Speedie and Dub Jones, three great receivers, and he also got the ball downfield pretty well. What made Otto even more dangerous was his ability to run. Like Waterfield, he had been an All-America tailback in college, at Northwestern. The true measure of Graham's talent, besides his spot in the Hall of Fame, is that he had his team in the championship game every year that he played.

Lou Groza really typified the players at that time. We battled each other, but there was great respect among all of us. Intimidation never worked; nor did mouthy guys stay around too long. Part of the reason was that most of us had been through a war, so playing football was placed in its proper perspective. We all looked at the game as a great opportunity to get something extra.

Still, I had some great individual battles during my time with the Rams. Groza was just one of them. George Connor, also in the Hall of Fame, was another when we played the Bears twice a year. He played offensive tackle and linebacker, and he was smart. He worked you over and tried to set you up, letting you think you could beat him and then springing a trap. He was always a gentleman, no dirty stuff, but I had to battle like hell against him.

Lou Creekmur of the Lions was another great confrontation. He was a big, strong, tough player who had leg-whipping, then legal, down to a science. We hammered each other twice a year, and he was fierce, but not unlike the entire Detroit team. The Lions were tough, the NFL's "Bad Guys" at that time. Detroit and the 49ers were our foremost rivals, and in 1952 we tied the Lions for the National Conference title and lost a playoff, 31-21.

Detroit didn't win entirely on toughness. They had great players like Doak Walker, Bobby Layne and Leon Hart. Layne was the show, the motivator for that team. He made you want to play as hard as you could to get at him. I also thought that Hart was a helluva good player. Leon was a six-foot, five-inch, 261-pound tight end who came into the NFL as a Heisman Trophy winner with a big Notre Dame buildup, and people mistakenly expected him to win games on his own. He also played fullback in some situations, and he was a load to handle.

The 49ers were the equal of any team in the league when I was with the Rams. Frankie Albert was their quarterback the first couple of years, and he was a wizard with the ball. He was a lefthander, and about five-foot-nine, but no one ran the option better. Before one game, Red Hickey kept harping on stopping that option by not getting caught inside. As the game went on and nothing happened, I paid little attention. But in crunch time, I bit on a fake, and Frankie just wheeled outside and into the end zone for a touchdown.

Their greatest star was Hugh McElhenny, a running back who was dubbed "The King." And he was—he and Jimmy Brown were the best I ever played against. Mac could embarrass you on the field with his moves and change-of-pace running style. He beat us once with twenty seconds to play by taking a screen pass 80 yards for a touchdown. No other team, needing a TD to win, ever threw a screen pass with twenty seconds to play. McElhenny changed the rules because he was so effective in the open field. Hugh was a member of the Giants in 1963, but his skills were at an end—though he gave us a big boost when injuries cut down our runners.

The 49ers also had a great runner in Joe Perry, a tough fullback who, like McElhenny, is in the Hall of Fame, and a pair of great receivers in Billy Wilson, who Emlen Tunnell once told me was the best he ever covered, and Gordy Soltau. After Albert retired, Y. A. Tittle came on, and the 49ers never skipped a beat. If they ever had a strong defense in those years, no one could have beaten them.

The loss to the Lions in a 1952 National Conference playoff was a bitter blow to coach Hampton Pool, who took over from Stydahar after the first game of the season. The two of them had gotten into a battle of hurt feelings after the 1951 championship season. Pool felt he didn't receive enough public recognition for the team's success, and Stydahar felt that Hamp got too much public notice, lessening his own image as a head coach. Joe admitted later this jealousy drove him to reclaim both the offensive and defensive coaching jobs in 1952, but he simply could not handle the creative aspects, which began to affect our performance. When Dan Reeves urged Stydahar to return to the other system, Joe balked, and he issued an ultimatum that either he or Pool had to go. Reeves wouldn't be cornered, so Stydahar left.

Joe was a gregarious person who understood the professional football player from his days as a Hall-of-Fame tackle with the Bears, but he really had no aptitude for the X's and O's that were beginning to break new horizons in professional football. Had he been content, as Jim Lee Howell was when he was head coach of the Giants, to take whatever credit any successful head coach will receive while at the same time recognizing the contributions of talented assistants, as Jim Lee did with Vince Lombardi and Tom Landry, there would have been no problem. At the same time, if Pool had the same confidence as Lombardi and Landry to exist in this fashion, the rift also could have been avoided.

As it turned out, both men, and the Rams, suffered. Stydahar's role as the man who kept law and order, and who knew how to handle pro football players, was sorely missed because Hamp was very distant, more content to create than to build a personal rapport with the team. Through the course of a season, players need someone like Stydahar who can understand the peaks and valleys yet not tolerate excuses for losing; and who can keep a team on an even keel by dealing evenly with all of the diverse personalities. We never really had that leadership during Hamp's tenure, and he finally resigned after the 1954 season.

During his three seasons, though, he acquired some spectacular players. Dick (Night Train) Lane intercepted 14 passes in his rookie 1952 season, and in 1953 a six-foot, five-inch, 272-pound giant named Gene (Big Daddy) Lipscomb made the club. He was Big Daddy even then, but a gentle guy and a fine player who got better after he left the Rams. I got along fine with him, and he used to come to our apartment for lunch quite often during the season.

In 1954 linebacker Les Richter joined the Rams after costing us eleven players in a trade with the Dallas Texans. He had been an All-America player at the University of California and came to us with a very big reputation as well as a huge local following. Les thought that would get him by, but it didn't because he didn't work at the game as a rookie. In a game at San Francisco he was so tired he just staggered back to the huddle. Don Paul watched this for a couple of plays and then exploded:

"Listen, rookie, either you are the first one up on every play and forming that huddle for me, or one of us is going to leave this field in a horizontal position. And it sure as hell isn't going to be me."

Richter got the message and stepped up his intensity, though he yapped too much on the field. Later that season he and lineman Don Joyce of the Colts got into a wrestling match on a kickoff return after Les gave him a verbal shot. Joyce finally ripped off Richter's helmet and clubbed him with it, sending Les to the hospital to get fourteen stitches over his right eye. In a 1955 game he hooked Eagles tight end Pete Pihos to the ground, and Pihos chased him across the field to kick him squarely in the ass. The older Les got, the harder he played, but he didn't light up the LA sky as much as he thought during his first two seasons with the Rams.

When Pool resigned, the Rams hired Sid Gillman from the University of Cincinnati, and Sid in turn hired college assistants, including Jack Faulkner, still with the team as administrator of football operations, and Joe Thomas, who gained a reputation for tearing down and rebuilding some NFL teams in the sixties and seventies. But Gillman's biggest job at the start was selling the players on the fact that a group of college coaches could be effective in professional football. He really catered to us in order to win our hearts, and it worked for a year because he was a refreshing change from the moodiness of the previous two years.

Tex Schramm really took a big gamble orchestrating that choice, but Tex never flinched from anyone or any problem. He really ran the Rams for Reeves, who spent most of his time at his stock brokerage in Los Angeles, and Tex, as much as anyone, was responsible for setting the great tone of excellence. However, he was also a very hard-nosed businessman, and perhaps a bit insensitive to the players in those matters. I contrast him with Wellington Mara. If there was a conflict between Tex and a player, Tex would not give in to the player; if there was one between Wellington and a player, Well agonized over it until it was resolved.

The difference was that Tex was a pure businessman, and he saw everything in that dimension. Wellington had a feeling for the player and always tried to work things out, regardless of the bottom line, and as I'll discuss later, it often cost him dearly.

I negotiated with both men, and Tex was tougher. My rookie year I made $4,200; I asked for $6,500 for 1952. He wanted to pay me $5,500, though I had been named outstanding rookie and we had won the title. He must have called me fifty times in Stamford trying to get it worked out, and the phone bills probably were several hundred dollars.

"Why don't you just give me the four or five hundred dollars that it's costing you in phone calls?" I finally asked.

"Because that's not part of the deal," he replied. "That's a cost of doing business."

It was a principle with him, and that is how he ran the team—on cold, strict principles, all geared to being fiscally responsible, yet never sacrificing the areas that gave the Rams a great image or the players a sense of pride. It is obvious that he has run the Cowboys the same way because you rarely find one of their players among the top fifty in salary, yet the image—America's Team—always has shone brightest.

Schramm left the Rams in 1956 and joined CBS in New York before moving to the Cowboys, and I was later told that Reeves fired him because he traded me to the Giants prior to that season. His successor as Rams general manager was Pete Rozelle, who had been our publicity director for a few years. I had a good relationship with Pete when he held that job, but after I had left the team, we had a run-in during his first year as GM.

In 1957 the Rams stayed at Bear Mountain, New York, about fifty miles from New York City, between a two-game swing through the East. I went up to visit some of my old teammates one evening, and a day or so later I heard that Pete ripped into me for keeping some of his players out after curfew. He even threatened to send Duane Putnam, a guard and one of my good friends, back to Los Angeles because of a dispute on the matter. This was all nonsense to me, and I said so when asked by the press to comment on Pete's charges. When I was in Los Angeles to play in the Pro Bowl after the season, I went to the Rams office to clear up the matter face-to-face, telling him in effect that he had no right, nor did I appreciate, his trying to make me a public scapegoat because some of his players missed a curfew. The incident left a bit of distaste between us at the time.

There were no problems during 1955. The Rams had only eleven players from their 1951 world championship team, and only Don Paul and I were left from that defensive unit. But that year our number-two draft choice, running back Ron Waller of Maryland, was a gem, though Gillman almost blew it. He drafted Waller as a defensive back, though he was a runner at Maryland, then spent most of the preseason trying to make him a wide receiver. Ron even opened the season at that spot before being told to learn all the running plays. He was a tough little guy who finished the year with a rookie record 719 yards. Moreover, he played every offensive down, as well as every punt and kickoff return.

Duane Putnam, our best offensive lineman, John Hock, another guard, and McLaughlin were my closest friends on the team. Putter's daughter later married the son of President Ronald Reagan.

There were other pleasant surprises that year, in Frank Fuller, a defensive tackle, who filled a big hole, and rookie defensive back Don Burroughs, nicknamed "The Blade" because he resembled one with his six-foot, four-inch frame barely covered by about 170 pounds. He had nine interceptions, and Will Sherman led the NFL with his 11.

Van Brocklin had the quarterback job to himself and still had Hirsch, Fears, Boyd and Skeets Quinlan, a tough little Texan. Larry Morris, our number-one draft choice and an All-America linebacker at Georgia Tech, was converted to running back for that year. He did a great job of blocking and some pretty good running considering that he had not carried the ball since his freshman year in college.

But there was a big difference between this team and the 1951 team. In 1951 we were primarily a veteran team at the key spots, very well-organized, very dedicated and disciplined. In 1955 Gillman assembled a group of players and then tried to make winners of them. We played with more of a college spirit than with the great confidence that we could win on our own. It worked, though, thanks to a four-game unbeaten string at the end of the year that helped us edge the Bears by a half-game for the Western Conference title. The game I best recall was our 27-14 win against the 49ers, when I intercepted one of Y. A. Tittle's screen passes and ran for a touchdown. As soon as he started back, I sensed a screen and ducked through the blockers. He saw me too late and as soon as he threw the ball, I heard him say, "Oh-oh." It was my sixth—and last— TD for the Rams, the other five from fumble recoveries and blocked punts.

The Browns beat us, 38-14, in the championship game, but we certainly helped them with six interceptions and an entirely new defensive setup for that game that never matched up well against their double-flanker offense. Our regular defense would have been more effective, and we urged the coaches to stay with it, but to no avail. All of this helped Otto Graham play his final NFL game in a blaze of glory. As it turned out, it was my final game too—for the Rams. But though I'm a Giant forever, I have never really lost my Rams horns.

2 Coming to the Giants: A Dynasty Begins

Until July of 1956, the New York Football Giants were just another NFL team to me. People who say, "It must have been a dream come true to come to the Giants," can't quite understand when I say it wasn't, even though I grew up within an hour's drive of their home field, the Polo Grounds. Pro football was not any big deal when I was a kid, and our interest in the sport was centered on our local high school and Notre Dame, whose exploits we could follow on the radio each Saturday afternoon. I didn't do much of that either, because my mother had first call on my services helping her clean Sacred Heart Church, and the rest of my free time was spent playing football, not listening to it.

I really never followed any professional football team until my college years. Then the New York Yankees of the All-America Football Conference aroused my interest after I visited their training camp one day at Cheshire, Connecticut, and talked with a couple of their players. I never forgot a 28-28 tie they played in 1948 with the Cleveland Browns because they blew a 28-0 lead, and it was incredible to me that any team could lose a four-touchdown lead. A couple of years after the AAFC and the NFL merged, the Yankees (then the New York Yanks) were moved to Dallas and became, for one season, the Texans. During my five seasons in Los Angeles, I was more thrilled playing against the Texans than I was when the Rams twice played against the Giants. One of those games was in the Polo Grounds in 1955, and my friends from Stamford honored me before the game.

Throughout the 1955 off-season I had no inkling that Sid Gillman and his staff were planning to tear apart and rebuild the Rams. Until the 1955 championship game, Sid had leaned on the veteran players for as much help as they could give because he and his staff knew little about the pro game. But even before that game the handwriting was on the wall; they constructed a plan that didn't have a chance to succeed and then rejected our suggestions to make some reasonable changes. Sid obviously felt he knew it all after one season in the NFL, and he blueprinted the Rams of the future in terms of players' sizes. When it came to defensive ends, he thought that Bud McFadin, a six-three, 245-pound guard-linebacker, was better suited than I was at six-one, 230 pounds to play defensive end. That change really never worked out; Bud went off to play in Canada after 1956 before finishing his career in the American Football League in the early sixties.

However, my future with the Rams—and the Giants—really was settled in a telephone call in mid-July of 1956. Andra, our fourth child, was born a week before I was scheduled to report to training camp, so I called Sid and said I would be a couple of days late because I wanted to wait until Jean was home from the hospital and was able to care for the new baby as well as our other three children.

"I've got a team to worry about, not your family," Sid told me.

"Well, I've got some kids to worry about, and I've got to do what's right for me," I replied. "And what the hell, it's only a couple of days."

"I don't care whether it's a couple of days or not," he replied. "You get your ass out here, that's all I can tell you."

"Sid," I told him bluntly, "I'll be out there as soon as my home situation is settled."

Of course, that wasn't the first time I had tasted this insensitivity. The previous year we had played the Redskins in Washington and my father passed away that weekend after a long bout with cancer. I told Sid that after the game I had to go home to Connecticut for the funeral.

"Well, if you must, then you must," he said rather impatiently. "But you get back to Los Angeles as quickly as possible."

I went home in time for the wake, attended my dad's funeral the next morning and was on a plane that afternoon for the West Coast. Looking back a couple of years later, I was furious at myself for allowing Gillman to bulldoze me at such a very tender time for our family. Sid was trying to put the team first, but how important was one day of practice? Was ordering me not to miss any time an indication of a need in himself to show he was the head coach? And that no one, under any conditions, should expect special consideration? It didn't take me long to find out for certain during that July.

A couple of days after my conversation with Gillman, my family was just about settled and I was preparing to leave for the Rams' training camp, when I got a phone call from Wellington Mara.

"I've been talking to the Rams about you," he told me, "and they're willing to trade you."

Wellington might have been stunned if he had seen me at that moment, because I almost buckled over from shock. Being traded had never entered my mind.

"I know that you're thirty years old, but do you think you could play two or three more years?" he asked me.

"I'll try to play as long as I can, but I don't know how long that will be," I told him, trying to sound calm.

"Well, if you tell me that you can play, or at least will try to play for that long, then I think I can make a trade for you."

"Go ahead and make the deal," I told Well, thinking to myself about the Rams, "Well, if you want to trade me, to hell with you. I might as well go with the Giants."

Well called me back a short time later and said the deal was made, and that I was to report to the Giants' training camp at St. Michael's College in Winooski Park, Vermont. The Giants gave the Rams a first-round draft choice which they retrieved in 1961 in the person of Del Shofner.

I never solicited that trade, though there were times during the five years of relocating my family across the country when I thought, "God, I'd love to be playing in New York and not have to go through all this." When it happened, it was a blow. I was perfectly happy with the Rams, content to play with them for the rest of my career. I bled Rams blue, and those horns were very special to me. I really was hurt at being rejected by the team that I loved so much, and for whom I performed with such dedication.

Even though I was facing new people, different philosophies and new surroundings, going to the Giants was not very traumatic. First, there were some former Ram teammates there, such as Herb Rich, Harland (Swede) Svare, Eddie Hughes and Ben Agajanian. Swede and I had been very close during the two seasons we played together in Los Angeles—in 1953 and 1954—and he had been my unofficial tour guide to some of the inside gatherings of the LA-Hollywood set. Coming to the Giants was like a grand reunion and to Swede, like the godfather coming home. We formed a close bond, which exists to this day. On the field he was my alter ego, and there we built a different kind of bond, one of great confidence, respect and feeling for each other, which was so very necessary as we mastered Tom Landry's defensive concepts.

St. Michael's was also like old home week for me—many up there still recalled that 1950 game between Arnold and St. Michael's College, and they treated me like a long-lost hero. Perhaps at that time I also needed to be remembered to salve the hurt feelings and rejection that are natural whenever an athlete is traded for what he perceives to be no good reason. It is almost like being able to say to new teammates, "See, I must be worth something because these people still remember me."

No one on the Giants ever did anything to make me feel anything but welcome—and needed. Having finished the 1955 season with five victories in its last seven games, the team had begun to build confidence in itself. In Jim Lee Howell's third season as head coach, this was also a team still in transition. I was part of a wave of ten new players that included Hughes, Dick Modzelewski, who had played for the Redskins and Steelers, and such rookies as Jim Katcavage, Sam Huff and Don Chandler.

I came to the Giants with a little better reputation than I deserved, thanks to the Rams mystique of the time that accompanied their players whenever they joined another team. I had played on a world championship team; I had been to the Pro Bowl; and I had made some all-pro teams. My quality as a player was known, if somewhat inflated, but I really believe my most important contribution at the outset was the nonfootball qualities that had sustained me with the Rams. I was a leader, I was a fighter and, as far as my defensive teammates were concerned, I helped solidify a good group of people, on and off the field. I used my contacts in the Stamford area to help many of them find places to live. Within a year or so we had quite a contingent of players and coaches living in southern Connecticut.

At that time the team really was a part of what was called the "Giants Family"—the players, coaches and front office, as well as a number of priests, doctors, lawyers and other close friends of the Mara family, which was headed by Tim Mara, Sr., and his sons, Jack and Wellington. Tim had founded the team in the mid-twenties and then nurtured it through good and bad times, like so many of the original NFL owners. Though we rarely ever saw him, we knew he believed in the "family" concept because he was a sportsman by nature; and football was something to be enjoyed, and the talents of its participants to be appreciated.

Mr. Mara had by that time turned over the day-to-day operations to Jack and Wellington, and there never was a more perfect partnership in pro football. Jack was the team's president, and he ran the nonfootball side of the business. We rarely ever saw him during the week, but he was no less rabid in his love for the team. If we lost, I always thought that Jack took it hardest of all; he often sat on a trunk in one end of our Yankee Stadium locker room and looked as if his world had come apart in one afternoon.

Wellington, the team's vice president at the time, handled all football matters. No one in the NFL was more competent or knowledgeable, as his trades and drafts that helped form our dynasty years attest. He was always at training camp, and he attended most of our weekly practices, but he never buddied around with any of the players because he also negotiated our contracts. He had a feeling for a player's needs, but you could never overinflate your own value. He knew exactly what you had accomplished, and in that sense he was a fair, though firm, negotiator.

When I joined the team Jack's son, Tim Jr., was just finishing school and about to join the front office. He soon developed close off-the-field relationships with some of the older offensive stars such as Frank Gifford, Charlie Conerly, Pat Summerall, Alex Webster and others whom we called the "downtown group" because they maintained a visible presence around New York City. Tim seemed to enjoy this kind of hero worship, though I often wondered what common ground there was between him and these older players.

My first coach with the Giants, Jim Lee Howell, was much like Joe Stydahar of the Rams. He was an administrator who delegated specific coaching duties to his chief defensive and offensive coaches, Tom Landry and Vince Lombardi, and to other assistants, end coach Ken Kavanaugh and offensive line coach Ed Kolman. Jim Lee allowed them to do their work freely, much as Stydahar let Hampton Pool exercise domain over the Rams' offense and defense.

To those on the outside, Jim Lee often appeared a jolly, easygoing Southern gentleman (he was from Arkansas, where he lived and maintained his ranch in the off-season). He was very gracious with outsiders, and he bestowed accolades on his assistants without any hesitation or fear that they were usurping his role as head coach. In fact, with two future great head coaches like Lombardi and Landry doing most of the work, he had the perfect setup, and the team won as a result.

Jim Lee often described his job as "sending in the punter on fourth down and being sure the kickoff and return teams were on the field." That was a bit of an oversimplification; Landry and Lombardi consulted with him on all of their plans. During the game, if it came to a decision on fourth down whether to punt the ball or try for a first down—such as happened in the 1958 NFL title game against the Colts—he made the call. In so doing, he took all the responsibility when a play turned out to be controversial.

But Jim Lee was also an ex-Marine who had seen combat during World War II, and he ran the team as if we were all members of his unit. He was tough on the players and he browbeat us when we needed to be browbeaten. He had the Marine drill sergeant approach of doing precisely what was called for, and he was adamant about conditioning—particularly in training camp, which some ex-Marine players said were like mini-boot camps. This wasn't all bad, and in fact we had a lot of fun. Jim Lee yelled and screamed a lot, giving us plenty of ammunition to mimic him and draw off some of the drudgery. He stressed running after practice, and that was tough at the end of a double session when our legs were so tired. We had to start at our practice field, circle a small shed located about 400 yards away and then return.

One day Dick Modzelewski got to the house and hid behind it while the rest of the players made the return run. Mo felt pretty good about his ploy, sitting back there while we did the running, kibitzing with us as we staggered past. All of a sudden, he looked down and saw a very familiar pair of legs—those belonging to Jim Lee, who stood there and looked at him. Mo didn't say a word, but he got up and started running. When we finished that day, Dick was still at it under Howell's watchful eye. Actually, that shed became a diversion for us. We went out every night and moved it about ten feet closer to our practice field—great mental therapy because even though we had to run, we felt we were putting something over on the coach, and that made us feel better.

One of Jim Lee's greatest virtues was that he was evenhanded in his criticism. While he may not have known all the technical secrets of football, he certainly tolerated nothing less than a full effort, and he was absolutely bearish on anyone making mistakes. No one was immune, and that even included Gifford, the acknowledged star of the team. When he referred to "those Hollywood characters," everyone knew there was true justice; and when anyone from the offense got their butt chewed, it kind of tickled the defense because we thought they should have been chewed all along. Ironically, Jim rarely got on the defense; I don't think he fully understood all we were doing in Tom Landry's system, though he sat in on some meetings every week in case Tom missed a game because of sickness. He wanted to be somewhat familiar with our coordinated schemes.

Those schemes were Landry's exclusive brainchild, and they were packaged into a revolutionary system that really changed the way the game was played and how it was watched and appreciated. I'll go into some of the specifics later, but when we had mastered it, the defensive player suddenly became a hero and Yankee Stadium rang with a new cheer: *DEEEEFENSE, DEEEEFENSE.* Up to that time, people had only cheered long runs and catches. Touchdowns were the real measuring stick of how well a team played. Look back at the newspaper accounts of the Giants' games in the fifties, and even into the early sixties, and you'll see only meager mention of the number of times we sacked the quarterback, or what we did to hold teams to under a hundred yards rushing (which happened innumerable times), or why we accumulated so many turnovers. People who covered football, as well as those who watched, simply didn't understand the defensive side of the game.

Landry's 4-3 defense ultimately changed all of that because we used it to win championships, and we did it in Yankee Stadium, where the whole nation tuned in and believed it was important. The defensive player was lionized when CBS made the television documentary, "The Violent World of Sam Huff," putting a microphone on Sam, our middle linebacker, and filming him throughout a game. Never before had people heard so clearly the noise of scrimmage combat. But we had raised the awareness of people to such heights that they wanted to know more. Tom's basic concepts of playing a coordinated defense and his teaching us to accept and carry them out with great confidence produced astounding results. There is little doubt that the *concept*—not the people—was responsible for our success. Tom could have been the defensive coach of the Washington Redskins or Chicago Cardinals at the time, and those teams would have been similarly successful. A team can get more from lesser-talented players who are willing to work in a coordinated fashion than defenses that depend on people physically dominating other people. In all honesty, had we not played Tom's system we would not have been a good football team—his defense allowed good ballplayers to become better.

Few, including many football people, ever understood what we did in this defense. The basic framework was fourfold. Tom had pursued a graduate degree in people management, so he became very dedicated to learning about human behavior and the tendencies people have to act and react to certain situations. This interest developed into his theory for the 4-3 defense, which said, in effect, that in a given situation an opponent probably favors one play above all others. He had studied the tendencies and habits of a coach and quarterback in similar situations by breaking down the film and charting the team's plays by down, distance, placement of the ball on the field and near the hashmarks, and by evaluating the strengths and weaknesses of its personnel.

He then established a system of "keys," or clues that told us what the offense was apt to do. For example, he knew from film study that if the fullback lined up behind the tackle on second and six, we might expect a sweep—because he was placed closest to the defensive end or outside linebacker, he was probably there to block to clear a path for the halfback. If we saw the fullback lined up behind the center on second and four, that team might try an inside play with either the fullback acting as lead blocker for the halfback or vice versa. On third and nine, when the two backs were split—what is called the pro set formation—then our linebackers knew, according to the team's tendencies, they might be flaring into the short areas as pass receivers, because they were set in the backfield where they could quickly get into a pass pattern or stay in as pass blockers because they were lined up to take on the outside pass rush. When we saw these various formations we added the down and distance tendencies, and thus had a good idea of what play was coming. We then called an appropriate defense. This is common practice now, but it was Landry who started the trend in such a sophisticated fashion.

Reading and recognizing the keys was followed by a third step in which Tom's system coordinated the movements of each of the four linemen and three linebackers so they were responsible for controlling seven of the eight gaps along the line of scrimmage. This required tremendous discipline because defensive players love to chase the football, and we had to overcome that instinct lest the coordination break down.

For example, if defensive tackle Rosie Grier made an inside move into the gap between the guard and center, he had to hold that ground even if the play went around the opposite end. If Rosie chased the ball too quickly, then he left his area uncovered because the men on either side and behind him also had definite assignments. When we all got into the gaps and controlled them, there was no place to run.

What about that eighth hole that remained uncovered? We set our alignment so that a bigger defensive lineman covered two gaps by playing head-on against an offensive lineman. He moved either inside or outside according to how the man tried to block him. If it was to the outside of the gap, the defensive man had to fight his way to the inside, and vice versa. We called that move a "Tilly." Sometimes we also covered that open gap with one of the defensive backs, but only if we could get him into the least important of those gaps—with his lack of size he was vulnerable to being run over by bigger linemen. The first time Landry explained the system, that open hole looked like the Lincoln Tunnel to me.

"But Tom," I said, "suppose they go to that open hole?"

"They won't," he replied.

"But suppose they do?" I insisted.

"I know they won't," he said calmly, "But if they do, I'll adjust."

The adjustments were the fourth part of that defense. In 1956 this concept was in its infancy, but as Tom saw all of the ploys used to beat it, and the mistakes we made using it, he had accumulated enough adjustments to cover every situation. We even adjusted on the run during a game, as our coaches in the spotting booth noted the various alignments being used against us. Later, Wellington started taking Polaroid camera shots—the Giants were years ahead of other NFL teams in this innovation—and tossing them down from the third-deck booth in Yankee Stadium to our bench area. When I was a player-coach in the sixties, I adjusted right in the huddle by asking our guys how they were being blocked. We knew that defense so well, with all of its variations, that we could adjust between plays.

As with everything in football, the final key to our success was total execution. We had total confidence that our defense was unbeatable if we played it properly, and this really motivated us to be perfect. We had to be. If, for example, our two defensive tackles played an inside defense—both moving in the same direction to fill the gaps in the center of the line—they knew they had to control that area because our middle linebacker had another gap to fill. If those tackles failed, there was nothing but open field for 20 yards.

As I noted, the concept—not the people—was most important to our success, and physical strength was not an overriding factor. The biggest people don't win in a 4-3 defense. If they did, then a perfect mix would have been a pair of six-six, 285-pound Rosie Griers in the middle, or a Sam Huff weighing 240 pounds so he could take the center's block alone and control the outside hole in the middle. Instead, we had a 220-pound Huff whose main responsibility was the inside hole, while the front four worked to keep blockers away from him so he could make so many plays. When they didn't, he was in trouble.

Tom also developed other packages of stunts that worked very well in this defense. Our blitz package was deadly (you still see him using it in Dallas). We labeled each of our linebacking positions—Wanda was the weak-side backer, Meg the middle and Sam the strong-side linebacker. All of them were geared to the opposition's tendencies—when and where they left backs in for pass protection; how deep and how quickly their quarterbacks took pass drops in certain situations; how able certain backs were to handle a rushing linebacker. We used single, double and triple (or all-out) blitzes. We even blitzed our cornerbacks at times (you still see the Cowboys doing that), and many times we used extra defensive backs, years before "nickel" and "dime" backs became fashionable.

When we got into goal-line defense situations, we lifted free safety Jimmy Patton and one of the linebackers and inserted offensive tackles

Rosey Brown and Jack Stroud, the two biggest and strongest offensive linemen on our team. . . and the two toughest. We went to a six-man front in this defense so that every offensive lineman and the tight end were covered—and so was every gap. Our goal-line stands—and we had so many of them—were the ignition points that turned people on to our defense and began to make it so popular. Yankee Stadium actually shook from the thunderous cheers we received when we trotted off the field after one of those stands. There is no real way to describe how it feels to hear 62,000 people cheering for you, except to say that it is the closest I have ever felt to being absolutely unbeatable. So did the other guys—and perhaps that is why we played that way so often.

When our defense did make mistakes it was usually because, overanxious to make a play, we overplayed our positions; or one of our linemen, facing a bigger, stronger opponent, didn't get into his gap quickly enough and got overpowered. Sometimes a team came in with a plan that was difficult to solve during the game, and we had to spend much of the game playing our automatic defense with very little change-up. Landry usually had the problem solved when we came in for film study on Tuesday, and we soon had the adjustments as part of our system should the problem arise again.

In 1956, when we won the NFL championship with a thundering 47-7 victory over the Bears, we were tops in the league in rushing defense and sacking the quarterback. The following year, we allowed the fewest first downs from passing; and in 1958 we repeated that mark and were also the stingiest team in rushing average, passing yardage and percentage of completed passes. In 1959 we led the league in all major rushing defense categories. I cite those figures only to underscore our consistency, which we maintained even after teams had had a couple of seasons to solve our defensive schemes. While the 1956 NFL championship, with its mighty Yankee Stadium backdrop, initially magnified what we did, two more conference titles in the next three seasons proved that under Tom Landry we were a great defense that could dominate other teams.

No one on the Giants knew Landry and his system better than I did. For three years he and I rode to work every day during the season. He had rented an apartment in Stamford from a friend of mine, and our drive time was always spent discussing our defensive plans. (Howard Cosell, who is still a good friend of mine, lived nearby and often rode with us. I'm sure our conversations, and his friendships with many of the players who lived in the Stamford area at the time, helped him learn something about the game.)

Landry said to us in his first meeting, "We're going to put our boat in the water, and we have three choices when we check the current. We can fight it and row upstream; we can study it and understand what it is about and follow it downstream with little fear of failure; or we can simply lay out in the middle, trying to go upstream and then downstream, but doing nothing but going around in circles. We're not going to do that. We're going to learn what that stream is about and go with it; and if there are times when we can't figure it out, we're going to go like hell in one direction or the other; but no matter which way we go, we're going to believe it's the right way and we'll still get someplace.''

We believed because Landry made us believe with his meticulous teaching and the absolute confidence he had in his system. Just as he had when I questioned him on covering that eighth hole on the offensive line, he always guaranteed we never had to worry, and this attitude typified his preparations. Unlike Vince Lombardi, who used his own emotional personality to motivate players, Tom always believed in thorough preparation as the best motivator. We had enough personal pride and inner fire to get ourselves up emotionally, but there was no substitute for going into a game knowing everything that was apt to happen; and knowing too that we had the ability to adjust to anything new.

Landry was tolerant of our mistakes because all of them were correctable. But if a player screwed up too often in a game, or in practice, he was out of the lineup. If we lost, Tom wasn't moody like Lombardi, who considered a defeat a personal affront and might not speak to anyone for two or three days (though we knew he was anything but quiet with the offense!). Tom's strongest urgings were, "Okay, you know what went wrong. Now it's up to you guys to do it right.''

Tom was a tremendous teacher, and that teaching process never stopped. Our classroom sessions were intense, and during the week we made the offense work harder than some of them might have liked because we always went full-speed. There was no pitty-patting, no gently nudging the guy out of the way. We believed in the motto You Play Like You Practice, and that was one of the great keys to our consistent record of success.

Landry often seemed very preoccupied with his work during the week, and he paid attention only to the players who would perform on Sunday. Dick Modzelewski had to miss a game one week because of an injury, so he was not practicing. He never got over the fact, though, that during a break, when he and Landry were standing next to each other at adjoining urinals finishing their business, Tom never said a word to him. "I guess because I wasn't going to play, he really had nothing to tell me," Dick said later. "Yet last week, when I played, he had plenty to say to me.''

But that was Tom—totally into the game and fully able to block out all that was unimportant or unnecessary. He never meant to be rude or uncaring, because he was anything but; yet he got so wound into his work that he could walk past you in the hallway and not say a word because he didn't even see you.

During a game he was under complete control, stoic and unanimated, regardless of the situation. He was no different after we stuffed an offense on our one yardline than if someone ran 60 yards for a touchdown. In both cases he moved to make corrections or adjustments, and then he allowed us to play. It was almost as if emotion had no place in the most emotional part of football—the defense—a far cry from when he was a

30

cornerback for the Giants, from 1950 until 1955, during which time he also was a defensive coach. When the Rams played the Giants in a preseason game in New York City in my rookie year, Tom worked over Glenn Davis all afternoon until Glenn finally beat him for a touchdown by nearly ten yards. But Landry never stopped running, and when he got close to Glenn in the end zone, Davis threw the ball at him and then took off for our bench with Tom in hot pursuit.

"When I crossed the goal line, I could still hear him coming after me," Glenn told us later. "I knew he wanted to punish me, so I heaved the ball at him and I yelled, 'You wanted it all afternoon, now you've got it.' He was so mad I'll bet he'd have killed me if I hadn't made it to the bench."

One of the unintended benefits of his defensive system was its galvanizing effect on our unit. Because we learned to adjust on the field and to tolerate each other off the field, we were like a family. When we intercepted a pass, the first question always was: Who forced it? There never was any fingerpointing or moaning when someone made a mistake, and no alibis because mistakes are instantly recognizable in a coordinated system. Instead, we admitted our mistakes and used them to improve. After a while we really became a team unto ourselves, and for most of their great seasons in the fifties, the New York Giants were two separate teams—the offense and the defense.

But this did not divide the team. Our locker room was always relatively free of backbiting and personality clashes, and we never disliked any of the offensive players. In fact, we "adopted" some of the linemen who, like us, were down-and-dirty guys who never received any of the glory or the goodies that went to the visible stars. The offensive unit also wasn't as tightly knit as we were, and many of its members went their own ways as individuals. Yet on the field we always played with the offense in mind. We delighted in giving them good field position, and we rationed our timeouts in case they needed them.

The real change occurred when the defense became the darlings of Yankee Stadium. Until then, football belonged to the offense and so did all of the cheers. For the first time, the cheers went to the defense every time we came off the field, and even before the game. One season, we were introduced before a couple of games, and then the offense got its chance, only to be met with a chorus of boos. That was the last time they were introduced that season. There is no doubt we exalted in this, but we had also earned it. I never worried that the offense might have resented our intruding onto their glory path; my feeling was: Go out and do it yourselves.

We weren't bashful about our status either. The offense went through a five-game dry spell in the 1959 season, but we allowed only two touchdowns, and the Giants won all of the games. Late in that streak, while running off the field after stopping an opponent for about the tenth time that afternoon, one of our guys shouted to the offense, "Hold 'em till we get back," the classic plea the offense usually makes to the defense. Another time, we passed the offense going onto the field and yelled, "Don't score too quickly. We love the pressure."

We did, too, not only because we played better in the pressure of a tight game, but also because we got exasperated at times when no points went on the board for us. I know that Pat Summerall never appreciated my barking at him one day after he had missed two straight field goals that would have given us a lead. "Come on, Pat," I yelled. "What the hell are you doing? We're busting our ass out there and you can't even kick a field goal."

When Y. A. Tittle came to us in 1961, a lot of this feeling broke down because he had the personality to bring everyone together. He never hung out with one group, though I think he favored ours. I know that Al Sherman didn't like the idea of two teams, and he tried to force a change when he became head coach in 1961. I disapproved of any forced change because loyalty cannot be legislated, and true loyalty cannot be ordered. The ferociousness that we projected and the pride we accumulated were our fuel.

Even today when we see each other there still is that special feeling. Ask Sam Huff, who played and coached for the Redskins, who now is one of their broadcasters and probably has great feeling for them, how he feels about our defensive team. I'll wager that when Sam cuts himself shaving, the blood that runs is Giants red, not Redskins burgundy.

Much of that feeling and success was due to a perfect mix of personalities. Modzelewski was the old-fashioned type of player, a plugger whose uniform always was dirty because he found a hundred different ways to do his job, but whose spirit was always upbeat. Sam was like the brazen brat in the family, and he'd fly high until Mo set him down. Kat was like a big, eager kid, and Rosie became everyone's special project. I believe I had the respect of everyone and I became the problem-solver. Taken together, all of the pieces fit perfectly, mirroring our system. If each of us had played on different teams, none would have been as successful.

Huff, of course, got the most notoriety, but that was the end product of our 4-3 system that funneled him to the point of attack because he most often keyed the gap where our frequencies indicated the play was likely to go. He made most of the tackles and he became the star—we became the semistars—but Sam never once accepted all the credit for himself. He always tried to point out that he was just part of an overall plan where a lot of people worked to get him to the ball carrier. That system worked well enough to get him into the Hall of Fame; and he worked hard enough to complement our system where the middle linebacker, regardless of who it was, was the focal point. We never resented his publicity because we were part of the reflection, and Sam never changed as a person. To us, he was just one-eleventh of our unit, expected to carry out his assignments, and if he erred, he dug in like all of us to become better.

Huff, of course, almost didn't make the Giants as a rookie in 1956. He was an All-America tackle at West Virginia, but in training camp he was bounced around from offensive guard (he was too slow) to offensive tackle (he was too small) to defensive tackle (still too small) and finally to middle linebacker. All of that bouncing, plus Lombardi's yelling and Jim Lee's boot-camp atmosphere, was too much for him and another rookie running back, Babe Chandler, and they decided after two weeks to forget pro football and pursue their life's work. One night they packed their bags and headed for the airport. Lombardi heard about it quite by accident and hurried out to intercept both of them because he knew the staff had already decided they were good prospects. Vince gave them a good lecture about not quitting—I could appreciate that from my days with Joe Stydahar—and he ordered them back to camp.

Huff's big break was replacing incumbent middle linebacker Ray Beck, who had injured his leg, in an exhibition game against the Cardinals. Sam always contended this was more of a whim on Landry's part to satisfy a hunch—great coaching decisions are often made that way. Huff showed immediately that he had all the natural ingredients to play the position in the coordinated defense. He never was indecisive in filling a hole because he read his keys so well, and his great anticipation kept him from being fooled too often. He became the pioneer prototype middle linebacker that was so visible for the next two decades.

Landry gets a lot of the credit for that, too, because as soon as he recognized Sam's natural talents, he made him his own pet project. Both of them lived in the Concourse Plaza Hotel, a couple of blocks from Yankee Stadium, during the 1956 season, and many evenings, Tom would call Sam's room.

"Sam," he'd often say, "I have a couple of reels of film I'd like to show you for a moment or two. Could you come to my place?"

Naturally Sam would go, but those "couple of moments" usually stretched into two or three hours of intense film study. Sam got better a lot faster than anyone thought; but to his credit, he was an eager student and a very willing worker who couldn't seem to get enough football learning. The result: He really wrote the book on how to play middle linebacker in a 4-3 defense. He also had the emotional tools; like Dick Butkus and Ray Nitschke, two other Hall-of-Fame middle linebackers who followed him as stars of their teams' defenses, he was fiercely competitive. Well Mara once said he'd kick a guy in the head if that's what it took to win, but if he ever did, it was only in the spirit of competition and not because he was ever a dirty player. Sam played hard, but he was never malicious, and while it appeared he sometimes arrived late at the scene of a tackle, he was always within the nature of the game. The only guy who ever openly bitched was Jim Taylor of Green Bay, and he resented anyone who tackled him. Jim liked to intimidate people but he didn't like to be intimidated, so he and Sam had some real jousts, particularly in the 1962 title game at Yankee Stadium when they battled each other so fiercely.

His battles with Jim Brown really helped propel his fame, and the press tried to make their meetings into a personal war. This was nonsense because it never was Jim Brown versus Sam Huff; it was Jim Brown and the Cleveland Browns versus the New York Giants defense, and Sam was the man who often filled the holes where Jim ran. They rarely spoke on the field, and if so, it generally was Jim who might say after a good hit, "Nice tackle, Big Sam." This drove Huff crazy; many times he said he wished that Brown could have been nastier—as Taylor was—because he found it so difficult to play angry against him, part of Sam's personal motivation. There were also disgraceful instances when the media insinuated that Sam's southern heritage and Jim's black heritage were also a factor in the rivalry. In fact, after one game against the Browns at Yankee Stadium, Sam was getting dressed, with his son, Little Sam, standing next to him in his cubicle, when a columnist from a Long Island newspaper walked up to him and asked whether the fact that Jim was black and Sam was white and from the south made their battles all the more personal.

"If you don't get away from me this instant, I'll throw you through that door," Sam told the man, pointing to the locker room entrance. The fury in his voice was evident, but his feelings became even more obvious when he instinctively reached down and hugged his son around the shoulders.

My roommate with the Giants was Dick Modzelewski. In addition to being one of the steadiest and most dependable players, he also was one of the funniest. Mo came from coal mine country in western Pennsylvania, and he spun stories by the hour about his dad and the coal miners he grew up with. Dick never forgot where he came from, and this was reflected in his work ethic on the field. He was not the biggest player, at six feet and about 250 pounds, but he was one of the most tenacious. When he filled a hole, it stayed filled, regardless of the size of the player across from him; and he was so good at playing his position, he covered up for Grier and Huff if they didn't get into their gaps quickly enough.

He was the prime example of someone who totally believed in Landry's defense, and he pretty much memorized his playbook to learn as much as he could. In turn, he became a big help on the field to Jim Katcavage and Grier because he knew their roles as well as his own. He was just as adept as cooking his favorite Polish dishes, and when he lived at the Concourse Plaza Hotel during the season, an invitation to his apartment was much sought because no one put out a better meal. Maybe it was also because he did the dishes!

When we played in Pittsburgh, Mo always brought Kat, Rosie and me to his parents' home for Saturday night dinner. He never tired of his mother's cooking, for which I couldn't blame him. I know that even when his parents were in their eighties and still living in their home, Dick made sure he got that Saturday night meal whenever the team he was coaching got to Pittsburgh.

Katcavage was, as I noted before, like a big, raw-boned kid brother to us, but he was a super player, and was probably a better defensive player than I. If he had played in my spot, on the right where there rarely was a tight end's block to contend with, he might have had much more recognition. He certainly was as quick as any defensive end who ever played, helping to mitigate a relative lack of size (six-three, 240) when he always faced a bigger offensive tackle. We nicknamed him "Kat" not as much for his last name, but because of that quickness, which was the biggest obstacle that he had to overcome initially. He was so fast that he sometimes carried himself past his area of responsibility. But once he learned to control that quickness, I believe the two of us played as blueprinted twins in our defense. Kat's big area of responsibility was the "trap gap," and here his quickness helped him to close quickly after he read the keys. With his ability, he saved us from being burned on many potential big plays.

One of my most striking memories of Jim occurred after a play in which he was buried in the midst of several bodies, and he began to scream, "My shoulder, my shoulder." He staggered out of that pile and started to head for the sidelines.

"Where the hell are you going?" I asked him.

"My shoulder, my shoulder," he gasped again. "I don't know if it's broken."

"To hell with your shoulder," Mo said. "It's going to be fine. You stay here, we've got a defense to play and we need you."

Jim stayed and played the rest of the game, and afterward, X-rays showed the shoulder was indeed broken. I sometimes wondered, "Were we being cruel to him making him play with a broken shoulder?" At the time, it never occurred to me because playing the game was all-important. Now, I don't know.

Roosevelt Grier was a real study. He was a rookie in 1955, from Penn State, and often the toughest battles he fought were with his weight. Sometimes it ballooned over 300 pounds, and then all hell broke loose around the locker room. He spent every summer in training camp at the "fat man's table," where overweight players were rationed with salads and gelatin. Rosie went through all of that without saying a word, but we knew he went out at night after our meetings and loaded up with a plateful of goodies that undid all that he had achieved from two-a-days and three sparse meals. During the season, his stamina suffered when his weight went above 300 pounds and he always looked for timeouts on the field. "We can't, Ro, we can't," I'd tell him. "We have to save them for the offense." One time we got one, and when it ended, he wanted another. We almost strangled him.

If Grier, who was a big, lovable guy, had kept himself in some semblance of shape all the time, he would be in the Hall of Fame. In those times when he was around 280 pounds, no offensive lineman in the league could handle him one-on-one. There never has been a quicker inside lineman, and like Kat, he had to condition himself to control his gap and not overrun it. He had great agility and an amazing ability to spin off a block and catch a running back before he barely reached the hole. When he spent the 1957 season in the military, we missed him, and his absence was part of the reason why we didn't repeat as champions. Kat played inside much of the time, and he was not as effective at tackle.

Early in his NFL career, Rosie still used a technique of sticking his hand in the face of the offensive lineman while making his charge. When we played a preseason game against the 49ers, he tried that on Bob St. Clair, San Francisco's great tackle, and got buried. He tried it twice more and again St. Clair just leveled him.

"I'm quitting, Andy," he told me when he came back to the sidelines. "That man is going to kill me."

"Keep your hand out of his face. No wonder he's mad," I told him.

Rosie didn't listen. When we went back out again, he tried the same routine, and St. Clair again bashed him.

"I'm through, Andy," he said when we were on the sidelines again. "That man is dangerous."

The next time we went out on the field, Grier made three tackles and the 49ers had to relinquish the ball. As we were walking off the field I said to him, "You finally get St. Clair, Ro?"

"Oh no," he said with a big grin. "I'm smiling because he wasn't in there this time."

You couldn't help liking him; he was always very pleasant, and it was hard to ruffle him. He took a lot of kidding about his weight, but even the more serious comments seemed to disappear into what was a very large sense of humor. In 1959 Walt Yaworksy had gone down to Philadelphia to scout the Eagles, and some disparaging remarks about their ability were attributed to him. As soon as Jim Lee saw them in the paper, he called a team meeting.

"I'm afraid we have the Eagles all riled up," he told us. "They'll be so mad they'll be playing over their heads. The big question is: What are we going to do about it?"

From the middle of the room, up spoke Rosie.

"I have a suggestion, coach. Maybe we should call them up and apologize."

He broke up the meeting.

Part of our summer camp routines always seemed to be listening to— or sometimes it was enduring—Rosie as he honed his musical skills on a guitar. His warblings could be heard throughout the dorm. I particularly like his rendition of "Moonlight in Vermont," but not between double sessions, coaches' meetings and other duties when quiet was more appropriate to our ears.

All four of us made our contributions to the defense. In my own case, I always believed that while I was a spectacular player with the Rams with intercepted passes, blocked punts and running for touchdowns with fumble recoveries, I was an even better all-around player with the Giants. My reputation was built, in part, on my ability to make the so-called "big play," like sacking the quarterback on the third down, forcing a fumble near our goal line or getting a key tackle. I did all of those things, but they really were the residue of working as hard as I could on every play, always believing that I could make something good happen. That belief developed a positive attitude, and often that was the little edge I needed to get that big play.

For example, there never was any doubt in my mind that I could get the passer on third and eighteen. Most of the time I never did, but I usually got him when it counted, and those are the times that people still seem to remember. Some people used to say, "Oh, you just lay back, take it easy, and then save it all up for one play. How do you know when the big play is going to come?"

I never argued because it was clear they were watching only certain plays, and I wouldn't get into a situation where I had to defend myself against someone who didn't know what was happening. All of us played with great intensity because our defense demanded a total effort, lest the coordination be broken.

Some in the New York media nicknamed us the Fearsome Foursome. Rosie probably took that big tag out to Los Angeles when he was traded to the Rams for John Lovetere after the 1962 season. The media out there immediately hung it on the Rams' front line of Deacon Jones, Merlin Olsen, Lamar Lundy and Rosie, and it got more prominence with them than with us. But we never were much concerned with nicknames or labels, and during all our dynasty years that Giants team never really had one.

That dynasty really began in 1956, and it was then that I understood the difference between playing on the two coasts. The Rams, and even the 49ers four hundred miles to the north, represented the laid-back style of their areas with the always-favorable weather and the more relaxed approach to life that seemed to be the tenor of this rapidly growing area of the country. Both teams used a finesse style of football, preferring to outscore an opponent than take it by the throat and throttle it to death. The Giants, on the other hand, came from an area tempered by hot and cold in one football season, where mud, snow and frozen playing surfaces had to be a factor and where life was not so laid back, but rather lived at a fast pace. Results mattered above all else. This intensity was seen in the way we played football; our offensive style, relished by Lombardi, was to knock teams on their collective asses and run over them. We had the same kind of power running game that Vince used at Green Bay, complemented with a very modest passing offense. Our defense, with Landry's 4-3 coordinated scheme, was designed to choke off an opponent and force him to do everything that it had hoped to avoid. Domination was the key, and you learned to dominate or you failed.

In 1956 the New York Giants were the only major football show in New York City. Columbia still played, but it had deemphasized its program from its intersectional appeal to adhere to the new Ivy League approach. Fordham, the last of a half-dozen city schools that once played teams from across the nation before and after World War II, had abandoned the sport after the 1954 season; Army made only one appearance each season; and where there had been three professional teams less than a decade before, only the Giants remained.

That left a huge vacuum for thousands of fans who really had no one to support, and if proper timing is important to ultimate success, then the Giants won the gold medal that season. The first step was small in distance—from the Polo Grounds on the west bank of the Harlem River in upper Manhattan to the east bank of that river and Yankee Stadium in the Bronx. That stadium was the nation's preeminent outdoor sports arena, where legend and lore were partners with the familiar facade that swept around its roof and made it so distinctive and so special.

Still, no one had an inkling the Giants of 1956 were of championship caliber, or that all of the changes from 1955 would have any great effect, until we returned to play our first game at home in mid-October. At training camp there was no media to report day-to-day happenings; our exhibition games were played around the country and none of the local papers covered them, relying instead on bare-boned wire service reports; and we spent the final part of the preseason on the West Coast, where we opened against the 49ers in San Francisco.

Instead, the city focused on the Yankees and Dodgers that year, with Brooklyn fighting for its pennant to the final day of the season. The World Series then occupied all of the media attention, so we worked in absolute privacy, which really wasn't too bad. To some who had been with the club for several seasons, the most notable event of the preseason was the disappearance of the team's solid red jerseys, which I'm certain many Giants fans have long since forgotten or never even knew existed. Their last appearance was against the 49ers in a preseason game. Some of them were from the forties because the numerals were so small; others were newer with medium-sized numbers; and finally there were four we borrowed from San Francisco because we didn't have enough of our own. The 49ers had just gotten new ones, with wide, white stripes on the sleeves and huge numbers on the front and back. They didn't match ours at all, so our equipment people tried dying the sleeves red to wipe away the white stripes. The result was a red jersey with pink sleeves, but we won the game—which went to prove further that clothes don't make the team. But those old red jerseys never made it back from California.

We won two of our first three games, against the 49ers and Steelers, and in both victories linebacker Bill Svoboda played superbly. He was the leader of the defense when I joined the Giants, a fiery, peppery guy who chewed on guys if they messed up; he screamed and hollered and he got people to play. He was one tough player who played best against the run and he had a helluva season for us.

One of our most memorable games was against the Browns when Paul Brown tried to send in plays to his quarterback with a radio transmitter beamed to a receiver in the player's helmet. The NFL has resurrected this idea recently to combat crowd noise, but we had the answer that day in Cleveland when a friend of Wellington's, who had worked with radio detection during the war, set up a receiver on our bench. Bob Topp, one of our reserve ends, intercepted the Browns' signals. That idea disappeared before the end of the game, and Brown later claimed crowd noise drowned out the transmission. His quarterback, Tom O'Connell, also said he picked up a taxi dispatcher sending out calls for empty cabs.

We broke a first-place tie with the Chicago Cardinals in the Eastern Conference in early November, beating them 23-10. We took a lead in the first quarter after I blocked a punt and Kat fell on it in the end zone. Our defense held Ollie Matson, a great running back, to just 43 yards that day before 62,410 persons at the Stadium, the largest crowd ever to see the Giants play to that time.

Two weeks later the Bears tied us, 17-17, but we blew a 17-0 lead when Chicago scored 14 points in the last quarter. George Blanda was their quarterback and he threw the tying touchdown to Harlon Hill in the final minutes. Hill made one of the greatest catches I ever saw when defender Jimmy Patton tipped the ball away and Hill somehow maneuvered his body as he fell and caught the ball while lying flat on his back. Finally, we clinched the title on the final weekend, beating the Eagles, 21-7, with Don Heinrich at quarterback. Don was our "shock team" quarterback— he started games so our offense could see what the opposing defense was doing, before giving way to Charlie Conerly, who was a bit more accurate passer. Our defense held the Eagles to just 73 rushing yards and 101 passing, but long before this game I saw the team come together. It wasn't any one thing, but an almost unexplainable feeling of harmony and cohesiveness. I felt it not only on the field, but away from it. I had this tremendous sense that we were like one person, and not the two distinct units that came to be later on. The defense was still gaining an identity at that time, but the cheers and the headlines still favored the offense, though we now had everyone's attention.

In the championship game, the Bears returned to Yankee Stadium. This time, they never had a chance to get back into a game where we led, 34-7, at halftime. The weather was our biggest concern that day, and one of my major contributions was supplying sneakers for all our players that made traction on the hard, frozen surface much easier.

A few days before the game, Frank Yohan, a salesman for Keds sneakers, was in my sporting goods shop in Cos Cob and raved about the suction on a new line of sneakers. "These are great on frozen surfaces," he said, without any apparent reference to the game on Sunday. But I told my partner, Eddie Clark, "Get Frank to deliver a couple of cases of sneakers and I'll take them to the Stadium. If we wear them, then we'll be using the Keds name."

I brought enough to the Stadium for all the players, and when the temperatures that Sunday morning hovered around fifteen degrees, Jim Lee dispatched Eddie Hughes, wearing conventional cleats, and Gene Filipski, wearing the sneakers, onto the field to test the traction. Hughes slipped and fell the moment he tried to cut. Gene said he had no problems.

"We all go with sneakers," Howell declared.

I don't know whether the sneakers did it, but after the game Chicago coach Paddy Driscoll thought they did because he claimed ours had thicker soles than those worn by some of his players, and hence gave us better traction. I believe we could have played in bare feet that day and beaten the Bears because we were a dedicated team. In fact, before the game we seemed so loose and confident that Jim Lee started to fret that perhaps we didn't give Chicago enough respect, and that the weather was a factor that could hurt us.

When we returned from our pregame warmups, Lombardi went to Howell and suggested, "Let's keep it simple," and Jim Lee agreed immediately. That was best suited for our fullback, Mel Triplett, a hard, tough runner who liked to run right at people. He was 220 pounds with huge legs, and when he ran he seemed to be all knees and elbows. In a game against the Cardinals that season, he told Lombardi, "Run 99, run 99." Vince laughed becaue he knew that was Mel's pet play—a drive over Jack Stroud, who wore jersey number 66. With Mel's number 33, their numbers added up to 99. Vince sent in the play, Jack stood up in front of the defensive lineman across from him, and Triplett knocked both of them headlong into the end zone with the force of his drive.

That's how he played against Chicago. On our first possession, following Filipski's 58-yard kickoff return, he blew apart the Bears' defense and ran 17 yards for a touchdown. I recovered a fumble by Rick Casares on Chicago's first series, and Ben Agajanian, my former teammate on the Rams who had come out of retirement from the Giants to help our kicking situation (Gifford and Chandler had done some early work), kicked a field goal for a 10-0 lead. He added another one after Patton intercepted a pass, and then our defense completed a "triple" by stopping J.C. Caroline on a fourth and one late in the first quarter, setting up Alex Webster's score for a 20-0 lead early in the second. I blocked a punt late in that quarter and a rookie, Henry Moore, fell on the ball in the end zone for a touchdown and a 34-7 halftime lead.

By that time the Bears had abandoned a running game that netted them only 67 yards that day, and they tried 47 passes. We sacked their quarterbacks a half-dozen times and their work netted them just five yards per passing attempt. There was no doubt after that game that the New York Giants' defense had an orbit all its own, and some 60,000 fans gave us a thunderous ovation when our day's work had ended. I was named the most valuable defensive player. As luck had it, they didn't start giving out cars to MVPs until the next year. But in all honesty, that was the only "unlucky" thing that happened to me that season. And a great deal more good fortune still lay ahead.

3 Vince Lombardi and His Offense

No one on the Giants in the mid-fifties considered himself a revolutionary, but in fact, we had begun a revolution in professional football that, within less than a decade, raised the game to the top of the public's popularity charts and really paved the way for the great surge of riches and acclaim that has surrounded the sport over the last three decades.

But revolutions don't begin with victory parades, and when ours began, it was game-by-game, season-by-season. It is nice to look back and know I was a part of that time; and it is even a bit heady at times to be credited with changing the way the sport is played and viewed by the public. Yet in all honesty, we did not even know it was happening, and to this day, I don't believe any of us from those teams consider ourselves the founding fathers of anything. Don't get me wrong about our feelings, though. We have great pride in all that we accomplished and how we did it; and we also are very protective of the niche we eventually carved for ourselves in the history of the game. If all of us played as members of the Giants in the atmosphere of popularity and materialism that surrounds pro football today, I doubt whether our approach to the game would be any different. I'm certain that that approach in itself would give us the potential to begin a dynasty such as we established from 1956 through 1963, despite the claims of the so-called experts who say conditions are no longer conducive to dynasty-building.

Three decades ago, none of us ever thought in such historical terms because we did not set out to change history. We all lived week-by-week for five months, and at the end of the season we looked back and toted up all that we accomplished to judge whether or not we had been successful. In 1958 and 1959 we were successful to a point—we got to the NFL championship game, but we didn't win. Forget all the historical business about the 1958 game against Baltimore and how great it was; it wasn't great for me because we lost. All that we accomplished that season didn't mean too much to me when I walked out of Yankee Stadium an hour after Alan Ameche scored the winning touchdown in the fifth quarter of that game. I'll look at that in greater detail later in the book.

In 1957 we were a half-game behind the Browns with three games to

43

play before the wheels came off. To this day, I still don't know what happened, and I don't get any sure-fire solutions from anyone else either. Looking back three decades later, I can point to a training camp that began nearly three weeks earlier than usual because, as defending NFL champions, we played the College All-Stars in mid-August, winning, 22-12. Then we played five exhibition games around the country, plus our regular schedule. Early in the season, Charlie Conerly injured his right hand and never again seemed comfortable handling the ball. The 49ers and Y. A. Tittle gunned us down, 27-17, and that put us a game and a half behind the Browns with two to play. We then lost to Pittsburgh in the mud of Forbes Field and our title hopes were ended.

Still, our little revolution continued to make an impact, and professional football was solidly entrenched as Sunday's game in New York. Tom Landry's defensive system had clicked in smoothly and the cheers were ringing louder and longer than in our 1956 championship season. It was at this point that we had begun to become two distinct teams—in fact if not in execution. The public was never aware of this dichotomy because, while the defense had at last received its recognition, the offense was still the medium by which the team was judged.

Don't get me wrong, we had a fine offensive team and we were their biggest rooters. As I said, there was never any backbiting or bickering in our locker room between the two units. When we began to dominate teams, as was happening at this time, we also began to flex the power that comes with any domination. The public, though, expected the offense to dominate other defenses, and if we lost, or the game sometimes was closer than people expected, then they got the zingers.

The person who felt this most was Vince Lombardi, our offensive coach. Vince was a very sensitive person despite all that has been said and written about his so-called ferocity when he was an NFL head coach. He had come to the Giants in 1954 from Army, where he worked for Earl (Red) Blaik for five seasons in what he always described as "the graduate school of my football education." Blaik was a master of organization who stressed teaching as the ultimate form of coaching. Vince was a high school teacher and coach in New Jersey prior to his stint at West Point, and he always was proud of that teacher's role, telling us often that "a coach really is nothing but a teacher whose classroom is outdoors and who conducts a final exam every Sunday afternoon."

If Lombardi got his graduate degree in football education at West Point, he received his Ph.D. with the Giants. For five seasons Jim Lee Howell allowed him to run the offense with very little interference, and Jim felt so positive about his performance that he refused to allow Al Sherman to make any drastic changes after Sherman succeeded Vinny as offensive coach in 1959.

The image of Lombardi as a martinet with overwhelming presence is more characteristic of his time as head coach in Green Bay and Washington

44

than his tenure in New York. As an assistant with the Giants he did not project that overwhelming presence, but he was the dominant personality on our coaching staff. It was my impression that Landry even looked at him differently—not as an assistant coach judging one of his peers, but as one who saw Vince as the head coach he would become, even before Tom himself thought about a similar position. There was something about his presence, and the respect it engendered among players and coaches alike, that set him apart at that time. That was an important distinction because even though our defensive unit never dealt with him as intimately as we did with Landry, we were very aware of him.

There was no hiding his volatility. We heard it on the field when the offense made a mistake or when one of his players wasn't paying attention. He bullied them somewhat, but as he did in Green Bay, he always knew who could take public criticism and who had to be dealt with in private. He never specifically embarrassed Conerly or Frank Gifford, our two offensive stars, because he understood their status among the players and he wanted their hearts on Sunday. Again, Jim Lee played his role, and his "Hollywood characters" references spoke volumes when he felt it was time for some ass-chewing of the stars.

The offensive players always praised Lombardi's teaching ability, and like Landry he made them believe that if they followed his dictums they would succeed. But Vinny's offense was built on power and dominance, and it did not try to fool people until it has set them up to be fooled. It was as if he was telling an opponent, "We practiced all week to run off tackle against you, and that's what we're going to do—but with some wiggles here and there if it looks like you might stop us." In the meantime he had drilled his players: "By God, you'll run off tackle all afternoon, whether that other defense likes it or not," and their job was to see that it happened. He kept those "wiggles" in reserve for just the right moment, a tribute to his Brooklyn street smarts.

Lombardi was the visible architect of this offensive style, with its basic passing offense, and he got much of the credit and the attention from the press. It is to Howell's credit that he never exhibited any hurt feelings, either among us or publicly, about the credit that Vinny accumulated; and Jim passed much of it to him in his own dealings with the media. It also is to Lombardi's credit that he never flaunted his position to make Jim Lee seem anything but the boss, the man who was responsible for everything the offense achieved. Like Landry, Vinny had a healthy ego, but again like Tom, he knew his job and his place, and that was where he operated. But he ran his offensive unit as he did the Packers—tough, unrelenting and very demanding.

If Lombardi had been the defensive coach, with Landry's schemes but his own fiery disposition, it wouldn't have bothered me one bit. Maybe it was because two guys of Italian heritage understood the emotions that are part of our makeup; but more likely it was because both of us wanted to win so badly. We were even dissatisfied with a "dirty" victory—a game where we played badly but still won. I know that most who played for him revere him, and I can fully appreciate their feelings because he never did anything other than try to make his players, and his team, the best.

His personal philosophy has often been deliberately misrepresented. He is usually quoted as saying, "Winning isn't everything, it's the only thing." But he didn't say that—he said, "Winning isn't everything, but *making the all-out effort to win* is the most important thing." Vinny always stressed effort; that is why he drove his players to reach their fullest capacities. Certainly, losing upset him; he saw it as a personal affront. But that was as much due to his wounded pride when his team did not emerge from a game as the best, as it was from blaming himself when his players may not have worked to the level he felt possible. Whenever they did, and were beaten by a better team, Vince was reasonably satisfied. He never criticized players who did their best, regardless of the outcome of a game, and he ardently believed that if they always gave a total effort, they would succeed more often than fail.

That is why he drove them so hard, and why they won far more often than they lost. He was never embarrassed by success or the effort it took, as some are who still ridicule his philosophy. To me, those who say it is better to compete than to win—and totally disregard making the fullest effort to win or be the best—are life's real losers, be they in sports, in business or in public life. The acceptance of this weak-kneed philosophy is one reason why our nation is lagging further and further behind others in achieving our potential; and why we have slipped from once being the world's most powerful country to one that is scrambling to keep up and allowing itself to be bedeviled by those within who are afraid to be number one.

The key to Vince's success lay in the way he treated his players. He taught them well and proved to them that by following his dictums they could be successful; and then he was tough enough to scare them a little. The big lesson I learned from him, though, was that you could be very demanding—with teammates, employees and even your kids—and they still can have the capacity to jump up on your lap and love you. He browbeat, pushed, bullied and harassed his players, but he also had the ability to get them back to his side and make them believe all of that was for their own good. He was emotional in his approach, but he never failed to pick his players up when all of the browbeating and ass-chewing was over. Sometimes he apologized; sometimes he did it with humor when he saw they got the message; but he never left them down, or hanging by their thumbs. Others might use Lombardi's approach but walk away, leaving people in a psychological heap. Soon it becomes clear that those people are selfish, emotional animals who can only beat people down, and they are failures as leaders.

There is little doubt that for as long as he coached with the Giants, Lombardi was the leader of the offense. No single player ever stepped forward to take the job until Y. A. Tittle came to us, but it is a tribute to the team that it could still be successful without a bona fide player-leader. Gifford was the acknowledged star of the team, but it appeared to me that he never wanted the leadership role. Conerly, as the quarterback, had it to some degree, but he was content to apply it during the game.

Actually, all of us looked up to Conerly in one degree or another because we knew he really linked us to the days when Coach Steve Owen used the A-formation and the T-formation, with Charlie as his main man. Everyone was aware that for many of those years he had taken some terrible physical beatings playing with woeful Giants teams, and as is the lot of every quarterback, he had become the object of scorn by the fans in those down times. It wasn't until the team began its dynasty run in 1956 that he finally got some positive recognition. But Conerly was as unflappable in those good times as he was when he was getting worked over by the fans—and opponents. He was a soft-spoken Southern gentleman, perhaps the classic pro football star of the day. He was ruggedly handsome, with tinges of gray offsetting a tanned, slightly leathered face. He became the symbol for Marlboro cigarettes when they tried to project a typical, rugged male symbol for their product, and for years he appeared in their ads, dressed in western attire astride a horse.

Charlie had torn up the college record books with his passing at the University of Mississippi, but a series of injuries with the Giants left him with just average arm strength. He threw best to the medium-range areas, but he knew exactly where and when to throw because he was a smart quarterback who knew his own limitations so well that he maximized his many attributes in the very picturesque, sometimes methodical way he threw the football.

I always believed his most productive season, in the six I was his teammate, was in 1959 when he won the NFL passing title; not because of his 1,700 yards and 14 touchdowns but because he threw only four interceptions over an entire season. He attempted 194 passes that year, which gave him one interception for every 49 passes—a remarkable average that underlined his fine ability always to do the correct thing with the ball (in 1956 he had led the league in fewest interceptions with seven in 134 throws). Charlie led NFL passers in that key area three times in his career, including that championship 1956 season, and he proved to me that he always cared more for his team than racking up impressive personal yardage statistics. In that respect, he was a most unselfish player, and he sometimes paid a fearsome price by eating the ball rather than making a dumb or careless play.

His 1956 season was his all-around best, but that year he had a healthy supporting cast for most of the year. In 1959, when we won a third Eastern Conference title, our offense, with a new coordinator in Al Sherman, ebbed and flowed all year. But when the flow went well, Charlie was the reason. Early in our first game that year against the Rams in LA, he passed 67 yards to Bob Schnelker for a touchdown; and then he came back with that same play with just three minutes left in the game for a 35-yard completion on fourth and eleven that set up Pat Summerall's game-winning field goal. When we clinched the title that year with a rollicking 48-7 victory over Cleveland at Yankee Stadium, Charlie threw three touchdown passes. He still holds the Giants' team records for most attempts (2,833), completions (1,418), yards (19,488) and touchdown passes (173), but perhaps his most significant statistic is, despite having to play with weak and sometimes undermanned teams for part of his career, he has the lowest career interception rate.

That last figure was a tribute to his approach to the game, and it always puzzled me why he sat on the bench at the start of a game while Don Heinrich worked the first quarter—a sort of "shock troops" approach. Both of them had the same passing style and arm strength, but Lombardi somehow felt that Don could get a feel of the game more quickly and find out what the other team was doing, and then turn everything over to Charlie and work with him from the sidelines for the rest of the day.

This system took two special people to make it work, and there never was any friction or animosity between them because of their less-than-definitive roles during Heinrich's four seasons with us. I think Don also endured the situation because he believed he was heir apparent to Conerly. But the Giants traded him before Charlie retired. Heinrich was a tough cookie and once, when one of the players tried to suggest a play, he snapped at him: "Shut up. I'm running this ball club out here." He did too, and he had a good mind for the game.

Conerly also did a great job of setting up another passing weapon—the halfback option pass that Frank Gifford used so effectively for much of his career. This play was Lombardi's pet "gadget," and he, of course, used it with much effectiveness in Green Bay with Paul Hornung, who had the benefit of once being a Heisman Trophy quarterback. Conerly got great mileage from Gifford around the ends and off the tackles, but when our power sweeps were going well and Frank was flashing for big yards, Charlie always seemed to know just the right moment to spring his trap with the option pass.

Gifford was the perfect player for such trickery. An excellent athlete, perhaps the team's best-ever all-around player, Frank came from the University of Southern California as an offensive player and wound up playing in the defensive backfield during some of the early years of his career. As I mentioned, he also did some of our placekicking in 1956, but his most productive time was as an offensive back.

He did not have great speed, but he did possess a very fluid running style and the ability to see the field around him as he ran. He always moved to where he could make yardage. He was a gliding, sliding runner, the kind that is often harder for a defense than the power guy, or even the speedster, because he never gives you a big target; nor is anticipation much good because that kind of runner rarely winds up where you expect. This style suited Gifford best; he was not a brutish type of runner who could pound away inside, even on short-yardage plays where he had to push the pile. If he broke a play inside, it was usually because the defense expected him to go outside so that our interior linemen got a good pop on guys leaning the wrong way. If Gifford wasn't used on missed key third- or fourth-down plays, as happened in the 1959 title game against the Colts, giving Baltimore the momentum to gain the lead, the second-guessers had a field day, saying that Frank should have gotten the ball. But he wasn't the man for that job, and we had our greatest success with him as a runner when he got to the outside.

After he missed the 1961 season following a serious head injury in 1960, Sherman put him outside as a flanker, and while he made some big plays at that position, I always felt he was less productive than at running back. The idea, of course, was to get him the ball and allow his running skills to take over, but how many times can that happen to a flanker in one game? Consequently, in those seasons we always were searching for a halfback.

Frank was also the first of our era to really take advantage of the publicity and notoriety that pro football began to offer. He had the "star" syndrome from his days at Southern California, along with the handsome features, and he had set his sights on a movie and television career. He worked in both areas and then got into broadcasting while he was a player. Frank, like Charlie Conerly, was also an intimate member of the Giants "family" that was highly visible around New York City during the season, particularly when Tim Mara, Jr., joined the entourage. Now, of course, Gifford has become a very successful television sportscaster and applied some of those "elusive" skills to weather the storms and adversities that seem to mark *Monday Night Football*.

But on the football field Gifford was a perfect partner for Alex Webster, who had the physical power and determination to take on anyone. Alex came to the Giants in 1955 from the Canadian Football League, where he had led the Montreal Allouettes to the Grey Cup title, was the game's MVP, and the league's leading rusher—all of that after being cut by the Washington Redskins, where he had been ticketed to play safety. At the time the Canadian League was raiding the NFL and luring some of its better players with more money. So, I was told, Tim Mara, Sr., said, "Let's stop this nonsense and get one of their stars." Mr. Mara knew all about Webster from Montreal's coach, Peahead Walker, who was a close friend. Walker had coached against Alex when he played at North Carolina State and Peahead was head coach at Wake Forest.

No physically tougher player has ever worked in the NFL; nor has there been one with more love and enthusiasm for the game. He seemed to live to play football, and maybe he appreciated it more than most back then because it was his ticket out of the smog and hard life of Kearney, New Jersey, a mill town behind Jersey City that, while less than five miles from the glitter of Manhattan, is a million miles away in its way of life.

Alex was always a bit different from the so-called "Hollywood types" on the offense, and Sam Huff once said he belonged with the defense because he was so tough. In our camp scrimmage we often took delight in sticking some of the glamour guys, but we probably treated Alex with more respect because he gave as good as he got. He was that way in the locker room too—if someone on the offense got out of line, or wasn't in the spirit of the team, Alex called the guy aside and gave him the word. He also took rookies aside and let them know what was expected of them.

But Webster set a bigger example with his playing. He was always the one guy on the offense you could count on once he stepped on the field, and there were many Sunday afternoons when his battered body belonged anyplace but on a football field. He was a gutty player, not very fast and not a particularly good pass receiver, but he gained yards and he caught passes. He stuck his nose into the tight areas, and when it was third and two and he was in the game as the fullback, there was no doubt who would get the call and who would get the yardage. Howell called him the best short-yardage back he ever saw, and that was more a tribute to his determination than any great running skill.

Alex was a smart runner who never seemed to go fast, but who had great peripheral vision and the ability to make people miss with a quick move here, another there—and just when it seemed he was about to be nailed, he always seemed to have one more move left to get another few yards. Years later, when he was head coach of the Giants and Ron Johnson was accumulating his thousand-yard seasons, Alex tried to convince Johnson he could do the same. It galled him to see Ron run out of bounds when a defender was near rather than using a move to make the defender miss, and then go on for more yardage. He tried to convince Ron, without much success, to "shift gears" when he ran, to set up defenders with changes of pace before turning on the quick bursts or utilizing the speed Webster never had. Alex knew what he was talking about—he had made his living with this style of running, and it is why he is the team's all-time rushing leader with more than 4,600 yards.

Webster certainly knew how to run with the ball and work defenders in the open field after he caught a pass. He had a bit of shake-and-bake, but he also had great ability to utilize his blockers. Gifford did too, but Frank had more quickness to burst into seams or openings that his blockers provided for him. Alex stayed with his blockers to the point of impact, then he made his moves.

Alex also was the consummate team man. If he was a lead blocker, he did it with as much enthusiasm as if he were carrying the ball. In a game against Baltimore he got kicked in the ribs by Colts defensive back Johnny

Sample on a running play and then heard Sample brag about it. On the next play he became a lead blocker and chased Sample halfway down the field before he evened the score. When he was called on to pass block, he took on Gino Marchetti with the same gusto he took on a smaller back like Sample.

Webster also had great tolerance for pain, but a severe distaste for going to hospitals to make it disappear. In 1957 he missed a game against Philadelphia because of an infected ear that forced Doc Sweeney to put him into St. Elizabeth's Hospital for treatment. It ultimately cost him the use of that ear, but at the time all that concerned Alex was getting out and playing against the 49ers. Doc wasn't hearing any of that so Alex finally called Jack Mara.

"Jack, let's make a deal," he said over the phone. "If you give me permission to leave the hospital and play on Sunday, I promise you I'll go right back in after the game."

"I can't do that, Alex," Jack replied. "You're Doc Sweeney's patient, and you stay in the hospital until he tells you to leave."

Alex stayed and we lost the game, for a variety of reasons, but his not being there certainly was one of them. I also believe that as head coach of the Giants in 1970 and 1972 he utilized his great inner determination to help produce better teams than seemed possible with such limited talent. Granted, in 1970 Fran Tarkenton was the team's quarterback, but Alex had the capacity to get him, for one of the few times in his career, to work for the team's benefit rather than solely for his own glory. In 1972 he also helped Norm Snead have the only great season of his career.

Kyle Rote had the same way of relating with people, perhaps better than anyone on those teams. Everyone liked him, and I guess you could say that he was everybody's buddy. But he also commanded a great deal of respect as a person, which is why so many players named children after him. Kyle had a very quiet, soft-spoken manner, but he always seemed to have time for everyone who spoke to him. In a sense, he was charming without ever trying to be, and this genuine quality made him a lot of friends in and out of the game.

He was also a very gifted football player. When I came to the Giants in 1956, he had been a wide receiver for two seasons, after knee injuries affected his running-back skills. Actually, he says Tom Landry was the one who suggested the move to Jim Lee Howell. As a player, Tom had worked against him in practice and saw his great natural receiving ability. Even with the success he had for seven seasons as a split end and flanker, I always believed that, like Gifford, he was a better running back, though I know he didn't believe his knees could have withstood the punishment. Still, I thought it was a waste to put him outside with that great talent. He was so natural running with the ball, making cuts and doing all of the things he always did so well as a halfback.

I just never understood the logic of putting great running backs outside, where they still got tackled—and pass receivers got worse jolts from defensive backs than running backs ever received because those blasts often came with their backs turned and their bodies in full extension—and where they still made cuts and did all of the physical actions they once did running the football. I know that Kyle had some fine seasons for us out there, but as in Gifford's case, he got the ball only a few times each game. That meant there were about 80 percent of the plays when either of them didn't see it. That's a huge chunk of nonaction for talented runners, and I always took the pragmatic—and maybe not too Christian—view that, instead of worrying about a guy's knees, you should worry about the people who have to open the hole and make sure they do their job to lessen the beating the guy with bad knees has to take.

But Rote was such a tremendous team player that he did everything he was asked, on and off the field. Though he led by example on the field, he probably was too nice a guy off it to cope with many who claimed to be his friends but who really had their own self-interests at heart. Kyle was almost too nice to ever say no to the attention and all the bright lights that shone on him. When we were assistant coaches under Sherman, I saw some of Rote's vulnerability, that gentle, sensitive nature that was the antithesis of the grind-'em-up life in New York. Kyle was very happy being the Giants' offensive coordinator, and with his job as sports director for radio station WNEW. In fact, his coaching talents, particularly in helping to design our offense, were excellent, and he played a key role in the offense that Y. A. Tittle used so spectacularly in 1962 and 1963.

After Rote left the Giants, he had fine success for several years as a football broadcaster for NBC. When that career ended, I helped him and another friend of mine get together and form an air freight company, Forty-Four Air Freight. Kyle's son, Kyle Jr., of course, became a very talented and renowned professional soccer star and followed his dad's footsteps into broadcasting.

The other offensive force during that time was Mel Triplett, the man who was all arms and elbows when he ran. He had excellent power, but he also considered himself Conerly's personal bodyguard and took great pride in the very unglamorous task of pass protection. Mel had a big upper chest but thin calves, and he was really a smaller type fullback. The biggest mystery about him was his pass receiving—whether he would catch the ball. In one 1956 game against the 49ers they didn't even bother to cover him on one play, and he caught the ball and ran for a touchdown. Mel also had a tendency to fumble the ball at times, but this was due more to his tenacity as a runner than sheer carelessness. He had good, quick feet, and once he got going he was a real load for any defense.

Our offense at the time was bulwarked by a fine front five, perhaps underrated because they worked in the shadow of the stars. As is still the case, no one—media or fans—really knew what they did. I did because I worked against that unit in practice, and I was particularly well-versed on Roosevelt Brown, our great left tackle. We worked against each other every day, and as so often happens, we helped make each other better, and, I guess, we helped each other into the Hall of Fame. No matter who we played, I never faced a better offensive tackle than Rosey, so my work against him meant I was always going against the best, and he kept me sharp for any other competition. I tried to do the same thing for him in every drill, and what we did for each other often happens when great players on the same team work together. There is no greater learning tool than working against a great player. There is something in the nature of both men that makes each go harder against the other.

Rosey, of course, was a twenty-seventh-round draft pick from Morgan State College in Baltimore. Wellington picked him sight unseen in the 1953 draft after seeing him listed on the black college All-America team. That pick, of course, turned into one of the great rags-to-riches stories in pro football history when Rosey became a starter his rookie season and stayed there until his retirement in 1965. He made nine Pro-Bowl teams, most in the team's history, and went to his first one with me in 1956.

By current standards, Rosey was not a big player, and seeing him today, he actually looks undersized for an offensive tackle. He was six-two, 240 pounds, but back in the fifties and early sixties he was one of the league's biggest tackles. Brown was the perfect physical specimen, with a thirty-one-inch waist bisecting a marvelously sculpted upper body that just rippled with a natural muscle structure and included a pair of arms like the drive shafts of a steam locomotive. His legs were perfectly proportioned to his torso so that he was always perfectly balanced and in the correct line with his blocking angle. He was not only a tenacious pass blocker, but he also had tremendous speed and could pull from his left tackle spot for sweeps going around right end, right out front in perfect timing with the runner. On the punting teams he was often the first man down under a kick to make a play, as happened in a game in 1959 against Green Bay when he downed a 55-yard punt by Don Chandler on the three yardline. Tackles just aren't supposed to do those things, but Ro was no ordinary tackle.

Rosey and Jack Stroud were guys who belonged on the defense because they were like us; and as I said, we used them in goal-line defense situations. The huge Yankee Stadium crowd always let out a mighty roar when Rosey and Jack ran onto the field for this special duty. If we tossed the opposing team outside the five yardline, we took them out and the crowd rocked the place with cheers. With his quick feet and great strength, Brown could have played defense with the same agility and ferocity that he played offensive tackle.

Rosey's greatest legeacy was that he worked so hard to come from an almost nondescript draft pick—we used to kid each other about coming into the league at the tail end of a draft where the bonuses and salaries were sparse—to being such a great player who made it to the Hall of Fame. If any player who signs as a free agent or is a low-round draft pick ever wonders whether he has a chance, let him talk to Rosey. Better still, let him look at some of his game films...then go out and work as hard.

Jack Stroud should be in the Hall of Fame because he was a great offensive lineman—and a magnificent team player. Probably the only reason he hasn't made it yet is that he was moved around so much during his career that he never got the recognition at one position that Rosey Brown did at left tackle. Jack played both guard and both tackle spots during his career—and in 1962, he played them all—and his performance never fluctuated. He was a coach's dream, an in-between size lineman who could adjust to both positions, thus saving a roster spot, but one who always gave top performances.

Jack was the first player on the Giants to use weightlifting in the off-season to build up his strength, and we thought he was crazy to expend all of that effort. No one had any kind of organized strength programs in those days, and all we did was run some before camp to get our legs in shape and then use the blocking sleds to build up our strength, with drills designed to help us play a particular position. For instance, I used them for quickness but never for bulk or strength because I didn't have to pick up a guy and throw him aside. I had to get out of his way, be able to spin right or left and use my hands or forearms as leverage to get off the blocker.

But Stroud had it all figured out for himself. All of that weight work enabled a man, not quite six feet, one inch, to move outside to tackle and take on bigger defensive ends; and also play guard and handle bigger defensive tackles. He was a smart, heady player, who, when he wore his glasses in the locker room, looked professorial with his serious demeanor and businesslike way he approached his job. Jack was another who gravitated to the defense, and we began a close friendship that lasts to this day. In fact, when I was head coach of the Brooklyn Dodgers of the Continental Football League in 1966, Stroud was my offensive coordinator and line coach, and he showed me a great capacity to teach when he took a group of undersized players who played mostly for fun and formed a fine unit at that level of play.

Jack was the captain of his University of Tennessee team in 1950 under Bob Neyland, one of college football's legendary coaches and a renowned disciplinarian. He also served two tours in the Army, before and after college, so he brought a great sense of the real world into our team, and I, for one, certainly appreciated it. I guess what really attracted me was that he didn't tag along with the Hollywood types. He seemed more comfortable with those of us who might sit around and bitch a bit and see the beauty of knocking someone down as being at least the equal of scoring a touchdown or making a big run.

Jack was also a ferocious battler on the field, and if one of our guys—particularly one of the quarterbacks—got into a jam or started jawing at someone for a late hit, Jack was always there as the enforcer. When he showed up, the matter was ended, but he did have this unusual rivalry with Darris McCord, a defensive lineman for the Detroit Lions and, ironically, also a Tennessee graduate. In fact, during Jack's early seasons with the Giants, he and McCord both lived in Knoxville, Tennessee, site of the university, and both used to work out together.

Somehow, after McCord cracked one of Stroud's teeth that togetherness wore off, and whenever we played the Lions thereafter, the two of them really went after each other. We played a preseason game in Cleveland against the Lions in 1962, when the Browns ran doubleheaders, and after a draw play, Jack was straightening up when McCord slammed him in the back. Since the play was over, Jack was not expecting the blow, and the two of them had some words. Our offensive line coach, Ed Kolman, saw the confrontation from the sidelines, and he immediately took Jack out of the game.

"What did you do that for, Ed?" Jack asked when he reached the bench.

"Because you were going to hit him," Kolman replied.

"Well, I'm going to hit him anyway," Jack said.

"Now Jack," Kolman pleaded. "Calm down, it's only an exhibition game."

That didn't mollify Jack one bit, and he bided his time on the sidelines until there were about forty-five seconds to play. Suddenly, he ran into the game, threw his substitute out of the huddle, and then trotted to the line of scrimmage for what was probably the final play of the game. McCord was a bit astonished to see him.

"What do you have for us this time, Jack?" he asked, as all defensive players do when an offense is killing the clock in the final seconds.

"I'll show you," Jack replied, and when the center snapped the ball, he hauled off and whaled him with an uppercut.

Both of them went at it until players and officials pulled them apart. Jack had his arms pinned and McCord was still swinging away until the referee stopped him and led him to the sidelines and out of the game. In those days that was an automatic fifty-dollar fine—something that Pete Rozelle instituted when he became commissioner because he felt fighting demeaned the game. When Bert Bell was commissioner, he felt the same way, but he never minded too much during the exhibition season. If you got tossed out, it was a freebie.

As McCord was being led away, no one said anything to Jack, and he thought he got the best of the deal. But the referee walked back into the Giants' huddle and said, "Okay, number 66, you're out of the game, too."

Jack gave him his most innocent look and said, "Who, me?" as he was led to the sidelines and thus also fined fifty dollars.

"You know," he told me with a laugh after the game, "I just paid eight dollars to play in an exhibition game and fight Darris McCord."

"What do you mean?" I asked.

"We get fifty dollars for playing the game, but after taxes it comes to forty-two dollars," he replied. "I have to pay the league fifty bucks for getting tossed out of the game, so that means I'm eight bucks behind...eight bucks to play and fight in front of 80,000 people!"

Jack always saw the humor in such zany situations, and this great spirit, as well as his own inner tenacity, helped him overcome the tragic loss of his son, Jack Jr., who died suddenly several years ago after a preseason football practice at Tennessee.

That offensive line was anchored by Ray Wietecha, our center and one of the best all-around athletes ever to play for the Giants. One of the smartest centers I ever saw, Ray always had the game under control. As a defensive player, I had an opportunity to see how other centers adjusted the blocking schemes for their offensive linemen, and no one did a better job of this than Wietecha. He was alert to even the subtlest nuances of an opposing defense.

Actually, Ray's coming to the Giants was another coup for Well Mara. The Chicago Bears thought they were the only team that knew Ray had played a year at Michigan State before transferring to his alma mater, Northwestern. Ray was eligible to be drafted in 1953, though he still had a year's eligibility remaining even though his original Michigan State class had graduated, so the Bears told him he would be picked by them in the twentieth round. But Wellington also knew Wietecha's status, and he selected him as a "future" choice in the twelfth round.

However, Ray also had signed a baseball contract with the Washington Senators' organization, and he was sent to their Charlotte, North Carolina, farm club that summer. With great power, he led the league in home runs and runs batted in, but batted only .260—*only* .260 today might get him into the major leagues.

He began to wonder whether the road to the big leagues might be too slow compared to being able to play professional football right away. Before he could make any decision, the Marines called him to active duty during the Korean War, and he spent two years as a captain. When he was discharged, he decided to forgo baseball and signed a contract with the Giants. Senators' owner Calvin Griffith accused the club of tampering. NFL commissioner Bert Bell ordered him out of camp, and Ray went home to East Chicago with both his baseball and football careers in limbo. But the Giants were determined to get him. John Rapacz, their starting center, was coming to the end of his career, and they finally got an okay from the NFL office.

However, Ray had told his grandmother to use her native Polish to answer the telephone, so repeated calls by Wellington and Jack Mara, as well as from coach Steve Owen, simply didn't get through. Finally, Well brought in Kolman, who also spoke Polish, and one of the most interesting transactions in Giants history was finished.

While Ray gained his fame with the Giants as their starting center for eight seasons, he spent his first two as a linebacker in passing situations, subbing for Jack Cannady, as well as an offensive end and defensive back. Ray had a distinguished coaching career in the NFL, including time with Vince Lombardi's NFL champions; he also spent five years with the Giants as offensive line coach, three of them when I was director of operations.

Don Maynard also came to us as a rookie in 1958, but he made his biggest splash in New York two years later when he joined the New York Titans of the new American Football League and became a star wide receiver. Don, of course, was just inducted into the Hall of Fame after becoming one of pro football's all-time great receivers, though there was no way to tell that could happen when he was with us for just one season. He was primarily a punt returner, but not a very steady receiver because he was intimidated by Lombardi. As often happens, he became so afraid of making a mistake that if affected his concentration.

Taken together, that offense was fine in its time, but it was not nearly as spectacular as the one that Y. A. Tittle ran during the 1961-63 seasons. But then, Vince Lombardi never was a flamboyant person, just a helluva great coach who knew how to win...and to make others around him become winners. That was his legacy with the Giants as it was every place he coached.

4 A Dynasty Continues through Sudden Death

Memories of people, not games and plays, tackles and sacks, are the riches I brought from my playing days in the NFL. I'm still asked about certain games or certain plays, but nearly everything that happened on the field back then really has become an elusive target for my memory, though some of my teammates still remember them in great detail and relish the retelling. I must admit, I always enjoy the remembering.

Still, there are some things I have never forgotten. Our rivalries with the Cleveland Browns and Baltimore Colts, and all that went with them, are still very vivid for me. I guess that is true of anyone who became emotionally involved with the Giants back in the late fifties. Our rivalry with those two teams really was the place from which an entire nation—not just a city or a section of the country—started a love affair with pro football. I'm certain the younger generation of fans may tire at times of hearing their elders talk about those games and their participants; they really can't relate to them, nor to the impact they had on all of us. But mention Jimmy Brown, Johnny Unitas or Raymond Berry...Paul Brown, Week Ewbank or Gino Marchetti to any older Giants fan, and the lights go up. Mine, too, because they were some of the principals during the 1958 and 1959 seasons who totally involved our team and determined to a large degree its destiny, as well as the destiny of the game of professional football.

So, too, did the relatively new medium of television. All of the events involving the Giants and those teams and their principals were seen by millions across the nation. That is commonplace now, but thirty years ago not that many people were aware of the marvelous drama that pro football can present. After our NFL title game against the Colts in 1958, it exploded into view and sent the sport on its upward spiral. Until then, the game still was behind college football and major league baseball in popularity, but neither of them ever spellbound a nation as dramatically as we did in just a handful of games against the Browns and Colts.

As far as I'm concerned, the setting was perfect: the Giants' defense against the offensive power of the Cleveland Browns and their master coach, Paul Brown...and then against the amazing feats of a young, daredevil quarterback named Johnny Unitas...and the Giants' offense with a grand old quarterback named Charlie Conerly forming a neat backdrop against which all of this was presented.

I'm not taking anything away from our offense when I say that the Giants' defense became the focal point of these dramas. In 1958, and in 1959 when we again won the conference title, our defense finally became recognized as a new, dominant force in the game. Tom Landry had perfected his system in 1956 and 1957, and when the 1958 season began we felt that no one could match us—though it didn't seem that easy at first when we split our first four games. Tom put the final cog in place when Cliff Livingston became the strongside, or left, linebacker and worked so well with Sam Huff and Swede Svare. Livvy had been a sub for most of his first four seasons with the Giants, after following his brother Howie to the team. He was an excellent player against the run, and at six feet, three inches, and 218 pounds, he was strong enough to take on the tight end. Cliff also had fine quickness, and perhaps his most famous play occurred early in the second half of the 1958 title game against the Colts, when he stepped in and threw Alan Ameche for a five-yard loss on fourth down, at our one yardline, when Ameche was looking for a receiver on a fullback-option pass. He was also an excellent role player who took his football seriously and disciplined himself on the field to play well next to Kat and Mo in our coordinated defense.

Cliff also knew how to enjoy thoroughly the good life in New York. He won $10,000 on the TV quiz show, "Name That Tune" in 1958, and he usually attended most theater openings, often arriving in his Mercedes 300SL. There was no mistaking his Californian background; his hair always had a blond tint, and he seemed perpetually tanned. One day we were just about set to fly out of Dallas without him when he came rushing on board the plane clad only in a bathing suit. He told us he had fallen asleep in his hotel with the bathing suit on, and while he was sleeping someone had stolen all of his clothes. You can imagine the reaction to that story!

When Cliff joined Huff and Svare our package of blitzes became so spectacular that someone made them members of the "Red Dog Society of America." I never found out what that was, but a *Red Dog* was one of the terms used to describe a blitz. I always preferred the term *blitz* to describe those stunts, and that pretty much became universal. In fact, our kids had a pet German shepherd whom we named Blitz, and he looked the part!

Svare played with me on the Rams, where he was a defensive end and linebacker. He and Don Paul are the two linebackers whom I most credit for helping me have a long and productive career: Don because of his tutelage during my rookie year; Swede because of the winning bond we formed on the field that allowed me to make so many eye-catching plays. When I released from my position I never worried whether he had everything covered. Because of that great confidence and respect we had for each other's abilities, and because each of us knew Tom Landry's system so intimately, we formed the perfect partnership. In fact, when Tom left to become head coach of the Cowboys in 1960, Svare became our defensive coach and I became defensive line coach while continuing to play.

Swede had great skills to be an outside linebacker, a position that demands a player be a combination defensive end, tackle and defensive back as well as linebacker. He also had to be the best blitzer on the team because the most deadly pressure on the passer always comes from the weak side, where there is no tight end to block. Most teams are predominantly right-handed and keep their tight end on that side. Most quarterbacks are right-handed as well, so when they drop back to pass their heads are turned away from the left, making it difficult to pick up the weak-side linebacker's blitz immediately. When we went on the all-out blitz, teams had some tough blocking choices to make very quickly; and running backs staying in to block often found the package too tough to handle. Swede also exhibited great anticipation in his pass drops and played excellent position in the short areas. He was quick enough to handle some backs or tight ends on his side as well. In a 1959 game against the Eagles, he deftly stepped in front of a Norm Van Brocklin pass and raced 80 yards for a touchdown.

But when we talk about intercepting passes and making spectacular plays, no one can overlook Emlen Tunnell. The fact that he is in the Hall of Fame and is number two in NFL career interceptions with 79 is proof enough of his greatness. But you had to be around him as a teammate to really appreciate Emlen the man, as well as Emlen the player. First of all, there is something special about someone who hitchhikes from Philadelphia to New York City and arrives for a tryout with a buck fifty in his pocket because he is so certain he will get the job. Emlen did that in 1948 when he first visited Wellington Mara.

"If you have enough guts to come in here and ask for a job, I'm going to give you a chance," Well told him, and he did, signing him as the Giants' first black player.

Emlen is one of those rare players who transcends his time. He was not the biggest guy in the world, at slightly over six feet, and 200 pounds, but he was a natural strong safety in Landry's defense. His best seasons actually were behind him when Landry put in this defense, but Em still accumulated thirteen interceptions in three seasons before moving on to Green Bay in 1959. There was not a smarter, sharper or more cunning defensive back in the NFL. What some call a "lurker," he always looked to the quarterback as if he were out of position. But as soon as the pass was thrown in that area Emlen would suddenly be up on the receiver and in perfect position to make the play.

Tunnell almost seemed a contradiction, a tough player who was very loose and unassuming—but not on the field. Once the game began, he was aggressive and sometimes fanatical in the way he played; and no one ever questioned his toughness since he did nearly all of the team's punt returns until Gene Filipski came to the team in 1956. And even at age thirty-six he shared the job. In the locker room he sometimes reminded me of Deacon Dan Towler, with his sage philosophy delivered in a very laid back style that again belied his fiery competitiveness. Emlen coached the Giants secondary for many years, establishing "Emlen's Gremlins" in the mid-sixties when Spider Lockhart, Willie Williams, Clarence Childs and Henry Carr were young players, and for long after that he went out of his way to help the young players.

When Vince Lombardi became Green Bay's head coach, his first trade was to get Tunnell, not only because Emlen knew Landry's defensive system, but because Vince needed a veteran player to give leadership to a team that had never won anything. Em played through 1961, the year the Packers beat us for their championship. That game was played on New Year's Eve afternoon in Green Bay, and that evening, a friend once told me, he saw Emlen standing at the end of a festive downtown bar, beseiged by happy Packer fans. One of them clapped him on the back and said, "Emlen isn't this the greatest city you ever saw?"

"Aw man," he said, "I'm from New York. That's the greatest city I ever saw."

"But what about the Packers?" the man persisted. "We just won the NFL championship today."

"Hey, that's great," Emlen said. "But I'm still a New York Giant."

And he was, right to the day nearly ten years ago when he died suddenly of a heart attack in our training camp at Pace College.

Though Emlen might have been past his prime when Landry installed his system, he was exactly the kind of player Tom needed to help solidify it...and the Cleveland Browns were exactly the team we needed to beat to make us famous. All of the shutouts, sacks and skimpy yardage figures really didn't mean much against Washington, Philadelphia or the Chicago Cardinals. But when we handled the mighty Browns, coached by Paul Brown, everyone noticed. When I joined the Giants, their rivalry with Cleveland had long been the most intense in the NFL, and it only got hotter when we started our dynasty years because the Browns were our chief rivals for dominance of the Eastern Conference.

But what I remember most about the Browns isn't any one player or any one game, but all that went with them. The trips to Cleveland to play the Browns are still unforgettable, not so much for the games we won but for what we had to overcome. For example, when we went to Washington to play the Redskins, it was a joyride. We played cards all the way down on the train, looked forward to going to Duke Ziebert's that night for a good dinner, thought of creaming the Redskins the next day, and finally, took a happy train ride home.

It was totally different when we played the Browns. When we took the train to Cleveland, the overnight trip ended in an awesome stadium filled with fans who made you feel that you didn't have a friend in the world, and you had to fight them as well as their team. There was the cold, damp weather, icy winds whipping in off Lake Erie and, if we played in Cleveland late in the season, a rutted, frozen field that was like a gravel road. Finally, though we may have had all the keys to beat the Browns, there still was the specter of Paul Brown coaching against you, with all of his knowledge and resourcefulness...and of course, Jim Brown with his great supporting cast. In short, it was a bitch!

Conventional defensive thinking did not work against the Browns' great offense. Because the Browns were our chief rival in the conference, Landry had to develop his coordinated defense; we had to find a way to beat them before we could win any titles. Tom later said that he had to match wits with Paul Brown, and in so doing, Brown forced him to become a better coach since Tom had to develop a system that neutralized everything Cleveland's offense did so well. Contrary to what many may have thought, the Browns never tried to overpower a team physically, though they had big, powerful fullbacks like Marion Motley, Curley Morrison, Ed Modzelewski and of course Jim Brown. Instead, they always tried to take advantage of an opponent's poor defensive positioning. A defensive lineman could be firing so far across the line of scrimmage that he took himself out of the play without even being blocked. The freed offensive player then helped to double-team another defender.

Another scheme depended on the positioning of the defensive end and outside linebacker. If they lined up inside the farthest offensive player on the line of scrimmage, Cleveland automatically pitched the ball to a halfback after blocking down on them. If those defensive players moved outside the farthest offensive player on the line, they faked the pitch, cross-blocked the end and came inside where there was no linebacker.

When we got into the gaps and closed down the holes along the line of scrimmage, Tom's concept worked against these options and effectively bottled up their great running game, which, from 1957 on, was built around Jim Brown. Actually, Cleveland had to depend on Brown for nearly all of its offense. After Otto Graham retired in 1955, they never had a great passer to worry our defense. Milt Plum was the starter from 1957 through 1961, but he was always easy picking because he did not have a strong arm and he was so easy to read. If he backpedaled without turning his back, we knew he was going to throw to the short areas, to his backs or tight end. When he sprinted back into the pocket, he immediately faced the way he was going to throw, so our defensive backs read the way he was facing and quickly moved to that side. Even when he had time to throw, we knew that, because he mistrusted his own arm strength, he often came off the long pattern to dump the ball to outlet receivers for short gains. In the end, we pretty much held the Brown's passing game in disdain and turned the bulk of our energies to shutting down Jim Brown and Bobby Mitchell.

Since the Browns didn't seem to challenge us physically along the line of scrimmage with their position game, and because they rarely changed their blocking patterns, we often became lethargic as the game progressed, when it always seemed as if there really was no hard contact. We became frustrated, and frustration led to breakdowns—which was a part of their thinking—when we forgot our responsibilities and abandoned or overran an area of responsibility. That was when they made big plays.

As a sort of tonic for those frustrating times, we developed our "40 Blast" defense, an all-out rush by the front four and the three linebackers. Whether it was the right call didn't matter; the idea was to get going, run over someone and feel as if we were doing something. Then we went back to our coordinated defense. But if we didn't do something drastic at times, playing Cleveland was like swimming in a school of bluefish—they nipped and bit at you until you found yourself bleeding to death without even knowing it was happening.

Stopping the run was only Phase One of Landry's plan against the Browns. Phase Two was getting into Paul Brown's mind and thinking along with him. Because he sent in all the plays, with the help of his coaches in the spotting booths, the human element was very important in each game. Landry tried to predict the human element, picking up the tendencies by down, distance, place on the field, time of game, score and the other ingredients the Browns used in their decision-making. We perfected our system against Cleveland to the point that when they lined up we knew from their formation, and from the frequencies we had charted, exactly where they were going to run. You can't imagine how confident we felt when we knew everything they would do at any time of the game. Ironically, there were many lesser teams in the NFL that scared us to death because they were so unpredictable.

Paul Brown knew what we were doing, but he never changed his tactics. From all I know of him, his great singlemindedness and total belief that his system was correct led him to assume that you would make the big mistake and fall into his traps. We did occasionally, but only our overzealousness to get to Jim Brown allowed him to break a big play, such as in the second game of the 1958 season when he ran 65 yards up the middle for a touchdown on the first play of the game.

We hadn't wasted any time in getting to know Jim—we played against him in his first NFL game in 1957, and he nicked us for 89 yards in 21 carries as Cleveland won, 6-3, on Lou Groza's field goal in the closing seconds. We learned a big lesson immediately: though we held the Browns to just 122 yards rushing and only 40 passing, we allowed Brown's running to dominate, and we lost. But for as long as I played and coached against him, Jim Brown had good days against us only if we didn't maintain the discipline in our defense and became too anxious to get him. If we left our gaps, he had the tremendous skill to change pace and direction without losing any speed and bounce into that opening for a big play.

Because we had mastered the way Cleveland used Brown to the point where each of us could diagram every one of his plays, we did a better job against him than any other NFL team. When he lined up behind the center with a halfback on the left, we could expect him to run what we called the A series; when the halfback was on his right, he ran the B series; when he was offset from the center he ran another series, and so on. Sam Huff simply looked at the formation, stood up and signaled us by touching his shoulder, and we knew exactly what defense to use because we knew where the play was going.

Huff did not key Jim's every move—only when he was in certain formations. Otherwise, the Browns could have "cross-keyed" us, that is, gotten Huff to follow Brown without the ball, opening up room for Mitchell, a world-class sprinter who, on a good field, was the NFL's best outside runner. Late in the season, particularly in Cleveland Stadium when the turf became so bad, Mitchell was not effective, and we concentrated totally on Brown. It was this handicap that eventually led Paul Brown to draft Ernie Davis, a runner with Jim Brown's speed and strength, who he figured would force defenses to spread their concentration. Ernie, of course, died before he could play in the NFL.

Taking nothing away from Walter Payton of the Bears and all that he has achieved, I believe Jim Brown was the greatest. He did everything—and that included blocking. He was often criticized because he wouldn't pass block, or was lackadaisical as a lead-run blocker, but that's all bunk. I ran into him enough to assure the skeptics that he was a fine blocker, and while he might not have done it with reckless abandon on every single play, how much do you want out of a guy? I know that some of the Cleveland players resented the halfhearted way he did calisthenics two days after a game, and criticized Paul Brown for relaxing his rigid code of having players raise their legs to a certain height. But Paul was correct when he later said, "How could I criticize someone who had just carried the ball 20 or 25 times two days before, and had taken a terrible beating in helping us to win, because he didn't raise his legs six inches higher than anyone else?"

Jim, who entered the Hall of Fame the same year I did, was really a powerful fullback with a halfback's speed. Though he weighed 220 pounds, he was as fast as Bobby Mitchell and far more powerful. He could burst through the middle of a defense and run 70 yards for a touchdown without even being touched once he passed the line of scrimmage. He could run into a pile, break free and take off in a different direction so quickly that the defense often was caught moving the wrong way. That was one major reason why we had to maintain our defensive positions.

He was not as shifty as Hugh McElhenny in the open field, but Mac could not withstand the beatings Jim took. But Brown had a great change of pace that turned around defensive backs getting ready to tackle him while he kept going untouched. His favorite ploy was giving the limp leg to tacklers, and when he felt them relax their grip when they thought he was going down, he exploded from their grasp. He had such great acceleration from an almost standing start that he was in full stride within a few steps.

Still, it was rare that you really got a good one-on-one tackle on him, unlike Jim Taylor of the Packers, who loved to challenge defensive people and believed he could punish them. With his myriad of sideways, spinning moves that didn't allow one person to put him down, Brown rarely gave you the head-on shot. But if you got to him one-on-one, his raw power simply shook your body from top to bottom.

For all of the beatings he took from us, coupled with the great emotion of our rivalry, I recall only one scrap, in 1963 with Tom Scott, our right linebacker. The whole deal began a couple of series before the fight, when Tommy was blitzing and Jim tried to block him. Scotty probably gave him a little extra on the way in, and Jim retaliated with a little extra on the way out. Then they started bitching at each other on every play, and Tom, who was one tough person, wasn't about to back down. Finally, after Scott tackled him, they both jumped up and started to fight, and both were ejected from the game.

The greatest season in this rivalry was 1958, when we beat the Browns in both regular-season games, the second on Pat Summerall's memorable 49-yard field goal through the snow, and then in a conference playoff game the next week, 10-0. However, the Detroit Lions had made all of that season-ending drama possible, tightening the race by beating the Browns the week after we defeated Cleveland in our first meeting, and then giving us a great break when we played Detroit in our next-to-last game, trailing the Browns by a game. Detroit led 17-12 in the fourth quarter when, on fourth and twenty-one at their 44 yardline, coach George Wilson inexplicably called for a fake punt-run by kicker Yale Lary. Cliff Livingston tackled him after just a one-yard gain, and we moved to the winning touchdown when Conerly made his biggest play of the year, a 34-yard pass to Bob Schnelker on fourth and ten. That set up Gifford's two-yard touchdown for a 19-17 victory that really wasn't sealed until Svare blocked Jim Martin's field goal with less than two minutes to play. Ironically, it also was Lou Creekmur Day in Detroit, and I was more than happy to see one of my chief antagonists going home for good.

The next week at Yankee Stadium, all the Browns had to do to win the conference title was to tie or beat us. Thanks in part to Brown's 65-yard touchdown run, Cleveland led, 10-3, going into the final quarter when, with ten minutes to play, I recovered Jim's fumble at Cleveland's 45 yardline.

Earlier in the game, Kyle Rote had told Gifford and Conerly that, by changing a pass route from the sideline to the middle of the field, he could split the Brown's zone defense. Charlie sat on it until the first play following the fumble recovery, before he had Gifford toss that pet halfback option pass to Kyle to the six yardline. Then he did it again to Schnelker two plays later for the tying touchdown.

We moved to the Browns 25 on our next possession, but Summerall, who had gotten kicked in the thigh the week before and didn't know whether he could even kick until pregame warmups, missed a 33-yard field goal. We held the Browns again and forced them into a bad punt that gave us good field position near midfield. But on third down Alex Webster dropped a perfect touchdown pass, and with two minutes left, it was decision time.

Jim Lee Howell wanted to try a field goal, but Lombardi was against it. He wanted to try another pass on fourth down. Jim Lee vetoed it, and sent Summerall and the field goal unit out to try again. When we got onto the field, the offense looked at us and said, "What are you out here for?"

"He wants a field goal," Pat said.

"Are you kidding?" one of the guys said. "It's 49 yards away."

But there was no kidding when Summerall struck the ball—it sailed mightily through a lazily falling snow and right through the goalposts with such velocity that he might have been successful from 60 yards. Of course, with that kick we won the game, and Summerall is remembered for all time. No one can forget the dramatic photograph of his body outlined against the falling snow and the darkness of that late December Sunday, his head down and leg fully extended right after the ball had been kicked. However, when he returned to the bench amidst absolute bedlam, Lombardi finally walked over to him and said, "You know you can't kick a ball that far, don't you?" And Vince just walked away, shaking his head.

In the locker room, Webster, who had been close to tears after dropping that sure touchdown pass, walked up to Pat and said, "If I had caught that ball, no one ever would have heard of you."

Everyone around them laughed, but we had to go out and do it again the following week. There were no doubts this time, nor any last minute dramatics, because we smothered the Browns and Jim Brown. No one could have beaten us that day; our defense was letter-perfect. We shut down Jim Brown, and when Cleveland went to Plum to pick up the slack, we got him too. At one point the Browns reached our four yardline, and when Plum tried to pass, I sacked him for a 12-yard loss an instant before he was to release the ball to an open receiver in the end zone. On the next play he tried to throw across our defense, and Huff intercepted the ball. That was the end of Cleveland for the day.

From that game, of course, came a little bit of history: the 1958 NFL championship game against Baltimore that everyone still calls the "greatest" ever played. I don't, not by any stretch of the imagination, because we lost a game we should have won; and I say that in all deference to what this game has meant to the growth of pro football, and even to how it elevated our team to new heights. There were no highs for me when I left our locker room on that late December Sunday afternoon in 1958. In fact, I never felt worse. We had let the world championship slip away

In fact, I never felt worse. We had let the world championship slip away from us, 23-17, and we did it in the first overtime game ever played.

Many still forget that we had beaten the Colts earlier that season, 24-21, before more than 71,000 fans at Yankee Stadium, in a game worthy of championship billing. Summerall won that one, too, on a 28-yard field goal with two minutes and forty seconds to play. Conerly's 63-yard touchdown pass to Schnelker put the Giants ahead, 7-0, and after Baltimore tied the score, we stopped them on four plays at our one yardline. Conerly's 25-yard pass to Rote and a 13-yard run by Gifford in the third quarter gave us a 21-14 lead, but George Shaw, playing for an injured Unitas, threw another TD pass for a tie. Conerly then marched the Giants to their winning field goal on the next drive.

That same day, the Lions beat the Browns, and we were tied for first place until the next week, when we were upset by the Steelers. That one-game difference lasted until the Browns game, but what lasted even longer was the memory of the great game against the Colts. When we played for the NFL title, they had rested for a couple of weeks during our playoff game, they had Unitas back, and they were the favorites. Much has been said, even by some of our players, about being emotionally and physically drained from the two consecutive games against Cleveland, but I never believed that. When you play for the NFL championship emotional fatigue disappears quickly as the challenge of the big game takes over, and while we may have been nicked up a bit physically (Rosie Grier couldn't finish the game), we had enough to get the lead and control of the game for most of the second half. In short, we had no excuses for losing when we had the Colts flat out beaten with two minutes to play.

Baltimore led at the half, 14-3, scoring twice after recovered fumbles. They threatened to put the game away early in the second half when they drove for a first down at our three yardline. We stopped three runs, and then Livingston stepped in and made his great tackle on Ameche. This sequence totally turned the game in our direction. Three plays later, Conerly, on third and two, passed down the middle to Rote, who ran 62 yards before fumbling the ball. But Webster was right behind him, and Alex scooped it up on the run and made it to the one yardline. Triplett burst over for a touchdown and our team came alive. Early in the fourth quarter, Conerly connected on a 46-yard pass to Schnelker, and then threw one of fifteen yards for a touchdown to Gifford for a 17-14 lead.

In the meantime, our defense had taken the Colts by the throat. When Baltimore got to our 27 yardline, with five minutes to play, Kat and I sacked Unitas and turned the ball over to the offense. On a third-down play, Gifford followed Rosey Brown around end, and he was tackled by Gino Marchetti. From where I stood on the sidelines, directly opposite from where Frank went down, Gifford had already made the first down. Linesman Charley Berry ruled otherwise, moving the ball backward to where it was a half-foot shy of the marker. But Berry blew that play; there were moving players between him and Gifford, and it was clear that he didn't have a clear look at where Frank's forward progress really ended. He also got no help from the other officials—that wouldn't happen today—so he really had to guess where the ball belonged. Unfortunately it was a bad guess—game films later proved the point—and instead of keeping the ball and perhaps running out the clock, or at least depriving Baltimore of enough time to get any points, Don Chandler had to punt.

Second-guessers then, and others through the years, said we should have gone for it. I disagree. The ball was in our end of the field where, if Baltimore stopped us on fourth down, it wouldn't have taken much for a field goal. Howell made the correct call on the spot—he didn't have the luxury of second-guessing—in ordering Chandler's punt, which went to the Colts' 14 yardline and could not have been better. Jim Lee also had seen our defense dominate in the second half, so he had every right to expect that we could hold the lead in the last two minutes.

Why didn't we?

Give the credit to Unitas. He used to his advantage the one ingredient that was so important to all his performances—pressure. In the final drive, which ended with Steve Myhra kicking a tie-making field goal with seven seconds to play, he did everything we tried to prevent. When we rushed in, he dumped the ball off to Lenny Moore, and when we didn't get a decisive rush on him, he hit three curls and square-ins to Ray Berry for a total of 63 yards. Some have said we were too conservative in our defensive scheme, but that isn't true either. Taking away the outside, so he couldn't get his receivers out of bounds after a catch, we forced him to throw to the middle and keep the clock going. Unfortunately for us, he had time to make some big plays in the middle, helped, I've always believed, by Grier's absence, which cut down our pass rush. His replacement, Frank Youso, wasn't nearly as strong, so the Colts didn't keep an extra back in for protection and gave our secondary and linebackers one more man to cover.

But being conservative or radical doesn't mean much against a quarterback like Unitas. His pass release was so quick that he could wait until the last second, and a couple of times he was just about to go down when he got the ball away to Berry. The Colts also were fanatical about protecting him, and one of my most vivid memories of that game is how tough it was to play against tackle Jim Parker that day. Though I got to Unitas a couple of times, it wasn't because I overwhelmed Jim—he was bigger and stronger than I. It took all of the quickness and guile I had to get past him, but that was the case every time I played against him.

In the sudden death we got the kickoff and missed a first down by another six inches when Conerly scrambled on third down, and only a sideways tackle by Colts linebacker Don Shinnick stopped his forward motion. Once more Chandler got off a magnificent punt to the Colts' 20 yardline, and once more we should have been able to stop the Colts. But we didn't.

Why?

Again, give Unitas the credit. He said afterward, "The clock was in our favor," meaning he had all the time in the world. He had no pressure this time, so he did anything he wished and he did it methodically. At one point I thought we had the Colts. Mo had sacked Unitas to set up a third and fifteen, but John got a hook pass to Berry after Carl Karilivicz slipped and fell on the coverage. Poor Carl! For years thereafter he blamed himself for our losing the game because he couldn't make that play, but that was not the case. On the next play, John spotted Huff cheating backward and to the left a bit to anticipate helping on pass coverage, so he called a trap play. As I noted, if we didn't fill the gaps quickly there was nothing but open country, and this time Sam couldn't get up fast enough to avoid a good block. Ameche rambled 23 yards to our 20 yardline. Five plays later, including a gutty sideline-out pattern to tight end Jim Mutscheller against coach Weeb Ewbank's orders, Ameche barreled into the end zone for a one-yard touchdown with six minutes and fifteen seconds played in the first sudden death game in NFL history.

That was it. The world of professional football was forever changed by that one game, but for me, it was a lousy way to make history. Still, I often have wondered: Suppose we had stopped the Colts and prevented the drama of those final minutes, and thus deprived a mesmerized national TV audience of that finish? What then would have been the impact of the sport on the public? Where would that game stand in pro football history? Questions for the ages...

I wasn't even thinking about any answers a couple of nights later when a group of Giants played the Harlem Globetrotters at Madison Square Garden. We lost again—never an upset against the Globies—but at least I had the consolation of scoring three points and throwing a "touchdown" pass to Kyle Rote when we lined up in a five-man T-formation. Actually it was a six-man formation because Kyle ran off the bench and caught it. It was good for a lot of laughs, and all of us needed a few at that point.

In 1959 Lombardi left to become head coach in Green Bay, and Al Sherman became our offensive coach. While I'll discuss his impact on the Giants in the next chapter, I don't believe Al ever really coped with the memory of Lombardi's time in New York, with the dynamic impression he left so firmly ingrained in the psyche of the offensive team, particularly when it became known two years later that the Giants wanted Vince to return as head coach after Howell retired. When Sherman replaced Lombardi, he sought immediately to make his own mark, which is only natural for any new coach, but Jim Lee resisted a total offensive makeover.

We did a couple of new things, such as moving our backfield setup behind the guards instead of behind the tackles, as Vince had done. Gifford had been the beneficiary of Lombardi's wider set; he got outside more quickly than under Sherman's system. But Al also used his system to get Frank more involved as a pass receiver in the middle of the field, against slower linebackers, as he tried to make us more pass-oriented. Conerly responded to the changes by winning his NFL passing title, thanks also to those meager four interceptions. Gifford gained more than 770 yards receiving and 540 rushing, the fourth straight season he led us in both categories. There is little doubt that he was a producer when he became our biggest offensive threat.

Defensively, we were never better than in 1959, and there was no doubt that we were the Darlings of Yankee Stadium. I think this bothered Sherman, who felt the pressure of replacing a popular coach like Lombardi. Later in the year he ran into a firestorm of criticism and heard his unit booed when it couldn't score a touchdown in two straight games. In the meantime the cheers for the defense got louder and louder every time we came off the field. But he could do nothing about it at the time, though I believe the impact certainly determined some of his actions after he became head coach. We beat the Browns, 10-6, in our first game against them, Lindon Crow's interception of a Milt Plum pass triggering our winning touchdown drive. The next week we held the Steelers to just 33 yards rushing and won the game when Huff scooped up Larry Krutko's fumble and rolled five yards for the winning touchdown.

Two weeks later we started a string of keeping opposing teams under 200 yards of total offense in five of six games, including one against the Cardinals that was played in Minneapolis—the Cards then played in Chicago and were shopping for a new city before eventually landing St. Louis—when we allowed zero yards passing. Chicago completed six passes, but our barrage of sacks on King Hill and John Roch wiped out their passing yardage, and the Cards finished with only 96 total yards. The following week we held the Redskins to 181 and clinched our title, and the week after that we blasted the Browns, 48-7, at Yankee Stadium in a game interrupted with about two minutes to play when thousands of drunken fans overran Cleveland's bench and forced Paul Brown to take his team off the field. At that point, the emotion of this rivalry had gone too far, and we could have lost the game on a forfeit had not the police been able to clear the field. It marked the last time the Giants ever sold field seats.

Two weeks after we defeated the Redskins for a 10-2 record, we played the Colts for the NFL title. . .and again we lost, this time 31-16. There was none of the high drama of the 1958 season. We clinched our conference title with two games to play, but Baltimore didn't get there until the final Sunday because they were in a neck-and-neck race with the Bears. Of course everyone was looking for a replay of the 1958 game, but those gems come along only once, especially when the events that precede are as dramatic as the game itself.

This time our defense played tremendous football. We stopped Baltimore's running game, allowing only 73 yards, and didn't do a bad job on Unitas, who gained 264 yards. We sacked him six times, and I got four of them, but all of this didn't mean much because Baltimore's defense shut down our offense when it had to. Part of the reason was our indecision, and even Howell noted after the game that the offense never seemed comfortable or in synch during the game, even though it outgained Baltimore.

The problem—which would plague us in future championship games—was Al Sherman's penchant for changing the offense, in the belief that he was surprising the oppostion, instead of going with all of the things that got us into the title game. That approach isn't unusual; Sid Gillman had done that with the Rams in our 1955 title game against Cleveland, and it has happened many times in Super Bowls. Why, I never have figured, because it doesn't make any sense to go away from something which has been successful, which your team feels comfortable in doing. Besides, the only person a coach fools with these brainstorms is himself, and the loser becomes his team.

In our 1959 game the Colts took a 7-0 lead on Unitas's touchdown pass to Lenny Moore, but we shut them down. Going into the fourth quarter the Giants led, 9-7, on three field goals by Summerall. The crucial play for us was the failure to make a first down on fourth and one late in the third quarter. The Colts correctly figured we would run Webster over Rosey Brown's position, and they stacked the area. From there they began the winning touchdown drive, which ended with Unitas keeping the ball for a four-yard touchdown run early in the fourth quarter. He followed that up with another touchdown pass, helped in part by Jimmy Patton's absence for the entire second half with an injured foot. Unitas took advantage of that with his great third-down completions. Once he needed 17 yards after being sacked, and he got 29; another time he needed 21, and he got 31. When Baltimore went up 21-9, we had to open up our offense, and Johnny Sample picked off a pass and ran it in for a touchdown.

After the game, Howard Cosell accompanied me to the hospital to view Mike, our eighth. He joined Rick, Bob, Tina, Tom, Laura, Andra, Chris and later, John. Jeanne got a private recap of the game...live with Cosell.

In any one game a defense can do only so much, and in a championship game it cannot do everything. But we wanted that game badly because we knew it was Tom Landry's last with the Giants. He was leaving to coach the new Dallas Rangers (who became the Cowboys before the start of the 1960 season), and to us there was no better going-away gift than a game ball. Instead, we had to settle for a large silver football...and a whole lot of great memories of mastering a system that helped to continue the dynasty long after he was gone.

5 A Giant New Look

The Giants began the sixties with both the team and professional football about to undergo some profound changes.

While we returned to training camp in Vermont, elsewhere in New England the Boston Patriots opened their camp as members of the brand new American Football League, and the New York Titans weren't too far away either, preparing to open their season at the Polo Grounds.

None of this really impacted much on us at the time, though for the first time in a decade the NFL had some competition for the vast New York metropolitan area audience. As players, we looked on with mild interest, wondering whether another league would be successful and what benefit might accrue. A year earlier NFL commissioner Bert Bell had told a congressional committee investigating the monopolistic practices of the NFL that he welcomed competition: the more teams playing professional football, he said, the better it would be for the sport.

At that time Lamar Hunt had tried to purchase the Chicago Cardinals from the Bidwell Family and move the team to Dallas, but the owners refused to sell, and the league didn't wish to be rushed into expansion. But Hunt, like Arch Ward, the father of the All-America Football Conference, thought that pro football should be structured like major league baseball, with a new American League to compete against an established National League. He then set in motion the formation of the AFL, after which the National League decided it indeed was time to expand, and targeted Dallas and the Twin Cities of Minneapolis-St. Paul for its new franchises.

But our chief concern at Winooski wasn't geography; we were trying to capture our third straight Eastern Conference championship and get the NFL title we had missed the previous two seasons. But Jim Lee Howell had already decided that 1960 would be his last season as head coach, and speculation was rife throughout the year about who would replace him. I believe Jim Lee never was consumed with being an NFL head coach. He must have really felt the loss of both Tom Landry and Vince Lombardi and what they meant to the team. He had two great future head coaches working as his assistants; he knew their temperaments and work habits;

and he had reached a level of confidence in them where they almost shared the head coaching job of the Giants. When they left, it meant breaking in new assistants, with new ideas and different personalities, and trying from scratch to establish the relationship and confidence that his particular situation required.

In 1960 Swede Svare replaced Landry as our defensive coach, I became the defensive line coach, and Jimmy Patton tutored the defensive backs. All of us continued as full-time players, though Tom Scott saw increased time in Swede's slot, which he took over in 1961 when Svare became a full-time coach. Regardless of who was coaching, Landry's system stayed in place, and we had a good year with our unit, though not quite as consistent as in 1959 when the Giants were the top defensive team in the NFL.

The Giants' major problems in 1960 were caused by injuries that, in the end, kept us from getting that third straight title. Instead, we watched Philadelphia win the NFL championship over Green Bay. Actually, it was an almost nightmarish year, beginning with the preseason when Charlie Conerly injured his elbow and missed the first five games at quarterback. During three of those games he became the punter. Don Chandler injured his leg in the opener against the 49ers and couldn't work until mid-October. George Shaw, who we had gotten from the Colts in 1959, became the quarterback, and despite his lack of size and strength he did a pretty good job of keeping us in a tight race with the Eagles. As it turned out, Conerly only played four games that year. In addition, Alex Webster missed the first four games of the year, and Kyle Rote played the second half of the season with a broken hand.

The biggest loss came at Yankee Stadium. During the fourth quarter of our first game against Philadelphia, Frank Gifford was carried off the field with a severe concussion after a hard tackle by linebacker Chuck Bednarik. The Eagles had gone ahead when Jimmy Carr picked up Mel Triplett's fumbled handoff and ran it in for a touchdown (doesn't that sound familiar!). We came right back and missed a touchdown on a dropped pass in the end zone. On the next play, Gifford fully extended himself to catch one in the middle of the field, and Bednarik crashed into him. The impact knocked Frank out and jarred the ball loose. Bednarik fell on the fumble, then jumped up and, in his exuberance over making the play, appeared to be doing a victory dance over the prone Gifford. He wasn't, of course, but the whole scene raised the passions of Giants fans to a boiling point, and through the next week some of the media fired those passions even further.

The events surrounding Gifford captured everyone's attention, but they also were an example of the bad luck that dogged us that season. The turning point in that game really occurred in the third quarter when we failed to score from Philly's nine yardline. Triplett got five yards, then another yard on second down, but he injured his foot and had to leave the game. Gifford twice tried to buck into the end zone, but he was repulsed from the two yardline. Triplett, the man we needed, wasn't there, and we wound up losing that game, 17-10. It was by far one of the most bizarre days I have ever spent in the NFL. At the moment Frank was being carried into our locker room with his serious injury, a special policeman on duty there succumbed to a heart attack. That game was also the one in which Jim Katcavage suffered his separated shoulder—the one we made him endure when he wanted to leave the game.

We also played Philadelphia the next week in Franklin Field and jumped to a 17-0 lead by scoring the first three times we had the ball, including a 71-yard pass from Shaw to Rote on the game's first play. But we ended up losing, 31-23, as the Eagles got all of their points following five turnovers, and we were out of the race for good.

The highlight of the year occurred in Cleveland when we beat the Browns, 17-13, and held them to just 95 yards—only six rushing, and just four by Jim Brown. Later that season, Rote, Jack Mara and I received medallions at a City Hall ceremony as part of a New York Football Giants Week. It was the first time the club ever had been honored by the city, which I'm certain was totally forgotten when Mayor Koch snubbed the Giants in 1986 and refused to offer them a victory parade for a Super Bowl victory.

The search for a new head coach began before the 1960 season, and it became something of a soap opera that continued after the season ended. The Maras wanted Vince Lombardi to return as head coach, and Vince wanted the job because he and his wife, Marie, were born-and-bred New Yorkers who simply missed the pace of the city. But Vinny had a long-term contract with Green Bay, and after he had taken them to the NFL title game that year the Packers' board of directors balked at letting him go. When push came to shove on the matter, Lombardi backed off and decided to stay in Green Bay, which ruffled some feelings inside the Giants' front office for a while. It believed Vince could have forced the move had he remained insistent. Had Tom Landry not taken the Cowboys' job in 1960, he would have become the head coach.

So Al Sherman got the job, and thus started an era of agony and ecstasy for all of us connected with the Giants—the agony often taking place in our locker room while the fans were in ecstasy over the wonderous feats our team performed, and for which Sherman took full credit.

But Al had to contend with his own agonies. In a sense he was part of the Giants' "family," with an affiliation that went back to Steve Owen's staff in the late forties and early fifties before a coaching stint in Canada, but I don't believe he ever felt anything familial about his place in the organization. The fact that he was not the Maras' first choice to replace Howell, but only a reluctant second after Lombardi, dented his ego. Having already been haunted by Lombardi's ghost when he replaced him as offensive coach, he now had to deal again with that specter, which seemed to loom larger and larger in his life after he became head coach.

In fairness to Al, he had two strikes against him the moment he joined

Howell's staff in 1959. One came when his very presence opened up comparisons to Lombardi immediately; the other when he had to work in the shadow of Landry, who was being acclaimed as a coaching genius for his defensive work. So, going in, Sherman had to overcome one legend and then try to coexist with a genius. The only person who could have pulled that off, without ever achieving those heights, was another Lombardi.

He certainly was not another Lombardi, though.

Everything Sherman did was compared to Vince. Many who look back on the excitement that the Giants' offense generated during his first three seasons as head coach must wonder about such comparisons. Primarily, it was one of style, both in a football sense and in his relations with the players. Any successful coach must be a good salesman and convince his players that his methods, as well as his game plans, will be successful. Sherman had his own ideas about offense, but it is hard for a new coach to sell new ideas to a veteran team that still reveres its former coach. Those players had tasted great success with Lombardi's driving, dominating, crunching style, and tough football from a drill sergeant like Vince was no big deal. He had taken us through the pro football wars and we had emerged as winners.

Here, the approaches became distinct, and they seemed to doom Sherman's acceptance by many of the players from the beginning, particularly those who had worked under Lombardi. Where Lombardi was blunt, Sherman tried to sell his style with slick jargon. Al used a wide variety of X's and O's flying all over blackboards; Vince's offensive diagrams featured more straight lines, meaning he wanted to overpower a team before he tried to fool it. Sherman drew up plays that predicted definite reactions by the defense to make them successful; Lombardi guaranteed success only if a defender was laid flat. For example, for one championship game Sherman installed a "slow" sweep that had as its key for success our flanker blocking down on the outside linebacker. Sherman guaranteed the play would succeed because the linebacker would react to a fake before the ball was handed off and drop five yards off the line of scrimmage, where the flanker had to go. In the game the linebacker didn't take the fake at all, he didn't drop five yards, and he wasn't blocked by the flanker, who had gone to the prescribed spot. Instead, he wound up throwing the runner for a loss. Lombardi never depended on the opposing defense for anything. A player was assigned to block someone and he had to get him.

Lombardi and Sherman both were Brooklyn born-and-bred, and both had played collegiate football in New York. Vince was a member of Fordham's famed Seven Blocks of Granite line in the thirties; Al was an undersized, gritty quarterback for Brooklyn College in the forties. When Lombardi spoke, you knew he was from Brooklyn; Sherman spoke with a contrived Southern accent that all of us knew wasn't Brooklyn, and that, in itself, turned off much of his message to the team. When he succeeded

Howell as head coach, Sherman was victimized by his own physical stature. Jim Lee towered over most of us, and when he spoke, his word was law. His ass-chewings had the mark of a drill sergeant. Sherman was a much smaller person in physical stature, and he never came across as a drill sergeant. When he chewed on us, the effect always fell far short of what he intended. When he tried to play the tough guy he often alienated the team. Lombardi, as I noted, could tear you down, but he never left you there. Sherman tore you down, too, but he left you down, and the rebuilding had to come from within the player. This was sometimes a slow, painful process that left open wounds and bitter feelings.

I guess Al tried to keep his offense tough by pitting it against the negative attitude he perceived the defense felt about that unit. But we never really challenged the offense, never really chastized them. We were separate, we were proud, we were different, but Al misread those feelings. He didn't understand that, while we may have still been two distinct teams under one name until Y. A. Tittle's influence finally knitted the break, we all were friends. As such, we freely wondered whether the head coach had a hang-up about the defense, and after a while we simply accepted the fact that we would never be his favorite. It was plain to us that he couldn't handle the defense's notoriety. In fact, in training camp there were times during our scrimmages when, before each play, the defense had to tell the offense what defense it would run. Obviously, this helped the offense in practice, but in the long run it was not really fair; it would not have defensive plays relayed to it in a game. But we always felt it was one more way to favor the offense. As it was, we controlled most of the scrimmages anyway.

Sherman was a very knowledgeable offensive coach, but he certainly was not the genius the media and his friends always portrayed him as. In the 1961 preseason, when he finally could install his own system, we tried three different running offenses, all different in the placement of backs from those the team had used under Lombardi. None of them produced very much. Finally, after losing our opening game to St. Louis, 21-10, Sherman called the offense together and threatened to make wholesale changes. Many players felt he was blaming them for his own inability to devise a system to fit our personnel. In the aftermath of Al's threats, there were some violent rumblings until cooler heads prevailed and got everyone to settle down and accept the system. But Sherman's credibility as an offensive innovator had suffered before the season had hardly begun.

His problem was not unique. It is one that seems to affect many new coaches who take over successful teams and feel they must immediately institute their own systems, regardless of whether the personnel are adaptable. I always thought that Don Shula had it figured out. His first couple of seasons as head coach at Baltimore he, too, had distinct ideas for offense, but the Colts did not have the players to make them work.

So he stayed with the system that best fit their talents and gradually changed people to fit his ideas. That's one reason why Don is one of the game's great coaches.

I had an opportunity to judge Sherman's skills up close when I was the defensive coach for three years, from 1962 through 1964. I know that during those years Kyle Rote, our offensive coordinator, played an important role in much of what our offense accomplished; as was the case in 1961 when Don Heinrich was offensive coordinator. But the biggest key to our offensive success and the tremendous excitement that it generated came from quarterback Y. A. Tittle. In 1962 and 1963 he had some input into our weekly game plans. He also became a coach on the field—as Van Brocklin was with the Eagles in 1960—where Y. A. combined that knowledge with his own competitiveness, guile and experience to lend stability to the team in times when none was forthcoming from the sidelines.

My role as coach offered me a unique perspective as well as some agonizing dealings with Sherman. I have no axe to grind; I never really had any personal confrontations with him. But I never felt comfortable on his staff either. Al was not the kind of person with whom you could disagree and feel it was for the good of the team. Sherman never allowed his younger assistants the creativity that is so necessary for good staff work. So there was never a time in our general discussion when, if I disagreed with something, I could say, "That's not correct." That was a tough situation for me because I felt one of the prerequisites of being a good assistant coach was to express freely an opinion that was based on experience and knowledge. After this went on for some time, I finally said to Sherman, "More and more, I find myself holding back my honest opinions on some of the things we are doing as a team because I don't believe you want to hear anybody who disagrees with your ideas. Even if I did, I have to wonder if they would be accepted in the right spirit. You only want to hear what pleases you, and it's hard to work that way."

As a playing coach I was also in a unique, often-times difficult situation in our staff meetings. When the defense was discussed there was often talk of trades and players' abilities. It was difficult hearing other coaches rip into guys without any basis in fact. At those times I didn't hesitate voicing my honest opinions, but again, I never felt that Sherman understood that if I said things he didn't like to hear, or didn't agree with, I wasn't being disloyal. In effect, I was serving two masters—the head coach and my defensive unit, and I was part of that unit.

Don't get me wrong. I was as honest in my postgame critiques of the defense as I could be, and I pointed out mistakes and presented my solutions for correcting them. That was good and proper. But I also was in the huddle with them during the games, playing and breaking my ass while they did the same, so I resented someone tearing down players who were working and doing the best job possible. When I tried to put that situation into focus, I was considered disloyal to the head coach. But I had to defend them when I knew I was right.

There were a few times during the heat of a game when Sherman came up to me and said, "What the hell are you doing out there?"

"I'm doing what I think is best," I would reply. "Tell me what you think we should be doing."

He never did tell me, yet I always made it a point to discuss our defensive game plan with him before each game, and very rarely did he change anything or make even slight alterations.

The real key to our offensive success during Sherman's first three seasons was Tittle, whom we acquired from the San Francisco 49ers only a few weeks before the 1961 season began. In fact, we played against him in an exhibition game in Portland, Oregon, only a few days before he joined us. Y. A. came into the game late in the second half and our guys kept telling each other, "Hey, don't hit him, don't touch him. He's ours." Somehow the word had slipped out that a deal for Yat had been made, or was about to be made, but the 49er players didn't know what we were talking about. What always puzzled me was why, if San Francisco had agreed to the deal or was about to do so, they even put him in a game, risking an injury that could have ended matters. An injury would also have been disastrous for the Giants considering all that Y. A. achieved for us, though at that time we primarily wanted a veteran to bulwark a very shaky quarterback situation.

Conerly wanted to retire after the 1960 season. He was forty years old and had been through a rough, injury-plagued year, so the game had become much less fun for him, much more painful. But because of his feeling for the Giants, he reluctantly returned for 1961, letting it be known that, while he would give the starting job his best shot, he would not complain if the team broke in another starter. The question was, who?

George Shaw, who started most of the games in 1960, had been traded to the Vikings for a number-one draft pick. Lee Grosscup, once considered the quarterback of the future, had already spent one season on the taxi squad and then saw little action in 1960, so his credentials were tarnished. The first solution was signing Sam Etcheverry, who had played for the Montreal Alouettes in the Canadian League, but Commissioner Pete Rozelle nullified the pact when St. Louis pointed out they held prior rights to him. Ironically, he was the Cardinals' quarterback in our opening-day loss to them. His nickname, "The Rifle," never held up because he came to the NFL with a chronically sore arm, unknown to any of us, and had a very undistinguished and brief career.

With no Etcheverry, Well Mara was forced to look elsewhere. Out in San Francisco my old Rams line coach, Red Hickey, who had become head coach of the 49ers, had decided to scrap the T-formation and go with a shotgun set-up to utilize the all-around running and passing skills of Billy Kilmer, Bobby Watters and John Brodie. Tittle, at age thirty-four, became the odd man out, and Well got him in exchange for lineman Lou Cordileone, who had been our top draft pick the previous year. Lou's reaction to the trade will forever be remembered as the epitome of understatement; when he was notified that he was being sent to the 49ers, his obvious first question was, "Who did they get for me?"

"Y. A. Tittle," he was told.

"Is that all?" he asked, with deep wonder in his voice.

Of course, in San Francisco Y. A. asked the same question, and he was told about Cordileone.

"I said to myself, 'Tittle for a guard named Cordileone. What a comedown,'" Y. A. told me some years later.

Still, Cordileone's reaction was probably the more common—thirty-four-year-old quarterbacks weren't supposed to have much left. With his bare pate, Y. A. looked far older than his years, causing even more doubt when fans in New York first saw him. Yat always took some ribbing about his lack of hair, but he always turned it into a joke or lighthearted remark that left people laughing. However, I'm sure he was stunned after a game in Cleveland when he boarded our charter and asked for a soft drink.

"I'm sorry sir," the flight attendant said, glancing at his bald head, "our orders are that we can only serve the football players now. You'll just have to wait."

"But I am a player," Y. A. said, noting her preoccupation with his head and giving her a bit of a fish-eyed look. "I just don't like hair falling in my eyes."

Looks aside, there was still much skepticism about the trade from those on the outside, particularly after Y. A. broke two bones in his back on his first play for us in an exhibition game against the Rams. He couldn't play for five weeks, and many began to wonder what the Giants had done. I certainly never doubted the wisdom of that trade—no one who had ever played against him did. I faced him many times when the Rams and 49ers played each other twice a year in the Western Conference. The memory of how he carved us up in the 1957 game that helped take the Giants out of the title race was still very fresh in the minds of all who played that day. I know the trade stunned the Browns, our foremost conference rival, who ironically once owned his rights in the old All-America Football Conference. They desperately wanted a quarterback and would have snapped him up in an instant.

And why not? Tittle was the best, the epitome of what anyone can expect of a quarterback. Everyone still raves about what he did on the field, but few really know how important he was to the team off the field. His great competitiveness and enthusiasm affected everyone, and I never met a more positive person in my life. He never, ever felt we would lose a game. Y. A. never once doubted his own ability nor that of anyone who played with him, and he inspired everyone to play to his utmost for the overall good of the team. He brought the team together with his spirit, viable because he formed no cliques and ran with none. He had as much time for the defensive players as he had for his offensive teammates; and he treated the stars of the team no differently from the last guy on the bench. After Y. A. became one of our leaders, the split between the offense and defense quickly healed, and we won or lost as a team, not as individual units. This made Sherman's job a great deal easier, too, because Al never could have closed that breach by himself.

Y. A. walked into our locker room carrying those old hightop shoes and a pair of battered old shoulder pads that he had used since his college days at LSU. When he flung his helmet to the ground in moments of frustration, that bald head shone like a beacon in Yankee Stadium and lit up the crowd as much as any long, arching 60-yard touchdown pass to Del Shofner. On the field, he was a master at play-calling, seeming always to do what the opposing defense least expected. His bootlegs for touchdowns were classics—after faking a handoff to Alex Webster or Phil King going one way, he deftly hid the ball on his hip, wheeled and sometimes ran untouched the other way into the end zone. Sometimes he didn't, and he paid a fierce physical price for his chicanery.

There has never been a more superb practitioner of the screen pass. He absolutely sold the play the way he stumbled back into the pocket and looked downfield while the onrushing defensive linemen hungrily closed in. It always seemed he had waited too long, but he never did. At just the right moment he lofted the pass to one of his backs, often taking his punishment from those onrushing linemen. His play-calling, as I said, was akin to having a coach on the field. Jim Lee Howell once said that he found it almost impossible to chart Y. A.'s tendencies while watching him during a game. "The closest I came was to believe he simply did exactly the opposite of what was expected," Jim Lee said.

But Y. A. was more than just an efficient quarterback. His personality carried over to the field, where there was no doubt who was in charge. Halfback Bobby Gaiters, our number-one draft pick in 1961, found that out. Though he had tremendous speed, he had developed a habit of not hitting a hole until he saw it open, rather than timing his run to get there the moment the opening occurred. Too often Gaiters was caught behind the line, or got nothing because the hole was closed before he arrived. Finally, Tittle could take no more, and when Bobby was trapped for a loss during a game against the Cowboys, Y. A. got right down on the ground next to him and yelled, "That's the last time you ever do that. Bust in there!"

But he always listened to his players. In a game against Pittsburgh in 1961, Webster had beaten linebacker George Tarasovic on a pass pattern, but Y. A. had gone elsewhere with the throw. Alex told Y. A. what happened and, later in the game, he sent his wide receivers and tight end running patterns to the right, isolated Webster on Tarasovic and passed to him for a touchdown.

Y. A. also retained his naturalness on the field. One time he threw a wobbling pass toward Shofner that fell off target. When he returned to the huddle Del said, in his best Texas twang, "Duck season is open and I just saw a lame duck heading my way. But the poor thing died before he reached me. Right Y. A.?"

His furry eyebrows rising a couple of notches, Tittle looked at Shofner. "The next one will be alive. Just make sure you catch it."

Some NFL quarterbacks couldn't have taken that needling because they took themselves too seriously, and with them Shofner might not have seen a pass for the rest of the day. But not Tittle.

During a game against the Redskins Yat complained to center Ray Wietecha that he was setting up the huddle only eight yards off the ball instead of the customary twelve.

"Yat, that saves me four yards of walking on every play, and that could add up to thousands of miles over a career," Ray replied. Tittle just looked at him and shook his head, but later in that game, he walked the eight yards to the line of scrimmage and almost panicked.

"Ray," he screamed, "I've forgotten the count."

"It's 'three' old buddy," Wietecha replied as he grasped the ball. Naturally, the Redskins linemen believed this was only a ruse to draw them offside, so they did not move until the ball was snapped—on the count of three, naturally—and Webster rolled through for a big gain.

When the team returned to the huddle, Wietecha nudged Tittle.

"Aren't you glad I set up the huddle eight yards off the ball? If I set it up where you wanted, you not only would have forgotten the snap count by the time you reached the line of scrimmage, you'd have forgotten the play as well," Ray said, and Tittle just laughed.

Y. A. saw his first action for the Giants in the second game of the 1961 season against Pittsburgh, when Conerly was injured and had to leave the game. We trailed, 14-10, but Yat's performance in a 17-14 victory simply was a preview of coming attractions because he completed ten of twelve passes for 123 yards, including four-for-four and 42 yards in the winning touchdown drive. Immediately, the New York media began its open speculations about whether Conerly was finished and Tittle should be the starting quarterback—with all of the negatives that those speculations could bring to the team.

Sherman was squarely on the spot, and he moved to deflect the speculation by calling both of them in to plead his case. He told them he understood both of them had been long-time starters, but he had to make a decision on when, where and how to use them; and he asked them to go along with his judgements and avoid doing anything to polarize the team. Of course, both agreed, and they worked in perfect harmony all season. Tittle was the consummate team player, and Charlie had already indicated he did not expect a blank check as the starting quarterback. But when he was replaced, he certainly expected to be treated with the dignity befitting someone who had given so much for the team and who had agreed to answer its plea for help.

That is exactly what did *not* happen the following week in Washington when we helped the Redskins christen D. C. (now Robert F. Kennedy) Stadium. Sherman allowed Conerly to start the game, though Charlie was hurting pretty good from the first two games. Midway through the first quarter, though, Al had Tittle throwing behind the bench, the worst thing any coach can do to a starting quarterback who has a game under control, especially when the game is in its early stages. You can imagaine what that does for the starting quarterback's confidence level, but with a veteran such as Conerly, it was tantamount to saying, "I'm starting you only because of who you are, but I don't have much faith that you can really do the job."

Charlie was doing the job in the game, getting us a 7-0 lead with a touchdown pass to Rote. Washington tied the score, but, on the next series Conerly underthrew Shofner and the ball was intercepted by Dale Hackbart, who returned it for a touchdown and a 14-7 lead. When we got the ball again Conerly started out on the field, but Sherman waved him back and sent in Y. A. Charlie was steaming as he walked past Sherman, slammed down his helmet and sat at the far end of the bench. Rarely had he ever displayed that kind of anger. All of us knew it was directed at Sherman, who he felt had given him an extraordinarily quick hook because of one bad play and had embarrassed him by allowing him to start the game and then calling him out.

Sherman claimed he squared the situation with Conerly after the game by explaining to him that he planned to use Tittle anyway, and that he did not yank him because of the interception. Whether he did or he didn't doesn't matter now, but at the time the fuse had been lit for a potentially explosive situation had Charlie chosen to exploit it. He never did, nor did he ever display one iota of jealousy, resentment or disappointment at having to be the number-two quarterback. Both players ignored the intermittent "Who should be the starter?" controversies concocted by the media. Their ability to work together really helped knit the breach, so that we won or lost as a team.

Conerly started only one more game that year—against the Cowboys at Yankee Stadium on Kyle Rote Day. That game came a week after he had relieved Y. A. in the fourth quarter of a game against the Rams and thrown a pair of touchdown passes to Shofner and Rote for a 24-14 victory. Against the Cowboys the magic just wasn't there, and he was relieved by Tittle, but too late to prevent a 17-16 loss that came on a last-minute field goal by Allen Green, whom we had traded to the Cowboys before the start of the season.

The week following the Washington game, Y. A. started his first game, a 24-9 victory over the Cardinals, and for the next three seasons the Tittle Era generated waves of excitement that still exist. No offensive player in the team's history has ever had such a long-lasting effect on its fans. The memories of all he achieved in just three seasons was, I always believed, one of the major reasons why Giants Fever never abated in New York and why the team survived some terrible seasons without ever losing its season-ticket holders. (Of course, the other reason was the excitement generated by our defense, which gave birth to Giants Fever.) People who saw him play told their children about his feats, and while the kids might not have any idea who Y. A. Tittle was and what he did, they know that after a quarter century his feats still are legendary, proof enough that he was a dominant figure in the team's history.

Perhaps the one great moment that epitomized his status occurred in 1968, four years after his retirement, when he accompanied the 49ers, with whom he coached at the time, to Yankee Stadium for a game. When San Francisco came out for a pregame practice, the Stadium was almost filled, and as soon as Y. A. walked out of the dugout and onto the field, everyone in the Stadium—nearly 60,000 strong—stood and gave him a five-minute ovation. I dare say that should he walk across the field at Giants Stadium on any Sunday now, he would receive the same welcome from those who remember—and those who have only heard.

If the latter group should still wonder, a quick glance into the record book will show what he achieved in just four seasons when teams played only fourteen games a year. Over that time he completed 731 of 1,308 passes for 10,439 yards, an average of over fourteen yards per completion. No Giants passer has ever done that well. (By comparison, Phil Simms is just under ten yards per completion thus far in his eight-season career.) Tittle's 36 touchdown passes in 1963 and 33 in 1962 still rank one-two; so do his seven TD passes in one game against Washington and six against Dallas, in 1962; and no Giants passer has surpassed his mark of throwing at least one touchdown pass in thirteen consecutive games. He achieved all this at a time when the rules did not favor a passing game, as they do today.

But my memories of Y. A. are not built around his statistics. To anyone who played with him or who watched him play he was truly a unique person in all he did. But he never called attention to himself; all of his actions on the field were spontaneous. One moment still stands out from his first game against Pittsburgh. Watching from the sidelines that day, I recall him bringing the team up to the line of scrimmage for a play and barking out the number three, which was the signal for an audible. Then nothing happened. Suddenly, I saw some of our linemen laugh before Y. A. ran the play.

"What happened?" I asked Jack Stroud after the game.

"Y. A. got to the line, gave the audible signal, and then he forgot the play," Jack replied. "We waited and I figured he would call time out. After a few seconds, I heard him say 'Aw, nuts!' and I couldn't help but laugh." A few seconds after that, he called the play.

And two plays later he threw his first touchdown pass to Del Shofner, triggering the beginning of the most potent passing combination the Giants have ever known. The Giants got Shofner at the urging of Tittle, who had not only seen him play often for the Rams, but who was also a teammate when they played in the Pro Bowl. "Get him, if you can," he urged Sherman and Well Mara. "He's the best receiver I ever threw to, and I played with some great ones in San Francisco."

Actually, the trade came about almost by accident. On the day we acquired Tittle from the 49ers, Don Smith, the Giants' publicist, was in Los Angeles to advance a game, and he had lunch with Elroy Hirsch, then the Rams' general manager. The Rams wanted the top draft pick that year so they could get quarterback Roman Gabriel of North Carolina State, but the Giants held the pick after their trade of George Shaw to the expansion Vikings.

"What would it take for us to get that pick?" Hirsch asked Smitty, obviously believing he had more decision-making power than was possible. Don had no idea, so he tried to think quickly of a couple of Ram stars.

"I'd say Del Shofner or Jon Arnett," Smith said off the top of his head. He said later they were the first two players who popped into his mind, but he didn't know at the time that Del was in the Rams' doghouse because some muscle problems had made him a stop-and-go player. Some in the LA organization felt he might be dogging it. They obviously didn't know Shofner.

Hirsch and Well Mara got together and, with Tittle's urgings still fresh in his mind, Well made the trade. But there was something personal in it for me, too, because it wound up being a part of the original deal by which I came to the Giants. New York had given the Rams a number-one draft pick to get me, which Los Angeles used to pick Shofner in 1957. Shofner brought that pick back to the Giants, so the 1956 deal really wound up being Del and me for a number-one pick.

Regardless of the complexity it was a great deal by the Giants. There has never been a wide receiver in the team's history who had such an overwhelming effect on its championship potential. Del was a lean, wiry Texan who, at six-three and 180 pounds, looked as if he could be snapped in two with one good hit. Everyone kidded him about his lean frame, but he was nicknamed "The Blade" because he was tough enough to play as a running back for Baylor and in the secondary for the Rams in his rookie season before moving to wide receiver. He was also tough enough as a receiver; he never flinched on patterns down the middle, nor when he was crunched from behind while reaching for a pass. Del had great speed and ran in such a relaxed manner that he seemed to glide along the ground. When he changed directions he never seemed to make any sharp cuts, appearing to flow from one angle to the next. His track coach at Baylor, where he was a championship sprinter, had taught him that running relaxed gained him more speed than if he stayed tight. In 1962, his second season with us, Rote and Ken Kavanaugh helped him develop some deception in his moves, so that he did not have to rely solely on speed to get into the open.

Del might have looked like a beanpole, but he had unusually powerful leg drive for such a skinny guy. That drive helped him break tackles after he had made a catch. He also had an excellent sense of balance, unusual for someone with such speed, that helped him stay on his feet when he got into heavy traffic around the ball. I have likened his pass-catching to Hirsch's in the way he could catch a ball coming directly over his head without breaking stride. On other tosses he was a "cherry-picker"—he just plucked them out of the air and brought them to his body. The NFL receiver who most resembles him in style and talent today is Cris Collinsworth of the Cincinnati Bengals.

Shofner and Tittle were roommates from their first training camp, and not only did they become good friends, they established that special rapport that is so unique—but so important—to quarterback and receiver. They seemed able to complete passes in the dark. It is little wonder that Tittle always said that Del was the best receiver with whom he ever worked, and Shofner's statistics for the 1961-1963 seasons bear him out. He caught 185 passes for 3,439 yards and 32 touchdowns, and he averaged over 18.5 yards per catch. Considering the terror he inflicted on opposing secondaries, he was Y. A.'s single greatest offensive weapon in those seasons.

Joe Walton, called by many "the world's smallest tight end," was another player who added much to the offense. At five-ten and 180 pounds he might have been the smallest, but he also might have been the smartest, and one of the toughest. He had to be both to survive, and Tittle once called him "the best third-down receiver in the game, bar none." If anything, he was an overachiever who did a better job run-blocking than he was supposed to and always managed to find an open area in his pass routes, which is why he was such a good third-down receiver. He caught 95 passes in our three championship seasons, 17 of them for touchdowns, and he gained over 1,300 yards. In a game of relative giants, Joe had a tough time, and his smallish body was often overcome by the pounding of bigger defensive linemen. Only in 1962 did he play all fourteen games. The injuries finally took their toll, forcing him to retire after sitting out the 1964 season.

Perhaps his biggest moment—among many big moments—came in 1962 when he caught Y. A.'s then record-setting 33d touchdown pass against the Cowboys in the final game of the year. Interestingly, Joe preceded Mike Ditka as starting tight end at Pitt, where both were All-Americans, and now both are NFL head coaches. Walton has said, though, that it was Tittle who influenced him the most in structuring his passing game and trying to keep a total offensive picture. Joe used that knowledge well as an offensive coach on Alex Webster's staff, and later for George Allen in Washington.

Thus, in 1961, we had all of the offensive elements in place to begin some high-powered moves back to the top of our conference. We also anchored our defensive secondary with the acquisition of cornerback Erich Barnes from the Rams in a three-way deal that also involved the Bears. Erich was a tough cookie, the prototype of what coaches look for in today's cornerbacks. He was good enough to play man-for-man against opposing flankers, many of whom were smaller, and he often just beat them up— or plain flat-out beat them. Six-two, 205 pounds, he was a fine athlete with tremendous quickness and anticipation. We needed him to cope with Tommy McDonald of the Eagles and Bobby Mitchell of the Redskins, two of the NFL's speediest flankers on teams that were key rivals. The first time Erich ever faced McDonald, in a 1961 game at Yankee Stadium, he held him to three catches and only 26 yards. When they met in the second game that season, he did another good job. In 1962, when he first faced Mitchell, he intercepted two passes intended for him and also incurred a couple of interference calls. But that's how Erich played— always close to the line, with such aggressive coverage that opposing teams began going elsewhere with their patterns.

The other cornerback was Dick Lynch, who had come to us in 1959 from the Redskins and easily settled into the starting role that season. He was a helluva player with the perfect temperament and athletic skills to play that position. Dick, who has been a Giants broadcaster for many years, is still the same delightful, charming guy with an unflappable air that he was as a player. In those years he seemed to prefer playing the happy-go-lucky guy who didn't give a damn. Much of that was a facade, his way of challenging himself to produce or be forced to choke on his own cockiness—and he was a producer.

But Lynch also challenged me when I became defensive coach, and he didn't win. I benched him in one game because I was fed up with his apparent lack of concentration. I had threatened him a couple of times, hoping to shake him up, but Dick's attitude was, "You'll never do it because you need me too much." We needed him, but with his mind straight—so he sat down. It almost cost us the game, but it also shook him up enough to get his attention (I also put him back in the game in the fourth quarter). Every time Dick started to slide back to his old ways, a quick reminder snapped him back into shape. Lynch still says I'm the only coach who ever benched him, but I'm also the only coach who got three successive great seasons from him.

Dick was another "lurker" in the secondary who looked like he could be beaten but always came into the play. He didn't seem to have great speed, but he had enough to return four interceptions for touchdowns; he didn't seem to be quick, yet he picked off nine passes in both the 1961 and 1963 seasons to lead the NFL. Twice in 1961, against St. Louis and Philadelphia, he had three interceptions in one game. Like Barnes he was tough, and he had a fiery Irish temper that never allowed him to back down from any confrontation.

He took a lot of heat from fans and the media about Buddy Dial of Pittsburgh and Dallas, his biggest nemesis. But much of it was sour grapes: the Giants had released Dial, when he was a rookie number-two draft pick in 1959, and as so often happens, he returned and had some good games against us. Dick didn't do badly either—in one 1961 game against the Steelers he intercepted a couple of passes and blocked a field goal. He was also one of our best punt blockers, and he always seemed to come through when we needed the big play to save a game or turn one around.

In 1961 my biggest problem as a defensive coach wasn't Dick Lynch—it was trying to fathom Tom Landry's multiple offense in Dallas. Landry had invented our 4-3 defense, so he also knew how to beat it—by interrupting the keys or clues that told where a play was apt to go. He did this by moving his backs around before the ball was snapped, a feature that is still part of his offense. I spent hours watching film before our first game against the Cowboys, and it wasn't until after midnight of the day we were to leave for Dallas that I finally stopped looking at all the movement and paid attention to where the backs lined up before the ball was snapped. It turned out that Dallas ran from the same formations as everyone else, and everything else—including having their offensive linemen stand up just before they set themselves to run the play—was camouflage. The action by the linemen was to mask the final set for just an instant and, they hoped, prevent the defense from getting that final key.

Going into that game I told our defense, "Let him do what he wants with his backs, we'll get into our gaps and force them to change." It worked; be beat Dallas, 31-10, but it was scary using a plan we hadn't practiced. Erich ran a record-setting 102 yards with an interception in that game, stepping in front of Lee Murchison two yards deep in the end zone to grab Eddie LeBaron's pass. It all happened so quickly that by the time he reached our 40 yardline he was in the clear.

Our other memorable defensive game was the usual donnybrook against the Browns. We held Jim Brown to minus four yards in the second half after he had scorched us for 72 in the first two quarters, and we won the game, 37-21. Barnes struck again, this time returning one of Len Dawson's passes 35 yards for the go-ahead touchdown early in the fourth quarter. On one play I saw that Cleveland was going to pitch the ball to Brown, so I gambled and tried to intercept it. I missed, and Jim made some yards through my position. After the game Jim Katcavage was all over me.

"The luckiest thing that happened to us was you're not getting away with that gamble and getting the ball for a touchdown," he jibed. "If you had made it, you'd be crowing over us for a week."

I probably would have been, though it would have been even tougher to reconcile telling my players never to leave their gaps when I left mine to try and make a big play. As I said, when we played the Browns it got so frustrating that we sometimes tried something outlandish, and we often paid for it.

That game against the Browns was one of four truly big games we played in 1961. Two others were against the Eagles, the first of which was on November 12, the day when the Pete Previte Special became a cherished part of the Giants legend. It was a play that was suggested by Pete Previte, one of the attendants in our locker room—which also was the Yankees' clubhouse (why do football players use a locker room and baseball players use the same room and call it a clubhouse?). Pete had worked for years at Yankee Stadium, and he was far more familiar with baseball than football, particularly some of the special plays, the use of fast pinch-runners when teams had rallies going in the late innings, for example.

"If baseball teams use their fastest runners off the bench in certain situations, why doesn't football do the same?" he asked our offensive coach, Don Heinrich.

"What do you mean?" Heinrich replied.

"Why can't you come up with a pass play to use all of your fastest players in the game at one time and get a big play," he said. Heinrich said that sounded intriguing, but nothing happened. So Pete mentioned it to Svare, and then specifically cited Erich Barnes and Jimmy Patton, our two fastest defensive backs. Swede, looking at the defensive problems a team would suddenly have if faced with defending against five speedsters, believed it would work, so he took the idea to Sherman. Al took this suggestion, and the coaches cooked up a splendid play that spread five receivers over the field. Barnes and Patton, replacing running backs Bob Gaiters and Alex Webster, joined Shofner, Rote and Walton. Barnes went into the slot next to Shofner on the left side, and Patton was in the slot between Rote and Walton on the right. We practiced it just briefly on Friday and decided to save it for a time when it would have the greatest impact.

It was one of those delightful gadgets that a team needs in a big game, and since both teams were tied for the conference lead, any edge was important. Tittle got touchdowns on our first two series with passes to Shofner and Rote, and then got lucky later on when Del fumbled a handoff on a reverse but picked up the ball and tossed it back to Y. A. That surprised Tittle, but Yat stunned the Eagles even more when he then tossed it to Gaiters for an 18-yard touchdown. Gaiters was just as lucky; he also fumbled a handoff at the Philly five yardline but kept the ball in front of him and fell on it in the end zone for another touchdown. Even Rote's TD pass had a bit of trickery. When he was running his pattern he suddenly stopped, dropped his arms and said, "Oh, hell!," then looked over at Shofner. Bobby Freeman and Don Burroughs, who were covering Kyle, did the same, and at that instant Rote made a quick break into the corner of the end zone and caught a 12-yard scoring pass.

But all of those crazy things paled when, just before the half, the Pete Previte Special came alive. Patton and Barnes streaked onto the field and right into position as Tittle lined up in the shotgun. Before the Eagles even had a chance to see what was happening, five guys were running down the field. Y. A. looked first at Patton, who with Walton and Rote had run underneath patterns, but Jimmy was covered. Shofner took off down the sidelines and got double coverage; but Barnes, who never had played one down of offense in the NFL, headed diagonally across the field, and he was open. So Tittle sent the ball to him, and Erich caught it on the run and scored. Yat and Erich were always on the same side during our Tuesday touch football game, so this hook-up was a natural.

While Yankee Stadium rocked with more than 62,000 fans going absolutely crazy and the Eagles were still trying to figure out what happened, Pete Previte leaned on his broom in our locker room, where he heard the play on the radio, and just smiled. When we came galloping into the room a couple of minutes later, few even knew the idea was his. After we won the game, 38-21, (Tom Scott got our last score with a 65-yard interception return after Jim Katcavage had tipped the ball), I gave the game ball to Sherman. It wasn't until later that I found out that Pete's idea produced the play, and had I known earlier, without question he would have gotten the ball.

Pete worked in our locker room with Peter Sheehy, who we called Big Pete, and they were as professional in their jobs as we were in ours. For two bucks a week, they made a player a sandwich every day for lunch, got his coffee, shined his shoes and kept his personal locker clean. But even in performing what could be considered menial tasks, they had a certain class about them that reflected the Yankee Stadium atmosphere. They were special people to us, not just a couple of guys pushing a broom. We knew they were a part of the Yankee tradition. We looked at Big Pete in awe because he had known Babe Ruth and Lou Gehrig when they were Yankee players, and he could keep us spellbound when he talked about them. He also had great stories about Red Ruffing, Lefty Gomez and his personal favorite, Joe DiMaggio. When we asked him about many of the other great players from the Yankees dynasties one thing became apparent: if Big Pete liked them, he talked about them for as long as we wanted to listen; if he didn't, he quickly dropped the subject, but he never bad-mouthed them. We knew that when the Yankee players asked about us, we got the same treatment.

Both of them considered it a privilege to work in Yankee Stadium, and I always considered it very special to play there. Part of the reason was growing up in the area and knowing the great tradition of that ballpark. That is why it was a tremendous feeling to go there on the day of a game, park the car and walk into the Stadium through hundreds of people all shouting words of encouragement and letting us know they considered the Giants something special. I felt a responsibility to live up to their expectations, and I believe that feeling was shared by nearly everyone in our locker room.

The greatest moments always occurred when we came out to be introduced before the game. I always stood atop the Yankee dugout steps while the cheers from the crowd for us built gradually into a huge roar. Involuntarily, my eyes swept around that stadium—few people realize how big it was or what 62,000 people look like. You had to stand down there and see the immensity of that spectacle. There is no doubt that it energized all of us; and for me, it was the last, necessary, emotional ingredient in the pregame tension that accompanied the realization that I was physically going to battle another person over the next three hours. There is no real way to describe all of that in mere words, except to say that I never have felt anything like it since I finished playing there. Yankee Stadium could do that to you, and if any of us, or the Yankees for that matter, couldn't appreciate it, then they had no soul.

Our two other big games that year were both away from that supportive Yankee Stadium atmosphere, and both were crucial to our clinching the conference title. On December 3 we played the Packers in Milwaukee and needed a victory to clinch the title. But we lost, 20-17, and dropped back into a tie with the Eagles. Most people recall the Packers setting up their winning touchdown when Jess Whittenton stole the ball from Webster on Green Bay's 23 yardline as Alex was being tackled. Webster was fighting for some extra yardage when two Packers players just pinned his arms. Unable to shift the ball away from Whittenton, he was powerless to prevent Jess from stealing it and running to our 30 yardline. Green Bay scored four plays later.

However, we drove to Green Bay's 27 on our next possession, primarily with short passes and straight-at-them runs, something we always did well against the Packers. But Pat Summerall missed a potential tying 34-yard field goal. When we got the ball again we used the same offensive schemes to reach their 20, and we were in a position to win the game, or certainly tie it with a field goal. But that week Sherman had installed a reverse that began with halfback Bobby Gaiters leading Webster to the right then quickly reversing his field, taking the ball from Alex and going back to the left. There simply wasn't enough time in the play for Gaiters, who was not always sure-handed, to get enough space between Webster and himself to make his reverse run and cleanly take the handoff. They continually messed it up in the practice, and when it finally worked one time, Sherman declared the play part of the game plan, and we never worked on it again that week.

Here, Al, displaying that misguided certainty that the defense would react precisely as he determined, did not assign anyone to block Green Bay's left end, Willie Davis. In fact, in practice Jim Katcavage, who was playing Willie's role in our drills, turned to Jack Stroud and said:

"Who gets me?"

"No one," Stroud told him.

"What is Davis supposed to do while all of this is going on?" Jim wanted to know.

"He's supposed to be chasing the play on the other side of the line of scrimmage," Jack told him.

"Well," Kat said, "I know Green Bay plays its defense much like we do, and I'm certain that Davis is going to stay put to guard against anything coming back. He'll be there right in the middle of the play."

When that was pointed out to Sherman, he waved off the point.

"Don't worry," he said, "they'll do it just like we have planned."

He didn't convince anyone, so when we got down to Green Bay's 20 yardline with our basic offensive plan, in came Gaiters. "Coach said run the reverse," Bobby told Y. A.

"When?" Y. A. asked him.

"Now," Gaiters replied.

"This play?" Yat said, with a tone of disbelief and disappointment in his voice.

"That's what the man said," Gaiters told him.

Tittle rarely ever swore, but he let out a big "Damn!" and reluctantly called the play. Sure enough, Willie Davis grabbed the fumbled handoff between Gaiters and Webster and the Packers ran out the clock. After the game, Sherman insisted there was nothing wrong with the play, but he never convinced us.

We went to Philadelphia the following week, tied with the Eagles for first place, and during the week Tittle wanted Sherman to alter Walton's pass routes to go into the middle of the field on the patterns called for Shofner. Y. A. felt certain Philadelphia would double-cover Del in situations when they knew he would be a primary receiver and leave only a linebacker covering our tight end. Al refused, saying he knew the Eagles defense well enough to know they wouldn't feature Shofner so much in their coverge. Y. A. was correct; Philadelphia did a good job of taking Del out of the offense in the first quarter, and Tittle had a wide open middle with no receivers coming into the area. The Eagle's defense had us hamstrung, so Sherman sent in Conerly. But before doing so, he made the changes in Walton's pass routes that Y. A. had wanted in the first place, and he told the offense that we now had an audible for a pattern to the tight end every time the quarterback saw double coverage coming on Shofner. On this first series Conerly hit Walton for a touchdown and hit him often enough when Shofner was double-covered that the Eagles had to switch their coverages. Del caught three touchdown passes in that game, Charlie had a helluva day, and we beat the Eagles, 28-24, to gain first place for good.

Of course the game against the Eagles is also remembered for a couple of other reasons. During the week Bednarik was quoted as calling Sam Huff "an overrated hillbilly who never wore shoes until he reached New

York." Chuck was full of himself in those days because he had gotten so much acclaim for having played both center and middle linebacker for a few games toward the end of the 1960 season and in the title-game victory over Green Bay. Bednarik had returned to full-time linebacking duties in 1961, and at that time he had begun to talk a better game than he played.

Our defense made the big plays that day. Dick Modzelewski's fumble recovery set up Conerly's second TD pass to Shofner at the start of the second half, and later in the third quarter, with the Giants ahead, 21-10, Philadelphia had a first and goal at our four yardline, but we pushed them back to the ten, and on fourth down we sacked Jurgensen. Of course the play that grabbed everyone's attention occurred in the last quarter with the Giants ahead, 21-17. The Eagles' John Nocera was charged with roughing Don Chandler on a punt that allowed us to keep possession and drive for the clinching touchdown, an 11-yard pass from Conerly to Shofner. Referee Ron Gibbs, the NFL's best at that time, made the roughing call, but the Eagles have forever insisted that Chandler did a superb job of acting. Looking at the films, Don got a pretty good lick from Nocera, and I thought it was a proper call.

From there, we tied Cleveland, 7-7, on the final game of the season, and then went to Green Bay to play the title game. That was a 37-0 disaster that wasn't made any easier to avoid when Sherman decided to radically alter our offense and try to "surprise" the Packers. A pattern, which had first surfaced when he was the offensive coach in our 1959 championship game against Baltimore, had developed; he became almost fanatic about fooling teams in title games instead of going with the strengths that got us there.

We didn't lose only because Sherman changed our offense, though any radical departure from what a team does best only erodes its confidence. That was partly the case with us. Even on the bus ride out to City Stadium in Green Bay, Y. A. and some of the offense were still trying to straighten out some of the changes. That was obvious when Green Bay intercepted four of our passes, but it didn't account for missed tackles and blown assignments. Some have said that the result might have been different had Rote not missed a sure touchdown pass early in the game when he was momentarily blinded by the sun, or if Gaiters hadn't overthrown him on a halfback option pass when he was wide open in the end zone. Of course, that just brought to mind Sammy Baugh's classic retort after his Redskins were beaten, 73-0, by the Bears in the 1940 NFL title game, when he was asked what would have happened if one of his players hadn't muffed a sure touchdown pass on the first series of plays.

"We'd have gotten beat 73-7," Baugh replied.

Maybe we would have lost 37-7, or 37-14, but as Y. A. said after the game, "We couldn't have beaten them if we used twenty-two men at once."

Green Bay had all the advantages—playing at home; the relentless driving of Lombardi, who, still smarting from having lost the title game the year before, had vowed his team never would lose another; injuries that cost us key defensive people and forced us to use Joe Morrison as our starting strong safety (which wasn't fair to him, but he was all we had); and the advantage that Lombardi brought to his offensive planning in knowing our defensive secrets so well from working on Howell's staff. Vince knew the weaknesses in that defense, so not only did we have to react to what we knew Green Bay did well, but we also had to react to what they did differently, based on Lombardi's special knowledge. We never did come to grips with it that day, a fatal flaw when your opponent plays what amounts to an almost perfect game.

At one point in the game one of the Packers said to Rote, "Everything right is happening for us, and all that could go wrong is happening to you."

That was it. Green Bay scored on four of its five possessions in the first half and got 24 points in the second quarter. Paul Hornung, on a weekend pass from the Army, set a playoff record by scoring 19 points. Our defense never made the big plays that would have given our offense a shot for an easy score or two to get back into the game, so Green Bay lived up to its nickname for that day: Titletown U.S.A.

We still had other great days ahead of us, but losing a championship in the final game of the year made for a difficult off-season. It was tough continually trying to explain 37 to 0! Still, considering all of the changes that occurred in 1961, I guess we didn't do too badly for a team with a "bald" new look.

6 Bombs Away— Almost

That "bald" look continued through the 1962 and 1963 seasons when Y. A. Tittle forever etched himself into Giants legend with a quarterbacking job that may be unmatched in NFL history. That may sound a bit prejudiced—he was my teammate and friend—but you only have to look at what he achieved to know that he had no peer at his position at that time. He carried an offensive team that, save for Del Shofner, had average talent and made it the most powerful in the NFL in those two years.

While that tremendous offensive firepower was producing record numbers of points and yardage, we also began to change our defensive personnel and some of our concepts so that we too had some exciting and dramatic moments during those seasons. Teams had begun to figure out ways to combat our 4-3 defense, but the beauty of Tom Landry's system was its flexibility. We could change the way we did things and force the opposition to begin an entirely new process of problem-solving without really having to stray from our basic concepts. In 1963, for example, when the NFL began keeping official records for sacking the quarterback, we led the league with 57, but no one seemed to notice too much since we had always done that so well. One year, playing only a twelve-game season, our own film studies showed we had 69 sacks before teams began changing their protection setups, but no one kept records of those statistics.

Yet with all of our success in those seasons, the question of age seemed to be the one thread that ran through any discussion of the Giants. Always it seemed we won because of "experience" and lost because of "age." In 1962 and 1963 we did give up about five points more a game than in previous years, but the problem was not age, it was new people. Yet this was never pointed out. I believe much of that "age" talk had its origins in the head coach's office. Sherman has been quoted many times since then as saying that we were an "old" defense that needed to be rebuilt. What is probably closer to the truth is that the age talk was part of an attempt to tear down a unit that had achieved its own popular identity and did not pay homage to its head coach. Paying homage in those days to the head coach by other coaches and players became a very big thing with the Giants, and that smokescreen became a grim reality after the 1963 season.

There was far more involved in that situation than simply replacing aging players or even adjusting our defensive plans. For one thing, we made some changes in 1962 and 1963, plugging in new people where they were needed but maintaining the integrity of our unit as well as—and this is very important—the ability of everyone to function within the coordinated system. From both a technical and psychological standpoint, Sherman never understood what made our defense so successful. A player simply could not move into our unit and, in a matter of a few games or even in one season, pick up all that we did. Major changes should have been carefully planned and executed. We also needed players willing to discipline themselves and sacrifice their individual glory and statistics to make our system function. Again, not just any defensive lineman or linebacker could fit right in. We discovered that in 1964, and even Landry has experienced it in some off-seasons at Dallas when he turned over his defensive unit.

The key to our defense, as I've said, was the ability of middle linebacker Sam Huff to slide into the gaps and make the play. Offenses had begun to change some of their blocking schemes so that a light backer like Sam was becoming vulnerable to larger lineman. We had either to protect him or replace him with a bigger, stronger linebacker. We chose to protect him by altering the way we filled the gaps, and Sam remained effective in these altered schemes. However, we also changed some personnel, affecting team performance. For instance, Sam had to work with three different strong-side linebackers in 1962 and 1963 after Cliff Livingston was traded to the Vikings. Naturally, team cohesiveness was altered somewhat. First, Bill Winter, an unknown, unsung rookie from St. Olaf's College in Minnesota, who became our rookie of the year, was Livingston's replacement in 1962. Bill was a tough-nosed, hungry kid, who at six-three and 220 was big enough to handle the tight end and take on pulling guards. In 1963 he was injured early in the season, so Bob Simms, who came to us as a tight end from Rutgers, replaced him and, despite his inexperience, gave us a fine effort for a few games before Jerry Hillebrand took over the job in midseason. Jerry was our number-one draft pick in 1962, coming from Colorado where he was an All-American tight end, but he didn't have the speed to break into our offense. He did have the size and aggressiveness to play linebacker, however, so we put him on the taxi squad for a year to learn the system. It wasn't until past midseason of 1963 that he finally showed any mastery of his position. Winter never did recover from his injury to reclaim a starting role.

So for two seasons, during which we won a pair of conference titles, we had three players filling one position, learning on the run. Clearly the problem was one of inexperience, not of age.

We coped with similar dilemmas in our defensive line and in the secondary. In 1963 we took a major gamble by breaking up our front four—and all of the cohesiveness we had established—by trading Rosie Grier to the Rams for defensive tackle John Lovetere. Rosie simply would not control his weight, often ballooning up to 340 pounds, and he became less effective. This trade meant breaking in another player and going through all of the problems a new man must endure as he fits into a system that runs counter to anything he has ever done before. But Lovetere was an all-out worker, a tough, determined guy who, at six-feet-four, 280 pounds, allowed us to keep great power up front. Those great efforts were offset by the mistakes during his learning process, but some saw the big plays by opponents and said age had caught up to us. Nonsense! I am sure that if John hadn't suffered a knee injury in 1964 that ended his playing career, he would have been the equal of anyone who ever played that position for the Giants. As it was, Grier had some fine seasons with the Rams. When he suddenly realized that everyone in the game is expendable, he got his weight problem under control.

We also made some changes in the secondary. Dick Pesonen, Allan Webb and Eddie Dove played at strong safety. Webb, now an executive with the 49ers after a coaching stint with the Giants in the late sixties and seventies, had played minor league football in Connecticut and just needed a chance to prove his ability, so I recommended that we sign him. Webby gave us some good seasons; he could play both corners and strong safety, and he also returned punts and kickoffs in 1963. Pesonen did a good job for us whenever we used him. Dick had to replace Erich Barnes when we beat the Eagles in a 1963 game and was promptly burned by Tommy McDonald on a 64-yard touchdown pass. But he shut down McDonald, who made only one reception for the rest of the game.

I point all of this out only to indicate that our defense had not grown old or inefficient during the early sixties and that we were replacing it the only sensible way—one man at a time, who could learn his job and quickly become an efficient part of the team. As we'll see later in this chapter, when Sherman traded Huff and Modzelewski, he not only tore the emotional fabric of the team, but he also lost two players who were keys to its on-the-field success.

I suppose, though, that when the age question is raised, I should point out that I was our oldest defensive player in 1962 and 1963. But age in football is relative, as we have seen with so many great players—George Martin of the Giants being the most recent after his performance during the 1986 season. I always kept myself in top physical condition, and I never missed a game with the Giants. In fact, during my time in the NFL, I missed only the last game of the 1951 season with the Rams. My last four seasons with the Giants were my best, in my estimation, because I was more efficient than at any time in my career. I had to prepare myself so I could prepare our team, so there never was a game when I was surprised by an opponent's plan or did not know how we could counter it. We did all of this on the field, without the benefit of any sideline coaching, and during those two seasons, we also had to give some extra care to the new players so they understood exactly what was happening.

The man who caused us the most problems was Cardinal coach Wally Lemm. Someone on his staff really had us figured out, and he made us work like hell to keep up with his changing offense.

They really gave us a run for our money in 1962, when we squeaked by them, 31-28. That was a big game for me: I caught a 28-yard pass from Ralph Guglielmi on a fake field goal play to set up one of the touchdowns. It was my only catch as a Giant (I had a 49-yard catch with the Rams). On the play I was the only receiver in the pattern because the Cardinals went to an eleven-man rush; though for once free safety Larry Wilson dropped off just as the ball was snapped. But I ran past him and got into the clear before he reacted. Alex Webster scored a couple of plays later, but we still had to scramble to win the game as Tittle tossed a 20-yard TD pass to Webster in the final minutes. St. Louis quarterback Charley Johnson bedeviled us that day and kept bringing the Cards back into the lead, particularly with his passes to Sonny Randle, who tortured Dick Lynch with 16 catches for over 250 yards. But Dick hung in, blocked a field goal and then clinched the win by intercepting a pass deep in our territory with less than two minutes to play.

But as good as Lynch and Erich Barnes played at cornerback, Jimmy Patton, our free safety, really was the glue that kept that secondary together. When we beat the Bears, 26–24, to clinch the conference title in 1962, Jimmy had three interceptions in the first half, only one of many big games during his career. Jimmy shared the defensive coaching duties with me during my last three seasons, but the added work never interfered with his play. He was a tough, wiry little guy who never weighed more than 185 pounds, but he took on everyone. An ideal free safety, he had fine speed, but best of all he had tremendous judgment for where the play would go and the range to get to that spot. Patton was as quiet as he was tough. There are no great Jimmy Patton stories because he came to work every day, did his job and then went home. Jim's work was always precise, and we formed a close bond coming up with our game plans. I don't believe he ever received enough recognition for his work—defensive backs seem to be noticed only when they are beaten for touchdowns, or when they intercept the ball. But in our system the secondary had to work in a coordinated manner with our front seven, and they also had definite coverage responsibilities, often man-for-man. And long before "nickel" and "dime" defenses came into vogue he juggled coverages to get more defenders on the field. He did it in his own quiet way and his innovations never got much publicity.

Because of his ability to get to double coverage responsibility from the free safety position, Patton was the best friend his secondary mates ever had. He allowed Erich Barnes to be aggressive in his coverage because Barnes knew he often had help deep or in the middle of the field, so he could take more chances. So did Dick Lynch; Patton was always there to help out. Jim's 52 interceptions, 40 during our championship seasons, tell much about his contribution, and he is second to Em Tunnell in lifetime interceptions. Jim died suddenly several years ago in an auto accident.

Patton and Lynch made a good combination, particularly on special teams. When we beat the Eagles, 29–13, in Philadelphia in 1962, we blocked three field goals. On the final one Patton got the block, picked up the ball and was at Philly's 35 yardline when tacklers closed in. He lateralled to Lynch—who was yelling for the ball—and Dick finished off the score with some of that fancy running he had learned at Notre Dame. In that game Sonny Jurgensen threw 57 times, but we intercepted three of them, all of which led to touchdowns. Jurgensen certainly is one of the NFL's all-time great passers, as his Hall-of-Fame status attests, but we had some good days against him. Part of the reason was his almost three-quarter sidearm throwing motion that meant he had to bring the ball up and over the pash rush. When I played against him, Sonny did not always get good pass protection, so we always had people on him.

Two weeks later Huff blocked a punt by St. Louis's Sam Etcheverry, and Lynch picked it up and ran it in for a touchdown with just one second to play in the first half. We won the game, 31–14, but our Mickey Walker will never forget it because he backed up too far while lined up in punt protection, and Babe Chandler kicked the ball right into his back. No one was more redfaced than Walker, but he always made up for any mistakes with his all-out play. Mickey was a free agent from Michigan State when he made the club in 1961 with aggressiveness and sheer tenacity. His body, which had to stretch to hit six feet and barely weighed 220 pounds, earned him the nickname "Toy Bulldog," and that is about how he played. He worked primarily at guard and linebacker but also filled in at center. But Mickey gained his greatest fame and became one of the "darlings" of Yankee Stadium with his wedge-busting on kickoffs. Walker was like a bowling ball when he slammed into and scattered the lead group of blockers like so many loose ten pins. But he never stopped there. He would jump up and look to make a tackle or knock someone else down. With utter disregard for his body, he seemed to get great delight from a job that usually causes other players to hide behind the bench.

In one game, during a sideline huddle prior to a kickoff, the players urged Chandler to kick the ball out of the end zone. Not Mickey. "Kick it anywhere you want," he said. "We'll get the guy."

"You mean, *you'll* get the guy," one of the players said. "It would break your heart if that ball went out of the end zone."

Mickey formed a close allegiance with Greg Larson, another talented and versatile player. Greg was much bigger, and before he finally moved into the center position following Ray Wietecha's retirement after the 1962 season—the position he was drafted to play—he played his rookie 1961 season at tackle and his second year at guard. Greg was the baby-faced assassin among the offensive linemen, his cherubic looks belying a toughness that often had defensive linemen checking out his whereabouts when they came after Tittle. Never content just to keep them from out of the passing pocket, he preferred to knock them down...hard!

He took on Alex Karras, the Detroit Lions' All-Pro defensive tackle, in a 1962 game at Yankee Stadium and all but played him off his feet in one of that season's most memorable games. The Lions came to New York with a highly touted defense, but if anyone wondered whether ours was becoming too old, we answered those questions once and for all. We controlled the game, particularly in the second half, when we shut out the Lions and preserved the final three-point margin after Chandler's tie-breaking field goal early in the third quarter. It was set up by Lynch's interception after Erich Barnes tipped away a pass from Milt Plum to Gail Cogdill at our five yardline. Huff saved another touchdown by Cogdill after Gail broke free on a completed pass and ran to our ten, where Sam caught him and forced him to fumble as he made the tackle, Patton recovering.

The Lions always thought of themselves as the bully boys of the NFL, with players such as Karras, Roger Brown, Joe Schmidt, Darris McCord, Wayne Walker and Night Train Lane, but we were tougher that day in a game in which they knocked Tittle to the bench for a while after he had bootlegged a four-yard TD pass. Shofner, who was supposed to be out for a couple of weeks with a separated shoulder, also came off the bench to play. The following week, when we played the Redskins for first place in the conference, Del caught a then team record 11 passes for 269 yards, while Yat got a record seven touchdown passes, three to Joey Walton, and 505 yards in our 40-34 win. When Tittle and Shofner saw the Redskins a few weeks later, they hooked up for three touchdowns in a 42-24 victory.

Johnny Counts was another electrifying force against the Redskins that day. Counts had the Stadium jumping all during the 1962 season, and on this day he returned the opening kickoff 90 yards for a touchdown. His kickoff returns became an explosive weapon that year; he simply roared out of our end of the field and beyond the 20 yardline before the opposing coverage got near him. He was not a flashy runner, and he never played long enough to learn the nuances of hitting the precise hole at the precise time. He just took the ball and ran, but his great initial burst of speed within the first ten yards got him so much momentum that he didn't have to be precise. Johnny averaged 30 yards per return in 1962, less than a half-yard from the all-time record for one season, but more importantly he consistently set up the offense with excellent field position. His two-year average of 28.7 yards per return is tops among all Giant returners, but he lacked only nine returns to qualify in the record book.

Perhaps our best all-around defensive effort in 1962 came against the Cowboys, the highest scoring team in the NFL at the time. We held them to ten points and 89 yards rushing while Tittle and Shofner again teamed up for three touchdown passes in a 41-10 win. We scored first, but on the Cowboys' first play I recovered a fumble, and Yat came right back in to throw a 19-yard TD pass to Shofner and we were off and running. Not bad for a bunch of old guys!

We beat the Bears, 26-24, to clinch our second straight title, Chandler kicking four field goals for the second time that season, and Patton picking off three of Billy Wade's passes in the first half. I sacked Wade for a ten-yard loss near midfield with a minute to play and the Bears needing only a field goal to tie. In what was supposed to be a meaningless game against the Cowboys to end the season, we won, 41-31. Tittle made it more significant when he broke the NFL season record of 32 touchdown passes, held by Jurgensen and Johnny Unitas, late in the game on a play that almost didn't happen. After he had thrown his fourth TD pass of the day—Webster caught two in a ten-catch afternoon—Sherman took him out of the game and allowed Guglielmi to clean up. Al might have known Yat was one away from the record, but he rightly didn't want to risk any foolish injuries with a title game coming up in two weeks. But Guglielmi had to come out of the game when he was injured—we carried only two quarterbacks on our active roster with another on the unavailable taxi squad—so Tittle had to go back in, risks and all. When we got down to the four yardline, Tittle wanted to call a running play, but as had happened in his seven-TD game against the Redskins, he met with some firm opposition inside the huddle.

"Forget it Y. A.," Webster told him. "Go for the record. Throw the damn ball."

"We could probably run it in just as easy," Yat argued. "They have to know we're thinking about a pass."

"We didn't bring you this far to have you run it," Shofner said. "Throw it. We only have a three-point lead, and you never can tell what might happen."

On that basis Tittle threw the record-setting touchdown pass to Walton, who coincidentally also had caught Y. A.'s record-making seventh TD pass earlier that year against Washington.

That was a terrific way to end the season, and it sent us into the title game against the Packers fully confident that we could win. We had all of our weapons in good shape, including a running game that had produced more than 1,000 yards between Webster and Phil King, so Green Bay's defense could not gang up on Tittle. We also felt that playing in Yankee Stadium and away from the frozen conditions of Green Bay would also be to our advantage. After all, New York can be cold at the end of December, but it has to be better than Green Bay, right?

Certainly...until Sunday, December 30, dawned with a sky that was ice blue and a forty-mile-per-hour wind that turned bodies the same color with a wind chill factor of twenty-five degrees below zero and conditions so bad that the wind literally picked up empty benches and hurled them onto the field. The Yankee Stadium gridiron, bare between the 20 yardlines from seven home games and daily practice, was like concrete. Footing was uncertain. It was no day for a team that relied heavily on the forward pass, but when we walked into the locker room we weren't too concerned. Our running game was strong, and we always ran well against Green Bay when we attacked them straight-on. However, before the game Sherman decided that the cold, windy conditions would not alter his game plan, and we went out and tried to pass as if it were a mid-October Indian summer day.

We were finished even before the kickoff. There was no way a passing game could have succeeded in those conditions. Tittle attempted 41 passes and completed only 18 for 197 yards, and we lost, 16–7. Time and again his passes sailed or dove according to the vagaries of the wind. Once he had Webster wide open in the end zone and a pass that he had completed dozens of time was suddenly scooped up by the wind and carried into the seats. He tried everything he knew to control the ball, but it was impossible under these conditions. Our only touchdown came midway in the third quarter when Erich Barnes blocked Max McGee's punt and rookie end Jim Collier recovered in the end zone, and we still trailed, 10–7.

We had some chances, but bad luck and faulty execution spoiled them. In the first quarter, trailing 3–0, we drove to the Packers' 16. Tittle then had Joe Walton clear in the end zone, but linebacker Ray Nitschke barely tipped his pass, and Dan Currie intercepted the ball. Later in the first half, following Jim Taylor's seven-yard touchdown run, Counts returned the kickoff 50 yards to the Packers' 41, and only Willie Wood's tackle stopped him from going for a touchdown.

We had our final opportunity in the third quarter when Wood, charged with pass interference at the Packers' 18, was so incensed at the call that he knocked down the official and was thrown out of the game. But we were hit with two consecutive 15-yard penalties and never recovered. In a 16–7 game, teams also have to be lucky, and Green Bay had some of that, too. One of Jerry Kramer's three field goals certainly did not look good from where I stood in the middle of the field, and McGee knocked two of his six punts dead at our five and seven yardlines. Those are tough holes from which to dig out.

On the other hand, Packers coach Vince Lombardi had more respect for the playing conditions and kept his passing game as sparse as possible. Bart Starr threw only 21 times and completed just nine for 85 yards. Lombardi said later that the only reason he threw that often was because we had such control of his running game that he had to do something to try and loosen up our defense. As it was we held the NFL's leading rushing offense, which had averaged more than 175 yards per game, to just 148 yards, or three yards per try, and Jim Taylor, the NFL's rushing champion that season, to just 85 yards, or under three yards a carry.

One false perception that remains from that game is that there was a personal or grudge duel between Huff and Taylor. Taylor carried the ball 31 times that day, and the way we played our defense he and the middle linebacker collided on nearly every play, so we went after him the same way we went after Jim Brown. In the second half, as the game became more ferocious with all that was at stake, matters got a bit personal between Taylor and Huff, but mainly because Jim went into a yelling and screaming act every time he got tackled. He thought we were treating him too roughly. Since Sam was there most of the time, Taylor made him the object of his wrath. Did he expect us to treat him with kid gloves? He was his team's best runner, and in that game Green Bay used him to control the ball in the second half when the weather dictated a more conservative game. Taylor bitched a lot on the field, and the more he yelled and screamed at us the more we wanted to get at him. Maybe that's how he challenged himself—I always thought he was too good a player to resort to those tactics—but if it was, then he had to pay the price. Everything he got from us that day came within the nature of the game, and the officials would have stepped in if there had been flagrant or deliberately dirty play. They didn't . . . and there wasn't.

Everyone's principal recollection of that game was the brutal weather conditions. Players on both teams suffered frostbite, and Jack Stroud still feels the effect from frostbitten toes. He later told me that, although he was wearing gloves, his hands were so cold that when he placed them in our charcoal warming bucket on the bench, he didn't even know his gloves had caught fire until he saw them begin to smolder.

That title game was the kind Starr excelled at: very controlled, methodical, with little flash or dash because of the weather. Bart was a very astute quarterback, but one who excelled only when surrounded by a great team and a great coach. When you saw the Packers, you didn't think immediately of Bart Starr, but of Taylor and Paul Hornung, and of course, Vince Lombardi, because Starr was a part of what they represented, a team that functioned mechanically because it had all the parts and was directed by Lombardi. Starr was the perfect quarterback for that situation because he had the temperament to withstand Lombardi's driving personality and do all that Vince wanted without too much dissent.

Quarterbacks are supposed to be the preeminent players on a team, but they are not necessarily the most dominant. So much of their success hinges on the respect they command. For example, Johnny Lujack, the Notre Dame legend who played for the Bears in the early fifties, was never as good as his reputation, but he had a great presence on the field. Regardless of how talented his team was, when the Bears came on the field you looked at him first. When teams played the Giants, they looked at Tittle first because he made us go; when Charlie Conerly was the quarterback, they looked at him, but they also saw Webster, Gifford and Rote—no one dominant player.

However, when we prepared for John Unitas, Norm Van Brocklin or

Bobby Layne, we knew each could take a less talented team and make it successful, as Layne did with the Steelers for a couple of years in the sixties, and as Van Brocklin had done in driving the Eagles to the 1960 title. Van Brocklin and Tittle could make any receiver look good, and any of them could take a team and, by sheer dint of his personality and talent, drive it the length of the field to win a game. There never was any doubt in my mind that if Van Brocklin had been the Packers' quarterback, they would have been twice as good; if Bob Waterfield had been with Lombardi in his prime, then Green Bay would have been three times as good. Bob was exactly what Starr was—only a much better quarterback— and Bart was good!

Speaking of quarterbacks, I always liked Charley Johnson when he played for the St. Louis Cardinals and directed those Wally Lemm teams that gave us so much trouble. A driver, he'd fight, scratch, scream and holler during a game to get things done. Not only did he fire up his own players, but he tried to intimidate our defense by screaming and shouting at it. He was completely opposite off the field, a very scholarly man gifted in mathematical sciences. On the field his only drawback was lack of size; he was barely six feet tall.

Eddie LeBaron, when he played for the Cowboys, was another small guy who gave us problems, much like the 49ers' Frankie Albert had done to the Rams. Both were magicians handling the ball, but since they could not throw well from a stationary pocket, they had to roll out a few yards and then decide what to do with the ball. Often LeBaron rolled a running back to the weak side, either for a delayed screen pass or as a downfield receiver. He wanted us to stay with that back and lessen our pass rush from his blind side. We developed a "bite his ass" call: we had the weak-side defensive end ignore the back and put pressure on LeBaron as fast as possible. The weakside linebacker then slid in and stationed himself near the back to take away the screen pass or cover him if he slipped out as a pass receiver. This forced Eddie to throw quickly downfield and took the back out of any play. Sometimes we resorted to all-out blitzes, as we did in our 37-21 victory in 1963. We trailed, 21-17, at the half, and our blitzing tactics forced him to set up quickly and unload the ball, helping us to shut him out in the second half.

Roll-out quarterbacks were a pain only if we allowed them to become one. They wanted a defense to play only the side of the field where they were rolling, figuring half the defense would stay put or not pursue too hard. The toughest were those who, once back in the pocket, could deftly roll to either side or stay put. You could never count on them being at one particular spot all the time. Knowing they would hit that pocket seven yards behind the center most of the time, we zeroed in our rush on that spot. The problems occurred when they started back and then rolled right or left to set up; or when they scrambled out of the pocket to throw. Unitas and Johnson were always threats that way, and so was Frank Ryan of

Cleveland, who carried the ball more than 60 times one season. Add Billy Wade of the Bears and Roman Gabriel of the Rams to that list.

But I wouldn't have traded any of them for Tittle, in the 1963 season or any other time. Yat was truly amazing, from his very first game that year, when he brought us back from an 18-point deficit in the second half, our first victory ever against a Unitas-led Baltimore team. Against the Colts he ran a nine-yard keeper for the go-ahead score and paid for it with rib injuries that forced him to miss the rest of that game and the next one as well. But he snapped back and, now so in synch with Shofner, produced offense in giant gobs throughout the season, allowing the defense time to get our new people settled in and working efficiently. This was important because the Browns got off to a 5-0 start. We were 3-2 after losing to Cleveland, 35-24, when Jim Brown blasted us for 209 rushing yards plus a couple of touchdown passes. But we got our revenge two weeks later by holding him to just 40 yards in nine carries and so dominating the Browns' offense that it got into our territory just once in the entire game. In the meantime we scored the first seven times we had the ball and won going away, 33-6. At that point the season had become a four-team race, with the Cards and Steelers in hot pursuit of the Browns and us, and it stayed that way until the very last week.

After that first Cleveland loss, Tittle went on a tear, throwing 16 touchdown passes in the next five games—all wins—beginning with four in the 37-21 win over the Cowboys. Tom Landry had begun to alternate LeBaron and Don Meredith at quarterback on nearly every play, and Lynch burned Meredith with an 82-yard touchdown interception. We gave Don the same blitzing treatment we gave LeBaron, and at one point our moving around got him so rattled that he finally looked up from behind his center and yelled, "Aw, c'mon you guys, will you please hold still so I can run this play?" Two weeks later, Tittle somehow conned the doctor into allowing him to leave his sick bed, and he threw four touchdown passes against the Cardinals in a 38-21 win. We intercepted four passes, setting up four scores, and sacked the St. Louis quarterbacks six times.

We gained a first-place tie with a 42-14 win over Philadelphia. Shofner caught a half-dozen passes for 119 yards and Tittle seared the Eagles in the first half with 13 for 15 passing, 214 yards and two TDs. We allowed the Eagles only 101 yards, and Hillebrand finally proved his worth with a fine game. Someone asked me afterward if I was at all anxious about the change, and I said, "I didn't have to worry about him. Everyone else seemed to be doing it for me." Tittle celebrated a reunion of sorts with his old 49er teammates the following week. When we checked into our midtown Manhattan hotel on Saturday afternoon, Y. A. had a message to call his good friend Matt Hazletine, the 49ers' fine linebacker.

"Hey Y. A.," Matt said, "I can't believe the prices here. It costs four or five bucks for a sandwich. You know this city. Where can we get a good meal at a reasonable price?"

Y. A. thought he would have a little fun with his friends, so he told Hazletine, "Matt, there's a great place called the Four Seasons on 52nd Street, just off Park Avenue. It's just what you're looking for."

Of course that restaurant was one of New York's most expensive dining spots, and the 49er players must have really gotten socked because the next day, after a play in which Hazletine put Tittle on the ground with some overenergetic force, he said to him, "That's part payment, old buddy, for that twenty-six dollar dinner you cost me last night."

Yat had the last laugh, though, because he threw four more TD passes, and Shofner caught seven passes for 159 yards as our offense produced 568 yards in a 48-14 victory. The defense held San Francisco to just 34 rushing yards and sacked John Brodie a half-dozen times to help us get first place for at least a week. After that, we went on a roller coaster of sorts that none of us will ever forget.

Two of the most memorable weekends were, of course, when President John F. Kennedy was assassinated, two days before we were to play the Cardinals at the Stadium, and the following weekend when we went to Dallas to play the Cowboys. I found out the President had been killed when I arrived at my travel business in Stamford and one of the girls came running out screaming, "President Kennedy was just assassinated, President Kennedy was just assassinated!" Like everyone else, I was stunned. We had just gone through our practice at the Stadium and left without any inkling of the tragedy.

That, of course, triggered a chain of events in which we were only bit players in a much larger drama. The entire nation went into mourning, and there immediately arose the question of whether the NFL would play its games that Sunday. Many colleges canceled or postponed their games the day after the assassination, and the American Football League soon announced it would not play. We found out the NFL would play its games when we showed up for our light practice on Saturday, and I believe everyone was in agreement with that decision. There was no open dissent. Most of us believed that despite that terrible event life still had to go on. I'm certain that all of us, in our own personal way, prayed for him, and that was as much as we could do. One of the players put the matter into a perspective that all of us understood. "From what I knew of President Kennedy," he said, "I believe that if he was here today and was asked whether we should play a game, he probably would say yes."

I never met Kennedy, but I knew he loved the game, so that struck me as a pretty reasonable explanation. Outside our confines, though, the controversy raged, particularly in the media, and there were some thunderous opinions handed down from many sides. Red Smith, the distinguished sports columnist for the *New York Herald Tribune* at that time, was vehemently opposed, and to the day he died he never forgave Rozelle for his decision to maintain the NFL schedule.

No NFL games were televised that day—and ours was not on radio, either—so only those at the Stadium witnessed our 24-17 defeat. Though the Giants offered refunds for any unused tickets, the place was full, and none were ever redeemed. The crowd was subdued at the start, obviously emotionally exhausted from the previous two days where all they saw and heard about was the assassination. But it didn't take too long for them to get into the game, an important one for us because we were tied for first place with the Cardinals and the Browns.

There are some who have claimed we lost because we were too preoccupied with the events swirling around us, but I have always disagreed. Other mean-spirited media people said we deserved to lose because we dared to play football when a slain President lay unburied, as if we, as a team or as individual players, had any impact on such decisions. There was no question that it was a tough day, and it was very hard to concentrate with all that had happened over the previous forty-eight hours. That had some bearing on our performance, but the St. Louis players were affected too. They apparently handled it better because they made the big defensive plays in the final quarter to beat us after going ahead for good with nine and a half minutes to play.

Of course we then had a week to digest all that happened before we left to play the Cowboys in Dallas. We flew into Love Field, the same airport where the President had landed on that fateful day. It had already become a national landmark of sorts, etched in all of our minds as many of us sought to identify the area where Air Force One had been parked at that time. Our route to the hotel took us right past Dealey Plaza where the Texas Book Depository building sat, and everyone in our bus was silent as we passed, heads craned to look at the fatal spot that had become so familiar during that week.

Dick Modzelewski and I went out to dinner that evening, as we always did before a game, and afterward we stood on a street corner in downtown Dallas waiting for a patrolman directing traffic to wave us across. At that moment a caravan of cars came past, young people inside of them yelling, "Kennedy is dead, and Johnson is next! Kennedy is dead, and Johnson is next!" I couldn't believe the whole scene, particularly when the policeman, who was supposed to uphold the law, allowed these people to hurl these terrible slurs. He did nothing about it, so infuriating me that for a moment I wished I was him—I would have been tempted to pull out my gun and shoot the sons of bitches! Why, at least, didn't he stop those cars and tell those people to shut up? It was a disgusting sight.

Did those events make us want to go out the next day and beat the ass off Dallas? No, but it stirred up some deep personal feelings in me that showed that prejudice has many faces, going all the way back to 1951, when the Rams played an exhibition game in Little Rock and the elevator operator in our hotel refused to carry the black players. We told him, "You take this friggin' elevator up with all of us on it, or we'll throw you right out of here." He did, too, but that cop didn't even flinch when those people yelled those terrible things, and that told me that philosophical differences can't be overcome by one tragic event. There was a lesson to be learned from what happened at Dealey Plaza, but there also was a bigger lesson in what happened on that street corner in Dallas.

We did beat the Cowboys, coming from a 27-14 halftime deficit as Tittle broke Bobby Layne's all-time NFL touchdown pass record. One of those scores was a winning throw to Shofner with five minutes to play after our defense had taken control of the game and held Dallas to just 65 yards rushing and 70 passing in the second half.

Two weeks later, after the defense had scored three touchdowns in a 44-14 romp over Washington and I recovered two fumbles to set up another pair of scores, we played Pittsburgh for the conference title. Back then, ties counted as no game played, and the Steelers came into the Stadium with a record of seven wins, three losses and three ties. We had a 10-3 record. If the Steelers won, their percentage would have been figured on an 8-3 record or .727 while ours would have been figured on a 10-4 mark and .714. That became academic when we won, 33-17. Our defense never played better, and we had control of the game from start to finish. We stopped five Pittsburgh drives near the goal line, and on another drive, when Pittsburgh needed a foot for a first down at our 14 yardline, we slammed them on two consecutive plays and took away the ball. We also intercepted three passes and recovered two fumbles, including one by Gary Ballman at our one yardline that shifted the momentum our way. Tittle had a marvelous day, completing 17 passes for 306 yards. His first touchdown pass went to Del Shofner and his last two to Joe Morrison, giving Yat an NFL season record of 36 that lasted until Dan Marino's 48 in 1984. The catch everyone remembers was Frank Gifford's third-down, diving, one-handed grab of a slant-in, keeping alive a third-quarter drive that ended two plays later with one of Tittle's touchdown passes to Morrison that put the game out of reach.

Morrison was our leading rusher that day, but in this, his fifth season with the Giants, he had long established himself as the team's most versatile performer, a distinction he holds to this day. During his thirteen-year career he played right and left halfback, fullback, flanker, split end, tight end and, as I mentioned, strong safety in the final three games and the championship game of 1961. Oh yes, he also was our emergency quarterback, and every week he took snaps just in case he was needed. In Joe's case, the word versatile was interchangeable with unselfish; he never balked when he was moved around, taking it all in stride as part of the job.

If it wasn't for Ed Kolman's savvy when he went to scout a game between Joe's alma mater, the University of Cincinnati, and Tulsa, Joe might never have played for us. Ed had gone to look at Tulsa's Ron Morris, but Morrison's all-around performance sent Kolman to the phone. He told the club to forget about Morris, but be sure to draft Joe in the early rounds. We picked him in the third round of the 1959 draft, and he played a key role in our winning the conference title when he made the club as a rookie.

Joe was everything you looked for in a player. At 190, he wasn't big; he wasn't really strong; he didn't have blinding speed; he often wasn't good enough to knock people out of starting jobs; but he was always good enough to play when the team needed help. He took a beating every season. During much of the 1963 season, when Alex Webster was injured and missed so much playing time, Joe filled in at fullback. I'm sure there are players in the NFL today (probably some Giants players) who tire of hearing people say, "Boy, they sure don't make 'em today like used to" —and I get a little tired of people saying to me, "Oh, you old-timers!"— but show me any player today who can match what Joe Morrison did for his team over thirteen seasons. Not points, yards or catches, but his willingness to be so versatile and then go out and produce.

Our final opportunity to win an NFL championship in the Tittle Era fell short two weeks after the Pittsburgh game. With the temperature at ten degrees and the footing very icy we lost to the Chicago Bears in Wrigley Field, 14-10. This game was replayed in TV clips and in print a couple of years ago when the Giants played the Bears in the NFC playoffs, and the blame for our loss always seemed to fall on Shofner because he failed to catch a touchdown pass in the first half when we were ahead, 7-0. Why do people still point to that play as the reason we lost? How about the players who missed blocks that forced Tittle to throw early and miss other touchdowns? How about those who didn't pick up the blitzes that caused him to be injured? How about the rookie quarterback who wasn't well prepared that day and missed open receivers? Or the defensive back who didn't close quickly enough on a run and allowed a big gain? Blaming Del Shofner is all baloney; there was much more to losing that game than one missed pass, and believe me, none of us have ever felt that he should ever have been, in any way, held accountable. If he hadn't made some great catches in October and November, we wouldn't have played that game in late December. Blaming one player is too obvious, and blaming him because his feet slipped in an icy end zone as he reached for the ball, slightly off balance, isn't even mentioned. Sure, Del always said he should have caught it, but that was Del—no excuses, no alibis.

One more thing about Shofner and championship play. He was always rapped because he didn't have big days in those title games, and players like Jess Whittenton and Dave Whitsell were given all the credit for their coverage. Their jobs were made a helluva lot easier when Shofner came into a game as the foil—a decoy who would fool the other team, which had prepared to stop him.

There is no doubt the chief reason we lost the Bears game was the injury to Tittle's left knee halfway through the second quarter. Bears linebacker Larry Morris slammed into him on a blitz, and Y. A. left for the rest of the half. In the second half he could not plant it properly to get any power or accuracy on his throws. Chicago picked off four of them in the second half, and our offense all but died. At the same time we lost Phil King for part of the game, though he still wound up as our leading rusher, and Morrison took such a pounding playing fullback that he too had to come out of the game. We also lost guard Bookie Bolin with a concussion, so our offense became a shell of the unit that had become the second highest scoring team in NFL history.

When we saw Tittle hobble off the field and into the locker room we knew it would be a tougher day, but not an impossible one. There was no letdown by the defense. Right away, the feeling was: "We've got to go twice as hard—and how can you do that when you're going as hard as you can?—but no one can look over his shoulder and expect a miracle. If we shut them out the rest of the way we win." Well, we didn't, but we didn't allow the Bears to drive past the 50 yardline on their own steam, either. As was the case the year before against the Packers, I don't believe the defense ever played any better. In two NFL title games we allowed only three touchdowns, and two of those by Chicago were the result of intercepted screen passes that became scoring drives of six and 24 yards.

There also were a couple of planning lapses in our preparations. Sherman again decided to revamp our offense over the previous two weeks to "surprise" Bears defensive coach George Allen, but in so doing he kept in our goal-line offense a couple of slow-developing sweeps to the right and left, with the tackles on the opposite side from where the play was to be run, pulling out and helping form the interference. Because Allen had seen these plays in our films, he knew that none of our other linemen blocked back to take away the pursuit, so he ordered his defensive ends to chase the runner at top speed.

In the first quarter Tittle passed 13 yards to Gifford for our only touchdown. We drove to the Bear's two yardline early in the second quarter, but when the offense got into the huddle to run a short goal-line play, Tittle said, "I've got to get a timeout because I'm not certain what to call here."

"Run a wedge play up the middle and we'll score," someone suggested.

"That's the problem," Y. A. replied. "We don't have a wedge play in our goal-line offense."

"Run it," came the suggestion again. "We know what to do."

"I can't," he said. "Sherman raises hell when we run a play that isn't in the offense. I've got to call time and go talk to him about it."

Finally, Jack Stroud, our offensive captain, told Tittle he would request the officials to measure how much we needed for a first down (we could make one and still not score). That got an automatic clock stoppage, and Tittle hurried over to talk to Sherman. He brought back orders to run the two sweeps—first to the left, and if we didn't score or get a first down, next to the right.

110

Morrison, our only healthy back that day, ran the first one as ordered, but it developed so slowly by design that the Bears' right defensive end Ed O'Bradovich caught Joe from behind for a loss. Tittle called the sweep to the right on the next play, and Doug Atkins, the Bears' left end, made the tackle. Stroud had driven O'Bradovich into the end zone with his block, and if Atkins hadn't run the play down from behind, Morrison most likely would have scored. Ever since, Jack has second-guessed himself for asking for the measurement. Jack felt that with the clock running, Y. A. would have had no option but to call the wedge play. The question is, of course, why didn't we have the most common of all goal-line plays? Instead of being up, 14-7, we wound up with Don Chandler kicking a field goal for a 10-7 lead.

When Tittle left the game with his injured knee, rookie Glynn Griffing was the only quarterback we had, but he simply wasn't ready for this role. During the 1963 season we did not carry a backup veteran quarterback. Several teams carried these quarterbacks, and the Bears had Rudy Bukich behind Billy Wade. We had one until Ralph Guglielmi, following a poor performance in a 31-0 loss to Pittsburgh, was traded to the 49ers after the second week of the season. Ralph also had a spotty preseason, but he had still proven himself more capable of handling the club than a rookie, and we were simply lucky that nothing happened to Tittle during the season or our title hopes would have been long gone. When we really needed a savvy guy in the biggest game of the year, there was none. It was obvious to all of us that Y. A. really shouldn't have played in the second half, but he forced himself because he knew there was no one else. Chalk it up to poor planning.

It turned out that Tittle had severe ligament damage to his left knee, bad enough that he wouldn't have been able to play for several weeks had the season continued, and the Bears' fans really endeared themselves to me when they cheered his injury as he limped off the field, the most despicable act any group of spectators could do. Their seats all but nudged our bench, and when that happened some of our guys turned around and started to scream at them. I thought for a moment that some of the players were going into the seats to get those obnoxious boors.

If matters worked out, the Bears game would have been my last as a player for the Giants. I wanted to turn all of my energies toward full-time coaching, even though I had some serious reservations about how much my contributions would be accepted. A couple of years before, when I was at the Pro Bowl, I had a long talk with Vince Lombardi about my future as an NFL coach, based on the fact that I did not wish to leave the New York City area.

"Your odds are very slim of ever being anything other than an assistant coach," he told me. "It means the head coach has to get fired, or leave for some reason, and management wants you to become his successor. There is no guarantee that will happen. It also means that you wind up

111

hoping your boss gets fired or gets another job. Either way, you are being unfair to him, and to yourself."

When we finished talking it was apparent that the odds of becoming the head coach of the Giants at any time soon were stacked against me. I had already learned from my work as an assistant coach that it would not be a happy life working under Sherman—the aggressive way that I wanted to coach and the dedication I wanted to bring to the job for the benefit of the entire team and organization simply would not be accepted. Even when I started working as a full-time defensive coach in training camp in 1964, it was apparent that my coaching ambitions could not be realized with the Giants, and I made up my mind that that season would be my last.

As matters turned out, Sherman obviously believed I was as valuable to him as a player as a full-time coach, so when we had problems filling holes on our team with the season less than a month away, he asked me to play the dual role again, and I happily accepted. Admittedly, the transition from player to full-time coach was very difficult for me. I wasn't part of the players' lives, and I couldn't be with them on the same basis as before. Had the future held more promise as a coach I would have overcome those problems, but when it became apparent that was not to be in the future, then I was happy in my former role.

Of course, I missed two good friends in 1964; Sherman had begun to dismantle the defense in the off-season by trading Dick Modzelewski and Sam Huff. Because assistant coaches worked at other jobs during the off-season, we had no serious discussions about these moves. As the defensive coach, I was never consulted about the effect of such changes, except for a single phone call from Sherman asking whether I thought Jerry Hillebrand could play middle linebacker. That call came while I was making a sales call at the Pennsylvania Railroad offices, where Sherman had left a message for me to call him. When I did, he asked about Hillebrand's ability to fill Huff's position, and I told him:

"With a lot of hard work anyone with the specific skills could play the position."

"Well," Sherman said, "I'm seriously thinking of trading Sam Huff."

"Seriously thinking," nothing. I knew at that moment Sam was gone, but I didn't try to talk Al out of it because I knew he had already made up his mind. It wasn't a question of me getting Sherman to reconsider; I never had the kind of relationship with him that I felt had to be a part of good staff work. It just wasn't there...and neither was Sam Huff.

His departure caused a firestorm of criticism; though from a pure football side the trade might have made some sense if there wasn't so much personal stuff involved. I knew that Sherman was trying to build his own defense rather than live with the fact that he had inherited it from Tom Landry, and that its allegiance was to a system, not to the head coach. That system had problems at times when teams caught up to our inside

4-3 defense. When we shifted to the outside 4-3 defense, the adjustment took some time. Sam incurred some of the pain by getting knocked on his ass more often than in the past as we worked to perfect it while building in new people as well. Still, it wasn't as if he couldn't play. We did well enough to win a couple of conference titles and to play dynamically in two title games. Sam, of course, played with the Redskins, and earned a place in the Hall of Fame.

Sherman also traded Dick Modzelewski to the Browns, and I often wondered whether part of the reason was my close friendship with him. From a football standpoint it made no sense. Dick was still playing well, something he proved in Cleveland when he did so much to solidify the Browns' defense with maturity and on-the-field leadership, helping them win the 1964 NFL title and the 1965 Eastern Conference title. Trading Huff and Mo also took away some of those leadership intangibles that had knit us together as a unit. Sam was the firebrand and the hot-shot; but his was the Violent World of Sam Huff, the vehicle of national prominence that brought recognition to our defense. Mo kept everyone together with his own personal style, and the fun he got from the game was contagious. Those moves, which netted the Giants three journeymen—tight end Bobby Crespino from Cleveland, and defensive end Andy Stynchula and running back Dickie James from Washington— also kept the rest of the players off-balance. Naturally, they felt that if a Sam Huff and Dick Modzelewski could be traded, their futures could be in jeopardy. Throughout the 1964 season, when we won just two of fourteen games (we tied two others), I could sense the players' uneasiness, almost as if they were asking, "Damn it, what's happening to us? We're a championship team and yet this so-called rebuilding is tearing us down. Maybe I'll be next." The consequence of that questioning was a lessening of mental alertness and overall confidence, the very qualities you need to ride out the storms in tough times, and a great deal of frustration on everyone's part.

From a football standpoint, we lost two key veteran players who knew our system and played it well, which shook everyone up. There was no way we could be as efficient as in past years. Players know when trades are made for the good of the team, when a player simply isn't doing the job on the field, for example, or when he becomes so much of a pain in the ass that he is hurting the team with his attitude. No one minded when Rosie Grier was traded to the Rams; his refusal to keep his weight under control had lessened his ability. Players also know that trading players still capable of helping the team is a disservice to the team. While the head coach might say trades are his prerogative, he must be sensitive to the effect they have on the team's performance and personality. Sherman tore the Giants apart to satisfy the whim of being able to say he now had *his* team. The record shows he did better with the team he largely inherited.

Coupled with the team's loss of confidence that year was a string of serious injuries. After he was injured in the second game of the season in Pittsburgh, Tittle was in and out of the lineup. The picture of Y. A. kneeling on the ground, helmet off, looking downcast as blood ran from his head, still hurts me. That picture typifies our 1964 season; all of us who were left tried extremely hard, and for our efforts we were bloodied and battered, having to endure the heartbreak of going from champions to last place in one year because trades never worked out and the rookies who replaced departed and injured veterans were simply overmatched. Y. A. did all he could that year, but he played with injuries so severe that he could hardly lift his arm above the shoulder. On defense, Lou Slaby, a rookie, replaced Sam Huff, and he worked hard to do the job. But you don't replace a Huff in one season with a rookie, and you don't surround that rookie with new people totally unfamiliar or incapable of playing with your system and hope to survive, let alone win.

But there are enough good memories from six championship seasons and one NFL title to help blot out that one bad experience. Like everyone else who caught a strong case of Giants Fever from those years, I still consider those memories very special, a part of the team's tradition that might never be duplicated. Certainly, they will never be matched in the minds of all who were participants...and celebrants.

At the same time, all of those great seasons still left unfulfilled a desire to do something more for my team. In 1964 I really didn't know what that was. I had cut off my coaching career with them, and any lingering hopes of getting called back were all but squashed in 1965 when Sherman signed a ten-year contract. That still didn't dampen my desire to be a coach, but as I said, my decision to build my life in Stamford all but ruled out anyplace other than New York City. I had been contacted by Sonny Werblin of the Jets in 1963 about the possibility of coaching his team, but nothing ever came of that. So my options seemed nil. Someplace in the back of my mind, however, I had still left room for fulfilling a role in the Giants' existence. In all honesty, I didn't really think it would ever come...but I never really gave up.

And it came...boy, did it ever!

114

Andy as a senior at Stamford High, 1942.

Water-tender and antiaircraft gunner during WWII.

116

Andy was number 84 with the Rams. . . and very much in love with those Ram horns.

Still in a Rams uniform, Andy is honored in the Polo Grounds in 1955, prior to a game against the Giants. Andy's parents (at left) are being greeted by his friend J. Walter Kennedy, later commissioner of the NBA.

Andy stops Cleveland's great back Jim Brown, with an assist by Sam Huff (70).

Andy once considered a professional baseball career. Here he poses with his favorite Yankee, Joe DiMaggio.

Andy (right) and Jim Katcavage smother Sonny Jurgensen while Dick Modzelewski moves in to help.

Conferring with head coach Allie Sherman during a game.

121

Vikings quarterback Fran Tarkenton finds no room to scramble as Andy closes in for a sack.

Andy takes aim at Redskins quarterback Norm Snead during a game at Yankee Stadium.

122

The Giants' great Fearsome Foursome of 1956-1962: from left, Andy, Rosie Grier, Dick Modzelewski and Jim Katcavage.

The Giants' coaching staff at the start of 1964 training camp. From left, Kyle Rote, head coach Allie Sherman, Ken Kavanaugh, Ed Kolman and Andy.

Director of Operations, 1976.

124

Part 2
Trying to Rebuild a Fallen Giant

7 A Giant Once More

On the weekend before Christmas 1973, most of Connecticut and Westchester County was embedded in several inches of ice after a monstrous storm swept through the area. The destruction was rampant, and hundreds of thousands of persons, including the Robustelli household in Stamford, were without power for several days—no heat, no water for daily showers, no lights for reading or life's other niceties. But inside the den of Wellington Mara's home, on the day after the 1973 season ended, it was cozy and warm, and the inconveniences that strapped so many nearby seemed very distant.

The team had won only two games and tied a third that year, a disaster that brought me to that den on that December Monday and had me deeply involved in discussions about becoming the director of operations for the Giants.

The organization really had cleared the decks. At rock bottom as far as its football future was concerned, it needed a plan that would revitalize its football life. Since Alex Webster had announced the previous week that he would not return as head coach, there was a grand opportunity to forge a new direction, with a revamped internal structure and a new coaching staff that could begin to work together on this mighty task.

I had had little contact with the club or Wellington since my departure in 1964, so I really never figured I would be considered for the job. Yet here I was, discussing the team's problems and what I saw as my role to help turn it around. Also involved in the discussion was Tim Mara, Well's nephew and the team's vice president, who represented the one-half ownership that had belonged to his late father, Jack. When Jack died in 1965, Tim had taken his role in the front office, overseeing all of the nonfootball operations.

During the previous week Well and Tim had discussed what might be done to revive the team, and Tim suggested that someone with a football background was needed to run that side of the operation. When Wellington and Jack ran the team, Well was vice president, but in effect his duties were those of a director of football operations, a major reason for the Giants' success.

When he succeeded Jack as president, Wellington thought he could continue to specialize in that area and allow Tim to take over the business side; as club president, Well would continue to oversee as necessary. Those plans fell apart when everyone in the organization turned to Wellington to solve every problem, and instead of devoting nearly 100 percent of his time to the football side, as he once did, he found himself spending no more than 40 percent on that end. This happened at a period when the NFL was going through some of its most profound changes during the AFL-NFL war, and their subsequent merger and realignment. As new people came into the sport, the way in which clubs did their business with each other was radically altered. Suddenly, the means by which the Giants had gained such preeminence were all but gone, a major reason why the team slumped so drastically on the field to its 1973 low point.

Obviously something had to be done to alleviate the problem, so Well and Tim decided to hire someone to fill that specialized football role. Well's first choice was Jim Finks, then general manager of the Minnesota Vikings, but he was under contract. Both agreed it would have taken so much time to get him cleared from that job and into the Giants that the impetus for change would have been lost. Then, Wellington told me later, Tim surprised him by suggesting me.

During that fall, I had had conversations with Tim and his brother-in-law, Dick Concannon, a Park Avenue lawyer, about the team and some of the Giants' problems. Those conversations were casual, the result of a big flap earlier in the season when quarterback Randy Johnson walked out and went home to Florida because he was miffed that Norm Snead was named the starting quarterback—even though Norm had gone to the Pro Bowl after the 1972 season. The walkout was a big headache at the time, and in a sudden surge of old Giant loyalty I responded by calling Tim and telling him that as I was going to Florida on a business trip I would be glad to intercede on the club's behalf if he thought it would do any good. My services were politely declined, but in the weeks following, as the Giants continued to lose, Tim called me a few times, asking me to meet with him and discuss the club's fortunes. Concannon was always with him, and they both asked pointed questions about how the football side could be run better and what solutions I might have for the problems that had arisen. I had not followed the team that closely, so in the spirit of general discussion only I voiced my opinions, mostly on management technique and assessment of playing skills, emphasizing that I did so without any of the privileged inside information to make specific judgments.

They were obviously intrigued by my suggestions, and after one of the meetings Tim asked me about the possibility of my joining the team to help oversee the football side—noting that he felt Well was spending far too much time in that area. I'm certain that was the time he and his brother-in-law began to formulate the position of director of operations. So when

Tim offered my name to his uncle, it had been after some serious consideration on his part, though he never told Wellington about any of our discussions. I never even thought about them the day Well, Tim and I discussed the job. I assumed this was a matter that had been discussed by both of them.

I'm certain now that all of those meetings I had with Tim and his brother-in-law had two distinct aims. Firstly, Tim wanted to showcase me for Concannon, hoping to elicit his approval so the idea of my overseeing the football operations could be sold to his side of the ownership. That 50 percent relied on Dick's advice for its every move, the final step before an agreement. Secondly, they were seeking someone to do their bidding and make their half of the ownership more dominant, something that became apparent to me about a year after I was on the job, when I began to see some of the things that took place to push Well aside. I had no idea such maneuvers were in the offing. By taking the job as director of operations I felt I could equalize the involvement of everyone—Tim, Well and myself— in our respective areas, helping to strike a good balance of responsibilities in the team's management. That wasn't what Tim had in mind. I discovered after a while that he would do almost anything to get Well out of a decision-making position.

This Machiavellian atmosphere smothered us throughout most of my tenure as director of operations, seriously impeding the team's resurgence. Tim's side of the ownership thought first about how it could control every move, rather than how the moves could help the team.

Being offered the job was a surprise to many. I had been away from football and the Giants for nine years, so the fact that I was not current on the teams and people in the NFL was very apparent. I guess I was a bit surprised, too, because I had never had especially close ties to Well Mara. I was rarely in his company; until that December Monday I had never been in his home. I dealt with him as a player negotiating my contract, and as I said, he was firm but fair. I believe he respected my football background and knowledge. He sat in on meetings when I discussed defensive game plans with Al Sherman, and he had assessed their effectiveness each week when he watched films of our games. He was also privy to my defense of our system and my defensive teammates when Sherman or other coaches tried to take them apart. He knew that I was always well prepared to state a case and prove it. Likewise, I had always respected him, but we were pretty much strangers to each other on that Monday. Yet he was willing to allow me to step into his organization and become a guiding force for its most visible side. That Tim was in favor of the move also helped; Well was still sensitive to the needs of the other half of the ownership, and he would do nearly anything he could to make an accommodation if it meant the team would benefit.

The thorniest question we discussed that day was not the future of the team, but what title would be given to Ray Walsh, the team's general manager. In reality, he was the business manager. Unlike most general managers in professional sports, he did not deal with players' contracts, make trades or involve himself in any way with the football operation. As director of operations, that would be my domain, so to delineate our responsibilities Well and Tim named him a vice president, with the same nonfootball responsibilities. They decided to leave the general manager's title open, keeping our areas separate and distinct. In fact, the general manager's job should have encompassed both areas; the people running the football and business sides should have been responsible to someone who, in turn, should have reported to the president on day-to-day matters, forming a direct line of authority from the top. In that way the president, not having to worry about the nuts and bolts of each segment, would have been able to lend leadership, judgment and guidance to the organization as a whole. The lack of such a structure would haunt the Giants, but with a fifty-fifty ownership split, it was almost impossible to build.

When we discussed the job that day, I was not concerned about a title, and I never even mentioned salary or any of the other conditions of the contract. In effect, I was to be like a consultant, stepping in and suggesting changes and methods of operating that would get the football side of the club back to an efficient state. I made it clear, and they agreed, that I wanted to stay only two or three years. My own business had just begun to expand, and in the end I really wanted to return and devote the rest of my life to it.

When our discussion turned to the team's problems, I demurred on specific solutions until I had all of the information at hand, but I did indicate my plan to combine my knowledge of football with the sound business principles I had learned through my own experiences to form the basis of my operation. Of course, I had no idea of the complexities of the job, nor of the roadblocks that lay ahead. I had only their word that all of us were in this together, and that we would all work to turn the organization around and make it an on-the-field winner once more. But I had no illusions about Super Bowls or titles, and I certainly had no inkling that my tenure would be the great adventure that it ultimately became.

Actually, when I left the Giants' locker room after the final game of the 1964 season, I never expected to be affiliated with the team again, and it hurt a bit. My NFL coaching ambitions all but abandoned, I was more or less content to follow the team from afar...more or less, I stress, because the Giants were in my blood, just as the Rams had been, and I never really got them out of my system. As the years passed, and my business grew, I realized more and more that much of the opportunity afforded me came from my time with the Giants, so in that sense I owed the team a debt of sorts. More than that, there also was a deep, abiding love that retiring as a player never really snuffed out, so when I was asked to return to help, I found it impossible to refuse.

Though I had been away from the NFL since 1964, my life was far from empty. I had accumulated enough experience to equip me somewhat for my return to the game, particularly in the business side, where the building of an organization, its backbone and structure, is so important. The consistently successful professional sports teams all have solid internal structures, run by sound and sensible principles that combine the nuances of the sport with the nuts and bolts of commerce. What I lacked coming back to the Giants was a personal rapport with the principals involved in pro football and some of the procedures by which the game operated. Those I picked up during my tenure; what I brought to the team was learned the hard way in the noninsulated business world.

There was never a time during my playing career when I was not involved in some business venture. None of us made enough money from playing football to support our families for an entire year. Actually, I began during my years at Arnold College. Each week I took a sackful of athletic equipment from Eddie Clark's store, sold the various items to students, kept a 10 or 15 percent commission and returned the next week with more wares. Eddie and I became partners when I invested my two-thousand dollar winner's share after the Rams' 1951 NFL title game, and we struggled to expand our business during the next five years. One of our coups was getting permission from every NFL club-owner to recreate their uniforms, and we sold them publicly, the first exposure of team identification of each NFL team, and a forerunner of the concept of NFL Properties.

In 1957, while at the College All-Star game in Chicago, I had a reunion with an old Navy buddy, Dick Johnston. He ran a fabricating company with his father that manufactured railroad cars, and he convinced me I could handle his business in New York City. So I became a manufacturer's rep and saw instantly that professional athletes had an entrée to business that was unique. I made as much selling to the railroads as I did from playing football, which enabled me to plow all of my sporting goods profits back into the business, helping Eddie and me broaden its base.

In 1964 I also took an option to purchase a travel agency in Stamford from my friend Bill Fugazy, and when my career with the Giants ended, the travel and sporting goods businesses became full-time occupations. Soon afterwards I also established a marketing firm, National Professional Athletes, Inc., to implement a program for what was then the Allied Chemical Corporation in which a group of professional football players became involved in sales, promotion, advertising and marketing for Allied's new Fibers Division. It all began when the firm's merchandising manager, Ted Picard, asked me to get a couple of athletes together for a father and son dinner, and the affair was a smash. I then sold him on carpeting the locker room in Yankee Stadium with his company's product, the first for any major league locker room. We also convinced him to have a couple of athletes sitting on the carpet and to use the picture as a sales promotion tool. In turn, the athletes got their homes carpeted, and that also became part of the marketing package. Allied was so pleased by the reaction to this concept that NPA was signed to handle more of this kind of business.

Using players like Merlin Olsen of the Rams, Pete Retzlaff of the Philadelphia Eagles, Nick Pietrosante of the Lions, Gino Cappelletti of the Patriots, Joe Morrison of the Giants and a half-dozen others, we kept this team more or less intact for some seven years, while building other facets of our business.

In 1965, the year after I left the Giants, Chet Simmons of NBC hired me to do color commentary on his network's telecasts of American Football League games. The war between the two leagues was in full swing, and hiring former NFL players was a good marketing tool for the AFL. Having their league praised on the air before millions of viewers gave their product legitimacy (certainly no one was going to knock it and say it was inferior to the NFL). I tried not to be prejudiced, but my loyalties to my old league made me a bit uncomfortable.

The job was frustrating in itself. Though hired as an analyst, I never felt I had the opportunity to analyze the game properly in the fifteen seconds I had between Charley Jones's play-by-play. Sometimes I found myself saying things that didn't mean anything just because I knew I couldn't explain complex situations in such a brief time. My most enjoyable moments came when they let me talk to the players or their families and put something of a human touch into my work. I also tried to convince the network people to arrange special classes for directors and cameramen that would educate them about the game of football and make them familiar with what happens in certain situations. Many times I would pick out a team's tendencies, describe what was going to happen, then lose the whole effect because the director and cameraman didn't know what to look for while it was happening. I wanted them to know how these plays were run from the beginning so they could be on top of them. Now you see isolated cameras on these kind of plays, but it took about twenty years for TV to get into the game, and there is still much they do not cover.

But even with building my businesses and doing TV, one of the most enjoyable times in my life was the six-month period in 1966 when I was head coach of the Brooklyn Dodgers of the Continental Football League, which played all but one of its home games at Downing Stadium on Randalls Island, next to the Triborough Bridge. We lasted only one season, but so much of what we did—building an organization from scratch, hiring loyal coaches, getting kids who wanted to play football, giving them a philosophy and getting them to believe in it—really gave me a direction to follow when I returned to the Giants as director of operations. On a personal basis, being head coach of the Dodgers was all I ever imagined myself doing had I become an NFL head coach.

Jack Stroud was one of my coaches, along with my boyhood friend, Carmine Tosches, and John Maher, a longtime successful high school coach in Darien, Connecticut. All of us were stunned by the response to our team by kids who dreamed of playing pro football and saw us as their one last chance. We held a couple of free agent tryout camps in the early summer that year, and more than three hundred applicants showed up, some from as far away as Texas—and we tried to discourage them because they had to pay their own way. These kids were more dedicated than the team's owners, some of whom were millionaire businessmen who liked the idea of being involved with pro football, but not of paying for the privilege. Before we even opened the season, most them had fled after just a minimal investment, leaving others less financially endowed to try and support us. It didn't work out, and the league took us over in midseason.

Still, we had some memorable adventures. When we played a preseason game in Orlando, Florida, during an airlines strike, the team was able to fly down but unable to get a return flight. So after the game we loaded ourselves onto a couple of chartered buses and rode home—twenty-two hours—looking forward to playing again. One of our owners ran a large supermarket chain in New York, and we ran a minimum purchase-for-ticket deal for a preseason home game. We "sold" over 20,000 tickets, but hardly half that number got into the stadium that evening because the traffic to the game was so jammed up along the Triborough Bridge. Thousands of ticket holders spent the night going nowhere.

Our players were comprised mostly of people who, drafted and cut by pro football teams, sought another chance. Others were former NFL players such as lineman George Bednar, who had spent a season with the St. Louis Cardinals; quarterback Sonny Gibbs, a six-foot-seven Texan who had been a top draft pick of the Cowboys; wide receivers Bob Reed and Bob Lacey from the Vikings and Giants; and linebacker Tom Costello, who had been one of my teammates on the 1964 Giants. Our quarterback, Tom Kennedy, was signed by the Giants midway through the 1966 season, when injuries decimated their quarterback corps. He finished as their starting quarterback and returned to the team in 1967.

In a personal sense, we were successful. Besides Kennedy, several of our players were signed to NFL contracts the next season, which was really all we had to offer them. It certainly wasn't the money—four hundred dollars per game was the top salary, and only two or three players got that much. We also had the personal satisfaction of saving one kid from taking his life during some tough domestic times. We were all he had to turn to, and it was enough to help him get a handle on his life.

In a football sense, we were an expansion team (the club had played in Providence, Rhode Island, the previous year) that came together to form a closeness similar to what I had experienced as a Giants player. Some of that came from adversity, some from achievement. We lost one game to Richmond on the old "phantom" play when a player sneaked off the bench and ran down the field to catch the winning touchdown pass in the final seconds. Our finest moment came in the last game of the season when we knew the team was finished and would likely be moved (it was—to Akron, Ohio), when we upset the Toronto team and cost it the division title. We were a very good football team at that point, the result of following

133

a sound plan of development.

In a financial sense, I paid for the privilege of coaching the team. We practiced at night because most of our players held full-time jobs in the Metropolitan area, and I continued to run my own firm. I had a contract that offered me 50 percent of the purchase price the team would receive for any player purchased by the NFL, but I never received a penny. Still, I believe our league was an ideal developmental program for the NFL, and it worked for many players: Tom Kennedy; defensive tackle Otis Sistrunk, who played for the Oakland Raiders; Sam Wyche, a quarterback who played with a number of NFL teams and now coaches the Cincinnati Bengals; running back Charley Leigh, who played with the Miami Dolphins during their Super Bowl years; and others who needed only to prove their worth over a full season rather than under the hectic and often brief conditions of training camp. Our Dodgers group gets together from time to time, and that special feeling that all of us shared is as strong today as it was then. So are the laughs.

When my Dodgers career ended, my football life was pretty much confined to television, occasional games at Yankee Stadium and, for two years before returning to the Giants, a weekly television show with Sam DeLucca that covered the Giants and Jets. I didn't enjoy watching the games in person. I found myself looking at them much too analytically, much too critically to enjoy the game for itself. My greatest Sunday joys during this time were sitting by my pool on warm September afternoons, listening to the Giants on the radio; or, as the fall came, riding through the New England countryside enjoying the foliage, something I hadn't been able to do for the sixteen years I was involved with the game. And if I had it to do over again under those conditions, I would still sit in the sun by my pool, still view the foliage. I go to a game or two at Giants Stadium now, but it is still as different as it was during the years between my jobs with the team. The games played then, and now, aren't my games, and I stay away from things that are not my business so I won't be tempted to become a critic.

But all of those experiences during those nine years away from the Giants had a direct influence on my actions when I returned as director of operations. I had an opportunity to get a perspective on the real world, of which football is only a segment. For the six months I was with the Dodgers I saw clearly that Tom Landry had the right approach to management: Get everything organized, give people the responsibility to do their jobs, then oversee the operation carefully. That is how Landry built his defense; that is how we built what really was a strong organization with the Dodgers despite a bare-bones budget; and ultimately it is what I tried to do with the Giants.

The Giants job was the ultimate test. When I sat in Well Mara's den on the December Monday in 1973, I had no idea how much had to be accomplished and how many obstacles had to be overcome. Since I left the Giants, the organization had simply not kept up with the way pro football had changed. In the past, owners freely helped each other with players. We got Y. A. Tittle in 1961 when Lou Spadia, the 49ers owner, called Well and told him the club was changing its offense and Y. A. was available if the Giants wanted to talk about a deal. Friends helped friends in those days and the deal was made. New people coming into the game had none of those old ties, and they were intent on going their own way. However, they also introduced new and more up-to-date methods of operating a football franchise, which they had used successfully in other business ventures. The old-guard NFL owners, of whom the Maras were among the pioneers, suddenly found themselves trailing the field, and, as we have seen over the past couple of decades, it took some new methods to get back on track, not only with the Giants but also with the Bears and Steelers. There are still old-guard NFL teams which have not caught up.

In a nutshell, the problem with the Giants during their down years was lack of an organizational structure where everyone had defined areas of responsibility and had to answer for those duties. When Well assumed the presidency and Tim took over the business side, there was never an equal distribution of responsibilities. Instead of insisting that everyone make his own decisions and accept the consequences, Wellington allowed himself to become the man who had to solve everyone's problems. No one wanted the consequences, so the end result was no input of fresh ideas, no healthy dialogue where everyone would have to prove the worth of new ideas. The club was literally run by one man for a decade, though Wellington never acted with anything but its best interests as his sole aim. He was so caught up in the team that he was often blinded by his own devotion—not unusual for someone who was raised to carry on its existence. He was always so close to the players and coaches that he failed to recognize that the old ways had to change as pro football rose to greater heights. The Giants did so much to change the game with our achievements in the late fifties, punctuated by the 1958 overtime championship game, that it is ironic Well Mara became a victim of his own success.

Everything changed when the American Football League was born in 1960. The Giants were on top then, and Wellington has admitted they sacrificed some younger talent at that time to stay there. That policy ultimately caught up with them when it came time to remake the team. There were also a couple of other factors. Al Sherman was given a ten-year contract in 1965, so his urgency to get back on top was softened by that cushion, though that is not to say he was satisfied with not winning. Another factor was the inability of Sherman and the staff of coaches he hired to develop new, young talent. With all due respect to Al, I don't believe he felt developing players was going to be a chore; nor did he recognize that every time you build with a new player, you are in effect starting over at that position. He wanted to build a new house, but he had no foundation.

So when it came time to replace older players, there were no man-for-man replacements, and the team's fortunes dipped. Quick fixes were tried, such as getting veteran players whose best days were past in exchange for draft picks that could have produced younger, more talented players over the long run. The biggest quick fix was acquiring quarterback Fran Tarkenton in 1967 from the Vikings for a couple of number-one draft picks. Those picks could have been used to give the team a better talent base, perhaps even a quarterback who could have carried the team through the seventies.

Another reason for the acquisition of Tarkenton was the Giants' competition with the Jets for supremacy in New York City. The Jets had quarterback Joe Namath, and the Giants needed someone—or so they thought—to match him. Tarkenton was good, but he never had the talented cast around him that Namath did for the two or three seasons when the Jets pushed the Giants.

The Giants also failed to realize that players had changed, that their loyalties and attitudes were less intense. The mentality toward the game and the team did not meet the standards of those years in the fifties when the championship teams were being built. In those years one man, with a good knowledge of physical talent, could handle such matters. But after the game grew more complex, teams needed an organization to match all of the changes in talent development. The ability to trade to maintain a top standing diminished severely after the AFL and NFL merged, as did the talent pool with so many clubs participating in the draft. The philosophy of development needed to cope with these changing times was not in place on the Giants, and the patching and filling through the sixties and early seventies, combined with poor back-to-back drafts in 1971 and 1972, left the club desperately needing better players.

Actually, the Tarkenton trade set the tone for the Giants' personnel makeup. They tried to surround him with an offense that suited his scrambling style. When I became director of operations, I surveyed the NFL and found the team's biggest problem was a very, very small offensive line. In their thinking at the time, the Giants may have believed a big line was not needed to protect a quarterback who did not rely on the passing pocket. Also, the overall quality of personnel was well below the top teams in the NFL, which suggested to me that the choices in the draft were more coach- and front-office picks than personnel department choices. Maybe being a member of the Giants family had meant not disagreeing with the coach or the boss. Maybe nobody wanted to rock the boat. It seemed the motto was: Let the other guy make the decisions. Instead of engaging in discussion about the merits of the decisions, most in the organization were satisfied not to be wrong. When those decisions didn't work out, there was some snippy criticism from some who should have been more involved, but never face-to-face with the team's president and coach, as it should have been.

Of course, the fingers of blame pointed toward Wellington Mara, the architect of this philosophy. Some of those fingers came from within the front office, even though everyone there should have shared some of the responsibility; they had avoided making decisions on matters clearly within their domain. He should have chewed some ass around the office and gotten people into the spirit of the team, but Well always believed that everyone was pulling together. In fact, only one oar was doing any rowing, and the ship was going around in circles instead of going forward.

But there was more to the problem. Well was so in love with his team and so positive that he had the solutions to its football problems that no one challenged him with different ideas. Instead, they became awestruck by his reasoning, which was based as much on his willing his team to be successful as it was motivated by his absolute devotion to it.

Until I became director of operations, I never saw this great obsession with his football team. His enthusiasm was scary because it made him certain that all of his judgments were correct. I fought him on some matters where I believed he was wrong. Some battles I won, some I lost, but we never had a problem, and he never intimidated me. No one had ever done that with him before, and I'm certain it brought him up short at the start of my tenure, but when he saw that my questioning had as its only purpose the betterment of the team, he appreciated this dialogue of different ideas.

To really understand all that went on with the Giants, you must first understand what moves Wellington Mara. He is a very private, almost shy person who is totally in love with his wife, his family and his team, in that earthly order. He is rarely given to public outbursts, and you'll never see him posturing or wooing the media for his own self-promotion. Many of the assumptions about him are based on rumor, hearsay or false conclusions. He is a very tough-minded person, but also a very sensitive one to the feelings of those who are loyal to his organization—and loyalty plays a key role in his life, and in the Giants family.

He can get upset, but he tries to confine this side of his personality to the business side of his life, though he has lashed out publicly when someone has taken an unfair shot. Yet he will answer every letter—good or bad—and when someone is critical of the team or its operation, he often takes great pains to explain his side of the story.

In a football sense, Well will do anything for his team; and sometimes he does too much. He was often generous to a fault with his players and coaches, to the point of going overboard with suggestions that they felt obliged to follow. Losing cut him like a sharp knife, and if Giants fans think they suffered through the lean years, they have no idea how much Well Mara agonized over his team's failures. I almost gag when people tell me he cared only about making money, and not winning. Money has always been secondary to winning with him, and I know that he raised ticket prices during the losing years only after a great deal of agonizing— and for sound fiscal reasons. He did not feel the fans should have to pay more to see an unsuccessful team. Contrary to what many may think, the Giants made only a modest profit during those years. Money was never a big deal with him, though there were others in the organization who grumbled one year when the profit-sharing was down.

There is another side of Well that never is seen publicly—his tremendous feeling for the good of the game. He is one of the few old-guard owners left, one of those men who built professional football by sublimating personal interests for the overall good of the NFL. Wellington has always done that. At league meetings, after getting raked over by club owners like Al Davis who clearly were putting self-interest ahead of everything else, I'd sometimes say to him, "Those guys don't care a damn about the league. When are you going to not give a damn about the league before everything else?"

"Well," he'd say with that quiet determination that is apparent when he knows he is right and will not back down, "that's the way I am. I still have a feeling for the league, and the league needs us to try and convert those people to seeing we're all in this together and that the future of the game is in our hands."

I often got exasperated when I heard that.

"You're not going to convert them, and you know it, Well," I said. "You've got to play their game."

"No," he'd insist, "I'm doing what I think is correct." A good example of his attitude occurred the time we got Larry Csonka, who, though a free agent after the World Football League folded, was once the property of the Miami Dolphins. Wellington insisted that we reimburse the Dolphins with a pair of number-three draft picks. I looked at other teams who had signed ex-NFL free agents from the WFL, and they weren't giving up a thing. I recall Cleveland owner Art Modell saying after he signed wide receiver Paul Warfield that he would give the Dolphins draft-choice compensation too, but I believe he gave them $50,000 and kept the draft pick and Warfield for himself.

I tried to get Well to do the same, but he wouldn't budge—though he did get upset when the Dolphins' owner, Joe Robbie, tried to muscle him and get the two picks in one year, contrary to the original deal. Robbie got his picks in successive years because Wellington felt it was the right thing to do and would keep some sort of status quo in these matters. Don't get me wrong, I never felt that Well should do what he couldn't live with, but I wanted him to be a little street smart once in a while and deal with the street guys on their own level. It's just not in his makeup to do that, and the NFL is damn lucky to have someone who still feels as strongly about the good of the game as he does, though I often wonder if it does any good.

My conclusions about the state of the team and my own personal profile of Wellington were the result of my time as director of operations. When I took the job my opinions of what should be done to turn things around were not solicited. I said at the start that I hadn't been following the team very closely, and even if I had I had no access to privileged information.

I wanted to look into the situation myself and draw my own conclusions so I could present them with some plan of operation. Within the first couple of weeks I completed a memo to Well and Tim that outlined what my philosophy and approach to the job would be. In that memo I keyed in on consistency, hard work, rebuilding from the bottom, patience and avoiding the quick fix.

At the same time, I made it clear that my job was to stimulate all areas of the football operation, and that meant pointing fingers at people not used to having fingers pointed at them. Like it or not, they had to contest my opinion of what was good or bad for the team. I strongly suggested to Well that the best way to begin to change the way the team operated was for him to stay out of the day-to-day decision-making of each department head. "Let them make their own decisions and survive on their own competence and experience," I urged him. "If they do, fine, and we as a team will get better. If they need you to make all their decisions, then we will not go forward." It had to be that way, I added, because we had a long way to go to catch up, and I needed everyone to be aware of just what changes had to take place.

Weighing all of this now, I don't think the Giants should have hired me because I had to work at a huge disadvantage. Had I intended to stay with the Giants forever I could have blasted out all of the inbreeding and faulty methods and established a permanent system. But I was going to make recommendations, institute changes and then leave. Two things could happen. One, someone else could inherit the system. If he liked it, fine; if he didn't, then he would make his own changes, and the organization would march in place until they were accomplished. Or, two, there could be a continuity, which is why I eventually pushed for an assistant director of operations who could learn the system and then help maintain it when I left so the club would not march in place. We tried the second option, hiring Terry Bledsoe, who had worked on the NFL Management Council. But that move, as we'll see, triggered the firestorm from Tim's side of the ownership that resulted in the big blowup and split in 1978.

One of the moves I suggested was, over a five-year period, phasing out all of those who reached retirement age but still retaining their know-how and experience with special assignments. We would pay them a retainer for that work which, when added to their retirement benefits, would not seriously impact on their salary structure. At the same time we would bring in new people who were knowledgeable and receptive to the new techniques and systems that were changing the face of every business at that time. My five-year plan began in our locker room with one of our trainers, John Dziegiel, a wonderful guy who simply wasn't in touch with the new training methods and equipment, and moving right up into the front office to include director of personnel Jim Lee Howell. Of course, those I had targeted were resentful, and when Jim Lee eventually found out—I'm certain that Tim told him; the plan was privy only to Wellington and him—I became the bad guy and *change* became a dirty word.

The area that needed the most change was our personnel department, where things were done in the mid-seventies as they had been in 1950, principally because Wellington made all the decisions and Jim Lee insisted on his own antiquated notebook-and-file-card method of record-keeping. He was very comfortable doing things his way, with help from our scouting combine reports, but there was little creativity or hands-on scouting from which we could make solid, up-to-date judgments. Well into the computer age, many teams had refined their systems so they could break down every bit of information and have it instantly accessible. Further, their personnel directors, by constantly looking at people, working with the scouts and gathering their own information to supplement the reports, kept their teams abreast of the best talent. With the talent pool so diluted, and our personnel needs so critical, it was imperative that our decisions be as mistake-free as possible, not only for our drafting, but for those times when players were available from other teams.

Jim Lee never seemed to accept that his methods would not meet these ends, partly because he was so used to Wellington running his department and making key decisions. If there were going to be any changes, they almost had to come from Well rather than me—exactly what I was trying to prevent. He fought the system vigorously, and I often wonder if the old coach-player relationship—he was my coach, I was his player—was a factor in his attitude. Also, he knew that no matter what he did, or didn't do, it really didn't matter—his loyalty to Wellington and the organization was beyond question, and his job was secure. The only answer was to work around him, which we did for five unsatisfying years, but this situation did not accelerate our rebuilding process or the football operation.

I wanted Jerry Shay, then in his early years as a scout, to take over the job, but he didn't want to leave California for New York. So we made him our chief scout, and he really grew in the job. He wasn't afraid to offer an opinion and he didn't worry about getting shot down. We also revamped the assignments of our other scouts so they would cover the areas where they lived rather than flying all over the country looking at people. The latter was very expensive and counterproductive. If each man concentrated on a single geographic area, I reasoned, he got to know the schools, the coaches and the players on a more intimate basis. He then became privy to the inside information needed to make the best possible judgments. That took a couple of years to accomplish.

But one of the things that always bothered me was the relationship between scouts and coaches, who also had scouting responsibilities. Coaches often took their brief tours and quickly rejected prospects scouts had looked at all year. Right away, the scout's judgment was in question—and whether or not to draft the player became a problem. Some say you need many opinions; I never believed that. Unless they are stacked on one side or the other, too many opinions muddy the process. I wanted our scouts to stay at training camp and track their prospects, and I wanted our coaches to call on the scout's knowledge of the player as they made their decisions. Further, if they believed the coaches were making wrong decisions, I wanted our scouts to speak up and fight them on what they knew to be mistaken or overlooked. It is not unusual for a coach to justify his prior opinion of a player, which may have run counter to that of the scout, by giving up on him at the first mistake, rather than working with the player and helping him improve. A scout on the scene can stop that situation short, or at least call the judgment into question to see that it is better resolved for the benefit of the team.

Jim Trimble, former head coach of the Eagles, was our director of pro personnel. He was another executive very set in his methods, but he was also very wise after three decades of coaching in pro football. I valued his counsel; he had tremendous contacts throughout the NFL, the Canadian Football League and college football, and he knew more about personnel in the league than any of us because he studied all the films that came in and was our advance game scout. But he kept most of his information in his head, and I continually urged him to put it into our system so we would have access when he wasn't around. My urgency didn't register; he simply was more comfortable with his own system. I also wanted him, instead of the coaches, to evaluate the waiver wire every day and, if he saw someone who might help us, get everyone stirred up until we made a decision. But coaches—not only our coaches, *all* coaches— think they know more about a player than the scouts. Personnel men of Jim's experience are more knowledgeable, and I knew he bridled when the coaches turned away his recommendations. But he should have fought like hell for people he believed could help. He often depended too much on Well's assessment, which again was something I wanted to get away from. Well, who was a good judge of talent, always made suggestions about players, but I wanted those suggestions to come through me so I could pass them on to Jim, and we could then both act on his appraisal.

Of course, I realized that this approach was new to people on the football side, who had to get used to my way of doing things as well as an entirely new coaching staff in 1974. At the same time, we were charting our future in another way: we had been given the opportunity to move into a brand new stadium in New Jersey, which meant the Giants, as New York City knew them, were about to change.

The first order of business was a new full-time practice site and training camp. In 1973 the team had its preseason base at Monmouth College in New Jersey. Since we were going to relocate permanently in that state in a couple of years, I wanted to move the practice site to New York so we wouldn't have the image of being an exclusively New Jersey team. So we returned to Fairfield University, feeling it was at least a familiar place. To retain our New York image into the season, I searched also for an in-season practice site and found an old monestary in Yonkers that seemed ideal. We couldn't make that deal, but Pace University, which had been a lower Manhattan school since its founding, had opened a new campus in Westchester County's Pleasantville, and it was looking for someone to help them develop some of the land it had acquired for athletic facilities.

Our negotiations with them were very difficult. They did not seem to appreciate what we would do for them: build a full-time facility, maintain and improve playing fields, give them something they could use themselves, and provide all of the benefits their association with the Giants would bring in the form of publicity and people visiting their campus to watch us practice. After giving us proposals and options they would back down or become scratchy about a proposal. Finally I told them to forget everything and we'd go elsewhere. This jolted them a bit, and we soon worked out the matter with a very good arrangement for both parties. We got a fifteen-year lease at a very low rate, but we paid them up front and amortized it over the term of the contract.

With our football facility in Westchester County we rented office space in White Plains for all but our football operations, which we moved into our building at Pace College. The Pace facility kept me almost totally occupied through the first six months of 1974. I did all the on-site work with the Pace College people and the architects, including laying out the playing fields and getting them ready for use after we left Fairfield. But when we finished, we had a dandy facility, more up-to-date than the team had when it used Yankee Stadium, and a world of difference from the rundown facility the team had used the previous year at Roosevelt Stadium in Jersey City. We at least had begun to take on the semblance of a first-class football organization.

The new look didn't stop there. Next came the uniforms, beginning with the helmet that for years had the familiar *NY* on the side. The Giants needed to be a little more modern in their look without departing entirely from the idea that we still were the New York Giants. So we let it be known a change was in the wings, and we solicited plenty of designs before settling on that modernized version of *NY* which we used in 1974 and 1975 when we played in New Haven and Shea Stadium, respectively. Of course, the GIANTS logo became standard when we moved into Giants Stadium in New Jersey in 1976, but I found out that fans don't always like change, and our mail indicated that as many people wanted to retain the old helmets and, later, the old uniform designs, as wanted the changes.

But more than helmets and uniforms were changing. After nine years away from the game I noticed that the attitudes of players had also shifted dramatically. These attitudes have changed even more over the decade since I left the Giants, and the evolution has not been for the overall good of the game. There have been two basic causes: the growth of the players' union, and the tremendous amount of money being paid to the players, some of whom simply do not have the ability to merit such compensation;

and each of these causes is abetted by changes in the attitudes of people toward life itself.

I am not against players organizing or being fairly compensated. What bothers me are the influences that have spun off from both areas and affected some of the "people" aspects of a team sport that, more than any other game, is vitally dependent upon the feelings of the participants for each other. Some coaches will use unconventional means to achieve this, such as Bum Phillips, when he coached the Houston Oilers, having a pizza and beer bash for his team every Thursday night during training camp so the team would get to know each other better. "When it's fourth and one on the goal line with ten seconds to play and we need a touchdown to win the game, I figure a guy might block just a bit better for someone he likes than for someone he doesn't know very well," Bum said, explaining this radical departure from standard training camp life.

When the union became stronger in the seventies and eighties, the idea that everyone was together for some kind of cause seemed to lessen the degree teammates were willing to sacrifice for each other or play as hard against the guys across from them. All part of one group, they seemed to forget they played for different teams. Nothing burns me up more than seeing a player helping up his opponent after he had just knocked him down. He was supposed to knock him down, and he is supposed to keep knocking him down until the other guy, tired of being knocked down, begins to quit a bit. Then the battle is won. That is what football is about—physical domination played within a rules structure that allows people to be knocked down but says nothing about helping them up again. The so-called brotherhood of football players should be confined to a player's locker room and off-season friendships. When the game begins the guy in the other colored jersey cannot be a buddy, nor should he be part of a "cause."

The influence of money on pro football has been even more pervasive and more destructive, fostering many of the recent negative developments in the sport. Players look at salaries differently. Eight or nine thousand dollars used to be a lot of money. Now players make no distinction between fifty and a hundred thousand dollars, and some scoff at the idea of a $400,000 salary. Everything is in terms of million-dollar-plus contracts over two or three years, incentive clauses that are supposed to reward athletes for performing duties for which they are paid a salary, and the stated desire to make enough money from football "so I'll never have to work again." That is short-term, foolish thinking, considering that a player may have forty years of his life ahead of him after football. It is also the breeding ground for future problems.

When I negotiated contracts for the Giants I saw some of the results of players getting so much money. Were they happier? Not really. Were they satisfied? The more they got, the more they wanted. Many players make as much in training camp compensation as we made for an entire season. When I joined the Rams we got ten bucks a week for laundry money and nothing for playing in preseason games. Later, we got fifty bucks per exhibition game. Somehow, though, we stretched that ten bucks to cover laundry and a couple of beers each night after our meetings. From it we built up a team spirit that did everything Bum Phillips's beer and pizza parties hoped to achieve. What so many of us who played in the fifties and early sixties missed more than anything after we left the game was the camaraderie of an evening of splitting the beer tab, singing our lungs out and then all going back to camp together. When we have reunions, we recount those times, rarely plays or games.

Fans seem to understand this point more than today's players, who look upon us as a bunch of old goats whose time has long passed. Perhaps our time as players has passed, but the things we stood for—some call them the eternal verities: loyalty, integrity, honesty—never will, and I believe today's players are missing much happiness from their pro football experience. The game itself is missing much of the feeling that helped make it so attractive to the public because, in a word, the players are spoiled.

The way players feel for each other often determines how well they do on the playing field; it was certainly a big reason for the success of my Rams and Giants teams. The trauma of fighting a war, the experience of many players who came into the game after World War II and the Korean War, contributed a lot to team feeling. Guys would pick each other up and show a little more concern for each other; life had taken on a new meaning after facing the daily possibility of death. It didn't lessen the all-out way we played the game, however; we played fair, hard and tough; we didn't mickey mouse around with little things; we didn't complain about what was fair or unfair. The few locker room lawyers didn't last too long. There was no griping about money, no sulking or holding back because of perceived financial inequity. A player didn't discuss his salary because he was embarrassed to let a teammate know he might be making five bucks more a game.

Team togetherness also meant being willing to sacrifice a player's own whims, fancies and desires for self-glory for the good of everyone. In a word it meant discipline, from being accountable for himself off the field—mention the word *curfew* to players today and some of them laugh at you—as well as on the field: paying attention to the snap count; checking the ball before getting into a stance and not lining up offside; knowing assignments so you don't go to the left when you should have gone to the right. I wasn't exaggerating when I said we could beat the Browns whenever our defense was disciplined. We knew the moment any of that discipline broke down, we were dead.

With the caring for self comes the caring for a team. Too often during my tenure as director of operations I found a player's individuality, his play-my-own-game-and-leave-me-alone attitude, eclipsing the impulse to take command or control and be accountable for everyone playing for

144

the good of the team. Today, the message seems to be that "everyone is his own leader." That is not team leadership. If a team is effectively led it will, if necessary, slap the hell out of someone who uses drugs or abuses alcohol. A team leader on the old Giants would have confronted anyone with a drug problem and said to him, "You stupid son of a bitch, you've got to be the weirdest friggin' man in the world to screw up a great career by fooling around with drugs. Damn it, you're my friend and I won't let you do it! And I won't let you do it because you're hurting this team and we need you!"

It's apparent that no one does this anymore, but on the old Giants teams someone would have stepped in, just as we did to Jim Katcavage when he tried to leave the game with a separated shoulder in 1960 and we told him flat out, "Stay here and play. Forget the damn shoulder!" Were we crude? I don't think so, though we might have been a bit cruel. But with so much at stake no one thinks about being cruel or unfair.

Lack of personal feeling for each other is another offshoot of the riches athletes are being paid. In the seventies I never felt there was genuine respect between players. I never believed they wanted anyone around who preached about the importance of those things, or even someone who walked into the locker room after a loss and smashed a fist into a locker because he hated so much to lose. If I did anything like that during my years as director of operations players would have looked at me as if I were corny or crazy because I cared so much and vented my feelings.

I know a lot of players today get aggravated when they hear people of my generation say, "They don't make 'em like they used to," but I've yet to see one player who's made like Joe Morrison, who would do anything to help his team. And I get a little tired of hearing people say, "Oh, you old-timers..." That's okay; we are old-timers and we did what we had to do but we also used the same ball, played under primarily the same rules and had people like Hugh McElhenny and Morrison who had such a great feeling for the team.

Now, if a player is unhappy because he isn't playing enough or got his butt chewed by his coach, he is on the phone to his agent demanding that he be traded. I openly questioned the ability of players who frequently wanted to be traded. That was often a euphemism for quitting while they still deluded themselves that they were really trying and needed only the right "environment." These are the players fans should boo. They shouldn't boo Del Shofner because he muffed one pass, or Phil Simms because of one subpar game while he was doing everything expected of a quarterback. If fans want to boo someone, then let them boo the million-dollar player who's batting .240, or the snotty football player who doesn't appreciate what he's getting and sticks it to the club and fans with outlandish demands and less than his best effort. Players who are richly paid have an obligation to reward their teams and fans with equally rich effort and production. It sickened me to hear Simms booed all those years; he

145

is a perfect player who has earned everyting he's made, a classy example of what every player should be, and the fans should appreciate his every game.

Still, I don't think the average player looks at fans or anyone else and believes he owes them something. Instead, he assumes the fan and the organization owe him something over and above the ample compensation and adulation he receives. I don't blame the player as much as I blame the times in which we live, but neither do I excuse this attitude. When I played, the worst thing that happened to me was hearing fans boo our team. In the 1963 and 1964 seasons I couldn't believe my ears. I used to believe that a player who booted a ground ball should not be booed, but I look at that a bit differently now: when a player blows a game he must bear the responsibility. Sure, no one can lose a game on his own, but a player who also has a chance to become the hero and blows it has to wear the goat horns. When I disregarded Red Hickey's admonitions to guard against 49ers' quarterback Frankie Albert bootlegging around my side of the line (in the game to which I referred earlier) and he scored the go-ahead touchdown in the waning minutes, I went back to the bench and said a prayer that Dutch Van Brocklin would win the game for us and relieve me of the burden of knowing I had hurt our team. He did, too, but until it happened I was in despair. I don't know if that word really means much to many players in pro football who make mistakes that hurt their team. I never found much of it with the Giants in the seventies.

Nor did I find players as willing to play with injuries as we were. Players today want to protect themselves and their big salaries, so many of them will not extend themselves. When I was director of operations we had a tough special teams player named Mickey Zofko who injured an ankle and would not return until it was 100 percent; our fine defensive tackle, John Mendenhall, hurt his leg during a game against the Jets in 1974 and wouldn't play in an overtime period because he didn't want to take any chances. We lost the game. When we were at 2-7 in 1974 Bob Tucker said his knee was a little ouchy and wouldn't play.

In 1963, when Doc Sweeney refused to aspirate the fluid from my injured knee, I went to our trainer, John Dziegiel, and asked him to do it because I couldn't even bend my leg. He took a look at it and said, "You're not playing for three weeks."

"You're crazy John," I told him. "I can't sit out that long. I want to play this Sunday."

"No way," he told me.

"Well," I replied, "a miracle might happen and the knee will be okay."

So I went to my own doctor, who aspirated it and gave me a couple of painkillers. That was on Friday afternoon, and when I went to the Stadium the following day for our brief workout and didn't report for treatments, Dziegiel came after me. He looked at the knee and saw the marks left by my doctor's needle.

146

"This is impossible," he said, obviously upset that I had gone outside his jurisdiction.

"John, come on," I said, "I just had the water taken out of my knee. You don't have to say anything."

He didn't, and I played the next day, but I felt that was what I was supposed to do. In 1964 I separated two ribs after falling on a fumble and played the last eight games of the season with the injury, taking just a painkiller before the game to be more comfortable. We had guys who played with dislocated elbows, partially separated shoulders and dislocated fingers. If your finger went out you ran to the sidelines and had the trainer pull it back in place, though that was just a temporary cure. We didn't do this because we wanted to be tough but because we didn't want to leave the game, and there weren't too many replacements.

When athletes have as much money as they do nowadays, they often don't know what to do with it, and if they have cultivated a drug habit in high school or college they discover they can support it as a pro athlete without any regard for what it does to them physically or emotionally. Of course, it quckly ends the career that provides those riches. With so much free time away from the field, some NFL players look for adventure, and today that seems to be the drug scene. Some say athletes turn to drugs to alleviate the pressures of the game, but I don't buy that reasoning. For one thing, not every well-paid athlete delves into the drug scene; for another, the privilege of high pay brings with it the responsibility to care for oneself; and thirdly, that free time can be constructively used to begin an athlete's life's work or to return to school to complete his education.

As director of operations I addressed this problem directly by instituting a program of having players live in the area during the off-season and work out two or three times a week, something that never was done before. The problem was getting the players jobs so they could support themselves and their families. We never got much cooperation from employers; nor did we get much reality from the players, who thought they should be paid for shaking hands instead of digging into a business and becoming productive parts of the company. We never considered paying for off-season workouts as the Giants do now, though it would have made more sense when average salaries were about one-third of what players make today. I'm not certain I would have favored that idea had it been proposed back then because I believe it is part of a player's obligation to himself and his team to keep in shape in the off-season and build himself up if that is what is required. I look at what the players are making today—an average of $200,000 a season—and I still wonder why any team should pay them to work out. What do they think that huge salary is about?

But back in 1974 I was thinking more about our immediate needs: an in-house film department, weight-training facilities, classrooms and office space for the coaches, all of which went on the drawing boards for our Giants Stadium facility that was still two years away. I'm proud of all that we accomplished in this regard. In just two years we brought the Giants into the modern era of the NFL with a football facility without comparison.

My second objective was to set in place some specific rules of operation to guide me over the four- or five-year span that I felt was needed to get the team back as a contender. As such, I wanted to delineate areas of responsibility, beginning with my own as director of operations. I made myself responsible for the activities of the coaches, the college and pro scouts, training camp, purchasing of equipment, the signing of current and new players, trades, the acquisition of free agents and the modernization of our football department. I instituted constant communication among everyone on the football side. I started weekly meetings with the coach so all of us could keep current on the team's problems. That was the easy part. I discovered before too long on the job that I was serving two very different owners, Wellington, who sometimes became overly involved in the football side of the business, and Tim, who had totally different aims and never seemed at all interested in getting involved with Well and me in getting the team and the organization turned around. I needed some guidelines to help me fulfill my job, but I also wanted a way to solve the differences that were bound to arise when someone from outside a very cozy organization begins to institute change. Change, under those conditions, usually brings disagreement. I broached that fact with Wellington.

"I don't think that will ever be a problem," he replied, "because we've worked very close since I've been running the club, and we've never had a problem. We've always been able to work things out, and I'm sure it will be no different with you here."

I realized later that they never disagreed because Tim never confronted him. In my many discussions with him during my five years with the team, I always said that if he wanted to be 50 percent of the show, then he had better stay on stage and be a part of the show and not hang back in the wings waiting for curtain calls. That little allegory never made much of an impression, and many of the unresolved matters became fodder for discussion within his 50 percent of the ownership. Dark clouds had begun to form on the horizon, but they were still five years away from exploding in the split between the two men.

But Well's promise of peace didn't satisfy me. I knew it was tough for three people to agree on everything, particularly when two of them were equal partners and principals in the team's operation. So I said to Well, "Don't you have a clause in your buy and sell agreement with each other that settles areas of disagreement?"

"Jack and I never had a buy and sell agreement, and when Tim took over, we never felt there was any need for such an agreement," he said.

"But there are going to be conflicts," I insisted, "because I know I'm going to cause some now and then. I'm also going to have to satisfy two people, and in times of conflict, that isn't going to always happen, so how are we going to resolve that problem?

"Now, Well," I continued, "if you can make that decision, that's fine. But what happens when you can't make the decision? Then what do I do? What means will be in place for those times?"

I had determined from the start that any problems I needed solved would be laid in the lap of the president, not the vice president. If Well Mara offered the solution then, as far as I was concerned, that was it. But there also were some exceptions to that rule that worried me; with a fifty-fifty split in ownership no one really runs the organization on an absolute basis, and if one-half of the ownership makes a decision, the other half must agree that it will benefit his side as well. What happens if there is a disagreement? Or, a more common problem, what happens if I needed a decision rendered and Wellington was not around, as was so often the case during 1974 and 1975 when he was immersed in the NFL Management Council as it sought to hammer out a new agreement with the Players Association? I didn't want to have to run to Tim for every answer, particularly after I saw that his motives for effecting change were different from Well's and mine. I didn't want to have to run to Well for every little decision, either, because in each case that ran contrary to my insisting that everyone run his own show.

This really was a minefield of sorts. I saw my role as a catalyst between the two Maras, raising issues, suggesting changes, offering solutions to problems. They would either have to agree or disagree with me. A fifty-fifty ownership split, combined with a third decision-making party, would sometimes result in one half-owner in the business being outvoted.

In getting decision-making power for my own use, I told them it would always be for the best interest of the club. What was the best interest of the club? Again, that had to be part of an up-front agreement so that when I made a decision I knew exactly where I stood afterwards. I wanted to make certain there was no second-guessing, no suggesting I had overstepped my authority. All of this had as its sole aim a system for keeping the peace in a situation that was fraught with problems, present and future, but there had to be rules to govern those times, and they had to be agreed upon by all of us.

Finally I said to Well, "I think from a very practical standpoint, someday something is going to happen where you will need a document to back you up. In a fifty-fifty business split, somebody is going to have to make a decision. There will be a vast difference between the way you'll operate in the future over how you've operated in the past, and there will be some problems that may come back to haunt you."

Well never did sign a formalized agreement. He simply could not foresee the fracturing of the organization that lay ahead; and Tim saw himself in a constant minority role when he began to realize that I had not taken the job to be his bully boy with Wellington or do his bidding because he did not have the courage to speak up on his own. It became clear to me after a while that he wanted me on the scene to be the ruthless guy who would force the changes that those on his side of the ownership were formulating. Tim saw me saying to Well, "You can't do this." I couldn't do that, if for no other reason than Wellington was the president of the club, and no employee can go around telling the president what to do. On the contrary, the relationship Wellington and I struck became very strong—if not always smooth. We did disagree, and I did challenge him on many of the things he had done in the past. But I did it on my own, not at Tim's behest, and when Tim saw that he would have to carry his own water those dark storm clouds began to get larger and larger.

As it turned out, Wellington could have used an agreement to keep Tim from fracturing the ownership in 1978 and putting the overseeing of the club's operations in the hands of the commissioner. It would have rightly established him as the chief operating officer, with all of the decision-making powers that went with the position, and forced Tim to either go along under the terms of the agreement or get out. It also would have saved a lot of bitterness and anguish since then, because for nearly the past ten years, Wellington has been president of a team without the full authority that a president should have.

With the matter unresolved I charted my own course over the first two or three years, gradually building a set of guidelines that involved consultation with the Maras on: never giving a player a raise of more than $25,000 per year; not trading a first-round draft pick; not signing anyone to more than a two-year contract; and never picking up a player on waivers who required some other kind of compensation or agreement. These guidelines made good business sense for them, but they also incited some lively discussions between the three of us, something that should have happened long before I got there.

In the course of my five years I also did some things without consulting them, but I was always fair to the team, the coach and management. For example, I signed Brad Van Pelt for ten thousand dollars more than we originally agreed upon so as not to lose him. That was being fair to the team. Being fair to the coach was arranging to take the team to Mexico City for a week so he could get extra work accomplished in the off-season with the players and generate some excitement and enthusiasm among them, all within budget. That was being fair to management, too, though Tim raised hell about both of those decisions. When I pointed out to him that they were within a reasonable set of guidelines and never cost the club any extra money, it didn't matter. Tim, in my opinion, didn't want to understand the football side of the business, and was always bitching about the spending on our side of the complex. He said I was too conservative in my own personal expenses, but he had a lower set of monetary standards for the team. The team, he said, had far too much money, and the players were always overpaid.

I don't know what was spent on the nonfootball side of the business, but early in 1974 I established a football budget of $4.25 million, based on what the club had spent the previous year plus 10 percent. The Giants had never had an operating budget for the football side, nor had they projected one for future seasons. When I left after the 1978 season, our football budget was $4,060,000, which included Larry Csonka's large salary, Brad Van Pelt's new $100,000 contract (big money nine years ago), the salary gains the players had made through the World Football League wars and a vastly expanded football department. I'll let those figures stand as proof of the efficacy of my management.

Once we got going, zeroing in on objectives with a minimal set of procedures, one of my biggest problems was holding Wellington back and keeping him from becoming intimately involved again with the football operation. Old habits die hard. He had solutions for every problem, particularly when we were looking for players or juggling lineups. I certainly understood his interest, but it gave the appearance of a lack of confidence in those making the decisions. Some of them still wanted him to make the decision for them, but I kept reminding him whenever possible that we had to allow them to sink or swim with their own solutions.

But Well was totally immersed in football and in his team, and at times he was not easily backed off. He was always objective in his discussing and understanding of problems, but when he wanted to get involved with the coach, I'd say, "Well, we can't influence the coach. He's there to make his own decisions and be comfortable with them." I didn't want to be the instrument for getting the coach to do what Wellington wanted, or what I wanted, for that matter. If the coach did everything we suggested then we should have coached the team ourselves.

I know many in all areas of the organization viewed me as intrusive. I questioned everything, and I know it shook up some of the old comfort zones. For example, getting ready to go to Seattle for a preseason game, we were having trouble chartering a plane. Now that was the domain of Ray Walsh on the business side, but Wellington became involved and came to me with the problem, perhaps not so much to solve it as to sound me out.

"Why do we have to deal with a company that is charging us $56,000 for a plane?" I asked him. "That's far overpriced."

"We use them all the time, and I hate going elsewhere for the business," he said.

"Hell," I replied, "they're not the only airline."

"I know," he said, "but they're our friends and we've been with them for so long."

"I'm sorry Well," I said, "if you want to pay a heavy price to have friends, that's your business. But if you want to do something about it, I'll get an airplane for us with just a phone call."

And I did...for $25,000, less than half the price we were going to pay. But did that make a difference? It certainly did to Wellington, but not to Ray and Tim. Pretty soon I heard a lot of bitching about interfering with that operation. After that, I just prayed the damn plane wouldn't go down!

Was that typical? Very much so. No one on that side of the operation had any impetus to change their ways of doing things (I must exclude the public relations department, which should have been under our control since it dealt almost exclusively with football, but over which Tim insisted keeping control). There was an arrogance of sorts, as if they defied anyone to change their procedures or to breathe new life into people whose motto seemed to be, "We've done it this way for years, so why should we change?" There was utter stagnation: no new ideas, no new ways of marketing the club's popularity among fans, who numbered in the millions. One season the club made no money at all, so I suggested we market watches with the Giants logo and take further advantage of the club's popularity. It started late; it was ill-conceived; consequently it did not produce the revenue we anticipated.

"I told you it wouldn't work," Ray Walsh said to me when the offer had expired. "We have our own way of doing things, and we're not interested in other ideas."

In other words, the messages to me were: "We don't try any gimmicks...Stay in the football end of the business...We know what we're doing." I also got a further message about the way the nonfootball and football sides of the team worked. The nonfootball side went its own way instead of trying to help Well through the difficult years. The lack of interaction in the business was critical. It seemed to me that Tim, his family and some selected friends and admirers were behind the scenes formulating blueprints of what they felt should be happening on the football side of the business. If they really had the good of the team at heart they should have confronted the president of the organization at the board of directors meetings and forge a new direction together. Instead, there never really were any policy-making officers within the organization. The "we" that I heard about so often became visible only in criticizing Wellington, who had to make all of the decisions because "we" didn't wish to.

Perhaps the saddest and most baffling part of this tawdry scene was the deterioration of the relationship between Well and Ray Walsh. They were longtime friends, beginning with their college days together at Fordham, but as Ray spent more and more time working with Tim and his brother-in-law, who was the club's counsel, on finalizing the Giants Stadium deal, he drew further and further away from Well, to the point where that friendship and close working relationship all but disappeared. There seemed to be a general feeling within the nonfootball side that you had to pick sides, which only built up the barrier between the two operations even further. I always thought the person who designed our offices at Giants Stadium must have known what was going to happen. There is a corridor that separates the football and nonfootball sides, and there were times when that hallway was a million miles long, just about as far as one part of the team was from the other.

It was certainly long enough to remind me not to offer advice—though never too long to keep them from coming into our area. Every time we won a game, so did they; when we lost, only the football side lost, and they had plenty to say about it. We were supposed to accept their criticisms, which rarely had any basis of fact. They knew very little about judging football talent or appraising the technical aspects of a game. A lot of that criticism was rooted in the unsuccessful years before my time there. When we tried to turn things around, it rocked them to see the old ways were being uprooted by an outsider.

All of this galled me from time to time. I knew this franchise had the potential to be the best in football, yet some people were not willing to give up their little fiefdoms. They were more worried about what side they lined up on, or even how to play both ends. I had never worked under those conditions before, mainly because I had always called my own shots in business, and there were times driving back and forth to Stamford when it seemed that the only friend I had in the world some days was the guy on the FM station who played that nice relaxing music. The two of us had some great conversations, though he never knew it. But it was the only way I could purge my gut of the frustration and bitterness I felt when I saw the selfishness gagging the club's ability to come from the depths. It made the struggle much harder and longer than it ever should have been. Ultimately it continued to build into those dark storm clouds that would irrevocably split the team—and a family.

It was a helluva situation for anyone to come into, and I know that neither I nor Bill Arnsparger had any inkling this warfare would increase when we made our plans to drag the Giants from the depths shortly after 1974 began. That was only the start of another series of adventures.

8 The Arnsparger Years

Changing the ways the Giants ran their football operation was a challenge, but rebuilding the team with available player resources, a new coaching staff and a new beginning with the draft was a task just as monumental. There were no easy answers, no shortcuts to the top, and I knew from the start that there would be no substitute for the hard work, determination to stick to a plan, patience and long suffering that would be a part of this process. In a personal sense, the process was difficult for me. I was used to success, for fourteen seasons as a player, and in the years following, when I followed my own instincts and experience to build and prosper in business.

But rebuilding the Giants was different. There were as many variables that depended on luck as on good planning and execution. Football is totally a "people" business, and as such, everyone in it is subject to the whims, fancies and vagaries of the human personality as well as the attitudes and outlooks of players and coaches who must eventually carry out the plans developed in the board rooms. I know fans don't really care too much about this; they are more interested in whether the team wins or loses than in why it happens. But they still have their own theories and solutions to problems, and by 1974 they were beginning to wonder if the Giants would ever return to their glory years. I believe their faith was bulwarked a bit when they saw the club willing to get new people and turn over much of the football operation to people outside the Giants family.

Their faith bought us some time—not as much as we needed, as it turned out—and gave us a basis we could use to try and prove that a brighter future was in the offing. However, rebuilding a team that did not foresee much success for a few seasons was going to be harder on the players. Many of them were frustrated at losing, frustrated at hearing that success was just another year away and frustrated at themselves for not being able to do much about all of these frustrations. I couldn't promise them or the fans any quick and easy solutions, only the fact that we were going to give the process a new and improved look that, if followed, would eventually bring success. At the same time I knew that most of those players wouldn't be around to enjoy any good years when they came, and as it turned out

155

I wasn't there either. But all that we began in 1974 helped to bring everyone who cared about the Giants to that pinnacle, though I must admit that when the journey began I didn't think it would be as long as it eventually turned out for me.

Hiring a head coach became my first priority. I had about three weeks to come up with a list of top prospects from the ranks of NFL assistants because the player draft was held in late February, and we wanted to give the new man at least a month to get to know his team. Having been away from the game for nine years I did not have a ready list of potential head coaches at my fingertips. I was even more unfamiliar with college coaches, so it was a step-by-step investigative process from the very start.

We had decided that, for the first time ever, the new coach would be from outside the Giants family, and that in itself made the process more complicated. Though he had a couple of suggestions, Wellington left the matter to me, and I called people I knew in the NFL, sounding out their opinions about who might be our man from within the ranks of assistant coaches. To make the selection process more orderly and get us the man I felt could begin the long, arduous process, I established some qualifications. I wanted someone who was defensively oriented. What little strengths the Giants had were on defense, and defense can sustain a team during a game and give it a chance to win. I also wanted a coach who stressed teaching and patience because we had a long, long way to go, and anyone looking for a quick shot of glory could forget us. I also wanted someone who could be something of a drill sergeant, someone who could get the players on a straight and narrow path; the comeback process simply had no room for anyone going his own way. We wanted to establish a solid base, with everyone into the spirit of the team and willing to work during some difficult times to help make it successful.

In the latter regard I considered Frank Kush, then the head coach at Arizona State. I knew his reputation for maintaining strong discipline and his tremendous record of success. But bringing in a college coach with no previous NFL experience is always chancy, and we couldn't afford to gamble at that point.

Of course, at that time Bill Arnsparger's name was on everyone's lips as the NFL assistant most likely to become a head coach. He had had great success as the defensive coordinator of the Miami Dolphins, who in 1973 had won their third straight American Conference title and were in the process of winning a second straight Super Bowl. He fit my defensive qualifications, and he was renowned for his teaching and patience. In the glare of Arnsparger's credentials, the field pretty much eliminated itself, so when the Dolphins won Super Bowl VIII, it took us only three days to finalize the deal and make him our head coach.

Bill's background was unique. He had been schooled thoroughly at the college and professional level, beginning with his playing career at Miami University in Ohio, the famed "Cradle of Coaches," which had produced, among others, Paul Brown, Weeb Ewbank, Red Blaik and three of Bill's teammates: Ara Parseghian, Paul Dietzel and Bo Schembechler. He played for Woody Hayes at Miami and then coached for him at that school and at Ohio State when Woody moved there in 1951.

His high school coach in Paris, Kentucky, was Blanton Collier, later a fine head coach of the Cleveland Browns in the sixties. Blanton became head coach at Kentucky in 1955 after having served on Paul Brown's staff at Cleveland since the birth of the Browns in 1946. Arnsparger jumped at the opportunity to join him, and that is where he first met Don Shula, also a member of a staff that included other future NFL head coaches: Chuck Knox, Howard Schnellenberger and John North, as well as Collier himself. Blanton was considered a great teacher, and Bill had an ideal situation to expand his knowledge of the game under the system that Blanton had learned from Brown.

Following two years at Tulane, Arnsparger joined Shula in Baltimore in 1964 and worked for Don until joining us as head coach. All of those credentials—no one had better breeding to become an NFL head coach— and his record of success in his defensive role made him the ideal choice to take over the monumental task of rebuilding an NFL team from scratch.

But it wasn't easy. He didn't have the experienced staff that he had worked with at Miami. A new coach simply can't go out and cull the best assistants he wants from other staffs. That group is usually pretty secure, part of successful programs. I couldn't offer much assistance because I didn't know the staffs that well, and we didn't have a football operation developed enough to lay out all that he needed. Bill and I were immediately aware that we had problems, and I told him that it was going to take some time before he could count on us to help solve them. In the meantime he would have to take more time than usual to develop both his coaching staff and his players, relying primarily on a group of eager, young assistants, who were hardworking and devoted to this monumental job. He also had to teach some of his teachers before they could teach the players, and with so few talented players, and so many new ones who had to learn on the run, that made his job even slower.

Bill became his own defensive coordinator, which meant he spent at least half his time coaching the defense instead of using all his time as head coach of the defense *and* the offense to maintain the overall perspective for both units that is so necessary for a developing team. However, he also got a fine young defensive assistant in 1975 by signing Marty Schottenheimer as linebacker coach. Marty, now the very successful head coach of the Browns, was only thirty-two. A coach at Portland in the World Football League the previous year, he was a dedicated, hardworking guy who had a tremendous hunger to learn all facets of the game. He made no bones about wanting to become an NFL head coach some day. He never stopped asking questions about anything to do with football. I gave him all my files on defensive football that I had accumulated over fourteen years because he could make better use of them. Marty was an excellent teacher and a no-nonsense coach. He helped develop Brian Kelley, Dan Lloyd and Brad Van Pelt. He was also a determined young man, often stubborn in his own beliefs, and we had some lively debates about our theories. His greatest contribution to the Giants was pressuring us to draft Harry Carson, who had played defensive end at South Carolina State, after some of our personnel people considered him only at his college position and gave him little opportunity of succeeding in the NFL. But Marty fought like hell to convince them that Harry could—and should—be switched to linebacker. That was the kind of dialogue that I wanted from our scouts. When we turned Carson over to Schottenheimer, Marty began to mold his talents during the two years he was his position coach. Harry probably owes the most to him for his overall development as a potential Hall-of-Fame player.

Bill's biggest staff problem was on offense. He retained Ray Wietecha as line coach, and hired Ted Plumb and Hunter Enis to run the offense. After working for five seasons with the Denver Broncos, Enis had been out of football for a couple of years. Plumb had six seasons as a college assistant. Ted is now a fine, experienced assistant with the Eagles, but in 1974 this group was weak on the offensive know-how needed to give us a bit of zip, and throughout Bill's tenure our offense always lagged. We tried to convince Bill to hire another veteran offensive coach to provide more guidance, particularly since he had chosen to spend so much time with the defense. He refused, and ultimately it became one of the factors that proved to be his undoing.

We had no real way of knowing what Bill would be like as a head coach, though Shula had assured me that he had all the qualifications and potential to be a good one. While that didn't come to pass with us, it did in the early eighties, when he became head coach at Louisiana State. Why it didn't happen in New York was due to a matter of circumstances. Bill was very stubborn about many things and very fixed in his ways, often unwilling to change or even compromise. He was often difficult to work with. Within a short time of taking the job he began to hide behind an inner shield that allowed no one to get close to him. He often became moody, severing the lines of communication as he simply refused to discuss some situations that needed fixing. When we got into crisis situations and needed his decisions, we often found he had moved off a previous position, and we were left to try and find another basis for solving the problem. If was exasperating at times. While he could be patient and fixed to a goal, the job as head coach—at least in New York—may have been too much for him, with all the attendant pressures, the publicity and the well-known expectations of millions of fans who were expecting him to recreate the Miami Dolphins' championship teams in one season. Working with Don Shula had been far different. Shula had taken all the heat and made many of the decisions. Shula knew every facet of his team's offense and defense and provided excellent coaches and talented players. Any skilled assistant coach can thrive under those conditions, but take him out of that situation and there are no guarantees he will succeed.

Bill was often contradictory in his relations with the front office and the players. Even people he had to work with away from the field felt his mood swings and stubbornness. For example, I made a couple of oblique references to my knowledge of Tom Landry and his system. I probably knew that system better than anyone outside the Cowboys' organization, because Landry had taught me everything he knew. I hoped that Bill would take the hint and call on my experience to help him solve some of the problems the Cowboys presented us twice a year. I would never have imposed my knowledge on him; I spent much of my time keeping Wellington and others in the football operation from doing the same thing. But he never once asked for anything, and in all but the first game he coached against Landry he came up just a little short of winning. Would anything I gave him have meant a difference? I always thought so. I certainly knew some of the things we planned against the Cowboys had no chance of succeeding. If I had gone to him and tried to make a case he would have turned me off. Then I would have put him in a position of having to take my advice or feel the consequences. The consequences had to be of his own making.

That gruff exterior and determined manner didn't always apply to the players. Though he always bent over backwards to bring them along and help them to develop a sense of confidence, he also allowed himself to be conned too much by them, and he was often too easy in cases where he should have been stern. Once a chartered flight was held up for an hour because Craig Morton was late for the plane. After we had waited for a while, I'd had enough. Everyone on the team was being affected.

"Bill," I said to him, "let's get this Goddamn plane going and leave Craig Morton here. Who the hell is he, to leave everyone sitting here waiting for him?"

"I know," Bill said in a very quiet tone, "but he's our quarterback and we really can't go without him."

I didn't press the issue, but it was probably the closest we ever came to a confrontation. Bill was dead wrong. Maybe I was wrong too for not insisting that Morton find his own way if he couldn't be on time. There were many coaches in the NFL—and from what I knew of Shula he was one of them—who would have locked up that plane at the appointed hour of departure so that anyone who missed it would have to pay his own way and be subject to a fine as well. I think there were times when Bill could not separate his compassion for a player and his willingness to give him the benefit of the doubt from what was really good for the team as a whole.

Of course, we had no inkling of these difficulties when Bill joined us. Our first order of business was to prepare for the draft. We knew going in that, with only a small nucleus of good veterans, that first draft would not have any dramatic results. We hoped that in our second draft we could continue to eliminate lesser players and establish a base of twenty good players by that time. If we did our work and were lucky, we would have a base of about twenty-eight players by the third year, and we could expect more positive on-the-field results. But I soon found out that hopes and plans don't always work out in the NFL.

In preparing for that first draft, we decided to concentrate on offensive linemen, and chose John Hicks, a lineman from Ohio State, as our top pick. We rated him just behind Ed "Too Tall" Jones after he won the Outland Trophy as the nation's outstanding collegiate lineman and finished second in the Heisman Trophy voting; and we picked Tom Mullen, whom we had rated seventeenth in the entire draft, in the second round.

Hicks and Mullen became starters immediately because they had to. Hicks became something of a darling of the crowd with his fist-waving and on-the-field exuberance, but that was only showtime. John might have thought he was a little better, but I think he let that top-pick notoriety go to his head, compounding a feeling that he did not believe he needed to work hard to get better, and he fell short of what we expected. I wasn't sold on him for other reasons. I felt he was top-heavy, and offensive lineman must have a solid base with strong legs so they don't get easily knocked over.

Mullen had great potential until a chronically bad shoulder ended his career in just three years. That was bad luck, not bad scouting. Playing with a talent-poor team like the Giants, an offensive lineman must pass-block a lot more than run-block. The chance of being injured is greater because a lineman must absorb blows rather than deliver them.

We picked thirteen players in that draft, and ten of them made the team. One of our pleasant surprises was wide receiver Ray Rhodes, a tenth-round pick who was a clever, intelligent receiver, but not especially fast. Still, he was a problem in man-for-man coverage. He became a starter in his second season, leading the NFL with his 20.7 yards per catch average, and was our top punt-returner. Two years later, when we needed help at cornerback, he moved over and won the starting job. Ray was a good example of a player who would have shone even more with better people around him, particularly at wide receiver where he could not be double-covered when used in special situations. With the Giants, he was one of the better people, and he had to survive on his own.

There was no more pleasant surprise than punter Dave Jennings. Dave had been cut by the Oilers in August, but since he lived in Connecticut, less than an hour away from Pace, we invited him to try out. Once he got there, he stayed for eleven seasons. I liked him from the very start and really took a personal interest in him. He was a very nice kid, he tried very hard, and he was the kind of person who you just knew would make your team better simply by being a part of it. I guess I saw a little of myself in him, too, because he came from St. Lawrence University, a very small school in upstate New York, and here he was competing with the big-money guys from bigger football programs. As it turned out, he joined Don Chandler as one of the best punters in the team's history, and he often was the one bright spot on some dreary afternoons.

Jennings, who beat out Tom Blanchard for the job, was one big plus we never counted on, but we also found some nuggets among some of those other ten drafted players in 1974, including eventual starters Bobby Brooks and Clyde Powers, who also were forced to play before they really were ready because our secondary was so poor.

Looking back on that draft, I think that if we had a better nucleus of veteran players to carry the load, the players we kept would have given us greater depth at that time, and put us much further ahead in our rebuilding program. A large disappointment in that first draft later turned out to be our fourth-round pick, quarterback Carl Summerell, a six-foot, four-inch former East Carolina player. He played a bit in 1974 and 1975, but we wanted him to learn and improve and fulfill his potential to become a starter. He started in the first preseason game of 1976, and he came away with a victory, further justifying our beliefs. Then, out of the blue, Carl disappeared, and when we finally tracked him down at his home in Virginia, he said personal family business had forced his move, and those problems had to be solved before he could consider returning to us. He returned only briefly and then left for good. We never heard from him again.

Quarterbacking was a problem right from the start of my tenure. Our holdover veterans, Norm Snead and Randy Johnson, were among a group of eleven players our personnel department had evaluated as our better players. "Snead," the report said, "is a quiet leader, dedicated, intelligent and well-experienced." While noting Johnson's physical ability, the report marked him down for his temperament, the careless way in which he threw the ball and poor practice habits. We eventually released Johnson, perhaps a bit too quickly, and he signed with the World Football League. Snead was troubled with bad knees. He gave it his best shot early in the season, but Norm simply was unable to play a full game, and he had no mobility at all against a pass rush. We had two options: Go to the bench or go to the market.

We had already gone to the market when Arnsparger pushed us to trade a third-round pick to Green Bay for Jim DelGaizo, a lefthanded quarterback who had been with the Dolphins for a season before Miami sent him to the Packers for a couple of second-round picks. This must have inflated his worth in Arnsparger's mind because his reputation for having a strong arm and being mobile and resourceful was totally without foundation. The first time I saw him throw I was shocked to see that he could do none of the things that Bill had touted. I knew at that moment we had made a grave error. Still, with Snead hobbling and ineffective, we had no choice but to give him a couple of starts. Nothing happened.

So we went back to the market, and this time we went big for Craig Morton of the Cowboys. He cost us a first- and second-round draft pick—something I said I would never do unless it was for an established quarterback I felt could help turn us around. To my mind Morton was not a quick fix. I felt he could do the job for six or seven years while helping the younger quarterbacks get ready. I pushed hard to get him because from some intensive film study, I liked his physical ability and I believed his experience as a starter for the Cowboys could help give us some stability. I was correct about most of his physical abilities; he did a good job for us at the start. But I was disappointed with him as a person, though I was told he needed some firm guidance. I figured Arnsparger would take care of that, but he didn't. He let him get away with too much. Craig often needed a kick in the ass to get his attention and let him know he couldn't call his own tune. Instead of being the positive influence I had sought, the opposite occurred, such as the time when we had a game upcoming against our bitterest rivals at the time, the Redskins, and he was three hours late for practice on the day when the offense put in its game plan. Arnsparger tolerated that, but I don't think he understood the negative effects those kinds of actions had on a young, struggling team. I take nothing away from Craig's football abilities, but he was not the kind of leader—and the quarterback must be a leader, particularly a veteran quarterback on a young team—that we sought. The players sensed that after a while, and they lost a lot of respect for him.

The question is, did we make a mistake? At the beginning, Morton brought a great rush of enthusiasm to the team, and I noticed immediately there was more poise and authority on the field when he played part of a game against the Cowboys, though he had less than a week's practice with us. In his first start in Kansas City, Craig took a terrible physical beating, but he hung in and got us our second—and last—win of the season.

We did not expect miracles from Craig. We knew he did not have the strong supporting cast that had helped him in Dallas, but we felt that his physical talent, poise and experience could compensate until we got better players around him. What we didn't foresee was his failure to rise to the task and playing to his full capabilities.

There are also other questions about that trade. Did Morton give us the time we needed to build the team and develop quarterbacks under him who could eventually become starters? None of our younger quarterbacks could have done as well as Craig during the time he played for the Giants. When Summerell left, and with DelGaizo simply incapable of being an NFL quarterback, we had no one ready to replace him. Had Morton stayed and played to his capability for a few more seasons, then we could have built up the position. In that sense, then, the trade did not work out, but we had no alternative. We finally traded him to Denver before the 1977 season because he had lost all credibility with the team, and he had begun to succumb to pressures put on him by increasingly hostile and impatient fans. Interestingly, when Craig went to the Broncos, he immediately led them to the Super Bowl, but in Denver he had none of the pressures that he had to shoulder with the Giants. I believe he finally grew up and realized that his career demanded a different approach.

When we began planning for the 1974 season, even before the draft, we knew there were huge problems other than finding a strong quarterback. I was given an evaluation of the returning veterans from 1973, and less than a dozen players from that team were considered to have any real talent. Only three, running back Ron Johnson, wide receiver Bob Grim and defensive end Jack Gregory, were considered championship caliber, but I always felt that tight end Bob Tucker, a tough, hard-nosed player who was an excellent receiver and a better-than-adequate blocker, also was in that category.

The report noted that Tucker could be as good as any tight end in the NFL. He had one unusual quality: "He plays better when he's angry...In 1973, he was not angry. He has a volatile personality; he's ill-tempered, often without using good judgment." The report, while noting Johnson's fine skills, also called him "spoiled and pampered," and after making my own observations I found the report accurate. It foretold some of the problems Arnsparger had with both of them during his tenure. Instead of becoming leaders on the offense they allowed their egos and disappointments to get in the way. They were frustrated by the team's lack of consistent success in the past and the possibility of continued failure until we got things turned around. The frustrations intensified when they were not featured in our new offensive system as they had been in past systems. Arnsparger wanted to model his offensive philosophy after the Dolphins, to establish a strong, basic offense rather than a system that dinked and dunked the ball all over the place as the Giants had done in previous seasons. We kept some of the dink-and-dunk style as part of the offense, but preferred something solid that got a defense back on its heels to give us the option of using everything; if our basic offense was stopped, we could go over to the other things.

This, of course, spread the ball around to everyone, and some of our veteran holdovers had problems accepting the new ways and coping with a coaching style that evidently was not nearly as laid back as what they had been used to on Alex Webster's staff. Johnson and Tucker were such outstanding players that their lack of intensity at times was clearly evident in the way they played. But it was also manifested off the field. At one point in 1974, Johnson lambasted the club in print; in turn Arnsparger lambasted him, and he was forced to apologize to the team for his remarks. Ron was wrong; throughout that season he never really seemed to get into the spirit of the team, and he never consistently displayed the talent that

163

had twice made him a thousand-yard rusher. I played on only one losing team in fourteen NFL seasons, but I tried to understand their frustrations. Still, I never accepted them giving less than their fullest, and in the end they became losers.

Johnson and Tucker were not the only ones with these attitudes on the team, and there were times when I got so frustrated with this group that I wanted to say, "Hey, you sonsuvbitches, leave the team if you're so unhappy." That underlined our absolute need to get people who wanted to win for the team, not for themselves, players willing in a losing situation to try and get better every day and become winners. The ideal situation was to have a team of guys like Dave Jennings, who could rally the team around them and have everyone thinking and acting positively. It certainly would have made our rebuilding process easier if some of the stars of the team had displayed that kind of leadership, but it didn't happen. We eventually waived Johnson in 1976. The Cowboys picked him up, but he was cut before the season began and retired from football to pursue a business career.

Tucker had led the NFC in pass receptions in 1971, and he had been the Giants' leading receiver for the past three seasons as the centerpiece of a predominately short-pass offense. His role changed in Arnsparger's system. Faced with the prospect of his new role and more losing seasons, Bob began to yearn to rejoin his pal, Fran Tarkenton, who was with the Vikings. They had formed a close association during the three seasons between 1969 and 1971. Tarkenton had forced a trade from the Giants because he wanted to become part of a winning system. I am told he began working on Tucker to do the same. I don't know how much effect this had on Bob, but his situation with us deteriorated to such a low point that by 1977 he had even lost credibility with the other players. When he went public and demanded to be traded, he lost me for good too. I didn't blame him for wanting out, but I resented his making this a public issue, putting us at a disadvantage as we tried to deal him.

Jack Gregory and John Mendenhall were our best defensive linemen, and our linebacking corps was pretty good, particularly Brian Kelley. Gregory, who wore my old number 81, had been to the Pro Bowl in 1972. Jack did a pretty good job for us, but like Johnson and Tucker he got caught up in the frustration of losing and not in the idea of working to get better and showing everyone else it was the only way we were going to succeed. But there are two kinds of leaders: Guys who are really sons of bitches because they harass people and get people moving without being perfect role models themselves—and we had a few of those on our great Giants teams—and role models, guys who do everything to their utmost but only for themselves and not consciously to have others follow them. The ideal is to have someone who encompasses a bit of both, and again, our best players fell short in both areas. Gregory could have been a helluva leader for us because he had the qualities that attracted people to him—a little of the con, now and then, too—but he never wanted to take the positive responsibilities that go with those qualities.

One of those he influenced the most was Mendenhall, who brought some tremendous skills and qualities to us. John was a "player." Not really big enough for the NFL, he always did a good job until he allowed some of the bitchers and moaners to get to him. But when he wanted to do the job, and worked at it with his quickness and strength, he was a good nose tackle at a time when that position had just begun to become a specialized position in the changing pro defenses. With a good team and a better surrounding cast he would have been a helluva player. He could have been a much better player with us, too, but he became disgruntled and dissatisfied with being good himself, and in time he played only for himself. He tried to influence others in a negative way, and he wound up not doing himself or the team any good.

One of John's continuing problems was that he never thought he was being paid enough, so we often were involved in a contract hassle. I worked like hell one year to get some of his salary deferred so he could avoid some ready-cash problems, but he got upset and thought I was trying to take advantage of him. Finally we got a deal worked out, and when he had signed a new contract I got up from my desk, went over to John and his wife, kissed her on the cheek and extended my hand to John, who said, "You didn't have to do that."

"John, I don't do things I don't have to do," I snapped at him. "I only did that because I wanted to. Don't give me any of that crap!"

I knew what he inferred by that remark...I never had any racial problems with the Giants; nor did the Giants, as a team. I grew up in a black neighborhood, and our family was the only white family in a six-family apartment house. I was eighteen years old when we moved, and I never knew the world had problems with whites or blacks...or in fact, with Italians.

When I looked at our linebackers prior to that first season, three names stuck out—Jim Files, who had been a number-one draft pick in 1969, Brian Kelley and Brad Van Pelt, who was a second-round pick in 1973. Files was already an excellent linebacker with room to improve. Though anchored in the middle, he was good enough to play any of the three positions. Unfortunately we never found out; Jim chose a life's career in the ministry and we lost him.

To my mind, Kelley was the best linebacker during my five years with the Giants. More consistent than Van Pelt, who went to the Pro Bowl many times, he kept improving every year, and he became a very steady, errorfree player, always a fierce hitter. Brian played all three positions, depending on our defenses, but he always looked as if he had been at each throughout his career.

Van Pelt had more talent than any of the linebackers, but he never improved his techniques, and he was never consistent. Brad had such

165

tremendous ability that he could get beaten early on a play, yet recoup and finish it off. My frustration with him was simple: if he was going to get beaten and still make the play, he would have been greater if he made the play from the start. Brad was a nice kid, but he could have been a sensational player if he had really worked at it. Assistant coach Marty Schottenheimer had him going in that direction before he left for another coaching job.

Other veterans included Grim and Walker Gillette, two pretty good wide receivers for us in 1974, offensive tackle Doug Van Horne, center Bob Hyland, and Spider Lockhart and Pat Hughes on defense. We supplemented our veteran nucleus for that first season with twenty-five new players. Two of the bright newcomers were running backs Joe Dawkins, who we got from the Broncos and who did his best work as a receiver coming out of the backfield, and rookie Doug Kotar. With Ron Johnson lagging all season, Kotar picked up the running slack, and he was just exceptional, considering his size and the fact that he was a free agent who was cut early by the Steelers.

Kotar was Jim Trimble's find. Somehow, Jim learned Pittsburgh was going to cut him. With some good information about his play at West Virginia, he recommended we sign him. Doug sparkled for us. He had good speed, and he was a tough, determined runner who was hungry to make the team. His first eye-popping performance came during a rookie scrimmage in Bridgeport one evening in July, and he forced his way into the lineup with a good performance in a close, opening-game loss against Washington. Doug, who died tragically a few years ago of a brain tumor, really was our best running back during my five years with the Giants, even better than Larry Csonka, whom he idolized in a way, and who in turn did some good blocking on his behalf for the three years they played together.

Our 1974 season reflected the transition to so many new players and the lack of a deep, talented team. Among our dozen losses (we beat a lackadaisical Cowboys' team, 14-6, as well as Kansas City), seven were by a touchdown or less, and one of those was in overtime to the Jets when Joe Namath rolled into the end zone for the winning touchdown. Our defensive game plan didn't allow for much blitzing against Namath, who at that point in his career was a stationary target without the talent he had during his Super Bowl season. The following week we lost by a point to the Lions in the final two seconds, and then came two more successive last-minute losses by a total of five points. In most games that year, we simply got overpowered on offense and defense. We were not physically strong enough to survive a learning process.

Overall, while I know the fans were disappointed with just two wins, I judged our value on how badly we had been beaten. After that first year, I believed we were starting to put some things together, that we had gotten onto the right track and had to stay there. The philosophy of "not losing as badly this week as we did last week'' had taken hold, so there was a nucleus of strength and hope. I thought that Arnsparger and his staff did a very good job in 1974. In reviewing the season, I wrote a memo to Well in which I said:

> I have my own ideas on player performance. I'll tell you right off, I don't run this club for the sake of running it, to be tough and create an image and all that goes with it. I've been hired to turn this team around, and I'm going to turn it around with people who want to work with me. I'm in between management and the coaching staff, and I have made up my mind there'll be no more looseness, easy money and spoiled brats. I'm also going to get out of management when *we* need to win.

What didn't help Arnsparger were the dual problems of the World Football League and the player's walkout and strike that spanned all of the 1974 season and the early part of 1975. Both ran concurrently, providing large-scale distractions to the team and to the NFL as a whole. There was constant talk of huge salaries available for players who joined the WFL, and naturally that had an immediate effect on our own salary talks with draftees and veterans. The agents jumped in right away and tried to use it as leverage, and we reacted to secure some of our better veterans whose contracts were up during this time. Remember, I am talking about contracts in the thirty-thousand-dollar range jumping to forty-five or fifty thousand dollars, which was considerable in the mid-seventies. Ticket prices were still in the seven-dollar range, and television revenues were about one-seventh of what teams get now. We got a double dose; in 1974 we played in the Yale Bowl and sold only about 35,000 season tickets, so the club did not make a profit that year even with the ancillary income.

What popped everyone's eyes were the million-dollar contracts given to three players from the Miami Dolphins' world championship team— Larry Csonka, Jim Kiick and Paul Warfield; and then the reports of contracts in the hundreds of thousands to other NFL players. It was only natural for everyone to believe the WFL was serious about challenging the NFL. Our players believed they would get that much from us or go and get it from them. Dreaming of riches distracts; players' loyalties are suddenly split between making a good deal with their current team or joining another.

In our case, most of the players were kidding themselves. The WFL went after some of the best NFL players, and we didn't have any whose contracts were in jeopardy. The most serious effect on us was that it delayed our rebuilding program by skimming off some young players and any good free agents.

The Players Association caused us far more serious problems in 1974 and 1975 with their contract negotiations, beginning with the veterans staying out of camp for a week prior to the start of training camp in 1974. Of course, while they walked a picket line at one gate, many of them were coming through another gate for treatments and general camaraderie. They picketed from ten in the morning until noon, took two hours for lunch in an air-conditioned trailer, then resumed another two hours of picketing before heading home. This schedule emphasized the differences between a real union and what the players labeled as their "union." In a trade union, all the members are paid the same hourly wage and have definite seniority rules as well as medical and pension programs that benefit each member equally—and that's it. In pro football, each player is an independent entrepreneur in that he negotiates his own salary (not exactly what craft union members receive), and has a benefits package negotiated by the union; and then he is eligible for varying pension and "walk away" benefits, depending upon his own longevity—or success—as a player.

As a member of management I had to maintain an official hands-off policy, though I did have several discussions with our player reps. But as a former player I believed that fairness is fairness, and to some degree the players have every right to expect anything within reason. What is within reason? That is always the basis of compromise between the two parties, though I don't believe the players ever fully know what is going on, and that is the biggest problem in reaching a settlement. I don't believe that players are unreasonable, but their attitudes can become unreasonable. If people make money, everyone has the right to share; but when people lose money, everyone involved should share in the losses, too. So far in pro football, or in any pro sport, a union has never offered to cut salaries proportionally to balance out the losses, and there are teams in the NFL today—just as there were ten years ago—that are losing money. Thus the financial risk is all on one side.

When I heard about the free-agency demands, or so-called freedom issues, from team reps in 1974 and 1975, I told them that pro football depended on rules to exist, not only on the field, where players do not have absolute freedom to do or say anything they please without risk of a penalty, but also in the way the league is structured. Maintaining equal competition...the "on any given Sunday" quality that gives every fan and every team, regardless of its record, some hope...gives the game its appeal.

The players are fortunate to have such great opportunities for establishing a financial base, but that is contingent only on the owners staying in business. A player, or his union, is no different from a bricklayer: both make demands on the basis of their talent. But if the contractor who is getting the bricklayer's demands doesn't build the building, the man is out of a job. So the key has to be working for the mutual benefit of each other.

When people say to me, "What about the salaries when you played?" I simply tell them, "Hey, the best I had was twenty-four-thousand dollars in my final season as a full-time player and coach, after being in more than a half-dozen Pro Bowls and playing on two world championship teams and in six other NFL championship games.''

"Did it upset you?" I am often asked next.

"If it upset me," I've said, "I wouldn't have gotten done what I had to get done. What's the sense of being upset when there is no other football alternative? And what's the sense of being upset when you do have something else to do away from the game that brings in more, thanks in part to being a well-known pro football player?''

That is the kind of reasoning people like Dan Goich, who became a lone picket when the veterans returned in 1974, never understood. Goich was the last player who should have been picketing if he was serious about continuing what was a very mediocre career. He had moved from a thirteen-thousand-dollar-a-year contract as an eighth-round draft pick in 1967 to thirty-five thousand dollars a year in 1972 (not far below the average salary level) with his fourth team—and he kept complaining about "no freedom." After playing only fifty-four minutes during the entire 1972 season because of injury, he asked the Giants for fifty thousand dollars, and when the club refused he played out his option for a 10 percent cut. When he became a free agent he wrote me a letter asking for a four-year, no-cut, no-trade contract worth three hundred and fifty thousand dollars, with extra monies to be paid for preseason games. We refused, and he walked up and down that picket line before fading away, but with the knowledge that he would, at that time, be eligible for a pension of more than seven hundred dollars a month at age fifty-five, much more if he decided to wait until sixty-five.

Of course, that strike was orchestrated by Ed Garvey, the head of the Players Association, whose motives I always felt were for his own self-interest, as was also the case in 1982 when the player staged their nine-game walkout. I had prior experience with Garvey in my travel business. He had brushed me off when I tried to get the Players Association to allow us to book all of its travel and lodging. I approached him not only on the basis of a straight business deal, but as one of the few former NFL players—and an original member of the union—who was in the travel business. I believe the fact that I was an ex-player and could do him no immediate good in his union activities was the reason for the snub.

We got through 1974 without the contract hassle bothering us, but once we got to training camp in 1975, the problems never ceased. Our players were meeting constantly, and sometimes the reps, Doug Van Horne and John Mendenhall, had to go into Manhattan from Pace College for other meetings. This was a huge distraction as we tried to get our team ready for the season. Wellington was part of the owners' negotiating team, so he was away in meetings all the time, but he called every day with a progress report, and I kept Arnsparger up-to-date.

However, the NFL wanted team management to maintain a hands-off policy, to avoid influencing players or being seen as strikebusters. Even so, Bill tried subtly to give the players an opposing view, but he was not as arrogant in his approach as I was. I was upset at the training camp disruption, and I felt they were doing themselves, the Giants and pro football as a whole a grave injustice. I had no real informants I could use to transmit my thinking, though I managed at times to get my points across in meetings with Van Horne and Mendenhall.

I urged them to talk about all the issues, using information from both sides, and to include Arnsparger and myself in the discussions so we could try to effect a balance. The players didn't really know what was happening, and in training camp they were more concerned about making the team than about how strong their union was or what issues were facing them. But the bottom line for us was that we were a team struggling to rise from the depths, and boycotts and strikes were the last thing our players should have been worrying about. There were times when I was tempted to say to them, "Hey, we're losers, and you can gain all you want from the contract, but you're not gaining anything for yourselves because some of you are not going to be around here since we'll continue to lose, and everyone will have to go. There is no big gain for the losers; only the winners keep winning in these situations." All of this, I knew, was eventually going to lead to a gigantic blowup where they became the victims.

And it did...in the Orange Bowl in Miami before our last 1975 exhibition game against the Dolphins. Our team voted to delay for thirty minutes going on the field and Miami coach Don Shula, his quarterback Bob Griese and the Dolphins team captains had to come into our locker room to urge our players to fulfill an obligation. It was the most disgusting and embarrassing situation I was ever associated with in football, and one that had its roots in Garvey's office. He had already convinced the New England Patriots and the Jets, two other perennial losers, to call off an exhibition game at the Yale Bowl. Now he wanted support from the other New York team, thus making a big publicity splash. This whole matter cooked throughout the day, but neither Wellington nor I were aware of it until just before the game, when we were summoned from the press box to the locker room to confront the issue.

Arnsparger had already been asked to leave the locker room so the players could vote, and when it was over they announced their half-hour boycott. Bill, of course, was mortified. He had returned to the city where he had made his reputation, and now his team was thumbing its nose at his former team and its fans. Emotions got hot and heavy. Wellington told the players that any delay was tantamount to a strike, and added that if the game wasn't played they would not get paid and not be able to practice until the new collective bargaining agreement was signed. Shula, of course, wanted the game played because he had a big crowd in the stadium and it meant a lot of money, but it was also as much a principle to him as it was to us. Don told our players his team wouldn't wait a half-hour to play, and Griese told them the strike would be against the fans, not the NFL, and that it would be no sympathy gesture for the Jets or Patriots.

I was much less tactful. I told Wellington, Bill and Shula, "If these guys don't get out on that field, let's leave the sons of bitches here and let them pay their own way home. Then let's see if they want to talk about a strike." I then jumped up on a table in the middle of the room and I vented those same feelings to the team, only in much harsher terms. They finally relented and played the game, but they did not like being threatened—not that I cared one bit—and I believe at that moment I lost some of the support of our better players. To that time, I had hoped they would help bring the team together, but when they showed absolutely no leadership and resented opposition to their tactics, I decided we would be better off looking more closely at the younger players and concentrate on developing them for our future. If the others wanted to join, that was okay too, but they were not going to be our future.

I don't believe the team ever recovered from that incident, and though we won our opener the following week against Philadelphia, there always seemed to be something missing in the way of leadership and the ability of the veterans to step out and take charge of a team that wanted to make a move. Throughout that year, there was an undercurrent of unrest and dissension, and that flared into the open one afternoon during a game at Shea Stadium, when a couple of the players got into a shoving match on the sidelines. That incident reflected the frustrations we were undergoing during a losing streak.

The 1975 season was a setback in other ways too, even though we won three more games than the previous year and turned the club over to the point where only twelve players remained from the 1973 team, nine of them starters. The top of our draft did not produce anything over the long run, and only George Martin, our eleventh pick, became a long-term starter. Our first pick went to Dallas in the Morton deal, and our second-round choice, offensive lineman Al Simpson, never worked out. That cost us throughtout the season. Our offensive line was a constant problem. We wanted Simpson to replace tackle Willie Young, who had given every ounce of his being for the Giants, and, never very big or strong, simply was worn down. I often wished everyone on the team had Willie Young's attitude; he was so conscientious and dedicated that he had blamed himself for some of the team's shortcomings when, in fact, if everyone had given the same effort the results would have been far different. Simpson was an adequate drive blocker, but he did not have the nimble feet needed to drop back for good pass-blocking position, meaning he could not play tackle, where we needed help. In 1976 he tried playing guard but couldn't handle the job there either. The domino effect was critical because we moved Tom Mullen, who was a splendid guard, to tackle. But his size at that position was inadequate, and Simpson couldn't pick up the slack at Tom's guard spot.

Consequently, Morton took a pounding for most of the season. He was the type of mechanical quarterback who threw the quick passes very well but was less efficient when he had to sit back and read a defense before making his choice of receiver. In other words, he needed more time than our line could provide. The flip side hurt us too. The lack of a strong line inhibited the running game that could have given Morton a bit more leverage. Hence, opposing defenses teed off on the passing game, which we also had hoped to strengthen with our third-round pick, wide receiver Danny Buggs, who didn't even catch a pass that year. Buggs's major problem was that he expected more out of himself than he had to give, and this led to his developing a complex that coaches were against him when they tried to help him improve. We traded him to Tampa Bay early in 1977.

So we really got little from the draft until Martin's spot, after which we also added a couple of good short-term players in running back Marsh White, our twelfth pick, and Rondy Colbert, our final pick. But George Martin has become something special for the Giants. He still has the same dedication that he brought to the team as a rookie, and George the Person is better than George the Player, which is saying a lot since the player is a marvelously gifted athlete, with size and speed, who was as conscientious about his playing as he was about all the off-the-field activities for which he has been widely recognized. Perhaps I appreciated George a bit more because of smooth playing style. All of his moves were effective without being overly rough or illegally aggressive.

George would have been an even better player in our 4-3 defense than in the 3-4 concept because he could have used that great athletic ability much more effectively in a gap defense. Linemen in the 3-4 play directly over an offensive lineman rather than in the gaps, and the linebackers are used to fill the gaps. Proponents of the 3-4 say the linemen can slide into the gaps, but I don't think they do it with the same effectiveness. In the 4-3 a defensive lineman is a yard off that offensive blocker, and the defender can get into the gap without being solidly blocked. This may be a technical argument, but I think it explains why the 3-4 doesn't really explode into an offense. I never favored it, and perhaps it explains why many NFL teams are now returning to the 4-3.

With all of the changes we made in 1975, probably the most important was moving back to New York City and playing in Shea Stadium. The club appreciated Yale University allowing it to play at the Bowl for a couple of years, but in a constantly losing situation—the Giants won only once in that time—the situation there became horrendous. The players, whose locker rooms were some distance from the stadium, were subject to a lot of harassment from the fans. I've never been called more dirty names in my life than during the seven Sundays I made that trek to and from the locker room; and seven "home" games there really meant an entire season of road games. Every week I became more convinced that we belonged back in Yankee Stadium where we had built so much of our legacy, and once there, I never wanted us to leave. When we finally moved into Giants Stadium it still wasn't the same to me. Nothing ever compared to Yankee Stadium, but in 1975 any permanent move was at least a year away, and we needed an immediate psychological boost.

New York City was having serious financial and self-image problems in 1975, so I suggested several times to Wellington that our returning might prove something of a boost—to the City as well as to the team. "New York is broke and this would be a good opportunity for us to give some hope to the City in at least a small way with the revenues our games would produce," I said to him. He and Tim finally agreed. With the help of a friend in city hall, Tim got us a one-year lease at Shea Stadium, as cotenants with the Jets.

Did it help? We won a couple of games there. Though the playing conditions got worse and worse each week, at least we were a New York team again. Our biggest win that year came on the road against another New York team, the Buffalo Bills, in a nationally televised Monday night game, when we staged a furious second-half comeback and beat the favored Bills, 17-14, (one Buffalo writer predicted we would lose, 63-7) on George Hunt's field goal in the final six seconds, his only bright spot all season. But as I said to Well after the game, it was also a super way to feature a team which was growing, which had been ridiculed by many of its so-called friends, including some in our own front office.

There were a couple of other bright spots as well, including a pair of season-ending victories over New Orleans and San Francisco that gave us hopes for a better 1976 season. We had become the youngest team, in terms of experience, in the NFL, and while improving in nearly every statistical category in 1975, we had also been in contention until late in the game in five of our nine losses. They are history, but I still believe that without the lingering effects of the strike on the attitudes of many veterans, we might have overcome some of our inexperience and won three or four of those games. Still, we had probably taken a step backward in trying to rebuild with new, young talent. Our deficiencies were glaring: lack of a strong offensive line, a good running attack and a consistent quarterback. On defense we needed one more talented rookie lineman to go with Mendenhall and George Martin, and more physical linebackers.

The first step toward curing those ills followed the folding of the World Football League in 1976, when we signed fullback Larry Csonka, the offensive star of Miami's 1973 and 1974 Super Bowl champions. Arnsparger, who knew Larry from their time together in Miami, fully concurred with that decision, in spite of Csonka's injury-weakened knee. Larry's agent, Ed Keating, who had handled Brad Van Pelt's new contract the previous year, came to us with the proposal after the Dolphins had turned down a deal that would have brought Larry back to them. Keating told me from the start that his numbers where high, something that got Well and Tim Mara a bit uptight when I relayed the news to them, but Well was as interested as I in pursuing the negotiations. He saw Csonka primarily as a great football addition to the team; I agreed with that, but I felt we could make some promotional hay and even erase a long-standing erroneous impression that the organization was unwilling to spend money to improve itself. And Keating had his motives too; he wanted to get some exposure in New York City with a big score.

We were not willing to pay just any price, either in salary or compensation to the Dolphins, but we wanted to pursue the issue as far as we could take it. The negotiations went very well; Keating was fair to us and to Csonka. He was firm, and he had a thorough knowledge of all the necessary facts. Never once did he leave us hanging or give us an ultimatum. In fact, the only impasse was their demand to include Kiick, but we weren't interested in him. My feeling was that if we packaged both Csonka and Kiick we'd be bringing back a Butch Cassidy-and-Sundance Kid combination who would have been seen as a constant tandem, perhaps stifling other players who felt they had a chance to play with Csonka too. Kiick was a helluva kid, and if the circumstances with us had been different, we might have taken the chance. I refused to budge from that point, however, and they finally backed down. They did ask for a bit more money—about 5 percent of the average $200,000 annual salary in the three-year deal (with an optional fourth year), and I agreed rather than spoil the deal for such a relatively small amount of money. We also agreed to some other goodies which brought the contract's worth to over a million dollars.

Wellington became more and more enthusiastic as the negotiations progressed—I dealt with Keating, but always kept Well informed—and kept urging me to get it finalized. Tim Mara was another matter. He didn't even involve himself in the negotiations despite my urgings. I wanted him to be around in case we needed a quick decision, especially since there was a lot of money involved and Well would spend anything to get a good player. But Tim remained absent and never inquired about the negotiations.

However, when the deal was signed he blew up.

"I thought you weren't going to sign him?" he said to me.

"I said I wasn't going to sign him if the price was outrageous," I told him. "Wellington thought the contract was fair to us and to Csonka."

"Well, that's an outrageous price to me," he said of the final salary package, telling me he thought first of money, not of improving the team at what was a reasonable cost.

It was the same after we signed Van Pelt. Prior to negotiating that deal with Keating, I proposed to Tim and Well a five-year package that called for a salary of $70,000, followed by $85,000, $100,000, $115,000 and $140,000, an average of $100,000 for each of the seasons. In so doing,

I pointed out to both of them that we had to give Brad good money in appreciation for all that he had done on what was really a very nominal first contract. Both agreed, so when Keating asked me at our first meeting for may proposal, I demurred. "I'm here to lay the cards on the table and not spend hours and hours conning each other," I told him. "Just give me your numbers."

He did—$100,000 to start, with a $5,000 raise for each of the next four seasons, for a total package of $550,000, an average of $110,000 per season, plus a $15,000 incentive for each Pro Bowl appearance.

"I know it's high," he said rather apologetically.

"No it's not, I'll take it," I told him, and he almost dropped over. But I wasn't going to bargain a guy down for $10,000 a year and get into a big hassle with all of the negative fallout when I could reasonably accommodate the player and give him an added incentive to play better for us. He did, too, making that Pro Bowl incentive four times during that five-year contract. Tim blew up over the Van Pelt deal, claiming I had betrayed the club by signing a deal worth $625,000 (if all the incentives were realized) when I indicated I was going no higher than $500,000. Even when I pointed out the average salary difference was only $10,000, he was not mollified.

Hypocritically, Tim was always carping about why we weren't a better team, yet during the Csonka negotiations, he chose to be a "convenient" owner—one who was visible in the good times but never around to help make the tough decisions or take his share of the flack when things went badly. I believe his nonparticipation in the Csonka negotiations was strategic; he left himself in a perfect position to second-guess the move, which he frequently did. As it was, the deal did not hurt the team financially, and it was structured in such a way that even some of the goodies in Larry's contract, such as endorsements, returned some money to the team.

Ideally, Wellington and Tim should have argued like hell with each other, while I acted as a sort of devil's advocate, thrashing out all of the problems and getting some sort of record of where everyone stood on this matter, particularly on the problem of giving a couple of third-round picks to Miami as compensation which, as I noted in the previous chapter, Well insisted on doing over my opposition. Tim, of course, said later that he was opposed to that, too, but he never was around to tell us beforehand.

Was the Csonka deal a good one? I believe so. We got a very good football player; everyone around the team got excited; we got some positive publicity when we needed it; and the fans were pepped up, though at times I believe that expectations were based too much on what they recalled Larry doing for the Dolphins, forgetting that we were a lesser team than those world championship teams he played on in Miami. Still, I think Larry gave the Giants everything he could, and he was always a credit to us. As to how much we got from him in a football sense, I'm not so sure that from time to time we could have used him a little differently. The biggest plus was his leadership. He was also a recognizable person on and off the football field, though after we had spent a day together on business in New York City, we walked down Fifth Avenue, counting all the people who recognized him and all who recognized me. I won, and I kidded him, "Did I make a mistake? They don't even know you."

Csonka wasn't the only former WFLer we brought in. We signed his head coach, John McVay, and twenty ex-WFL players. Five-sixths of Larry's offensive line at Memphis came to us, including tight end Gary Shirk, the only player who made it. My optimum dream was the front line starting for us en masse, eliminating a three- or four-year development period. No way, I quickly discovered. While Memphis had gathered the best talent in that league, for the most part the best of the WFL players were not as good as the last people on our roster, so one plan to accelerate our growth quickly faded.

Our growth came from the draft, and in 1976 we scored with top pick Troy Archer, a defensive lineman who tragically lost his life in an auto accident back in 1979. He could have become one of the best ever to play for the Giants. He had all the ingredients to be a great defensive lineman—he was big, tough and quick. Randy White, now heading for the Hall of Fame, had begun to star for the Dallas Cowboys as a defensive tackle at that time, but Troy showed me in just three seasons that he was every bit as good. We also picked linebackers Harry Carson in the fourth round, and Dan Lloyd in the sixth.

As I noted earlier, Carson, a defensive end in college, was Marty Schottenheimer's pet project. Marty's instincts were right: Harry fit the physical profile of what a good linebacker—and not a defensive end—should be. One of Harry's great assets, besides the fact that he is such a smart player, is his excellent balance; you never see him on the ground, but always moving parallel to the line of scrimmage, or low enough so that he can penetrate and remain upright to meet a block or make a tackle. It took Harry three or four years to become a solid player, and Lloyd was approaching the same level when he was forced to leave the game after just four seasons because of his battle against cancer. Dan, who was perfectly suited to play outside linebacker, was a more ferocious hitter than Carson, and just as tough and smart. I looked at Dan playing outside linebacker at that time, and I could see myself at the same position if I had been playing then. Though I had about ten pounds on him, we were almost the same size. With my agility, I might have been better dropping off in pass protection, but maybe not as tough sticking my head into the hole. Dan was fearless, but I'm pretty sure I would have figured out a way to get there before it opened. That's how I survived as a defensive end for fourteen seasons without getting pounded to bits.

We also thought for a time we had a nugget in quarterback Jerry Golsteyn, our twelfth-round pick. Jerry was a very intelligent quarterback with good mechanics and an adequate arm. He grasped our offense quickly and made good decisions on the field when the situations were pat. But he played cautiously, and he never gave the impression that he could take the team by the seat of the pants and drive it down the field. He was better suited to play with a team talented at every position, a team which didn't need to do explosive things all the time to survive. He won the starting job in his second season, but he was injured in the opening game and couldn't reclaim it again from Joe Pisarcik.

With the improved draft and the new people beginning to get a better grasp—particularly without the distraction of a strike and fewer disgruntled veterans—we sailed through the 1976 exhibition season with four wins in six games, one of those over defending Super Bowl champion Pittsburgh, which used its front-liners for most of the game. Expectations of a winning season were high, starting with the opening game at Washington. The players and coaches had primed themselves; beating George Allen had become such a big thing. Arnsparger believed George had stuck it to us a couple of times in 1975, and I never saw any of his teams as pumped up for a game as we were were that early September Sunday. But it was not to be—Washington drove for the winning touchdown in the final seconds, and we lost by two points, the margin provided by a safety the Redskins had scored when they trapped Morton in the end zone. The loss was a crushing blow to the players, one from which they never fully recovered: we lost our first seven games, and Arnsparger lost his job.

Looking back, there were several factors that ultimately led to our being forced to release Bill, and not all of them were his fault. After the good preseason, I believe everyone on his staff had overinflated our true worth. We still had some of the basic weaknesses that had plagued us for two years—a ho-hum offense, including a weak passing attack; a weak pass rush and sub-par pass defense; and Morton's inconsistency. Still, they used the positive feelings from that winning preseason to help build the team's self-esteem going into the season. Veteran teams can gauge their own value; teams wanting desperately to become winners, like ours at that time, don't keep a solid perspective, and after losing a game to Washington that they so dearly wanted to win, the effect was shattering.

A fiery coach like Vince Lombardi could have gotten the team rekindled; or a solid nucleus of leaders could have done the same thing in the locker room. Bill, like Tom Landry, believed that preparation was the prime motivator, but sometimes a team needs fire and brimstone from the boss to get it moving. Bill was not that way, and that missing ingredient was compounded by the fact that the team simply did not believe that Morton could produce victories. All of this was apparent the following week, when we lost to an inferior Eagles team, and there we were, still struggling, when the full brunt of a killer schedule hit us. We had to play the first four games of the season on the road while the finishing touches were applied to Giants Stadium, and the last two of those started a string of six straight games against teams that were in the 1975 playoffs. Under optimum conditions, any of the NFL's best teams at that time would have been hard-pressed to break even in that run, but we never had a chance to shake the doldrums that had befallen us. I will not use the schedule as an excuse for our failures, but I still question why the NFL schedule-makers, who claim they take into account the strengths and weaknesses of all teams in making the pairings, would give an obviously weaker team such a stretch of games. I supposed they figured our first two games were ones we could have won, and they were correct; but why not sprinkle them, and have another even match or two among that string of superior opponents to give us a chance to prevent such an extended losing streak?

So we were like a heavy rock in a pool, sinking faster and faster, with a 24-10 loss to the Rams. That week Bill called a team meeting, and every player had to stand up and give his opinion of what was wrong. I wondered if instead of asking them what was wrong he should have told them, but I guess he was trying to get everyone to take some responsibility by acknowledging their faults. Again, a Lombardi or Landry never did this, but everyone has his own management style. Things got worse the following week when we lost to the Cards, 27-21, a game we could have won had not Walker Gillette dropped an end zone pass from Morton in the final seconds. We were 0-4, but only five seconds from being 2-2.

We opened Giants Stadium the following week against the Cowboys, and the emotion and excitement were at a fever pitch. But the Cowboys punctured our balloon at the start when they ran the opening kickoff to midfield. They controlled the game, thanks in part to our elementary mistakes, which cut off some good offensive drives, and a rather passive, methodical defense that did nothing to take away the Cowboys' offense. Jimmy Robinson scored the first Giants touchdown in the Stadium on a pass from Morton, but that is the only positive memory in a 24-14 loss.

In that game we finally turned to Norm Snead—I had claimed him on waivers near the end of the preseason, and in so doing I had my only serious conflict with Wellington. Snead had a no-cut contract, and normally I consulted with Well before taking a player with such a contract. But he wasn't around when the decision had to be made, so I checked with Tim and he felt we should do it. Bill was pressing me to get him some veteran quarterback help behind Morton, so with five minutes remaining before the waivers closed I claimed Snead. Wellington's displeasure revolved around the money commitments we undertook and the fact that we didn't turn to our two young quarterbacks, Jerry Golsteyn and Dennis Shaw, when we were committing ourselves to a rebuilding program. But there are certain positions where you can't wait forever, and quarterback is one of them. My job was to help the coach get what he believed he needed to turn things around, not to stifle those aims, and with Morton having become iffy, I agreed with his wishes.

Snead got the chance the following week when he started against the

Vikings, but at that point even Y. A. Tittle in his best years probably couldn't have helped us. We were stuck, and Minnesota won easily, 24-7. I knew then there was only the slimmest chance—beating Pittsburgh at home the following week—that Bill could survive, and I drew up a scenario, even before we left Minneapolis, in case Wellington wanted to change coaches immediately. Both of us were concerned lest the situation get so serious that all that we had gained could disappear, yet we were hoping that he could turn things around. It didn't happen against Pittsburgh, either, and the next morning Well, Tim and I met at Wellington's home, and we decided a change had to be made.

I'm sure Bill knew it was coming. After the Pittsburgh game, when I was asked by the media if I was going to change coaches, I simply said, "I'm going to sleep on it," though I knew at the time we had to make a move. The easy part was deciding—the hard part was telling him. When I walked into his office at Pace he looked up from his desk and said, "Well, did you have your big meeting and make a decision?"

"Come on, Bill," I replied, "don't make it rough. You know some things have to be done, and there was no stopping the slide. I hate like hell to even have to say that, but you know we're just going to have to make a change."

That was it, though I believe he had prepared himself for it and had made some alternate plans, because almost immediately he was back in Miami with the Dolphins as defensive coach. That was the toughest thing I ever had to do, and it was even tougher the next day when Bill's wife, Betty Jane, came in to return their season tickets and asked me why I couldn't have given him just one more week.

When I spoke to the players the next day, there seemed to be an atmosphere of relief, but also a realization that their dreams weren't the only ones to be shattered. I told them:

> It's not easy standing here, but I guess it hasn't been easy for you either. It hasn't for any of us, particularly Bill. Yesterday was a very, very difficult day, and I hope that you share in the sorrow. . . and maybe some of the responsibility because we're all in this together.
>
> As a group, you've worked like hell. As in all groups, we get some good and some bad. But we have a lot of good. We've got to suck up our guts and start all over. Some of you are going to ask, "How many times do I start over?" The answer is: "Everytime I break the offensive or defensive huddle." Now, if you don't want it that way, get out!
>
> I don't expect miracles. The miracle workers are each and every one of us. . . .

Could there have been any miracles with Bill Arnsparger as coach? Probably not. As I noted earlier, some factors were beyond his control. Still, Bill was a very honorable coach, and he never put himself before the organization. He stayed on the rebuilding target and never put pressure on anyone to make moves that would have been short-term solutions. I believe all of us on the football side did everything possible to help him, and he probably would have been more successful if the Giants had a sound football operation when he came. But he still would have had to rebuild a team that had only a few good players. Bill's teaching style and low-key demeanor were better suited to a team much more advanced than ours. He would have been more successful with veteran players who had not been beaten down by continuous failure. As it was, when the prospect of immediate success did not occur, our players simply didn't feel any further effort was worthwhile.

Our single biggest failure on his behalf was not coming up with a solid quarterback. Had Morton come in and did all we anticipated, we might have been a much better team, even without the strong supporting cast that he obviously needed. With few exceptions, it never happened, and that hurt us—and Bill—as much as anything.

Should I have done anything differently to help his situation?

Bill was not an easy person to deal with on a one-on-one basis, and he preferred to remain aloof, seeming to put himself above some of us who did not have his football background. I was in football long enough to know that football coaches often become very narrow in their thinking and get too introspective, while at the same time preaching to their players about correcting faults. But sometimes they never seem to accept the fact that they, too, have correctable faults.

I always felt my relationship with Arnsparger was sincere, but I never felt that we could sit and have a beer after a game and really open up to each other, or that I could say, "Bill, you did a couple of really stupid things out there today." Even if I forced the issue, I don't think it would have been accepted in the spirit in which it was offered. I believe he even resented me looking at the game films. I reviewed them each week and then met privately with him to discuss some of the things we did, but never to second-guess any of the strategy decisions he and his staff had made during a game. But Bill put up that protective shield, and allowed his coaches to perpetuate bad decisions rather than acknowledging their mistakes, stepping in and ordering the changes. Though I realized the sensitivity of this oversight, when the moves didn't come, and the team continued to suffer, our discussions became more direct and so did my questions, but I never ordered him to make any changes. If I did, he had every right to tell me to come down and coach the team.

In fact, his frequent retort to me was, "Why don't you come down on the field during a game?" Why he wanted that I don't know. Maybe he thought I would get a better feel for the game by being on the sidelines. That, of course, would have been disastrous for a number of reasons. It gives the appearance to the players and coaches that the head coach really isn't in charge of the team. Also, the bench area is the worst possible place to get a true perspective of what is really happening. In the heat of a game, objectivity often disappears. A coach sees only the things happening on the field, not why or how they are happening. I sat with Wellington in the press box at Giants Stadium, directly across from our bench and next to the coaches in the spotting booth. From my vantage point, I heard and saw how the coaches on the field and in the booth worked with each other; I watched how the coaches on the sidelines worked with players; and in general had a more panoramic picture of exactly what we were doing, good and bad.

There also is a tendency when you stay close to the coaches to second-guess coaching decisions during a game. My own coaching experience and knowledge of the game made it much more difficult for me to stay out of the way, particularly when I knew that what we had planned wasn't going to work very well. I'd have to close my eyes and say to myself, "I hope I'm wrong." There also were times when I saw obvious mistakes during a game, such as when we had ten or twelve men on the field, or when people were coming into the game late, creating a penalty. In those situations I wanted to knock on that window and tell the coaches to order the bench to shape up. Well saw the same thing, and I could see his anxiety or hear his oblique suggestion that I step in at that moment. "It's not our job to coach," I'd remind him. "So even if we see some things going bad, we must let the coaches pick them up."

So being on the field wasn't the answer. The answer was an open dialogue so Bill and I could exchange views, not to order him to make changes but to give him a different perspective. None of this ever happened, and perhaps the reason went back to the beginning of our time together with the Giants, when he asked me about some players and I had honestly to tell him that I didn't know about them because I had not been that close to the game. Right away, we missed an opportunity for "football" rapport, and I always felt that he believed he knew more about the game and those who played it than I did. He didn't seem to feel confident that he could seek my help, as in my giving him all I knew about Landry's system with the Cowboys. I would much rather he said at the beginning, "Hey, you don't know anything about what's been going on," and I would have said, "You're probably right; I haven't been around the game for nine years, but give me a chance. Teach me, and then we'll work together." He was not the kind of person to do that, and even when he asked about something he always seemed to muse on the answer rather than giving the impression that he had found the information he sought.

All of that was no longer of any account on that October Monday morning in 1976. It was time to pick up and go on...upward, we hoped.

9 Changing the Guard Once More

Bill Arnsparger's departure on a Monday meant that we had to have a new head coach for Tuesday, and I came the closest I ever did to fulfilling my dream of becoming a head coach in the National Football League.

The subject came up at Well's home when we agreed that Bill would be released. I immediately suggested that research and development director John McVay be named his replacement. He had impressed everyone with his great enthusiasm and sense of organization, but Well wasn't ready to move that quickly.

"Before we get into that kind of permanent change, you can take the team over," he said.

"I guess for the interim that might be okay," I said.

Tim hemmed and hawed about the idea, though I would have preferred for him to say to me straight out, "It's a mistake." But I read the mood, and eager not to get involved in another controversy within the ownership to make it appear we had returned to the ex-Giant syndrome, I said, "Under the circumstances, I think it's best that we take John McVay, who has been on the field as a head coach." I don't know that I actually believed that. After McVay's appointment was made official a couple of the assistant coaches told me they were certain I would have taken the job.

Looking back, and without wishing to appear arrogant, I believe I could have stayed and delivered winning seasons for the Giants for as long as I had wished to be a head coach. At the time of decision, though, we had proceeded with the belief that the Giants had to step into the modern era, unafraid to hire people from outside the organization. Had I inserted myself as head coach I would have recanted the direction that I had so ardently been trying to sell.

One big reason why Wellington would have allowed me to step into the job, though, was his belief that every time a team changes coaches it takes at least three years for the team to resume an upward course. Taking into account the attitude of the players, that new nucleus that had started to form, we saw a lot of good things happening that we didn't wish to undo. Since I had been part of establishing the new system, that changeover period could have been lessened had I been named coach, and there would not have been as much upheaval.

With me out of the running, McVay got the job, and at the time he was a good choice. My reasons for hiring him were centered on his considerable experience as a college head coach at Dayton University, and the fact that he had done a good job with Memphis of the WFL, where he had managed to bring players into a growth situation and still maintain a winning record in the face of all the controversy surrounding that league. On top of that, in just a few short months with us John had displayed a charisma that was in sharp contrast to Arnsparger's demeanor, and it rubbed off on everyone. I saw immediately that people would bust their butts to work for him because they liked him, and we needed that for our team.

Away from football he had the unique personality that is demanded of anyone who must work in the eye of New York's media watch, and he easily interfaced with all of the media covering our team. At that time, with matters so down and gloomy, we needed someone who could project some positive feeling and lift some of the dark clouds that had encased us.

McVay, of course, had come to the Giants on Arnsparger's recommendation. They had been teammates at Miami University, and old school ties, particularly from the Cradle of Coaches, bind tightly. But I concurred in the move because John also brought to us extensive knowledge of a whole group of WFL players who might help us—and at that time, I was looking for every edge I could get to help our rebuilding—and he did a good job for us in the newly established post of research and development director. We hired him as head coach on an interim basis for the rest of the 1976 season. I did not know the specifics of his talents, but I was more interested in his obvious ability to pick people up and get them going so that we could at least finish on a positive note.

"I don't know what's going to happen when we finish the season," I said in offering him the job. "But until it is over, I want to give you as much help and cooperation as I can, and I want you to do all you can to get this turned around and have the players and fans believing we are still making progress."

True to our wishes, John did not change our football system very much, and the way the other coaches and players reacted to him was a change for the better. His presence and command were very upbeat, in contrast to the methodical Bill, who didn't drive his players into the ground but didn't lift them up either. He expected people to mature and do their job. John had a bit more fire, a "gooser" I called him, and he always seemed to know just what to do to get people moving without making a big deal about it. It wasn't too long before everyone, including the players, were really impressed with John and wanted to play for him. Our level of play began to reflect those feelings, and we won three of our last five games, losing one by a point to Denver and the other by a late field goal to St. Louis.

Perhaps his biggest splash was finally beating the Redskins for the first time since 1970 and ending our season-long nine-game losing streak on the same afternoon. You might have thought we had won the title that day. That victory, and the way he made some discrete changes in our offensive structure (we beat the Lions at a time when their defense had dominated some opponents), showed us John was fully capable of handling the job. The new enthusiasm around the team convinced us he could be our head coach, so we gave him the job on a full-time basis even before the season had ended.

John's reaction to the challenge and the response from the enthusiasm that he engendered also underscored my determination to do all possible to help make up some lost ground from the past two seasons, and that meant trying to get every possible edge to accelerate our growth. Getting an edge in the NFL meant different things to different people. Some simply nodded at the rules and went about stashing players; others looked for loopholes in the NFL rules and worked around established procedures that way. Wellington insisted that we stick by the spirit of the rules, but he agreed that as long as we were never in violation of them we should get whatever edge possible.

By the rules in 1977 we were allowed two veteran mini-camps because we had a new head coach. The usual procedure was to hold them in early and late spring. But I saw possibilities beyond that and arranged through my friend, Mac Cimas, Minister of Sport in Mexico, for the Giants to be invited as guests of that country for a week, during which they would put on some clinics and allow people to watch their practices. That was one of our allowable mini-camps, though it was a week long; the other was a three-day affair at Giants Stadium. But we got much more accomplished during the week in Mexico, and to me it was the edge I wanted to give John McVay to work with his players.

What I didn't forsee were the internal disruptions the trip would create within our organization—yet another example of what happens to people who suddenly find themselves doing something new and different. It began when I sent Jim Trimble to Mexico City to arrange the details for the week-long trip. Jim went down knowing the Mexican government wanted us to be their guests, so he naturally believed everything we needed would be easily arranged and handed to us carte blanche. When that didn't happen, and he found an environment unlike any he had experienced, he returned and painted such a gloomy picture of this venture that it fueled the disbelievers in our organization and started them clucking their way around the office like a group of doomsayers, predicting nothing but the most dire consequences (Tim even spoke of our team being a ripe target for mad bombers!).

Suddenly, a very simple venture became a major crisis, and I had to step in and hold the line, pointing out that I knew from my travel-business dealings with the Mexicans that it takes some sweet-talking, some negotiation and more than a bit of selling before the package comes as neatly wrapped as you want it. But it took a strongly worded memo to Well and Tim to finally get it done:

> Why Mexico? Why anywhere? I firmly believe in John, and if we accomplish our football objective, that's great. How about faith, enthusiasm, a new beginning, being a team again and maybe even hard fields, small lockers and the unsophistication of our lifestyle? Remember, most of our players come from less than Mexico will offer us. Just maybe they will appreciate what they have.
>
> I believe when we stop believing we can do something, we do nothing. I believe our team can benefit by being together as a group in an exciting new situation. I do not believe we ever had total management faith in each other, and in this case, in me.
>
> If I have the authority and responsibility I assume I do, and I have cleared with Well (I assume Well and Tim discuss such matters as this), then I would expect faith in the projects in which I am involved.

The trip came off in grand fashion, costing us less than $20,000, compared to $28,000 we had spent to bring in the veterans for one camp the previous year. The coaches came back well-satisfied with the results. Most importantly, we established a knitting process that brought everyone together after the tumultuous events of the previous two seasons, particularly the newer players who had become our future.

I don't mean to be hypercritical of the Giants for their reaction to the new and the different; many NFL clubs reflect the institutional nature of pro football, where change is often a foreign word. While some cheated and others found loopholes, no one seemed willing to come up with means of developing players that would benefit everyone equally and take away the rule-breaking and stretching.

At the 1975 league meeting, for example, I proposed to the NFL owners that they establish an off-season developmental league in Europe where each NFL team could send a specific number of players to play a six- or eight-week schedule with plenty of teaching in between. In my season in the Continental League I saw many players who had NFL potential but needed more time to develop. Why not give them an opportunity in a structured environment, supported and stocked by the NFL, with additional talent from among the quarter-million servicemen stationed in Europe? Free agent prospects could work there as well. I looked at our player development costs—we spent $100,000 on first-round draft pick John Hicks and then found that George Martin was the steal of the century as a twelfth-round pick. How many George Martins were out there? Even one or two would make a big difference to any team, and there was no denying the cost effectiveness of the program.

My proposal got nowhere. But today the NFL is actively cultivating the European market with an annual game in London and plans to play even more preseason games abroad. Perhaps NFL football will eventually become an international sport, a feasible possibility in this era of global communications. Look at the hundreds of millions on every continent who watch the Super Bowl each year.

To get the Giants an edge—which really was at the heart of my proposal for a European league—I tried to organize a group to tour Europe and seek out soccer-style kickers. I even drew up a manual to illustrate the salient points of American football as they applied to kicking. That was shot down too.

I also proposed to the Giants that we switch from filming our practices to using videotapes. Our filmings, all one-time operations, were very expensive. Videotape, even ten years ago, was reusable. (Vince Lombardi had used it when he was head coach of the Redskins in 1969 and was enthralled at its possibility as an on-the-field teaching tool.) It also helped the coaches use their time better by giving them immediate access to the tool; films took three hours to be developed. The reaction was no different from what I had heard about the watches or the Mexico trip: "Oh, we never did this before"..."we don't have the equipment"..."what's wrong with film?" And I'm talking about coaches as well as some in the front office. Yet today videotape is mandatory throughout the NFL, and it eventually will save millions in expenses.

Though pro football was enjoying more and more popularity, advertising itself as the sport of now *and* the future, it was still operating in the past, unreceptive to the practical ideas that helped teams but didn't happen to be ideal public relation tools for image-building. To me, image-building comes from winning; with the Giants, I wanted most of all to get us working efficiently, to the benefit of everyone. That is why I proposed we hire someone who understood the nuances of the evolving world of money management, with deferred contract payments, annuities, better utilization of profits for the long-term benefit of the organization and the other financial instruments that were becoming so popular. When we discussed contracts with agents, they came prepared to talk in such terms, but we had no one who could deal with those new ideas. As far as the Giants were concerned, that was the province of Tim Mara and Ray Walsh, and all proposals I made for such improvements simply fell on deaf ears.

Agents had become a very important part of the football business, and a club's management simply was hamstrung unless it could deal on equal conditions. In five years I found many more good agents than bad ones; but perhaps more marginal ones than the other two categories combined. Some were friends of players and not prepared to negotiate; others were trying to become agents without any of the necessary background in finance or law or any of the know-how to help the player merchandise his ability away from football. Ed Keating was a very good agent; so was Jack Mills of Colorado. Some clubs had problems with Howard Slusher, but he was very reasonable with me in the three or four dealings we had.

But I had the advantage of being an ex-player with considerable experience in business, a profile different from what most of them were used to. I didn't go by the Harvard Business School approach, where if you went fishing and pulled up a tire, you looked upon yourself as a bad fisherman. If I went fishing and pulled up a tire I sold the tire, and the day was not a complete waste. I really enjoyed working with agents because I had great confidence in my own business instincts and in my resolve always to do what was best for the Giants.

I talked to an agent first to get a feel of him as a person. With contract demands I always made my game plan clear: we drafted the player because we wanted him; we don't want him to come to us unhappy over a contract squabble; but at the same time we expect reasonable proposals and negotiations with a minimum of posturing and foolish nonsense. Negotiations have to be fair, and once we make a commitment to each other there should be no changes or further finagling.

In 1977 we made Gary Jeter our top draft pick, and after one conversation with his agent I knew we were going to have tough negotiations. He wanted an outlandish contract. Rather than go back and forth over the phone, I flew to California, went to his office and said, "Look, I'm out here because I want to be fair and as reasonable as possible. I want you to do the same thing. You gave me numbers that I can't live with, so I'm telling you that if those still are your numbers, then we're going to have a problem."

"Well," he replied, "those still are the numbers."

"Okay," I said. I closed my briefcase and walked out of the office, just as I had planned if he stayed with the original offer. If he wanted to negotiate reasonably, I was prepared to do that too. The trip was a gamble of sorts that did not produce immediate results, but it let him know that I was adamant about our position. We eventually got the contract worked out to the satisfaction of both of us, but not to the detriment of the team, nor to the point where Jeter came to us disgruntled and unhappy.

Interestingly, the day before I left for California to see Jeter's agent I talked to Jack Kemp, a member of our 1958 team who was then early in his Congressional career. Noting that I would have five or six hours between flights, I mentioned that I would like to visit former President Richard Nixon, who then was living in San Clemente. I had first met Nixon when he was Vice President. After our 1959 title game in Baltimore he visited our locker room, and I was the first person he saw. I was standing stark naked when he walked over to shake hands and console me a bit. "Sorry I'm not better dressed," I mumbled as I took his hand. "Don't worry about it," he said with a laugh. "There's never a towel around when I need one, either."

We had kept in touch from time to time after that, and I did some volunteer work for him during his two Presidential campaigns. In 1977 he was beginning to re-emerge into public life, and following my phone conversation with Kemp, Jack must have called him because I got a call back saying that Nixon would enjoy a visit. When I went down to San Clemente it was tough for the first five minutes to get into any kind of conversation, but we got going after a while and covered a lot of ground, including my feelings about Lowell Weicker, the Republican senator from Connecticut who had been such an outspoken critic of his administration during the Watergate hearings. Nixon didn't seem as upset with Weicker's grandstanding as I had been, or with his leftist stands on most issues. Politicians learn to accept such things, which is probably one good reason why I wouldn't be a very good politician.

Nixon, an ardent Giants fan who has always maintained a keen interest in football, was very conversant about Gary Jeter when I explained the purpose of my trip, and he didn't seem as surprised as many Giants fans when we made a defensive lineman our top draft pick for the second straight year. Jeter was considered a premium player, but he fit the John Hicks mold in that he didn't work to justify his top-draft-choice status during the two seasons we were together with the Giants. He had tremendous size, and he was strong and quick—all the necessary ingredients for an outstanding defensive lineman—but he lacked that sense of urgency that would have made him work every day to get better. With us he had to be able to start and play well right from the start. Consequently, I believe he has not become the great player that was his potential. He has seemed content to be a situation player, used mostly in pass-rushing situations, as has been his role over the last few seasons with the Giants, and lately with the Rams. Without the luxury of talent that allowed for situation substitutions, we wanted him to be a full-time player, and he just never filled that role as we expected.

The 1977 draft was interesting. In addition to Jeter, we picked up wide receiver Johnny Perkins in the second round, Emery Moorehead in the fifth and Al Dixon in the seventh. Perkins stayed with the Giants for seven seasons. He had great speed and catching ability, but he had trouble adjusting on the run to changing defenses or unanticipated coverages, so he never had the superb career he could have had. Moorehead, of course, later became the Bears' starting tight end in the eighties, and Dixon went on to have some productive seasons with Kansas City. The Giants saw him only as a wide receiver who needed time to learn to play, and he never really got that time. He became a better blocker after he left the Giants. Dixon should have been better; he had great physical attributes, but he couldn't knock off Gary Shirk, who was slower, smaller and not nearly as physically talented. But Gary ran a lot of people off because he worked harder, was smarter, and was willing to do anything to survive. Shirk and J. T. Turner were the best of the players who came from the WFL. Turner had been a defensive lineman in the WFL but played as an offensive guard for six of his seven seasons with the Giants. J. T. was a helluva kid and smart, which is why he made the change from defense to offense so easily

189

and then played so well.

Jim Trimble, who was very knowledgeable about players, also found Joe Pisarcik, who had played three seasons with the Calgary Stampeders of the Canadian League. Pisarcik was a very methodical, strong-armed quarterback who was never going to be exceptional, but he was tough and he'd fight right to the end of the game. I liked him from the start because I thought he was the right kind of player for our situation—someone who could hang tough and absorb some pounding while we bought time, upgraded other positions and got ourselves the star quarterback of the future. He started the 1977 training camp as our number-five quarterback, but he eventually gained the starting job in both the 1977 and 1978 seasons in a battle with Jerry Golsteyn.

Joe did a good job for us, considering that we still were an emerging team, and he had to learn about the NFL while also trying to learn about his teammates. He had some charisma, too, and in one self-deprecating bit of humor he noted that Joe Namath was "Broadway Joe" during his years in New York City, but he, Joe Pisarcik, was "Patterson Plank Road Joe," after a road that ran past one edge of the Meadowlands sports complex. But that was Joe—no airs, blue collar, a take-what-you-find kind of player who was something of a throwback to another era of the game when quarterbacks weren't so deified.

Joe and wide receiver Jimmy Robinson, another free agent, were very alike in their outlooks on the field. Trimble used to say that Robinson, at five-nine and 160 pounds, was so small that "he had to stand on a brick to kick a duck in the ass," but he was tough and resourceful, and led the Giants in pass receiving in both the 1977 and 1978 seasons. He was our top kickoff returner in 1976 and returned punts in addition to his other duties.

We also hit the free-agent jackpot late in the 1977 season by signing Brad Benson, who had been an eighth-round pick of the Patriots that season. My old Rams teammate, Leon McLaughlin, line coach of the Pats at that time, gave him a tremendous recommendation, noting that he simply needed work and seasoning. He became a starter at both guard and tackle in 1978. Of course, Brad is one of the survivors from that time who celebrated the Super Bowl and a Pro Bowl after the 1986 season, and he has run off a lot of higher priced, more physically gifted players. Our team in 1977 and 1978 had a two-tone look—half of the players were comprised of draft choices, but none later than 1972, when John Mendenhall was a third-round choice; and nearly half were free agents, all but Doug Van Horne signed from 1974 on.

Our draft over the past four years had cost us $1.5 million. For our money we had twenty pretty good players. However, our free agents cost us very little and brought us about twenty players, about eight of whom were equal in quality to our drafted players. We only had five players acquired by trade, but one of those, Joe Danelo, obtained from Green

Bay, kicked a thirty-yard field goal in the final three seconds to give us a 20-17 opening-game victory over Washington in 1977, providing another measure of delight for our long-suffering fans, who watched George Allen lose for the first time ever on an opening day. Jerry Golsteyn quarterbacked us all the way in that game, but the following week he was one of several players who couldn't survive the hundred-degree heat in Dallas when we lost to the Cowboys. We had a couple of bad scares after the game. Brian Kelley collapsed in the locker room, and on the plane home Troy Archer collapsed and had to spend the night in the hospital. Keeping quarterbacks healthy became a real problem, but we also faced the culmination of Bob Tucker's unhappiness with the Giants early in October 1977 when he publicly demanded to be traded. As I've said, I didn't blame him for wanting to be with a winner, but he should have kept his mouth shut because we had all but finalized a deal with the Vikings to trade him for a third-round pick. But once he went public our bargaining power shrank considerably, and McVay had become so disgusted that he wanted me to put him on waivers and forget any deal. When Mike Lynn, the general manager of the Vikings, saw our predicament, he reneged on the deal and falsely claimed we had broken off negotiations. Lynn lacked reliability and, in my mind, honor as we tried to work something out. Tucker further exacerbated the situation the next Sunday when he claimed he was injured and could not play during our 20-17 victory over the 49ers. Four days later we finally traded him to Minnesota for a fifth-round draft pick—a big difference on draft day from our original deal. A day after that his mysterious leg injury must have disappeared because I was told he was running full tilt in drills with his new team.

The Tucker problem was like a volcanic eruption, but some of our coaching problems had more far-reaching consequences. These problems centered around McVay's preoccupation with some of his old friends and players from the World Football League who had joined the team in 1976 and 1977. Bill Arnsparger had hired Jay Fry (who had played at Miami University during Bill's time there and later coached in Canada and with McVay at Memphis) to be our line coach in 1976. John kept him on the staff in 1977, when he also added former WFL coaches Lindy Infante and Bob Gibson. In 1978 he added Joe Galat, another former Memphis coach, to succeed Marty Schottenheimer as linebacker coach, and Dick Modzelewski had returned to the Giants as defensive coordinator. I could not dictate his choice of coaches at the start because every head coach must get people with whom he is compatible professionally and personally, but after a while I saw our staff had become woefully inexperienced compared with other NFL teams. Too often they equated the old WFL with the NFL, two very different worlds.

Our biggest failing was in the offensive line, where Fry insisted on using Ralph Hill at center. Ralph was one of the nicest young men you'd ever want to know, but he was simply too small to play in the NFL. Our quarterbacks were getting mauled because of poor pass protection in the middle, and opponents were piling up four and five sacks a game against us. I pushed John to make a change, and unlike Arnsparger he sat and listened to my comments; but nothing happened. Obviously he felt he was usurping Jay's coaching domain. But there are times when the head coach must make some command decisions and forget friendship and loyalty to individuals for the overall betterment of the team. Finally, ignoring the sensitivities involved, I stepped in and all but ordered him to replace Hill with Karl Chandler, a radical move on my part because I had been so insistent with Wellington about staying out of the coaches' business.

"I know you believe in your coaches," I said to John, "but how long is Ralph Hill going to play center? We're getting our asses kicked, and while it's great to be loyal to the coaches, at some point you're going to have to say to them, 'Hey, you're not doing me any favors by resisting my suggestions.' Otherwise, you also ought to consider that they ultimately may be responsible for hanging your ass."

I don't believe John ever felt comfortable with such confrontations, and I know that he reluctantly allowed Fry to become the conditioning coach in 1978 while Jerry Wampfler moved in as line coach. He didn't agree with our replacing Gibson as offensive coordinator after the infamous "fumble" game against the Eagles that same year, but more about that later.

Gibson had been a defensive coach at Charlotte of the World League and backfield coach for the Lions in 1976 before joining us, but he and Infante, our receivers coach, were so limited in pro experience that our offense really suffered, and we became a boring team to watch. Our young defense was playing reasonably well, and I was willing to do anything to help take off some of the pressure and give us more flair and punch. At one point I suggested to John that he hire Norm Van Brocklin as our offensive coordinator. Dutch had a fantastic mind for offense, and in my estimation we desperately needed someone of his ability. I pushed pretty hard for that one. John, still strong in his loyalty to friends, pushed just as hard in the other direction, to the point of near-confrontation. I backed off and allowed him to stay status quo. I still voiced my strong opposition to his path and reminded him that he alone would have to face the consequences for his decision. Later, I also tried to convince him to hire Joe Morrison, who then had spent several years as a successful head coach at the University of Tennessee at Chattanooga and who I knew always had a fine mind for implementing an NFL-style offense. I got nowhere on that one either.

Finally, sensing I would not get him to hire anyone on a full-time basis, I set up a series of coaching clinics for his offensive staff. I brought in such outstanding offensive innovators as Bill Walsh, now head coach of the 49ers (where McVay is club president). Bill was head coach at Stanford, and I'm sure he would have taken a job as our offensive coordinator had he been asked. I know he wanted to get back into the NFL. Blanton Collier, the former coach of the Browns, Bill McPeak, former offensive coordinator for the Lions and Redskins, and Sid Gillman, my old Rams coach who was renowned for his knowledge of pass offense, were also at these clinics.

Through all of this I pointed out to McVay that everyone who came in had been with the NFL for a long time, and that kind of knowledge was absolutely necessary to survive and be successful. "We're missing that ingredient," I told him flatly. "You can't surround yourself with a lack of experience by taking a lot of people who were in the World Football League and expect to go out and match wits with people such as those who have been helping your staff. We don't need part-time instructors; we need full-time experienced coaches. While you and your coaches might think they have the NFL all figured out, they have a long way to go just to get even, and after that they have to know it even better."

I still wanted to be a stimulating source of ideas rather than an adversarial or interfering overseer. It was difficult because I was familiar with our game plan each week and knew exactly what was working and what was not; and I doublechecked my opinions and observations with my own film study. John was always cordial in our discussions, unlike Arnsparger, and he always left me with a sense that he understood the problems too, yet he never really did much to solve them. I always offered to give him specific instances of our shortcomings, but again, obviously feeling it would be disloyal to his coaches, he never asked for them.

What made that all the more frustrating was that we had considerably improved, and we were now competitive enough that some extra punch could get us some victories and overcome some of the misfortunes that always dog young, emerging teams. In a 1977 game at Cleveland, we seemingly broke a 7-7 tie when Bobby Hammond caught a 68-yard touchdown pass, but the play was nullified by a penalty. A couple of plays later Golsteyn had one of his passes picked off and returned for a touchdown, so instead of being ahead, 14-7, we were behind, 14-7, and wound up losing, 21-7. We then smothered the Cardinals, 27-7, with our best all-around performance of the year, and a week later we were just one play and four seconds from beating the Eagles. Philadelphia had a fourth down at our one yardline. Marty Schottenheimer correctly figured out what play Philadelphia would call—a bootleg run by quarterback Ron Jaworski after a fake to the fullback—and set up a prearranged defense to counter it, one we had practiced against that specific play during the week. Still, one of our cornerbacks missed his assignment, and Jaworski scored for a 17-14 victory.

The following week, at Giants Stadium, we played a courageous game before losing to the Bears, 12-9, with just nine seconds to play in overtime. An icy rain fell throughout the game, and for once the coaches allowed Csonka to hammer at the defense. He had his only one-hundred-yard rushing game of the year.

There was always a lot of discussion about the way we used, or didn't use, Larry, and there were times when he was not too happy about what he considered his role as the "highest paid blocker on the team." Larry proved before and after he played with us, in his two terms with the Dolphins, that he was an effective runner only when his team was ahead or in contention. His greatest attribute was controlling the ball, hence the clock. He also worked best with a good all-around offense which featured a number of other weapons, and with a defense that got the ball back in fairly good field position most of the time.

When we first signed him I envisioned a better offense and defense. That didn't work out. In his first season a gimpy knee he brought from the WFL hampered him somewhat. Over the next two years our offense did not consistently put us in a position to make the proper use of him. With a team that jumped to early leads he could have been more effective. Sometimes he had those opportunities with the Giants, sometimes he didn't. I would have liked to have seen our game plans built a little more strongly around his running. Again, I don't believe our coaching staff at that time saw the importance of integrating all of our offensive weapons in a more rounded approach, though on their behalf we still had not emerged with an offensive line that could consistently knock people backwards. Later in the 1978 season, this began to happen and there were times when Csonka worked very well in a system that spread the load around with our other backs. Through all of this I still believe that Larry was a credit to himself and to the team in all that he did.

He certainly rose to the battle in the 1977 season finale against the Bears, when Walter Payton came to Giants Stadium with a lot of fanfare, needing less than two hundred yards to set an NFL single-season rushing mark. Many conceded he'd get it against us, but our defense allowed him less than fifty. Though we lost the game (some sure touchdown passes were dropped in the end zone), it still was a great way to finish. I felt at the time that our team had finally come together, and by a matter of just thirteen seconds over the final two games we missed a break-even record while still suffering from a stuttering offense that was hampered all year by offensive-line problems. We had to contend with inadequate coaching and lineup mistakes. Also, the end of the John Hicks and Tom Mullen era—having become unmanageable, Hicks was ultimately traded before the 1978 season, and Mullen's shoulder finally gave out, ending his NFL career—required patching and filling among the front five.

I didn't recognize another brush fire that had begun to ignite at the time—our frustration had begun to spread to the fans. After so many losing seasons, all of those close losses were beginning to take their toll on patience and endurance, made worse by the obvious perception that we had turned around some of the woeful ways and could have won some close games. A team is sometimes better off getting blown out consistently than forcing everyone to endure agonizingly close losses. The "what ifs" and "should haves" of heartbreaking losses feed frustrations and often make people lose perspective and a measurement of just how far a team has come. A new generation of fans were beginning to attend Giants games, and they didn't have the emotional underpinnings of past championship seasons to sustain them until the rebuilding job was completed. They wanted immediate success, and their tolerance of close defeats was not very high. I don't believe they realized just how far the team's fortunes had sunk only four years before, and I don't think they were too interested in all that had been accomplished internally to help revive them. The Tucker affair, the obvious problems we had with the offensive line, the occasional disappearance of Csonka from the offense and the tough learning process and problems that Pisarcik suffered had become sticking points to many impatient for winning seasons. Those became part of the backdrop to the series of tumultuous events that rocked the franchise a year later. There is no doubt in my mind that had we been able to win some of those close games, we could have bought more time and probably withstood the furies that descended on us after the infamous "fumble game" in 1978. Of course, the fans were not the only ones who were part of this backdrop; there were some within our own organization who, in 1977, were already starting to beat their own drums of discontent, though they should have known better.

In 1978 we tried to lessen those frustrations in two ways: revamping our coaching staff and adding people with more NFL experience. When Marty Schottenheimer resigned in January 1978, I recommended—but never pressured McVay to sign—Dick Modzelewski to replace him as defensive coordinator. Jerry Wampfler, who had five seasons as an NFL offensive line coach, succeeded Fry at that post. Mo had been an assistant coach at Cleveland since his retirement in 1967, and in recommending him to John McVay I simply stated what I thought he might be able to do for us and left the decision up to him. "I don't want you to be influenced by this recommendation, nor do I expect you to be." I'm sure he wasn't. Dick brought a 3-4 defensive look to the Giants, surprising many who thought he would come in with the 4-3 concept he knew so well from his playing days with the great Giants defenses.

Mo, who I believe did a fine job in the one season he was defensive coordinator, was not unlike many coaches who see the successful use of a philosophy or style by other coaches and adapt it for their needs. Personally, I would have wished the Giants had used the 4-3; I believed in it, and I also felt we had the kind of talent to make it successful: four good down linemen (Jack Gregory, Troy Archer, John Mendenhall and George Martin) and some good linebackers (Harry Carson, Brad Van Pelt, Brian Kelley and Dan Lloyd for special situations). Some coaches—and I guess Mo was one of them—believed Landry's original 4-3 had outlived its usefulness, and that the 3-4 offered more flexibility. Marty Schottenheimer and I always had this argument whenever we got into our discussions about defense, and my point was always that the 4-3, as an accumulation of changes based on current offensive styles, could never be totally dominated by an offensive system because it always has the flexibility to change. Tom proved that in Dallas when he came up with a different version of the "flex"—moving a lineman a yard off the ball—from the version he used with us, and made quick, strong tackles like Bob Lilly and Randy White absolutely devastating inside players against both the run and the pass. Actually, to be effective in the 3-4 a team needs better players than in the 4-3; the 3-4 is supposed to harass people with the linebackers rather than with the linemen, while the 4-3 coordinates the efforts of seven people—the four linemen and three linebackers. As I mentioned earlier, with the passing game now so pervasive, there is a greater need to get as much pressure on the passer as possible, and four big linemen can still do the best job. Teams are now often moving big, quick linebackers, such as Lawrence Taylor or Andre Tippett, into the line on passing situations as a fourth, or sometimes a fifth, down lineman.

But systems and philosophies aside, Mo did a good job for us. He worked very well with Wampfler, an important relationship since both units can learn so much from working with each other. Of course, the personalities of both men helped. They never felt the need to be a top dog on the coaching staff because they were so secure in their own knowledge and experience. Jerry, in addition to his NFL experience in Philadelphia and Buffalo, had been a head coach at Colorado State. He was probably the best assistant coach I ever knew in pro football. He had great consideration for the players under his control, and he was very knowledgeable. As a teacher he was bright, creative and enthusiastic, and he gave us the best front five the Giants had during my tenure as director of operations. I thought so highly of him that I signed him to a long-term contract before I left, but that didn't work out when Ray Perkins became head coach. Jerry then left to join Dick Vermeil on the Eagles staff. The move cost Philadelphia a sixth-round draft pick, but it also helped them into the Super Bowl two years later.

Jerry also had some better players to work with than his predecessors with the Giants had. Tackle Gordon Gravelle, obtained from Pittsburgh in 1977, finally stabilized our left tackle spot. In 1978 the most important person in Wampfler's unit became center Jim Clack, who, like Gravelle, had been part of two world championships with the Steelers. We traded Hicks to Pittsburgh even-up for Clack, the best trade I made during my tenure. Not only did Jim help to solidify our line that season, he was the glue that held that unit together right through the team's 1981 playoff season. Jim was like Ray Wietecha: a fine blocker who also knew a lot about changing assignments at the line of scrimmage and gave strong, on-the-field direction to younger players. After what we had endured for parts of two previous seasons, the actual improvement at that position seemed stark, but it also was genuine.

Another offensive acquisition that year pleased me—Dan Doornick, a six-foot-three, 210-pound fullback from Washington State who was our seventh-round draft pick. He was absolutely perfect in everything he did— he was smart, he ran well, he blocked well, he caught the ball—and he was a gentleman in every sense of the word, someone like George Martin who made the team better just by being a part of it. He was perhaps the closest we ever came to having the genuine All-American boy. Dan had all of the attributes that would have made him a superstar in New York City. Along with his great talent and way with people, he also was a good-looking kid, the kind Madison Avenue and the networks look for when they seek someone with star quality. It didn't take me long to realize how lucky we were to get him in the seventh round. Scouting reports claimed he was a bit of a timid runner in college, but I never saw that when he was with us, or during the games I saw him play on television during his fine career with the Seattle Seahawks. He was probably someone whom the Giants should have found a way to keep throughout his career, especially as he was prepared from the beginning to pursue his medical studies in the East, if necessary, and not return to the Northwest, as has been reported.

Our top draft pick in 1978 was offensive tackle Gordon King of Stanford, who had problems with his run-blocking because he was not an aggressive blocker. He came from an offensive system that featured the pass, and pass-blocking depends on more passive reactions. All else being equal, I prefer an offensive lineman who is an aggressive blocker; he can help the running game and spin off to help make play-action passing much more effective as well. These plays depend on an aggressive blocking technique that must sell the possibility of a running play to the defense to give the quarterback and receivers time to get a jump. For part of that 1978 season Ron Mickolajczyk (another former WFLer we obtained in 1977 in a trade with Oakland) started at right tackle until he injured his knee. He was replaced by Brad Benson when King could not do a consistent job.

Still, heading into the 1978 season we felt the team had finally stabilized to the point where we had some talent at all our starting positions as well as some better backup depth, especially considering that eight of the twenty-two draft picks on the team were starters. All five of the players we acquired by trade also started, as did eleven of the twenty free agents. We started by winning three of our first four games, and our offensive performances had been good enough to offset the defense's learning process as it adapted to its new 3-4 philosophy. Doing everything we anticipated, Pisarcik continued to improve, and there was every reason at midseason, after a mighty 17-6 victory over Washington for a 5-3 record, to believe that we finally had turned the corner. In that game Pisarcik completed only three passes, but one went for a touchdown and another set up a score in the first half. Our running game, with Csonka, Kotar and Bobby Hammond, dominated the Redskins' defense, and our defense stuffed Washington's comeback attempts in the second half.

Then, as often happens to young quarterbacks, Pisarcik ran into a slump. A string of interceptions were instrumental in our losing the next three games, the third one 16-13 in overtime at Washington. The following week, however, we got back on track against the Eagles...and for fifty-nine minutes and twenty-nine seconds we had a hard-fought game in our pocket. Then came the darkest moment in the team's history since Alan Ameche tumbled into the end zone to end our overtime NFL title game in 1958, a moment that stunned...shocked...befuddled...and angered Giants fans everywhere.

It was *THE FUMBLE.*

Nine years after Csonka and Pisarcik collided on a handoff and lost the ball to the Eagles' Herman Edwards for his now-famous 26-yard touchdown return with just thirty-one seconds to play and the Giants ahead, 17-12, that play still plunges into my heart like a dagger. In the course of a few seconds, everything we had worked to achieve, all the gains we had made, were blurred in the minds of millions of Giants fans, and the futility that had seemed to dog the franchise for so many years suddenly erupted in an agonizing sequence.

Quite frankly, I really don't like to talk about that moment. The hurt has not disappeared after all of these years. Yet, let's face it, there was no excuse for it ever to happen. It can never be replayed correctly, but there are times when I think of it and wish I could yell, "Stop! Don't run the ball. Just lay on it." That's all that Pisarcik had to do that day, and that awful moment never would have occurred...or the domino effect of franchise-shattering events that flashed into view during the four weeks that followed.

The scene, as you might remember, had the Giants in possession of the ball as the clock rolled past the one-minute mark. We had just stopped the Eagles' fourth-down pass play inside our 30 yardline. That defensive stand was a significant moment; at last we had taken the ball away from an opponent late in the game and prevented a winning score. We ran the ball on first down and made a few yards, after which the Eagles used their final timeout with about a minute to play.

Using the clock in the final minutes of a game is a delicate art, even when your team has the ball and your opponents have no timeouts. Plays must be called that use a maximum of time with a minimum of risk until the clock reaches a point where the quarterback needs only take the snap from center and drop on the ground. The clock must be past the thirty-second mark so he will not have to call another play. In that case, what happens to reach that point is as important as the final play itself, and on that November Sunday, Bob Gibson, the offensive coordinator who was sending down plays from the spotter's booth to Lindy Infante on the sideline, called for Larry Csonka to run off tackle on second down to gain as many seconds as possible. Gibson called all the plays for Pisarcik that season, using a tight end shuttle system, so Infante sent in the play, and Csonka did what he did best—he hammered for about four yards as the clock spun past the fifty-second mark.

However, that play required Pisarcik to make a reverse spin—that is, he took the ball and spun in the opposite direction from where Csonka was running before wheeling around and placing the ball in his hands. A more basic move is for the quarterback to take the ball, step in the direction of the back and slip him the ball. The idea of the reverse pivot, the execution of which must be perfect, is to move the middle linebacker to an area away from where the runner is supposed to go when he finally gets the ball; the defender will believe initially there will be a direct handoff to the side where the quarterback first steps. When he sees the quarterback wheeling around with the ball he has to move a couple of yards back to his original position, by which time the offense usually has a blocker in his path to seal him off from making the play.

That's all well and good during a game, but not in the final seconds when the linebacker is likely to keep his position. The bottom line was that the game was about to end, no handoff of any kind should have been attempted. We should have allowed the quarterback to lay on the ball while the clock ticked off the seconds, and if we still had to run another play, do it again.

I cringed when I saw that first reverse pivot. I would have accepted even the simple handoff with its smaller margin of error, particularly with a back like Csonka who had done it thousands of times in his career. I could hear Gibson and the other coaches, who were seated in a booth next to us, making the calls, but neither Well nor I could, in our wildest dreams, ever imagine anything other than Pisarcik being told to lay on the ball for the final play. Even now, nine years after the event, anything else seems impossible and unbelievable.

Yet it happened. Gibson sent down another off-tackle run by Csonka, in which Pisarcik again had to do a reverse pivot before handing off the ball. Infante never questioned it; or if he did, he never admitted to it. Instead, he gave it to the tight end Al Dixon to take into the game to Pisarcik. The players in the huddle knew they had the game won, and when Al reached the huddle and told Joe about the play, several of the players were irate. "Forget it, Joe," they told him. "Just lay on the ball and let's get out of here."

Pisarcik hesitated. "I can't," he told the players. "I've got to use what he calls." Joe obviously worried more about his coach's reaction to a refusal than the possibility of a fumble. I doubt any coach would bitch at a quarterback for ignoring a call in that situation, and if he did, the quarterback had every right to bitch right back. There are times when a quarterback must be given his right of refusal, and it must be recognized as legitimate. Even as I recount that incident I don't see how there would have been any repercussions...just as I do not understand why a coach would not recognize that no play needed to be called for the quarterback in that situation.

McVay said he was unaware of the call, though it was his responsibility to know what went into the huddle, particularly with the game now in our grasp. He had walked away from Infante at the time, obviously believing Pisarcik would be told to lay on the ball. Again, John did not interfere in the actions of his assistants or take a direct hand in even the most mundane sequence of events. Hindsight says he should have signaled Pisarcik to lay down, while telling Infante to forget any more plays. Infante himself should also have known enough to question the call and suggest to Gibson that Joe be allowed to end the game on his own, something that the 76,000 fans in the stands believed was going to happen. So did I . . . and so did the Eagles. When the Giants lined up, the Eagles obviously just assumed we were going to fall on the ball, a common procedure that saves a lot of needless bashing in hopeless situations. But you never know for certain; some teams play it soft, and some battle you till the final whistle. Since we had decided to go after them the Eagles really had new life, and they lined up to make a desperation play instead of just going through the motions. Pisarcik took the ball and started his reverse pivot, but he and Csonka collided, and the ball flew out of Joe's hands and bounced onto the artificial turf. As often happens on the carpet, it bounced perfectly into the hands of Edwards, who had crashed into the play from the right side. He was going full speed in the direction of the end zone when the ball popped into his hands, and he scored before anyone seemed to know what had happened.

After Csonka's second-down run, and with the clock winding down to the thirty-second mark, I didn't pay much attention to any conversations between the coaching booth and the field. I had gathered my notes, and Well and I had prepared to leave. We had our backs half turned to the field when we heard a huge roar. At first I thought Pisarcik had ended the game, and the crowd was saluting the fact that we were winners. Then I saw some of our players running toward the end zone and saw an official's hands go up, signaling a touchdown. Well and I simultaneously looked at each other.

"What the hell happened?" I asked. I had not seen Pisarcik and Csonka collide and fumble the ball; I hadn't even seen Edwards pick it up and begin his run to the end zone. But in an instant I realized the disaster that had befallen us, and I was stunned to the point where I didn't want to believe that the impossible had actually happened. It was as if someone had taken a sledgehammer and slammed it into my middle. My first thought was not, "How did it happen?" but, "why did it have to happen to us?"

Going to the locker room after a loss is always tough, but going in that day was almost terrifying. I wanted to duck, to leave and believe the whole disaster hadn't occurred. It was ugly. Players were outraged; some threw helmets across the room, some verbally abused the media as they vented their frustration and embarrassment. I walked down the hall toward the coaches' offices and spotted Pisarcik sitting alone in a room, his head buried in his hands. He had fled the media as soon as he came into the locker room, but I knew that wasn't the answer.

"Come on, Joe," I said to him, "you have to face up to it."

He followed me out of the room to a huge group of interviewers awaiting him. "I hope you guys will be a little sensitive," I said. "What happened to him was very traumatic, and he really doesn't want to talk about it. But he's agreed to come out and try to handle it the best way he can. So try and give him a break."

Then I talked to McVay to find out what happened and why it happened. Nothing he said reassured me. He did not criticize Gibson's decision, simply noting that he gave him the authority to call the play and that was it. While he was as shocked as everyone about the play's outcome, he didn't seem to believe there was a coaching problem. If he did, that blind loyalty would not allow him to acknowledge its seriousness. Perhaps he preferred to believe that one bad call did not take away from Gibson's countering of a good Eagles defense all day long.

Gibson's decision is still a mystery to me. Even with as little NFL experience as he had accumulated, I thought Bob was a bright, innovative guy. In the nearly two seasons he was our offensive coordinator he was still learning how to apply that experience with the personnel at hand. But he didn't seem to appreciate any outside advice or assistance, even when we ran our "clinics" for his benefit. I know he bridled at meetings when others critiqued his game plans and offenses, a reflection of the protective shield that McVay had thrown around his coaches. Pisarcik's fear of going against Gibson's orders, even when Joe knew the play was unnecessary, also said something about the system.

The consequences surfaced that evening at Wellington's home, when we discussed the entire sequence and decided without dissent that Gibson could not stay around the team. Our major concern was to avoid the total collapse that something so traumatic can trigger.

I met with McVay the next morning and told him, "John, you have to relieve Gibson of the offensive coordinator duties, and we'll find something for him in the scouting area and just ease him out of here. We can't have him around the players because he would only be a reminder of this horrible situation."

"I won't do that," McVay told me, maintaining blind loyalty to a coach who had betrayed his confidence with a stupid decision. He refused to acknowledge that the decision had been lethal.

"Well, I'm going to do it," I told John. "I'll fire him and that will be it."

"Do you want both of us to go to make it easier?" McVay replied.

"I don't want you to go," I said. "You and I are both going to have to stand together and face the music, and after that, you're going to have to find a way to pick up the team and get it back up again. We have come too far to allow something like this to spoil everything, and there is still time this season to get us going upward again.''

While McVay was unalterably opposed to Gibson's removal, he let him go reluctantly, making little effort to hide his displeasure when he met the media later that day to announce the move. I don't blame him for feeling bad about having to dismiss a close associate, but I still believe he should have felt more displeasure with Gibson for putting him into such a situation and causing the organization and the players so much embarrassment.

Afterward, I issued a public statement in which I said:

> In any organization, personnel changes are sometimes found to be necessary, but they're never pleasant. They're painful not only to the person relieved of his duties but also to the person who has to do the relieving, and they're potentially upsetting to the organization.
>
> In the last analysis, a personnel change reflects a decision that *no* action would be more upsetting to the organization—in our case, the football team—than some action. The play at the end of the Philadelphia game, and the turmoil that preceded and followed it, was the immediate reason for our conclusion that action was required—not to cause a conflict, but to resolve one.
>
> Unfortunately, our offense and our quarterbacks have been inconsistent. Two of them have suffered through a pretty rough season, as has our entire football team. As of the last two games, Joe has done pretty well, but at the end of the Eagles game he was caught in a situation he shouldn't have had to be in—caught between a play his coach called, and a play his teammates wanted him to ignore.
>
> He was forced to try to satisfy everyone, and couldn't, and wound up unable to execute as a professional.
>
> It was our judgement that such a situation could not be permitted to continue, else it completely destroy a lot of hard work and suffering done by a lot of people...including Bob Gibson. The relationship between an offensive coordinator and his unit, and especially between him and his quarterbacks, is a vital key to success.
>
> The faith must be mutual, the belief of the players in what they are instructed to do must be total.
>
> It was for those reasons that we felt a change must be made.

In another note to myself I wrote:

> The "fumble" was one of life's most important happenings to come by luck or chance. Luck can either ruin a team or make it. It depends not on luck, but how well a team handles that happening!

I was disturbed with the fans, too, but I also get disturbed with my children. Yet I love them both!

The media had a field day with all of those events, yet with one exception they did a fair and accurate job in explaining events that were as bizarre to the fans as they were to us. That exception was a column by Mike Lupica of the *Daily News* a day later. He quoted some of my explanation for Gibson's firing and the rationale that led to that decision. As is his privilege in writing a column, he presented his own views on the situation. I have never quarrelled with the right of a columnist to present a fair and measured opinion, or of a reporter to present the facts at hand, as long as they were accurate and fairly presented. However, Lupica painted word pictures of how I made my case as if he were present, when in fact he picked up his quotes from a tape recording of the original press conference that our public relations department provided. He never showed up to ask any questions in person, nor did he find out from those who were party to all of the events exactly what moved us to make our decision. Friends of mine in the media later told me that was nothing but lazy journalism. I would have had more respect and acceptance for what he wrote had he confronted me directly and asked if we were making Gibson a scapegoat instead of relying on tape recordings of a press conference and his own preconceived notions that he obviously feared might not stand up to the facts at hand.

On the other hand, a couple of days later Dick Young, another *Daily News* columnist who had once questioned my appointment as director of operations because of my friendship with Howard Cosell, whom he disliked, put the entire situation into perspective when, in referring to the feelings of the fans, he wrote:

> There is good reason to be irate. They have taken so much for so long, these suffering Giants fans. They have been told things are getting better, hang in there. And then, just when it looks as though that really is true, comes a frustration that defies credibility, a dum-dum play that turns a five-point victory into a two-point defeat when a handoff is made to the other team.
>
> It is more than frustrating. It is depressing. But the wonderful thing about sports is there is always tomorrow, always next Sunday. Emotions subside. Reason takes over. Professionalism survives.
>
> There will be some changes after the season but they will be made on the solid structure general manager [*sic*] Andy Robustelli has built. The quarterback problem must be solved. Overall, the Giants are a better team, much better.

We were, but we didn't show it totally for the rest of the season, losing the following week in Buffalo when the defense collapsed in the fourth quarter after we had a 17-7 lead. To that point the players seemed as if they had totally shrugged off that awful game, but we got wiped out when the Bills scored 27 points and won, 34-17. Ironically, with McVay calling the plays Pisarcik had his best passing day of the season. The following week we led the Rams, 17-10, going into the fourth quarter. Again, we faltered and lost, 20-17.

While our players had obviously recovered from "the fumble," the fans had not, and losing twice in the last quarter on consecutive weeks simply fueled the discontent that had been building over those kinds of late-game losses for some time. The media, particularly the radio sports talk shows and television, were quick to jump into the cauldron when some fans began forming groups to protest the club's policies. A cry to boycott the next game, as if that would do any good, reached groundswell proportions. There were 24,000 no-shows at our last home game against St. Louis, though the weather and the fact that the club was out of the race also had an effect. Then there was the famous ticket-burning ceremony outside the stadium that day when a group of fans got together and burned tickets over a charcoal cooker while the TV cameras rolled and photographers clicked away. After that little ceremony, the TV people packed up their gear and left. They should have stayed around and followed some of those self-righteous "protesters" into the stadium where they sat and enjoyed our 17-0 victory over St. Louis.

Of course, the protest that still seems to live was the airplane that towed the sign. It was then I wished I had my old 20 mm. antiaircraft gun handy, just as I had wished a few weeks earlier that Mike Lupica was an opposing quarterback standing in the pocket with me lined up on the other side of the line of scrimmage. In both cases, I wouldn't have missed, though I'm sure Mike probably has a different sense of the Giants now that he has matured somewhat as a journalist. Recently, he became a part of the literary brigade that collaborated with some of them to write books after their Super Bowl victory.

I am still irate about such things, not because I disagree with the right of protest, but because I felt our players and management were lashed at unfairly. All of our achievements over five years were dismissed because of one play. The team and the coaches, to their credit, did not use that Eagles' loss as an excuse to bag the rest of the season; they played even harder than before and truly deserved better than one victory in their four remaining games (Philly beat us in the finale, 20-3). We finished the season with a 6-10 record, but three of those losses, including the first Eagles game, were by a total of just eight points, so we were that close to being a winning team. No other Giants team came close to a winning season until 1981, when the team finally made the playoffs. Interestingly, fourteen of the twenty-four starters from 1978 (including two kickers) also started during that season, and in the playoffs.

However, if you thought the 1978 season had its interesting and often agonizing turn of events on the field, some of what went on behind the floor-to-ceiling glass walls of the Giants' offices was even more intriguing. Eventually that behind-the-scenes action impacted on the future of the team much more than any game we played that season. And as we shall see, the impact was not always for the best.

10 *A Different Game & Good-Bye*

The game of football is meant to be played on the field. It is a tough, grueling experience punctuated by moments of excitement, personal achievement and failure that send fans into highs of exhilaration or lows of depression. They love to watch...to cheer...and to talk about all they see, real or imagined.

But during my five seasons as director of operations, the games played behind the games played on Sunday were far tougher and costlier to the franchise than anything that ever happened on the field. Even with the ownership split, which at that point had not exploded publicly, the 1978 season had been going along well. But after the "fumble" it came from all corners. It's bad enough having players separating themselves from the team—it's even worse when the organization itself becomes divided. Like the games on the field, there were soon two teams in our office.

Tim considered everyone who hadn't firmly sided with him to be on Well's team; so in his mind I was also on Well's team. In my mind I wasn't on anyone's team but the Giants', trying to give 100 percent of my efforts to each 50 percent of the ownership. But even that neutral stance dimmed when my efforts to bridge both groups were thwarted by Tim's frequent references to my "being on Well's side." Ultimately he accepted little of what I suggested or attempted to do for the overall good of the organization.

The infamous "fumble game" has often been portrayed by the media, including the writer of a *New York Times* article prior to the Giants' Super Bowl XXI appearance, as the impetus for Tim's seizing the moment and forcing a change in the team's operation. He has been credited—incorrectly, I might add—with being responsible for much of the team's success in the mid-eighties. Nothing could be further from the truth. Neither was that fateful game the reason why I left the Giants as director of operations. Both events were significant, but they were far beyond Tim's scope or impact, as was anything achieved by the Giants football team since 1978.

In fact, my leaving was set in motion long before Larry Csonka and Joe Pisarcik collided on that ill-fated handoff. From the day I agreed to take the job, I had always intended to return to my own business. Even before the end of my first year as director of operations I had begun construction of a new building to house the varied adjuncts of my travel business, with a blueprinted plan to expand them and develop other areas. I did not alter any of those plans when I joined the Giants. My veteran staff, overseen by my son Rick, my brother Lou and my personal secretary Pat Walsh, could keep things marching along. I also thought that after my daily Giants duties were finished I could give some time to tying up loose ends and setting a direction.

That didn't work out. I found out that, despite the best efforts and loyalties of those left in charge, absentee ownership doesn't really work. In our case, it might have worked better had there not been a severe economic downturn in the mid-seventies that blasted businesses from coast to coast. Considering I wasn't present on any regular basis to give impetus to what I wanted done, those who ran my business did a good job. If anything, I handicapped them by my absence. I thought I could help Well and Tim get the Giants back on track within two years by helping to streamline the organization and set up procedures that would achieve the ends I established. That was a gross miscalculation. After just two months on the job I saw it was a mistake for me to be there unless I intended to do the job for the rest of my life. I realized that I was setting up a set of procedures that made sense to me, and under which I could comfortably function, but what about the person who came after me?

I also didn't realize the extent of the team's personnel problems and front-office inbreeding. These problems could not be solved with the flash of an idea or the creation of a flow chart. The failure of Bill Arnsparger was another setback, but overriding all was the ownership split that started to tear us apart. Differences of opinion are healthy, but only if they surface immediately. I'll say it again, Wellington's did and Tim's did not. The result was a series of unfinished projects away from the field and an unfinished product on the field. So I kept delaying my return to private business, hoping to get matters to a point where I could leave with at least my basic objectives accomplished and the Giants once more fully competitive.

When I left football after my fourteenth season as a player and coach, I felt I was leaving the greatest opportunity of my life, and that running my own business would not match being in pro football. But I soon discovered that I enjoyed working for myself far more than for two bosses. I also found that an NFL team, like the NFL itself, is an institution. Things move slowly, more subject to the past than to new ideas for the future. I like new ideas, new projects and ventures, and I found the pro football atmosphere often like being tied to a chair. With the Giants, those feelings were magnified. Total dedication by others to get better or to re-energize the organization was missing. I found out that after five years I was no longer a "football person"—one who finds total satisfaction poring over scouting reports, spending hours looking at films of college players or other NFL teams, and having a consummate desire to improve blocking schemes, pass routes or individual techniques.

I really enjoyed the business aspects of football: negotiating contracts, structuring an organization and trying to steer those within my orbit onto correct paths. I also enjoyed setting up our Pace College facility and getting the team turned toward its future back in the New York area. The Giants wanted me to combine my business function with a revamping and maintaining of the football side. But the future that really concerned me was in Stamford; my business there just couldn't succeed without direct leadership. I couldn't do that by coming in for a couple of hours a night a few times a month, or on a free Saturday; and it wasn't fair asking people to wait around until seven o'clock in the evening to see whether I would get there. Greg Michie, Paul Salvatore and John Henry, in my business, had a rotating schedule of days waiting for me to discuss their problems. If I didn't get there before seven o'clock, they went home—but they still had to wait, often without result. I was absolutely unselfish in my time with the Giants, and no one from my own business was allowed to call me at the Giants' offices. Others had to solve the problems or leave them until I got around to them, but I soon found that pro football is a seven-day-a-week operation from July through December, and not much less in the off-season with meetings, trips, signings and the myriad of other details that wrap up one season and begin another.

Since from the beginning I had not intended to make the job a career, early in 1977 I began the necessary steps toward forging solutions to the problems I faced with the Giants, primarily by attempting to get Well and Tim working together. I explained my need to leave to both of them. I also said that others would have to leave with me so the organization could have a fresh start at all levels of operation. In a memo I spelled out what I foresaw as a course of action to achieve those objectives:

A YARD AT A TIME!

One of the easiest procedures in reconstructing an organization is wiping it clean and starting from scratch. With such a method, the architect is fully responsible, from the foundation to the point where the organization succeeds or fails. In all candor, we are trying to break down, convert, change attitudes, protect and fight for every inch of progress we make.

We still stand divided. Being together has not changed us; only winning will change us—until we lose again. Then the same people will have caused the loss and the same people will be pointing to what should have been done!

We are divided and must recognize that fact, above all. So again, I submit changes that will continue to bring us a yard or so closer to breaching the problem of reconstruction—not only as a football team, but more importantly, as an organization.

207

DIRECTOR OF OPERATIONS

The Director of Operations operates within the following guidelines:

1) He must have full control of coordinating the football operation;

2) He should be at the same level as the head coach in line of authority, operating as the link between the football operation and management;

3) He should have experience in all areas of his responsibility, making sure all departments operate under the guidelines set for them by the executive committee;

4) He should directly receive reports from the director of each area of responsibility, including pro personnel, college personnel, college scouting, medical matters, films, equipment and team maintenance. Each of these directors should control all budgets and procedures as well as other responsibilities.

EXECUTIVE DIRECTORS

As members of the policy board or the board of directors, the Executive Directors are two independent persons who will act as a review organ. They should not be a part of top management, but available to it to act with knowledge in directing the club, but also to make recommendations and help make decisions in any crisis situation.

They must look critically at the planning of the team, its policies and its budgets. They must not be afraid to step up and be counted. They are a voice of outside spirit and progress. They are the watchdogs of the development of objectives.

Management needs to look at itself and not become isolated with internal or external pressures or problems. The Executive Directors or the football operating committee need not be salaried, but should have access to expense accounts in order to travel when necessary.

BOARD OF DIRECTORS

Distribution of stock can never really make this board a visible force since legally no one can or really does control the destiny of the Giants. It is essential that a board of directors become that force.

In order to satisfy both parties, a nonvoting executive member should be elected from each 50-percent stockholder, or a separate committee can be set up as the football operating committee. In either case, this is the board that sets the parameters for how the team will operate.

All football control will be handled by the Director of Operations, who will work directly on a day-to-day basis with the president. Both will be guided by the predetermined boundaries of responsibilities set by the board.

CONCLUSION

My coming to the Giants has started a new era for management. Over the past four years it would have been difficult for any outsider to succeed me. Now, I believe we are ready to make the transition without much difficulty.

Regardless of whatever direction the stockholders take, new people coming into any situation must not be a party to any organizational infighting. They need the opportunity to contribute with open mind and open heart. My mind and heart have been open with 100 percent spirit and desire.

I believe that I have contributed in two primary areas: Control of spending and my honest attempt to discuss the organization as I see it, with no influence by either party.

We have a long way to go to catch up with the organizations that are ahead of us—in the office and on the playing field.

It is with sorrow that I can't look forward to football as my full-time career, but I have only scratched the surface of the Giants and my own business. I must face up to where my future lies...

Ideally, I should hire and help the new Director of Operations, who will benefit from my being here during the turnover, but I leave that decision to others.

The hiring of a new director of operations seemed a logical step to both Well and me, but neither of us knew at the time that in the eyes of Tim's group it was like a hurricane warning. In proposing the idea, I envisioned a hiring process similar to my own, where both principals would concur on my successor. But I discovered later that Tim and his group—or certainly Tim himself—wanted someone to do their bidding. Tim simply wouldn't sit down in meetings and join Well and me in decision-making discussions. Often he sat mute, as he had done in the Csonka contract discussions, and then came back the next day with his repetitive "my mother and my sister don't think..." or "we don't think..." line. After a while I knew that he was probably not getting his advice from his mother and sister but probably his brother-in-law and some of his friends on the outside.

My ideas for change encompassed nearly every department. I suggested we hire new, energetic and reasonably experienced people under fifty years of age to head these areas so they would be with the club over the next couple of decades, when the ownership itself would undergo some sort of change at the top. The main push was to avoid a last-minute surge of new people without some definite plan whereby they could settle in and become familiar with new sets of procedures.

Two of my early prospects were Bobby Beathard, then the personnel director of the Miami Dolphins, whom I wanted to head our personnel department; and Jan Van Duser, head of personnel in the NFL office, whom I felt could become a director of administration on the football side of our business. Making no promises to either man, I sounded them out. Each was a splendid example of the kind of person we needed in our organization. Bobby became general manager of the Redskins the following year, but I know he preferred the personnel end of that job. He spent months out of the office looking at college players. I wanted someone to spend more time directing the scouts and becoming familiar with the college prospects so he could run the draft each spring. Van Duser had strong administrative experience, and he was also very knowledgeable of the often-complicated procedures surrounding the NFL's waivers and trading rules. He could have given us extra expertise in those areas.

However, the restructuring did not begin until about a year later. Wellington hired Terry Bledsoe as assistant director of operations with my complete concurrence, and with the expectation that we would begin to fill the other jobs later in 1978. That included my own successor, who in the spring of 1978 I envisioned as John McVay, providing he produced a winning season and presented a positive image that would give the Giants a sleek, modernized look heading into the eighties. If that happened, then my goal of restructuring our football operation would be completed, and my work finished.

Oh, how wrong I was!

Wellington's hiring of Bledsoe blew the whole plan away. Tim's group was totally opposed to any appointments that didn't pass their muster, that is, anyone who they thought would not represent their views on a day-to-day basis with Wellington, which they thought I was going to do when I took the job. Terry was a former sportswriter from Milwaukee who had spent some four years working with Well as a staff member on the NFL Management Council. Well had come to know and admire him for his knowledge of the minefield that rests between the covers of the agreement between the Players Association and the owners. He was a bright, articulate man who had worked on the volatile union contract, and he was also adept at representing all areas of that emerging area of sports management to the NFL owners at their annual meetings. He had skills we needed, particularly since so much of our time and effort would be centered around the complicated area of player relations. His knowledge would relieve some of the burdens that consumed much of my time and took me away from more important football matters. Terry had no technical football background, so his duties would have to be limited to the administrative, including union-management affairs and the media. There never was any intention, as Tim has since claimed, that Bledsoe succeed me as director of operations.

McVay was the perfect person to move into my post after the completion of the 1978 season. John had the football background; he had been a long-time administrator in college and a general manager in the WFL; he knew our organization; and he was a tremendously personable man with impeccable relations with the huge media corps that covers the Giants. Moving him up was also an exercise in continuity within the organization, and having Terry in place to master the other nitty-gritty details over a season was an ideal situation. Of course, "the fumble" ruined that plan. John left us and went to the San Francisco 49ers as an executive, where he has helped guide the fortunes of that organization to a pair of NFL championships. Terry, of course, worked for me during the 1978 season and then stayed on after I left as George Young's principal deputy, covering the specific areas that Well and I had laid out for him from the very start. His coming to the Giants helped the organization step out of the administrative dark ages, and Terry matured and learned well enough to be later named the general manager of the Buffalo Bills.

Tim, of course, has tried to justify the flap over Bledsoe's hiring by claiming that Terry was to be groomed to replace me as director of operations, but Well made it absolutely clear from the beginning that this would not be the case. When he laid out Terry's qualifications, I had no objection, and Tim said nothing. Soon after, he came back with the "after talking it over..." routine, but Wellington saw that as a clear incursion into his powers as president and hired Bledsoe anyhow.

The next thing we knew, the matter landed on the desk of NFL Commissioner Pete Rozelle. In a May 17, 1978, letter, Tim said his group would not agree to Bledsoe's hiring and asked the league not to approve his contract:

> We want to be on record as of this date that 50 percent of the board of directors and 50 percent of the stockholders of the New York Football Giants do not approve of the hiring of Mr. Terry Bledsoe as an employee or assistant director of operations of the New York Football Giants.
>
> He was not approved by the board of directors of the New York Football Giants, and we ask that the National Football League not accept his contract when or if submitted.
>
> Under no circumstances does Mr. Bledsoe have the authority or the power of the board to represent the New York Football Giants in signing any personnel to be employed by the New York Football Giants including coaches, players, scouts, etc. Mr. Bledsoe does not have the right to vote for or represent the New York Football Giants on any National Football League matters or at National Football League meetings.

The next day Tim and I had a fiery meeting in which he brought up his favorite topic: Which 50 percent of the ownership did I favor? He demonstrated clearly that his view was totally limited to self-interest. The following day I sent him this memo:

Friday—5/19/78

Tim—

I take offense to your statement yesterday that "you didn't care what 50 percent I favor"!

This is a gross insult to me, and a statement I cannot accept. If I would, then I would be prostituting myself.

I was hired to work for 100 percent of the New York Giants. Every decision I have made, right or wrong, good or bad, was made in everyone's interest—not yours or Well's but in an attempt to try to get the team on a better course.

In your mind I have failed. In my mind I see some daylight in a situation that cannot be changed as quickly as you would like it to change. Therefore, shortly I will formally submit to 100 percent of the stockholders an account of my stewardship...and my termination.

Within a week I submitted a lengthy memo to both Wellington and Tim, in which I laid out not only an overview of all that I had achieved, but also some overall impressions of the organization, and how it operated, that I had gathered during my time as director of operations. Of all the memos I submitted to them during those years, this one best epitomized what happened. Here are its high points:

The Beginning. In my quest for organizational improvement, any of my criticisms or judgments, so necessary to the development of any organization, were taken very lightly. Our operating committee—Well, Tim and I—should have concerned itself with overall problems, large or small, short-term or long-term, but the only time there was a real concern for details was during crisis situations.

The End. What might seem like a sudden account of my performance and eventual termination was the result of a crisis—a crisis in which I had no direct part but later became a means used by Tim to cast doubt on my credibility and on my ability to handle a complex problem without showing favoritism to either 50 percent of the ownership.

Let me reiterate: all of my decisions were made with full concern for 100 percent of the organization, and never, ever to favor either involved party.

Football World. This is a business based on negotiation and compromise, as is all business. My role was coordinator of all that wasn't working, unfinished or never attempted! We really had no organization. What we had was an outmoded structure with one man taking all the responsibilities and making all the decisions.

Now we are starting from scratch. The strength of any organization is the role of management...only this time, the crisis is management itself!

1974. I came into a situation with no illusions, no timetable, no immediate expectations. My blind entrance was on faith, love and spirit. I never wore Giants blue on the outside; I never publicly praised the Mara family; I did not depend on or feel part of the inner circle. I was a player who never missed a game, worked harder than most players, did my job, got paid, received no favors and asked for none.

I came on the scene not as a miracle worker, but as what most writers referred to as another member of the Giants Family. I really didn't know what Wellington expected of me; I felt that Tim thought I'd be tough and ruthless, then maybe the team would turn around quickly...

In retrospect I didn't really know or realize how far behind we were as an organization...how desperately we needed to overhaul our entire organization. But I realized it had to be done within the framework of its president who wanted to be loyal and faithful to certain people, as well as a vice president who had similar loyalties. Clean house? No way! So we kept the framework of the Giants and the family intact.

The house was torn down and rebuilt in every department, working around all of the obstacles by attempting to get the best results from all the people involved in this family situation.

But no family in these complex, changing times can survive without faith and spirit. Our team was no different. Everyone looked for the quick win, blamed everyone but themselves, yet were unwilling to "suck up their guts" and believe in the unselfish total team concept. Suffer and sink, or swim together!

My Account. This team needed a complete overhaul, and that it got—slowly but properly! Our football operational expenses did not appreciably increase in a highly inflatable four-year period.

People started to make decisions, without always running to Mr. Mara; we had better medical records, better staff...John McVay can and does make his own decisions...Jerry Shay has gotten better...and our drafts are 1000 percent better.

Director of Operations. He cannot be everything to everyone...he should be the voice and control for top management. Coaches should coach; scouts should scout; doctors should operate!

As I look back on my contributions, only you, the stockholders, can assess my productivity. I can only tell you that I gave 100 percent effort for the total cause. I gave it love, I tried to give it spirit, and I still have faith!

I will continue to work 100 percent for the New York Giants until December 31, 1978. Then I will officially terminate my relationship.

By that time, the split between Well and Tim had become the unbreachable gap that exists to this day. Judging by his public comments, I don't believe Tim fully understood—or even cared to understand—that Bledsoe was not going to replace me. We sat in Well's office and discussed various people, and Wellington concluded the meeting by saying that he would hire Terry as my assistant. Tim never said a word—then came his letter to the league and his request to the NFL not to approve Bledsoe's contract. Tim's 50 percent tried to remove Wellington from any decision-making capacity. Six weeks later, after Rozelle had stepped into the situation, Tim agreed to Bledsoe's hiring under the same condition Wellington had originally proposed. In a letter to Wellington, Rozelle said:

> Tim Mara has agreed to waive the objections raised in his letter of May 17 relative to this contract upon the understanding that Terry's duties as an employee will not be appreciably altered nor will he be signed to a new contract or extension without board approval in accordance with by-law procedures now being developed.

Wellington, in his role as club president, had every right to tell Tim and his group to go to hell when they tried to dictate who and what kind of people he could hire. He should have carried that same stance into Rozelle's office and insisted upon his right as president to make those appointments and have that right arbitrated in court, if necessary, where a determination would be binding. Tim would have done it to him if their roles were reversed, but Well, at that time, stopped short of going to the wall when he felt the good of the league could be affected.

That decision has meant that since 1978 the team operates within the confines of an agreement signed by both Well and Tim, under the aegis of Rozelle. Wellington's only real power as president is to speak and vote for the team at league meetings, or to designate someone to do it for him.

This fued between the Maras was not spontaneous; it was not caused by one fumble or contract settlement. It had probably been building for more than a decade without the principals even realizing it. There were too many losing seasons, and Tim's half of the ownership did little to alleviate them. Instead of being a 50-percent participant who accepted the responsibilities accompanying the prerogatives of power, Tim and his group allowed Wellington to make all of the decisions and do all of the work and then blamed him for all that went wrong. Never, to the best of my knowledge, did they ever publicly acknowledge their own culpability. They told the world that getting Wellington away from decision-making responsibilities was for the good of the team. The fact that their decision-making capacity also was lessened by the agreement with the league meant nothing because they never wanted to get involved anyhow. That group is still content to allow George Young to use certain mandates from the commissioner's office because it keeps them off the hot seat. Some in the media have gobbled up Tim's claim that he used this course of action to save the franchise, and they have allowed the perception to stand that his moves were in the team's best interest. It's my belief that Tim was obsessed with getting Wellington out completely, and that was not for the good of the team.

If Wellington had been allowed to proceed with our plans for restructuring the football side, there is little doubt in my mind—and he has also said as much—that the Giants would have become a title contender, perhaps sooner than actually happened. All of the conditions under which the team operated would have been controlled from within their offices, not the commissioner's. Wellington has to share some of the blame in this matter, if only because he took years of criticism and allowed others to escape their responsibilities. But it is not Well's nature to fight back when team or family would be exposed to public scrutiny, just as it was not Tim's nature to become fully involved and willing to accept responsibility.

Yet during all of this, I noticed that Wellington had indeed changed his attitudes about how the team should be run, and I believe he finally realized he had to remove himself from the daily grind of being involved in every decision. At this point he was willing to bring bright young people into the organization who were experienced in football or sports management, and who certainly did not share Tim's closed-end view that self-interest ruled above all else. In so doing, Wellington is the person to whom credit should be given for establishing a form of excellence that carried the Giants onward and upward into the eighties.

At one point I even suggested to Well that he should consider Don Shula for his job as president and become chairman of the board himself. Don had talked from time to time about leaving the pressure of coaching, and with his background he would have been a helluva president. I don't know whether they ever had any discussions (Well was always very careful to avoid tampering), but I'm sure Don knew that he always had a place to land if he wanted to leave Miami and become a football executive.

That Well didn't dismiss the idea out of hand showed me he realized he no longer could be as consumed with all of the details, and that he had to be willing to allow others to take up the slack, at least on the football side of the operation. But Tim was so blinded by his "them against us" stance that he missed that change, and in so doing he also missed a golden opportuntity to become an equal partner in practice as well as in fact. Ironically, he also failed to take advantage of the one thing he had wanted all along: Well's willingness to draw back from the daily operation. Instead, he caused a needless split and all of the internal organizational problems are no different today than a decade ago, with the added personal burden of a family forever sliced in two and with scant chance of reconciliation.

The inanity of this tragedy was that the vice president of a team and half of its board of directors were telling the president and the other half of the board what could be done. I don't know of any organization where the board of directors votes on everything that happens in the organization. No business can run that way...which says a lot in itself about Tim's view of how he believes the Giants should be run. While he was allegedly raised to the game—his father was passionately involved in the sport and always wanted his son to become part of it—Tim never showed me the slightest inclination to become involved in any of its aspects, unlike the sons of other owners, like the Rooney boys in Pittsburgh, Bill Bidwell in St. Louis, George Halas's late son, Mugsy, and now his grandson, Mike McCaskey, and Paul Brown's son, Mike, in Cincinnati, all of whom now form the cornerstone of the next generation of NFL leadership. To the best of my knowledge, he was never part of the various committees that oversee and formulate policy within the NFL, as the members of those other pioneer families do. His view of the game went no further than the ownership share of the Giants franchise that he represented. That is selfish. The good of the game depends on the accumulated experience and actions of all who are involved in its management.

For years, when Tim should have been learning about the football business, he allowed Well to make all the decisions. He did not demand reasons and answers or offer his own ideas. He never negotiated a contract or talked to an agent, and he never familiarized himself with the tenor of the times as pro football moved through its consolidation after the AFL-NFL war or coped with the incursion of the World Football League that began to change the way in which the sport did its business. When we sat in our meetings to make decisions, Well and I wound up doing most of the talking or brainstorming when we also needed Tim's considered opinions that should have been founded on his own experiences and knowledge. His principal interest in the club's affairs surfaced only when we got into major contract-proposal discussions that involved substantial contract settlements, and then his only concern was sticking to a proposed bottom-line money figure. Had he known anything about contract negotiations he would have recognized that there must be some leverage, particularly if you are bidding against another team.

A perfect example were our negotiations with linebacker Ted Hendricks, who had played out his option in Green Bay and was deciding between us and the Oakland Raiders. Ted was a great player, and one we desperately needed, so before the negotiations began Tim, Well and I set an average annual salary package of $165,000—$20,000 more than Hendricks made in Green Bay. Knowing Tim's feelings on the matter I stayed with it, proposing also that Ted could increase that income with varied promotional outlets I would arrange for him in the New York City area. But when you negotiate against Al Davis, there can be no restrictions until all reasonable overtures are exhausted, so when we broached our $165,000 figure, the Raiders went higher. Hendricks's lawyer wasn't too impressed with potential income from promotional deals. He preferred a set cash figure, so we had to drop out. Tim didn't try to understand the need for some leverage if it meant getting a player who could help us get better (we would also have had to give up some compensation to Green Bay), but Wellington was much more flexible. As I said, with him money was no object—not always a sound policy, either. He was more interested in helping the team on the field. Yet in handling those negotiations I gave total consideration to the interests of each half of the franchise—doing all I could to get Well his player and adhering to Tim's budgetary limitation. Once more, the need for that set of procedures I so dearly wanted was underlined, and once more lack of it cost us. Those procedures would have given me the direction I needed to serve the best overall interests of the team. I did this more or less on my own in later dealings. In the Csonka and Van Pelt negotiations I balanced Tim's primary budget considerations against Well's pay-anything-it-takes approach to complete the deals for what were reasonable figures.

The financial philosophy of the Giants was only one part of the split between the two, though an important part in Tim's mind. In an era when salaries began to escalate, he became obsessed with how much we planned to spend. There was little an enlightened pro-football management could do except approach the problem realistically, with a sense of fairness to both sides. But Tim's lack of experience and involvement didn't allow him to realize that the days of "This is it! Take it or leave it!" were gone. If an NFL executive or owner was spoiled or selfish and refused to recognize the changing times without proposing solutions to the problems, then it also made the situation thorny for all who had to carry out his biding.

Fiscal disagreement wasn't my only bone of contention with Tim during my time with the Giants, nor were we in a constant state of disagreement during my first three seasons. If he was so opinionated in certain areas, he should have shown it with all of us and fought for the 50 percent of his opinion. From the start I had urged him to become more involved. I would have relished his input as a full-time participant because the three of us would at leat have been working in one direction. Once, while flying out to California shortly after he had remarried, I said to his new wife, "You've got to get this guy to become more involved in the team. He's got to know the reasons why he says what we shouldn't be doing; or if he's going to carry matters back to the board of directors for decisions, then he's got to know a little about the business."

Of course, she agreed, but it made no difference. Tim continued to roll around our offices like a loose cannon, constantly carping and criticizing the football team without a basis of knowledge or, worse still, without any viable solutions. I said to him on many occasions, "If you're going to criticize your own organization, be a part of it. If you're not a part of it, then don't criticize it. But if you do criticize, do it constructively and know what the hell you're talking about."

My words were wasted. Despite being around the sport all of his life, he didn't know the first thing about the technical elements of the game, and his criticisms reflected his lack of knowledge. His only solution to our on-the-field problem was "Get rid of him." At one point I said to him, "If we got rid of everyone you wanted, we'd have no one left. It takes more than getting rid of someone. It takes patience and teaching and learning to become better." I still don't belive he understood what I meant.

When we won, it was "their" team; when we lost it was Well's team. Our fans showed us more loyalty than some on Tim's side of the organization, yet instead of sitting down and trying to find out what we were doing and how we were doing it, as many fans did in letters Well and I received (and answered), abuse became the order of the day. Beginning in 1977 our confrontations became more frequent and more explosive. One day, during a meeting, Tim castigated John McVay because we weren't scoring enough, and I said to him, "Everyone knows that. *Why* aren't we scoring enough?"

"I don't know for certain, except that he's using the same plays all the time," he replied.

"What plays should he be using then?" I asked.

There was no answer, but I had had enough of this approach, so I continued:

"I'll tell you why we're not scoring enough. We have a center who isn't effective and a guard who can't pull very well to lead some of our running plays. We have some other problems, too, that need time to fix. But I've been talking to John about the situation. Now do you want me to go tell the coach not to use that center? That he can't use that guard? If that's what you want, then I might as well tell the coach to leave, that I'm taking over because I'm telling him how to run his football team."

He still looked at me blankly, so I added:

"Our role up here is to try and convince the coach there may be areas of weakness that he simply doesn't face up to and perhaps we can convince him to make changes. We've been through a couple of situations where we didn't think players were going to make it, and they turned out to be pretty good. Suppose we had followed your suggestions and forced the coach to get rid of them. Do we keep running back to the coach to apologize? We can't do that. We have to be like a conscience and help get the coaches what they need, while allowing them to do their jobs and make reasonable suggestions based on our own experience.

"When you start to talk about our whole organization, you overlook the fact that the nonfootball side also has many weaknesses, but you never suggest we look at them as well. Why don't we look at them?"

"Well," he said, "that's different. It doesn't show up in the newspapers."

"Making the newspapers isn't the true test of an organization," I told him. "Everything we do in this business should be the same, whether it's on the field or on the nonfootball side. Let's develop some continuity where we can feed in and feed out and get the best from everyone."

All of this contention had its own ramifications with the players and coaches. They also had tasted Tim's disdain for them first-hand. I don't think Marty Schottenheimer will ever forget that someone came up to him during a game at Giants Stadium and told him his car was being towed away because it wasn't parked in the right spot. At first Marty thought it was an ill-timed joke in the middle of a very tense situation, but he later found out it was true. The same thing happened to players during games on orders from Tim, whose jurisdiction included team-parking areas.

One time I said to him, "You always look at the team two ways—*we* and *us*. The players don't look at it that way. They look at us as *we*. I can't be dishonest with the coach when he says 'they (up there) don't really have any feeling for us.' I can't tell him that he's wrong when you and some of the others in your group go around openly criticizing them or doing things to make their lives miserable."

And ten years later nothing seems to have changed. In late 1986 I received permission from Well to use the Giants' locker room as a site to shoot commercials for an antidrug campaign. We scheduled the shoot for a day when there was no practice. But Wellington wasn't in his office at the Stadium, and as we were going into the weight room to set up, Tim's secretary walked by and saw us. A short time later one of the team's locker room attendants showed up and told us to leave. When I protested that we had permission from Well Mara, it did no good. The man said, "There's been a mix-up, and some of the players want to use the room." A "mix-up". . . or a coincidence of my being there? I have my own idea.

Even the Super Bowl victory didn't dim the pettiness. The Giants' team and front-office executives were invited to the White House to be greeted by President Reagan several weeks after winning Super Bowl XXI, and it was within Tim's scope—the promotion department—to coordinate all of the arrangements between the organization and the White House, including setting an agenda for the President's use. When it came time to make the presentation, the President incredibly invited George Young, the team's general manager, to receive it, instead of Wellington, as the team's president. The President, following a prearranged script, was an innocent party to a terrible snub. That was a deliberately orchestrated slap in Wellington's face, something I know embarrassed him thoroughly and did not relfect very well on the organization.

This atmosphere plagued us in 1978 as we began looking for new people to step into the football side. Following his dumping of the Bledsoe hiring into Rozelle's lap, it was clear that Tim was going to oppose anyone Well and I proposed, regardless of his merits. For example, I suggested that Jack Butler, head of the NFL's BLESTO scouting combine at the time and one of the NFL's best personnel people, be considered as our personnel director. But I couldn't offer him the job; I could only suggest he discuss it. If he was interested, Well and I would have to get Tim's acquiescence. That was embarrassing to the organization, so I put it aside while hoping for a resolution to the problem, though at the time Jim Lee Howell had gotten a whiff of our plan from Tim, and he started to balk about being moved out.

Then there was the matter of hiring a new head coach. One way or the other, McVay was not going to return to that job after 1978. Until "the fumble," I had hoped he could move into my job. One of my top choices was Joe Paterno of Penn State. When we began considering candidates Joe was into his own season, so we dropped a feeler with his brother George, who then was head coach at the Merchant Marine Academy. But "the fumble" and the subsequent ownership blowup soon followed, and Joe publicly disavowed any interest in the job. Bill Walsh, in his final season as head coach at Stanford and itching to become an NFL head coach, was also interested in the job, even *after* "the fumble." Bill's interest was piqued during the previous spring when he came in for one of our quarterback seminars. I discussed the possibility of a change and wanted to consider him part of that change. Of course, Bill and John McVay have made a helluva team with the 49ers, and I don't think much has to be left to the imagination to know what would have happened with the Giants had Walsh become head coach in 1979.

I had received impressive reports on Darryl Rodgers, then head coach at Michigan State, who has since become head coach of the Detroit Lions. From our own staff I also saw that Jerry Wampfler would have been a top candidate, one reason why I signed him to another contract before leaving my job.

The toughest part of the head-coach search was telling my old roommate, Dick Modzelewski, that I could not recommend him for the job. Mo badly wanted to become an NFL head coach, and he asked to be considered strictly on his own merits and without hint of our friendship or past relationship as teammates.

"I just don't think the circumstances are right," I told him. "I want you and Jerry to stay with us because the team needs you and you work so well together. Forget the damn fumble; we are still not a bad team, and we're getting better. But the worst thing we can do is to bring in someone as head coach who will destroy what we've built, so you and Jerry are two who can help keep it together.

"But I can't go to Wellington and tell him to hire you as head coach. With all that's happened, this club cannot stand another ex-Giant. That's going backwards. You could be the best coach in the world, but because you're an ex-Giant, and there has been so much talk about us hiring only ex-Giants, you'd come in with three strikes against you. We can't take that chance."

Of course, that entire selection process went right out the window after "the fumble," and about the only thing left for me to do was to wrap up the loose ends of the season and prepare to leave the Giants. Inside the Giants' office only Tim and Wellington knew of my absolute decision to leave. Norm Miller of the *Daily News,* to whom I had mentioned it during a casual conversation that fall, also knew. I had originally submitted my letter of resignation in June, after that aforementioned memo to Tim, making it effective on December 31. However, when we got off to our good start, Well asked me to stay three or four months past the deadline to help put the finishing touches on what both of us thought would be an orderly transition and infusion of new people. The NFL had not yet placed any restrictions on our hiring a coach or other personnel, so Well felt that if I did it for the club it might head off a potential lawsuit by Tim, who he felt would go to any lengths to prevent him from exercising that power. I agreed to stay, and Well wrote me a confirming memorandum. He sent a copy to Tim, as neither was speaking to the other.

Tim blew his stack, and in quick step came a letter:

> Confirming our conversation yesterday, I have checked with my mother and my sister about the written resignation you submitted in June to take effect December 31, 1978.
>
> We were completely unaware that you and Well had reopened this subject and that he prevailed upon you to reconsider. Since you were the one who initiated your resignation, we feel that it is irrevocable no matter how you feel at this time.

Of course, Tim also signed an agreement later that allowed me to stay on "in an interim basis until we have employed a director of operations," who was to be chosen by the board of directors. That never happened because matters deteriorated so badly that the entire hiring process was dumped into the commissioner's lap, and I left as scheduled, publicly announcing my resignation on December 15. I summarized my achievements in a public statement that read in part:

> I am satisfied that I have accomplished the primary objective spelled out by Well Mara when I took the post nearly five years ago—namely to upgrade and improve the interior football operations of the Giants and to put them, at least, on a par with the best teams in the National Football League.
>
> The foundation for that operation has been established with the revitalization and reorganization of our scouting areas; the introduction and use of extensive computer and information systems; and the continued upgrading of the team's talents where, despite its final 1978 record, it has become competitive on the field with any team in the league. All of this has consumed my total attention and energy during the past five years.
>
> During my tenure, Mr. Mara has been totally supportive of

everything I sought to accomplish, and he allowed me free rein to establish all the new procedures which have strengthened our football operation. I have appreciated his support and assistance, and that of everyone within the Giants organization who responded to my efforts to rebuild the excellence I had known here as a player.

However, I also prepared a series of final memos wrapping up the season and made several proposals for improving the team in 1979. Foremost was getting a quarterback, and during the fall of 1978 both Phil Simms and Jack Thompson of Washington State were the top candidates to fill our needs. From preliminary reports, my first choice was Simms, who had demonstrated fine arm-strength and passing touch as well as the important toughness factor. I knew any young quarterback coming to the Giants was going to take a pounding for a bit unless Joe Pisarcik could play well enough to allow him to develop. I guess the only ones who were surprised with Simms as first pick in 1979 were the fans. He was no dark horse in our scouting department, which was very high on him even before the 1978 season ended, and he certainly has justified those expectations.

My final submission prior to a very quiet departure was to reissue to Wellington that memo I wrote to them in May that said I was leaving, and detailed every aspect of my time as director of operations. Much of what was contained in it has already been detailed in this chapter, but there were also some final personal thoughts:

> The past was built on faith, love and spirit. How long can this type of organization survive? Only when 100 percent of the company has that love, faith and spirit.
>
> These were the instruments that held the corporation together. Now we must put love aside and try to reconstruct, for the first time, a truly businesslike organization. Hopefully, faith and spirit...necessary to grow, not to satisfy 50 percent of this or 50 percent of that, but 100 percent of something we currently don't have.
>
> Faith and spirit...are a two-way street. Don't expect it in your staff, coaches and players if you don't have it in each other!
>
> Whoever comes in after me will find a much improved football organization. I hope he finds that faith, love and spirit which is so necessary to the success of our total organization...

After that I walked out of Giants Stadium as if it were the end of another workday, without so much as a "good-bye and good luck." For many reasons it was an unforgettable day, but what I warmly recall was receiving a phone call from my friend Harry Greene shortly before I left, and his telling me that he had heard of my departure. "I'm with Art Richardson, Harry Turpin, Jack Craham and Sandy Granowicz, and we'd like you to have dinner with us," Harry said. All were people whom I liked very much, so I joined them and I will never forget what they did that evening to help soften the intense emotions I felt about leaving the Giants, a step I knew would never be reversible...the end of a dream, so to speak.

A bit later that evening I joined our company's employees who were having their annual Christmas party, and if faith, love and spirit could be measured, it would have exploded constantly from the feelings present at that party. It was just as it had been with my old teammates during my playing days—and rarely, if ever, during my five years with the Giants as director of operations.

That faith, love and spirit were in great measure the ingredients that propelled the Giants to the World Championship in Super Bowl XXI...just as they were the ingredients that pushed our Giants teams and those before me to similar glories...and they are the ingredients that always made me feel that once a Giant, always a Giant.